263 482

THE WORLD'S CLASSICS

ROMOLA

GEOR[illegible]IOT was born Mary Anne Evans on 22 Nov[illegible] 1819 near Nuneaton, Warwickshire, on the Arb[illegible] estate of the Newdigate family, of which her [illegible] agent. At the age of nine she was imbued with [illegible] Evangelicalism that dominated her life until [illegible] twenty-two. Removing to Coventry with her [illegible] 1841, she became acquainted with the family of [illegible] Bray, a free-thinker, and was persuaded to translate [illegible]ss's *Life of Jesus* (1846). After her father's death [illegible] 1849 she spent six months in Geneva, reading widely. On her return she lived in London in the house of the publisher John Chapman, editing the *Westminster Review*. Here, at the focus of many radical ideas, she met George Henry Lewes, a versatile journalist, whose marriage was irretrievably ruined but divorce impossible. In 1854 she went to Germany with him, and for 24 years lived openly with him as his wife. Through his encouragement at the [illegible] 37 she began to write fiction. *Scenes of Clerical* [illegible] serialized in *Blackwood's Magazine*, and reprinted [illegible] under the *nom de plume* George Eliot, was an [illegible] success. *Adam Bede* (1859) became a best seller; [illegible] declared that 'its author takes rank at once [illegible] masters of the art'. In *The Mill on the Floss* [illegible] the five novels that followed George Eliot, [illegible] skill, continued the subtle probing of [illegible] that leads many modern critics to regard [illegible] greatest novelist of the nineteenth century. [illegible]th in 1878 was a devastating blow that ended her writing career. On 6 May 1880 she married John Walter Cross, a banker, 20 years her junior, and on 22 December died at 4 Cheyne Walk, London.

ANDREW BROWN, editor of the Clarendon Edition of *Romola* (1993), is Director of Humanities Publishing at Cambridge University Press.

ROMOLA

GEORGE ELIOT was born Mary Anne Evans on 22 November 1819 near Nuneaton, Warwickshire, on the Arbury estate of the Newdigate family, of which her father was agent. At the age of nine she was imbued with an intense Evangelicalism that dominated her life until she was twenty-two. Removing to Coventry with her father in 1841, she became acquainted with the family of Charles Bray, a free-thinker, and was persuaded to translate Strauss's *Life of Jesus* (1846). After her father's death (1849) she spent six months in Geneva, reading widely. On her return she lived in London in the house of the publisher John Chapman, editing the *Westminster Review*. Here, at the focus of many radical ideas, she met George Henry Lewes, a versatile journalist, whose marriage was irretrievably ruined but divorce impossible. In 1854 she went to Germany with him, and for 24 years lived openly with him as his wife. Through his encouragement at the age of 37 she began to write fiction. *Scenes of Clerical Life*, serialized in *Blackwood's Magazine*, and reprinted (1858) under the nom de plume George Eliot, was an instant success. *Adam Bede* (1859) became a best seller. [illegible] assured that its author takes rank at once among the masters of the art'. In *The Mill on the Floss* (1860) and the five novels that followed George Eliot, with increasing skill, continued the subtle probing of [illegible] that leads many modern critics to regard her as the greatest novelist of the nineteenth century. Lewes's death in 1878 was a devastating blow that ended her writing career. On 6 May 1880 she married John Walter Cross, a banker, 20 years her junior, and on 22 December died at 4 Cheyne Walk, London.

ANDREW BROWN, editor of the Clarendon Edition of *Romola* (1993), is Director of Humanities Publishing at Cambridge University Press.

THE WORLD'S CLASSICS

GEORGE ELIOT

Romola

Edited with an Introduction by
ANDREW BROWN

Oxford New York
OXFORD UNIVERSITY PRESS
1994

Oxford University Press, Walton Street, Oxford OX2 6DP

Oxford New York Toronto
Delhi Bombay Calcutta Madras Karachi
Kuala Lumpur Singapore Hong Kong Tokyo
Nairobi Dar es Salaam Cape Town
Melbourne Auckland Madrid
and associated companies in
Berlin Ibadan

Oxford is a trade mark of Oxford University Press

Editorial material © Andrew Brown 1994
First published as a World's Classics paperback 1994

All rights reserved. No part of this publication may be reproduced, stored in a retrieval system, or transmitted, in any form or by any means, without the prior permission in writing of Oxford University Press. Within the UK, exceptions are allowed in respect of any fair dealing for the purpose of research or private study, or criticism or review, as permitted under the Copyright, Designs and Patents Act, 1988, or in the case of reprographic reproduction in accordance with the terms of the licences issued by the Copyright Licensing Agency. Enquiries concerning reproduction outside these terms and in other countries should be sent to the Rights Department, Oxford University Press, at the address above

900263482

This book is sold subject to the condition that it shall not, by way of trade or otherwise, be lent, re-sold, hired out or otherwise circulated without the publisher's prior consent in any form of binding or cover other than that in which it is published and without a similar condition including this condition being imposed on the subsequent purchaser

British Library Cataloguing in Publication Data
Data available
ISBN 0-19-282964-5

Library of Congress Cataloging in Publication Data
Data available
ISBN 0-19-282964-5

Set by Hope Services (Abingdon) Ltd.
Printed in Great Britain
by BPC Paperbacks,
Aylesbury,
Bucks

CONTENTS

INTRODUCTION

Romola always occupied a special place in George Eliot's affections. 'I felt some wonder that anyone should think I had written anything better,' she confided to a friend; 'I could swear by every sentence as having been written with my best blood.' In an obvious sense *Romola* (1862–3) is strikingly different from anything she wrote before or after. Its setting is not the familiar one of rural England, but Italy in the last decade of the fifteenth century, the Renaissance Florence of Machiavelli and Michelangelo. The action opens in the *annus mirabilis* of 1492, as Columbus sets sail for the New World and the Grand Inquisitor Torquemada scourges the Old. In Milan Leonardo da Vinci enjoys the patronage of the tyrant Ludovico Sforza; in Rome the murderous Rodrigo Borgia becomes Pope; in Florence, centre of classical learning and the most cultured city in Europe, supreme power passes to a Dominican monk named Girolamo Savonarola who burns books on a 'Bonfire of Vanities'. The story of Romola de' Bardi is closely bound up with the shaping forces of these tumultuous times: the *realpolitik* of the Medici, the humanist philosophy of the new Platonists, the religious fundamentalism of Savonarola. For all its exotic period specificity, however, *Romola*'s main concerns are unmistakably those of George Eliot's other mature novels: the moral pre-eminence of social duty, the vital relationship between self-fulfilment and the health of the wider community which the gifted individual helps to define. It is a complex and erudite work, rooted in historical particularities, yet deeply personal in its abiding preoccupations. No less a critic than Henry James pronounced it 'the finest thing she wrote'.

The genesis of *Romola* can be dated with unusual accuracy. Following the completion of *The Mill on the Floss* in March 1860, George Eliot and George Henry Lewes took a long-anticipated holiday in Italy. After several weeks in Rome and Naples, they arrived in Florence on 17 May and were immediately enchanted. On the 21st, while reading a guidebook, it struck Lewes that the life and times of Savonarola would make excellent material for a historical novel. George Eliot, he noted in his journal, 'at once caught at the idea with enthusiasm'. The very next day they visited the Dominican monastery of San Marco, of which Savonarola had been Prior, only to find that since it was still a religious foundation entrance was forbidden to women. Undeterred, Lewes toured the interior making notes which were later used in the novel, while George Eliot waited in the chapter-house admiring Fra Angelico's fresco of the Crucifixion, one of the supreme glories of Florentine art. On their way back to the hotel she stopped at a bookshop and bought a biography of Savonarola. The seed had been planted; she wrote to her publisher John Blackwood that Florence 'has stimulated me to entertain rather an ambitious project . . . It will require a great deal of study and labour, and I am athirst to begin.'

On her return to England, however, she began to doubt her ability to carry off so different a work of fiction from those she had previously undertaken. She decided to turn her attentions instead to another tale of rural English life, and in September 1860 she started work on *Silas Marner*. Within days of its completion, in April 1861, her thoughts turned again to the 'ambitious project' of an Italian historical romance. She and Lewes promptly set out on another visit to Florence, and for five weeks immersed themselves in the sights and sounds, the art and monuments of the city. They returned home in June 1861 with an enhanced sense of place and a fund of local details, but George Eliot remained convinced that 'a great deal of study and labour' was required to bring the project to fruition, and she settled down to a protracted course of reading on the social and political history of fifteenth-century Florence. In October Lewes remarked that she was still 'buried in musty old antiquities', while he had become 'a sort of Italian Jackal, hunting up rare books and vellum bound unreadabilities in all the second hand bookstalls of London'. George Eliot consulted over 200 volumes in her preparations for the novel The notebooks she kept indicate the breadth of her research: on buildings and battles, customs and costumes, fairs and funerals, state officials and religious orders; on topics as diverse as usury, the wool-trade, horse-racing, and the manufacture of spectacles; on politicians, philosophers, clerics, scholars, artists, and poets.

As things turned out, the more she studied the more convinced she became that she was not yet ready to start writing. Her trepidation at attempting so different a work from her previous novels paralysed her creative faculties and, as if by way of compensation, the relentless acquisition of background details became an end in itself, almost an obsession. Instead of writing a novel, Lewes reflected gloomily, she was compiling an encyclopaedia, and making herself ill with worry in the process. George Eliot suffered attacks of diffidence during the composition of each of her novels, but never more acutely than in the case of *Romola*. Many years later she told her husband John Cross, in a distinctive phrase, that it had 'ploughed into her' more than any of her other books. Her journal for the period records a depressing succession of headaches, nausea, and nervous debility. For days on end she was too sick to work, and on a number of occasions she considered abandoning the project altogether.

Eventually, after fully six months of concentrated study, and with a fine sense of timing, she began writing *Romola* on New Year's Day 1862. Three weeks later she received a visit from the publisher George Smith, senior partner of the firm of Smith, Elder & Co., who offered her the quite unprecedented sum of £10,000 for the copyright to the novel. In 1860 Smith had launched a new literary periodical, the *Cornhill Magazine*, which proved such a success that it soon reached a monthly sale of 100,000 copies. By the beginning of 1862, however, the circulation had dipped alarmingly, and Smith recognized that he needed to sign a star author in order to revive its fortunes. By any reckoning the terms he proposed to George Eliot were princely (as indeed they had to be to persuade her to desert her previous publishers, Blackwoods): £10,000 was four or five times more than any author had hitherto been offered for a single work of fiction. By way of comparison it is worth noting that Anthony Trollope was paid just £1,000 for *Framley Parsonage*, whose serialization in the *Cornhill* (January 1860–April 1861) was one reason for the magazine's early success. Remarkably, Smith's initial offer for *Romola* was rejected. He wanted the novel to start appearing in the *Cornhill* in April or May 1862, and to make the most of its drawing power it should extend to 16 parts (of 24 pages each); George Eliot was unable to guarantee its being ready before August or September, and felt besides that it would damage the structure of the story to divide it into so many episodes. Smith, Lewes records, was 'much put out'. He was also a shrewd and persistent negotiator. With the assistance of Lewes, whom in the meantime he had appointed as editor of the *Cornhill*, a compromise was struck: *Romola* would be published in 12 parts of 32 pages each commencing in July 1862. George Eliot's fee was reduced to £7,000, for which Smith also acquired a seven-year exclusive right to publish the novel in book form when the serialization was completed.

When George Eliot accepted Smith's revised offer for *Romola* in May 1861 she had written only eight chapters—enough for just one-and-a-half of the 12 parts specified in the agreement, though the book was scheduled to begin publication within two months. Clearly, the paralysing doubts and delays had to be put behind her. Indeed, it may be that this pressing practical obligation was exactly what she needed. The contract was signed, and public announcements made in the press; now she had to deliver the goods. She began writing with a new sense of purpose, though in her journal she reports regular attacks of migraine, 'malaise', 'dreadful palsy', and 'uneasy incapacitating sensations' throughout the period of composition. These ailments were clearly exacerbated by the unaccustomed pressure of monthly deadlines, and she resolved never again to publish in serial form. Notwithstanding, she was generally able to deliver copy for each part to the printer around six weeks in advance of its scheduled appearance in the magazine. In January 1863, after finishing part 9, she realized that she could not in fact complete the book in the 12 parts she had earlier insisted on limiting it to. With Smith's agreement, but with no suggestion of increasing her fee, she decided to extent it to 14 parts, with the result that as printed in the *Cornhill* the novel is some 13 per cent longer than originally contracted for.

Romola was serialized in the *Cornhill Magazine* between July 1862 and August 1863 (its effect on the circulation figures was minimal). After reading the first episode Anthony Trollope wrote a letter to George Eliot which anticipated the reactions of the majority of critics at the time. On the one hand he expressed deep admiration for the scale and beauty of the novel's artistic design; on the other he worried that its sheer weight of historical reference would 'fire too much over the heads' of average readers and thus disaffect them. A few days later, as if in response, George Eliot confided to her friend Sara Hennell that 'Of necessity, the book is addressed to fewer readers than my previous works, and I myself have never expected—I might rather say *intended*—that the book should be as "popular" in the same sense as the others.' If this was indeed her expectation of the novel's likely reception, she must in the main have been gratified at the verdict of the reviews when *Romola* was published in book form in July 1863. 'It will never be George Eliot's most popular book,' remarked the *Spectator*; 'it seems to us, however, much the greatest she has yet produced.' 'It cannot be denied that *Romola* is less popular than its predecessors,' agreed the *Westminster Review*, 'but we do not hesitate to say that it is the author's greatest work.' 'It is not likely to be popular', *The Times* pronounced, but 'it impresses one with a sense of sublime power'. The principal reason for its lack of popularity, the critics agreed, was its excessive erudition—what the *Saturday Review* termed its pervasive sense of 'instructive antiquarianism'. As the *Athenaeum* put it, 'the amount of reading that the author must have achieved to get up the minute details of time, place, circumstance and costume is marvellous, and the reader feels as though he were ungrateful, in not being better entertained by all that has cost so much time and labour'. The *British Quarterly Review* was rather blunter in its conclusion, arguing that the distracting minutiae of Florentine history had 'no interest for the general reader'. Many of its most distinguished readers, however, had nothing but praise for the novel. George Eliot reported with delight that she had received 'a great deal of pretty encouragement from immense big-wigs—some of them saying "Romola" is the finest book they ever read'. Robert Browning, for example, wrote to her describing it as 'the noblest and most heroic prose-poem that I have ever read'. Among others who expressed particular admiration for the book were Tennyson and Gladstone, the painter John Everett Millais, and the Italian leader Mazzini. Twenty years later Henry James was to single out *Romola* as 'the most important of George Eliot's works . . . the one in which the largest things are attempted and grasped'.

Though George Eliot is most commonly associated with novels set during her own lifetime, it is no surprise that she was attracted to the idea of historical fiction, which from Sir Walter Scott onwards had established itself as one of the dominant genres of the age. In the thirty years between Scott's death and the publication of *Romola*, best-sellers such as William Harrison Ainsworth and G. P. R. James had successfully exploited the mass-market appeal of costume adventures set in times of old, while the phenomenally popular Edward Bulwer Lytton had sold even more copies of voluminous historical sagas which used past events to cast new light on current political concerns. Lewes shrewdly anticipated that George Eliot would 'probably do something in historical romance rather different in character from what has been done before', though in suggesting the project to her he was doubtless aware of its commercial as well as artistic possibilities. Neither is it surprising that an Italian subject should have been chosen for her foray into the genre. The history of Italy held a particular fascination for George Eliot's contemporaries. The stirring exploits of Garibaldi, Cavour, and Mazzini during the *Risorgimento* of the 1850s had promoted in the cultivated English imagination a romantic interest in the past glories as well as the current aspirations of the country. Newspapers and magazines ran articles about Italian history, art, and civilization; poets such as Browning, painters such as Frederic Leighton (who illustrated *Romola* for the *Cornhill*) were producing much of their best work on Italian historical themes. Widely read in the classics of Italian literature, and a devoted amateur of Italian art and opera, George Eliot epitomized the English enthusiasm for Italian history and culture which reached its zenith in the early 1860s. For all the difficulties it caused her, *Romola* was thus in many ways a timely venture.

The fact that the story was set in the distant past in no sense disqualified it, to George Eliot's way of thinking, from speaking to perennial or timeless concerns. As the narrator is at pains to insist, there is a 'likeness' in the human condition that is 'broader and deeper than all possible change' (p. 4). Indeed, given the essential constancy of human nature, a sensitive reconstruction of historical events may permit the novelist to examine moral issues of universal significance under what amount to laboratory conditions. Much in the manner of Bulwer Lytton, whose influential Italian historical novel *Rienzi, The Last of the Tribunes* (1835) she read during her preparations for *Romola*, George Eliot deliberately eschewed the merely anecdotal or picturesque in her portrayal of past events, and aimed instead for what she termed 'the exercise of a veracious imagination in historical picturing . . . using all extant evidence and supplying deficiencies by careful analogical creation'. Her compilation and deployment of documentary historical evidence were prodigious, for an accurate reconstruction of the cultural milieu of

Renaissance Florence was essential if the idiom in which her characters moved was to be properly 'veracious'—'The fortunes of Tito and Romola', the narrator remarks, 'were dependent on certain grand political and social conditions which made an epoch in the history of Italy' (p. 195). To the historian's empirical research, however, is added the novelist's special prerogative of 'analogical creation', which involves the attribution of motives which history inadequately explains, according to the unalterable laws of human behaviour. It is an ingenious concept: the creative writer will always present a more completely 'veracious' picture than the mere chronicler because she is uniquely justified in hypothesizing the likely springs of human action. Complementarily, the novelist's investigation of the growth of the representative individual mind may be symbolic of the development of society in general.

To implement such a strategy, the period of history chosen for consideration must be especially susceptible to the drawing of typical or universal implications. George Eliot's selection of the life and times of Savonarola, whatever the impulse behind Lewes's initial suggestion of the subject, must surely have chimed with some nascent intellectual scheme in her own mind. For Florence at the end of the fifteenth century stood at a crossroads in the intellectual history of Europe. Under the patronage of Lorenzo de' Medici—Lorenzo 'the Magnificent', first among the great Renaissance princes—scholars of classical literature and philosophy had flocked to the city and made it an unrivalled centre of the newly awakened interest in the civilization of the ancients. This new and essentially secular learning had the effect of undermining many of the most basic tenets on which medieval Christian society was founded. Instead of reiterating the divinely ordained providential arrangement of the universe, it stressed self-reliance and the potential for self-determination in each individual. Man became the measure; the age of humanism was dawning. Temporal power, as the Florentine Niccolò Machiavelli was soon to argue, could be decoupled from the Christian commandments. The perfection of the human soul, as scholars such as the Florentine Marsilio Ficino were teaching, could be approached through the study of Plato as surely as that of Christ. Then, in April 1492, four months before Columbus set sail on the voyage that was forever to alter man's perception of the world, Lorenzo the Magnificent died. In the ensuing upheavals, as if alarmed at the implications of the changes it had helped set in train, Florence turned to a leader whose reactionary principles of government harked back to that same medieval world order which the ascendant spirit of the times was fast making untenable. The conjunction was a potent one: on the one hand the charismatic figure of the monk Savonarola, ascetic and authoritarian, insisting that Florence should be governed in strict obedience to divine laws as he himself was guided by divine visions; on the other the nexus of social, political, and philosophical currents that were heralding a new order for Europe. It is as a city of such conflicts and contradictions that the Florence of April 1492 is described in the Proem to *Romola*—caught, 'in the unrest of a new growth', in a 'strange web of belief and unbelief'.

Underpinning this specific historical conjunction is a broader philosophical view of the development of Western society, based on the tripartite division of the nature of human knowledge by the French philosopher Auguste Comte (1798–1857), whose influence on George Eliot's cast of mind is well documented. According to Comte's formulation, in the first or 'theological' state of society all inexplicable phenomena are simply ascribed to supernatural forces, whether pagan or Christian. The second or 'metaphysical' state is characterized by the critical enquiry of the intellect into the hitherto unfathomable nature of the universe. The third or 'positive' state is founded on the scientific observation and objective analysis of natural laws. The age of positivism, which represents the final ascent of human society, was to be brought about in the nineteenth century. It was the Renaissance, according to Comte, that marked the shift from the theological to the metaphysical state: a transitional period in which man worships nothing higher than the abstractions of his own mind, and in which the forces of affection and reverence that bind society together are fragmented by an undisciplined and essentially self-centred spirit of enquiry. The 'epoch in the history of Italy' which *Romola* chronicles is thus a crucial turning-point in the development of the modern European mind.

Of the leading characters, it is the young Greek scholar Tito Melema who is most obviously conceived as a representative of this particular moment in history. Recognizing neither moral order nor divine purpose in the universe, Tito is an object lesson in unrestrained egotism, and is thus inevitably hostile to the higher ideals on which human society is founded. He arrives in Florence on the very day of Lorenzo de' Medici's death, displaying, like Lucifer, 'the air of a fallen prince'. Though this Satanic connection is further developed in Dino's vision of him as 'the Great Tempter', the image with which he is most persistently associated is that of the Roman fertility god Bacchus. Like a force of nature, elemental, undisciplined, and without moral conscience, he values nothing beyond his own selfish desires. In pseudo-Epicurean terms he defines the object of life simply as personal pleasure. What others condemn as his heartless treachery, he sees as a course of action to which there is no sensible or rational alternative. He is not malicious by nature; rather, amoral and atheistic, he is a criminal without consciousness of crime. 'It is good', the narrator observes, quoting the *Eumenides* of Aeschylus, 'that fear should sit as the guardian of the soul, forcing it into wisdom . . . else, how shall [men] learn to revere the right' (p. 112). Like the Bacchus of classical mythology, Tito experiences no such fear, for the concept of Nemesis means no more to him than that of Christian retribution. Rather, he typifies that brand of intellectual scepticism and ruthless self-seeking which has come to be associated with his Florentine contemporary Niccolò Machiavelli.

In social terms Tito is a vicious outsider who must be seen to suffer his just deserts. Accordingly, much as his moral bankruptcy proceeds from the limitations of his philosophy, so his amoral behaviour carries within it the seeds of his own destruction. He sees life simply as a series of opportunities to be grasped and exploited to his own ends. In his headlong pursuit of the main chance he ignores the simple fact that every action has its reaction, and that no one can avoid the social consequences of their deeds. He does so at his peril, for like all men he is subject to the 'inexorable law of human souls' that it is 'the reiterated choice of good or evil which gradually determines character' (p. 212). His failure to recognize this only adds to the deliberate irony surrounding the circumstances of his death, for he is struck down at the last by a force whose very existence he has denied, a force of retributive justice fashioned from his own reiterated choice of evil. By clear implication his story shows that the individual can never separate himself entirely from the life of the social unit, or the moral considerations that define its welfare.

Unlike Tito, Savonarola is an actual historical figure, but in this most premeditated of novels he too is pressed into service as the representative of a particular world-view. In one sense, indeed, he is the exact antitype of Tito. Where Tito is a soulless materialist who repudiates all manifestations of the supernatural, Savonarola's whole being depends upon his belief in the divine order of the universe. Where Tito's unprincipled secularism implies a philosophy of every man for himself, Savonarola preaches a doctrine of brotherly love as the basis for social life. If Tito is an extreme version of Renaissance man—self-reliant, self-serving, and amoral—Savonarola epitomizes the spiritual values and moral certainties of medieval Christianity. For George Eliot, despite her own agnosticism, Savonarola's Christian ideals are clearly preferable to the social divisiveness and moral degeneracy of Tito's self-seeking. It is the supernatural framework to the Christian ethic that she questions. Savonarola's nobility of purpose is beyond doubt: he preaches freedom through social responsibility, and social commitment through love. Boldly challenging the prevailing secular tendencies of the age, such as Tito so extremely represents, he seeks to bring men to a realization of their duty both to themselves and to their fellows. His moral philosophy, however, is founded on what for George Eliot are untenable metaphysical assumptions: that world events are directed in accordance with God's divine plan, and that that plan is specially revealed to himself, as God's prophet, in mystical visions. Moreover, to implement his moral agenda he must involve himself in the business of politics, and the power politics of Renaissance Florence inevitably prove corrupting. He comes to identify all who oppose him with the enemies of God, and as his theological model of society is compromised by exposure to temporal realities, so his pious ideals are increasingly expressed in terms of the most peremptory egotism. For all his lofty ideals, his philosophy is shown in the end to be scarcely less narrow and restricting, scarcely less inappropriate to the continuing welfare of society, than that of the radically amoral Tito. Stern and unlovable by nature, in sharp contrast to the pliant young Greek, he too fails to provide an adequate framework for social reconstruction, for all the apparent rectitude of his moral programme. Ironically, it is the very integrity of his purpose that marks him out for eventual failure in a world that has turned away from the fundamentalist beliefs which inform his every action. As the narrator sadly observes, he is confounded 'not because of his sins, but because of his greatness—not because he sought to deceive the world, but because he sought to make it noble' (p. 541).

Though the public story of Savonarola clearly dominates the action of the book, it is in Romola's personal journey of self-fulfilment that its deepest preoccupations are articulated. It is instructive that *Romola* is the only one of George Eliot's novels to be named after its heroine. Indeed, in its dramatization of a proud and gifted woman's struggle with male (most often patriarchal) authority, it is perhaps also her most autobiographical; while in its overarching philosophical scheme there is a ringing endorsement of Comte's argument that 'it is from the feminine aspect only that human life can really be comprehended as a whole'.

Romola's upbringing in a single-parent household, removed from all female company beyond that of her amiable but bird-brained cousin Brigida, has imbued in her the strict Stoical principles of her severe and joyless father Bardo. Self-opinionated, tetchy, and aloof, Bardo makes no attempt to disguise how much he would have preferred her to have been a boy. Though his physical blindness is readily symbolic of a still more serious lack of moral vision, his daughter feels herself inadequately equipped to fulfil her filial duties to him. It is a barren and wintry life that Romola leads in and around Bardo's library, surrounded only by the dusty relics and classical learning of the past. In her brother Dino, disowned by their father since he left the family home to become a monk, she finds only a bleak excess of religious devotion which "places visions before natural duties" (p. 148) and subjects all sympathetic impulses to an unbending external rule. Ironically, father and son—pagan enthusiast and Christian zealot alike—remain inextricably linked in their equally narrow but entirely incompatible certitudes. Blinkered by doctrinaire principles, and driven by masculine assertiveness, each has ignored the familial obligations which Romola instinctively recognizes as the basis of human society, the 'human sympathies which are the very life and substance of our wisdom' (p. 155). Given the sterility of her past life, it is hardly surprising that Romola should be so utterly overwhelmed by Tito, who bursts into her cloistered world with all the spontaneous energy of the fertility god Bacchus. Shrewdly adapting to the circumstances of the moment, he becomes first her replacement brother and then her husband, thus uniting familial and erotic love in an irresistible combination. When he goes on to betray both her father's trust and her own, Romola is left doubly desolate.

As Tito's abdication of moral principles is measured primarily by his dealings with his adoptive father Baldassarre, so Romola comes to define the purpose of her own life in relation to a surrogate, spiritual father in Savonarola. Lonely and bewildered following Bardo's death and Tito's treachery, she is drawn to Savonarola at once by the sheer force of his personality and by his ringing call for the renunciation of self in favour of a society based on brotherly love. Here is a great soul in which to believe, and a great cause to which she can devote her life. In time, however, she finds herself repelled by his inflexible demand for the subjugation of inner feelings to external law. Though his moral programme is in itself beyond reproach, the means by which he seeks to enforce it run contrary to Romola's most basic sense of social justice, for 'Justice', as the narrator observes, 'is not without us as a fact, it is within us as a great yearning' (p. 517). His authoritarian theology makes no concession to the sacredness of the individual conscience, that innate moral sense by which Romola feels herself naturally guided. Accordingly, in the climactic confrontation with Savonarola in Ch. 59, Romola defends the primacy of common affections over abstract doctrine: the kingdom of God, she insists, is more compassionate than Savonarola's systematic dogmatism will allow—"else, let me stand outside it with the beings that I love" (p. 464). It is the individual's moral conscience that must decide his or her true path; 'the soul must dare to act on its own warrant' (p. 442), even when this runs counter to the code of established religion, for the compassionate and charitable soul is the greatest of God's gifts to mankind.

For George Eliot, the progress of society depends on a moral orientation which can control the selfish impulses of Tito without recourse to the authoritarian abstractions of Savonarola. That orientation derives from the power of love, and love, as the novel makes abundantly clear, is most powerfully centred in the family: in ties to parents, to spouses, and above all to children. When Romola appears in the plague village nursing an abandoned child, she is specifically identified with the Blessed

Virgin, but in practice she has long since established herself as a sister of mercy and, as 'The Visible Madonna' (Ch. 44), a saintly lady, who ministers to the needy of Florence in general. She becomes, in effect, a feminine ideal of compassionate love, and in this role she at last finds a productive outlet for her talents. In the prelude to *Middlemarch* George Eliot famously acknowledges that in an age such as her own, lacking any 'coherent social faith and order', it is hard to achieve that 'rapturous consciousness of life beyond self' which alone can bring about a 'constant unfolding of far-resonant action'. This consciousness is precisely what Romola attains following her symbolic baptism on the waters of the Mediterranean, in which she seeks for the oblivion of death but is mysteriously awakened to a new life. It is fair to say, though, that for all the deliberate metaphorical play that attends the event (Romola reborn from the depths of the sea as Tito, who had once survived drowning, dies in the shallows of the Arno) her conversion is scarcely believable in dramatic or psychological terms. The Romola who attains at a stroke the requisite 'rapturous consciousness' (the 'self-renouncing beneficent strength', p. 399) to inspire a life of 'far-resonant action' tends inevitably towards an unrealistic paragon of virtue. The conclusion to the novel is thus deeply flawed, but it serves all the more to accentuate the instructive moral of the book: namely, that the essence of Christianity is duty to mankind, and that, as Romola herself explains to Lillo, Tito's natural and her adopted son: "We can only have the highest happiness . . . by having wide thoughts, and much feeling for the rest of the world, as well as ourselves" (p. 547).

Though the setting is historically specific, the action of the novel aspires to the universal significance of a fable, and from this derives the sense of premeditation and contrivance that suffuses the narrative. For example, at the broadest structural level there is the heavily accented theme of filial relations: two 'lost' sons, each of whom has unnaturally rejected his stern and unforgiving father; and a daughter who devotes herself to no fewer than four fathers in turn—to Bardo, Bernardo del Nero, Savonarola, and Baldassarre (the narrative wheel thus coming full circle as she nurtures the same father whom her husband has abandoned). Eventually, as Romola becomes an adoptive parent to a small boy saved from the sea, the corrupted filial relations of the previous generation are brought to a dramatic conclusion in filicide as Baldassarre strangles Tito. At a more local level, the plot unfolds through a deliberate pattern of coincidences and parallel events: Tito is recognized by Dino in the streets of Florence because he is wearing a ring, a gift from Baldassarre, whose device is superstitiously believed to 'restore lost things'; to rid himself of this dangerous encumbrance Tito then sells the ring to a man whom Baldassarre chances to meet in the streets of Genoa; as a result Baldassarre sets out for Florence, but is overtaken by historical events and actually arrives in the city as a prisoner of the invading French army (personal and public events thus coinciding: see note to p. 206); he escapes from his captors and quite literally bumps into Tito on the steps of the Cathedral—that which was lost is indeed restored, with the most extreme dramatic irony. Such devices, however blunt, are intrinsic to George Eliot's purpose: events occur not so much because they are likely in themselves as because, as in a fable, they are necessary to the unfolding of the book's moral design. By a similar token, Fra Luca's vision of Romola's marriage to the 'Great Tempter' is uncannily enacted in the fantastic procession she happens upon on her betrothal day, while Piero di Cosimo's apparently whimsical decision to paint Tito in the guise of Sinon deceiving Priam is doubly vindicated when the encounter outside the Cathedral prompts him to select Baldassarre as the model for Priam. To read *Romola* as 'realistic' or 'naturalistic' fiction is to mistake George Eliot's intentions. As she herself acknowledged, 'there is scarcely a phrase, an incident, an allusion, that did not gather its value to me from its supposed subservience to my main artistic objects'.

Those objects, perhaps more clearly so than in any other of her novels, are unashamedly didactic: showing the means to social reformation (perhaps a more appropriate word would be *renaissance*) through moral altruism and the spiritual rebirth of the individual. Significantly, the individual concerned is a woman, who learns from her encounters with patriarchal authority—familial, political, and clerical—finely to distinguish self-serving from charitable motives. From close experience of the inadequacies of the two dominant cultures, the pagan and Christian traditions represented in extreme form by Bardo and Savonarola, Romola is seen to fashion a new and positivist perspective for the modern world. She comes to exemplify a feminine principle of instinctive concern at once for the family and for the wider social unit, a concern based neither on inherited superstition nor on self-generated abstractions (respectively, in Comte's scheme, the 'theological' and 'metaphysical' stages of human development), but simply on natural fellow-feeling and on the binding power of love—

She felt that the sanctity attached to all close relations, and, therefore, pre-eminently to the closest, was but the expression in outward law of that result towards which all human goodness and nobleness must spontaneously tend; that the light abandonment of ties, whether inherited or voluntary, because they had ceased to be pleasant, was the uprooting of social and personal virtue. (p. 442)

George Eliot's reputation today is so closely bound up with her novels of nineteenth-century English life that at first glance *Romola* may seem a curiously uncharacteristic work. Indeed, though widely hailed at the time as her greatest achievement, its critical standing has since suffered a serious eclipse, as the taste for historical fiction in general has declined. It was certainly conceived of by George Eliot herself as a radical new departure in her writing career. She was acutely conscious of the difficulties inherent in such an experiment but, as she confided to Sara Hennell, she was resolved 'not to be a machine always grinding out the same material or spinning the same sort of web'. In the event, she rose with extraordinary energy to the challenge of re-creating life in Renaissance Florence, and we should not minimize the degree of artistic accomplishment that she herself attached to this process. One of her clear aims in the novel was to reconstruct a significant passage in European history as accurately and comprehensively as possible, in order to share with her readers her own profound fascination for the period. This was, however, but *one* of her aims. In the final reckoning, for all its erudition and encyclopaedic accumulation of historical detail, *Romola* is not so much a novel about the past as one which makes use of the past—to exemplify experiences universal to the human condition. The public events it so meticulously records are interwoven throughout with the private lives of its leading characters. Though deliberately set at a representative moment in history, its overriding concern is with a group of representative human beings, whose actions are prompted by the unconscious internal forces which George Eliot considers typical determinants of the historical process. It is not the pastness of the past, or what specially distinguishes it from the present, that most attracts George Eliot, but rather the timeless truths it can be used to illustrate. If 'far-resonant action' seemed impossible in her own age, a narrative set in a remote and quite different time could legitimately provide an exemplary and inspiring alternative. *Romola* is a novel about history itself, and the forces which bring about change and progress in human society. Far from being an anomaly in the George Eliot canon, it can be recognized as her most ambitious attempt to chart the relationship between the moral conduct of individuals and the welfare of society at large. Freed from the narrative constraints of verisimilitude to contemporary life, it operates at a level that is at once archival and symbolic. By analogy, the spiritual rebirth of Romola de' Bardi indicates the true basis for a lasting renaissance in the society whose highest aspirations she comes to embody. The most experimental and programmatic of George Eliot's novels, *Romola* is also her most adventurous. Chronologically, it represents the mid-point of her career as a novelist; artistically and intellectually too, it can fairly claim a central place in the register of her achievements.

NOTE ON THE TEXT

Romola first appeared in the *Cornhill Magazine* in 14 monthly parts between July 1862 and August 1863, with 24 illustrations by Frederic Leighton. It was published complete, in three volumes at one-and-a-half guineas, in July 1863 by Smith, Elder & Co., the proprietors of the *Cornhill.* The first one-volume edition was issued by Smith, Elder & Co. in 1865 at 6*s.* and was subsequently reprinted from stereotype plates as a 'New Edition' selling for 2*s.* 6*d.* Almost 15,000 copies had been sold in this cheap format by 1878, the year that William Blackwood and Sons published both their 'Cabinet Edition' of the novel, in 2 volumes at 10*s.* the set, and their one-volume 'Stereotyped Edition' at 3*s.* 6*d.* Over 10,000 copies of this latter had been sold by the time of GE's death in December 1880. The last British edition published during GE's lifetime was Smith, Elder & Co.'s two-volume de luxe edition, limited to 1,000 copies at five guineas the set, which appeared in October 1880. Five editions of the novel were published in the USA during GE's lifetime, the first by the New York firm of Harper and Brothers in August 1863.

The autograph manuscript of *Romola*, which served as setting copy for the *Cornhill* serialization, is in the British Library (Add. MSS 34,027–9). Showing clear signs of being the working draft rather than a fair copy, it is shot through with all manner of minor stylistic irregularities and inconsistencies of presentation. Most of these were attended to by the printer, who sought to tidy up the oddities or anomalies of the author's punctuation, capitalization, italicization, and so on before sending out the proofs. Such a process of 'normalization' was standard practice at the time; as an experienced author GE would have expected it in the case of *Romola*, as a service which rendered what amounted almost to shorthand manuscript copy into a form more suitable for publication. GE then had to read proof for each of the monthly parts while she was still at work on the next one, but she took the opportunity to revise extensively and in all made almost 1,000 substantial alterations on the *Cornhill* proofs. She subsequently introduced several hundred further changes, some of them quite significant, to the three-volume edition of 1863, the one-volume edition of 1865, and the 'Cabinet Edition' of 1878. She saw proof for none of the American editions, nor for the 'Stereotyped Edition' of 1878 or the de luxe edition of 1880.

The text of this World's Classics edition, like that of the

Clarendon edition from which it is taken, is based on the first printing of the novel—the *Cornhill* serialization, for which GE corrected proof in 1862–3. It incorporates the changes GE herself made to the resettings of 1863, 1865, and 1878, but removes the cumulative layers of restyling and the hundred or more verbal miscopyings by the printers of these later editions, which have been reproduced in virtually all printings of the novel until now. For a record and analysis of variants in the different printed editions, and of GE's deletions and additions in the manuscript, together with a full account of the composition and publication of the novel, the interested reader should consult the Clarendon edition.

SELECT BIBLIOGRAPHY

The primary sources are *George Eliot's Life as Related in her Letters and Journals*, ed. John W. Cross, 3 vols. (1885), and *The George Eliot Letters*, ed. Gordon S. Haight, 9 vols. (1954–78). Haight also wrote the standard life, *George Eliot: A Biography* (1968). Primary material relating to *Romola* can be found in George Eliot's notebooks (see p. 549), of which two have been published: *George Eliot: A Writer's Notebook 1854–1879*, ed. Joseph Wiesenfarth (1981), and *Some George Eliot Notebooks: An Edition of the Carl H. Pforzheimer Library's George Eliot Holograph Notebooks*, volume ii—MSS 707–11, ed. William Baker (1984). Additional material may be found in the introduction to Guido Biaggi's edition of *Romola*, 2 vols. (1907), in Maria Tosello, *Le Fonti Italiane della 'Romola' di George Eliot* (1956), Gennaro Anthony Santangelo's dissertation 'The Background of George Eliot's Romola' (University of North Carolina, 1962), and in the introduction and notes to the Clarendon edition of the novel (ed. Andrew Brown, 1993).

The most important critical study devoted to *Romola* is Felicia Bonaparte's *The Triptych and the Cross: The Central Myths of George Eliot's Poetic Imagination* (1979). Other books with major sections on the novel include Avrom Fleishman, *The English Historical Novel* (1971), Andrew Sanders, *The Victorian Historical Novel, 1840–1880* (1978), Hugh Witemeyer, *George Eliot and the Visual Arts* (1979), K. M. Newton, *George Eliot: Romantic Humanist: A Study of the Philosophical Structure of her Novels* (1981), Alexander Welsh, *George Eliot and Blackmail* (1985), Gillian Beer, *George Eliot* (1986), Mary Wilson Carpenter, *George Eliot and the Landscape of Time: Narrative Form and Protestant Apocalyptic History* (1986), and David Carroll, *George Eliot and the Conflict of Interpretations* (1992). Essays worth consulting include George Levine, '*Romola* as Fable', in Barbara Hardy (ed.), *Critical Essays on George Eliot* (1970); Gennaro Anthony Santangelo, 'Villari's *Life and Times of Savonarola*: A Source for George Eliot's *Romola*', *Anglia* (1972); J. B. Bullen, 'George Eliot's *Romola* as Positivist Allegory', *Review of English Studies* (1975); and Hugh Witemeyer, 'George Eliot's *Romola* and Bulwer Lytton's *Rienzi*', *Studies in the Novel* (1983). For a more detailed list of further reading see Constance Marie Fulmer, *George Eliot: A Reference Guide* (1977) and George Levine, *An Annotated Critical Bibliography of George Eliot* (1988).

Contemporaneous reviews of *Romola* can be found in *A Century of George Eliot Criticism*, ed. Gordon S. Haight (1965); *George Eliot and Her Readers*, ed. Laurence Lerner and John Holmstrom (1966); and *George Eliot: The Critical Heritage*, ed. David Carroll (1971).

A CHRONOLOGY OF GEORGE ELIOT

1819 Born 22 November at South Farm, Arbury, Warwickshire, the youngest of three children of Robert Evans's second marriage, to Christiana Pearson; 29 November baptized Mary Anne Evans at Chilvers Coton.

1820 Family moves to Griff House where her father was agent for the Arbury estate of Francis Newdigate.

1825–7 At Miss Lathom's School, Attleborough, with her sister Christiana.

1828–32 At Mrs Wallington's School, Nuneaton, where she becomes friendly with Miss Lewis, the principal governess and a strong evangelical.

1832–5 At the Miss Franklins' School, Coventry, run by the daughters of the Baptist minister.

1835 Leaves school finally at Christmas.

1836 Her mother dies 3 February. GE takes charge of her father's household, learns Italian and German from a Coventry teacher, and reads Greek and Latin with the headmaster of Coventry Grammar School.

1840 Her first publication, a religious poem, appears in the *Christian Observer* in January.

1841 Her brother Isaac marries, and takes over the house at Griff. In March Robert Evans and his daughter move to a house in Foleshill Road, Coventry. Later in the year GE forms a friendship with Charles Bray and his wife Caroline, Coventry free-thinkers, through whom she makes contact with Sara Hennell and her brother, Charles Hennell, author of *An Inquiry into the Origins of Christianity* (1838). GE's religious faith challenged.

1842 Refuses to attend church with her father from January to May, but finally agrees to accompany him at the end of what she called their 'Holy War'.

1843 Visits Dr Brabant of Devizes in November with his daughter, who had undertaken a translation of David Friedrich Strauss's work of historical criticism, *Das Leben Jesu* (1835), but who discontinued it on her marriage to Charles Hennell.

1844 GE takes over the translation of Strauss.

1846 *The Life of Jesus* published in three volumes in June after much labour and many complaints of being 'Strauss-sick'.

1849 Her father dies 31 May. Goes abroad in June with the Brays, and stays in Geneva by herself for eight months.

1850 Returns to Coventry and lives with the Brays for seven months.

1851 Goes to London to assist John Chapman in editing the *Westminster Review*, and contributes a review of Mackay's *The Progress of the Intellect* to the January number. In March GE is driven away from 142 Strand by the jealousy of Chapman's wife and mistress. In September she returns to edit the journal.

1852 Friendship with Herbert Spencer leads to rumours of an engagement; through him she meets the versatile George Henry Lewes, at this time editor of the *Leader*.

1854 Her translation of Ludwig Feuerbach's radical critique of orthodox belief, *The Essence of Christianity*, published in July; in the same month she and Lewes leave for Germany together, first visiting Weimar, and then spending the winter in Berlin where GE begins the translation of Spinoza's *Ethics*. Lewes could not obtain a divorce because he had condoned his wife's adultery.

1855 They return to England in March, when Lewes's *Life of Goethe* is published to general and lasting acclaim; settle in Richmond, and GE writes regularly for the *Leader* and *Westminster Review*.

1856 Visit Ilfracombe for Lewes's research into marine biology (later published as *Sea-side Studies*, 1858), and then on to Tenby in Wales where in July GE begins writing her story, 'The Sad Fortunes of the Rev. Amos Barton', the first of the *Scenes of Clerical Life*.

1857 Part I of 'Amos Barton' appears in *Blackwood's Edinburgh Magazine*, and she assumes the pseudonym 'George Eliot'. Begins writing *Adam Bede* in October.

1858 *Scenes of Clerical Life* published in two volumes in January. In April they go to Munich and Dresden for a stay of five months.

1859 *Adam Bede* published in three volumes in February to critical acclaim; 16,000 copies sold in the first year. In the same month they settle at Holly Lodge, Wandsworth, where GE forms a close relationship with the positivists, Mr and Mrs Richard Congreve.

1860 *The Mill on the Floss* published in three volumes in April as they leave for a holiday in Italy where, in May, GE projects a historical novel based on the life of Savonarola. Abandons the project in September in favour of *Silas Marner*.

1861 *Silas Marner* published in April, and they revisit Florence to collect more material for an Italian historical novel. On their return GE buries herself in background research and makes several false starts on the novel.

1862 Starts writing *Romola* on 1 January. Smith and Elder offer the unprecedented sum of £10,000 for the new novel (GE eventually accepted £7,000) which begins to appear in fourteen parts in the *Cornhill* in July.

1863 *Romola* published in three volumes in July: 'I began it a young woman,—I finished it an old woman.' In August they move to The Priory, Regent's Park, the house associated with the novelist's most famous years.

1864 Visits Italy in May. In June GE begins work on *The Spanish Gypsy*, a tragic play in blank verse; becomes ill and abandons the work.

1865 In March begins *Felix Holt*.

1866 *Felix Holt* published in three volumes in June but sales disappointing; *The Spanish Gypsy* taken up again, and they set off for Spain in December to collect material.

1868 *The Spanish Gypsy* published in April.

1869 March and April spent in Italy; in Rome GE meets the stockbroker John Walter Cross for the first time. Begins writing 'Middlemarch' (the Featherstone-Vincy part) in August. Lewes's second son, Thornton, returns from Natal in May with spinal tuberculosis, and dies in October. GE writes the poems eventually published as *The Legend of Jubal and Other Poems* (1874).

1870 Puts aside 'Middlemarch' in despair, and in November begins a new story 'Miss Brooke' which develops rapidly.

1871 Combines the two narratives early in the year to create the first section of *Middlemarch*, to be published in eight parts. Book I published in December.

1872 *Middlemarch* concludes with Book VIII in December and is also published in four volumes.

1873 In November GE is 'simmering towards another book'.

1874 Makes her first 'Sketches towards Daniel Deronda' in January. *The Legend of Jubal and Other Poems* published.

1876 *Daniel Deronda* begins publication on the same plan as *Middlemarch* in February, with the last part appearing in September. In December they buy The Heights at Witley in Surrey as a summer residence.

1878 Lewes dies on 30 November. GE refuses to see anyone for several weeks and occupies herself in completing and preparing his major philosophical work, *Problems of Life and Mind*, for the press.

1879 Agrees to see Cross in February, and helps him to learn Italian. *Impressions of Theophrastus Such* published in June.

1880 In April agrees to marry Cross. Married in May, upon which her brother Isaac writes to congratulate her after twenty-three years of estrangement. Moves to Cheyne Walk. GE catches a chill at a concert, and dies on 22 December. Buried in Highgate Cemetery.

Romola

[*JULY 1862*]

PROEM

MORE than three centuries and a half ago, in the mid springtime of 1492, we are sure that the angel of the dawn, as he travelled with broad slow wing from the Levant to the Pillars of Hercules,* and from the summits of the Caucasus across all the snowy alpine ridges to the dark nakedness of the western isles, saw nearly the same outline of firm land and unstable sea—saw the same great mountain shadows on the same valleys as he has seen to-day—saw olive mounts, and pine forests, and the broad plains green with young corn or rain-freshened grass—saw the domes and spires of cities rising by the river sides or mingled with the sedge-like masts on the many-curved sea coast, in the same spots where they rise to-day. And as the faint light of his course pierced into the dwellings of men, it fell, as now, on the rosy warmth of nestling children; on the haggard waking of sorrow and sickness; on the hasty uprising of the hard-handed labourer; and on the late sleep of the night-student, who had been questioning the stars or the sages, or his own soul, for that hidden knowledge which would break through the barrier of man's brief life, and show its dark path, that seemed to bend no whither, to be an arc in an immeasurable circle of light and glory. The great river-courses which have shaped the lives of men have hardly changed; and those other streams, the life-currents that ebb and flow in human hearts, pulsate to the same great needs, the same great loves and terrors. As our thought follows close in the slow wake of the dawn, we are impressed with the broad sameness of the human lot, which never alters in the main headings of its history—hunger and labour, seed-time and harvest, love and death.

Even if, instead of following the dim daybreak, our imagination pauses on a certain historical spot and awaits the fuller morning, we may see a world-famous city, which has hardly changed its outline since the days of Columbus, seeming to stand as an almost unviolated symbol, amidst the flux of human things, to remind us that we still resemble the men of the past more than we differ from them, as the great mechanical principles on which those domes and towers were raised must make a likeness in human building that will be broader and deeper than all possible change. And doubtless, if the spirit of a Florentine citizen, whose eyes were closed for the last time while Columbus was still waiting and arguing for the three poor vessels with which he was to set sail from the port of Palos,* could return from the shades and pause where our thought is pausing, he would believe that there must still be fellowship and understanding for him among the inheritors of his birthplace.

Let us suppose that such a Shade has been permitted to revisit the glimpses* of the golden morning, and is standing once more on the famous hill of San Miniato, which overlooks Florence from the south.

The Spirit is clothed in his habit as he lived: the folds of his well-lined black silk garment or *lucco* hang in grave unbroken lines from neck to ancle; his plain cloth cap, with its *becchetto*, or long hanging strip of drapery, to serve as a scarf in case of need, surmounts a penetrating face, not, perhaps, very handsome, but with a firm, well-cut mouth, kept distinctly human by a close-shaven lip and chin. It is a face charged with memories of a keen and various life passed below there on the banks of the gleaming river; and as he looks at the scene before him, the sense of familiarity is so much stronger than the perception of change, that he thinks it might be possible to descend once more among the streets, and take up that busy life where he left it. For it is not only the mountains and the westward-bending river that he recognizes; not only the dark sides of Mount Morello opposite to him, and the long valley of the Arno that seems to stretch its grey low-tufted luxuriance to the far-off ridges of Carrara; and the steep height of Fiesole, with its crown of monastic walls and cypresses; and all the green and grey slopes sprinkled with villas which he can name as he looks at them. He sees other familiar objects much closer to his daily walks. For though he misses the seventy or more towers that once surmounted the walls, and encircled the city as with a regal diadem, his eyes will not dwell on that blank; they are drawn irresistibly to the unique tower springing, like a tall flower-stem drawn towards the sun, from the square turreted mass of the Old Palace in the very heart of the city—the tower that looks none the worse for the four centuries that have passed since he used to walk under it. The great dome,* too, greatest in the world, which, in his early boyhood, had been only a daring thought in the mind of a small quick-eyed man—there it raises its large curves still, eclipsing the hills. And the well-known bell-towers—Giotto's, with its distant hint of rich colour, and the graceful-spired Badia,* and the rest—he looked at them all from the shoulder of his nurse.

"Surely," he thinks, "Florence can still ring her bells with the solemn hammer-sound that used to beat on the hearts of her citizens and strike out the fire there. And here, on the right, stands the long dark mass of Santa Croce,* where we buried our famous dead, laying the laurel on their cold brows and fanning them with the breath of praise and of banners. But Santa Croce had no spire then: we Florentines were too full of great building projects to carry them all out in stone and marble; we had our frescoes and our shrines to pay for, not to speak of rapacious condottieri, bribed royalty, and purchased territories, and our façades and spires must needs wait. But what architect can the Frati Minori* have employed to build that spire for them? If it had been built in my day, Filippo Brunelleschi or Michelozzo* would have devised something of another fashion than that—something worthy to crown the church of Arnolfo."

At this the Spirit, with a sigh, lets his eyes travel on to the city walls, and now he dwells on the change there with wonder at these modern times. Why have five out of the eleven convenient gates been closed? And why, above all, should the towers have been levelled that were once a glory and defence? Is the world become so peaceful, then, and do Florentines dwell in such harmony, that there are no longer conspiracies to bring ambitious exiles home again with armed bands at their back? These are difficult questions: it is easier and pleasanter to recognize the old than to account for the new. And there flows Arno, with its bridges just where they used to be—the Ponte Vecchio, least like other bridges in the world, laden with the same quaint shops where our Spirit remembers lingering a little, on his way, perhaps, to look at the progress of that great palace which Messer Luca Pitti had set a-building with huge stones got from the Hill of Bogoli* close behind, or, perhaps, to transact a little business with the cloth-dressers in Oltrarno.* The exorbitant line of the Pitti roof is hidden from San Miniato; but the yearning of the old Florentine is not to see Messer Luca's too ambitious palace which he built unto himself; it is to be down among those narrow streets and busy humming Piazze where he inherited the eager life of his fathers. Is not the anxious voting with black and white beans still going on down there? Who are the *Priori* in these months, eating soberly-regulated official dinners in the Palazzo Vecchio, with removes of tripe and boiled partridges, seasoned by practical jokes against the ill-fated butt among those potent signors? Are not the significant banners still hung from the windows—still distributed with decent pomp under Orgagna's Loggia* every two months?

Life had its zest for the old Florentine when he, too, trod the marble steps and shared in those dignities. His politics had an area as wide as his trade, which stretched from Syria to Britain, but they had also the passionate intensity, and the detailed practical interest, which could belong only to a narrow scene of corporate action; only to the members of a community shut in close by the hills and by walls of six miles' circuit, where men knew each other as they passed in the street, set their eyes every day on the memorials of their commonwealth, and were conscious of having not simply the right to vote, but the chance of being voted for. He loved his honours and his gains, the business of his counting-house, of his guild, of the public council-chamber; he loved his enmities too, and fingered the white bean which was to keep a hated name out of the *borsa** with more complacency than if it had been a golden florin. He loved to strengthen his family by a good alliance, and went home with a triumphant light in his eyes after concluding a satisfactory marriage for his son or daughter under his favourite loggia in the evening cool; he loved his game at chess under that same loggia, and his biting jest, and even his coarse joke, as not beneath the dignity of a man eligible for the highest magistracy. He had gained an insight into all sorts of affairs at home and abroad: he had been of the "Ten" who managed the war department, of the "Eight" who attended to home discipline, of the *Priori* or *Signori* who were the heads of the executive government; he had even risen to the supreme office of *Gonfaloniere*;* he had made one in embassies to the Pope and to the Venetians; and he had been commissary to the hired army of the Republic, directing the inglorious bloodless battles in which no man died of brave breast-wounds—*virtuosi colpi*—but only of casual falls and tramplings.* And in this way he had learned to distrust men without bitterness; looking on life mainly as a game of skill, but not dead to traditions of heroism and clean-handed honour. For the human soul is hospitable, and will entertain conflicting sentiments and contradictory opinions with much impartiality. It was his pride, besides, that he was duly tinctured with the learning of his age, and judged not altogether with the vulgar, but in harmony with the ancients: he, too, in his prime, had been eager for the most correct manuscripts, and had paid many florins for antique vases and for disinterred busts of the ancient immortals—some, perhaps, *truncis naribus*,* wanting as to the nose, but not the less authentic; and in his old age he had made haste to look at the first sheets of that fine Homer* which was among the early glories of the Florentine press. But he had not, for all that, neglected to hang up a waxen image* or double of himself under the protection of the Madonna Annunziata, or to do penance for his sins in large gifts to the shrines of saints whose lives had not been modelled on the study of the classics; he had not even neglected making liberal bequests towards buildings for the *Frati*, against whom he had levelled many a jest.

For the Unseen Powers were mighty. Who knew—who was sure—that there was *any* name given to them behind which there was no angry force to be appeased, no intercessory pity to be won? Were not gems medicinal, though they only pressed the finger? Were not all things charged with occult virtues? Lucretius might be right—he was an ancient, and a great poet; Luigi Pulci, too, who was suspected of not believing anything from the roof upward (*dal tetto in su*),* had very much the air of being right over the supper-table, when the wine and jests were circulating fast, though he was only a poet in the vulgar tongue. There were even learned personages who maintained that Aristotle, wisest of men (unless, indeed, Plato were wiser?), was a thoroughly irreligious philosopher;* and a liberal scholar must entertain all speculations. But the negatives might, after all, prove false; nay, seemed manifestly false, as the circling hours* swept past him, and turned round with graver faces. For had not the world become Christian? Had he not been baptized in San Giovanni, where the dome is awful with the symbols of coming judgment,* and where the altar bears a crucified Image disturbing to perfect complacency in oneself and the world? Our resuscitated Spirit was not a pagan philosopher, nor a philosophizing pagan poet, but a man of the fifteenth century, inheriting its strange web of belief and unbelief; of Epicurean levity* and fetichistic dread; of pedantic impossible ethics uttered by rote, and crude passions acted out with childish impulsiveness; of inclination towards a self-indulgent paganism, and inevitable subjection to that human conscience which, in the unrest of a new growth, was filling the air with strange prophecies and presentiments.

He had smiled, perhaps, and shaken his head dubiously, as he heard simple folk talk of a Pope Angelico, who was to come by and by and bring in a new order of things, to purify the Church from simony, and the lives of the clergy from scandal—a state of affairs too different from what existed under Innocent the Eighth* for a shrewd merchant and politician to regard the prospect as worthy of entering into his calculations. But he felt the evils of the time, nevertheless; for he was a man of public spirit, and public spirit can never be wholly immoral, since its essence is care for a common good. That very Quaresima or Lent of 1492 in which he died, still in his erect old age, he had listened in San Lorenzo, not without a mixture of satisfaction, to the preaching of a Dominican Friar, named Girolamo Savonarola, who denounced with a rare boldness the worldliness and vicious habits of the clergy, and insisted on the duty of Christian men not to live for their own ease when wrong was triumphing in high places, and not to spend their wealth in outward pomp even in the churches, when their fellow-citizens were suffering from want and sickness. The *Frate* carried his doctrine rather too far for elderly ears; yet it was a memorable thing to see a preacher move his audience to such a pitch that the women even took off their ornaments, and delivered them up to be sold for the benefit of the needy.

"He was a noteworthy man, that Prior of San Marco," thinks our Spirit; "somewhat arrogant and extreme, perhaps, especially in his denunciations of speedy vengeance. Ah, *Iddio non paga il Sabato**—the wages of men's sins often linger in their payment, and I myself saw much established wickedness of long-standing prosperity. But a Frate Predicatore* who wanted to move the people—how could he be moderate? He might have been a little less defiant and curt, though, to Lorenzo de' Medici, whose family had been the very makers of San Marco: was that quarrel ever made up? And our Lorenzo himself, with the dim outward eyes and the subtle inward vision, did he get over that illness at

Careggi?* It was but a sad, uneasy-looking face that he would carry out of the world which had given him so much, and there were strong suspicions that his handsome son would play the part of Rehoboam.* How has it all turned out? Which party is likely to be banished and have its houses sacked just now? Is there any successor of the incomparable Lorenzo, to whom the Great Turk is so gracious as to send over presents of rare animals, rare relics, rare manuscripts, or fugitive enemies,* suited to the tastes of a Christian Magnifico who is at once lettered and devout—and also slightly vindictive? And what famous scholar is dictating the Latin letters of the Republic—what fiery philosopher is lecturing on Dante* in the Duomo, and going home to write bitter invectives against the father and mother of the bad critic who may have found fault with his classical spelling? Are our wiser heads leaning towards alliance with the Pope and the *Regno*,* or are they rather inclining their ears to the orators of France and of Milan?

"There is knowledge of these things to be had in the streets below, on the beloved *Marmi* in front of the churches, and under the sheltering Loggie,* where surely our citizens have still their gossips and debates, their bitter and merry jests as of old. For are not the well-remembered buildings all there? The changes have not been so great in those uncounted years. I will go down and hear—I will tread the familiar pavement, and hear once again the speech of Florentines."

Go not down, good Spirit! for the changes are great, and the speech of Florentines would sound as a riddle in your ears. Or, if you go, mingle with no politicians on the *Marmi*, or elsewhere; ask no questions about trade in the Calimala;* confuse yourself with no inquiries into scholarship, official or monastic. Only look at the sunlight and shadows on the grand walls that were built solidly, and have endured in their grandeur; look at the faces of the little children, making another sunlight amid the shadows of age; look, if you will, into the churches, and hear the same chants, see the same images as of old—the images of willing anguish for a great end, of beneficent love and ascending glory; see upturned living faces and lips moving to the old prayers for help. These things have not changed. The sunlight and shadows bring their old beauty and waken the old heart-strains at morning, noon, and even-tide; the little children are still the symbol of the eternal marriage between love and duty; and men still yearn for the reign of peace and righteousness—still own *that* life to be the highest, which is a conscious voluntary sacrifice. For the Papa Angelico is not come yet.

BOOK I

CHAPTER I.

The Shipwrecked Stranger

The Loggia de' Cerchi stood in the heart of old Florence, within a labyrinth of narrow streets behind the Badia, now rarely threaded by the stranger, unless in a dubious search for a certain severely simple door-place, bearing this inscription:

QUI NACQUE IL DIVINO POETA.*

To the ear of Dante, the same streets rang with the shout and clash of fierce battle between rival families; but in the fifteenth century, they were only noisy with the unhistorical quarrels and broad jests of wool-carders in the cloth-producing quarters of San Martino and Garbo.

Under this loggia, in the early morning of the 9th of April, 1492, two men had their eyes fixed on each other: one was stooping slightly, and looking downward with the scrutiny of curiosity; the other, lying on the pavement, was looking upward with the startled gaze of a suddenly-awakened dreamer.

The standing figure was the first to speak. He was a grey-haired, broad-shouldered man, of the type which, in Tuscan phrase, is moulded with the fist and polished with the pickaxe; but the self-important gravity which had written itself out in the deep lines about his brow and mouth seemed intended to correct any contemptuous inferences from the hasty workmanship which Nature had bestowed on his exterior. He had deposited a large well-filled bag, made of skins, on the pavement, and before him hung a pedlar's basket, garnished partly with small woman's-ware, such as thread and pins, and partly with fragments of glass, which had probably been taken in exchange for those commodities.

"Young man," he said, pointing to a ring on the finger of the reclining figure, "when your chin has got a stiffer crop on it, you'll know better than to take your nap in street corners with a ring like that on your forefinger. By the holy 'vangels! if it had been anybody but me standing over you two minutes ago—but

Bratti Ferravecchi* is not the man to steal. The cat couldn't eat her mouse if she didn't catch it alive, and Bratti couldn't relish gain if it had no taste of a bargain. Why, young man, one San Giovanni,* three years ago, the Saint sent a dead body in my way—a blind beggar, with his cap well lined with pieces—but, if you'll believe me, my stomach turned against the money I'd never bargained for, till it came into my head that San Giovanni owed me the pieces for what I spend yearly at the Festa: besides, I buried the body and paid for a mass—and so I saw it was a fair bargain. But how comes a young man like you, with the face of Messer San Michele,* to be sleeping on a stone bed with the wind for a curtain?"

The deep guttural sounds of the speaker were scarcely intelligible to the newly-waked, bewildered listener, but he understood the action of pointing to his ring: he looked down at it, and, with a half-automatic obedience to the warning, took it off and thrust it within his doublet, rising at the same time and stretching himself.

"Your tunic and hose match ill with that jewel, young man," said Bratti, deliberately. "Anybody might say the saints had sent *you* a dead body; but if you took the jewels, I hope you buried him—and you can afford a mass or two for him into the bargain."

Something like a painful thrill appeared to dart through the frame of the listener, and arrest the careless stretching of his arms and chest. For an instant he turned on Bratti with a sharp frown; but he immediately recovered an air of indifference, took off the red Levantine cap which hung like a great purse over his left ear, pushed back his long dark-brown curls, and glancing at his dress, said, smilingly,

"You speak truth, friend: my garments are as weather-stained as an old sail, and they are not old either, only, like an old sail, they have had a sprinkling of the sea as well as the rain. The fact is, I'm a stranger in Florence, and when I came in foot-sore last night I preferred flinging myself in a corner of this hospitable porch to hunting any longer for a chance hostelry, which might turn out to be a nest of blood-suckers of more sorts than one."

"A stranger in good sooth," said Bratti, "for the words come all melting out of your throat, so that a Christian and a Florentine can't tell a hook from a hanger.* But you're not from Genoa? More likely from Venice, by the cut of your clothes?"

"At this present moment," said the stranger, smiling, "it is of less importance where I come from than where I can go to for a mouthful of breakfast. This city of yours turns a grim look on me just here: can you show me the way to a more lively quarter, where I can get a meal and a lodging?"

"That I can," said Bratti, "and it is your good fortune, young man, that I have happened to be walking in from Rovezzano this morning, and turned out of my way to Mercato Vecchio to say an Ave* at the Badia. That, I say, is your good fortune. But it remains to be seen what is *my* profit in the matter. Nothing for nothing, young man. If I show you the way to Mercato Vecchio, you'll swear by your patron saint to let me have the bidding for that stained suit of yours, when you set up a better—as doubtless you will."

"Agreed, by San Niccolò,"* said the other, laughing. "But now let us set off to this said Mercato, for I feel the want of a better lining to this doublet of mine which you are coveting."

"Coveting? Nay," said Bratti, heaving his bag on his back and setting out. But he broke off in his reply, and burst out in loud, harsh tones, not unlike the creaking and grating of a cart-wheel: "*Chi abbaratta—baratta—b'ratta—chi abbaratta cenci e vetri—b'ratta ferri vecchi?*"*

"It's worth but little," he said presently, relapsing into his conversational tone. "Hose and altogether, your clothes are worth but little. Still, if you've a mind to set yourself up with a lute worth more than any new one, or with a sword that's been worn by a Ridolfi,* or with a paternoster* of the best mode, I could let you have a great bargain, by making an allowance for the clothes; for, simple as I stand here, I've got the best-furnished shop in the Ferravecchi, and it's close by the Mercato. The Virgin be praised! it's not a pumpkin I carry on my shoulders. But I don't stay caged in my shop all day: I've got a wife and a raven to stay at home and mind the stock.* *Chi abbaratta—baratta—b'ratta?*. . . . And now, young man, where do you come from, and what's your business in Florence?"

"I thought you liked nothing that came to you without a bargain," said the stranger. "You've offered me nothing yet in exchange for that information."

"Well, well; a Florentine doesn't mind bidding a fair price for news: it stays the stomach a little, though he may win no hose* by it. If I take you to the prettiest damsel in the Mercato to get a cup of milk—that will be a fair bargain."

"Nay; I can find her myself, if she be really in the Mercato; for pretty heads are apt to look forth of doors and windows. No, no. Besides, a sharp trader, like you, ought to know that he who bids for nuts and news, may chance to find them hollow."

"Ah! young man," said Bratti, with a sideway glance of some admiration, "you were not born of a Sunday—the salt shops were open* when you came into the world. You're not a Hebrew, eh?—come from Spain or Naples, eh? Let me tell you the Frati Minori are trying to make Florence as hot as Spain for those dogs of hell that want to get all the profits of usury* to themselves and leave none for Christians; and when you walk the Calimala with a piece of yellow cloth in your cap, it will spoil your beauty more than a sword-cut across that smooth olive-cheek of yours.—*Abbaratta, baratta—chi abbaratta?*—I tell you, young man, grey cloth is against yellow cloth;* and there's as much grey cloth in Florence as would make a gown and cowl for the Duomo, and there's not so much yellow cloth as would make hose for Saint Christopher—blessed be his name, and send me a sight of him* this day!—*Abbaratta, baratta, b'ratta—chi abbaratta?*"

"All that is very amusing information you are parting with for nothing," said the stranger, rather scornfully; "but it happens not to concern me. I am no Hebrew."

"See, now!" said Bratti, triumphantly; "I've made a good bargain with mere words. I've made you tell me something, young man, though you're as hard to hold as a lamprey. San Giovanni be praised! a blind Florentine is a match for two one-eyed men. But here we are in Mercato."

They had now emerged from the narrow streets into a broad piazza, known to the elder Florentine writers as the Mercato Vecchio, or the Old Market. This piazza, though it had been the scene of a provision market from time immemorial, and may perhaps, says fond imagination, be the very spot to which the Fesulean ancestors* of the Florentines descended from their high fastness to traffic with the rustic population of the valley, had not been shunned as a place of residence by Florentine wealth. In the early decades of the fifteenth century, which was now near its end, the Medici and other powerful families of the *popolani grassi*, or commercial nobility, had their houses there, not, perhaps, finding their ears much offended by the loud roar of mingled dialects, or their eyes much shocked by the butchers' stalls, which the old poet Antonio Pucci accounts a chief glory, or *dignità*,* of a market that, in his esteem, eclipsed the markets of all the earth beside. But the glory of mutton and veal (well attested to be the flesh of the right animals; for were not the skins, with the heads attached, duly displayed, according to the decree of the Signoria?) was just now wanting to the Mercato, the time of Lent not being yet over. The proud corporation, or "Art," of butchers was in abeyance, and it was the great harvest-time of the market-gardeners, the cheesemongers, the vendors of macaroni, corn, eggs, milk, and dried fruits: a change which was apt to make the women's voices predominant in the chorus. But in all seasons there was the experimental ringing of pots and pans, the chinking of the money-changers, the tempting offers of cheapness at the old-clothes' stalls, the challenges of the dicers, the vaunting of new linens and woollens, of excellent wooden-ware, kettles, and frying-pans; there was the choking of the narrow inlets with mules and carts, together with much uncomplimentary remonstrance in terms remarkably identical with the insults in use by the gentler sex of the present day, under the same imbrowning and heating circumstances. Ladies and gentlemen, who came to market, looked on at a larger amount of amateur fighting than could easily be seen in these later times, and beheld more revolting rags, beggary, and rascaldom, than modern householders could well picture to themselves. As the day wore on, the hideous drama of the gaming-house might be seen here by any chance open-air spectator—the quivering eagerness, the blank despair, the sobs, the blasphemy, and the blows: –

> "E vedesi chi perde con gran soffi
> E bestemmiar colla mano alla mascella,
> E ricever e dar dimolti ingoffi."*

But still there was the relief of prettier sights: there were brood-rabbits, not less innocent and astonished than those of our own period; there were doves and singing-birds to be bought as presents for the children; there were even kittens for sale, and here and there a handsome *gattuccio*, or "Tom," with the highest character for mousing; and, better than all, there were young, softly rounded cheeks and bright eyes, freshened by the start from the far-off castello* at daybreak, not to speak of older faces with the unfading charm of honest goodwill in them—such as are never quite wanting in scenes of human industry. And high on a pillar in the centre of the place—a venerable pillar, fetched from the church of San Giovanni—stood Donatello's stone statue of Plenty,* with a fountain near it, where, says old Pucci, the good wives of the market freshened their utensils, and their throats also—not because they were unable to buy wine, but because they wished to save the money for their husbands.

But on this particular morning a sudden change seemed to have come over the face of the market. The *deschi*, or stalls, were indeed partly dressed with their various commodities, and already there were purchasers assembled, on the alert to secure the finest, freshest vegetables and the most unexceptionable butter. But when Bratti and his companion entered the piazza, it appeared that some common preoccupation had for the moment distracted the attention both of buyers and sellers from their proper business. Most of the traders had turned their backs on their goods, and had joined the knots of talkers who were concentrating themselves at different points in the piazza. A vendor of old clothes, in the act of hanging out a pair of long hose, had distractedly hung them round his neck in his eagerness to join the nearest group; an oratorical cheesemonger, with a piece of cheese in one hand and a knife in the other, was incautiously making notes of his emphatic pauses on that excellent specimen of *marzolino*; and elderly market-women, with their egg-baskets in a dangerously oblique position, contributed a wailing fugue of invocation.

In this general distraction, the Florentine boys, who were never wanting in any street scene, and were of an especially mischievous sort—as who should say, very sour crabs* indeed—saw a great opportunity. Some made a rush at the nuts and dried figs, others preferred the farinaceous delicacies at the cooked-provision stalls—delicacies to which certain four-footed dogs also, who had learned to take kindly to Lenten fare, applied a discriminating nostril, and then disappeared with much rapidity under the nearest shelter; while the mules, not without some kicking and plunging among impeding baskets, were stretching their muzzles towards the aromatic green-meat.

"*Diavolo!*" said Bratti, as he and his companion came, quite unnoticed, upon the noisy scene; "the Mercato is gone as mad as if the Most Holy Father had excommunicated us again.* I must know what this is. But never fear: it seems a thousand years* to you till you see the pretty Tessa, and get your cup of milk; but keep hold of me, and I'll hold to my bargain. Remember, I'm to have the first bid for your suit, specially for the hose, which, with all their stains, are the best *panno di garbo*—as good as ruined, though, with mud and weather stains."

"*Olà*, Monna Trecca," Bratti proceeded, turning towards an old woman on the outside of the nearest group, who for the moment had suspended her wail to listen, and shouting close in her ear, "Here are the mules upsetting all your bunches of parsley: is the world coming to an end, then?"

"Monna Trecca" (equivalent to "Dame Greengrocer") turned round at this unexpected trumpeting in her right ear, with a half-fierce, half-bewildered look, first at the speaker, then at her disarranged commodities, and then at the speaker again.

"A bad Easter and a bad year* to you, and may you die by the sword!" she burst out, rushing towards her stall, but directing this first volley of her wrath against Bratti, who, without heeding the malediction, quietly slipped into her place, within hearing of the narrative which had been absorbing her attention; making a sign at the same time to the young stranger to keep near him.

"I tell you I saw it myself," said a fat man, with a bunch of newly-purchased leeks in his hand. "I was in Santa Maria Novella, and saw it myself. The woman started up and threw out her arms, and cried out and said she saw a big bull with fiery horns coming down on the church to crush it. I saw it myself."

"Saw what, Goro?" said a man of slim figure, whose eye twinkled rather roguishly. He wore a close jerkin, a skull-cap lodged carelessly over his left ear as if it had fallen there by chance, a delicate linen apron tucked up on one side, and a razor stuck in his belt. "Saw the bull, or only the woman?"

"Why, the woman, to be sure; but it's all one, *mi pare*: it doesn't alter the meaning—*va!*" answered the fat man, with some contempt.

"Meaning? no, no; that's clear enough," said several voices at once, and then followed a confusion of tongues, in which "Lights shooting over San Lorenzo for three nights together"—"Thunder in the clear starlight"—"Lantern of the Duomo struck with the sword of St. Michael"—"*Palle*"*—"All smashed"—"Lions tearing each other to pieces"*—"Ah! and they might well"—"*Boto* caduto in Santissima Nunziata!*"—"Died like the best of Christians"—"God will have pardoned him"—were often-repeated phrases, which shot across each other like storm-driven hailstones, each speaker feeling rather the necessity of utterance than of finding a listener. Perhaps the only silent members of the group were Bratti, who, as a new-comer, was busy in mentally piecing together the flying fragments of information; the man of the razor; and a thin-lipped, eager-looking personage in spectacles, wearing a pen-and-ink case at his belt.

"*Ebbene*, Nello", said Bratti, skirting the group till he was within hearing of the barber. "It appears the Magnifico is dead—rest his soul! and the price of wax will rise?"

"Even as you say," answered Nello; and then added, with an air of extra gravity, but with marvellous rapidity, "and his waxen image in the Nunziata fell at the same moment, they say; or at some other time, whenever it pleases the Frati Serviti,* who know best. And several cows and women have had still-born calves this Quaresima; and for the bad eggs that have been broken since the carnival, nobody has counted them! Ah! a great man—a great politician—a greater poet than Dante. And yet the cupola didn't fall, only the lantern. *Che miracolo!*"

A sharp and lengthened "Pst!" was suddenly heard darting across the pelting storm of gutturals. It came from the pale man in spectacles, and had the effect he intended; for the noise ceased, and all eyes in the group were fixed on him with a look of expectation.

"'Tis well said you Florentines are blind," he began, in an incisive high voice. "It appears to me, you need nothing but a diet of hay to make cattle of you. What! do you think the death of Lorenzo is the scourge God has prepared for Florence? Go! you are sparrows chattering praises over the dead hawk. What! a man who was trying to slip a noose over every neck in the Republic that he might tighten it at his pleasure! You like that; you like to have the election of your magistrates turned into closet-work, and no man to use the rights of a citizen unless he is a Medicean. That is what is meant by qualification now: *netto di specchio** no longer means that a man pays his dues to the Republic: it means that he'll wink at robbery of the people's money—at robbery of their daughters' dowries; that he'll play the chamberer and the philosopher by turns—listen to bawdy songs at the Carnival, and cry 'Bellissimi!'—and listen to sacred Lauds, and cry again, 'Bellissimi!' But this is what you love: you grumble and raise a riot over your *quattrini bianchi*"* (white farthings); "but you take no notice when the public treasury has got a hole in the bottom for the gold to run into Lorenzo's drains. You like to pay for footmen to walk before and behind one of your citizens, that he may be affable and condescending to you. 'See, what a tall Pisan we keep,' say you, 'to march before him with the drawn sword flashing in our eyes; and yet Lorenzo smiles at us. What goodness!' And you think the death of a man, who would soon have saddled and bridled you as the Sforza has saddled and bridled Milan*—you think his death is the scourge God is warning you of by portents. I tell you there is another sort of scourge in the air."

"Nay, nay, Ser Cioni, keep astride your politics, and never mount your prophecy; politics is the better horse," said Nello. "But if you talk of portents, what portent can be greater than a pious notary? Balaam's ass* was nothing to it."

"Ay, but a notary out of work, with his ink-bottle dry," said another bystander, very much out at elbows. "Better don a cowl at once, Ser Cioni; everybody will believe in your fasting."

The notary turned and left the group with a look of indignant contempt, disclosing, as he did so, the sallow but mild face of a short man who had been standing behind him, and whose bent shoulders told of some sedentary occupation.

"By San Giovanni, though," said the fat purchaser of leeks, with the air of a person rather shaken in his theories, "I'm not sure there isn't some truth in what Ser Cioni says. For I know I've good reason to find fault with the *quattrini bianchi* myself. Grumble, did he say? Suffocation! I should think we do grumble; and, let anybody say the word, I'll turn out into the piazza with the readiest, sooner than have our money altered in our hands as if the magistracy were so many necromancers. And it's true Lorenzo might have hindered such work if he would—and for the bull with the flaming horns, why, as Ser Cioni says, there may be many meanings to it, for the matter of that; it may have more to do with the taxes than we think. For when God above sends a sign, it's not to be supposed he'd have only one meaning."

"Spoken like an oracle, Goro!" said the barber. "Why, when we poor mortals can pack two or three meanings into one sentence, it were mere blasphemy not to believe that your miraculous bull means everything that any man in Florence likes it to mean."

"Thou art pleased to scoff, Nello," said the sallow, round-shouldered man, no longer eclipsed by the notary, "but it is not the less true that every revelation, whether by visions, dreams, portents, or the written word, has many meanings, which it is given to the illuminated only to unfold."

"Assuredly," answered Nello. "Haven't I been to hear the Frate in San Lorenzo? But then, I've been to hear Fra Menico in the Duomo too; and according to him, your Fra Girolamo, with his visions and interpretations, is running after the wind of Mongibello, and those who follow him are like to have the fate of certain swine* that ran headlong into the sea—or some hotter place. With San Domenico roaring *è vero* in one ear, and San Francisco screaming *è falso* in the other, what is a poor barber to do—unless he were illuminated? But it's plain our Goro here is beginning to be illuminated, for he already sees that the bull with the flaming horns means first himself, and secondly all the other aggrieved taxpayers of Florence, who are determined to gore the magistracy on the first opportunity."

"Goro is a fool!" said a bass voice, with a note that dropped like the sound of a great bell in the midst of much tinkling. "Let him carry home his leeks and shake his flanks over his wool-beating. He'll mend matters more that way than by showing his tun-shaped body in the piazza, as if everybody might measure his grievances by the size of his paunch. The burdens that harm him most are his heavy carcass and his idleness."

The speaker had joined the group only in time to hear the conclusion of Nello's speech, but he was one of those figures for whom all the world instinctively makes way, as it would for a battering-ram. He was not much above the middle height, but the impression of enormous force which was conveyed by his capacious chest and brawny arms bared to the shoulder, was deepened by the keen sense and quiet resolution expressed in his glance and in every furrow of his cheek and brow. He had often been an unconscious model to Domenico Ghirlandajo, when that great painter was making the walls of the churches reflect the life of Florence,* and translating pale aerial traditions into the deep colour and strong lines of the faces he knew. The naturally dark tint of his skin was additionally bronzed by the same powdery deposit that gave a polished black surface to his leathern apron—a deposit which habit had probably made a necessary condition of perfect ease, for it was not washed off with punctilious regularity.

Goro turned his fat cheek and glassy eye on the frank speaker with a look of deprecation rather than of resentment.

"Why, Niccolò," he said, in an injured tone, "I've heard you sing to another tune than that, often enough, when you've been laying down the law at San Gallo* on a festa. I've heard you say yourself, that a man wasn't a mill-wheel, to be on the grind, grind, as long as he was driven, and then stick in his place without stirring when the water was low. And you're as fond of your vote as any man in Florence—ay, and I've heard you say, if Lorenzo—"

"Yes, yes," said Niccolò. "Don't you be bringing up my speeches again after you've swallowed them, and handing them about as if they were none the worse. I vote and I speak when there's any use in it: if there's hot metal on the anvil, I lose no time before I strike; but I don't spend good hours in tinkling on cold iron, or in standing on the pavement as thou dost, Goro, with snout upward, like a pig under an oak-tree. And as for Lorenzo—dead and gone before his time—he was a man who had an eye for curious iron-work; and if anybody says he wanted to make himself a tyrant, I say, '*Sia*; I'll not deny which way the wind blows when every man can see the weathercock.' But that only means that Lorenzo was a crested hawk, and there are plenty of hawks without crests whose claws and beaks are as good for tearing. Though if there was any chance of a real reform, so that Marzocco* might shake his mane and roar again, instead of dipping his head to lick the feet of anybody that will mount and ride him, I'd strike a good blow for it."

"And that reform is not far off, Niccolò," said the sallow, mild-faced man, seizing his opportunity like a missionary among the too light-minded heathens, "for a time of tribulation is coming, and the scourge is at hand. And when the Church is purged of cardinals and prelates who traffic in her inheritance that their hands may be full to pay the price of blood and to satisfy their own lusts, the State will be purged too—and Florence will be purged of men who love to see avarice and lechery under the red hat and the mitre because it gives them the screen of a more hellish vice than their own."

"Ay, as Goro's broad body would be a screen for my narrow

person in case of missiles," said Nello; "but if that excellent screen happened to fall, I were stifled under it, surely enough. That is no bad image of thine, Nanni—or rather, of the Frate's; for I fancy there is no room in the small cup of thy understanding for any other liquor than what he pours into it."

"And it were well for thee, Nello," replied Nanni, "if thou could'st empty thyself of thy scoffs and thy jests, and take in that liquor too. The warning is ringing in the ears of all men: and it's no new story; for the Abbot Joachim* prophesied of the coming time three hundred years ago, and now Fra Girolamo has got the message afresh. He has seen it in a vision, even as the prophets of old: he has seen the sword hanging from the sky."

"Ay, and thou wilt see it thyself, Nanni, if thou wilt stare upward long enough," said Niccolò; "for that pitiable tailor's work of thine makes thy noddle so overhang thy legs, that thy eyeballs can see nought above the stitching-board but the roof of thy own skull."

The honest tailor bore the jest without bitterness, bent on convincing his hearers of his doctrine rather than of his dignity. But Niccolò gave him no opportunity for replying; for he turned away to the pursuit of his market business, probably considering further dialogue as a tinkling on cold iron.

"*Ebbene*," said the man with the hose round his neck, who had lately migrated from another knot of talkers, "they are safest who cross themselves and jest at nobody. Do you know that the Magnifico sent for the Frate at the last,* and couldn't die without his blessing?"

"Was it so—in truth?" said several voices. "Yes, yes—God will have pardoned him." "He died like the best of Christians." "Never took his eyes from the holy crucifix." "And the Frate will have given him his blessing?"

"Well, I know no more," said he of the hosen; "only Guccio there met a footman going back to Careggi, and he told him the Frate had been sent for yesternight, after the Magnifico had confessed and had the holy sacraments."

"It's likely enough the Frate will tell the people something about it in his sermon this morning; is it not true, Nanni?" said Goro. "What do you think?"

But Nanni had already turned his back on Goro, and the group was rapidly thinning; some being stirred by the impulse to go and hear "new things" from the Frate ("new things" were the nectar of Florentines); others by the sense that it was time to attend to their private business. In this general movement, Bratti got close to the barber, and said,—

"Nello, you've a ready tongue of your own, and are used to worming secrets out of people when you've once got them well-lathered. I picked up a stranger this morning as I was coming in from Rovezzano, and I can spell him out no better than I can the letters on that scarf I bought from the French cavalier. It isn't my wits are at fault,—I want no man to help me tell peas from paternosters,*—but when you come to foreign fashions, a fool may happen to know more than a wise man."

"Ay, thou hast the wisdom of Midas,* who could turn rags and rusty nails into gold, even as thou dost," said Nello, "and he had also something of the ass about him. But where is thy bird of strange plumage?"

Bratti was looking round, with an air of disappointment.

"*Diavolo!*" he said, with some vexation. "The bird's flown. It's true he was hungry, and I forgot him. But we shall find him in the Mercato, within scent of bread and savours, I'll answer for him."

"Let us make the round of the Mercato, then," said Nello.

"It isn't his feathers that puzzle me," continued Bratti, as they pushed their way together. "There isn't much in the way of cut and cloth on this side the Holy Sepulchre that can puzzle a Florentine."

"Or frighten him, either," said Nello, "after he has seen an Englander or a German."

"No, no," said Bratti, cordially; "one may never lose sight of the Cupola and yet know the world, I hope. Besides, this stranger's clothes are good Italian merchandise, and the hose he wears were dyed in Ognissanti* before ever they were dyed with salt water, as he says. But the riddle about him is—"

Here Bratti's explanation was interrupted by some jostling as they reached one of the entrances of the piazza, and before he could resume it, they had caught sight of the enigmatical object they were in search of.

CHAPTER II.
A Breakfast For Love

AFTER Bratti had joined the knot of talkers, the young stranger, hopeless of learning what was the cause of the general agitation, and not much caring to know what was probably of little interest to any but born Florentines, soon became tired of waiting for Bratti's escort; and chose to stroll round the piazza, looking out for some vendor of eatables who might happen to have less than the average curiosity about public news. But as if at the suggestion of a sudden thought, he thrust his hand into a purse or wallet that hung at his waist, and explored it again and again with a look of frustration.

"Not an obolus,* by Jupiter!" he murmured, in a language which was not Tuscan or even Italian. "I thought I had one poor piece left. I must get my breakfast for love, then!"

He had not gone many steps farther before it seemed likely that he had found a quarter of the market where that medium of exchange might not be rejected.

In a corner, away from any group of talkers, two mules were standing, well adorned with red tassels and collars. One of them carried wooden milk-vessels, the other a pair of panniers filled with herbs and salads. Resting her elbow on the neck of the mule that carried the milk, there leaned a young girl, apparently not more than sixteen, with a red hood surrounding her face, which was all the more baby-like in its prettiness from the entire concealment of her hair. The poor child, perhaps, was weary after her labour in the morning twilight in preparation for her walk to market from some castello three or four miles off, for she seemed to have gone to sleep in that half-standing, half-leaning posture. Nevertheless, our stranger had no compunction in awaking her, but the means he chose were so gentle that it seemed to the damsel in her dream as if a little sprig of thyme had touched her lips while she was stooping to gather the herbs. The dream was broken, however, for she opened her blue baby-eyes, and started up with astonishment and confusion to see the young stranger standing close before her. She heard him speaking to her in a voice which seemed so strange and soft, that even if she had been more collected she would have taken it for granted that he said something hopelessly unintelligible to her, and her first movement was to turn her head a little away, and lift up a corner of her green serge mantle as a screen. He repeated his words—

"Forgive me, pretty one, for awaking you. I'm dying with hunger, and the scent of milk makes breakfast seem more desirable than ever."

He had chosen the words "*muoio di fame*," because he knew they would be familiar to her ears; and he had uttered them playfully, with the intonation of a mendicant. This time he was understood; the corner of the mantle was dropped, and in a few moments a large cup of fragrant milk was held out to him. He paid no further compliments before raising it to his lips, and while he was drinking, the little maiden found courage to look up at the long dark curls of this singular-voiced stranger, who had asked for food in the tones of a beggar, but who, though his clothes were much damaged, was unlike any beggar she had ever seen.

While this process of survey was going on, there was another current of feeling that carried her hand into a bag which hung by the side of the mule, and when the stranger set down his cup, he saw a large piece of bread held out towards him, and caught a glance of the blue eyes that seemed intended as an encouragement to him to take this additional gift.

"But perhaps that is your own breakfast," he said. "No, I have had enough without payment. A thousand thanks, my gentle one."

There was no rejoinder in words; but the piece of bread was pushed a little nearer to him, as if in impatience at his refusal; and as the long dark eyes of the stranger rested on the baby face, it seemed to be gathering more and more courage to look up and meet them.

"Ah, then, if I must take the bread," he said, laying his hand on it, "I shall get bolder still, and beg for another kiss to make the bread sweeter."

His speech was getting wonderfully intelligible in spite of the strange voice, which had at first almost seemed a thing to make her cross herself. She blushed deeply, and lifted up a corner of her mantle to her mouth again. But just as the too presumptuous stranger was leaning forward, and had his fingers on the arm that held up the screening mantle, he was startled by a harsh voice close upon his ear.

"Who are *you*—with a murrain to you?* No honest buyer, I'll warrant, but a hanger-on of the dicers—or something worse. Go! dance off, and find fitter company, or I'll give you a tune to a little quicker time than you'll like."

The young stranger drew back and looked at the speaker with a glance provokingly free from alarm and deprecation, and his slight expression of saucy amusement broke into a broad beaming smile as he surveyed the figure of his threatener. She was a stout but brawny woman, with a man's jerkin slipped over her green serge gamurra or gown, and the peaked hood of some departed mantle fastened round her sunburnt face, which, under all its coarseness and premature wrinkles, showed a half-sad, half-ludicrous maternal resemblance to the tender baby face of the little maiden—the sort of resemblance which often seems a more croaking, shudder-creating prophecy than that of the death's head.

There was something irresistibly propitiating in that bright young smile, but Monna Ghita was not a woman to betray any weakness, and she went on speaking, apparently with heightened exasperation.

"Yes, yes, you can grin as well as other monkeys in cap and jerkin. You're a minstrel or a mountebank, I'll be sworn; you look for all the world as silly as a tumbler when he's been upside down and has got on his heels again. And what fools' tricks hast thou been after, Tessa?" she added, turning to her daughter, whose frightened face was more inviting to abuse. "Giving away the milk and victual, it seems; ay, ay, thou'dst carry water in thy ears for any idle vagabond that didn't like to stoop for it, thou silly staring rabbit! Turn thy back, and lift the herbs out of the panniers, else I'll make thee say a few Aves without counting."

"Nay, Madonna," said the stranger, with a pleading smile, "don't be angry with your pretty Tessa for taking pity on a hungry traveller, who found himself unexpectedly without a quattrino. Your handsome face looks so well when it frowns, that I long to see it illuminated by a smile."

"*Va via!* I know what paste you are made of. You may tickle me with that straw a good long while before I shall laugh, I can tell you. Get along, with a bad Easter! else I'll make a beauty spot or two on that face of yours that shall spoil your kissing on this side Advent."

As Monna Ghita lifted her formidable talons by way of complying with the first and last requisite of eloquence,* Bratti, who had come up a minute or two before, had been saying to his companion, "What think you of this pretty parrot, Nello? Doesn't his tongue smack of Venice?"

"Nay, Bratti," said the barber in an under-tone, "thy wisdom has much of the ass in it, as I told thee just now; especially about the ears. This stranger is a Greek, else I'm not the barber who has had the sole and exclusive shaving of the excellent Demetrio,* and drawn more than one sorry tooth from his learned jaw. And this youth might be taken to have come straight from Olympus—at least when he has had a touch of my razor."

"*Orsù!* Monna Ghita!" continued Nello, not sorry to see some sport; "what has happened to cause such a thunder-storm? Has this young stranger been misbehaving himself?"

"By San Giovanni!" said the cautious Bratti, who had not shaken off his original suspicions concerning the shabbily-clad possessor of jewels, "he did right to run away from *me*, if he meant to get into mischief. I can swear that I found him under the Loggia de' Cerchi, with a ring on his finger such as I've seen worn by Bernardo Rucellai* himself. Not another rusty nail's worth do I know about him."

"The fact is," said Nello, eying the stranger good-humouredly, "this *bello giovane* has been a little too presumptuous in admiring the charms of Monna Ghita, and has attempted to kiss her while her daughter's back is turned; for I observe that the pretty Tessa is too busy to look this way at present. Was it not so, Messer?" Nello concluded, in a tone of courtesy.

"You have divined the offence like a soothsayer," said the stranger, laughingly. "Only that I had not the good fortune to find Monna Ghita here at first. I begged a cup of milk from her daughter, and had accepted this gift of bread, for which I was making a humble offering of gratitude, before I had had the higher pleasure of being face to face with these riper charms which I was perhaps too bold in admiring."

"*Va, va!* be off, every one of you, and stay in purgatory till I pay to get you out, will you?" said Monna Ghita, fiercely, elbowing Nello, and leading forward her mule so as to compel the stranger to jump aside. "Tessa, thou simpleton, bring forward thy mule a bit—the cart will be upon us."

As Tessa turned to take the mule's bridle, she cast one timid glance at the stranger, who was now moving with Nello out of the way of an approaching market-cart; and the glance was just long enough to seize the beckoning movement of his hand, which indicated that he had been watching for this opportunity of an adieu.

"*Ebbene*," said Bratti, raising his voice to speak across the cart; "I leave you with Nello, young man, for there's no pushing my bag and basket any farther, and I have business at home. But you'll remember our bargain, because if you found Tessa without me, it was not my fault. Nello will show you my shop in the Ferravecchi, and I'll not turn my back on you."

"A thousand thanks, friend!" said the stranger, laughing, and then turned away with Nello up the narrow street which led most directly to the Piazza del Duomo.

CHAPTER III.

The Barber's Shop

"To tell you the truth," said the young stranger to Nello, as they got a little clearer of the entangled vehicles and mules, "I am not sorry to be handed over by that patron of mine to one who has a less barbarous accent, and a less enigmatical business. Is it a common thing among you Florentines for an itinerant trafficker in broken glass and rags to talk of a shop where he sells lutes and swords?"

"Common? No: our Bratti is not a common man. He has a theory, and lives up to it, which is more than I can say for any philosopher I have the honour of shaving," answered Nello, whose loquacity, like an over-full bottle, could never pour forth a small dose. "Bratti means to extract the utmost possible amount of pleasure, that is to say, of hard bargaining, out of this life; winding it up with a bargain for the easiest possible passage through purgatory, by giving Holy Church his winnings when the game is over. He has had his will made to that effect on the cheapest terms a notary could be got for. But I have often said to him, 'Bratti, thy bargain is a limping one, and thou art on the lame side of it. Does it not make thee a little sad to look at the pictures of the Paradiso? Thou wilt never be able there to chaffer for rags and rusty nails: the saints and angels want neither pins nor tinder; and except with San Bartolommeo, who carries his skin* about in an inconvenient manner, I see no chance of thy making a bargain for second-hand clothing.' But God pardon me," added Nello, changing his tone, and crossing himself, "this light talk ill beseems a morning when Lorenzo lies dead, and the Muses are tearing their hair*—always a painful thought to a barber; and you yourself, Messere, are probably under a cloud, for when a man of your speech and presence takes up with so sorry a night's lodging, it argues some misfortune to have befallen him."

"What Lorenzo is that whose death you speak of?" said the stranger, appearing to have dwelt with too anxious an interest on this point to have noticed the indirect inquiry that followed it.

"What Lorenzo? There is but one Lorenzo, I imagine, whose death could throw the Mercato into an uproar, set the lantern of the Duomo leaping in desperation, and cause the lions of the Republic to feel under an immediate necessity to devour one another. I mean Lorenzo de' Medici, the Pericles* of our Athens—if I may make such a comparison in the ear of a Greek."

"Why not?" said the other, laughingly; "for I doubt whether Athens, even in the days of Pericles, could have produced so learned a barber."

"Yes, yes; I thought I could not be mistaken," said the rapid Nello, "else I have shaved the venerable Demetrio Calcondila to little purpose; but pardon me, I am lost in wonder: your Italian is better than his, though he has been in Italy forty years—better even than that of the accomplished Marullo, who may be said to have married the Italic Muse in more senses than one, since he has married our learned and lovely Alessandra Scala."*

"It will lighten your wonder to know that I come of a Greek stock planted in Italian soil much longer than the mulberry-trees which have taken so kindly to it. I was born at Bari, and my—I mean, I was brought up by an Italian—and, in fact, I am a Greek very much as your peaches are Persian.* The Greek dye was subdued in me, I suppose, till I had been dipped over again by long abode and much travel in the land of gods and heroes. And, to confess something of my private affairs to you, this same Greek dye, with a few ancient gems I have about me, is the only fortune shipwreck has left me. But—when the towers fall, you know, it is an ill-business for the small nest-builders—the death of your Pericles makes me wish I had rather turned my steps towards Rome, as I should have done, but for a fallacious Minerva* in the shape of an Augustinian monk. 'At Rome,' he said, 'you will be lost in a crowd of hungry scholars; but at Florence, every corner is penetrated by the sunshine of Lorenzo's patronage: Florence is the best market in Italy for such commodities as yours.'"

"*Gnaffè*, and so it will remain, I hope," said Nello. "Lorenzo was not the only patron and judge of learning in our city—heaven forbid! Because he was a large melon, every other Florentine is not a pumpkin, I suppose. Have we not Bernardo Rucellai, and Alamanno Rinuccini,* and plenty more? And if you want to be informed on such matters, I, Nello, am your man. It seems to me a thousand years till I can be of service to a *bel erudito* like yourself. And, first of all, in the matter of your hair. That beard, my fine young man, must be parted with, were it as dear to you as the nymph of your dreams. Here at Florence, we love not to see a man with his nose projecting over a cascade of hair. But, remember, you will have passed the Rubicon,* when once you have been shaven: if you repent, and let your beard grow after it has acquired stoutness by a struggle with the razor, your mouth will by and by show no longer what Messer Angelo* calls the divine prerogative of lips, but will appear like a dark cavern fringed with horrent brambles."

"That is a terrible prophecy," said the Greek, "especially if your Florentine maidens are many of them as pretty as the little Tessa I stole a kiss from this morning."

"Tessa? she is a rough-handed contadina: you will rise into the favour of dames who bring no scent of the mule-stables with them. But to that end, you must not have the air of a *sgherro*, or a man of evil repute: you must look like a courtier, and a scholar of the more polished sort, such as our Pietro Crinito*—like one who sins among well-bred, well-fed people, and not one who sucks down vile *vino di sotto* in a chance tavern."

"With all my heart," said the stranger. "If the Florentine Graces demand it, I am willing to give up this small matter of my beard, but—"

"Yes, yes," interrupted Nello. "I know what you would say.

It is the *bella zazzera*—the hyacinthine locks,* you do not choose to part with; and there is no need. Just a little pruning—ecco!—and you will look not unlike the illustrious prince Pico di Mirandola* in his prime. And here we are in good time in the Piazza San Giovanni, and at the door of my shop. But you are pausing, I see: naturally, you want to look at our wonder of the world, our Duomo, our Santa Maria del Fiore. Well, well, a mere glance; but I beseech you to leave a closer survey till you have been shaved: I am quivering with the inspiration of my art even to the very edge of my razor. Ah, then, come round this way."

The mercurial barber seized the arm of the stranger, and led him to a point, on the south side of the piazza, from which he could see at once the huge dark shell of the cupola, the slender soaring grace of Giotto's campanile, and the quaint octagon of San Giovanni in front of them, showing its unique gates of storied bronze,* which still bore the somewhat dimmed glory of their original gilding. The inlaid marbles were then fresher in their pink and white and purple than they are now, when the winters of four centuries have turned their white to the rich ochre of well-mellowed meerschaum; the façade of the Cathedral did not stand ignominious in faded stucco, but had upon it the magnificent promise of the half-completed marble inlaying and statued niches, which Giotto had devised a hundred and fifty years before; and as the campanile in all its harmonious variety of colour and form led the eyes upward, high into the clear air of this April morning, it seemed a prophetic symbol, telling that human life must somehow and some time shape itself into accord with that pure aspiring beauty.

But this was not the impression it appeared to produce on the Greek. His eyes were irresistibly led upward, but as he stood with his arms folded and his curls falling backward, there was a slight touch of scorn on his lip, and when his eyes fell again, they glanced round with a scanning coolness which was rather piquing to Nello's Florentine spirit.

"Well, my fine young man," he said, with some impatience, "you seem to make as little of our Cathedral as if you were the angel Gabriel come straight from paradise. I should like to know if you have ever seen finer work than our Giotto's tower, or any cupola that would not look a mere mushroom by the side of Brunelleschi's there, or any marbles finer or more cunningly wrought than these that our Signoria got from far-off quarries, at a price that would buy a dukedom. Come, now, have you ever seen anything to equal them?"

"If you asked me that question with a scimitar at my throat, after the Turkish fashion, or even your own razor," said the young Greek, smiling gaily, and moving on towards the gates of the Baptistery, "I daresay you might get a confession of the true faith from me. But with my throat free from peril, I venture to tell you that your buildings smack too much of Christian barbarism for my taste. I have a shuddering sense of what there is inside—hideous smoked Madonnas; fleshless saints in mosaic, staring down idiotic astonishment and rebuke from the apse; skin-clad skeletons hanging on crosses, or stuck all over with arrows, or stretched on gridirons; women and monks with heads aside in perpetual lamentation. I have seen enough of those wry-necked favourites of heaven at Constantinople. But what is this bronze door rough with imagery?* These women's figures seem moulded in a different spirit from those starved and staring saints I spoke of: these heads in high relief speak of a human mind within them, instead of looking like an index to perpetual spasms and colic."

"Yes, yes," said Nello, with some triumph. "I think we shall show you by and by that our Florentine art is not in a state of barbarism. These gates, my fine young man, were moulded half a century ago, by our Lorenzo Ghiberti, when he counted hardly so many years as you do."*

"Ah, I remember," said the stranger, turning away, like one whose appetite for contemplation was soon satisfied. "I have heard that your Tuscan sculptors and painters have been studying the antique a little. But with monks for models, and the legends of mad hermits and martyrs for subjects, the vision of Olympus itself would be of small use to them."

"I understand," said Nello, with a significant shrug, as they walked along. "You are of the same mind as Michele Marullo, aye, and as Angelo Poliziano himself, in spite of his canonicate,* when he relaxes himself a little in my shop, after his lectures, and talks of the gods awaking from their long sleep and making the woods and streams vital once more. But he rails against the Roman scholars who want to make us all talk Latin again: 'My ears,' he says, 'are sufficiently flayed by the barbarisms of the learned, and if the vulgar are to talk Latin I would as soon have been in Florence the day they took to beating all the kettles in the city because the bells were not enough to stay the wrath of the saints.' Ah, Messer Greco, if you want to know the flavour of our scholarship, you must frequent my shop: it is the focus of Florentine intellect, and in that sense the navel of the earth—as my great predecessor, Burchiello,* said of *his* shop, on the more frivolous pretension that his street of the Calimala was the centre of our city. And here we are at the sign of 'Apollo and the Razor.' Apollo, you see, is bestowing the razor on the Triptolemus* of our craft, the first reaper of beards, the sublime *Anonimo*, whose mysterious identity is indicated by a shadowy hand."

"I see thou hast had custom already, Sandro," continued Nello, addressing a solemn-looking dark-eyed youth, who made way for them on the threshold. "And now make all clear for this signor to sit down. And prepare the finest-scented lather, for he has a learned and a handsome chin."

"You have a pleasant little adytum* there, I see," said the stranger, looking through a latticed screen which divided the shop from a room of about equal size, opening on to a still smaller walled enclosure, where a few bays and laurels surrounded a stone Hermes. "I suppose your conclave of *eruditi* meets there?"

"There, and not less in my shop," said Nello, leading the way into the inner room, in which were some benches, a table, with one book in manuscript and one printed in capitals lying open upon it, a lute, a few oil-sketches, and a model or two of hands and ancient masks. "For my shop is a no less fitting haunt of the Muses, as you will acknowledge when you feel the sudden illumination of understanding and the serene vigour of inspiration that will come to you with a clear chin. Ah! you can make that lute discourse, I perceive. I, too, have some skill that way, though the serenata is useless when daylight discloses a visage like mine, looking no fresher than an apple that has stood the winter. But look at that sketch—it is a fancy of Piero di Cosimo's,* a strange freakish painter, who says he saw it by long looking at a mouldy wall."

The sketch Nello pointed to represented three masks—one a drunken laughing Satyr, another a sorrowing Magdalen, and the third, which lay between them, the rigid, cold face of a Stoic: the masks rested obliquely on the lap of a little child, whose cherub features rose above them with something of the supernal promise in the gaze which painters had by that time learned to give to the Divine Infant.

"A symbolical picture, I see," said the young Greek, touching the lute while he spoke, so as to bring out a slight musical murmur. "The child, perhaps, is the Golden Age, wanting neither worship nor philosophy. And the Golden Age can always come back as long as men are born in the form of babies, and don't come into the world in cassock or furred mantle. Or the child may mean the wise philosophy of Epicurus,* removed alike from the gross, the sad, and the severe."

"Ah! everybody has his own interpretation for that picture," said Nello; "and if you ask Piero himself what he meant by it, he says his pictures are an appendix which Messer Domeneddio has been pleased to make to the universe, and if any man is in doubt what they mean, he had better inquire of Holy Church. He has been asked to paint a picture after the sketch, but he puts his fingers to his ears and shakes his head at that: the fancy is past, he says—a strange animal, our Piero. But now all is ready for your initiation into the mysteries of the razor."

"Mysteries they may well be called," continued the barber, with rising spirits at the prospect of a long monologue, as he imprisoned the young Greek in the shroud-like shaving-cloth; "mysteries of Minerva and the Graces.* I get the flower of men's thoughts, because I seize them in the first moment after shaving. (Ah! you wince a little at the lather: it tickles the outlying limits of the nose, I admit.) And that is what makes the peculiar fitness of a barber's shop to become a resort of wit and learning. For, look now at a druggist's shop: there is a dull conclave at the sign of 'The Moor'* that pretends to rival mine; but what sort of inspiration, I beseech you, can be got from the scent of nauseous vegetable decoctions?—to say nothing of the fact that you no sooner pass the threshold than you see a doctor of physic, like a gigantic spider disguised in fur and scarlet, waiting for his prey; or even see him blocking up the doorway seated on a bony hack, inspecting saliva. (Your chin a little elevated, if it please you: contemplate that angel who is blowing the trumpet at you from the ceiling. I had it painted expressly for the regulation of my clients' chins.) Besides, your druggist, who herborises and decocts, is a man of prejudices: he has poisoned people according to a system, and is obliged to stand up for his system to justify the consequences. Now a barber can be dispassionate; the only thing he necessarily stands by is the razor, always providing he is not an author. That was the flaw in my great predecessor Burchiello—he was a poet, and had consequently a prejudice about his own poetry. I have escaped that; I saw very early that authorship is a narrowing business, in conflict with the liberal art of the razor, which demands an impartial affection for all men's chins. Ecco, Messer! the outline of your chin and lip is as clear as a maiden's; and now fix your mind on a knotty question—ask yourself whether you are bound to spell Virgil with an *i* or an *e*, and say if you do not feel an unwonted clearness on the point. Only, if you decide for the *i*, keep it to yourself till your fortune is made, for the *e* hath the stronger following in Florence.* Ah! I think I see a gleam of still quicker wit in your eye. I have it on the authority of our young Niccolò Macchiavelli, himself keen enough to discern *il pelo nell' uovo*,* as we say, and a great lover of delicate shaving, though his beard is hardly of two years' date, that no sooner do the hairs begin to push themselves, than he perceives a certain grossness of apprehension creeping over him."

"Suppose you let me look at myself," said the stranger, laughing. "The happy effect on my intellect is perhaps obstructed by a little doubt as to the effect on my appearance."

"Behold yourself in this mirror, then; it is a Venetian mirror from Murano, the true *nosce teipsum*,* as I have named it, compared with which the finest mirror of steel or silver is mere darkness. See now, how by diligent shaving, the nether region of your face may preserve its human outline, instead of presenting no distinction from the physiognomy of a bearded owl or a Barbary ape. I have seen men whose beards have so invaded their cheeks, that one might have pitied them as the victims of a sad, brutalizing chastisement befitting our Dante's *Inferno*, if they had not seemed to strut with a strange triumph in their extravagant hairiness."

"I seems to me," said the Greek, still looking into the mirror, "that you have taken away some of my capital with your razor—I mean a year or two of age, which might have won me more ready credit for my learning. Under the inspection of a patron whose vision has grown somewhat dim, I shall have a perilous resemblance to a maiden of eighteen in the disguise of hose and jerkin."

"Not at all," said Nello, proceeding to clip the too extravagant curls; "your proportions are not those of a maiden. And for your age, I myself remember seeing Angelo Poliziano begin his lectures on the Latin language when he had a younger beard than yours; and between ourselves, his juvenile ugliness was not less signal than his precocious scholarship. Whereas you—no, no, your age is not against you; but between ourselves, let me hint to you that your being a Greek, though it be only an Apulian Greek, is not in your favour. Certain of our scholars hold that your Greek learning is but a wayside degenerate plant until it has been transplanted into Italian brains, and that now there is such a plentiful crop of the superior quality, your native teachers are mere propagators of degeneracy. Ecco! your curls are now of the right proportion to neck and shoulders; rise, Messer, and I will free you from the encumbrance of this cloth. *Gnaffè!* I almost advise you to retain the faded jerkin and hose a little longer; they give you the air of a fallen prince."

"But the question is," said the young Greek, leaning against the high back of a chair, and returning Nello's contemplative admiration with a look of inquiring anxiety; "the question is, in what quarter I am to carry my princely air, so as to rise from the said fallen condition. If your Florentine patrons of learning share this scholarly hostility to the Greeks, I see not how your city can be a hospitable refuge for me, as you seemed to say just now."

"*Pian piano*—not so fast," said Nello, sticking his thumbs into his belt and nodding to Sandro to restore order. "I will not conceal from you that there is a prejudice against Greeks among us; and though, as a barber unsnared by authorship, I share no prejudices, I must admit that the Greeks are not always such pretty youngsters as yourself: their erudition is often of an uncombed, unmannerly aspect, and encrusted with a barbarous utterance of Italian, that makes their converse hardly more euphonious than that of a Tedesco in a state of vinous loquacity. And then, again, excuse me—we Florentines have liberal ideas about speech, and consider that an instrument which can flatter and promise so cleverly as the tongue, must have been partly made for those purposes; and that truth is a riddle for eyes and wit to discover, which it were a mere spoiling of sport for the tongue to betray. Still we have our limits beyond which we call dissimulation treachery. But it is said of the

Greeks that their honesty begins at what is the hanging-point with us, and that since the old Furies* went to sleep, your Christian Greek is of so easy a conscience that he would make a stepping-stone of his father's corpse."

The flush on the stranger's face indicated what seemed so natural a movement of resentment, that the good-natured Nello hastened to atone for his want of reticence.

"Be not offended, *bel giovane*; I am but repeating what I hear in my shop; as you may perceive, my eloquence is simply the cream which I skim off my clients' talk. Heaven forbid I should fetter my impartiality by entertaining an opinion. And for that same scholarly objection to the Greeks," added Nello, in a more mocking tone, and with a significant grimace, "the fact is, you are heretics, Messer; jealousy has nothing to do with it: if you would just change your opinion about leaven, and alter your Doxology* a little, our Italian scholars would think it a thousand years till they could give up their chairs to you. Yes, yes; it is chiefly religious scruple, and partly also the authority of a great classic,—Juvenal, is it not? He, I gather, had his bile as much stirred by the swarm of Greeks as our Messer Angelo, who is fond of quoting some passage about their incorrigible impudence—*audacia perdita*."

"Pooh! the passage is a compliment," said the Greek, who had recovered himself, and seemed wise enough to take the matter gaily—

> 'Ingenium velox, audacia perdita, sermo
> Promptus, et Isæo torrentior.'*

A rapid intellect and ready eloquence may carry off a little impudence."

"Assuredly," said Nello. "And since, as I see, you know Latin literature as well as Greek, you will not fall into the mistake of Giovanni Argiropulo, who ran full tilt against Cicero,* and pronounced him all but a pumpkin-head. For, let me give you one bit of advice, young man—trust a barber who has shaved the best chins, and kept his eyes and ears open for twenty years—oil your tongue well when you talk of the ancient Latin writers, and give it an extra dip when you talk of the modern. A wise Greek may win favour among us; witness our excellent Demetrio, who is loved by many, and not hated immoderately even by the most renowned scholars."

"I discern the wisdom of your advice so clearly," said the Greek, with the bright smile which was continually lighting up the fine form and colour of his young face, "that I will ask you for a little more. Who now, for example, would be the most likely patron for me? Is there a son of Lorenzo who inherits his tastes? Or is there any other wealthy Florentine specially addicted to purchasing antique gems? I have a fine Cleopatra cut in sardonyx, and one or two other intaglios and cameos,* both curious and beautiful, worthy of being added to the cabinet of a prince. Happily, I had taken the precaution of fastening them within the lining of my doublet before I set out on my voyage. Moreover, I should like to raise a small sum for my present need on this ring of mine" (here he took out the ring and replaced it on his finger), "if you could recommend me to any honest trafficker."

"Let us see, let us see," said Nello, perusing the floor, and walking up and down the length of his shop. "This is no time to apply to Piero de' Medici, though he has the will to make such purchases if he could always spare the money; but I think it is another sort of Cleopatra that he covets most.* . . . Yes, yes, I have it. What you want is a man of wealth, and influence, and scholarly tastes—not one of your learned porcupines, bristling all over with critical tests, but one whose Greek and Latin are of a comfortable laxity. And that man is Bartolommeo Scala, the secretary of our Republic. He came to Florence as a poor adventurer himself—a miller's son—a 'branny monster,'* as he has been nicknamed by our honey-lipped Poliziano, who agrees with him as well as my teeth agree with lemon-juice. And, by the by, that may be a reason why the secretary may be the more ready to do a good turn to a strange scholar. For, between you and me, *bel giovane*—trust a barber who has shaved the best scholars—friendliness is much such a steed as Ser Benghi's:* it will hardly show much alacrity unless it has got the thistle of hatred under its tail. However, the secretary is a man who'll keep his word to you, even to the halving of a fennel seed;* and he is not unlikely to buy some of your gems."

"But how am I to get at this great man?" said the Greek, rather impatiently.

"I was coming to that," said Nello. "Just now everybody of any public importance will be full of Lorenzo's death, and a stranger may find it difficult to get any notice. But in the meantime, I could take you to a man who, if he has a mind, can help you to a chance of a favourable interview with Scala sooner than anybody else in Florence—worth seeing for his own sake too, to say nothing of his collections, or of his daughter Romola, who is as fair as the Florentine lily before it got quarrelsome, and turned red."*

"But if this father of the beautiful Romola makes collections, why should he not like to buy some of my gems himself?"

Nello shrugged his shoulders. "For two good reasons—want of sight to look at the gems, and want of money to pay for them. Our old Bardo de' Bardi is so blind that he can see no more of his daughter than, as he says, a glimmering of something bright when she comes very near him: doubtless her golden hair, which, as Messer Luigi Pulci says of his Meridiana's, '*raggia come stella per sereno*.'* Ah! here come some clients of mine, and I shouldn't wonder if one of them could serve your turn about that ring."

CHAPTER IV.

First Impressions

"GOOD DAY, Messer Domenico," said Nello to the foremost of the two visitors who entered the shop, while he nodded silently to the other. "You come as opportunely as cheese on macaroni.* Ah! you are in haste—wish to be shaved without delay—ecco! And this is a morning when every one has grave matter on his mind. Florence orphaned—the very pivot of Italy snatched away—heaven itself at a loss what to do next. *Oimè!* Well, well; the sun is nevertheless travelling on towards dinner-time again; and, as I was saying, you come like cheese ready grated. For this young stranger was wishing for an honourable trader who would advance him a sum on a certain ring of value, and if I had counted every goldsmith and money-lender in Florence on my fingers, I couldn't have found a better name than Menico Cennini. Besides, he hath other ware in which you deal—Greek learning, and young eyes—a double implement which you printers are always in need of."

The grave elderly man, son of that Bernardo Cennini,* who,

twenty years before, having heard of the new process of printing carried on by Germans, had cast his own types in Florence, remained necessarily in lathered silence and passivity while Nello showered this talk in his ears, but turned a slow sideway gaze on the stranger.

"This fine young man has unlimited Greek, Latin, or Italian at your service," continued Nello, fond of interpreting by very ample paraphrase. "He is as great a wonder of juvenile learning as Francesco Filelfo or our own incomparable Poliziano. A second Guarino,* too, for he has had the misfortune to be shipwrecked, and has doubtless lost a store of precious manuscripts that might have contributed some correctness even to your correct editions, Domenico. Fortunately, he has rescued a few gems of rare value. His name is—you said your name, Messer, was—?"

"Tito Melema," said the stranger, slipping the ring from his finger, and presenting it to Cennini, whom Nello, not less rapid with his razor than with his tongue, had now released from the shaving-cloth.

Meanwhile the man who had entered the shop in company with the goldsmith—a tall figure, about fifty,* with a short trimmed beard, wearing an old felt hat and a threadbare mantle—had kept his eye fixed on the Greek, and now said abruptly,

"Young man, I am painting a picture of Sinon deceiving old Priam,* and I should be glad of your face for my Sinon, if you'd give me a sitting."

Tito Melema started and looked round with a pale astonishment in his face as if at a sudden accusation; but Nello left him no time to feel at a loss for an answer: "Piero," said the barber, "thou art the most extraordinary compound of humours and fancies ever packed into a human skin. What trick wilt thou play with the fine visage of this young scholar to make it suit thy traitor? Ask him rather to turn his eyes upward, and thou may'st make a Saint Sebastian of him that will draw troops of devout women,* or, if thou art in a classical vein, put myrtle about his curls and make him a young Bacchus, or say rather a Phœbus Apollo, for his face is as warm and bright as a summer morning; it made me his friend in the space of a 'credo.'"*

"Aye, Nello," said the painter, speaking with abrupt pauses; "and if thy tongue can leave off its everlasting chirping long enough for thy understanding to consider the matter, thou may'st see that thou hast just shown the reason why the face of

Messere will suit my traitor. A perfect traitor should have a face which vice can write no marks on—lips that will lie with a dimpled smile—eyes of such agate-like brightness and depth that no infamy can dull them—cheeks that will rise from a murder and not look haggard. I say not this young man is a traitor: I mean, he has a face that would make him the more perfect traitor if he had the heart of one, which is saying neither more nor less than that he has a beautiful face, informed with rich young blood, that will be nourished enough by food, and keep its colour without much help of virtue. He may have the heart of a hero along with it; I aver nothing to the contrary. Ask Domenico there if the lapidaries can always tell a gem by the sight alone. And now I'm going to put the tow in my ears, for thy chatter and the bells together are more than I can endure; so say no more to me, but trim my beard."

With these last words Piero (called "di Cosimo," from his master, Cosimo Rosselli) drew out two bits of tow, stuffed them in his ears, and placed himself in the chair before Nello, who shrugged his shoulders and cast a grimacing look of intelligence at the Greek, as much as to say, "A whimsical fellow, you perceive! Everybody holds his speeches as mere jokes."

Tito, who had stood transfixed, with his long dark eyes resting on the unknown man who had addressed him so equivocally, seemed recalled to his self-command by Piero's change of position, and, apparently satisfied with his explanation, was again giving his attention to Cennini, who presently said,—

"This is a curious and a valuable ring, young man. This intaglio of the fish with the crested serpent above it, in the black stratum of the onyx, or rather nicolo, is well shown by the surrounding blue of the upper stratum. The ring has, doubtless, a history?" added Cennini, looking up keenly at the young stranger.

"Yes, indeed," said Tito, meeting the scrutiny very frankly. "The ring was found in Sicily, and I have understood from those who busy themselves with gems and sigils, that both the stone and intaglio are of virtue to make the wearer fortunate, especially at sea, and also to restore to him whatever he may have lost.* But," he continued, smiling, "though I have worn it constantly since I quitted Greece, it has not made me altogether fortunate at sea, you perceive, unless I am to count escape from drowning as a sufficient proof of its virtue. It remains to be seen whether my lost chests will come to light; but to lose no chance of such a result, Messer, I will pray you only to hold the ring for a short space as pledge for a small sum far beneath its value, and I will redeem it as soon as I can dispose of certain other gems which are secured within my doublet, or indeed as soon as I can earn something by any scholarly employment, if I may be so fortunate as to meet with such."

"That may be seen, young man, if you will come with me," said Cennini. "My brother Pietro, who is a better judge of scholarship than I, will perhaps be able to supply you with a task that may test your capabilities. Meanwhile, take back your ring until I can hand you the necessary florins, and, if it please you, come along with me."

"Yes, yes," said Nello, "go with Messer Domenico, you cannot go in better company; he was born under the constellation that gives a man skill, riches, and integrity, whatever that constellation may be, which is of the less consequence because babies can't choose their own horoscopes, and indeed, if they could, there might be an inconvenient rush of babies at particular epochs. Besides, our Phœnix, the incomparable Pico, has shown that your horoscopes are all a nonsensical dream*—which is the less troublesome opinion. *Addio! bel giovane!* don't forget to come back to me."

"No fear of that," said Tito, beckoning a farewell, as he turned round his bright face at the door. "You are to do me a great service:—that is the most positive security for your seeing me again."

"Say what thou wilt, Piero," said Nello, as the young stranger disappeared, "I shall never look at such an outside as that without taking it as a sign of a loveable nature. Why, thou wilt say next that Lionardo, whom thou art always raving about, ought to have made his Judas as beautiful as St. John!* But thou art as deaf as the top of Mount Morello with that accursed tow in thy ears. Well, well: I'll get a little more of this young man's history from him before I take him to Bardo Bardi."

CHAPTER V.

The Blind Scholar and his Daughter

THE Via de' Bardi, a street noted in the history of Florence, lies in Oltrarno, or that portion of the city which clothes the southern bank of the river. It extends from the Ponte Vecchio to the Piazza de' Mozzi at the head of the Ponte alle Grazie; its right-hand line of houses and walls being backed by the rather steep ascent which in the fifteenth century was known as the Hill of Bogoli, the famous stone-quarry whence the city got its pavement—of dangerously unstable consistence when penetrated by rains; its left-hand buildings flanking the river and making on their northern side a length of quaint, irregularly-pierced façade, of which the waters give a softened loving reflection as the sun begins to decline towards the western heights. But quaint as these buildings are, some of them seem to the historical memory a too modern substitute for the famous houses of the Bardi family, destroyed by popular rage in the middle of the fourteenth century.

They were a proud and energetic stock, these Bardi: conspicuous among those who clutched the sword in the earliest world-famous quarrels of Florentines with Florentines, when the narrow streets were darkened with the high towers of the nobles, and when the old tutelar god Mars, as he saw the gutters reddened with neighbours' blood, might well have smiled at the centuries of lip-service paid to his rival, the Baptist.* But the Bardi hands were of the sort that not only clutch the sword-hilt with vigour, but love the more delicate pleasure of fingering minted metal: they were matched, too, with true Florentine eyes, capable of discerning that power was to be won by other means than by rending and riving, and by the middle of the fourteenth century we find them risen from their original condition of *popolani* to be possessors, by purchase, of lands and strongholds, and the feudal dignity of Counts of Vernio, disturbing to the jealousy of their republican fellow-citizens. These lordly purchases are explained by our seeing the Bardi disastrously signalized only a few years later as standing in the very front of European commerce—the Christian Rothschilds of that time—undertaking to furnish specie for the wars of our Edward the Third, and having revenues "in kind" made over to them; especially in wool, most precious of freights for Florentine Galleys. Their august debtor left them with an august deficit, and alarmed Sicilian creditors made a too sudden demand for the payment of deposits, causing a ruinous shock to the credit of the Bardi and that of associated houses, which was felt as a commercial calamity along all the coasts of the Mediterranean. But, like more modern bankrupts, they did not, for all that, hide their heads in humiliation; on the contrary, they seemed to have held them higher than ever, and to have been among the most arrogant of those grandees, who under certain noteworthy circumstances, open to all who will read the honest pages of Giovanni Villani,* drew upon themselves the exasperation of the armed people in 1343. The Bardi, who had made themselves fast in their street between the two bridges, kept these narrow inlets, like panthers at bay, against the oncoming gonfalons of the people, and were only made to give way by an assault from the hill behind them. Their houses by the river, to the number of twenty-two (*palagi e case grandi*), were sacked and burnt, and many among the chief of those who bore the Bardi name were driven from the city. But an old Florentine family was many-rooted, and we find the Bardi maintaining importance and rising again and again to the surface of Florentine affairs in a more or less creditable manner, implying an untold family history that would have included even more vicissitudes and contrasts of dignity and disgrace, of wealth and poverty, than are usually seen on the background of wide kinship.* But the Bardi never resumed their proprietorship in the old street on the banks of the river, which in 1492 had long been associated with other names of mark, and especially with the Neri, who possessed a considerable range of houses on the side towards the hill.

In one of these Neri houses there lived, however, a descendant of the Bardi, and of that very branch which a century and a half before had become Counts of Vernio: a descendant who had inherited the old family pride and energy, the old love of pre-eminence, the old desire to leave a lasting track of his footsteps on the fast-whirling earth. But the family passions lived on in him under altered conditions: this descendant of the Bardi was not a man swift in street warfare, or one who loved to play the signor, fortifying strongholds and asserting the right to hang vassals, or a merchant and usurer of keen daring, who delighted in the generalship of wide commercial schemes: he was a man with a deep-veined hand cramped by much copying of manuscripts, who ate sparing dinners, and wore threadbare clothes, at first from choice and at last from necessity; who sat among his books and his marble fragments of the past, and saw them only by the light of those far-off younger days which still shone in his memory: he was a moneyless, blind old scholar—the Bardo de' Bardi to whom Nello, the barber, had promised to introduce the young Greek, Tito Melema.

The house in which Bardo lived was situated on the side of the street nearest the hill, and was one of those large sombre masses of stone building pierced by comparatively small windows, and surmounted by what may be called a roofed terrace or loggia, of which there are many examples still to be seen in the venerable city. Grim doors, with conspicuous scrolled hinges, having high up on each side of them a small window defended by iron bars, opened on a groined entrance court, empty of everything but a massive lamp-iron suspended from the centre of the groin. A smaller grim door on the left hand admitted to the stone staircase, and the rooms on the ground floor. These last were used as a warehouse by the proprietor; so was the first floor; and both were filled with precious stores, destined to be carried, some perhaps to the banks of the Scheldt, some to the shores of Africa, some to the isles of the Egean, or to the banks of the Euxine.* Maso, the old serving-man, when he returned from the Mercato, with the stock of cheap vegetables, had to make his slow way up to the second story before he reached the door of his master, Bardo, through which we are about to enter only a few mornings after Nello's conversation with the Greek.

We follow Maso across the antechamber to the door on the left hand, through which we pass as he opens it. He merely looks in and nods, while a clear young voice says, "Ah, you are come back, Maso. It is well. We have wanted nothing."

The voice came from the farther end of a long, spacious room, surrounded with shelves, on which books and antiquities were arranged in scrupulous order. Here and there, on separate stands in front of the shelves, were placed a beautiful feminine torso; a headless statue, with an uplifted muscular arm wielding a bladeless sword; rounded, dimpled, infantine limbs severed from the trunk, inviting the lips to kiss the cold marble; some well-preserved Roman busts; and two or three vases from

Magna Græcia.* A large table in the centre was covered with antique bronze lamps and small vessels in dark pottery. The colour of these objects was chiefly pale or sombre: the vellum bindings, with their deep-ridged backs, gave little relief to the marble livid with long burial; the once splendid patch of carpet at the farther end of the room had long been worn to dimness; the dark bronzes wanted sunlight upon them to bring out their tinge of green, and the sun was not yet high enough to send gleams of brightness through the narrow windows that looked on the Via de' Bardi.

The only spot of bright colour in the room was made by the hair of a tall maiden of seventeen or eighteen, who was standing before a carved *leggio*, or reading-desk, such as is often seen in the choir of Italian churches. The hair was of a reddish gold colour, enriched by an unbroken small ripple, such as may be seen in the sunset clouds on grandest autumnal evenings. It was confined by a black fillet above her small ears, from which it rippled forward again, and made a natural veil for her neck above her square-cut gown of black rascia, or serge. Her eyes were bent on a large volume placed before her: one long white hand rested on the reading-desk, and the other clasped the back of her father's chair.

The blind father sat with head uplifted and turned a little aside towards his daughter, as if he were looking at her. His delicate paleness, set off by the black velvet cap which surmounted his drooping white hair, made all the more perceptible the likeness between his aged features and those of the young maiden, whose cheeks were also without any tinge of the rose. There was the same refinement of brow and nostril in both, counterbalanced by a full though firm mouth and powerful chin, which gave an expression of proud tenacity and latent impetuousness: an expression carried out in the backward poise of the girl's head, and the grand line of her neck and shoulders. It was a type of face of which one could not venture to say whether it would inspire love or only that unwilling admiration which is mixed with dread: the question must be decided by the eyes, which often seem charged with a more direct message from the soul. But the eyes of the father had long been silent, and the eyes of the daughter were bent on the Latin pages of Politian's *Miscellanea*,* from which she was reading aloud at the eightieth chapter, to the following effect:—

"There was a certain nymph of Thebes named Chariclo, espe-
"cially dear to Pallas; and this nymph was the mother of "Teiresias. But once when in the heat of summer, Pallas, in "company with Chariclo, was bathing her disrobed limbs in the "Heliconian Hippocrene, it happened that Teiresias coming as a "hunter to quench his thirst at the same fountain, inadvertently "beheld Minerva unveiled, and immediately became blind. For "it is declared in the Saturnian laws, that he who beholds the "gods against their will, shall atone for it by a heavy penalty. . . . "When Teiresias had fallen into this calamity, Pallas, moved by "the tears of Chariclo, endowed him with prophecy and length "of days, and even caused his prudence and wisdom to continue "after he had entered among the shades, so that an oracle spake "from his tomb: and she gave him a staff, wherewith, as by a "guide, he might walk without stumbling. . . . And hence "Nonnus, in the fifth book of the *Dionysiaca*,* introduces "Actæon exclaiming that he calls Teiresias happy, since, without "dying, and with the loss of his eyesight merely, he had beheld "Minerva unveiled, and thus, though blind, could for evermore "carry her image in his soul."

At this point in the reading, the daughter's hand slipped from the back of the chair and met her father's, which he had that moment uplifted; but she had not looked round, and was going on, though with a voice a little altered by some suppressed feeling, to read the Greek quotation from Nonnus, when the old man said—

"Stay, Romola; reach me my own copy of Nonnus. It is a more correct copy than any in Poliziano's hands, for I made emendations in it which have not yet been communicated to any man. I finished it in 1477, when my sight was fast failing me."

Romola walked to the farther end of the room, with the queenly step which was the simple action of her tall, finely-wrought frame, without the slightest conscious adjustment of herself.

"Is it in the right place, Romola?" asked Bardo, who was perpetually seeking the assurance that the outward fact continued to correspond with the image which lived to the minutest detail in his mind.

"Yes, father; at the west end of the room, on the third shelf from the bottom, behind the bust of Hadrian, above Apollonius Rhodius and Callimachus, and below Lucan and Silius Italicus."

As Romola said this, a fine ear would have detected in her clear voice and distinct utterance, a faint suggestion of weariness struggling with habitual patience. But as she approached her father and saw his arms stretched out a little with nervous excitement to seize the volume, her hazel eyes filled with pity; she hastened to lay the book on his lap, and kneeled down by him, looking up at him as if she believed that the love in her face must surely make its way through the dark obstruction that shut out everything else. At that moment the doubtful attractiveness of Romola's face, in which pride and passion seemed to be quivering in the balance with native refinement and intelligence, was transfigured to the most loveable womanliness by mingled pity and affection: it was evident that the deepest fount of feeling within her had not yet wrought its way to the less changeful features, and only found its outlet through her eyes.

But the father, unconscious of that soft radiance, looked flushed and agitated as his hand explored the edges and back of the large book.

"The vellum is yellowed in these thirteen years, Romola."

"Yes, father," said Romola, gently; "but your letters at the back are dark and plain still—fine Roman letters; and the Greek character," she continued, laying the book open on her father's knee, "is more beautiful than that of any of your bought manuscripts."

"Assuredly, child," said Bardo, passing his finger across the page, as if he hoped to discriminate line and margin. "What hired amanuensis can be equal to the scribe who loves the words that grow under his hand, and to whom an error or indistinctness in the text is more painful than a sudden darkness or obstacle across his path? And even these mechanical printers who threaten to make learning a base and vulgar thing—even they must depend on the manuscripts over which we scholars have bent with that insight into the poet's meaning which is closely akin to the *mens divinior** of the poet himself; unless they would flood the world with grammatical falsities and inexplicable anomalies that would turn the very fountains of Parnassus* into a deluge of poisonous mud. But find the passage in the fifth book, to which Poliziano refers—I know it very well."

Seating herself on a low stool, close to her father's knee, Romola took the book on her lap and read the four verses containing the exclamation of Actæon.

"It is true, Romola," said Bardo, when she had finished; "it is a true conception of the poet; for what is that grosser, narrower light by which men behold merely the petty scene around them, compared with that far-stretching, lasting light which spreads over centuries of thought, and over the life of nations, and makes clear to us the minds of the immortals who have reaped the great harvest and left us to glean in their furrows? For me, Romola, even when I could see, it was with the great dead that I lived; while the living often seemed to me mere spectres—shadows dispossessed of true feeling and intelligence; and unlike those Lamiæ,* to whom Poliziano, with that superficial ingenuity which I do not deny to him, compares our inquisitive Florentines, because they put on their eyes when they went abroad, and took them off when they got home again, I have returned from the converse of the streets as from a forgotten dream, and have sat down among my books, saying with Petrarca, the modern who is least unworthy to be named after the ancients, 'Libri medullitus delectant, colloquuntur, consulunt, et viva quadam nobis atque arguta familiaritate junguntur.' "*

"And in one thing you are happier than your favourite Petrarca, father," said Romola, affectionately humouring the old man's disposition to dilate in this way; "for he used to look at his copy of Homer and think sadly that the Greek was a dead letter to him: so far, he had the inward blindness that you feel is worse than your outward blindness."

"True, child; for I carry within me the fruits of that fervid study which I gave to the Greek tongue under the teaching of the younger Crisolora,* and Filelfo, and Argiropulo, though that great work in which I had desired to gather, as into a firm web, all the threads that my research had laboriously disentangled, and which would have been the vintage of my life, was cut off by the failure of my sight and my want of a fitting coadjutor. For the sustained zeal and unconquerable patience demanded from those who would tread the unbeaten paths of knowledge are still less reconcileable with the wandering, vagrant propensity of the feminine mind than with the feeble powers of the feminine body."

"Father," said Romola, with a sudden flush and in an injured tone, "I read anything you wish me to read; and I will look out any passages for you, and make whatever notes you want."

Bardo shook his head, and smiled with a bitter sort of pity. "As well try to be a pentathlos* and perform all the five feats of the palæstra with the limbs of a nymph. Have I forgotten thy fainting in the mere search for the references I needed to explain a single passage of Callimachus?"

"But, father, it was the weight of the books, and Maso can help me,—it was not want of attention and patience."

Bardo shook his head again. "It is not mere bodily organs that I want: it is the sharp edge of a young mind to pierce the way for my somewhat blunted faculties. For blindness acts like a dam, sending the streams of thought backward along the already-travelled channels and hindering the course onward. If my son had not forsaken me, deluded by debasing fanatical dreams, worthy only of an energumen* whose dwelling is among tombs, I might have gone on and seen my path broadening to the end of my life; for he was a youth of great promise. . . . But it has closed in now," the old man continued, after a short pause; "it has closed in now;—all but the narrow track he has left me to tread—alone, in my blindness."

Romola started from her seat, and carried away the large volume to its place again, stung too acutely by her father's last words to remain motionless as well as silent; and when she turned away from the shelf again, she remained standing at some distance from him, stretching her arms downward and clasping her fingers tightly as she looked with a sad dreariness in her young face at the lifeless objects around her—the parchment backs, the unchanging mutilated marble, the bits of obsolete bronze and clay.

Bardo, though usually susceptible to Romola's movements and eager to trace them, was now too entirely preoccupied by the pain of rankling memories to notice her departure from his side.

"Yes," he went on, "with my son to aid me, I might have had my due share in the triumphs of this century: the names of the Bardi, father and son, might have been held reverently on the lips of scholars in the ages to come; not on account of frivolous verses or philosophic treatises, which are superfluous and presumptuous attempts to imitate the inimitable, such as allure vain men like Panhormita, and from which even the admirable Poggio* did not keep himself sufficiently free; but because we should have given a lamp whereby men might have studied the supreme productions of the past. For why is a young man like Poliziano (who was not yet born when I was already held worthy to maintain a discussion with Thomas of Sarzana) to have a glorious memory as a commentator on the Pandects—why is Ficino,* whose Latin is an offence to me, and who wanders purblind among the superstitious fancies that marked the decline at once of art, literature, and philosophy, to descend to posterity as the very high priest of Platonism, while I, who am more than their equal, have not effected anything but scattered work, which will be appropriated by other men? Why? but because my son, whom I had brought up to replenish my ripe learning with young enterprise, left me and all liberal pursuits that he might lash himself and howl at midnight with besotted friars—that he might go wandering on pilgrimages befitting men who know of no past older than the missal and the crucifix?—left me when the night was already beginning to fall on me."

In these last words the old man's voice, which had risen high in indignant protest, fell into a tone of reproach so tremulous and plaintive that Romola, turning her eyes again towards the blind aged face, felt her heart swell with forgiving pity. She seated herself by her father again, and placed her hand on his knee—too proud to obtrude consolation in words that might seem like a vindication of her own value, yet wishing to comfort him by some sign of her presence.

"Yes, Romola," said Bardo, automatically letting his left hand, with its massive prophylactic rings,* fall a little too heavily on the delicate blue-veined back of the girl's right, so that she bit her lip to prevent herself from starting. "If even Florence only is to remember me, it can but be on the same ground that it will remember Niccolò Niccoli*—because I forsook the vulgar pursuit of wealth in commerce that I might devote myself to collecting the precious remains of ancient art and wisdom, and leave them, after the example of the munificent Romans, for an everlasting possession to my fellow-citizens. But why do I say Florence only? If Florence remembers me, will not the world remember me? . . . Yet," added Bardo, after a short pause, his voice falling again into a saddened key, "Lorenzo's untimely death has raised a new difficulty. I had his promise—I should have had his bond—that my collection should always bear my name and should never be sold, though the harpies might clutch everything else; but there is enough for them—there is more than enough—

and for thee, too, Romola, there will be enough. Besides, thou wilt marry; Bernardo reproaches me that I do not seek a fitting *parentado* for thee, and we will delay no longer, we will think about it."

"No, no, father; what could you do? besides, it is useless: wait till some one seeks me," said Romola, hastily.

"Nay, my child, that is not the paternal duty. It was not so held by the ancients, and in this respect Florentines have not degenerated from their ancestral customs."

"But I will study diligently," said Romola, her eyes dilating with anxiety. "I will become as learned as Cassandra Fedele:* I will try and be as useful to you as if I had been a boy, and then perhaps some great scholar will want to marry me, and will not mind about a dowry; and he will like to come and live with you, and he will be to you in place of my brother . . . and you will not be sorry that I was a daughter."

There was a rising sob in Romola's voice as she said the last words, which touched the fatherly fibre in Bardo. He stretched his hand upward a little in search of her golden hair, and as she placed her head under his hand, he gently stroked it, leaning towards her as if his eyes discerned some glimmer there.

"Nay, *Romola mia*, I said not so: if I have pronounced an anathema on a degenerate and ungrateful son, I said not that I could wish thee other than the sweet daughter thou hast been to me. For what son could have tended me so gently in the frequent sickness I have had of late? And even in learning thou art not, according to thy measure, contemptible. Something perhaps were to be wished in thy capacity of attention and memory, not incompatible even with the feminine mind. But as Calcondila bore testimony, when he aided me to teach thee, thou hast a ready apprehension, and even a wide-glancing intelligence. And thou hast a man's nobility of soul: thou hast never fretted me with thy petty desires as thy mother did. It is true, I have been careful to keep thee aloof from the debasing influence of thy own sex, with their sparrow-like frivolity and their enslaving superstition, except, indeed, from that of our cousin Brigida, who may well serve as a scarecrow and a warning. And though—since I agree with the divine Petrarca, when he declares, quoting the *Aulularia* of Plautus, who again was indebted for the truth to the supreme Greek intellect,* 'Optimam fœminam nullam esse, alia licet alia pejor sit'—I cannot boast that thou art entirely lifted out of that lower category to which Nature assigned thee, nor even that in erudition thou art on a par with the more learned women of this age; thou art nevertheless—yes, *Romola mia*," said the old man, his pedantry again melting into tenderness, "thou art my sweet daughter, and thy voice is as the lower notes of the flute, 'dulcis, durabilis, clara, pura, secans aëra et auribus sedens,' according to the choice words of Quintilian;* and Bernardo tells me thou art fair, and thy hair is like the brightness of the morning, and indeed it seems to me that I discern some radiance from thee. Ah! I know how all else looks in this room, but thy form I only guess at. Thou art no longer the little woman six years old, that faded for me into darkness: thou art tall, and thy arm is but little below mine. Let us walk together."

The old man rose, and Romola, soothed by these beams of tenderness, looked happy again as she drew his arm within hers, and placed in his right hand the stick which rested at the side of his chair. While Bardo had been sitting, he had seemed hardly more than sixty: his face, though pale, had that refined texture in which wrinkles and lines are never deep; but now that he began to walk he looked as old as he really was—rather more than seventy; for his tall spare frame had the student's stoop of the shoulders, and he stepped with the undecided gait of the blind.

"No, Romola," he said, pausing against the bust of Hadrian, and passing his stick from the right to the left that he might explore the familiar outline with a "seeing hand." "There will be nothing else to preserve my memory and carry down my name as a member of the great republic of letters—nothing but my library and my collection of antiquities. And they are choice," continued Bardo, pressing the bust and speaking in a tone of insistance. "The collections of Niccolò I know were larger: but take any collection which is the work of a single man—that of the great Boccaccio* even—mine will surpass it. That of Poggio was contemptible compared with mine. It will be a great gift to unborn scholars. And there is nothing else. For even if I were to yield to the wish of Aldo Manuzio* when he sets up his press at Venice, and give him the aid of my annotated manuscripts, I know well what would be the result: some other scholar's name would stand on the title-page of the edition—some scholar who would have fed on my honey and then declared in his preface that he had gathered it all himself fresh from Hymettus.* Else, why have I refused the loan of many an annotated codex? why have I refused to make public any of my translations? why? but because scholarship is a system of licensed robbery, and your man in scarlet and furred robe who sits in judgment on thieves, is himself a thief of the thoughts and the fame that belong to his fellows. But against that robbery Bardo de' Bardi shall struggle—though blind and forsaken, he shall struggle. I too have a right to be remembered—as great a right as Pontanus or Merula,* whose names will be foremost on the lips of posterity, because they sought patronage and found it; because they had tongues that could flatter, and blood that was used to be nourished from the client's basket.* I have a right to be remembered."

The old man's voice had become at once loud and tremulous, and a pink flush overspread his proud, delicately-cut features, while the habitually raised attitude of his head gave the idea that behind the curtain of his blindness he saw some imaginary high tribunal to which he was appealing against the injustice of Fame.

Romola was moved with sympathetic indignation, for in her nature too there lay the same large claims, and the same spirit of struggle against their denial. She tried to calm her father by a still prouder word than his.

"Nevertheless, father, it is a great gift of the gods to be born with a hatred and contempt of all injustice and meanness. Yours is a higher lot, never to have lied and truckled, than to have shared honours won by dishonour. There is strength in scorn, as there was in the martial fury by which men became insensible to wounds."

"It is well said, Romola. It is a Promethean word* thou hast uttered," answered Bardo, after a little interval in which he had begun to lean on his stick again, and to walk on. "And I indeed am not to be pierced by the shafts of Fortune. My armour is the *æs triplex** of a clear conscience, and a mind nourished by the precepts of philosophy. 'For men,' says Epictetus,* 'are disturbed not by things themselves, but by their opinions or thoughts concerning those things.' And again, 'whosoever will be free, let him not desire or dread that which it is in the power of others either to deny or inflict: otherwise, he is a slave.' And of all such gifts as are dependent on the caprice of fortune or of men, I have long ago learned to say, with Horace—who, however, is too wavering in his philosophy, vacillating between the precepts of Zeno and the less worthy maxims of Epicurus, and attempting, as we say, 'duabus sellis sedere'*—concerning such accidents, I say, with the pregnant brevity of the poet—

'Sunt qui non habeant, est qui non curat habere.'*

He is referring to gems, and purple, and other insignia of wealth; but I may apply his words not less justly to the tributes men pay us with their lips and their pens, which are also matters of purchase, and often with base coin. Yes, '*inanis*'*—hollow, empty—is the epithet justly bestowed on Fame."

They made the tour of the room in silence after this; but Bardo's lip-born maxims were as powerless over the passion which had been moving him, as if they had been written on parchment and hung round his neck in a sealed bag;* and he presently broke forth again in a new tone of insistance.

"*Inanis?* yes, if it is a lying fame; but not if it is the just meed of labour and a great purpose. I claim my right: it is not fair that the work of my brain and my hands should not be a monument to me—it is not just that my labour should bear the name of another man. It is but little to ask," the old man went on, bitterly, "that my name should be over the door—that men should own themselves debtors to the Bardi library in Florence. They will speak coldly of me, perhaps: 'a diligent collector and transcriber,' they will say, 'and also of some critical ingenuity, but one who could hardly be conspicuous in an age so fruitful in illustrious scholars. Yet he merits our pity, for in the latter years of his life he was blind, and his only son, to whose education he had devoted his best years—' Nevertheless, my name will be remembered, and men will honour me: not with the breath of flattery, puchased by mean bribes, but because I have laboured, and because my labour will remain. Debts! I know there are debts; and there is thy dowry, Romola, to be paid. But there must be enough—or, at least, there can lack but a small sum, such as the Signoria might well provide. And if Lorenzo had not died, all would have been secured and settled. But now. . . ."

At this moment Maso opened the door, and advancing to his master, announced that Nello, the barber, had desired him to say, that he was come with the Greek scholar whom he had asked leave to introduce.

"It is well," said the old man. "Bring them in."

Bardo, conscious that he looked more dependent when he was walking, liked always to be seated in the presence of strangers, and Romola, without needing to be told, conducted him to his chair. She was standing by him at her full height, in quiet majestic self-possession, when the visitors entered; and the most penetrating observer would hardly have divined that this proud pale face, at the slightest touch on the fibres of affection or pity, could become passionate with tenderness, or that this woman, who imposed a certain awe on those who approached her, was in a state of girlish simplicity and ignorance concerning the world outside her father's books.

[*AUGUST 1862*]

CHAPTER VI.

Dawning Hopes

WHEN Maso opened the door again, and ushered in the two visitors, Nello, first making a deep reverence to Romola, gently pushed Tito before him, and advanced with him towards her father.

"Messer Bardo," he said, in a more measured and respectful tone than was usual with him, "I have the honour of presenting to you the Greek scholar, who has been eager to have speech of you, not less from the report I made to him of your learning and your priceless collections, than because of the furtherance your patronage may give him under the transient need to which he has been reduced by shipwreck. His name is Tito Melema, at your service."

Romola's astonishment could hardly have been greater if the stranger had worn a panther-skin and carried a thyrsus;* for the cunning barber had said nothing of the Greek's age or appearance; and among her father's scholarly visitors, she had hardly ever seen any but middle-aged or grey-headed men. There was only one masculine face, at once youthful and beautiful, the image of which remained deeply impressed on her mind: it was that of her brother, who long years ago had taken her on his knee, kissed her, and never come back again: a fair face, with sunny hair, like her own. But the habitual attitude of her mind towards strangers—a proud self-dependence and determination to ask for nothing even by a smile—confirmed in her by her father's complaints against the world's injustice, was like a snowy embankment hemming in the rush of admiring surprise. Tito's bright face showed its rich-tinted beauty without any rivalry of colour above his black *sajo* or tunic reaching to the knees. It seemed like a wreath of spring, dropped suddenly into Romola's young but wintry life, which had inherited nothing but memories—memories of a dead mother, of a lost brother, of a blind father's happier time—memories of far-off light, love, and beauty, that lay embedded in dark mines of books, and could hardly give out their brightness again until they were kindled for her by the torch of some known joy. Nevertheless, she returned Tito's bow, made to her on entering, with the same pale proud face as ever; but, as he approached, the snow melted, and when he ventured to look towards her again, while Nello was speaking, a pink flush overspread her face, to vanish again almost immediately, as if her imperious will had recalled it. Tito's glance, on the contrary, had that gentle, beseeching admiration in it which is the most propitiating of appeals to a proud, shy woman, and is perhaps the only atonement a man can make for being too handsome. The finished fascination of his air came chiefly from the absence of demand and assumption. It was that of a fleet, soft-coated, dark-eyed animal that delights you by not bounding away in indifference from you, and unexpectedly pillows its chin on your palm, and looks up at you desiring to be stroked—as if it loved you.

"Messere, I give you welcome," said Bardo, with some condescension; "misfortune wedded to learning, and especially to Greek learning, is a letter of credit that should win the ear of every instructed Florentine; for, as you are doubtless aware, since the period when your countryman, Manuelo Crisolora,* diffused the light of his teaching in the chief cities of Italy, now nearly a century ago, no man is held worthy of the name of scholar who has acquired merely the transplanted and derivative literature of the Latins; rather, such inert students are stigmatized as *opici* or barbarians, according to the phrase of the Romans themselves, who frankly replenished their urns at the fountain-head. I am, as you perceive, and as Nello has doubtless forewarned you, totally blind: a calamity to which we Florentines are held especially liable, whether owing to the cold winds which rush upon us in spring from the passes of the Apennines, or to that sudden transition from the cold gloom of our houses to the dazzling brightness of our summer sun, by which the *lippi** are said to have been made so numerous among the ancient Romans; or, in fine, to some occult cause which eludes our superficial surmises. But I pray you be seated: Nello, my friend, be seated."

Bardo paused until his fine ear had assured him that the visitors were seating themselves, and that Romola was taking her usual chair at his right hand. Then he said:

"From what part of Greece do you come, Messere? I had

thought that your unhappy country had been almost exhausted of those sons who could cherish in their minds any image of her original glory, though indeed the barbarous Sultans have of late shown themselves not indisposed to engraft on their wild stock the precious vine which their own fierce bands have hewn down and trampled under foot. From what part of Greece do you come?"

"I sailed last from Nauplia,"* said Tito; "but I have resided both at Constantinople and Thessalonica, and have travelled in various parts little visited by Western Christians since the triumph of the Turkish arms. I should tell you, however, Messere, that I was not born in Greece, but at Bari. I spent the first sixteen years of my life in Southern Italy and Sicily."

While Tito was speaking, some emotion passed, like a breath on the waters, across Bardo's delicate features; he leaned forward, put out his right hand towards Romola, and turned his head as if about to speak to her; but then, correcting himself, turned away again, and said, in a subdued voice,—

"Excuse me; is it not true—you are young?"

"I am three and twenty," said Tito.

"Ah," said Bardo, still in a tone of subdued excitement, "and you had, doubtless, a father who cared for your early instruction—who, perhaps, was himself a scholar?"

There was a slight pause before Tito's answer came to the ear of Bardo; but for Romola and Nello it began with a slight shock that seemed to pass through him, and cause a momentary quivering of the lip; doubtless at the revival of a supremely painful remembrance.

"Yes," he replied; "at least, a father by adoption. He was a Neapolitan, and of accomplished scholarship both Latin and Greek. But," added Tito, after another slight pause, "he is lost to me—was lost on a voyage he too rashly undertook to Delos."

Bardo sank backward again, too delicate to ask another question that might probe a sorrow which he divined to be recent. Romola, who knew well what were the fibres that Tito's voice had stirred in her father, felt that this new acquaintance had with wonderful suddenness got within the barrier that lay between them and the alien world. Nello, thinking that the evident check given to the conversation offered a graceful opportunity for relieving himself from silence, said—

"In truth, it is as clear as Venetian glass that this fine young man has had the best training; for the two Cennini have set him to work at their Greek sheets already, and it seems to me they are not men to begin cutting before they have felt the edge of their tools; they tested him well beforehand, we may be sure, and if there are two things not to be hidden—love and a cough*—I say there is a third, and that is ignorance, when once a man is obliged to do something besides wagging his head. The *tonsor inequalis** is inevitably betrayed when he takes the shears in his hand; is it not true, Messer Bardo? I speak after the fashion of a barber, but, as Luigi Pulci says—

'Perdonimi s'io fallo: chi m'ascolta
Intenda il mio volgar col suo latino.' " *

"Nay, my good Nello," said Bardo, with an air of friendly severity, "you are not altogether illiterate, and might doubtless have made a more respectable progress in learning if you had abstained somewhat from the *cicalata* and gossip of the street-corner, to which our Florentines are excessively addicted; but still more if you had not clogged your memory with those frivolous productions of which Luigi Pulci has furnished the most peccant exemplar—a compendium of extravagancies and incongruities the farthest removed from the models of a pure age, and resembling rather the *grylli** or conceits of a period when mystic meaning was held a warrant for monstrosity of form; with this difference, that while the monstrosity is retained, the mystic meaning is absent; in contemptible contrast with the great poem of Virgil, who, as I long held with Filelfo, before Landino* had taken upon him to expound the same opinion, embodied the deepest lessons of philosophy in a graceful and well-knit fable. And I cannot but regard the multiplication of these babbling, lawless productions, albeit countenanced by the patronage, and in some degree the example of Lorenzo himself, otherwise a friend to true learning, as a sign that the glorious hopes of this century are to be quenched in gloom; nay, that they have been the delusive prologue to an age worse than that of iron*—the age of tinsel and gossamer, in which no thought has substance enough to be moulded into consistent and lasting form."

"Once more, pardon," said Nello, opening his palms outward, and shrugging his shoulders, "I find myself knowing so many things in good Tuscan before I have time to think of the Latin for them; and Messer Luigi's rhymes are always slipping off the lips of my customers:—that is what corrupts me. And, indeed, talking of customers, I have left my shop and my reputation too long in the custody of my slow Sandro, who does not deserve even to be called a *tonsor inequalis*, but rather to be pronounced simply a bungler in the vulgar tongue. So with your permission, Messer Bardo, I will take my leave—well understood that I am at your service whenever Maso calls upon me. It seems a thousand years till I dress and perfume the damigella's hair, which deserves to shine in the heavens as a constellation, though indeed it were a pity for it ever to go so far out of reach."

Three voices made a fugue of friendly farewells to Nello, as he retreated with a bow to Romola and a beck to Tito. The acute barber saw that the pretty youngster, who had crept into his liking by some strong magic, was well launched in Bardo's favourable regard; and satisfied that his introduction had not miscarried so far, he felt the propriety of retiring.

The little burst of wrath, called forth by Nello's unlucky quotation, had diverted Bardo's mind from the feelings which had just before been hemming in further speech, and he now addressed Tito again with his ordinary calmness.

"Ah! young man, you are happy in having been able to unite the advantages of travel with those of study, and you will be welcome among us as a bringer of fresh tidings from a land which has become sadly strange to us, except through the agents of a now restricted commerce and the reports of hasty pilgrims. For those days are in the far distance which I myself witnessed, when men like Aurispa and Guarino went out to Greece as to a storehouse, and came back laden with manuscripts which every scholar was eager to borrow—and, be it owned with shame, not always willing to restore; nay, even the days when erudite Greeks* flocked to our shores for a refuge, seem far off now—farther off than the on-coming of my blindness. But, doubtless, young man, research after the treasures of antiquity was not alien to the purpose of your travels?"

"Assuredly not," said Tito. "On the contrary, my companion—my father—was willing to risk his life in his zeal for the discovery of inscriptions and other traces of ancient civilization."

"And I trust there is a record of his researches and their results," said Bardo, eagerly, "since they must be even more precious than those of Ciriaco,* which I have diligently availed myself of, though they are not always illuminated by adequate learning."

"There *was* such a record," said Tito, "but it was lost, like everything else, in the shipwreck I suffered below Ancona. The only record left is such as remains in our—in my memory."

"You must lose no time in committing it to paper, young man," said Bardo, with growing interest. "Doubtless you remember much, if you aided in transcription; for when I was your age, words wrought themselves into my mind as if they had been fixed by the tool of the graver; wherefore I constantly marvel at the capriciousness of my daughter's memory, which grasps certain objects with tenacity, and lets fall all those minutiæ whereon depends accuracy, the very soul of scholarship. But I apprehend no such danger with you, young man, if your will has seconded the advantages of your training."

When Bardo made this reference to his daughter, Tito ventured to turn his eyes towards her, and at the accusation against her memory his face broke into its brightest smile, which was reflected as inevitably as sudden sunbeams in Romola's. Conceive the soothing delight of that smile to her! Romola had never dreamed that there was a scholar in the world who would smile at a deficiency for which she was constantly made to feel herself a culprit. It was like the dawn of a new sense to her—the sense of comradeship. They did not look away from each other immediately, as if the smile had been a stolen one; they looked and smiled with frank enjoyment.

"She is not really so cold and proud," thought Tito.

"Does *he* forget too, I wonder?" thought Romola. "Yet I hope not, else he will vex my father."

But Tito was obliged to turn away, and answer Bardo's question.

"I have had much practice in transcription," he said, "but in the case of inscriptions copied in memorable scenes, rendered doubly impressive by the sense of risk and adventure, it may have happened that my retention of written characters has been weakened. On the plain of the Eurotas, or among the gigantic stones of Mycenæ and Tyrins*—especially when the fear of the Turk hovers over one like a vulture—the mind wanders, even though the hand writes faithfully what the eye dictates. But something doubtless I have retained," added Tito, with a modesty which was not false, though he was conscious that it was politic—"something that might be of service if illustrated and corrected by a wider learning than my own."

"That is well-spoken, young man," said Bardo, delighted. "And I will not withhold from you such aid as I can give, if you like to communicate with me concerning your recollections. I foresee a work which will be a useful supplement to the *Isolario* of Cristoforo Buondelmonte, and which may take rank with the *Itineraria* of Ciriaco and the admirable Ambrogio Traversari.* But we must prepare ourselves for calumny, young man," Bardo went on with energy, as if the work were already growing so fast that the time of trial was near; "if your book contains novelties you will be charged with forgery; if my elucidations should clash with any priciples of interpretation adopted by another scholar, our personal characters will be attacked, we shall be impeached with foul actions; you must prepare yourself to be told that your mother was a fish-woman, and that your father was a renegade priest or a hanged malefactor. I myself, for having shown error in a single preposition, had an invective written against me wherein I was taxed with treachery, fraud, indecency, and even hideous crimes.* Such, my young friend—such are the flowers with which the glorious path of scholarship is strewed! But tell me, then: I have learned much concerning Byzantium and Thessalonica long ago from Demetrio Calcondila, who has but lately departed from Florence; but you, it seems, have visited less familiar scenes?"

"Yes; we made what I may call a pilgrimage full of danger, for the sake of visiting places which have almost died out of the memory of the West, for they lie away from the track of pilgrims; and my father used to say that scholars themselves hardly imagine them to have any existence out of books. He was of opinion that a new and more glorious era would open for learning when men should begin to look for their commentaries on the ancient writers in the remains of cities and temples, nay, in the paths of the rivers, and on the face of the valleys and mountains."

"Ah!" said Bardo, fervidly, "your father, then, was not a common man. Was he fortunate, may I ask? Had he many friends?" These last words were uttered in a tone charged with meaning.

"No; he made enemies—chiefly, I believe, by a certain

impetuous candour; and they hindered his advancement, so that he lived in obscurity. And he would never stoop to conciliate: he would never forget an injury."

"Ah!" said Bardo again, with a long, deep intonation.

"Among our hazardous expeditions," continued Tito, willing to prevent further questions on a point so personal, "I remember with particular vividness a hastily snatched visit to Athens. Our hurry, and the double danger of being seized as prisoners by the Turks, and of our galley raising anchor before we could return, made it seem like a fevered vision of the night—the wide plain, the girdling mountains, the ruined porticos and columns, either standing far aloof, as if receding from our hurried footsteps, or else jammed in confusedly among the dwellings of Christians degraded into servitude, or among the forts and turrets of their Moslem conquerors, who have their stronghold on the Acropolis."

"You fill me with surprise," said Bardo. "Athens, then, is not utterly destroyed and swept away, as I had imagined?"

"No wonder you should be under that mistake, for few even of the Greeks themselves who live beyond the mountain boundary of Attica know anything about the present condition of Athens, or *Setine*,* as the sailors call it. I remember, as we were rounding the promontory of Sunium, the Greek pilot we had on board our Venetian galley pointed to the mighty columns that stand on the summit of the rock—the remains, as you know well, of the great temple erected to the goddess Athena, who looked down from that high shrine with triumph at her conquered rival* Poseidon;—well, our Greek pilot, pointing to those columns said, 'That was the school of the great philosopher Aristotle.' And at Athens itself, the monk who acted as our guide in the hasty view we snatched, insisted most on showing us the spot where St. Philip baptized the Ethiopian eunuch,* or some such legend."

"Talk not of monks and their legends, young man!" said Bardo, interrupting Tito impetuously. "It is enough to overlay human hope and enterprise with an eternal frost to think that the ground which was trodden by philosophers and poets is crawled over by those insect-swarms of besotted fanatics or howling hypocrites."

"*Perdio*, I have no affection for them," said Tito, with a shrug; "servitude agrees well with a religion like theirs, which lies in the renunciation of all that makes life precious to other men. And they carry the yoke that befits them: their matin chant is drowned by the voice of the muezzin, who, from the gallery of the high tower on the Acropolis, calls every Mussulman to his prayers. That tower springs from the Parthenon itself; and every time we paused and directed our eyes towards it, our guide set up a wail, that a temple which had once been won from the diabolical uses of the pagans to become the temple of another virgin than Pallas—the Virgin Mother of God—was now again perverted to the accursed ends of the Moslem.* It was the sight of those walls of the Acropolis, which disclosed themselves in the distance as we leaned over the side of our galley when it was forced by contrary winds to anchor in the Piræus, that fired my father's mind with the determination to see Athens at all risks, and in spite of the sailors' warnings that if we lingered till a change of wind they would depart without us: but after all, it was impossible for us to venture near the Acropolis, for the sight of men eager in examining 'old stones'* raised the suspicion that we were Venetian spies, and we had to hurry back to the harbour."

"We will talk more of these things," said Bardo, eagerly. "You must recall everything, to the minutest trace left in your memory. You will win the gratitude of after times by leaving a record of the aspect Greece bore while yet the barbarians had not swept away every trace of the structures that Pausanias and Pliny described:* you will take those great writers as your models; and such contribution of criticism and suggestion as my riper mind can supply shall not be wanting to you. There will be much to tell; for you have travelled, you said, in the Peloponnesus?"

"Yes; and in Bœotia also: I have rested in the groves of Helicon, and tasted of the fountain Hippocrene.* But on every memorable spot in Greece conquest after conquest has set its seal, till there is a confusion of ownership even in ruins, that only close study and comparison could unravel. High over every fastness, from the plains of Lacedæmon to the straits of Thermopylæ, there towers some huge Frankish fortress, once inhabited by a French or Italian marquis, now either abandoned or held by Turkish bands."

"Stay!" cried Bardo, whose mind was now too thoroughly preoccupied by the idea of the future book to attend to Tito's further narration. "Do you think of writing in Latin or Greek?

Doubtless Greek is the more ready clothing for your thoughts, and it is the nobler language. But, on the other hand, Latin is the tongue in which we shall measure ourselves with the larger and more famous number of modern rivals. And if you are less at ease in it, I will aid you—yes, I will spend on you that long-accumulated study which was to have been thrown into the channel of another work—a work in which I myself was to have had a helpmate."

Bardo paused a moment, and then added,—

"But who knows whether that work may not be executed yet? For you, too, young man, have been brought up by a father who poured into your mind all the long-gathered stream of his knowledge and experience. Our aid might be mutual."

Romola, who had watched her father's growing excitement, and divined well the invisible currents of feeling that determined every question and remark, felt herself in a glow of strange anxiety: she turned her eyes on Tito continually, to watch the impression her father's words made on him, afraid lest he should be inclined to dispel these visions of co-operation which were lighting up her father's face with a new hope. But no! He looked so bright and gentle: he must feel, as she did, that in this eagerness of blind age there was piteousness enough to call forth inexhaustible patience. How much more strongly he would feel this if he knew about her brother! A girl of eighteen* imagines the feelings behind the face that has moved her with its sympathetic youth, as easily as primitive people imagined the humours of the gods in fair weather: what is she to believe in, if not in this vision woven from within?

And Tito was really very far from feeling impatient. He delighted in sitting there with the sense that Romola's attention was fixed on him, and that he could occasionally look at her. He was pleased that Bardo should take an interest in him; and he did not dwell with enough seriousness on the prospect of the work in which he was to be aided, to feel moved by it to anything else than that easy, good-humoured acquiescence which was natural to him.

"I shall be proud and happy," he said, in answer to Bardo's last words, "if my services can be held a meet offering to the matured scholarship of Messere. But doubtless"—here he looked towards Romola—"the lovely damigella, your daughter, makes all other aid superfluous; for I have learned from Nello that she has been nourished on the highest studies from her earliest years."

"You are mistaken," said Romola; "I am by no means sufficient to my father: I have not the gifts that are necessary for scholarship."

Romola did not make this self-depreciatory statement in a tone of anxious humility, but with a proud gravity.

"Nay, my Romola," said her father, not willing that the stranger should have too low a conception of his daughter's powers; "thou art not destitute of gifts; rather, thou art endowed beyond the measure of women; but thou hast withal the woman's delicate frame, which ever craves repose and variety, and so begets a wandering imagination. My daughter"—turning to Tito—"has been very precious to me, filling up to the best of her power the place of a son. For I had once a son . . ."

Bardo checked himself: he did not wish to assume an attitude of complaint in the presence of a stranger, and he remembered that this young man, in whom he had unexpectedly become so much interested, was still a stranger, towards whom it became him rather to keep the position of a patron. His pride was roused to double activity by the fear that he had forgotten his dignity.

"But," he resumed, in his original tone of condescension, "we are departing from what I believe is to you the most important business. Nello informed me that you had certain gems which you would fain dispose of, and that you desired a passport to some man of wealth and taste who would be likely to become a purchaser."

"It is true; for, though I have obtained employment as a corrector with the Cennini, my payment leaves little margin beyond the provision of necessaries, and would leave less but that my good friend Nello insists on my hiring a lodging from him, and saying nothing about the rent till better days."

"Nello is a good-hearted prodigal," said Bardo; "and though, with that ready ear and ready tongue of his, he is too much like the ill-famed Margites—knowing many things and knowing them all badly, as I hinted to him but now—he is nevertheless 'abnormis sapiens,'* after the manner of our born Florentines. But have you the gems with you? I would willingly know what they are—yet it is useless: no, it might only deepen regret. I cannot add to my store."

"I have one or two intaglios of much beauty," said Tito, proceeding to draw from his wallet a small case.

But Romola no sooner saw the movement than she looked at him with significant gravity, and placed her finger on her lips,

"Con viso che tacendo dicea, Taci."*

If Bardo were made aware that the gems were within reach, she knew well he would want a minute description of them, and it would become pain to him that they should go away from him, even if he did not insist on some device for purchasing them in spite of poverty. But she had no sooner made this sign than she felt rather guilty and ashamed at having virtually confessed a weakness of her father's to a stranger. It seemed that she was destined to a sudden confidence and familiarity with this young Greek, strangely at variance with her deep-seated pride and reserve; and this consciousness again brought the unwonted colour to her cheeks.

Tito understood her look and sign, and immediately withdrew his hand from the case, saying, in a careless tone, so as to make it appear that he was merely following up his last words, "But they are usually in the keeping of Messer Domenico Cennini, who has strong and safe places for these things. He estimates them as worth at least five hundred ducats."

"Ah, then, they are fine intagli," said Bardo. "Five hundred ducats! Ah, more than a man's ransom!"

Tito gave a slight, almost imperceptible start, and opened his long dark eyes with questioning surprise at Bardo's blind face, as if his words—a mere phrase of common parlance, at a time when men were often being ransomed from slavery or imprisonment—had had some special meaning for him. But the next moment he looked towards Romola, as if her eyes must be her father's interpreters. She, intensely preoccupied with what related to her father, imagined that Tito was looking to her again for some guidance, and immediately spoke.

"Alessandra Scala delights in gems, you know, father; she calls them her winter flowers; and the Segretario would be almost sure to buy any gems that she wished for. Besides, he himself sets great store by rings and sigils, which he wears as a defence against pains in the joints."

"It is true," said Bardo. "Bartolommeo has overmuch confidence in the efficacy of gems—a confidence wider than what is sanctioned by Pliny,* who clearly shows that he regards many beliefs of that sort as idle superstitions; though not to the utter denial of medicinal virtues in gems. Wherefore, I myself, as you observe, young man, wear certain rings, which the discreet Camillo Leonardi* prescribed to me by letter when two years ago I had a certain infirmity of sudden numbness. But thou hast spoken well, Romola. I will dictate a letter to Bartolommeo, which Maso shall carry. But it were well that Messere should notify to thee what the gems are, together with the intagli they bear, as a warrant to Bartolommeo that they will be worthy of his attention."

"Nay, father," said Romola, whose dread lest a paroxysm of the collector's mania should seize her father, gave her the courage to resist his proposal. "Your word will be sufficient that Messere is a scholar and has travelled much. The Segretario will need no further inducement to receive him."

"True, child," said Bardo, touched on a chord that was sure to respond. "I have no need to add proofs and arguments in confirmation of my word to Bartolommeo. And I doubt not that this young man's presence is in accord with the tones of his voice, so that, the door being once opened, he will be his own best advocate."

Bardo paused a few moments, but his silence was evidently charged with some idea that he was hesitating to express, for he once leaned forward a little as if he were going to speak, then turned his head aside towards Romola and sank backward again. At last, as if he had made up his mind, he said in a tone which might have become a prince giving the courteous signal of dismissal,—

"I am somewhat fatigued this morning, and shall prefer seeing you again to-morrow, when I shall be able to give you the secretary's answer, authorizing you to present yourself to him at some given time. But before you go"—here the old man, in spite of himself, fell into a more faltering tone—"you will perhaps permit me to touch your hand? It is long since I touched the hand of a young man."

Bardo had stretched out his aged white hand and Tito immediately placed his dark but delicate and supple fingers within it. Bardo's cramped fingers closed over them, and he held them for a few minutes in silence. Then he said,—

"Romola, has this young man the same complexion as thy brother—fair and pale?"

"No, father," Romola answered, with determined composure, though her heart began to beat violently with mingled emotions. "The hair of Messere is dark—his complexion is dark." Inwardly she said, "Will he mind it? will it be disagreeable? No, he looks so gentle and good-natured." Then aloud again,

"Would Messere permit my father to touch his hair and face?"

Her eyes inevitably made a timid entreating appeal while she asked this, and Tito's met them with soft brightness as he said, "Assuredly," and, leaning forward, raised Bardo's hand to his curls, with a readiness of assent which was the greater relief to her because it was unaccompanied by any sign of embarrassment.

Bardo passed his hand again and again over the long curls and grasped them a little, as if their spiral resistance made his inward vision clearer; then he passed his hand over the brow and cheek, tracing the profile with the edge of his palm and fourth finger, and letting the breadth of his hand repose on the rich oval of the cheek.

"Ah!" he said, as his hand glided from the face and rested on the young man's shoulder. "He must be very unlike thy brother, Romola: and it is the better. You see no visions, I trust, my young friend?"

At this moment the door opened, and there entered, unannounced, a tall elderly man in a handsome black silk *lucco*, who, unwinding his *becchetto* from his neck and taking off his cap, disclosed a head as white as Bardo's. He cast a keen glance of surprise at the group before him—the young stranger leaning in that filial attitude, while Bardo's hand rested on his shoulder, and Romola sitting near with eyes dilated by anxiety and agitation. But there was an instantaneous change: Bardo let fall his hand, Tito raised himself from his stooping posture, and Romola rose to meet the visitor with an alacrity which implied all the greater intimacy, because it was unaccompanied by any smile.

"Well, god-daughter," said the stately man, as he touched Romola's shoulder; "Maso said you had a visitor, but I came in nevertheless."

"It is thou, Bernardo," said Bardo. "Thou art come at a fortunate moment. This, young man," he continued, while Tito rose and bowed, "is one of the chief citizens of Florence—Messer Bernardo del Nero, my oldest, I had almost said my only friend—whose good opinion, if you can win it, may carry you far. He is but three and twenty, Bernardo, yet he can doubtless tell thee much which thou wilt care to hear; for though a scholar, he has already travelled far, and looked on other things besides the manuscripts for which thou hast too light an esteem."

"Ah, a Greek, as I augur," said Bernardo, returning Tito's reverence but slightly, and surveying him with that sort of glance which seems almost to cut like fine steel. "Newly arrived in Florence, it appears. The name of Messere—or part of it, for it is doubtless a long one?"

"On the contrary," said Tito, with perfect good humour, "it is most modestly free from polysyllabic pomp. My name is Tito Melema."

"Truly?" said Bernardo, rather scornfully, as he took a seat, "I had expected it to be at least as long as the names of a city, a river, a province and an empire all put together. We Florentines mostly use names as we do prawns, and strip them of all flourishes before we trust them to our throats."

"Well, Bardo," he continued, as if the stranger were not worth further notice, and changing his tone of sarcastic suspicion for one of sadness, "we have buried him!"

"Ah!" replied Bardo, with corresponding sadness, "and a new epoch has come for Florence—a dark one, I fear. Lorenzo has left behind him an inheritance that is but like the alchemist's laboratory when the wisdom of the alchemist is gone."

"Not altogether so," said Bernardo. "Piero de' Medici has abundant intelligence; his faults are only the faults of hot blood. I love the lad—lad he will always be to me, as I have always been 'little father' to him."

"Yet all who want a new order of things are likely to conceive new hopes," said Bardo. "We shall have the old strife of parties, I fear."

"If we could have a new order of things that was something else than knocking down one coat of arms to put up another," said Bernardo, "I should be ready to say, 'I belong to no party: I am a Florentine.' But as long as parties are in question, I am a Medicean, and will be a Medicean till I die. I am of the same mind as Farinata degli Uberti: if any man asks me what is meant by siding with a party, I say, as he did, 'To wish ill or well, for the sake of past wrongs or kindness.'"*

During this short dialogue, Tito had been standing, and now took his leave.

"But come again at the same hour to-morrow," said Bardo, graciously, before Tito left the room, "that I may give you Bartolommeo's answer."

"From what quarter of the sky has this pretty Greek youngster alighted so close to thy chair, Bardo?" said Bernardo del Nero, as the door closed. He spoke with dry emphasis, evidently intended to convey something more to Bardo than was implied by the mere words.

"He is a scholar who has been shipwrecked and has saved a few gems, for which he wants to find a purchaser. I am going to send him to Bartolommeo Scala, for thou knowest it were more prudent in me to abstain from further purchases."

Bernardo shrugged his shoulders and said, "Romola, wilt thou see if my servant is without? I ordered him to wait for me here." Then, when Romola was at a sufficient distance, he leaned forward and said to Bardo in a low, emphatic tone:—

"Remember, Bardo, thou hast a rare gem of thy own; take care no man gets it who is not likely to pay a worthy price. That pretty Greek has a lithe sleekness about him, that seems marvellously fitted for slipping easily into any nest he fixes his mind on."

Bardo was startled: the association of Tito with the image of his lost son had excluded instead of suggesting the thought of Romola. But almost immediately there seemed to be a reaction which made him grasp the warning as if it had been a hope.

"But why not, Bernardo? If the young man approved himself worthy—he is a scholar—and—and there would be no difficulty about the dowry, which always makes thee gloomy."

CHAPTER VII.

A Learned Squabble

Bartolommeo Scala, secretary of the Florentine Republic, on whom Tito Melema had been thus led to anchor his hopes, lived in a handsome palace close to the Porta Pinti, now known as the Casa Gherardesca. His arms—an azure ladder transverse on a golden field, with the motto *Gradatim** placed over the entrance—told all comers that the miller's son held his ascent to honours by his own efforts a fact to be proclaimed without wincing. The secretary was a vain and pompous man, but he was also an honest one: he was sincerely convinced of his own merit, and could see no reason for feigning. The topmost round of his azure ladder had been reached by this time: he had held his secretaryship these twenty years—had long since made his orations on the *ringhiera*, or platform, of the Old Palace, as the custom was, in the presence of princely visitors, while Marzocco, the republican lion, wore his gold crown on the occasion, and all the people cried, "Viva Messer Bartolommeo!"—had been on an embassy to Rome, and had there been made titular Senator, Apostolical Secretary, Knight of the Golden Spur; and had, eight years ago, been Gonfaloniere*—last goal of the Florentine citizen's ambition. Meantime he had got richer and richer, and more and more gouty, after the manner of successful mortality; and the Knight of the Golden Spur had often to sit with helpless cushioned heel under the handsome loggia he had built for himself, overlooking the spacious gardens and lawn at the back of his palace.

He was in this position on the day when he had granted the desired interview to Tito Melema. The May afternoon sun was on the flowers and the grass beyond the pleasant shade of the loggia; thc too stately silk *lucco* was cast aside, and a light loose mantle was thrown over his tunic; his beautiful daughter Alessandra and her husband, the Greek soldier-poet Marullo, were seated on one side of him: on the other, two friends, not oppressively illustrious, and, therefore, the better listeners. Yet, to say nothing of the gout, Messer Bartolommeo's felicity was far from perfect: it was embittered by the contents of certain papers that lay before him, consisting chiefly of a correspondence between himself and Politian. It was a human foible at that period (incredible as it may seem) to recite quarrels, and favour scholarly visitors with the communication of an entire and lengthy correspondence; and this was neither the first nor the second time that Scala had asked the candid opinion of his friends as to the balance of right and wrong in some half score Latin letters between himself and Politian, all springing out of certain epigrams written in the most playful tone in the world. It was the story of a very typical and pretty quarrel,* in which we are interested, because it supplied precisely that thistle of hatred necessary, according to Nello, as a stimulus to the sluggish paces of the cautious steed, Friendship.

Politian, having been a rejected pretender to the love and the hand of Scala's daughter, kept a very sharp and learned tooth in readiness against the too prosperous and presumptuous secretary, who had declined the greatest scholar of the age for a son-in-law. Scala was a meritorious public servant, and, moreover, a lucky man*—naturally exasperating to an offended scholar; but then—O beautiful balance of things!—he had an itch for authorship, and was a bad writer—one of those excellent people who, sitting in gouty slippers, "penned poetical trifles" entirely for their own amusement, without any view to an audience, and, consequently, sent them to their friends in letters, which were the literary periodicals of the fifteenth century. Now Scala had abundance of friends who were ready to praise his writings: friends like Ficino and Landino—amiable browsers in the Medicean park along with himself—who found his Latin prose style elegant and masculine; and the terrible Joseph Scaliger,* who was to pronounce him totally ignorant of Latinity, was at a comfortable distance in the next century. But when was the fatal coquetry inherent in superfluous authorship ever quite contented with the ready praise of friends? That critical, supercilious Politian—a fellow-browser, who was far from amiable—must be made aware that the solid secretary showed, in his leisure hours, a pleasant fertility in verses, which indicated pretty clearly how much he might do in that way if he were not a man of affairs.

Ineffable moment! when the man you secretly hate sends you a Latin epigram with a false gender—hendecasyllables* with a questionable elision, at least a toe too much—attempts at poetic figures which are manifest solecisms. That moment had come to Politian: the secretary had put forth his soft head from the official shell, and the terrible lurking crab was down upon him. Politian had used the freedom of a friend, and pleasantly, in the form of a Latin epigram, corrected the mistake of Scala in making the *culex* (an insect too well known on the banks of the Arno) of the inferior or feminine gender. Scala replied by a bad joke, in suitable Latin verses, referring to Politian's unsuccessful suit. Better and better. Politian found the verses very pretty and highly facetious: the more was the pity that they were seriously incorrect, and inasmuch as Scala had alleged that he had written them in imitation of a Greek epigram, Politian, being on such friendly terms, would enclose a Greek epigram of his own, on the same interesting insect—not, we may presume, out of any wish to humble Scala, but rather to instruct him; said epigram containing a lively conceit about Venus, Cupid, and the *culex*,* of a kind much tasted at that period, founded partly on the zoological fact that the gnat, like Venus, was born from the waters. Scala, in reply, begged to say that his verses were never intended for a scholar with such delicate olfactories as Politian, nearest of all living men to the perfection of the ancients, and of a taste so fastidious that sturgeon itself must seem insipid to him; defended his own verses, nevertheless, though indeed they were written hastily, without correction, and intended as an agreeable distraction during the summer heat to himself and such friends as were satisfied with mediocrity, he, Scala, not being like some other people, who courted publicity through the booksellers. For the rest, he had barely enough Greek to make out the sense of the epigram so graciously sent him, to say nothing of tasting its elegancies; but—the epigram was Politian's: what more need be said? Still, by way of postscript, he feared that his incomparable friend's comparison of the gnat to Venus, on account of its origin from the waters, was in many ways ticklish. On the one hand, Venus might be offended; and on the other, unless the poet intended an allusion to the doctrine of Thales,* that cold and damp origin seemed doubtful to Scala in the case of a creature so fond of warmth: a fish were perhaps the better comparison, or, when the power of flying was in question, an eagle, or, indeed, when the darkness was taken into consideration, a bat or an owl were a less obscure and more apposite parallel, &c. &c. Here was a great opportunity for Politian. He was not aware, he wrote, that when he had Scala's verses placed before him, there was any question of sturgeon, but rather of frogs and gudgeons: made short work with Scala's defence of his own Latin, and mangled him terribly on the score of the stupid criticisms he had ventured on the Greek epigram kindly forwarded to him as a model. Wretched cavils, indeed! for as to the damp origin of the gnat, there was the authority of Virgil himself, who had called it the "*alumnus* of the waters;"* and as to what his dear dull friend had to say about the fish, the eagle, and the rest, it was "nihil ad rem;"* for because the eagle could fly higher, it by no means followed that the gnat could not fly at all, &c. &c. He was ashamed, however, to dwell on such trivialities, and thus to swell a gnat into an elephant; but, for his own part, would only add that he had nothing deceitful or double about him, neither was he to be caught when present by the false blandishments of those who slandered him in his absence, agreeing rather with a Homeric sentiment* on that head—which furnished a Greek quotation to serve as powder to his bullet.

The quarrel could not end there. The logic could hardly get worse, but the secretary got more pompously self-asserting, and the scholarly poet's temper more and more venomous. Politian had been generously willing to hold up a mirror, by which the too-inflated secretary, beholding his own likeness, might be induced to cease setting up his ignorant defences of bad Latin against ancient authorities whom the consent of centuries had placed beyond question,—unless, indeed, he had designed to sink in literature in proportion as he rose in honours, that by a sort of compensation men of letters might feel themselves his equals. In return, Politian was begged to examine Scala's writings: nowhere would he find a more devout admiration of antiquity. The secretary was ashamed of the age in which he lived, and blushed for it. *Some*, indeed, there were who wanted to have their own works praised and exalted to a level with the divine monuments of antiquity; but he, Scala, could not oblige them. And as to the honours which were offensive to the envious, they had been well earned: witness his whole life since he came in penury to Florence. The elegant scholar, in reply, was not surprised that Scala found the Age distasteful to him, since he himself was so distasteful to the Age; nay, it was with perfect accuracy that he, the elegant scholar, had called Scala a branny monster, inasmuch as he was formed from the offscourings of monsters, born amidst the refuse of a mill, and eminently worthy the long-eared office of turning the paternal millstones (*in pistrini sordibus natus, et quidem pistrino dignissimus*)!*

It was not without reference to Tito's appointed visit that the papers containing this correspondence were brought out to-day. Here was a new Greek scholar whose accomplishments were to be tested; and on nothing did Scala more desire a dispassionate opinion from persons of superior knowledge than on that Greek epigram of Politian's. After sufficient introductory talk concerning Tito's travels, after a survey and discussion of the gems, and an easy passage from the mention of the lamented Lorenzo's eagerness in collecting such specimens of ancient art to the subject of classical tastes and studies in general and their present condition in Florence, it was inevitable to mention Politian, a man of eminent ability indeed, but a little too arrogant—assuming to be a Hercules, whose office it was to destroy all the literary monstrosities* of the age, and writing letters to his elders without signing them, as if they were miraculous revelations that could only have one source. And after all, were not his own criticisms often questionable and his taste perverse? He was fond of saying pungent things about the men who thought they wrote like Cicero because they ended every sentence with "esse videtur:"* but while he was boasting of his freedom from servile imitation, did he not fall into the other extreme, running after strange words and affected phrases? Even in his much-belauded *Miscellanea* was every point tenable? And Tito, who had just been looking into the *Miscellanea*, found so much to say that was agreeable to the secretary—he would have done so from the mere disposition to please, without further motive—that he showed himself quite worthy to be made a judge in the notable correspondence concerning the *culex*. Here was the Greek epigram which Politian had doubtless thought the finest in the world, though he had pretended to believe that the "transmarini," the Greeks themselves, would make light of it: had he not been unintentionally speaking the truth in his false modesty?

Tito was ready, and scarified the epigram to Scala's content. O wise young judge!* He could doubtless appreciate satire even in the vulgar tongue, and Scala—who, excellent man, not seeking publicity through the booksellers, was never unprovided with "hasty uncorrected trifles," as a sort of sherbet for a visitor on a hot day, or, if the weather were cold, why then as a cordial—had a few little matters in the shape of sonnets, turning on well-known foibles of Politian's, which he would not like to go any farther, but which would, perhaps, amuse the company.

Enough: Tito took his leave under an urgent invitation to come again. His gems were interesting; especially the agate, with the *lusus naturæ* in it—a most wonderful semblance of Cupid riding on the lion; and the "Jew's stone," with the lion-headed serpent* enchased in it; both of which the secretary agreed to buy—the latter as a reinforcement of his preventives against the gout, which gave him such severe twinges that it was plain enough how intolerable it would be if he were not well supplied with rings of rare virtue, and with an amulet worn close under the right breast. But Tito was assured that he himself was more interesting than his gems. He had won his way to the Scala Palace by the recommendation of Bardo de' Bardi, who, to be sure, was Scala's old acquaintance and a worthy scholar, in spite of his overvaluing himself a little (a frequent foible in the secretary's friends); but he must come again on the ground of his own manifest accomplishments.

The interview could hardly have ended more auspiciously for Tito, and as he walked out at the Porta Pinti that he might laugh a little at his ease over the affair of the *culex*, he felt that Fortune could hardly mean to turn her back on him again at present, since she had taken him by the hand in this decided way.

CHAPTER VIII.

A Face in the Crowd

It is easy to northern people to rise early on Midsummer morning, to see the dew on the grassy edge of the dusty pathway, to notice the fresh shoots among the darker green of the oak and fir in the coppice, and to look over the gate at the shorn meadow, without recollecting that it is the Nativity of Saint John the Baptist.

Not so to the Florentine—still less to the Florentine of the fifteenth century: to him on that particular morning the brightness of the eastern sun on the Arno had something special in it; the ringing of the bells was articulate, and declared it to be the great summer festival of Florence, the Day of San Giovanni.

San Giovanni had been the patron saint of Florence for at least eight hundred years—ever since the time when the Lombard Queen Theodolinda had commanded her subjects to do him peculiar honour; nay, says old Villani, to the best of his knowledge, ever since the days of Constantine the Great and Pope Sylvester,* when the Florentines deposed their Idol Mars, whom they were nevertheless careful not to treat with contumely; for while they consecrated their beautiful and noble temple to the honour of God and of the "Beato Messere Santo Giovanni," they placed old Mars respectfully on a high tower near the River Arno, finding in certain ancient memorials that he had been elected as their tutelar deity under such astral influences that if he were broken, or otherwise treated with indignity, the city would suffer great damage and mutation. But in the fifteenth century that discreet regard to the feelings of the man-destroyer* had long vanished: the god of the spear and shield had ceased to frown by the side of the Arno, and the defences of the Republic were held to lie in its craft and its coffers. For spear and shield could be hired by gold florins, and on the gold florins there had always been the image of San Giovanni.

Much good had come to Florence since the dim time of struggle between the old patron and the new: some quarrelling and bloodshed, doubtless, between Guelf and Ghibelline, between Black and White, between orthodox sons of the Church and heretic Paterini; some floods, famine, and pestilence; but still much wealth and glory. Florence had achieved conquests over walled cities once mightier than itself, and especially over hated Pisa,* whose marble buildings were too high and beautiful, whose masts were too much honoured on Greek and Italian coasts. The name of Florence had been growing prouder and prouder in all the courts of Europe, nay, in Africa itself, on the strength of purest gold coinage, finest dyes and textures, pre-eminent scholarship and poetic genius, and wits of the most serviceable sort for statesmanship and banking: it was a name so omnipresent that a Pope with a turn for epigram had called Florentines "the fifth element." And for this high destiny, though it might partly depend on the stars and Madonna dell' Impruneta,* and certainly depended on other higher Powers less often named, the praise was greatly due to San Giovanni, whose image was on the fair gold florins.

Therefore it was fitting that the day of San Giovanni—that ancient Church festival already venerable in the days of St. Augustine—should be a day of peculiar rejoicing to Florence, and should be ushered in by a vigil duly kept in strict old Florentine fashion, with much dancing, with much street jesting, and perhaps with not a little stone-throwing and window-breaking, but emphatically with certain street sights such as could only be provided by a city which held in its service a clever Cecca, engineer and architect, valuable alike in sieges and in shows. By the help of Cecca, the very saints, surrounded with their almond-shaped glory, and floating on clouds with their joyous companionship of winged cherubs, even as they may be seen to this day in the pictures of Perugino,* seemed, on the eve of San Giovanni, to have brought their piece of the heavens down into the narrow streets, and to pass slowly through them; and, more wonderful still, saints of gigantic size, with attendant angels, might be seen, not seated, but moving in a slow mysterious manner along the streets, like a procession of colossal figures come down from the high domes and tribunes of the churches. The clouds were made of good woven stuff, the saints and cherubs were unglorified mortals supported by firm bars, and those mysterious giants were really men of very steady brain, balancing themselves on stilts, and enlarged, like Greek tragedians, by huge masks and stuffed shoulders; but he was a miserably unimaginative Florentine who thought only of that—nay, somewhat impious, for in the images of sacred things was there not some of the virtue of sacred things themselves? And if, after that, there came a company of merry black demons well-armed with claws and thongs, and other implements of sport, ready to perform impromptu farces of bastinadoing and clothes-tearing, why, that was the demons' way of keeping a vigil, and they, too, might have descended from the domes and the tribunes. The Tuscan mind slipped from the devout to the burlesque, as readily as water round an angle; and the saints had already had their turn, had gone their way, and made their due pause before the gates of San Giovanni, to do him honour on the eve of his Festa. And on the morrow, the great day thus ushered in, it was fitting that the tributary symbols paid to Florence by all its dependent cities, districts, and villages, whether conquered, protected, or of immemorial possession, should be offered at the shrine of San Giovanni in the old octagonal church, once the Cathedral, and now the Baptistery, where every Florentine had had the sign of the cross made with the anointing chrism on his brow; that all the city, from the white-haired man to the stripling, and from the matron to the lisping child, should be clothed in its best to do honour to the great day, and see the great sight; and that again, when the sun was sloping and the streets were cool, there should be the glorious race or Corso, when the unsaddled horses, clothed in rich trappings, should run right across the city, from the Porta al Prato on the north-west, through the Mercato Vecchio, to the Porta Santa Croce on the south-east, where the richest of *Palii*, or velvet and brocade banners with silk linings and fringe of gold, such as became a city that half clothed the well-dressed world, were mounted on a triumphal car awaiting the winner or winner's owner.

And thereafter followed more dancing; nay, through the whole day, says an old chronicler* at the beginning of that century, there were weddings and the grandest gatherings, with so much piping, music and song, with balls and feasts and gladness and ornament, that this earth might have been mistaken for paradise!

In this year of 1492, it was, perhaps, a little less easy to make that mistake. Lorenzo the magnificent and subtle was dead, and an arrogant, incautious Piero was come in his room; an evil change for Florence, unless, indeed, the wise horse prefers the bad rider, as more easily thrown from the saddle; and already the regrets for Lorenzo were getting less predominant over the murmured desire for government on a broader basis, in which corruption might be arrested, and there might be that free play for everybody's jealousy and ambition, which made the ideal liberty of the good old quarrelsome, struggling times, when Florence raised her great buildings, reared her own soldiers, drove out would-be tyrants at the sword's point, and was proud to keep faith at her own loss. Lorenzo was dead, Pope Innocent was dying, and a troublesome Neapolitan succession, with an intriguing, ambitious Milan, might set Italy by the ears* before long: the times were likely to be difficult. Still, there was all the more reason that the Republic should keep its religious festivals.

And Midsummer morning, in this year 1492, was not less bright than usual. It was betimes in the morning that the symbolic offerings to be carried in grand procession were all assembled at their starting-point in the Piazza della Signoria—that famous piazza, where stood then, and stand now, the massive turreted Palace of the People, called the Palazzo Vecchio, and the spacious Loggia, built by Orgagna—the scene of all grand State ceremonial. The sky made the fairest blue tent, and under it the bells swung so vigorously that every evil spirit with sense enough to be formidable, must long since have taken his flight; windows and terraced roofs were alive with human faces; sombre stone houses were bright with hanging draperies; the boldly soaring palace tower, the yet older square tower of the Bargello,* and the spire of the neighbouring Badia, seemed to keep watch above; and below, on the broad polygonal flags of the piazza, was the glorious show of banners, and horses with rich trappings, and gigantic *ceri*, or tapers, that were fitly called towers—strangely aggrandized descendants of those torches by whose faint light the Church worshipped in the catacombs.* Betimes in the morning all processions had need to move under the midsummer sky of Florence, where the shelter of the narrow streets must every now and then be exchanged for the glare of wide spaces; and the sun would be high up in the heavens before the long pomp had ended its pilgrimage in the Piazza di San Giovanni.

But here, where the procession was to pause, the magnificent city, with its ingenious Cecca, had provided another tent than the sky; for the whole of the Piazza del Duomo, from the octagonal Baptistery in the centre to the façade of the Cathedral and the walls of the houses on the other sides of the quadrangle, was covered, at the height of forty feet or more, with blue drapery, adorned with well-stitched yellow lilies and the familiar coats of arms, while sheaves of many-coloured banners drooped at fit angles under this superincumbent blue—a gorgeous rainbow-lit shelter to the waiting spectators who leaned from the windows, and made a narrow border on the pavement, and wished for the coming of the show.

One of those spectators was Tito Melema. Bright, in the midst of brightness, he sat at the window of the room above Nello's shop, his right elbow resting on the red drapery hanging from the window-sill, and his head supported in a backward position by the right hand, which pressed the curls against his ear. His face wore that bland liveliness, as far removed from excitability as from heaviness or gloom, which marks the companion popular alike amongst men and women—the companion who is never obtrusive or noisy from uneasy vanity or excessive animal spirits, and whose brow is never contracted by resentment or indignation. He showed no other change from the two months and more that had passed since his first appearance in the weather-stained tunic and hose, than that added radiance of good fortune, which is like the just perceptible perfecting of a flower after it has drunk in a morning's sunbeams. Close behind him, ensconced in the narrow angle between his chair and the window-frame, stood the slim figure of Nello in holiday suit, and at his left the younger Cennini—Piero, the erudite, corrector of proof-sheets, not Domenico the practical. Tito was looking alternately down on the scene below, and upward at the varied knot of gazers and talkers immediately around him, some of whom had come in after witnessing the commencement of the procession in the Piazza della Signoria. Piero di Cosimo was raising a laugh among them by his grimaces and anathemas at the noise of the bells, against which no kind of ear-stuffing was a sufficient barricade, since the more he stuffed his ears the more he felt the vibration of his skull, and declaring that he would bury himself in the most solitary spot of the Valdarno* on a festa, if he were not condemned, as a painter, to lie in wait for the secrets of colour that were sometimes to be caught from the floating of banners and the chance grouping of the multitude.

Tito had just turned his laughing face away from the whimsical painter to look down at the small drama going on among the chequered border of spectators, when at the angle of the marble steps in front of the Duomo, nearly opposite Nello's shop, he saw a man's face upturned towards him, and fixing on him a gaze that seemed to have more meaning in it than the ordinary passing observation of a stranger. It was a face with tonsured head, that rose above the black mantle and white tunic of a Dominican friar—a very common sight in Florence; but the glance had something peculiar in it for Tito. There was a faint suggestion in it, certainly not of an unpleasant kind. Yet what pleasant association had he ever had with monks? None. The glance and the suggestion hardly took longer than a flash of lightning.

"Nello!" said Tito, hastily, but immediately added in a tone of disappointment, "Ah, he has turned round. It was that tall, thin friar who is going up the steps. I wanted you to tell me if you knew aught of him?"

"One of the Frati Predicatori," said Nello, carelessly; "you don't expect me to know the private history of the crows."

"I seem to remember something about his face," said Tito. "It is an uncommon face."

"What? you thought it might be our Fra Girolamo? Too tall; and he never shows himself in that chance way."

"Besides, that loud-barking 'hound of the Lord'* is not in

Florence just now," said Francesco Cei,* the popular poet; "he has taken Piero de' Medici's hint, to carry his railing prophecies on a journey for a while."

"The Frate neither rails nor prophesies against any man," said a middle-aged personage seated at the other corner of the window; "he only prophesies against vice. If you think that an attack on your poems, Francesco, it is not the Frate's fault."

"Ah, he's gone into the Duomo now," said Tito, who had watched the figure eagerly. "No, I was not under that mistake, Nello. Your Fra Girolamo has a high nose and a large underlip. I saw him once—he is not handsome; but this man . . ."

"Truce to your descriptions!" said Cennini. "Hark! see! Here come the horsemen and the banners. That standard," he continued, laying his hand familiarly on Tito's shoulder,—"that carried on the horse with white trappings—that with the red eagle holding the green dragon between his talons, and the red lily over the eagle—is the Gonfalon of the Guelf party, and those cavaliers close round it are the chief officers of the Guelf party. That is one of our proudest banners, grumble as we may; it means the triumph of the Guelfs, which means the triumph of Florentine will, which means triumph of the *popolani*."

"Nay, go on, Cennini," said the middle-aged man, seated at the window, "which means triumph of the fat *popolani* over the lean, which again means triumph of the fattest *popolano* over those who are less fat."

"Cronaca, you are becoming sententious," said the printer; "Fra Girolamo's preaching will spoil you, and make you take life by the wrong handle. Trust me, your cornices will lose half their beauty if you begin to mingle bitterness with them; that is the *maniera Tedesca* which you used to declaim against when you came from Rome. The next palace you build we shall see you trying to put the Frate's doctrines into stone."*

"That is a goodly show of cavaliers," said Tito, who had learned by this time the best way to please Florentines; "but are there not strangers among them? I see foreign costumes."

"Assuredly", said Cennini; "you see there the Orators* from France, Milan, and Venice, and behind them are English and German nobles; for it is customary that all foreign visitors of distinction pay their tribute to San Giovanni in the train of that gonfalon. For my part, I think our Florentine cavaliers sit their horses as well as any of those cut-and-thrust northerns, whose wits lie in their heels and saddles; and for yon Venetian, I fancy he would feel himself more at ease on the back of a dolphin.* We ought to know something of horsemanship, for we excel all Italy in the sports of the *Giostra*, and the money we spend on them. But you will see a finer show of our chief men by and by, Melema; my brother himself will be among the officers of the Zecca."

"The banners are the better sight," said Piero di Cosimo, forgetting the noise in his delight at the winding stream of colour as the tributary standards advanced round the piazza. "The Florentine men are so so; they make but a sorry show at this distance with their patch of sallow flesh-tint above the black garments; but those banners with their velvet, and satin, and minever, and brocade, and their endless play of delicate light and shadow!—*Va!* your human talk and doings are a tame jest; the only passionate life is in form and colour."

"Ay, Piero, if Satanasso could paint, thou wouldst sell thy soul to learn his secrets," said Nello. "But there is little likelihood of it, seeing the blessed angels themselves are such poor hands at chiaroscuro, if one may judge from their capo-d'opera, the Madonna Nunziata."*

"There go the banners of Pisa and Arezzo," said Cennini. "Ay, Messer Pisano, it is no use for you to look sullen; you may as well carry your banner to our San Giovanni with a good grace. 'Pisans false, Florentines blind'*—the second half of that proverb will hold no longer. There come the ensigns of our subject-towns and signories, Melema; they will all be suspended in San Giovanni until this day next year, when they will give place to new ones."

"They are a fair sight," said Tito; "and San Giovanni will surely be as well satisfied with that produce of Italian looms as Minerva with her peplos,* especially as he contents himself with so little drapery. But my eyes are less delighted with those whirling towers, which would soon make me fall from the window in sympathetic vertigo."

The "towers" of which Tito spoke were a part of the procession esteemed very glorious by the Florentine populace; and being perhaps chiefly a kind of hyperbole for the all-efficacious wax taper, were also called *ceri*. But inasmuch as hyperbole is impracticable in a real and literal fashion, these gigantic *ceri*, some of them so large as to be of necessity carried on wheels, were not solid but hollow, and had their surface made not solely of wax, but of wood and pasteboard, gilded, carved, and painted, as real sacred tapers often are, with successive circles of figures—warriors on horseback, foot soldiers with lance and shield, dancing maidens, animals, trees and fruits, and in fine, says the old chronicler,* "all things that could delight the eye and the heart;" the hollowness having the further advantage that men could stand inside these hyperbolic tapers and whirl them continually, so as to produce a phantasmagoric effect, which, considering the towers were numerous, must have been calculated to produce dizziness on a truly magnificent scale.

"*Pestilenza!*" said Piero di Cosimo, moving from the window, "those whirling circles one above the other are worse than the jangling of all the bells. Let me know when the last taper has passed."

"Nay, you will surely like to be called when the contadini come carrying their torches," said Nello; "you would not miss the country folk of the Mugello and the Casentino, of whom your favourite Lionardo would make a hundred grotesque sketches."*

"No," said Piero resolutely; "I will see nothing till the car of the Zecca comes. I have seen clowns enough holding tapers aslant, both with and without cowls, to last me for my life."

"Here it comes, then, Piero—the car of the Zecca," called out Nello, after an interval during which towers and tapers in a descending scale of size had been making their slow transit.

"*Fediddio!*" exclaimed Francesco Cei, "that is a well-tanned San Giovanni! some sturdy Romagnole* beggar-man, I'll warrant. Our Signoria plays the host to all the Jewish and Christian scum that every other city shuts its gates against, and lets them fatten on us like Saint Anthony's swine."*

The car* of the Zecca or Mint, which had just rolled into sight, was originally an immense wooden tower or *cero* adorned after the same fashion as the other tributary *ceri*, mounted on a splendid car, and drawn by two mouse-coloured oxen, whose mild heads looked out from rich trappings bearing the arms of the Zecca. But the latter half of the century was getting rather ashamed of the towers with their circular or spiral paintings, which had delighted the eyes and the hearts of the other half, so that they had become a contemptuous proverb, and any ill-painted figure looking, as will sometimes happen to figures in the best ages of art, as if it had been boned for a pie, was called a *fantoccio da cero*, a tower-puppet; consequently improved taste, with Cecca to help it, had devised for the magnificent Zecca a triumphal car like a pyramidal catafalque, with ingenious wheels warranted to turn all corners easily. Round the base were living figures of saints and angels arrayed in sculpturesque fashion; and on the summit, at the height of thirty feet, well bound to an iron rod and holding an iron cross also firmly infixed, stood a living representative of St. John the Baptist, with arms and legs bare, a garment of tiger-skins about his body, and a golden nimbus fastened on his head—as the Precursor was wont to appear in the cloisters and churches, not having yet revealed himself to painters as the brown and sturdy boy who made one of the Holy Family.* For where could the image of the patron saint be more fitly placed than on the symbol of the Zecca? Was not the royal prerogative of coining money the surest token that a city had won its independence? and by the blessing of San Giovanni this "beautiful sheepfold"* of his had shown that token earliest among the Italian cities. Nevertheless, the annual function of representing the patron saint was not among the high prizes of public life; it was paid for with something like ten shillings, a cake weighing fourteen pounds, two bottles of wine, and a handsome supply of light eatables; the money being furnished by the magnificent Zecca, and the payment in kind being by peculiar "privilege" presented in a basket suspended on a pole from an upper window of a private house, whereupon the eidolon* of the austere saint at once invigorated himself with a reasonable share of the sweets and wine, threw the remnants to the crowd, and embraced the mighty cake securely with his right arm through the remainder of his passage. This was the attitude in which the mimic San Giovanni presented himself as the tall car jerked and vibrated on its slow way round the piazza to the northern gates of the Baptistery.

"There go the masters of the Zecca, and there is my brother—you see him, Melema?" cried Cennini, with an agreeable stirring of pride at showing a stranger what was too familiar to be remarkable to fellow-citizens. "Behind come the members of the corporation of Calimala,* the dealers in foreign cloth, to which we have given our Florentine finish; men of ripe years, you see, who were matriculated before you were born; and then comes the famous Art of money-changers."

"Many of them matriculated also to the noble art of usury before you were born," interrupted Francesco Cei, "as you may discern by a certain fitful glare of the eye and sharp curve of the nose which manifest their descent from the ancient harpies,* whose portraits you saw supporting the arms of the Zecca. Shaking off old prejudices now, such a procession as that of some four hundred passably ugly men carrying their tapers in open daylight, Diogenes-fashion, as if they were looking for a lost quattrino, would make a merry spectacle for the Feast of Fools."*

"Blaspheme not against the usages of our city," said Piero Cennini, much offended. "There are new wits who think they see things more truly because they stand on their heads to look at them, like tumblers and mountebanks, instead of keeping the attitude of rational men. Doubtless it makes little difference to Maestro Vaiano's monkeys whether they see our Donatello's statue of Judith* with their heads or their tails uppermost."

"Your solemnity will allow some quarter to playful fancy, I hope," said Cei, with a shrug, "else what becomes of the ancients, whose example you scholars are bound to revere, Messer Piero? Life was never anything but a perpetual see-saw between gravity and jest."*

"Keep your jest then till your end of the pole is uppermost," said Cennini, still angry, "and that is not when the great bond of our Republic is expressing itself in ancient symbols, without which the vulgar would be conscious of nothing beyond their own petty wants of back and stomach, and never rise to the sense of community in religion and law. There has been no great people without processions, and the man who thinks himself too wise to be moved by them to anything but contempt is like the puddle that was proud of standing alone while the river rushed by."

No one said anything after this indignant burst of Cennini's till he himself spoke again.

"Hark! the trumpets of the Signoria: now comes the last stage of the show, Melema. That is our Gonfaloniere in the middle, in the starred mantle, with the sword carried before him. Twenty years ago we used to see our foreign *Podestà*,* who was our judge in civil causes, walking on his right hand; but our Republic has been over-doctored by clever *medici*.* That is the Proposto* of the *Priori* on the left; then come the other seven

Priori; then all the other magistracies and officials of our Republic. You see your patron the Segretario?"

"There is Messer Bernardo del Nero also," said Tito; "his visage is a fine and venerable one, though it has worn rather a petrifying look towards me."

"Ah," said Nello, "he is the dragon that guards the remnant of old Bardo's gold,* which, I fancy, is chiefly that virgin gold that falls about the fair Romola's head and shoulders; eh, my Apollino?" he added, patting Tito's head.

Tito had the youthful grace of blushing, but he had also the adroit and ready speech that prevents a blush from looking like embarrassment. He replied at once:—

"And a very Pactolus* it is—a stream with golden ripples. If I were an alchemist—"

He was saved from the need for further speech by the sudden fortissimo of drums and trumpets and fifes, bursting into the breadth of the piazza in a grand storm of sound—a roar, a blast, and a whistling, well befitting a city famous for its musical instruments, and reducing the members of the closest group to a state of deaf isolation.

During this interval Nello observed Tito's fingers moving in recognition of some one in the crowd below, but not seeing the direction of his glance he failed to detect the object of this greeting—the sweet round blue-eyed face under a white hood—immediately lost in the narrow border of heads, where there was a continual eclipse of round contadina cheeks by the harsh-lined features or bent shoulders of an old spadesman, and where profiles turned as sharply from north to south as weathercocks under a shifting wind.

But when it was felt that the show was ended—when the twelve prisoners released in honour of the day, and the very *barberi* or race-horses, with the arms of their owners embroidered on their cloths, had followed up the Signoria, and been duly consecrated to San Giovanni, and every one was moving from the window—Nello, whose Florentine curiosity was of that lively canine sort which thinks no trifle too despicable for investigation, put his hand on Tito's shoulder and said,—

"What acquaintance was that you were making signals to, eh, *giovane mio?*"

"Some little contadina who probably mistook me for an acquaintance, for she had honoured me with a greeting."

"Or who wished to begin an acquaintance," said Nello. "But you are bound for the Via de' Bardi and the feast of the Muses: there is no counting on you for a frolic, else we might have gone in search of adventures together in the crowd, and had some pleasant fooling in honour of San Giovanni. But your high fortune has come on you too soon: I don't mean the professor's mantle—*that* is roomy enough to hide a few stolen chickens, but—Messer Endymion minded his manners after that singular good fortune* of his; and what says our Luigi Pulci?

'Da quel giorno in quà ch' amor m' accese
Per lei son fatto e gentile e cortese.'"*

"Nello, *amico mio*, thou hast an intolerable trick of making life stale by forestalling it with thy talk," said Tito, shrugging his shoulders, with a look of patient resignation, which was his nearest approach to anger: "not to mention that such ill-founded babbling would be held a great offence by that same goddess whose humble worshipper you are always professing yourself."

"I will be mute," said Nello, laying his finger on his lips, with a responding shrug. "But it is only under our four eyes that I talk* any folly about her."

"Pardon! you were on the verge of it just now in the hearing of others. If you want to ruin me in the minds of Bardo and his daughter—"

"Enough, enough!" said Nello. "I am an absurd old barber. It all comes from that abstinence of mine, in not making bad verses in my youth: for want of letting my folly run out that way when I was eighteen, it runs out at my tongue's end now I am at the unseemly age of fifty. But Nello has not got his head muffled for all that; he can see a buffalo in the snow.* *Addio, giovane mio.*"

CHAPTER IX.

A Man's Ransom

TITO was soon down among the crowd, and, notwithstanding his indifferent reply to Nello's question about his chance acquaintance, he was not without a passing wish, as he made his way round the piazza to the Corso degli Adimari, that he might encounter the pair of blue eyes which had looked up towards him from under the square bit of white linen drapery that formed the ordinary hood of the contadina at festa time. He was perfectly well aware that that face was Tessa's; but he had not chosen to say so. What had Nello to do with the matter? Tito had an innate love of reticence—let us say a talent for it—which acted as other impulses do, without any conscious motive, and, like all people to whom concealment is easy, he would now and then conceal something which had as little the nature of a secret as the fact that he had seen a flight of crows.

But the passing wish about pretty Tessa was almost immediately eclipsed by the recurrent recollection of that friar whose face had some irrecoverable association for him. Why should a sickly fanatic, worn with fasting, have looked at *him* in particular, and where in all his travels could he remember encountering that face before? Folly! such vague memories hang about the mind like cobwebs, with tickling importunity—best to sweep them away at a dash: and Tito had pleasanter occupation for his thoughts. By the time he was turning out of the Corso degli Adimari into a side street he was caring only that the sun was high, and that the procession had kept him longer than he had intended from his visit to that room in the Via de' Bardi, where his coming, he knew, was anxiously awaited. He felt the scene of his entrance beforehand: the joy beaming diffusedly in the blind face like the light in a semi-transparent lamp; the transient pink flush on Romola's face and neck, which subtracted nothing from her majesty, but only gave it the exquisite charm of womanly sensitiveness, heightened still more by what seemed the paradoxical boy-like frankness of her look and smile. They were the best comrades in the world during the hours they passed together round the blind man's chair: she was constantly appealing to Tito, and he was informing her, yet he felt himself strangely in subjection to Romola with that simplicity of hers: he felt for the first time, without defining it to himself, that loving awe in the presence of noble womanhood, which is perhaps something like the worship paid of old to a great Nature-Goddess, who was not all-knowing, but whose life and power were something deeper and more primordial than knowledge. They had never been alone together, and he could frame to himself no probable image of love scenes between them: he could only fancy and wish wildly—what he knew was impossible—that Romola would some day tell him that she loved him. One day in Greece, as he was leaning over a wall in the sunshine, a little black-eyed peasant girl, who had rested her water-pot on the wall, crept gradually nearer and nearer to him, and at last shyly asked him to kiss her, putting up her round olive cheek very innocently. Tito was used to love that came in this unsought fashion. But Romola's love would never come in that way: would it ever come at all?—and yet it was that topmost apple on which he had set his mind. He was in his fresh youth—not passionate, but impressible: it was as inevitable that he should feel lovingly towards Romola as that the white irises should be reflected in the clear sun-lit stream; but he had no coxcombry, and he had an intimate sense that Romola was something very much above him. Many men have felt the same before a large-eyed, simple child.

Nevertheless, Tito had had the rapid success which would have made some men presuming, or would have warranted him in thinking that there would be no great presumption in entertaining an agreeable confidence that he might one day be the husband of Romola—nay, that her father himself was not without a vision of such a future for him. His first auspicious interview with Bartolommeo Scala had proved the commencement of a growing favour on the secretary's part, and had led to an issue which would have been enough to make Tito decide on Florence as the place in which to establish himself, even if it had held no other magnet. Politian was professor of Greek as well as Latin at Florence, professorial chairs being maintained there, although the university had been removed to Pisa; but for a long time Demetrio Calcondila, one of the most eminent and respectable among the emigrant Greeks, had also held a Greek chair, simultaneously with the too predominant Italian. Calcondila was now gone to Milan, and there was no counterpoise or rival to Politian such as was desired for him by the friends who wished him to be taught a little propriety and humility. Scala was far from being the only friend of this class, and he found several who, if they were not among those thirsty admirers of mediocrity that were glad to be refreshed with his verses in hot weather, were yet quite willing to join him in doing that moral service to Politian. It was finally agreed that Tito should be supported in a Greek chair, as Demetrio

Calcondila had been by Lorenzo himself, who, being at the same time the affectionate patron of Politian, had shown by precedent that there was nothing invidious in such a measure, but only a zeal for true learning and for the instruction of the Florentine youth.

Tito was thus sailing under the fairest breeze, and besides convincing fair judges that his talents squared with his good fortune, he wore that fortune so easily and unpretentiously that no one had yet been offended by it. He was not unlikely to get into the best Florentine society: society where there was much more plate than the circle of enamelled silver in the centre of the brass dishes, and where it was not forbidden by the Signory to wear the richest brocade.* For where could a handsome young scholar not be welcome when he could touch the lute and troll a gay song? That bright face, that easy smile, that liquid voice, seemed to give life a holiday aspect; just as a strain of gay music and the hoisting of colours make the work-worn and the sad rather ashamed of showing themselves. Here was a professor likely to render the Greek classics amiable to the sons of great houses.

And that was not the whole of Tito's good fortune; for he had sold all his jewels, except the ring he did not choose to part with, and he was master of full five hundred gold florins.

Yet the moment when he first had this sum in his possession was the crisis of the first serious struggle his facile, good-humoured nature had known. An importunate thought, of which he had till now refused to see more than the shadow as it dogged his footsteps, at last rushed upon him and grasped him: he was obliged to pause and decide whether he would surrender and obey, or whether he would give the refusal that must carry irrevocable consequences. It was in the room above Nello's shop, which Tito had now hired as a lodging, that the elder Cennini handed him the last quota of the sum on behalf of Bernardo Rucellai, the purchaser of the two most valuable gems.

"*Ecco, giovane mio!*" said the respectable printer and goldsmith, "you have now a pretty little fortune; and if you will take my advice, you will let me place your florins in a safe quarter, where they may increase and multiply, instead of slipping through your fingers for banquets and other follies which are rife among our Florentine youth. And it has been too much the fashion of scholars, especially when, like our Pietro Crinito, they think their scholarship needs to be scented and broidered, to squander with one hand till they have been fain to beg with the other. I have brought you the money, and you are free to make a wise choice or an unwise: I shall see on which side the balance dips. We Florentines hold no man a member of an Art till he has shown his skill and been matriculated; and no man is matriculated to the art of life till he has been well tempted. If you make up your mind to put your florins out to usury, you can let me know to-morrow. A scholar may marry, and should have something in readiness for the *morgen cap*.* Addio."

As Cennini closed the door behind him, Tito turned round with the smile dying out of his face, and fixed his eyes on the table where the florins lay. He made no other movement, but stood with his thumbs in his belt, looking down, in that transfixed state which accompanies the concentration of consciousness on some inward image.

"A man's ransom!"—who was it that had said five hundred florins was more than a man's ransom? If now, under this midday sun, on some hot coast far away, a man somewhat stricken in years—a man not without high thoughts and with the most passionate heart—a man who long years ago had rescued a little boy from a life of beggary, filth, and cruel wrong, had reared him tenderly, and been to him as a father—if that man were now under this summer sun toiling as a slave, hewing wood and drawing water, perhaps being smitten and buffeted because he was not deft and active? If he were saying to himself, "Tito will find me: he had but to carry our manuscripts and gems to Venice; he will have raised money, and will never rest till he finds me out"? If that were certain, could he, Tito, see the price of the gems lying before him, and say, "I will stay at Florence, where I am fanned by soft airs of promised love and prosperity: I will not risk myself for his sake"? No, surely not, *if it were certain*. But nothing could be farther from certainty. The galley had been taken by a Turkish vessel on its way to Delos: *that* was known by the report of the companion galley, which had escaped. But there had been resistance, and probable bloodshed; a man had been seen falling overboard: who were the survivors, and what had befallen them amongst all the multitude of possibilities? Had not he, Tito, suffered shipwreck, and narrowly escaped drowning? He had good cause for feeling the omnipresence of casualties that threatened all projects with futility. The rumour that there were pirates who had a settlement in Delos was not to be depended on, or might be nothing to the purpose. What, probably enough, would be the result if he were to quit Florence and go to Venice; get authoritative letters—yes, he knew that might be done—and set out for the Archipelago? Why, that he should be himself seized, and spend all his florins on preliminaries, and be again a destitute wanderer—with no more gems to sell.

Tito had a clearer vision of that result than of the possible moment when he might find his father again, and carry him deliverance. It would surely be an unfairness that he, in his full ripe youth, to whom life had hitherto had some of the stint and subjection of a school, should turn his back on promised love and distinction, and perhaps never be visited by that promise again. "And yet," he said to himself, "if I were certain—yes, if I were certain that Baldassarre Calvo was alive, and that I could free him, by whatever exertions or perils, I would go now—now I have the money: it was useless to debate the matter before. I would go now to Bardo and Bartolommeo Scala, and tell them the whole truth." Tito did not say to himself so distinctly that if those two men had known the whole truth he was aware there would have been no alternative for him but to go in search of his benefactor, who, if alive, was the rightful owner of the gems, and whom he had always equivocally spoken of as "lost;" he did not say to himself—what he was not ignorant of—that Greeks of distinction had made sacrifices, taken voyages again and again, and sought help from crowned and mitred heads for the sake of freeing relatives from slavery to the Turks. Public opinion did not regard that as an exceptional virtue.

This was his first real colloquy with himself: he had gone on following the impulses of the moment, and one of those impulses had been to conceal half the fact: he had never considered this part of his conduct long enough to face the consciousness of his motives for the concealment. What was the use of telling the whole? It was true, the thought had crossed his mind several times since he had quitted Nauplia that, after all, it was a great relief to be quit of Baldassarre, and he would have liked to know *who* it was that had fallen overboard. But such thoughts spring inevitably out of a relation that is irksome. Baldassarre was exacting, and had got stranger as he got older: he was constantly scrutinizing Tito's mind to see whether it answered to his own exaggerated expectations; and age—the age of a thick-set, heavy-browed, bald man beyond sixty, whose intensity and eagerness in the grasp of ideas have long taken the character of monotony and repetition, may be looked at from many points of view without being found attractive. Such a man, stranded among new acquaintances, unless he had the philosopher's stone, would hardly find rank, youth, and beauty at his feet. The feelings that gather fervour from novelty will be of little help towards making the world a home for dimmed and faded human beings; and if there is any love of which they are not widowed, it must be the love that is rooted in memories and distils perpetually the sweet balms of fidelity and forbearing tenderness.

"But surely such memories were not absent from Tito's mind? Far in the backward vista of his remembered life, when he was only seven years old, Baldassarre had rescued him from blows, had taken him to a home that seemed like opened paradise, where there was sweet food and soothing caresses, all had on Baldassarre's knee; and from that time till the hour they had parted, Tito had been the one centre of Baldassarre's fatherly cares.

And he had been docile, pliable, quick of apprehension, ready to acquire: a very bright, lovely boy, a youth of even splendid grace, who seemed quite without vices, as if that beautiful form represented a vitality so exquisitely poised and balanced that it could know no uneasy desires, no unrest—a radiant presence for a lonely man to have won for himself. If he were silent when his father expected some response, still he did not look moody; if he declined some labour—why, he flung himself down with such a charming, half-smiling, half-pleading air, that the pleasure of looking at him made amends to one who had watched his growth with a sense of claim and possession: the curves of Tito's mouth had ineffable good humour in them. And then, the quick talent to which everything came readily, from philosophic systems to the rhymes of a street ballad caught up at a hearing! Would any one have said that Tito had not made a rich return to his benefactor, or that his gratitude and affection would fail on any great demand? He did not admit that his gratitude had failed; but *it was not certain* that Baldassarre was in slavery, not certain that he was living.

"Do I not owe something to myself?" said Tito, inwardly, with a slight movement of his shoulders, the first he had made since he had turned to look down at the florins. "Before I quit everything, and incur again all the risks of which I am even now weary, I must at least have a reasonable hope. Am I to spend my life in a wandering search? *I believe he is dead.* Cennini was right about my florins: I will place them in his hands to-morrow."

When, the next morning, Tito put this determination into act he had chosen his colour in the game, and had given an inevitable bent to his wishes. He had made it impossible that he should not from henceforth desire it to be the truth that his father was dead; impossible that he should not be tempted to baseness rather than that the precise facts of his conduct should not remain for ever concealed.

Under every guilty secret there is hidden a brood of guilty wishes, whose unwholesome infecting life is cherished by the darkness. The contaminating effect of deeds often lies less in the commission than in the consequent adjustment of our desires—the enlistment of our self-interest on the side of falsity; as, on the other hand, the purifying influence of public confession springs from the fact, that by it the hope in lies is for ever swept away, and the soul recovers the noble attitude of simplicity.

Besides, in this first distinct colloquy with himself the ideas which had previously been scattered and interrupted had now concentrated themselves: the little rills of selfishness had united and made a channel, so that they could never again meet with the same resistance. Hitherto Tito had left in vague indecision the question whether, with the means in his power, he would not return, and ascertain his father's fate; he had now made a definite excuse to himself for not taking that course; he had avowed to himself a choice which he would have been ashamed to avow to others, and which would have made him ashamed in the resurgent presence of his father. But the inward shame, the reflex of that outward law which the great heart of mankind makes for every individual man, a reflex which will exist even in the absence of the sympathetic impulses that need no law, but rush to the deed of fidelity and pity as inevitably as the brute mother shields her young from the attack of the hereditary enemy—that inward shame was showing its blushes in Tito's determined assertion to himself that his father was dead, or that at least search was hopeless.

CHAPTER X.

Under the Plane-tree

ON the day of San Giovanni it was already three weeks ago that Tito had handed his florins to Cennini, and we have seen that as he set out towards the Via de' Bardi he showed all the outward signs of a mind at ease. How should it be otherwise? He never jarred with what was immediately around him, and his nature was too joyous, too unapprehensive, for the hidden and the distant to grasp him in the shape of a dread. As he turned out of the hot sunshine into the shelter of a narrow street, took off the black cloth berretta, or simple cap with upturned lappet, which just crowned his brown curls, pushing his hair and tossing his head backward to court the cooler air, there was no brand of duplicity on his brow; neither was there any stamp of candour: it was simply a finely formed, square, smooth young brow. And the slow absent glance he cast round at the upper windows of the houses had neither more dissimulation in it, nor more ingenuousness, than belongs to a youthful well-opened eyelid with its unwearied breadth of gaze; to perfectly pellucid lenses; to the undimmed dark of a rich brown iris; and to a pure cerulean-tinted angle of whiteness streaked with the delicate shadows of long eyelashes. Was it that Tito's face attracted or repelled according to the mental attitude of the observer? Was it a cipher with more than one key? The strong, unmistakable expression in his whole air and person was a negative one, and it was perfectly veracious; it declared the absence of any uneasy claim, any restless vanity, and it made the admiration that followed him as he passed among the troop of holiday-makers a thoroughly willing tribute.

For by this time the stir of the Festa was felt even in the narrowest side streets; the throng which had at one time been concentrated in the lines through which the procession had to pass, was now streaming out in all directions in pursuit of a new object. Such intervals of a festa are precisely the moments when the vaguely active animal spirits of a crowd are likely to be the most petulant and most ready to sacrifice a stray individual to the greater happiness of the greater number. As Tito entered the neighbourhood of San Martino, he found the throng rather denser; and near the hostelry of the *Bertucce*,* or Baboons, there was evidently some object which was arresting the passengers and forming them into a knot. It needed nothing of great interest to draw aside passengers unfreighted with a purpose, and Tito was preparing to turn aside into an adjoining street, when, amidst the loud laughter, his ear discerned a distressed childish voice crying, "Loose me! Holy Virgin, help me!" which at once determined him to push his way into the knot of gazers. He had just had time to perceive that the distressed voice came from a young contadina, whose white hood had fallen off in the struggle to get her hands free from the grasp of a man in the particoloured dress of a *cerretano*, or conjuror, who was making laughing attempts to soothe and cajole her, evidently carrying with him the amused sympathy of the spectators. These, by a persuasive variety of words, signifying simpleton, for which the Florentine dialect is rich in equivalents, seemed to be arguing with the contadina against her obstinacy. At the first moment the girl's face was turned away, and he saw only her light brown hair plaited and fastened with a long silver pin; but in the next, the struggle brought her face opposite Tito's, and he saw the baby features of Tessa, her blue eyes filled with tears, and her under-lip quivering. Tessa, too, saw *him*, and through the mist of her swelling tears there beamed a sudden hope, like that in the face of a little child, when, held by a stranger against its will, it sees a familiar hand stretched out.

In an instant Tito had pushed his way through the barrier of bystanders, whose curiosity made them ready to turn aside at the sudden interference of this handsome young signor, had grasped Tessa's waist, and had said, "Loose this child! What right have you to hold her against her will?"

The conjuror—a man with one of those faces in which the angles of the eyes and eyebrows, of the nostrils, mouth, and sharply defined jaw, all tended upward—showed his small regular teeth in an impish but not ill-natured grin, as he let go Tessa's hands, and stretched out his own backward, shrugging his shoulders, and bending them forward a little in a half-apologetic, half-protesting manner.

"I meant the *ragazza* no evil in the world, Messere: ask this respectable company. I was only going to show them a few samples of my skill, in which this little damsel might have helped me the better because of her kitten-face, which would have assured them of open dealing; and I had promised her a lapful of *confetti* as a reward. But what then? Messer has doubtless better *confetti* at hand, and she knows it."

A general laugh among the bystanders accompanied these last words of the conjuror, raised, probably, by the look of relief and confidence with which Tessa clung to Tito's arm, as he drew it from her waist and placed her hand within it. She only cared about the laugh as she might have cared about the roar of wild beasts from which she was escaping, not attaching any meaning to it; but Tito, who had no sooner got her on his arm than he foresaw some embarrassment in the situation, hastened to get clear of observers who, having been despoiled of an expected amusement, were sure to re-establish the balance by jests.

"See, see, little one! here is your hood," said the conjuror, throwing the bit of white drapery over Tessa's head. "*Orsù*, bear me no malice; come back to me when Messere can spare you."

"Ah! Maestro Vaiano, she'll come back presently, as the toad said to the harrow,"* called out one of the spectators, seeing how Tessa started and shrank at the action of the conjuror.

Tito pushed his way vigorously towards the corner of a side street, a little vexed at this delay in his progress to the Via de' Bardi, and intending to get rid of the poor little contadina as soon as possible. The next street, too, had its passengers inclined to make holiday remarks on so unusual a pair; but they had no sooner entered it than he said, in a kind but hurried manner, "Now, little one, where were you going? Are you come by yourself to the Festa?"

"Ah, no!" said Tessa, looking frightened and distressed again; "I have lost my mother in the crowd—her and my father-in-law.* They will be angry—he will beat me. It was in the crowd in San Pulinari*—somebody pushed me along and I couldn't stop myself, so I got away from them. Oh, I don't know where they're gone! Please, don't leave me!"

Her eyes had been swelling with tears again, and she ended with a sob.

Tito hurried along again: the church of the Badia was not far off. They could enter it by the cloister that opened at the back, and in the church he could talk to Tessa—perhaps leave her. No! it was an hour at which the church was not open; but they paused under the shelter of the cloister, and he said, "Have you no cousin or friend in Florence, my little Tessa, whose house you could find; or are you afraid of walking by yourself since you have been frightened by the conjuror? I am in a hurry to get to Oltrarno, but if I could take you anywhere near—"

"Oh, I *am* frightened: he was the devil—I know he was. And I don't know where to go—I have nobody: and my mother meant to have her dinner somewhere, and I don't know where. Holy Madonna! I shall be beaten."

The corners of the pouting mouth went down piteously, and the poor little bosom with the beads on it above the green serge gown heaved so, that there was no longer any help for it: a loud sob *would* come, and the big tears fell as if they were making up for lost time. Here was a situation! It would have been brutal to leave her, and Tito's nature was all gentleness. He wished at that moment that he had not been expected in the Via de' Bardi. As he saw her lifting up her holiday apron to catch the hurrying tears, he laid his hand, too, on the apron, and rubbed one of the cheeks and kissed the baby-like roundness.

"My poor little Tessa! leave off crying. Let us see what can be done. Where is your home—where do you live?"

There was no answer, but the sobs began to subside a little and the drops to fall less quickly.

"Come! I'll take you a little way, if you'll tell me where you want to go."

The apron fell, and Tessa's face began to look as contented as a cherub's budding from a cloud. The diabolical conjuror, the anger and the beating seemed a long way off.

"I think I'll go home, if you'll take me," she said, in a half whisper, looking up at Tito with wide blue eyes, and with something sweeter than a smile—with a child-like calm.

"Come, then, little one," said Tito, in a caressing tone, putting her arm within his again. "Which way is it?"

"Beyond Peretola*—where the large pear-tree is."

"Peretola? Out at which gate, pazzarella? I am a stranger, you must remember."

"Out at the Por del Prato," said Tessa, moving along with a very fast hold on Tito's arm.

He did not know all the turnings well enough to venture on an attempt at choosing the quietest streets; and besides, it occurred to him that where the passengers were most numerous there was, perhaps, the most chance of meeting with Monna Ghita and finding an end to his knight-errantship. So he made straight for Porta Rossa, and on to Ognissanti, showing his usual bright propitiatory face to the mixed observers who threw their jests at him and his little heavy-shod maiden with much liberality. Mingled with the more decent holiday-makers there were frolicsome apprentices, rather envious of his good fortune; bold-eyed women with the badge of the yellow veil;* beggars who thrust forward their caps for alms, in derision at Tito's evident haste; dicers, sharpers, and loungers of the worst sort; boys whose tongues were used to wag in concert at the most brutal street games: for the streets of Florence were not always a moral spectacle in those times, and Tessa's terror at being lost in the crowd was not wholly unreasonable.

When they reached the Piazza d'Ognissanti, Tito slackened his pace: they were both heated with their hurried walk, and here was a wider space where they could take breath. They sat down on one of the stone benches which were frequent against the walls of old Florentine houses.

"Holy Virgin!" said Tessa; "I am glad we have got away from those women and boys; but I was not frightened, because you could take care of me."

"Pretty little Tessa!" said Tito, smiling at her. "What makes you feel so safe with me?"

"Because you are so beautiful—like the people going into Paradise—they are all good."

"It is a long while since you had your breakfast, Tessa," said Tito, seeing some stalls near, with fruit and sweetmeats upon them. "Are you hungry?"

"Yes, I think I am—if you will have some too."

Tito bought some apricots, and cakes, and comfits, and put them into her apron.

"Come," he said, "let us walk on to the Prato, and then perhaps you will not be afraid to go the rest of the way alone."

"But you will have some of the apricots and things," said Tessa, rising obediently and gathering up her apron as a bag for her store.

"We will see," said Tito aloud; and to himself he said, "Here is a little contadina who might inspire a better idyl than Lorenzo de' Medici's *Nencia da Barberino*, that Nello's friends rave about; if I were only a Theocritus,* or had time to cultivate the necessary experience by unseasonable walks of this sort! However, the mischief is done now: I am so late already that another half hour will make no difference. Pretty little pigeon!"

"We have a garden and plenty of pears," said Tessa, "and two cows, besides the mules; and I'm very fond of them. But my father-in-law is a cross man: I wish my mother had not married him. I think he is wicked; he is very ugly."

"And does your mother let him beat you, poverina? You said you were afraid of being beaten."

"Ah, my mother herself scolds me: she loves my young sister better, and thinks I don't do work enough. Nobody speaks kindly to me, only the Pievano (parish priest) when I go to confession. And the men in the Mercato laugh at me and make fun of me. Nobody ever kissed me and spoke to me as you do; just as I talk to my little black-faced kid, because I'm very fond of it."

It seemed not to have entered Tessa's mind that there was any change in Tito's appearance since the morning he begged the milk from her, and that he looked now like a personage for whom she must summon her little stock of reverent words and signs. He had impressed her too differently from any human being who had ever come near her before, for her to make any comparison of details: she took no note of his dress; he was simply a voice and a face to her, something come from Paradise into a world where most things seemed hard and angry; and she prattled with as little restraint as if he had been an imaginary companion born of her own lovingness and the sunshine.

They had now reached the Prato, which at that time was a large open space within the walls, where the Florentine youth played at their favourite *Calcio*—a peculiar kind of foot-ball—and otherwise exercised themselves. At this midday time it was forsaken and quiet to the very gates, where a tent had been erected in preparation for the race. On the border of this wide meadow, Tito paused and said,

"Now, Tessa, you will not be frightened if I leave you to walk the rest of the way by yourself. Addio. Shall I come and buy a cup of milk from you in the Mercato to-morrow morning, to see that you are quite safe?"

He added this question in a soothing tone, as he saw her eyes widening sorrowfully, and the corners of her mouth falling. She said nothing at first; she only opened her apron and looked down at her apricots and sweetmeats. Then she looked up at him again, and said complainingly,—

"I thought you would have some, and we could sit down under a tree outside the gate, and eat them together."

"Tessa, Tessa, you little siren, you would ruin me," said Tito, laughing and kissing both her cheeks. "I ought to have been in the Via de' Bardi long ago. No! I must go back now; you are in no danger. There—I'll take an apricot. Addio!"

He had already stepped two yards from her when he said the last word. Tessa could not have spoken; she was pale, and a great sob was rising; but she turned round as if she felt there was no hope for her, and stepped on, holding her apron so forgetfully that the apricots began to roll out on the grass.

Tito could not help looking after her, and seeing her shoulders rise to the bursting sob, and the apricots fall—could not help going after her and picking them up. It was very hard upon him: he was a long way off the Via de' Bardi, and very near to Tessa.

"See, my silly one," he said, picking up the apricots. "Come, leave off crying, I will go with you, and we'll sit down under the tree. Come, I don't like to see you cry; but you know I must go back some time."

So it came to pass that they found a great plane-tree not far outside the gates, and they sat down under it, and all the feast was spread out on Tessa's lap, she leaning with her back against the trunk of the tree, and he stretched opposite to her, resting his elbows on the rough green growth cherished by the shade, while the sunlight stole through the boughs and played about them like a winged thing. Tessa's face was all contentment again, and the taste of the apricots and sweetmeats seemed very good.

"You pretty bird!" said Tito, looking at her as she sat eyeing the remains of the feast with an evident mental debate about saving them, since he had said he would not have any more. "To think of any one scolding you! What sins do you tell of at confession, Tessa?"

"Oh, a great many. I am often naughty. I don't like work, and I can't help being idle, though I know I shall be beaten and scolded; and I give the mules the best fodder when nobody sees me, and then when the *madre* is angry I say I didn't do it, and that makes me frightened at the devil. I think the conjuror was the devil. I am not so frightened after I've been to confession. And see, I've got a *Breve* here that a good father, who came to

Prato* preaching this Easter, blessed and gave us all." Here Tessa drew from her bosom a tiny bag carefully fastened up. "And I think the Holy Madonna will take care of me; she looks as if she would; and perhaps if I wasn't idle, she wouldn't let me be beaten."

"If they are so cruel to you, Tessa, shouldn't you like to leave them, and go and live with a beautiful lady who would be kind to you, if she would have you to wait upon her?"

Tessa seemed to hold her breath for a moment or two. Then she said doubtfully, "I don't know."

"Then should you like to be *my* little servant, and live with me?" said Tito, smiling. He meant no more than to see what sort of pretty look and answer she would give.

There was a flush of joy immediately. "Will you take me with you now? Ah! I shouldn't go home and be beaten then." She paused a little while, and then added more doubtfully, "But I should like to fetch my black-faced kid."

"Yes, you must go back to your kid, my Tessa," said Tito, rising, "and I must go the other way."

"By Jupiter!" he added, as he went from under the shade of the tree, "it is not a pleasant time of day to walk from here to the Via de' Bardi; I am more inclined to lie down and sleep in this shade."

It ended so. Tito had an unconquerable aversion to anything unpleasant, even when an object very much loved and desired was on the other side of it. He had risen early; had waited; had seen sights, and had been already walking in the sun: he was inclined for a siesta, and inclined all the more because little Tessa was there, and seemed to make the air softer. He lay down on the grass again, putting his cap under his head on a green tuft by the side of Tessa. That was not quite comfortable; so he moved again, and asked Tessa to let him rest his head against her lap; and in that way he soon fell asleep. Tessa sat quiet as a dove on its nest, just venturing, when he was fast asleep, to touch the wonderful dark curls that fell backward from his ear. She was too happy to go to sleep—too happy to think that Tito would wake up, and that then he would leave her, and she must go home. It takes very little water to make a perfect pool for a tiny fish, where it will find its world and paradise all in one, and never have a presentiment of the dry bank. The fretted summer shade, and stillness, and the gentle breathing of some loved life near—it would be paradise to us all, if eager thought, the strong angel with the implacable brow, had not long since closed the gates.

It really was a long while before the waking came—before the long dark eyes opened at Tessa, first with a little surprise, and then with a smile, which was soon quenched by some preoccupying thought. Tito's deeper sleep had broken into a doze, in which he felt himself in the Via de' Bardi, explaining his failure to appear at the appointed time. The clear images of that doze urged him to start up at once to a sitting posture, and as he stretched his arms and shook his cap he said,—

"Tessa, little one, you have let me sleep too long. My hunger and the shadows together tell me that the sun has done much travel since I fell asleep. I must lose no more time. Addio," he ended, patting her cheek with one hand, and settling his cap with the other.

She said nothing, but there were signs in her face which made him speak again in as serious and chiding a tone as he could command,—

"Now, Tessa, you must not cry. I shall be angry; I shall not love you if you cry. You must go home to your black-faced kid, or if you like you may go back to the gate and see the horses start. But I can stay with you no longer, and if you cry, I shall think you are troublesome to me."

The rising tears were checked by terror at this change in Tito's voice. Tessa turned very pale, and sat in trembling silence, with her blue eyes widened by arrested tears.

"Look now," Tito went on, soothingly, opening the wallet that hung at his belt, "here is a pretty charm that I have had a long while—ever since I was in Sicily, a country a long way off."

His wallet had many little matters in it mingled with small coins, and he had the usual difficulty in laying his finger on the right thing. He unhooked his wallet, and turned out the contents on Tessa's lap. Among them was his onyx ring.

"Ah, my ring!" he exclaimed, slipping it on the forefinger of his right hand. "I forgot to put it on again this morning. Strange, I never missed it! See, Tessa," he added, as he spread out the smaller articles, and selected the one he was in search of. "See this pretty little pointed bit of red coral—like your goat's horn, is it not? and here is a hole in it, so you can put it on the cord round your neck along with your *Breve*, and then the evil spirits can't hurt you: if you ever see them coming in the shadow round the corner, point this little coral horn at them, and they will run away. It is a 'buon fortuna,'* and will keep you from harm when I am not with you. Come, undo the cord."

Tessa obeyed with a tranquillizing sense that life was going to be something quite new, and that Tito would be with her often. All who remember their childhood remember the strange vague sense, when some new experience came, that everything else was going to be changed, and that there would be no lapse into the old monotony. So the bit of coral was hung beside the tiny bag with the scrap of scrawled parchment in it, and Tessa felt braver.

"And now you will give me a kiss," said Tito, economizing time by speaking while he swept in the contents of the wallet and hung it at his waist again, "and look happy, like a good girl, and then—"

But Tessa had obediently put forward her lips in a moment, and kissed his cheek as he hung down his head.

"Oh, you pretty pigeon!" cried Tito, laughing, pressing her round cheeks with his hands and crushing her features together so as to give them a general impartial kiss.

Then he started up and walked away, not looking round till he was ten yards from her, when he just turned and gave a parting beck. Tessa was looking after him, but he could see that she was making no signs of distress. It was enough for Tito if she did not cry while he was present. The softness of his nature required that all sorrow should be hidden away from him.

"I wonder when Romola will kiss my cheek in that way?" thought Tito, as he walked along. It seemed a tiresome distance now, and he almost wished he had not been so soft-hearted, or so tempted to linger in the shade. No other excuse was needed to Bardo and Romola than saying simply that he had been unexpectedly hindered; he felt confident their proud delicacy would inquire no farther. He lost no time in getting to Ognissanti, and hastily taking some food there, he crossed the Arno by the Ponte alla Carraja, and made his way as directly as possible towards the Via de' Bardi.

But it was the hour when all the world who meant to be in particularly good time to see the Corso were returning from the

Borghi, or villages just outside the gates, where they had dined and reposed themselves; and the thoroughfares leading to the bridges were of course the issues towards which the stream of sightseers tended. Just as Tito reached the Ponte Vecchio and the entrance of the Via de' Bardi, he was suddenly urged back towards the angle of the intersecting streets. A company on horseback, coming from the Via Guicciardini, and turning up the Via de' Bardi, had compelled the foot passengers to recede hurriedly. Tito had been walking, as his manner was, with the thumb of his right hand resting in his belt; and as he was thus forced to pause, and was looking carelessly at the passing cavaliers, he felt a very thin cold hand laid on his. He started round, and saw the Dominican friar whose upturned face had so struck him in the morning. Seen closer, the face looked more evidently worn by sickness and not by age; and again it brought some strong but indefinite reminiscence to Tito.

"Pardon me, but—from your face and your ring,"—said the friar, in a faint voice, "is not your name Tito Melema?"

"Yes," said Tito, also speaking faintly, doubly jarred by the cold touch and the mystery. He was not apprehensive or timid through his imagination, but through his sensations and perceptions he could easily be made to shrink and turn pale like a maiden.

"Then I shall fulfil my commission."

The friar put his hand under his scapulary, and drawing out a small linen bag which hung round his neck, took from it a bit of parchment, doubled and stuck firmly together with some black adhesive substance, and placed it in Tito's hand. On the outside was written in Italian, in a small but distinct character—

"*Tito Melema, aged twenty-three, with a dark, beautiful face, long dark curls, the brightest smile, and a large onyx ring on his right forefinger.*"

Tito did not look at the friar, but tremblingly broke open the bit of parchment. Inside, the words were—

"*I am sold for a slave: I think they are going to take me to Antioch. The gems alone will serve to ransom me.*"

Tito looked round at the friar, but could only ask a question with his eyes.

"I had it at Corinth," the friar said, speaking with difficulty, like one whose small strength had been over-taxed, "I had it from a man who was dying."

"He is dead, then?" said Tito, with a bounding of the heart.

"Not the writer. The man who give it me was a pilgrim, like myself, to whom the writer had entrusted it, because he was journeying to Italy."

"You know the contents?"

"I do not know them, but I conjecture them. Your friend is in slavery—you will go and release him. But I am unable to talk now." The friar, whose voice had become feebler and feebler, sank down on the stone bench against the wall from which he had risen to touch Tito's hand, adding,

"I am at San Marco; my name is Fra Luca."

[*SEPTEMBER 1862*]

CHAPTER XI.

Tito's Dilemma

WHEN Fra Luca had ceased to speak, Tito still stood by him in irresolution, and it was not till, the pressure of the passengers being removed, the friar rose and walked slowly into the church of Santa Felicità, that Tito also went on his way along the Via de' Bardi.

"If this monk is a Florentine," he said to himself—"if he is going to remain at Florence, everything must be disclosed." He felt that a new crisis had come, but he was not, for all that, too evidently agitated to pay his visit to Bardo, and apologize for his previous non-appearance. Tito's talent for concealment was being fast developed into something less neutral. It was still possible—perhaps it might be inevitable—for him to accept frankly the altered conditions, and avow Baldassarre's existence—but hardly without casting an unpleasant light backward on his original reticence as studied equivocation, in order to avoid the fulfilment of a secretly recognized claim, to say nothing of his quiet settlement of himself and investment of his florins, when, it would be clear, his benefactor's fate had not been certified. It was at least provisionally wise to act as if nothing had happened, and, for the present, he would suspend decisive thought; there was all the night for meditation, and no one would know the precise moment at which he had received the letter.

So he entered the room on the second story—where Romola and her father sat among the parchment and the marble, aloof from the life of the streets on holidays as well as on common days—with a face only a little less bright than usual, from regret at appearing so late: a regret which wanted no testimony, since he had given up the sight of the Corso in order to express it; and then set himself to throw extra animation into the evening, though all the while his consciousness was at work like a machine with complex action, leaving deposits quite distinct from the line of talk; and by the time he descended the stone stairs and issued from the grim door in the starlight, his mind had really reached a new stage in its formation of a purpose.

And when, the next day, after he was free from his professorial work, he turned up the Via del Cocomero, towards the convent of San Marco, his purpose was fully shaped. He was going to ascertain from Fra Luca precisely how much he conjectured of the truth, and on what ground he conjectured it; and, further, how long he was to remain at San Marco. And on that fuller knowledge he hoped to mould a statement which would in any case save him from the necessity of quitting Florence. Tito had never had occasion to fabricate an ingenious lie before: the occasion was come now—the occasion which circumstance never fails to beget on tacit falsity; and his ingenuity was ready. For he had convinced himself that he was not bound to go in search of Baldassarre. He had once said that on a fair assurance of his father's existence and whereabout, he would unhesitatingly go after him. But, after all, *why* was he bound to go? What, looked at closely, was the end of all life, but to extract the utmost sum of pleasure? And was not his own blooming life a promise of incomparably more pleasure, not for himself only, but for others, than the withered wintry life of a man who was past the time of keen enjoyment, and whose ideas had stiffened into barren rigidity? Those ideas had all been sown in the fresh soil of Tito's mind, and were lively germs there: that was the proper order of things—the order of Nature, which treats all maturity as a mere nidus* for youth. Baldassarre had done his work, had had his draught of life: Tito said it was *his* turn now.

And the prospect was so vague:—"I think they are going to take me to Antioch:" here was a vista! After a long voyage, to spend months, perhaps years, in a search for which even now there was no guarantee that it would not prove vain: and to leave behind at starting a life of distinction and love: and to find, if he found anything, the old exacting companionship which was known by rote beforehand. Certainly the gems and therefore the florins were, in a sense, Baldassarre's: in the narrow sense by which the right of possession is determined in ordinary affairs; but in that larger and more radically natural view by which the world belongs to youth and strength, they were rather his who could extract the most pleasure out of them. That, he was conscious, was not the sentiment which the complicated play of human feelings had engendered in society.

The men around him would expect that he should immediately apply those florins to his benefactor's rescue. But what was the sentiment of society?—a mere tangle of anomalous traditions and opinions, that no wise man would take as a guide, except so far as his own comfort was concerned. Not that he cared for the florins, save perhaps for Romola's sake: he would give up the florins readily enough. It was the joy that was due to him and was close to his lips, which he felt he was not bound to thrust away from him and so travel on, thirsting. Any maxims that required a man to fling away the good that was needed to make existence sweet were only the lining of human selfishness turned outward: they were made by men who wanted others to sacrifice themselves for their sake. He would rather that Baldassarre should not suffer: he liked no one to suffer: but could any philosophy prove to him that he was bound to care for another's suffering more than for his own? To do so, he must have loved Baldassarre devotedly, and he did *not* love him: was that his own fault? Gratitude! seen closely, it made no valid claim: his father's life would have been dreary without him: are we convicted of a debt to men for the pleasures they give themselves?

Having once begun to explain away Baldassarre's claim, Tito's thought showed itself as active as a virulent acid, eating its rapid way through all the tissues of sentiment. His mind was destitute of that dread which has been erroneously decried as if it were nothing higher than a man's animal care for his own skin: that awe of the Divine Nemesis which was felt by religious pagans, and, though it took a more positive form under Christianity, is still felt by the mass of mankind simply as a vague fear at anything which is called wrong-doing. Such terror of the unseen is so far above mere sensual cowardice that it will annihilate that cowardice: it is the initial recognition of a moral law restraining desire, and checks the hard bold scrutiny of imperfect thought into obligations which can never be proved to have any sanctity in the absence of feeling. "It is good," sing the old Eumenides, in Æschylus,* "that fear should sit as the guardian of the soul, forcing it into wisdom—good that men should carry a threatening shadow in their hearts under the full sunshine; else, how shall they learn to revere the right?" That guardianship may become needless; but only when all outward law has become needless—only when duty and love have united in one stream and made a common force.

As Tito entered the outer cloister of San Marco, and inquired for Fra Luca, there was no shadowy presentiment in his mind: he felt himself too cultured and sceptical for that: he had been nurtured in contempt for the tales of priests whose impudent lives were a proverb, and in erudite familiarity with disputes concerning the chief good, which had after all, he considered, left it a matter of taste. Yet fear was a strong element in Tito's nature—the fear of what he believed or saw was likely to rob him of pleasure; and he had a definite fear that Fra Luca might be the means of driving him from Florence.

"Fra Luca? ah, he is gone to Fiesole—to the Dominican monastery there. He was taken on a litter in the cool of the morning. The poor brother is very ill. Could you leave a message for him?"

This answer was given by a *fra converso*, or lay brother, whose accent told plainly that he was a raw contadino, and whose dull glance implied no curiosity.

"Thanks; my business can wait."

Tito turned away with a sense of relief. "This friar is not likely to live," he said to himself. "I saw he was worn to a shadow. And at Fiesole there will be nothing to recall me to his mind. Besides, if he should come back, my explanation will serve as well then as now. But I wish I knew what it was that his face recalled to me."

CHAPTER XII.

The Prize is Nearly Grasped

TITO walked along with a light step, for the immediate fear had vanished; the usual joyousness of his disposition reassumed its predominance, and he was going to see Romola. Yet Romola's life seemed an image of that loving, pitying devotedness, that patient endurance of irksome tasks, from which he had shrunk and excused himself. But he was not out of love with goodness, or prepared to plunge into vice: he was in his fresh youth, with soft pulses for all charm and loveliness; he had still a healthy appetite for ordinary human joys, and the poison could only work by degrees. He had sold himself to evil, but at present life seemed so nearly the same to him that he was not conscious of the bond. He meant all things to go on as they had done before, both within and without him: he meant to win golden opinions by meritorious exertion, by ingenious learning, by amiable compliance: he was not going to do anything that would throw him out of harmony with the beings he cared for. And he cared supremely for Romola; he wished to have her for his beautiful and loving wife. There might be a wealthier alliance within the ultimate reach of successful accomplishments like his, but there was no woman in all Florence like Romola. When she was near him, and looked at him with her sincere hazel eyes, he was subdued by a delicious influence as strong and inevitable as those musical vibrations which take possession of us with a rhythmic empire that no sooner ceases than we desire it to begin again.

As he trod the stone stairs, when he was still outside the door, with no one but Maso near him, the influence seemed to have begun its work by the mere nearness of anticipation.

"Welcome, *Tito mio*," said the old man's voice, before Tito had spoken. There was a new vigour in the voice, a new cheerfulness in the blind face, since that first interview more than two months ago. "You have brought fresh manuscript, doubtless; but since we were talking last night I have had new ideas: we must take a wider scope—we must go back upon our footsteps."

Tito, paying his homage to Romola as he advanced, went, as his custom was, straight to Bardo's chair, and put his hand in the palm that was held to receive it, placing himself on the cross-legged leather seat with scrolled ends, close to Bardo's elbow.

"Yes," he said, in his gentle way; "I have brought the new manuscript, but that can wait your pleasure. I have young limbs, you know, and can walk back up the hill without any difficulty."

He did not look at Romola as he said this, but he knew quite well that her eyes were fixed on him with delight.

"That is well said, my son." Bardo had already addressed Tito in this way once or twice of late. "And I perceive with gladness that you do not shrink from labour, without which, the poet has wisely said,* life has given nothing to mortals. It is too often the 'palma sine pulvere,'* the prize of glory without the dust of the race, that attracts young ambition. But what says the

Greek?* 'In the morning of life, work; in the midday, give counsel; in the evening, pray.' It is true, I might be thought to have reached that helpless evening; but not so, while I have counsel within me which is yet unspoken. For my mind, as I have often said, was shut up as by a dam; the plenteous waters lay dark and motionless; but you, my Tito, have opened a duct for them, and they rush forward with a force that surprises myself. And now, what I want is, that we should go over our preliminary ground again, with a wider scheme of comment and illustration; otherwise I may lose opportunities which I now see retrospectively, and which may never occur again. You mark what I am saying, Tito?"

He had just stooped to reach his manuscript, which had rolled down, and Bardo's jealous ear was alive to the slight movement.

Tito might have been excused for shrugging his shoulders at the prospect before him, but he was not naturally impatient; moreover, he had been bred up in that laborious erudition, at once minute and copious, which was the chief intellectual task of the age; and with Romola near, he was floated along by waves of agreeable sensation that made everything seem easy.

"Assuredly," he said; "you wish to enlarge your comments on certain passages we have cited."

"Not only so; I wish to introduce an occasional excursus,* where we have noticed an author to whom I have given special study; for I may die too soon to achieve any separate work. And this is not a time for scholarly integrity and well-sifted learning to lie idle, when it is not only rash ignorance that we have to fear, but when there are men like Calderino,* who, as Poliziano has well shown, have recourse to impudent falsities of citation to serve the ends of their vanity and secure a triumph to their own mistakes. Wherefore, my Tito, I think it not well that we should let slip the occasion that lies under our hands. And now we will turn back to the point where we have cited the passage from Thucydides, and I wish you, by way of preliminary, to go with me through all my notes on the Latin translation made by Lorenzo Valla,* for which the incomparable Pope Nicholas V.—with whose personal notice I was honoured while I was yet young, and when he was still Thomas of Sarzana—paid him (I say not unduly) the sum of five hundred gold scudi. But inasmuch as Valla, though otherwise of dubious fame, is held in high honour for his severe scholarship, whence the epigrammatist has jocosely said of him that since he went among the shades, Pluto himself has not dared to speak in the ancient languages, it is the more needful that his name should not be as a stamp warranting false wares; and therefore I would introduce an excursus on Thucydides, wherein my castigations of Valla's text may find a fitting place. My Romola, thou wilt reach the needful volumes—thou knowest them—on the fifth shelf of the cabinet."

Tito rose at the same moment with Romola, saying, "I will reach them, if you will point them out," and followed her hastily into the adjoining small room, where the walls were also covered with ranges of books in perfect order.

"There they are," said Romola, pointing upward; "every book is just where it was when my father ceased to see them."

Tito stood by her without hastening to reach the books. They had never been in this room together before.

"I hope," she continued, turning her eyes full on Tito, with a look of grave confidence—"I hope he will not weary you; this work makes him so happy."

"And me too, Romola—if you will only let me say, I love you—if you will only think me worth loving a little."

His speech was the softest murmur, and the dark beautiful face, nearer to hers than it had ever been before, was looking at her with beseeching tenderness.

"I do love you," murmured Romola; she looked at him with the same simple majesty as ever, but her voice had never in her life before sunk to that murmur. It seemed to them both that they were looking at each other a long while before her lips moved again; yet it was but a moment till she said, "I know *now* what it is to be happy."

The faces just met, and the dark curls mingled for an instant with the rippling gold. Quick as lightning after that, Tito set his foot on a projecting ledge of the book-shelves and reached down the needful volumes. They were both contented to be silent and separate, for that first blissful experience of mutual consciousness was all the more exquisite for being unperturbed by immediate sensation.

It had been as rapid as the irreversible mingling of waters, for even the eager and jealous Bardo had not become impatient.

"You have the volumes, my Romola?" the old man said, as they came near him again. "And now you will get your pen ready; for, as Tito marks off the scholia* we determine on extracting, it will be well for you to copy them without delay—numbering them carefully, mind, to correspond with the numbers in the text which he will write."

Romola always had some task which gave her a share in this joint work. Tito took his stand at the *leggio*, where he both wrote and read, and she placed herself at a table just in front of him, where she was ready to give into her father's hands anything that he might happen to want, or relieve him of a volume that he had done with. They had always been in that position since the work began, yet on this day it seemed new; it was so different now for them to be opposite each other; so different for Tito to take a book from her, as she lifted it from her father's knee. Yet there was no finesse to secure an additional look or touch. Each woman creates in her own likeness the love tokens that are offered to her; and Romola's deep calm happiness encompassed Tito like the rich but quiet evening light which dissipates all unrest.

They had been two hours at their work, and were just desisting because of the fading light, when the door opened and there entered a figure strangely incongruous with the current of their thoughts and with the suggestions of every object around them. It was the figure of a short stout black-eyed woman, about fifty, wearing a black velvet berretta, or close cap, embroidered with pearls, under which surprisingly massive black braids surmounted the little bulging forehead, and fell in rich plaited curves over the ears, while an equally surprising carmine tint on the upper region of the fat cheeks contrasted with the surrounding sallowness. Three rows of pearls and a lower necklace of gold reposed on the horizontal cushion of her neck; the embroidered border of her trailing black velvet gown and her embroidered long-drooping sleeves of rose-coloured damask were slightly faded, but they conveyed to the initiated eye the satisfactory assurance that they were the splendid result of six months' labour by a skilled workman; and the rose-coloured petticoat, with its dimmed white fringe and seed-pearl arabesques, was duly exhibited in order to suggest a similar pleasing reflection. A handsome coral rosary hung from one side of an inferential belt, which emerged into certainty with a large clasp of silver wrought in *niello*;* and, on the other side, where the belt again became inferential, hung a scarsella, or large purse of crimson velvet, stitched with pearls. Her little fat right hand, which looked as if it had been made of paste, and had risen out of shape under partial baking, held a small book of devotions, also splendid with velvet, pearls, and silver.

The figure was already too familiar to Tito to be startling, for Monna Brigida was a frequent visitor at Bardo's, being excepted from the sentence of banishment passed on feminine triviality, on the ground of her cousinship to his dead wife and her early care for Romola, who now looked round at her with an affectionate smile, and rose to draw the leather seat to a due distance from her father's chair, that the coming gush of talk might not be too near his ear.

"*La cugina?*" said Bardo, interrogatively, detecting the short steps and the sweeping drapery.

"Yes, it is your cousin," said Monna Brigida, in an alert voice, raising her fingers smilingly at Tito, and then lifting up her face to be kissed by Romola. "Always the troublesome cousin breaking in on your wisdom," she went on, seating herself and beginning to fan herself with the white veil hanging over her arm. "Well, well; if I didn't bring you some news of the world now and then, I do believe you'd forget there was anything in life but these mouldy ancients, who want sprinkling with holy water if all I hear about them is true. Not but what the world is bad enough nowadays, for the scandals that turn up under one's nose at every corner—*I* don't want to hear and see such things, but one can't go about with one's head in a bag; and it was only yesterday—well, well, you needn't burst out at me, Bardo, I'm not going to tell anything; if I'm not as wise as the three kings, I know how many legs go into one boot. But, nevertheless, Florence is a wicked city—is it not true, Messer Tito? for you go into the world. Not but what one must sin a little—Messer Domeneddio expects that of us, else what are the blessed sacraments for? And what I say is, we've got to reverence the saints, and not to set ourselves up as if we could be like them, else life would be unbearable; as it will be if things go on after this new fashion. For what do you think? I've been at the wedding to-day—Dianora Acciajoli's with the young Albizzi that there has been so much talk of—and everybody wondered at its being to-day instead of yesterday; but, *cieli!* such a wedding as it was might have been put off till the next Quaresima for a penance. For there was the bride looking like a white nun—not so much as a pearl about her—and the bridegroom as solemn as San Giuseppe.* It's true! And half the people invited were Piagnoni*—they call them Piagnoni now, these new saints of Fra Girolamo's making. And to think of two families like the Albizzi and the Acciajoli taking up such notions, when they could afford to wear the best! Well, well, they invited me—but they could do no other, seeing my husband was Luca Antonio's uncle by the mother's side—and a pretty time I had of it while we waited under the canopy in front of the house, before they let us in. I couldn't stand in my clothes, it seemed, without giving offence; for there was Monna Berta, who has had worse secrets in her time than any I could tell of myself, looking askance at me from under her hood like a Pinzochera,* and telling me to read the Frate's book about widows,* from which she had found great guidance. Holy Madonna! it seems as if widows had nothing to do now but to buy their coffins, and think it a thousand years till they get into them, instead of enjoying themselves a little when they've got their hands free for the first time. And what do you think was the music we had to make our dinner lively? A long discourse from Fra Domenico of San Marco, about the doctrines of their blessed Fra Girolamo—the three doctrines we are all to get by heart; and he kept marking them off on his fingers till he made my flesh creep: and the first is, Florence, or the Church—I don't know which, for first he said one and then the other—shall be scourged; but if he means the pestilence, the Signory ought to put a stop to such preaching, for it's enough to raise the swelling under one's arms with fright; but then, after that, he says Florence is to be regenerated; but what will be the good of that when we're all dead of the plague, or something else? And then, the third thing, and what he said oftenest, is, that it's all to be in our days: and he marked that off on his thumb, till he made me tremble like the very jelly before me. They had jellies, to be sure, with the arms of the Albizzi and the Acciajoli raised on them in all colours; they've not turned the world quite upside down yet. But all their talk is, that we are to go back to the old ways: for up starts Francesco Valori,* that I've danced with in the Via Larga when he was a bachelor and as fond of the Medici as anybody, and he makes a speech about the old times, before the Florentines had left off crying 'Popolo' and begun to cry 'Palle'—as if that had anything to do with a wedding!—and how we ought to keep to the rules the Signory laid down heavens knows when, that we were not to wear this and that, and not to eat this and that—and how our manners were corrupted and we read bad books; though he can't say that of *me*—"

"Stop, cousin!" said Bardo, in his imperious tone, for he had a remark to make, and only desperate measures could arrest the rattling lengthiness of Monna Brigida's discourse. But now she gave a little start, pursed up her mouth and looked at him with round eyes.

"Francesco Valori is not altogether wrong," Bardo went on. "Bernardo, indeed, rates him not highly, and is rather of opinion that he christens private grudges by the name of public zeal; though I must admit that my good Bernardo is too slow of belief in that unalloyed patriotism which was found in all its lustre among the ancients. But it is true, Tito, that our manners have degenerated somewhat from that noble frugality which, as has been well seen in the public acts of our citizens, is the parent of true magnificence. For men, as I hear, will now spend on the transient show of a *giostra* sums which would suffice to found a library, and confer a lasting possession on mankind. Still, I conceive, it remains true of us Florentines that we have more of that magnanimous sobriety which abhors a trivial lavishness that it may be grandly open-handed on grand occasions, than can be found in any other city of Italy; for I understand that the Neapolitan and Milanese courtiers laugh at the scarcity of our plate, and think scorn of our great families for borrowing from each other that furniture of the table at their entertainments. But in the vain laughter of folly wisdom hears half its applause."

"Laughter, indeed!" burst forth Monna Brigida again, the moment Bardo paused. "If anybody wanted to hear laughter at the wedding to-day they were disappointed, for when young Niccolò Macchiavelli tried to make a joke, and told stories out of Franco Sacchetti's book,* how it was no use for the Signoria to make rules for us women, because we were cleverer than all the painters, and architects, and doctors of logic in the world, for we could make black look white, and yellow look pink, and crooked look straight, and, if anything was forbidden, we could find a new name for it—Holy Virgin! the Piagnoni looked more dismal than before, and somebody said Sacchetti's book was wicked. Well, I don't read it—they can't accuse *me* of reading anything. Save me from going to a wedding again, if that's to be the fashion; for all of us who were not Piagnoni were as comfortable as wet chickens.* I was never caught in a worse trap but once before, and that was when I went to hear their precious Frate last Quaresima in San Lorenzo.* Perhaps I never told you about it, Messer Tito?—it almost freezes my blood when I think of it. How he rated us poor women! and the men, too, to tell the truth, but I didn't mind that so much. He called us cows, and lumps of flesh, and wantons, and mischief-makers—and I could just bear that, for there were plenty others more fleshy and spiteful than I was—though every now and then his voice shook the very bench under me like a trumpet; but then he came to the false hair, and, O misericordia! he made a picture—I see it now—of a young woman lying a pale corpse, and us light-minded widows—of course he meant me as well as the rest, for I had my plaits on, for if one is getting old, one doesn't want to look as ugly as the Befana,*—us widows rushing up to the corpse, like bare-pated vultures as we were, and cutting off its young dead hair to deck our old heads with. Oh, the dreams I had after that! And then he cried, and wrung his hands at us, and I cried too. And to go home, and to take off my jewels, this very clasp, and everything, and to make them into a packet, *fù tutt'uno*; and I was within a hair of sending them to the good men of St. Martin* to give to the poor, but, by heaven's mercy, I bethought me of going first to my confessor, Fra Cristoforo, at Santa Croce, and he told me how it was all the work of the devil, this preaching and prophesying of their Fra Girolamo, and the Dominicans were trying to turn the world upside down, and I was never to go and hear him again, else I must do penance for it; for the great preachers Fra Mariano and Fra Menico had shown how Fra Girolamo preached lies—and that was true, for I heard them both in the Duomo—and how the Pope's dream* of San Francesco propping up the Church with his arms was being fulfilled still, and the Dominicans were beginning to pull it down. Well and good: I went away *con Dio*, and made myself easy. I am not going to be frightened by a Frate Predicatore again. And all I say is, I wish it hadn't been the Dominicans that poor Dino joined years ago, for then I should have been glad when I heard them say he was come back—"

"Silenzio!" said Bardo, in a loud agitated voice, while Romola half started from her chair, clasped her hands, and looked round at Tito, as if now she might appeal to him. Monna Brigida gave a little scream, and bit her lip.

"Donna!" said Bardo, again, "hear once more my will. Bring no reports about that name to this house; and thou, Romola, I forbid thee to ask. My son is dead."

Bardo's whole frame seemed vibrating with passion, and no one dared to break silence again. Monna Brigida lifted her shoulders and her hands in mute dismay; then she rose as quietly as possible, gave many significant nods to Tito and Romola, motioning to them that they were not to move, and stole out of the room like a culpable fat spaniel who has barked unseasonably.

Meanwhile, Tito's quick mind had been combining ideas with lightning-like rapidity. Bardo's son was not really dead, then, as he had supposed: he was a monk; he was "come back:" and Fra Luca—yes! it was the likeness to Bardo and Romola that had made the face seem half-known to him. If he were only dead at Fiesole at that moment! This importunate selfish wish inevitably thrust itself before every other thought. It was true that Bardo's rigid will was a sufficient safeguard against any intercourse between Romola and her brother; but *not* against the betrayal of what he knew to others, especially when the subject was suggested by the coupling of Romola's name with that of the very Tito Melema whose description he had carried round his neck as an index. No! nothing but Fra Luca's death could remove all danger; but his death was highly probable, and after the momentary shock of the discovery, Tito let his mind fall back in repose on that confident hope.

They had sat in silence, and in a deepening twilight for many minutes, when Romola ventured to say—

"Shall I light the lamp, father, and shall we go on?"

"No, my Romola, we will work no more to-night. Tito, come and sit by me here."

Tito moved from the reading-desk and seated himself on the other side of Bardo, close to his left elbow.

"Come nearer to me, *figliuola mia*," said Bardo again, after a moment's pause. And Romola seated herself on a low stool and let her arm rest on her father's right knee, that he might lay his hand on her hair, as he was fond of doing.

"Tito, I never told you that I had once a son," said Bardo,

forgetting what had fallen from him in the emotion raised by their first interview. The old man had been deeply shaken and was forced to pour out his feelings in spite of pride. "But he left me—he is dead to me—I have disowned him for ever. He was a ready scholar, as you are, but more fervid and impatient, and yet sometimes rapt and self-absorbed, like a flame fed by some fitful source; showing a disposition from the very first to turn away his eyes from the clear lights of reason and philosophy, and to prostrate himself under the influences of a dim mysticism which eludes all rules of human duty as it eludes all argument. And so it ended. We will speak no more of him: he is dead to me. I wish his face could be blotted from that world of memory in which the distant seems to grow clearer and the near to fade."

Bardo paused, but neither Romola nor Tito dared to speak—his voice was too tremulous, the poise of his feelings too doubtful. But he presently raised his hand and found Tito's shoulder to rest it on, while he went on speaking with an effort to be calmer.

"But *you* have come to me, Tito—not quite too late. I will lose no more time in vain regret. When you are working by my side I seem to have a son again."

The old man, preoccupied with the governing interest of his life, was only thinking of the much-meditated book which had quite thrust into the background the suggestion, raised by Bernardo del Nero's warning, of a possible marriage between Tito and Romola. But Tito could not allow the moment to pass unused.

"Will you let me be always and altogether your son? Will you let me take care of Romola—be her husband? I think she will not deny me. She has said she loves me. I know I am not equal to her in birth—in anything; but I am no longer a destitute stranger."

"Is it true, my Romola?" said Bardo, in a lower tone, an evident vibration passing through him and dissipating the saddened aspect of his features.

"Yes, father," said Romola, firmly. "I love Tito—I wish to marry him, that we may be both your children and never part."

Tito's hand met hers in a strong clasp for the first time, while she was speaking, but their eyes were fixed anxiously on her father.

"Why should it not be?" said Bardo, as if arguing against any opposition to his assent, rather than assenting. "It would be a happiness to me; and thou, too, Romola, wouldst be the happier for it."

He stroked her long hair gently and bent towards her.

"Ah, I have been apt to forget that thou needest some other love than mine. And thou wilt be a noble wife. Bernardo thinks I shall hardly find a husband fitting for thee. And he is perhaps right. For thou art not like the herd of thy sex: thou art such a woman as the immortal poets had a vision of, when they sang the lives of the heroes—tender but strong, like thy voice, which has been to me instead of the light in the years of my blindness. . . . And so thou lovest him?"

He sat upright again for a minute and then said, in the same tone as before, "Why should it not be? I will think of it; I will talk with Bernardo."

Tito felt a disagreeable chill at this answer, for Bernardo del Nero's eyes had retained their keen suspicion whenever they looked at him, and the uneasy remembrance of Fra Luca converted all uncertainty into fear.

"Speak for me, Romola," he said, pleadingly. "Messer Bernardo is sure to be against me."

"No, Tito," said Romola, "my godfather will not oppose what my father firmly wills. And it is your will that I should marry Tito—is it not true, father? Nothing has ever come to me before that I have wished for strongly: I did not think it possible that I could care so much for anything that could happen to myself."

It was a brief and simple plea; but it was the condensed story of Romola's self-repressing colourless young life, which had thrown all its passion into sympathy with aged sorrows, aged ambition, aged pride and indignation. It had never occurred to Romola that she should not speak as directly and emphatically of her love for Tito as of any other subject.

"*Romola mia*!" said her father fondly, pausing on the words, "it is true thou hast never urged on me any wishes of thy own. And I have no will to resist thine; rather, my heart met Tito's entreaty at its very first utterance. Nevertheless, I must talk with Bernardo about the measures needful to be observed. For we must not act in haste, or do anything unbeseeming my name. I am poor, and held of little acount by the wealthy of our family—nay, I may consider myself a lonely man—but I must nevertheless remember that generous birth has its obligations. And I would not be reproached by my fellow-citizens for rash haste in bestowing my daughter. Bartolommeo Scala gave his Alessandra to the Greek Marullo, but Marullo's lineage was well known, and Scala himself is of no extraction. I know Bernardo will hold that we must take time: he will, perhaps, reproach me with want of due forethought. Be patient, my children: you are very young."

No more could be said, and Romola's heart was perfectly satisfied. Not so Tito's. If the subtle mixture of good and evil prepares suffering for human truth and purity, there is also suffering prepared for the wrong-doer by the same mingled conditions. As Tito kissed Romola on their parting that evening, the very strength of the thrill that moved his whole being at the sense that this woman, whose beauty it was hardly possible to think of as anything but the necessary consequence of her noble nature, loved him with all the tenderness that spoke in her clear eyes, brought a strong reaction of regret that he had not kept himself free from that first deceit which had dragged him into this danger of being disgraced before her. There was a spring of bitterness mingling with that fountain of sweets. Would the death of Fra Luca arrest it? He hoped it would.

CHAPTER XIII.

The Shadow of Nemesis

It was the lazy afternoon time on the seventh of September, more than two months after the day on which Romola and Tito had confessed their love to each other.

Tito, just descended into Nello's shop, had found the barber stretched on the bench with his cap over his eyes: one leg was drawn up, and the other had slipped towards the ground, having apparently carried with it a manuscript volume of verse, which lay with its leaves crushed. In a corner sat Sandro, playing a game at *mora** by himself, and watching the slow reply of his left fingers to the arithmetical demands of his right with solemn-eyed interest.

Treading with the gentlest step, Tito snatched up the lute, and bending over the barber, touched the strings lightly while he sang,—

"Quant' è bella giovinezza,
Che si fugge tuttavia!
Chi vuol esser lieto sia,
Di doman non c'è certezza."*

Nello was as easily awaked as a bird. The cap was off his eyes in an instant, and he started up.

"Ah, my Apollino! I am somewhat late with my siesta on this hot day, it seems. That comes of not going to sleep in the natural way, but taking a potion of potent poesy. Hear you, how I am beginning to match my words by the initial letter, like a *trovatore*? That is one of my bad symptoms: I am sorely afraid that the good wine of my understanding is going to run off at the spigot of authorship, and I shall be left an empty cask with an odour of dregs, like many another incomparable genius of my acquaintance. What is it, my Orpheus?" here Nello stretched out his arms to their full length, and then brought them round till his hands grasped Tito's curls, and drew them out playfully. "What is it you want of your well-tamed Nello? For I perceive a coaxing sound in that soft strain of yours. Let me see the very needle's eye of your desire, as the sublime poet says,* that I may thread it."

"That is but a tailor's image of your sublime poet's," said Tito, still letting his fingers fall in a light dropping way on the strings. "But you have divined the reason of my affectionate impatience to see your eyes open. I want you to give me an extra touch of your art—not on my chin, no; but on the *zazzera*, which is as tangled as your Florentine politics. You have an adroit way of inserting your comb, which flatters the skin, and stirs the animal spirits agreeably in that region; and a little of your most delicate orange scent would not be amiss, for I am bound to the Scala palace, and am to present myself in radiant company. The young Cardinal Giovanni de' Medici is to be there, and he brings with him a certain young Bernardo Dovizi of Bibbiena,* whose wit is so rapid, that I see no way of outrivalling it save by the scent of orange-blossoms."

Nello had already seized and flourished his comb, and pushed Tito gently backward into the chair, wrapping the cloth round him.

"Never talk of rivalry, *bel giovane mio*: Bernardo Dovizi is a keen youngster, who will never carry a net out to catch the wind;* but he has something of the same sharp-muzzled look as his brother Ser Piero,* the weasel that Piero de' Medici keeps at his beck to slip through small holes for him. No! you distance all rivals, and may soon touch the sky with your forefinger.* They tell me you have even carried enough honey with you to sweeten the sour Messer Angelo; for he has pronounced you less of an ass than might have been expected, considering there is such a good understanding between you and the secretary."

"And between ourselves, *Nello mio*, that Messer Angelo has more genius and erudition than I can find in all the other Florentine scholars put together. It may answer very well for them to cry me up now, when Poliziano is beaten down with grief, or illness, or something else; I can try a flight with such a sparrow-hawk as Pietro Crinito, but for Poliziano, he is a large-beaked eagle who would swallow me, feathers and all, and not feel any difference."

"I will not contradict your modesty there, if you will have it so; but you don't expect us clever Florentines to keep saying the same things over again every day of our lives, as we must do if we always told the truth. We cry down Dante, and we cry up Francesco Cei, just for the sake of variety; and if we cry you up as a new Poliziano, heaven has taken care that it shall not be quite so great a lie as it might have been. And are you not a pattern of virtue in this wicked city? with your ears double-waxed* against all siren invitations that would lure you from the Via de' Bardi, and the great work which is to astonish posterity?"

"Posterity in good truth, whom it will probably astonish as the universe does, by the impossibility of seeing what was the plan of it."

"Yes, something like that was being prophesied here the other day. Cristoforo Landino said that the excellent Bardo was one of those scholars who lie overthrown in their learning, like cavaliers in heavy armour,* and then get angry because they are over-ridden—which pithy remark, it seems to me, was not a herb out of his own garden; for of all men, for feeding one with an empty spoon and gagging one with vain expectation by long discourse, Messer Cristoforo is the pearl. Ecco! you are perfect now." Here Nello drew away the cloth. "Impossible to add a grace more! But love is not always to be fed on learning, eh? I shall have to dress the *zazzera* for the betrothal before long—is it not true?"

"Perhaps," said Tito, smiling, "unless Messer Bernardo should next recommend Bardo to require that I should yoke a lion and a wild boar to the car of the Zecca before I can win my Alcestis. But I confess he is right in holding me unworthy of Romola; she is a Pleiad* that may grow dim by marrying any mortal."

"*Gnaffè*, your modesty is in the right place there. Yet Fate seems to have measured and chiselled you for the niche that was left empty by the old man's son, who, by the way, Cronaca was telling me, is now at San Marco. Did you know?"

A slight electric shock passed through Tito as he rose from the chair, but it was not outwardly perceptible, for he immediately stooped to pick up the fallen book, and busied his fingers with flattening the leaves, while he said,

"No: he was at Fiesole, I thought. Are you sure he is come back to San Marco?"

"Cronaca is my authority," said Nello, with a shrug. "I don't frequent that sanctuary, but he does. Ah," he added, taking the book from Tito's hands, "my poor Nencia da Barberino! It jars your scholarly feelings to see the pages dog's-eared. I was lulled to sleep by the well-rhymed charms of that rustic maiden—'prettier than the turnip-flower,' 'with a cheek more savoury than cheese.'* But to get such a well-scented notion of the contadina, one must lie on velvet cushions in the Via Larga—not go to look at the Fierucoloni stumping in to the Piazza della Nunziata this evening after sundown."

"And pray who are the Fierucoloni?" said Tito, indifferently, settling his cap.

"The contadine who come from the mountains of Pistoia,* and the Casentino, and heaven knows where, to keep their vigil in the church of the Nunziata and sell their yarn and dried mushrooms at the Fierucola,* as we call it. They make a queer show, with their paper lanterns, howling their hymns to the Virgin on this eve of her nativity—if you had the leisure to see them. No?—well, I have had enough of it myself, for there is wild work in the Piazza. One may happen to get a stone or two about one's ears or shins without asking for it, and I was never fond of that pressing attention. Addio."

Tito carried a little uneasiness with him on his visit, which ended earlier than he had expected, the boy-cardinal Giovanni de' Medici, youngest of red-hatted Fathers, who has since presented his broad dark cheek very conspicuously to posterity as Pope Leo the Tenth,* having been detained at his favourite pastime of the chase, and having failed to appear. It still wanted half an hour of sunset as he left the door of the Scala palace, with the intention of proceeding forthwith to the Via de' Bardi; but he had not gone far when, to his astonishment, he saw Romola advancing towards him along the Borgo Pinti.

She wore a thick black veil and black mantle, but it was impossible to mistake her figure and her walk; and by her side was a short stout form which he recognized as that of Monna Brigida, in spite of the unusual plainness of her attire. Romola had not been bred up to devotional observances, and the occasions on which she took the air elsewhere than under the loggia on the roof of the house, were so rare and so much dwelt on beforehand, because of Bardo's dislike to be left without her, that Tito felt sure there must have been some sudden and urgent ground for an absence of which he had heard nothing the day before. She saw him through her veil and hastened her steps.

"Romola, has anything happened?" said Tito, turning to walk by her side.

She did not answer at the first moment, and Monna Brigida broke in.

"Ah, Messer Tito, you do well to turn round, for we are in haste. And is it not a misfortune?—we are obliged to go round by the walls and turn up the Via del Maglio, because of the Fair; for the contadine coming in block up the way by the Nunziata, which would have taken us to San Marco in half the time."

Tito's heart gave a great bound, and began to beat violently.

"Romola," he said, in a lower tone, "are you going to San Marco?"

They were now out of the Borgo Pinti and were under the city walls, where they had wide gardens on their left hand, and all was quiet. Romola put aside her veil for the sake of breathing the air, and he could see the subdued agitation in her face.

"Yes, *Tito mio*," she said, looking directly at him with sad eyes. "For the first time I am doing something unknown to my father. It comforts me that I have met you, for at least I can tell *you*. But if you are going to him, it will be well for you not to say that you met me. He thinks I am only gone to my cousin, because she sent for me. I left my godfather with him: *he* knows where I am going, and why. You remember that evening when my brother's name was mentioned and my father spoke of him to you?"

"Yes," said Tito, in a low tone. There was a strange complication in his mental state. His heart sank at the probability that a great change was coming over his prospects, while at the same time his thoughts were darting over a hundred details of the course he would take when the change had come,—and yet he returned Romola's gaze with a hungry sense that it might be the last time she would ever bend it on him with full unquestioning confidence.

"The *cugina* had heard that he was come back, and the evening before—the evening of San Giovanni—as I afterwards found, he had been seen by our good Maso near the door of our house; but when Maso went to inquire at San Marco, Dino, that is, my brother—he was christened Bernardino, after our godfather, but now he calls himself Fra Luca—had been taken to the monastery at Fiesole, because he was ill. But this morning a message came to Maso, saying that he was come back to San Marco, and Maso went to him there. He is very ill, and he has adjured me to go and see him. I cannot refuse it, though I hold him guilty: I still remember how I loved him when I was a little girl, before I knew that he would forsake my father. And perhaps he has some word of penitence to send by me. It cost me a struggle to act in opposition to my father's feeling, which I have always held to be just. I am almost sure you will think I have chosen rightly, Tito, because I have noticed that your nature is less rigid than mine, and nothing makes you angry: it would cost you less to be forgiving; though, if you had seen your father forsaken by one to whom he had given his chief love—by one in whom he had planted his labour and his hopes—forsaken when his need was becoming greatest—even you, Tito, would find it hard to forgive."

What could he say? He was not equal to the hypocrisy of telling Romola that such offences ought not to be pardoned; and he had not the courage to utter any words of dissuasion.

"You are right, my Romola; you are always right, except in thinking too well of me."

There was really some genuineness in those last words, and Tito looked very beautiful as he uttered them, with an unusual pallor in his face, and a slight quivering of his lip. Romola, interpreting all things largely, like a mind prepossessed with high beliefs, had a tearful brightness in her eyes as she looked at him, touched with keen joy that he felt so strongly whatever she felt. But without pausing in her walk, she said—

"And now, Tito, I wish you to leave me, for the *cugina* and I shall be less noticed if we enter the piazza alone."

"Yes, it were better you should leave us," said Monna Brigida; "for to say the truth, Messer Tito, all eyes follow you, and let Romola muffle herself as she will, every one wants to see what there is under her veil, for she has that way of walking, like a procession. Not that I find fault with her for it, only it doesn't suit my steps. And, indeed, I would rather not have us seen going to San Marco, and that's why I am dressed as if I were one of the Piagnoni themselves, and as old as Sant' Anna;* for if it had been anybody but poor Dino, who ought to be forgiven if he's dying, for what's the use of having a grudge against dead people?—make them feel while they live, say I—"

No one made a scruple of interrupting Monna Brigida, and Tito, having raised Romola's hand to his lips, and said, "I understand, I obey you," now turned away, lifting his cap—a sign of reverence rarely made* at that time by native Florentines, and which excited Bernardo del Nero's contempt for Tito as a fawning Greek, while to Romola, who loved homage, it gave him an exceptional grace.

He was half glad of the dismissal, half disposed to cling to Romola to the last moment in which she would love him without suspicion. For it seemed to him certain that this brother would before all things want to know, and that Romola would before all things confide to him, what was her father's position and her own after the years which must have brought so much change. She would tell him that she was soon to be publicly betrothed to a young scholar, who was to fill up the place left vacant long ago by a wandering son. He foresaw the impulse that would prompt Romola to dwell on that prospect, and what would follow on the mention of the future husband's name. Fra Luca would tell all he knew and conjectured, and Tito saw no possible falsity by which he could now ward off the worst consequences of his former dissimulation. It was all over with his prospects in Florence. There was Messer Bernardo del Nero, who would be delighted at seeing confirmed the wisdom of his advice about deferring the betrothal until Tito's character and position had been established by a longer residence; and the history of the young Greek professor, whose benefactor was in slavery, would be the talk under every loggia. For the first time in his life he felt too fevered and agitated to trust his power of self-command; he gave up his intended visit to Bardo, and walked up and down under the walls until the yellow light in the west had quite faded, when, without any distinct purpose, he took the first turning, which happened to be the Via San Sebastiano, leading him directly towards the Piazza dell' Annunziata. He was at one of those lawless moments which come to us all if we have no guide but desire, and if the pathway where desire leads us seems suddenly closed; he was ready to follow any beckoning that offered him an immediate purpose.

CHAPTER XIV.

The Peasants' Fair

THE moving crowd and the strange mixture of noises that burst on him at the entrance of the piazza, reminded Tito of what Nello had said to him about the Fierucoloni, and he pushed his way into the crowd with a sort of pleasure in the hooting and elbowing, that filled the empty moments, and dulled that calculation of the future which had so new a dreariness for him, as he foresaw himself wandering away solitary in pursuit of some unknown fortune, that his thought had even glanced towards going in search of Baldassarre after all.

At each of the opposite inlets he saw people struggling into the piazza, while above them paper lanterns, held aloft on sticks, were waving uncertainly to and fro. A rude monotonous chant made a distinctly traceable strand of noise, across which screams, whistles, gibing chants in piping boyish voices, the beating of drums, and the ringing of little bells, met each other in confused din. Every now and then one of the dim floating lights disappeared with a smash from a stone launched more or less vaguely in pursuit of mischief, followed by a scream and renewed shouts. But on the outskirts of the whirling tumult there were groups who were keeping this vigil of the Nativity of the Virgin in a more methodical manner than by fitful stone-throwing and gibing. Certain ragged men, darting a hard sharp glance around them while their tongues rattled merrily, were inviting country people to game with them on fair and open-handed terms; two masquerading figures on stilts, who had snatched lanterns from the crowd, were swaying the lights to and fro in meteoric fashion, as they strode hither and thither: a sage trader was doing a profitable business, at a small covered stall, in hot *berlingozzi*, a favourite farinaceous delicacy; one man standing on a barrel, with his back firmly planted against a pillar of the loggia in front of the Foundling Hospital (Spedale degl' Innocenti), was selling efficacious pills, invented by a doctor of Salerno, warranted to prevent toothache and death by drowning; and not far off, against another pillar, a tumbler was showing off his tricks on a small platform; while a handful of prentices, despising the slack entertainment of guerilla stone-throwing, were having a private concentrated match of that favourite Florentine sport at the narrow entrance of the Via de' Febbrai.

Tito, obliged to make his way through chance openings in the crowd, found himself at one moment close to the trotting procession of bare-footed, hard-heeled contadine, and could see their sun-dried, bronzed faces, and their strange fragmentary garb, dim with hereditary dirt, and of obsolete stuffs and fashions, that made them look, in the eyes of the city people, like a way-worn ancestry returning from a pilgrimage on which they had set out a century ago. Just then it was the hardy, scant-feeding peasant-women from the mountains of Pistoia, who were entering with a year's labour in a moderate bundle of yarn on their backs, and in their hearts that meagre hope of good and that wide dim fear of harm, which were somehow to be cared for by the Blessed Virgin, whose miraculous image, painted by the angels, was to have the curtain drawn away from it on this Eve of her Nativity, that its potency might stream forth without obstruction.

At another moment he was forced away towards the boundary of the piazza, where the more stationary candidates for attention and small coin had judiciously placed themselves, in order to be safe in their rear. Among these Tito recognized his acquaintance Bratti, who stood with his back against a pillar and his mouth pursed up in disdainful silence, eying every one who approached him with a cold glance of superiority, and keeping his hand fast on a serge covering, which concealed the contents of the basket slung before him. Rather surprised at a deportment so unusual in an anxious trader, Tito went nearer and saw two women go up to Bratti's basket with a look of curiosity, whereupon the pedlar drew the covering tighter, and looked another way. It was quite too provoking, and one of the women was fain to ask what there was in his basket?

"Before I answer that, Monna, I must know whether you mean to buy. I can't show such wares as mine in this fair for every fly to settle on and pay nothing. My goods are a little too choice for that. Besides, I've only two left, and I've no mind to sell them; for with the chances of the pestilence that wise men talk of, there is likelihood of their being worth their weight in gold. No, no: *andate con Dio*."

The two women looked at each other.

"And what may be the price?" said the second.

"Not within what you are like to have in your purse, buona donna," said Bratti, in a compassionately supercilious tone. "I recommend you to trust in Messer Domeneddio and the saints: poor people can do no better for themselves."

"Not so poor!" said the second woman, indignantly, drawing out her money-bag. "Come, now! what do you say to a grosso?"

"I say you may get twenty-one quattrini for it," said Bratti, coolly; "but not of me, for I haven't got that small change."

"Come; two, then?" said the woman, getting exasperated, while her companion looked at her with some envy. "It will hardly be above two, I think."

After further bidding, and further mercantile coquetry, Bratti put on an air of concession.

"Since you've set your mind on it," he said, slowly raising the cover, "I should be loath to do you a mischief; for Maestro Gabbadeo used to say, when a woman sets her mind on a thing and doesn't get it, she's in worse danger of the pestilence than before. Ecco! I have but two left; and let me tell you, the fellow to them is on the finger of Maestro Gabbadeo,* who is gone to Bologna—as wise a doctor as sits at any door."

The precious objects were two clumsy iron rings, beaten into the fashion of old Roman rings such as were sometimes disinterred. The rust on them, and the entirely hidden character of their potency, were so satisfactory, that the grossi were paid without grumbling, and the first woman, destitute of those handsome coins, succeeded after much show of reluctance on Bratti's part in driving a bargain with some of her yarn, and carried off the remaining ring in triumph. Bratti covered up his basket, which was now filled with miscellanies, probably obtained under the same sort of circumstances as the yarn, and moving from his pillar, came suddenly upon Tito, who, if he had had time, would have chosen to avoid recognition.

"By the head of San Giovanni, now," said Bratti, drawing Tito back to the pillar; "this is a piece of luck. For I was talking of you this morning, Messer Greco; but, I said, he is mounted up among the *signori* now—and I'm glad of it, for I was at the bottom of his fortune—but I can rarely get speech of him, for he's not to be caught lying on the stones now—not he! But it's your luck, not mine, Messer Greco, save and except some small trifle to satisfy me for my trouble in the transaction."

"You speak in riddles, Bratti," said Tito. "Remember, I don't sharpen my wits, as you do, by driving hard bargains for iron rings: you must be plain."

"By the Holy 'Vangels! it was an easy bargain I gave them. If a Hebrew gets thirty-two per cent., I hope a Christian may get a little more. If I had not borne a conscience, I should have got twice the money and twice the yarn. But, talking of rings, it is your ring—that very ring you've got on your finger—that I could get you a purchaser for—ay, and a purchaser with a deep money-bag."

"Truly?" said Tito, looking at his ring, and listening.

"A Genoese who is going straight away into Hungary, as I understand. He came and looked all over my shop to see if I had any old things I didn't know the price of; I warrant you, he thought I had a pumpkin on my shoulders.* He had been rummaging all the shops in Florence. And he had a ring on—not like yours, but something of the same fashion; and as he was talking of rings, I said I knew a fine young man, a particular acquaintance of mine, who had a ring of that sort. And he said, 'Who is he, pray? Tell him I'll give him his price for it.' And I thought of going after you to Nello's to-morrow; for it's my opinion of you, Messer Greco, that you're not one who'd see the Arno run broth, and stand by without dipping your finger."

Tito had lost no word of what Bratti had said, yet his mind

had been very busy all the while. Why should he keep the ring? It had been a mere sentiment, a mere fancy, that had prevented him from selling it with the other gems; if he had been wiser and had sold it, he might perhaps have escaped that identification by Fra Luca. It was true that it had been taken from Baldassarre's finger and put on to his as soon as his young hand had grown to the needful size; but there was really no valid good to anybody in those superstitious scruples about inanimate objects. The ring had helped towards the recognition of him. Tito had begun to dislike recognition, which was a claim from the past. This foreigner's offer, if he would really give a good price, was an opportunity for getting rid of the ring without the trouble of seeking a purchaser.

"You speak with your usual wisdom, Bratti," said Tito. "I have no objection to hear what your Genoese will offer. But when and where shall I have speech of him?"

"To-morrow, at three hours after sunrise, he will be at my shop, and if your wits are of that sharpness I have always taken them to be, Messer Greco, you will ask him a heavy price. For he minds not money; it's my belief he's buying for somebody else, and not for himself—perhaps for some great Signor."

"It is well," said Tito. "I will be at your shop, if nothing hinders."

"And you will doubtless deal nobly by me for old acquaintance' sake, Messer Greco, so I will not stay to fix the small sum you will give me in token of my service in the matter. It seems to me a thousand years now till I get out of the piazza, for a fair is a dull, not to say a wicked thing, when one has no more goods to sell."

Tito made a hasty sign of assent and adieu, and moving away from the pillar, again found himself pushed towards the middle of the piazza and back again, without the power of determining his own course. In this zigzag way he was carried along to the end of the piazza opposite the church, where, in a deep recess formed by an irregularity in the line of houses, an entertainment was going forward which seemed to be especially attractive to the crowd. Loud bursts of laughter interrupted a monologue which was sometimes slow and oratorical, at others rattling and buffoonish. Here a girl was being pushed forward into the inner circle with apparent reluctance, and there a loud-laughing minx was finding a way with her own elbows. It was a strange light that was spread over the piazza. There were the pale stars breaking out above, and the dim waving lanterns below, leaving all objects indistinct except when they were seen close under the fitfully moving lights; but in this recess there was a stronger light, against which the heads of the encircling spectators stood in dark relief as Tito was gradually pushed towards them, while above them rose the head of a man wearing a white mitre with yellow cabalistic figures upon it.

"Behold, my children!" Tito heard him saying, "behold your opportunity! neglect not the Holy Sacrament of matrimony when it can be had for the small sum of a white quattrino—the cheapest matrimony ever offered, and dissolved by special bull beforehand at every man's own will and pleasure. Behold the bull!" Here the speaker held up a piece of parchment with huge seals attached to it. "Behold the indulgence granted by his Holiness Alexander the Sixth, who, being newly elected Pope for his peculiar piety,* intends to reform and purify the Church, and wisely begins by abolishing that priestly abuse which keeps too large a share of this privileged matrimony to the clergy and stints the laity. Spit once, my sons, and pay a white quattrino! This is the whole and sole price of the indulgence. The quattrino is the only difference the Holy Father allows to be put any longer between us and the clergy—who spit and pay nothing."

Tito thought he knew the voice, which had a peculiarly sharp ring, but the face was too much in shadow from the lights behind for him to be sure of the features. Slipping as near as he could, he saw within the circle behind the speaker an altar-like table raised on a small platform, and covered with a red drapery stitched all over with yellow cabalistical figures. Half-a-dozen thin tapers burned at the back of this table, which had a conjuring apparatus scattered over it, a large open book in the centre, and at one of the front angles a monkey fastened by a cord to a small ring and holding a small taper, which in his incessant fidgety movements fell more or less aslant, while an impish boy in a white surplice occupied himself chiefly in cuffing the monkey, and adjusting the taper. The man in the mitre also wore a surplice, and over it a chasuble on which the signs of the zodiac were rudely marked in black upon a yellow ground. Tito was sure now that he recognized the sharp upward-tending angles of the face under the mitre: it was that of Maestro Vaiano, the mountebank, from whom he had rescued Tessa. Pretty little

Tessa! Perhaps she too had come in among the troops of contadine?

"Come, my maidens! This is the time for the pretty who can have many chances, and for the ill-favoured who have few. Matrimony to be had—hot, eaten, and done with as easily as *berlingozzi!* And see!" here the conjuror held up a cluster of tiny bags. "To every bride I give a *Breve* with a secret in it—the secret alone worth the money you pay for the matrimony. The secret how to—no, no, I will not tell you what the secret is about, and that makes it a double secret. Hang it round your neck if you like, and never look at it; I don't say that *that* will not be the best, for then you will see many things you don't expect: though if you open it (you may break your leg—*è vero*), but you will know a secret! Something nobody knows but me! And mark—I give you the *Breve*, I don't sell it, as many another holy man would: the quattrino is for the matrimony, and the *Breve* you get for nothing. *Orsù*, *giovanetti*, come like dutiful sons of the Church and buy the indulgence of his Holiness Alexander the Sixth."

This buffoonery just fitted the taste of the audience: the *fierucola* was but a small occasion, so the townsmen might be contented with jokes that were rather less indecent than those they were accustomed to hear at every carnival, put into easy rhyme by the Magnifico and his poetic satellites; while the women, over and above any relish of the fun, really began to have an itch for the *Brevi*. Several couples had already gone through the ceremony, in which the conjuror's solemn gibberish and grimaces over the open book, the antics of the monkey, and even the preliminary spitting, had called forth peals of laughter; and now a well-looking, merry-eyed youth of seventeen, in a loose tunic and a red cap, pushed forward, holding by the hand a plump brunette, whose scanty ragged dress displayed her round arms and legs very picturesquely.

"Fetter us without delay, maestro!" said the youth, "for I have got to take my bride home and paint her under the light of a lantern."

"Ha! Mariotto,* my son, I commend your pious observance. . . ." The conjuror was going on, when a loud chattering behind him warned him that an unpleasant crisis had arisen with his monkey.

The temper of that imperfect acolyth was a little tried by the over-active discipline of his colleague in the surplice, and a sudden cuff administered as his taper fell to a horizontal position, caused him to leap back with a violence that proved too much for the slackened knot by which his cord was fastened. His first leap was to the other end of the table, from which position his remonstrances were so threatening that the imp in the surplice took up a wand by way of an equivalent threat, whereupon the monkey leaped on to the head of a tall woman in the foreground, dropping his taper by the way, and chattering with increased emphasis from that eminence. Great was the screaming and confusion, not a few of the spectators having a vague dread of the maestro's monkey, as capable of more hidden mischief than mere teeth and claws could inflict; and the conjuror himself was in some alarm lest any harm should happen to his familiar. In the scuffle to seize the monkey's string, Tito got out of the circle, and, not caring to contend for his place again, he allowed himself to be gradually pushed towards the church of the Nunziata, and to enter amongst the worshippers.

The brilliant illumination within seemed to press upon his eyes with palpable force after the pale scattered lights and broad shadows of the piazza, and for the first minute or two he could see nothing distinctly. That yellow splendour was in itself something supernal and heavenly to many of the peasant-women, for whom half the sky was hidden by mountains, and who went to bed in the twilight; and the uninterrupted chant from the choir was repose to the ear after the hellish hubbub of the crowd outside. Gradually the scene became clearer, though still there was a thin yellow haze from incense mingling with the breath of the multitude. In a chapel on the left hand of the nave, wreathed with silver lamps, was seen unveiled the miraculous fresco of the Annunciation, which, in Tito's oblique view of it from the right-hand side of the nave, seemed dark with the excess of light* around it. The whole area of the great church was filled with peasant-women, some kneeling, some standing; the coarse bronzed skins, and the dingy clothing of the rougher dwellers on the mountains, contrasting with the softer-lined faces and white or red head-drapery of the well-to-do dwellers in the valley, who were scattered in irregular groups. And spreading high and far over the walls and ceiling there was another multitude, also pressing close against each other, that they might be nearer the potent Virgin. It was the crowd of votive waxen images, the effigies of great personages, clothed in their habit as they lived: Florentines of high name in their black silk *lucco*, as when they sat in council: popes, emperors, kings, cardinals, and famous condottieri with plumed morion seated on their chargers; all notable strangers who passed through Florence or had aught to do with its affairs—Mohammedans, even, in well-tolerated companionship with Christian cavaliers; some of them with faces blackened and robes tattered by the corroding breath of centuries, others fresh and bright in new red mantle or steel corslet, the exact doubles of the living. And wedged in with all these were detached arms, legs, hands, and other members, with only here and there a gap where some image had been removed for public disgrace, or had fallen ominously, as Lorenzo's had done six months before. It was a perfect resurrection-swarm of remote mortals and fragments of mortals, reflecting, in their varying degrees of freshness, the sombre dinginess and sprinkled brightness of the crowd below.

Tito's glance wandered over the wide multitude in search of something. He had already thought of Tessa, and the white hoods suggested the possibility that he might detect her face under one of them. It was at least a thought to be courted, rather than the vision of Romola looking at him with changed eyes. But he searched in vain; and he was leaving the church, weary of a scene which had no variety, when, just against the doorway, he caught sight of Tessa, only two yards off him. She was kneeling with her back against the wall, behind a group of peasant-women, who were standing and looking for a spot nearer to the sacred image. Her head hung a little aside with a look of weariness, and her blue eyes were directed rather absently towards an altar-piece* where the archangel Michael stood in his armour, with young face and floating hair, amongst bearded and tonsured saints. Her right hand, holding a bunch of cocoons, fell by her side listlessly, and her round cheek was paled, either by the light or by the weariness that was expressed in her attitude: her lips were pressed poutingly together, and every now and then her eyelids half fell: she was a large image of a sweet sleepy child. Tito felt an irresistible desire to go up to her and get her pretty trusting looks and prattle: this creature who was without moral judgments that could condemn him, whose little loving ignorant soul made a world apart, where he might feel in freedom from suspicions and exacting demands, had a new attraction for him now. She seemed a refuge from the threatened isolation that would come with disgrace. He glanced cautiously round, to assure himself that Monna Ghita was not near, and then, slipping quietly to her side, kneeled on one knee, and said, in the softest voice, "Tessa!"

She hardly started, any more than she would have started at a soft breeze that fanned her gently when she was needing it. She turned her head and saw Tito's face close to her: it was very much more beautiful than the archangel Michael, who was so mighty and so good that he lived with the Madonna and all the saints, and was prayed to along with them. She smiled in happy silence, for that nearness of Tito quite filled her mind.

"My little Tessa! you look very tired. How long have you been kneeling here?"

She seemed to be collecting her thoughts for a minute or two, and at last she said—

"I'm very hungry."

"Come, then; come with me."

He lifted her from her knees, and led her out under the cloisters surrounding the atrium, which were then open, and not yet adorned with the frescoes of Andrea del Sarto.*

"How is it you are all by yourself, and so hungry, Tessa?"

"The madre is ill; she has very bad pains in her legs, and sent me to bring these cocoons to the Santissima Nunziata, because they're so wonderful; see!"—she held up the bunch of cocoons, which were arranged with fortuitous regularity on a stem,—"and she had kept them to bring them herself, but she couldn't, and so she sent me because she thinks the Holy Madonna may take away her pains; and somebody took my bag with the bread and chestnuts in it, and the people pushed me back, and I was so frightened coming in the crowd, and I couldn't get anywhere near the Holy Madonna, to give the cocoons to the *padre*, but I must—oh, I must."

"Yes, my little Tessa, you shall take them; but first come and let me give you some *berlingozzi*. There are some to be had not far off."

"Where did you come from?' said Tessa, a little bewildered. "I thought you would never come to me again, because you never came to the Mercato for milk any more. I set myself *Aves* to say, to see if they would bring you back, but I left off, because they didn't."

"You see I come when you want some one to take care of you, Tessa. Perhaps the *Aves* fetched me, only it took them a long while. But what shall you do if you are here all alone? Where shall you go?"

"Oh, I shall stay and sleep in the church—a great many of them do—in the church and all about here—I did once when I came with my mother; and the *patrigno* is coming with the mules in the morning."

They were out in the piazza now, where the crowd was rather less riotous than before, and the lights were fewer, the stream of pilgrims having ceased. Tessa clung fast to Tito's arm in satisfied silence, while he led her towards the stall where he remembered seeing the eatables. Their way was the easier because there was just now a great rush towards the middle of the piazza, where the masqued figures on stilts had found space to execute a dance. It was very pretty to see the guileless thing giving her cocoons into Tito's hand and then eating her *berlingozzi* with the relish of a hungry child. Tito had really come to take care of her, as he did before, and that wonderful happiness of being with him had begun again for her. Her hunger was soon appeased, all the sooner for the new stimulus of happiness that had roused her from her languor, and as they turned away from the stall, she said nothing about going into the church again, but looked round as if the sights in the piazza were not without attraction to her now she was safe under Tito's arm.

"How can they do that?" she exclaimed, looking up at the dancers on stilts. Then, after a minute's silence, "Do you think Saint Christopher helps them?"

"Perhaps. What do you think about it, Tessa?" said Tito, slipping his right arm round her, and looking down at her fondly.

"Because Saint Christopher is so very tall; and he is very good: if anybody looks at him he takes care of them all day. He is on the wall of the church—too tall to stand up there—but I saw him walking through the streets one San Giovanni, carrying the little *Gesù*."*

"You pretty pigeon! Do you think anybody could help taking care of *you*, if you looked at them?"

"Shall you always come and take care of me?" said Tessa, turning her face up to him, as he crushed her cheek with his left hand. "And shall you always be a long while first?"

Tito was conscious that some bystanders were laughing at them, and though the licence of street fun, among artists and young men of the wealthier sort as well as among the populace, made few adventures exceptional, still less disreputable, he chose to move away towards the end of the piazza.

"Perhaps I shall come again to you very soon, Tessa," he answered, rather dreamily, when they had moved away. He was thinking, that when all the rest had turned their backs upon him, it would be pleasant to have this little creature adoring him and nestling against him. The absence of presumptuous self-conceit in Tito made him feel all the more defenceless under prospective obloquy: he needed soft looks and caresses too much ever to be impudent.

"In the Mercato?" said Tessa. "Not to-morrow morning, because the *patrigno* will be there, and he is so cross. Oh! but you have money, and he will not be cross if you buy some salad. And there are some chestnuts. Do you like chestnuts?"

He said nothing, but continued to look down at her with a dreamy gentleness, and Tessa felt herself in a state of delicious wonder; everything seemed as new as if she were being carried on a chariot of clouds.

"Holy Virgin!" she exclaimed again, presently; "there is a holy Father like the Bishop I saw at Prato."

Tito looked up too, and saw that he had unconsciously advanced to within a few yards of the conjuror, Maestro Vaiano, who, for the moment, was forsaken by the crowd. His face was turned away from them, and he was occupied with the apparatus on his altar or table, preparing a new diversion by the time the interest in the dancing should be exhausted. The monkey was imprisoned under the red cloth, out of reach of mischief, and the youngster in the white surplice was holding a sort of dish or salver, from which his master was taking some ingredient. The altar-like table, with its gorgeous cloth, the row of tapers, the sham episcopal costume, the surpliced attendant, and even the movements of the mitred figure, as he alternately bent his head and then raised something before the lights, were a sufficiently near parody of sacred things to rouse poor little Tessa's veneration; and there was some additional awe produced by the mystery of their apparition in this spot, for when she had seen an altar in the street before, it had been on Corpus Christi Day, and there had been a procession to account for it. She crossed herself, and looked up at Tito, but then, as if she had had time for reflexion, said, "It is because of the Nativitá."

Meanwhile Vaiano had turned round, raising his hands to his mitre with the intention of changing his dress, when his quick eye recognized Tito and Tessa who were both looking at him, their faces being shone upon by the light of his tapers, while his own was in shadow.

"Ha! my children!" he said, instantly, stretching out his hands in a benedictory attitude, "you are come to be married. I commend your penitence—the blessing of Holy Church can never come too late."

But whilst he was speaking, he had taken in the whole meaning of Tessa's attitude and expression, and he discerned an opportunity for a new kind of joke which required him to be cautiously solemn.

"Should you like to be married to me, Tessa?" said Tito, softly, half enjoying the comedy, as he saw the pretty childish seriousness on her face, half prompted by hazy previsions which belonged to the intoxication of despair.

He felt her vibrating before she looked up at him and said, timidly, "Will you let me?"

He answered only by a smile, and by leading her forward in front of the *cerretano*, who seeing an excellent jest in Tessa's evident delusion, assumed a surpassing sacerdotal solemnity, and went through the mimic ceremony with a liberal expenditure of *lingua furbesca* or thieves' Latin. But some symptoms of a new movement in the crowd urged him to bring it to a speedy conclusion and dismiss them with hands outstretched in a benedictory attitude over their kneeling figures. Tito, disposed always to cultivate goodwill, though it might be the least select, put a piece of four grossi into his hand as he moved away, and was thanked by a look which, the conjuror felt sure, conveyed a perfect understanding of the whole affair.

But Tito himself was very far from that understanding, and did not, in fact, know whether, the next moment, he should tell Tessa of the joke and laugh at her for a little goose, or whether he should let her delusion last, and see what would come of it—see what she would say and do next.

"Then you will not go away from me again," said Tessa, after they had walked a few steps, "and you will take me to where you live." She spoke meditatively, and not in a questioning tone. But, presently, she added, "I must go back once to the madre, though, to tell her I brought the cocoons, and that I'm married, and shall not go back again."

Tito felt the necessity of speaking now; and, in the rapid thought prompted by that necessity, he saw that by undeceiving Tessa he should be robbing himself of some at least of that pretty trustfulness which might, by and by, be his only haven from contempt. It would spoil Tessa to make her the least particle wiser or more suspicious.

"Yes, my little Tessa," he said, caressingly, "you must go back to the madre; but you must not tell her you are married—you must keep that a secret from everybody; else some very great harm would happen to me, and you would never see me again."

She looked up at him with fear in her face.

"You must go back and feed your goats and mules, and do just as you have always done before, and say no word to any one about me."

The corners of her mouth fell a little.

"And then, perhaps, I shall come and take care of you again when you want me, as I did before. But you must do just what I tell you, else you will not see me again."

"Yes, I will, I will," she said, in a loud whisper, frightened at that blank prospect.

They were silent a little while; and then Tessa, looking at her hand, said,—

"The madre wears a betrothal-ring. She went to church and had it put on, and then after that, another day, she was married. And so did the cousin Nannina. But then *she* married Gollo," added the poor little thing, entangled in the difficult comparison between her own case and others within her experience.

"But you must not wear a betrothal-ring, my Tessa, because no one must know you are married," said Tito, feeling some insistance necessary. "And the *buon fortuna* that I gave you did just as well for betrothal. Some people are betrothed with rings and some are not."

"Yes, it is true, they would see the ring," said Tessa, trying to convince herself that a thing she would like very much was really not good for her.

They were now near the entrance of the church again, and she remembered her cocoons which were still in Tito's hand.

"Ah, you must give me the *Boto*," she said; "and we must go in, and I must take it to the *padre*, and I must tell the rest of my beads, because I was too tired before."

"Yes, you must go in Tessa; but I will not go in. I must leave you now," said Tito, too feverish and weary to re-enter that stifling heat, and feeling that this was the least difficult way of parting with her.

"And not come back? Oh, where do you go?" Tessa's mind had never formed an image of his whereabout or his doings when she did not see him: he had vanished, and her thought, instead of following him, had stayed in the same spot where he was with her.

"I shall come back some time, Tessa," said Tito, taking her under the cloisters to the door of the church. "You must not cry—you must go to sleep, when you have said your beads. And here is money to buy your breakfast. Now kiss me, and look happy; else I shall not come again."

She made a great effort over herself as she put up her lips to kiss him, and submitted to be gently turned round, with her face towards the door of the church. Tito saw her enter; and then, with a shrug at his own resolution, leaned against a pillar, took off his cap, rubbed his hair backward, and wondered where Romola was now, and what she was thinking of him. Poor little Tessa had disappeared behind the curtain among the crowd of peasants; but the love which formed one web with all his worldly hopes—with the ambitions and pleasures that must make the solid part of his days—the love that was identified with his larger self—was not to be banished from his consciousness. Even to the man who presents the most elastic resistance to whatever is unpleasant, there will come moments when the pressure from without is too strong for him, and he must feel the smart and the bruise in spite of himself. Such a moment had come to Tito. There was no possible attitude of mind, no scheme of action, by which the uprooting of all his newly-planted hopes could be made otherwise than painful.

[*OCTOBER 1862*]

CHAPTER XV.

The Dying Message

WHEN Romola arrived at the entrance of San Marco she found one of the Frati waiting there in expectation of her arrival. Monna Brigida retired into the adjoining church, and Romola was conducted to the door of the chapter-house in the outer cloister, whither the invalid had been conveyed; no woman being allowed admission beyond this precinct.

When the door opened, the subdued external light blending with that of two tapers placed behind a truckle-bed showed the emaciated face of Fra Luca, with the tonsured crown of golden hair above it, and with deep-sunken hazel eyes fixed on a small crucifix which he held before him. He was propped up into nearly a sitting posture; and Romola was just conscious, as she threw aside her veil, that there was another monk standing by the bed, with the black cowl drawn over his head, and that he moved towards the door as she entered; just conscious that in the background there was a crucified form rising high and pale on the frescoed wall, and pale faces of sorrow looking out from it below.

The next moment her eyes met Fra Luca's as they looked up at her from the crucifix, and she was absorbed in that pang of recognition which identified this monkish emaciated form with the image of her fair young brother.

"Dino!" she said, in a voice like a low cry of pain. But she did not bend towards him; she held herself erect, and paused at two yards' distance from him. There was an unconquerable repulsion for her in that monkish aspect; it seemed to her the brand of the dastardly undutifulness which had left her father desolate—of the grovelling superstition which could give such undutifulness the name of piety. Her father, whose proud sincerity and simplicity of life had made him one of the few frank pagans of his time, had brought her up with a silent ignoring of any claims the Church could have to regulate the belief and action of beings with a cultivated reason; the Church, in her mind, belonged to that actual life of the mixed multitude from which they had always lived apart, and she had no ideas that could render her brother's course an object of any other feeling than incurious, indignant contempt. Yet the lovingness of Romola's soul had clung to that image in the past, and while she stood rigidly aloof, there was a yearning search in her eyes for something too faintly discernible.

But there was no corresponding emotion in the face of the monk. He looked at the little sister returned to him in her full womanly beauty, with the far-off gaze of a revisiting spirit.

"My sister!" he said, with feeble and interrupted but yet distinct utterance, "it is well thou hast not longer delayed to come, for I have a message to deliver to thee, and my time is short."

Romola took a step nearer: the message, she thought, would be one of affectionate penitence to her father, and her heart began to open. Nothing could wipe out the long years of desertion; but the culprit, looking back on those years with the sense of irremediable wrong committed, would call forth pity. Now, at the last, there would be understanding and forgiveness. Dino would pour out some natural filial feeling; he would ask questions about his father's blindness—how rapidly it had come on? how the long dark days had been filled? what the life was now in the home where he himself had been nourished?—and the last message from the dying lips would be one of tenderness and regret.

"Romola," Fra Luca began again, "I have had a vision concerning thee. Thrice I have had it in the last two months: each time it has been clearer. Therefore I came from Fiesole, deeming it a message from heaven that I was bound to deliver. And I gather a promise of mercy to thee in this, that my breath is preserved in order to—"

The difficult breathing which continually interrupted him would not let him finish the sentence.

Romola had felt her heart chilling again. It was a vision, then, this message—one of those visions she had so often heard her father allude to with bitterness. Her indignation rushed to her lips.

"Dino, I thought you had some words to send to my father. You forsook him when his sight was failing; you made his life very desolate. Have you never cared about that? never repented? What is this religion of yours, that places visions before natural duties?"

The deep-sunken hazel eyes turned slowly towards her, and rested upon her in silence for some moments, as if he were meditating whether he should answer her.

"No," he said at last; speaking, as before, in a low passionless tone, as of some spirit not human, speaking through dying human organs. "No; I have never repented fleeing from the stifling poison-breath of sin that was hot and thick around me, and threatened to steal over my senses like besotting wine. My father could not hear the voice that called me night and day; he knew nothing of the demon-tempters that tried to drag me back from following it. My father has lived amidst human sin and misery without believing in them: he has been like one busy picking shining stones in a mine, while there was a world dying of plague above him. I spoke, but he listened with scorn. I told him the studies he wished me to live for were either childish trifling—dead toys—or else they must be made warm and living by pulses that beat to worldly ambitions and fleshly lusts: for worldly ambitions and fleshly lusts made all the substance of the poetry and history he wanted me to bend my eyes on continually."

"Has not my father led a pure and noble life, then?" Romola burst forth, unable to hear in silence this implied accusation against her father. "He has sought no worldly honours; he has been truthful; he has denied himself all luxuries; he has lived like one of the ancient sages. He never wished you to live for worldly ambitions and fleshly lusts; he wished you to live as he himself has done, according to the purest maxims of philosophy, in which he brought you up."

Romola spoke partly by rote, as all ardent and sympathetic young creatures do; but she spoke with intense belief. The pink flush was in her face, and she quivered from head to foot. Her brother was again slow to answer; looking at her passionate face with strange passionless eyes.

"What were the maxims of philosophy to me? They told me to be strong, when I felt myself weak; when I was ready, like the blessed Saint Benedict, to roll myself among thorns,* and court smarting wounds as a deliverance from temptation. For the Divine Love had sought me, and penetrated me, and created a great need in me; like a seed that wants room to grow. I had been brought up in carelessness of the true faith; I had not studied the doctrines of our religion; but it seemed to take possession of me like a rising flood. I felt that there was a life of perfect love and purity for the soul; in which there would be no uneasy hunger after pleasure, no tormenting questions, no fear of suffering. Before I knew the history of the saints, I had a foreshadowing of their ecstasy. For the same truth had penetrated even into pagan philosophy: that it is a bliss within the reach of man to die to mortal needs, and live in the life of God as the Unseen Perfectness. But to attain that I must forsake the world: I must have no affection, no hope, wedding me to that which passeth away; I must live with my fellow-beings only as human souls related to the eternal unseen Life. That need was urging me continually: it came over me in visions when my mind fell away weary from the vain words which record the passions of dead men; it came over me after I had been tempted into sin, and had turned away with loathing from the scent of the emptied cup. And in visions I saw the meaning of the Crucifix."

He paused, breathing hard for a minute or two: but Romola was not prompted to speak again. It was useless for her mind to attempt any contact with the mind of this unearthly brother: as useless as for her hand to try and grasp a shadow. When he spoke again his heaving chest was quieter.

"I felt whom I must follow: but I saw that even among the servants of the Cross who professed to have renounced the world, my soul would be stifled with the fumes of hypocrisy, and lust, and pride. God had not chosen me, as he chose Saint Dominic and Saint Francis, to wrestle with evil in the Church and in the world. He called upon me to flee: I took the sacred vows and I fled—fled to lands where danger and scorn and want bore me continually, like angels, to repose on the bosom of God. I have lived the life of a hermit, I have ministered to pilgrims; but my task has been short: the veil has worn very thin that divides me from my everlasting rest. I came back to Florence that—"

"Dino, you *did* want to know if my father was alive," interrupted Romola, the picture of that suffering life touching her again with the desire for union and forgiveness.

"—that before I die I might urge others of our brethren to study the eastern tongues, as I had not done, and go out to greater ends than I did, and I find them already bent on the work. And since I came, Romola, I have felt that I was sent partly to thee—not to renew the bonds of earthly affection, but to deliver the heavenly warning conveyed in a vision. For I have had that vision thrice. And through all the years since first the Divine voice called me, while I was yet in the world, I have been taught and guided by visions. For in the painful linking together of our waking thoughts we can never be sure that we have not mingled our own error with the light we have prayed for; but in visions and dreams we are passive, and our souls are as an instrument in the Divine hand. Therefore listen, and speak not again—for the time is short."

Romola's mind recoiled strongly from listening to this vision. Her indignation had subsided, but it was only because she had felt the distance between her brother and herself widening. But while Fra Luca was speaking, the figure of another monk had entered, and again stood on the other side of the bed, with the cowl drawn over his head.

"Kneel, my daughter, for the Angel of Death is present, and waits while the message of heaven is delivered: bend thy pride before it is bent for thee by a yoke of iron," said a strong rich voice, startlingly in contrast with Fra Luca's. The tone was not that of imperious command, but of quiet self-possession and assurance of the right, blended with benignity. Romola, vibrating to the sound, looked round at the figure on the opposite side of the bed. His face was hardly discernible under the shadow of the cowl, and her eyes fell at once on his hands, which were folded across his breast and lay in relief on the edge of his black mantle. They had a marked physiognomy which enforced the influence of the voice: they were very beautiful and almost of transparent delicacy. Romola's disposition to rebel against command, doubly active in the presence of monks, whom she had been taught to despise, would have fixed itself on any repulsive detail as a point of support. But the face was hidden, and the hands seemed to have an appeal in them against all hardness. The next moment the right hand took the crucifix to relieve the fatigued grasp of Fra Luca, and the left touched his lips with a wet sponge which lay near. In the act of bending, the cowl was pushed back, and the features of the monk had the full light of the tapers on them. They were very marked features, such as lend themselves to popular description. There was the high arched nose, the prominent under-lip, the coronet of thick dark hair above the brow, all seeming to tell of energy and passion; there were the blue-grey eyes, shining mildly under auburn eyelashes, seeming, like the hands, to tell of acute sensitiveness. Romola felt certain they were the features of Fra Girolamo Savonarola, the prior of San Marco, whom she had chiefly thought of as more offensive than other monks because he was more noisy. Her rebellion was rising against the first impression, which had almost forced her to bend her knees.

"Kneel, my daughter," the penetrating voice said again, "the pride of the body is a barrier against the gifts that purify the soul."

He was looking at her with mild fixedness while he spoke, and again she felt that subtle mysterious influence of a personality by which it has been given to some rare men to move their fellows.

Slowly Romola fell on her knees, and in the very act a tremor came over her; in the renunciation of her proud erectness, her mental attitude seemed changed, and she found herself in a new state of passiveness. Her brother began to speak again.

"Romola, in the deep night, as I lay awake, I saw my father's room—the library—with all the books and the marbles and the *leggio,* where I used to stand and read; and I saw you—you were revealed to me as I see you now, with fair long hair, sitting before my father's chair. And at the *leggio* stood a man whose face I could not see—I looked, and looked, and it was a blank to me, even as a painting effaced; and I saw him move and take thee, Romola, by the hand; and then I saw thee take my father by the hand; and you went all three down the stone steps into the streets, the man whose face was a blank to me leading the way. And you stood at the altar in Santa Croce, and the priest who married you had the face of death; and the graves opened, and the dead in their shrouds rose and followed you like a bridal train. And you passed on through the streets and the gates into the valley, and it seemed to me that he who led you hurried you more than you could bear, and the dead were weary of following you, and turned back to their graves. And at last you came to a stony place where there was no water, and no trees or herbage; but instead of water, I saw written parchment unrolling itself everywhere, and instead of trees and herbage I saw men of bronze and marble springing up and crowding round you. And my father was faint for want of water and fell to the ground; and the man whose face was a blank loosed thy hand and departed; and as he went I could see his face; and it was the face of the Great Tempter. And thou, Romola, didst wring thy hands and seek for water, and there was none. And the bronze and marble figures seemed to mock thee and hold out cups of water, and when thou didst grasp them and put them to my father's lips, they turned to parchment. And the bronze and marble figures seemed to turn into demons and snatch my father's body from thee, and the parchments shrivelled up, and blood ran everywhere instead of them, and fire upon the blood, till they all vanished, and the plain was bare and stony again, and thou wast alone in the midst of it. And then it seemed that the night fell and I saw no more. . . . Thrice I have had that vision, Romola. I believe it is a revelation meant for thee—to warn thee against marriage as a temptation of the enemy—it calls upon thee to dedicate thyself—"

His pauses had gradually become longer and more frequent, and he was now compelled to cease by a severe fit of gasping, in which his eyes were turned on the crucifix as on a light that was vanishing. Presently he found strength to speak again, but in a feebler, scarcely audible tone.

"To renounce the vain philosophy and corrupt thoughts of the heathens: for in the hour of sorrow and death their pride will turn to mockery, and the unclean gods will—"

The words died away.

In spite of the thought that was at work in Romola, telling her that his vision was no more than a dream, fed by youthful memories and ideal convictions, a strange awe had come over her. Her mind was not apt to be assailed by sickly fancies; she had the vivid intellect and the healthy human passion, which are too keenly alive to the constant relations of things to have any morbid craving after the exceptional. Still, the images of the vision she despised jarred and distressed her like painful and cruel cries. And it was the first time she had witnessed the struggle with approaching death: her young life had been sombre, but she had known nothing of the utmost human needs; no acute suffering—no heart-cutting sorrow; and this brother, come back to her in his hour of supreme agony, was like a sudden awful apparition from an invisible world. The pale faces of sorrow in the fresco on the opposite wall seemed to have come nearer, and to make one company with the pale face on the bed.

"Frate," said the dying voice.

Fra Girolamo leaned down. But no other word came for some moments.

"Romola," it said next.

She leaned forward too: but again there was silence. The words were struggling in vain.

"Fra Girolamo, give her—"

"The crucifix," said the voice of Fra Girolamo.

No other sound came from the dying lips.

"Dino!" said Romola, with a low but piercing cry, as the certainty came upon her that the silence of misunderstanding could never be broken.

"Take the crucifix, my daughter," said Fra Girolamo, after a few minutes. "His eyes behold it no more."

Romola stretched out her hand to the crucifix, and this act appeared to relieve the tension of her mind. A great sob burst from her. She bowed her head by the side of her dead brother, and wept aloud.

It seemed to her as if this first vision of death must alter the daylight for her for ever more.

Fra Girolamo moved towards the door, and called in a lay Brother who was waiting outside. Then he went up to Romola and said in a tone of gentle command, "Rise, my daughter, and be comforted. Our brother is with the blessed. He has left you the crucifix, in remembrance of the heavenly warning—that it may be a beacon to you in the darkness."

She rose from her knees, trembling, folded her veil over her head, and hid the crucifix under her mantle. Fra Girolamo then led the way out into the cloistered court, lit now only by the stars and by a lantern which was held by some one near the entrance. Several other figures in the dress of the dignified laity were grouped about the same spot. They were some of the numerous frequenters of San Marco, who had come to visit the Prior, and having heard that he was in attendance on the dying brother in the chapter-house, had awaited him here.

Romola was dimly conscious of footsteps and rustling forms moving aside: she heard the voice of Fra Girolamo, saying, in a low tone, "Our brother is departed;" she felt a hand laid on her arm. The next moment the door was opened, and she was out in the wide piazza of San Marco, with no one but Monna Brigida, and the servant carrying the lantern.

The fresh sense of space revived her, and helped her to

recover her self-mastery. The scene which had just closed upon her was terribly distinct and vivid, but it began to narrow under the returning impressions of the life that lay outside it. She hastened her steps, with nervous anxiety to be again with her father—and with Tito—for were they not together in her absence? The images of that vision, while they clung about her like a hideous dream not yet to be shaken off, made her yearn all the more for the beloved faces and voices that would assure her of her waking life.

Tito, we know, was not with Bardo; his destiny was being shaped by a guilty consciousness, urging on him the despairing belief that by this time Romola possessed the knowledge which would lead to their final separation.

And the lips that could have conveyed that knowledge were for ever closed. The prevision that Fra Luca's words had imparted to Romola had been such as comes from the shadowy region where human souls seek wisdom apart from the human sympathies which are the very life and substance of our wisdom; the revelation that might have come from the simple questions of filial and brotherly affection had been carried into irrevocable silence.

CHAPTER XVI.

A Florentine Joke

EARLY the next morning Tito was returning from Bratti's shop in the narrow thoroughfare of the Ferravecchi. The Genoese stranger had carried away the onyx ring, and Tito was carrying away fifty florins. It did just cross his mind that if, after all, Fortune, by one of her able devices, saved him from the necessity of quitting Florence, it would be better for him not to have parted with his ring, since he had been understood to wear it for the sake of peculiar memories and predilections; still, it was a slight matter, not worth dwelling on with any emphasis, and in those moments he had lost his confidence in Fortune. The feverish excitement of the first alarm which had impelled his mind to travel into the future had given place to a dull, regretful lassitude. He cared so much for the pleasures that could only come to him through the good opinion of his fellow-men, that he wished now he had never risked ignominy by shrinking from what his fellow-men called obligations. But our deeds are like children that are born to us; they live and act apart from our own will. Nay, children may be strangled, but deeds never: they have an indestructible life both in and out of our consciousness; and that dreadful vitality of deeds was pressing hard on Tito for the first time.

He was going back to his lodgings in the Piazza di San Giovanni, but he avoided passing through the Mercato Vecchio, which was his nearest way, lest he should see Tessa. He was not in the humour to seek anything; he could only await the first sign of his altering lot.

The piazza with its sights of beauty was lit up by that warm morning sunlight under which the autumn dew still lingers and which invites to an idlesse undulled by fatigue. It was a festival morning too, when the soft warmth seems to steal over one with a special invitation to lounge and gaze. Here, too, the signs of the fair were present; in the spaces round the octagonal Baptistery, stalls were being spread with fruit and flowers, and here and there laden mules were standing quietly absorbed in their nose-bags, while their drivers were perhaps gone through the hospitable sacred doors to kneel before the Blessed Virgin on this morning of her Nativity. On the broad marble steps of the Duomo there were scattered groups of beggars and gossiping talkers; here an old crone with white hair and hard sunburnt face encouraging a round-capped baby to try its tiny bare feet on the warmed marble, while a dog sitting near snuffed at the performance suspiciously; there a couple of shaggy-headed boys leaning to watch a small pale cripple who was cutting a face on a cherry-stone; and above them on the wide platform men were making changing knots in laughing desultory chat, or else were standing in close couples gesticulating eagerly.

But the largest and most important company of loungers was that towards which Tito had to direct his steps. It was the busiest time of the day with Nello, and in this warm season and at an hour when clients were numerous, most men preferred being shaved under the pretty red and white awning in front of the shop rather than within narrow walls. It is not a sublime attitude for a man to sit with lathered chin thrown backward, and have his nose made a handle of; but to be shaved was a fashion of Florentine respectability, and it is astonishing how gravely men look at each other when they are all in the fashion. It was the hour of the day too when yesterday's crop of gossip was freshest, and the barber's tongue was always in its glory when his razor was busy; the deft activity of those two instruments seemed to be set going by a common spring. Tito foresaw that it would be impossible for him to escape being drawn into the circle; he must smile and retort, and look perfectly at his ease. Well! it was but the ordeal of swallowing bread and cheese pills* after all. The man who let the mere anticipation of discovery choke him was simply a man of weak nerves. But just at that time Tito felt a hand laid on his shoulder, and no amount of previous resolution could prevent the very unpleasant sensation with which that sudden touch jarred him. His face, as he turned it round, betrayed the inward shock; but the owner of the hand that seemed to have such evil magic in it broke into a light laugh. He was a young man about Tito's own age, with keen features, small close-clipped head, and close-shaven lip and chin, giving the idea of a mind as little encumbered as possible with material that was not nervous. The keen eyes were bright with hope and friendliness, as so many other young eyes have been that have afterwards closed on the world in bitterness and disappointment; for at that time there were none but pleasant predictions about Niccolò Macchiavelli, as a young man of promise, who was expected to mend the broken fortunes of his ancient family.

"Why, Melema, what evil dream did you have last night, that you took my light grasp for that of a *sbirro*, or something worse?"

"Ah, Messer Niccolò!" said Tito, recovering himself immediately; "it must have been an extra amount of dulness in my veins this morning that shuddered at the approach of your wit. But the fact is, I have had a bad night."

"That is unlucky, because you will be expected to shine without any obstructing fog to-day in the Rucellai Gardens. I take it for granted you are to be there."

"Messer Bernardo did me the honour to invite me," said Tito; "but I shall be engaged elsewhere."

"Ah! I remember, you are in love," said Macchiavelli, with a shrug, "else you would never have such inconvenient engagements. Why, we are to eat a peacock and ortolans* under the loggia among Bernardo Rucellai's rare trees; there are to be the choicest spirits in Florence and the choicest wines. Only as Piero de' Medici is to be there, the choice spirits may happen to be swamped in the capping of impromptu verses. I hate that game; it is a device for the triumph of small wits, who are always inspired the most by the smallest occasions."

"What is that you are saying about Piero de' Medici and small wits, Messer Niccolò?" said Nello, whose light figure was at that moment predominating over the Herculean frame of Niccolò Caparra. That famous worker in iron, whom we saw last with bared muscular arms and leathern apron in the Mercato Vecchio, was this morning dressed in holiday suit, and as he sat submissively while Nello skipped round him, lathered him, seized him by the nose, and scraped him with magical quickness, he looked much as a lion might if it had donned linen and tunic, and was preparing to go into society.

"A private secretary will never rise in the world if he couples great and small in that way," continued Nello. "When great men are not allowed to marry their sons and daughters as they like, small men must not expect to marry their words as they like. Have you heard the news Domenico Cennini, here, has been telling us?—that Pagolantonio Soderini has given Ser Piero da Bibbiena a box on the ear for setting on Piero de' Medici to interfere with the marriage between young Tommaso Soderini and Fiammetta Strozzi, and is to be sent ambassador to Venice as a punishment?"

"I don't know which I envy him most," said Macchiavelli, "the offence or the punishment. The offence will make him the most popular man in all Florence, and the punishment will take him among the only people in Italy who have known how to manage their own affairs."

"Yes, if Soderini stays long enough at Venice," said Cennini, "he may chance to learn the Venetian fashion, and bring it home with him. The Soderini have been fast friends of the Medici, but what has happened is likely to open Pagolantonio's eyes to the good of our old Florentine trick of choosing a new harness when the old one galls us; if we have not quite lost the trick in these last fifty years."

"Not we," said Niccolò Caparra, who was rejoicing in the free use of his lips again. "Eat eggs in Lent and the snow will melt. That's what I say to our people when they get noisy over their cups at San Gallo, and talk of raising a *romor* (insurrection): I say, never do you plan a *romor;* you may as well try to fill Arno with buckets. When there's water enough Arno will be full, and that will not be till the torrent is ready."

"Caparra, that oracular speech of yours is due to my excellent shaving," said Nello. "You could never have made it with that dark rust on your chin. Ecco, Messer Domenico, I am ready for you now. By the way, my *bel erudito,*" continued Nello, as he saw Tito moving towards the door, "here has been old Maso seeking for you, but your nest was empty. He will come again presently. The old man looked mournful, and seemed in haste. I hope there is nothing wrong in the Via de' Bardi."

"Doubtless, Messer Tito knows that Bardo's son is dead," said Cronaca, who had just come up.

Tito's heart gave a leap—had the death happened before Romola saw him?

"No, I had not heard it," he said, with no more discomposure than the occasion seemed to warrant, turning and learning against the door-post, as if he had given up his intention of going away. "I knew that his sister had gone to see him. Did he die before she arrived?"

"No," said Cronaca; "I was in San Marco at the time, and saw her come out from the chapter-house with Fra Girolamo, who told us that the dying man's breath had been preserved as by a miracle, that he might make a disclosure to his sister."

Tito felt that his fate was decided. Again his mind rushed over all the circumstances of his departure from Florence, and he conceived a plan of getting back his money from Cennini before the disclosure had become public. If he once had his money he need not stay long in endurance of scorching looks and biting words. He would wait now, and go away with Cennini and get the money from him at once. With that project in his mind he stood motionless—his hands in his belt, his eyes fixed absently on the ground. Nello, glancing at him, felt sure that he was absorbed in anxiety about Romola, and thought him such a pretty image of self-forgetful sadness, that he just perceptibly pointed his razor at him, and gave a challenging look at Piero di Cosimo, whom he had never forgiven for his refusal to see any prognostics of character in his favourite's handsome face. Piero, who was leaning against the other door-post, close to Tito, shrugged his shoulders: the frequent recurrence of such challenges from Nello had changed the painter's first declaration of neutrality into a positive inclination to believe ill of the much-bepraised Greek.

"So you have got your Fra Girolamo back again,* Cronaca? I suppose we shall have him preaching again this next Advent," said Nello.

"And not before there is need," said Cronaca, gravely. "We have had the best testimony to his words since the last Quaresima; for even to the wicked wickedness has become a plague; and the ripeness of vice is turning to rottenness in the nostrils even of the vicious. There has not been a change since the Quaresima, either in Rome or at Florence, but has put a new seal on the Frate's words—that the harvest of sin is ripe, and that God will reap it with a sword."

"I hope he has had a new vision, however," said Francesco Cei, sneeringly. "The old ones are somewhat stale. Can't your Frate get a poet to help out his imagination for him?"

"He has no lack of poets about him," said Cronaca, with quiet contempt, "but they are great poets and not little ones; so they are contented to be taught by him, and no more think the truth stale which God has given him to utter, than they think the light of the moon is stale. But, perhaps, certain high prelates and princes who dislike the Frate's denunciations, might be pleased to hear that, though Giovanni Pico and Poliziano and Marsilio Ficino, and most other men of mark in Florence reverence Fra Girolamo, Messer Francesco Cei despises him."

"Poliziano?" said Cei, with a scornful laugh. "Yes, doubtless he believes in your new Jonah;* witness the fine oration he wrote for the envoys of Siena, to tell Alexander the Sixth that the world and the Church were never so well off as since he became Pope."

"Nay, Francesco," said Macchiavelli, smiling, "a various scholar must have various opinions. And as for the Frate, whatever we may think of his saintliness, you judge his preaching too narrowly. The secret of oratory lies, not in saying new things, but in saying things with a certain power that moves the hearers—without which, as old Filelfo has said, your speaker deserves to be called, 'non *o*ratorem, sed *a*ratorem.'* And, according to that test, Fra Girolamo is a great orator."

"That is true, Niccolò," said Cennini, speaking from the shaving-chair, "but part of the secret lies in the prophetic visions. Our people—no offence to you, Cronaca—will run after anything in the shape of a prophet, especially if he prophesies terrors and tribulations."

"Rather say, Cennini," answered Cronaca, "that the chief secret lies in the Frate's pure life and strong faith, which stamp him as a messenger of God."

"I admit it—I admit it," said Cennini, opening his palms, as he rose from the chair. "His life is spotless: no man has impeached it."

"He is satisfied with the pleasant lust of arrogance," Cei burst out, bitterly. "I can see it in that proud lip and satisfied eye of his. He hears the air filled with his own name—Fra Girolamo Savonarola, of Ferrara; the prophet, the saint, the mighty preacher, who frightens the very babies of Florence into laying down their wicked baubles."

"Come, come, Francesco, you are out of humour with waiting," said the conciliatory Nello. "Let me stop your mouth with a little lather. I must not have my friend Cronaca made angry: I have a regard for his chin; and his chin is in no respect altered since he became a Piagnone. And for my own part, I confess, when the Frate was preaching in the Duomo last Advent, I got into such a trick of slipping in to listen to him, that I might have turned Piagnone too, if I had not been hindered by the liberal nature of my art—and also by the length of the sermons, which are sometimes a good while before they get to the moving point. But as Messer Niccolò here says, the Frate lays hold of the people by some power over and above his prophetic visions. Monks and nuns who prophesy are not of that rareness. For what says Luigi Pulci? 'Dombruno's sharp-cutting scimitar* had the fame of being enchanted; but,' says Luigi, 'I am rather of opinion that it cut sharp because it was of strongly-tempered steel.' Yes, yes; paternosters may shave clean, but they must be said over a good razor."

"See, Nello!" said Macchiavelli, "what doctor is this advancing on his Bucephalus?* I thought your piazza was free from those furred and scarlet-robed lacqueys of death. This man looks as if he had had some such night adventure as Boccaccio's Maestro Simone,* and had his bonnet and mantle pickled a little in the gutter; though he himself is as sleek as a miller's rat."

"A-ah!" said Nello, with a low, long-drawn intonation, as he looked up towards the advancing figure—a round-headed, round-bodied personage, seated on a raw young horse, which held its nose out with an air of threatening obstinacy, and by constant effort to back and go off in an oblique line showed free views about authority very much in advance of the age.

"And I have a few more adventures in pickle for him," continued Nello, in an under-tone, "which I hope will drive his inquiring nostrils to another quarter of the city. He's a doctor from Padua; they say he has been at Prato for three months, and now he's come to Florence to see what he can net. But his great trick is making rounds among the contadini. And do you note those great saddle-bags he carries? They are to hold the fat capons and eggs and meal he levies on silly clowns with whom coin is scarce. He vends his own secret medicines, so he keeps away from the doors of the druggists; and for this last week he has taken to sitting in my piazza for two or three hours every day, and making it a resort for asthmas and squalling *bambini*. It stirs my gall to see the toad-faced quack fingering the greasy quattrini, or bagging a pigeon in exchange for his pills and powders. But I'll put a few thorns in his saddle, else I'm no Florentine. Laudamus!* he is coming to be shaved; that's what I've waited for. Messer Domenico, go not away—wait; you shall see a rare bit of fooling, which I devised two days ago. Here, Sandro!"

Nello whispered in the ear of Sandro, who rolled his solemn eyes, nodded, and following up these signs of understanding with a slow smile, took to his heels with surprising rapidity.

"How is it with you, Maestro Tacco?" said Nello, as the doctor, with difficulty, brought his horse's head round towards the barber's shop. "That is a fine young horse of yours, but something raw in the mouth, eh?"

"He is an accursed beast, the *vermocane* seize him!" said Maestro Tacco, with a burst of irritation, descending from his saddle and fastening the old bridle, mended with string, to an iron staple in the wall. "Nevertheless," he added, recollecting himself, "a sound beast and a valuable, for one who wanted to purchase, and get a profit by training him. I had him cheap."

"Rather too hard riding for a man who carries your weight of learning: eh, maestro?" said Nello. "You seem hot."

"Truly, I am likely to be hot," said the doctor, taking off his bonnet, and giving to full view a bald low head and flat broad face, with high ears, wide lipless mouth, round eyes, and deep arched lines above the projecting eyebrows, which altogether made Nello's epithet "toad-faced" dubiously complimentary to the blameless batrachian.* "Riding from Peretola, when the sun is high, is not the same thing as kicking your heels on a bench in the shade, like your Florence doctors. Moreover, I have had not a little pulling to get through the carts and mules into the Mercato, to find out the husband of a certain Monna Ghita, who had had a fatal seizure before I was called in; and if it had not been that I had to demand my fees—"

"Monna Ghita!" said Nello, as the perspiring doctor interrupted himself to rub his head and face. "Peace be with her angry soul! The Mercato will want a whip the more if her tongue is laid to rest."

Tito, who had roused himself from his abstraction, and was listening to the dialogue, felt a new rush of the vague half-formed ideas about Tessa, which had passed through his mind the evening before: if Monna Ghita were really taken out of the way, it would be easier for him to see Tessa again—whenever he wanted to see her.

"*Gnaffè,* maestro," Nello went on, in a sympathizing tone, "you are the slave of rude mortals, who, but for you, would die like brutes, without help of pill or powder. It is pitiful to see your learned lymph oozing from your pores as if it were mere vulgar moisture. You think my shaving will cool and disencumber you? One moment and I have done with Messer Francesco here. It seems to me a thousand years till I wait upon a man who carries all the science of Arabia in his head and saddle-bags. Ecco!"

Nello held up the shaving-cloth with an air of invitation, and Maestro Tacco advanced and seated himself under a preoccupation with his heat and his self-importance, which made him quite deaf to the irony conveyed in Nello's officiously polite speech.

"It is but fitting that a great medicus like you," said Nello, adjusting the cloth, "should be shaved by the same razor that has shaved the illustrious Antonio Benevieni,* the greatest master of the chirurgic art."

"The chirurgic art!" interrupted the doctor, with an air of contemptuous disgust. "Is it your Florentine fashion to put the masters of the science of medicine on a level with men who do carpentry on broken limbs, and sew up wounds like tailors, and carve away excrescences as a butcher trims meat? *Via!* A manual art, such as any artificer might learn, and which has been practised by simple barbers like yourself—on a level with the noble science of Hippocrates, Galen, and Avicenna,* which penetrates into the occult influences of the stars, and plants and gems!—a science locked up from the vulgar!"

"No, in truth, maestro," said Nello, using his lather very deliberately, as if he wanted to prolong the operation to the utmost, "I never thought of placing them on a level: I know your science comes next to the miracles of Holy Church for mystery. But there, you see, is the pity of it"—here Nello fell into a tone of regretful sympathy—"your high science is sealed from the profane and the vulgar, and so you become an object of envy and slander. I grieve to say it, but there are low fellows in this city—mere *sgherri,* who go about in night-caps and long beards, and make it their business to sprinkle gall in every man's broth who is prospering. Let me tell you—for you are a stranger—this is a city where every man had need carry a large nail ready to fasten in the wheel of Fortune* when his side happens to be uppermost. Already there are stories—mere fables doubtless—beginning to be buzzed about concerning you, that make me wish I could hear of your being well on your way to Arezzo. I would not have a man of your metal stoned, for though San Stefano was stoned, he was not great in medicine like San Cosmo and San Damiano.* . . . "

"What stories? what fables?" stammered Maestro Tacco. "What do you mean?"

"*Lasso!* I fear me you are come into the trap for your cheese, maestro. The fact is, there is a company of evil youths who go prowling about the houses of our citizens carrying sharp tools in their pockets;—no sort of door, or window, or shutter, but they will pierce it. They are possessed with a diabolical patience to watch the doings of people who fancy themselves private. It must be they who have done it—it must be they who have spread the stories about you and your medicines. Have you by chance detected any small aperture in your door, or window shutter? No? Well, I advise you to look—for it is now commonly talked of that you have been seen in your dwelling at the Canto di Paglia, making your secret specifics by night: pounding dried toads in a mortar, compounding a salve out of mashed worms, and making your pills from the dried livers of rats which you mix with saliva emitted during the utterance of a blasphemous incantation—which indeed these witnesses profess to repeat."

"It is a pack of lies!" exclaimed the doctor, struggling to get utterance, and then desisting in alarm at the approaching razor.

"It is not to me, or any of this respectable company that you need to say that, doctor. *We* are not the heads to plant such carrots as those in. But what of that? What are a handful of reasonable men against a crowd with stones in their hands? There are those among us who think Cecco d'Ascoli* was an innocent sage—and we all know how he was burnt alive for being wiser than his fellows. Ah, doctor, it is not by living at Padua that you can learn to know Florentines. My belief is, they would stone the Holy Father himself, if they could find a good excuse for it; and they are persuaded that you are a necromancer, who is trying to raise the pestilence by selling secret medicines—and I am told your specifics have in truth an evil smell."

"It is false!" burst out the doctor, as Nello moved away his razor. "It is false! I will show the pills and the powders to these honourable signori—and the salve—it has an excellent odour—an odour of—of salve." He started up with the lather on his chin, and the cloth round his neck, to search in his saddle-bag for the belied medicines, and Nello in an instant adroitly shifted the shaving-chair till it was in the close vicinity of the horse's head, while Sandro, who had now returned, at a sign from his master, placed himself near the bridle.

"Behold, messeri!" said the doctor, bringing a small box of medicines and opening it before them. "Let any signor apply this box to his nostrils and he will find an honest odour of medicaments—not indeed of pounded gems, or rare vegetables from the East, or stones found in the bodies of birds; for I practise on the diseases of the vulgar, for whom heaven has provided cheaper and less powerful remedies according to their degree: and there are even remedies known to our science which are entirely free of cost—as the new *tussis** may be counteracted in the poor, who can pay for no specifics, by a resolute holding of the breath. And here is a paste which is even of savoury odour, and is infallible against melancholia, being concocted under the conjunction of Jupiter and Venus—and I have seen it allay spasms."

"Stay, maestro," said Nello, while the doctor had his lathered face turned towards the group near the door, eagerly holding out his box, and lifting out one specific after another; "here comes a crying contadina with her baby. Doubtless she is in search of you; it is perhaps an opportunity for you to show this honourable company a proof of your skill. Here, *buona donna*! here is the famous doctor. Why, what is the matter with the sweet *bimbo*?"

This question was addressed to a sturdy-looking, broad-shouldered contadina, with her head-drapery folded about her face so that little was to be seen but a bronzed nose and a pair of dark eyes and eyebrows. She carried her child packed up in the stiff mummy-shaped case in which Italian babies have been from time immemorial introduced into society, turning its face a little towards her bosom, and making those sorrowful grimaces which women are in the habit of using as a sort of pulleys to draw down reluctant tears.

"Oh, for the love of the Holy Madonna!" said the woman in a wailing voice; "will you look at my poor bimbo? I know I can't pay you for it, but I took it into the Nunziata last night, and it's turned a worse colour than before; it's the convulsions. But when I was holding it before the Santissima Nunziata, I remembered they said there was a new doctor come who cured everything; and so I thought it might be the will of the Holy Madonna that I should bring it to you."

"Sit down, maestro, sit down," said Nello. "Here is an opportunity for you; here are honourable witnesses who will declare before the Magnificent Eight that they have seen you practising honestly and relieving a poor woman's child. And then if your life is in danger, the Magnificent Eight will put you in prison a little while just to ensure your safety, and after that their *sbirri* will conduct you out of Florence by night, as they did the zealous Frate Minore who preached against the Jews.* What! our people are given to stone-throwing; but we have Magistrates."

The doctor, unable to refuse, seated himself in the shaving-chair, trembling, half with fear and half with rage, and by this time quite unconscious of the lather which Nello had laid on with such profuseness. He deposited his medicine-case on his knees, took out his precious spectacles (wondrous Florentine device!)* from his wallet, lodged them carefully above his flat nose and high ears, and lifting up his brows, turned towards the applicant.

"O Santiddio! look at him," said the woman with a more piteous wail than ever, as she held out the small mummy, which had its head completely concealed by dingy drapery wound round the head of the portable cradle, but seemed to be struggling and crying in a demoniacal fashion under this imprisonment. "The fit is on him! *Ohimè!* I know what a colour he is; it's the evil eye—oh!"

The doctor, anxiously holding his knees together to support his box, bent his spectacles towards the baby, and said cautiously, "It may be a new disease; unwind these rags, Monna!"

The contadina, with sudden energy, snatched off the encircling linen, when out struggled—scratching, grinning, and screaming—what the doctor in his fright fully believed to be a demon, but what Tito recognized as Vaiano's monkey, made more formidable by an artificial blackness, such as might have come from a hasty rubbing up the chimney.

Up started the unfortunate doctor, letting his medicine box fall, and away jumped the no less terrified and indignant monkey, finding the first resting-place for his claws on the horse's mane, which he used as a sort of rope-ladder till he had fairly found his equilibrium, when he continued to clutch it as a bridle. The horse wanted no spur under such a rider, and, the already loosened bridle offering no resistance, darted off across the piazza, with the monkey clutching, grinning and blinking, on his neck.

"*Il cavallo! Il Diavolo!*" was now shouted on all sides by the idle rascals who had gathered from all quarters of the piazza, and was echoed in tones of alarm by the stall-keepers, whose vested interests seemed in some danger; while the doctor, out of his wits with confused terror at the devil, the possible stoning, and the escape of his horse, took to his heels with spectacles on nose, lathered face, and the shaving-cloth about his neck, crying—"Stop him! stop him! for a powder—a florin—stop him for a florin!" while the lads, outstripping him, clapped their hands and shouted encouragement to the runaway.

The *cerretano*, who had not bargained for the flight of his monkey along with the horse, had caught up his petticoats with much celerity, and showed a pair of particoloured hose above his contadina's shoes, far in advance of the doctor. And away went the grotesque race up the Corso degli Adimari—the horse with the singular jockey, the contadina with the remarkable hose, and the doctor in lather and spectacles, with furred mantle outflying.

It was a scene such as Florentines loved,* from the potent and reverend signor* going to council in his *lucco*, down to the grinning youngster, who felt himself master of all situations when his bag was filled with smooth stones from the convenient dry bed of the torrent. The grey-headed Domenico Cennini laughed no less heartily than the younger men, and Nello was triumphantly secure of the general admiration.

"Aha!" he exclaimed, snapping his fingers when the first burst of laughter was subsiding. "I have cleared my piazza of that unsavoury flytrap, *mi pare*. Maestro Tacco will no more come here again to sit for patients than he will take to licking marble* for his dinner."

"You are going towards the Piazza della Signoria, Messer Domenico," said Macchiavelli. "I will go with you, and we shall perhaps see who has deserved the *palio* among these racers. Come, Melema, will you go too?"

It had been precisely Tito's intention to accompany Cennini, but before he had gone many steps, he was called back by Nello, who saw Maso approaching.

Maso's message was from Romola. She wished Tito to go to the Via de' Bardi as soon as possible. She would see him under the loggia, at the top of the house, as she wished to speak to him alone.

CHAPTER XVII.

Under the Loggia

THE loggia at the top of Bardo's house rose above the buildings on each side of it, and formed a gallery round quadrangular walls. On the side towards the street the roof was supported by columns; but on the remaining sides, by a wall pierced with arched openings, so that at the back, looking over a crowd of irregular, poorly-built dwellings towards the Hill of Bogoli, Romola could at all times have a walk sheltered from observation. Near one of those arched openings, close to the door by which he had entered the loggia, Tito awaited her, with a sickening sense of the sunlight that slanted before him and mingled itself with the ruin of his hopes. He had never for a moment relied on Romola's passion for him as likely to be too strong for the repulsion created by the discovery of his secret; he had not the presumptuous vanity which might have hindered him from feeling that her love had the same root with her belief in him. But as he imagined her coming towards him in her radiant beauty, made so loveably mortal by her soft hazel eyes, he fell into wishing that she had been something lower, if it were only that she might let him clasp her and kiss her before they parted. He had had no real caress from her—nothing but now and then a long glance, a kiss, a pressure of the hand; and he had so often longed that they should be alone together. They were going to be alone now; but he saw her standing inexorably aloof from him. His heart gave a great throb as he saw the door move: Romola was there. It was all like a flash of lightning: he felt, rather than saw, the glory about her head, the tearful appealing eyes; he felt, rather than heard, the cry of love with which she said, "Tito!"

And in the same moment she was in his arms, and sobbing with her face against his.

How poor Romola had yearned through the watches of the night to see that bright face! The new image of death; the strange bewildering doubt infused into her by the story of a life removed from her understanding and sympathy; the haunting vision, which she seemed not only to hear uttered by the low gasping voice, but to live through, as if it had been her own dream, had made her more conscious than ever that it was Tito who had first brought the warm stream of hope and gladness into her life, and who had first turned away the keen edge of pain in the remembrance of her brother. She would tell Tito everything; there was no one else to whom she could tell it. She had been restraining herself in the presence of her father all the morning; but now, that long pent-up sob might come forth. Proud and self-controlled to all the world beside, Romola was as simple and unreserved as a child in her love for Tito. She had been quite contented with the days when they had only looked at each other; but now, when she felt the need of clinging to him, there was no thought that hindered her.

"My Romola! my goddess!" Tito murmured with passionate fondness, as he clasped her gently, and kissed the thick golden ripples on her neck. He was in paradise: disgrace, shame, parting—there was no fear of them any longer. This happiness was too strong to be marred by the sense that Romola was deceived in him; nay, he could only rejoice in her delusion; for, after all, concealment had been wisdom. The only thing he could regret was his needless dread; if, indeed, the dread had not been worth suffering for the sake of this sudden rapture.

The sob had satisfied itself, and Romola raised her head. Neither of them spoke; they stood looking at each other's faces with that sweet wonder which belongs to young love—she with her long white hands on the dark brown curls, and he with his dark fingers bathed in the streaming gold. Each was so beautiful to the other; each was experiencing that undisturbed mutual consciousness for the first time. The cold pressure of a new sadness on Romola's heart made her linger the more in that silent soothing sense of nearness and love; and Tito could not even seek to press his lips to hers, because that would be change.

"Tito," she said, at last, "it has been altogether painful. But I must tell you everything. Your strength will help me to resist the impressions that will not be shaken off by reason."

"I know, Romola—I know he is dead," said Tito; and the long lustrous eyes told nothing of the many wishes that would have brought about that death long ago if there had been such potency in mere wishes. Romola only read her own pure thoughts in their dark depths, as we read letters in happy dreams.

"So changed, Tito! It pierced me to think that it was Dino. And so strangely hard: not a word to my father—nothing but a vision that he wanted to tell me. And yet it was so piteous—the struggling breath, and the eyes that seemed to look towards the crucifix, and yet not to see it. I shall never forget it; it seems as if it would come between me and everything I shall look at."

Romola's heart swelled again, so that she was forced to break off. But the need she felt to disburthen her mind to Tito urged her to repress the rising anguish. When she began to speak again, her thoughts had travelled a little.

"It was strange, Tito. The vision was about our marriage, and yet he knew nothing of you."

"What was it, my Romola? Sit down and tell me," said Tito,

leading her to the bench that stood near. A fear had come across him lest the vision should somehow or other relate to Baldassarre; and this sudden change of feeling prompted him to seek a change of position.

Romola told him all that had passed from her entrance in San Marco, hardly leaving out one of her brother's words which had burnt themselves into her memory as they were spoken. But when she was at the end of the vision, she paused; the rest came too vividly before her to be uttered, and she sat looking at the distance, almost unconscious for the moment that Tito was near her. *His* mind was at ease now; that vague vision had passed over him like white mist, and left no mark. But he was silent, expecting her to speak again.

"I took it," she went on, as if Tito had been reading her thoughts; "I took the crucifix; it is down below in my bedroom."

"And now, my Romola," said Tito, entreatingly; "you will banish these ghastly thoughts. The vision was an ordinary monkish vision, bred of fasting and fanatical ideas. It surely has no weight with you."

"No, Tito; no. But poor Dino, *he* believed it was a divine message. It is strange," she went on meditatively, "this life of men possessed with fervid beliefs that seem like madness to their fellow-beings. Dino was not a vulgar fanatic; and that Fra Girolamo, his very voice seems to have penetrated me with a sense that there is some truth in what moves them—some truth of which I know nothing."

"It was only because your feelings were highly wrought, my Romola. Your brother's state of mind was no more than a form of that theosophy which has been the common disease of excitable dreamy minds in all ages; the same ideas that your father's old antagonist, Marsilio Ficino, pores over in the New Platonists;* only your brother's passionate nature drove him to act out what other men write and talk about. And for Fra Girolamo, he is simply a narrow-minded monk, with a gift for preaching and infusing terror into the multitude. Any words or any voice would have shaken you at that moment. When your mind has had a little repose, you will judge of such things as you have always done before."

"Not about poor Dino," said Romola. "I was angry with him; my heart seemed to close against him while he was speaking;

but since then I have thought less of what was in my own mind and more of what was in his. Oh, Tito! it was very piteous to see his young life coming to an end in that way. That yearning look at the crucifix when he was gasping for breath—I can never forget it. Last night I looked at the crucifix a long while, and tried to see that it would help him, until at last it seemed to me by the lamplight as if the suffering face shed pity."

"My Romola, promise me to resist such thoughts; they are fit for sickly nuns, not for my golden-tressed Aurora,* who looks made to scatter all such twilight fantasies. Try not to think of them now; we shall not long be alone together."

The last words were uttered in a tone of tender beseeching, and he turned her face towards him with a gentle touch of his right hand.

Romola had had her eyes fixed absently on the arched opening, but she had not seen the distant hill; she had all the while been in the chapter-house, looking at the pale images of sorrow and death.

Tito's touch and beseeching voice recalled her, and now in the warm sunlight she saw that rich dark beauty which seemed to gather round it all images of joy—purple vines festooned between the elms, the strong corn perfecting itself under the vibrating heat, bright winged creatures hurrying and resting among the flowers, round limbs beating the earth in gladness, with cymbals held aloft; light melodies chanted to the thrilling rhythm of strings—all objects and all sounds that tell of Nature revelling in her force. Strange, bewildering transition from those pale images of sorrow and death to this bright youthfulness, as of a sun-god who knew nothing of night! What thought could reconcile that worn anguish in her brother's face—that straining after something invisible—with this satisfied strength and beauty, and make it intelligible that they belonged to the same world? Or was there never any reconciling of them—but only a blind worship of clashing deities, first in mad joy and then in wailing? Romola for the first time felt this questioning need like a sudden uneasy dizziness and want of something to grasp; it was an experience hardly longer than a sigh, for the eager theorizing of ages is compressed, as in a seed, into the momentary want of a single mind. But there was no answer to meet the need, and it vanished before the returning rush of young sympathy with the glad loving beauty that beamed upon her in new radiance, like the dawn after we have looked away from it to the grey west.

"Your mind lingers apart from our love, my Romola," Tito said, with a soft reproachful murmur. "It seems a forgotten thing to you."

She looked at the beseeching eyes in silence, till the sadness all melted out of her own.

"My joy!" she said, in her full clear voice.

"Do you really care for me enough, then, to banish those chill fancies, or shall you always be suspecting me as the Great Tempter?" said Tito, with his bright smile.

"How should I not care for you more than for everything else? Everything I had felt before in all my life—about my father, and about my loneliness—was a preparation to love you. You would laugh at me, Tito, if you knew what sort of man I used to think I should marry—some scholar with deep lines in his face, like Alamanno Rinuccini, and with rather grey hair, who would agree with my father in taking the side of the Aristotelians, and be willing to live with him. I used to think about the love I read of in the poets, but I never dreamed that anything like that could happen to me here in Florence in our old library. And then *you* came, Tito, and were so much to my father, and I began to believe that life could be happy for me too."

"My goddess! is there any woman like you?" said Tito, with a mixture of fondness and wondering admiration at the blended majesty and simplicity in her.

"But, dearest," he went on, rather timidly, "if you minded more about our marriage, you would persuade your father and Messer Bernardo not to think of any more delays. But you seem not to mind about it."

"Yes, Tito, I will, I do mind. But I am sure my godfather will urge more delay now, because of Dino's death. He has never agreed with my father about disowning Dino, and you know he has always said that we ought to wait until you have been at least a year in Florence. Do not think hardly of my godfather. I know he is prejudiced and narrow, but yet he is very noble. He has often said that it is folly in my father to want to keep his library apart, that it may bear his name; yet he would try to get my father's wish carried out. That seems to me very great and noble—that power of respecting a feeling which he does not share or understand."

"I have no rancour against Messer Bernardo for thinking you too precious for me, my Romola," said Tito; and that was true. "But your father, then, knows of his son's death?"

"Yes, I told him—I could not help it—I told him where I had been, and that I had seen Dino die; but nothing else; and he has commanded me not to speak of it again. But he has been very silent this morning, and has had those restless movements which always go to my heart; they look as if he were trying to get outside the prison of his blindness. Let us go to him now. I had persuaded him to try to sleep, because he slept little in the night. Your voice will soothe him, Tito; it always does."

"And not one kiss? I have not had one," said Tito, in his gentle reproachful tone, which gave him an air of dependence very charming in a creature with those rare gifts that seem to excuse presumption.

The sweet pink blush spread itself with the quickness of light over Romola's face and neck as she bent towards him. It seemed impossible that their kisses could ever become common things.

"Let us walk once round the loggia," said Romola, "before we go down."

"There is something grim and grave to me always about Florence," said Tito, as they paused in the front of the house, where they could see over the opposite roofs to the other side of the river, "and even in its merriment there is something shrill and hard—biting rather than gay. I wish we lived in Southern Italy, where thought is broken not by weariness, but by delicious languors such as never seem to come over the 'ingenia acerrima Florentina.'* I should like to see you under that southern sun, lying among the flowers, subdued into mere enjoyment, while I bent over you and touched the lute and sang to you some little unconscious strain that seemed all one with the light and the warmth. You have never known that happiness of the nymphs, my Romola."

"No; but I have dreamed of it often since you came. I am very thirsty for a deep draught of joy—for a life all bright like you. But we will not think of it now, Tito; it seems to me as if there would always be pale sad faces among the flowers, and eyes that look in vain. Let us go."

CHAPTER XVIII.

The Portrait

WHEN Tito left the Via de' Bardi that day in exultant satisfaction at finding himself thoroughly free from the threatened peril, his thoughts, no longer claimed by the immediate presence of Romola and her father, recurred to those futile hours of dread in which he was conscious of having not only felt but acted as he would not have done if he had had a truer foresight. He would not have parted with his ring; for Romola, and others to whom it was a familiar object, would be a little struck with the apparent sordidness of parting with a gem he had professedly cherished, unless he feigned as a reason the desire to make some special gift with the purchase-money; and Tito had at that moment a nauseating weariness of simulation. He was well out of the possible consequences that might have fallen on him from that initial deception, and it was no longer a load on his mind; kind fortune had brought him immunity, and he thought it was only fair that she should. Who was hurt by it? The results to Baldassarre were too problematical to be taken into account. But he wanted now to be free from any hidden shackles that would gall him, though ever so little, under his ties to Romola. He was not aware that that very delight in immunity which prompted resolutions not to entangle himself again, was deadening the sensibilities which alone could save him from entanglement.

But, after all, the sale of the ring was a slight matter. Was it also a slight matter that little Tessa was under a delusion which would doubtless fill her small head with expectations doomed to disappointment? Should he try to see the little thing alone again and undeceive her at once, or should he leave the disclosure to time and chance? Happy dreams are pleasant, and they easily come to an end with daylight and the stir of life. The sweet, pouting, innocent, round thing! It was impossible not to think of her. Tito thought he should like some time to take her a present that would please her, and just learn if her step-father treated her more cruelly now her mother was dead. Or, should he at once undeceive Tessa, and then tell Romola about her, so that they might find some happier lot for the poor thing? No: that unfortunate little incident of the *cerretano* and the marriage, and his allowing Tessa to part from him in delusion, must never be known to Romola, and since no enlightenment could expel it from Tessa's mind, there would always be a risk of betrayal; besides, even little Tessa might have some gall in her when she found herself disappointed in her love—yes, she *must* be a little in love with him, and that might make it well that he should not see her again. Yet it was a trifling adventure such as a country girl would perhaps ponder on till some ruddy contadino made acceptable love to her, when she would break her resolution of secrecy and get at the truth that she was free. *Dunque*—good-by, Tessa! kindest wishes! Tito had made up his mind that the silly little affair of the *cerretano* should have no further consequences for himself; and people are apt to think that resolutions taken on their own behalf will be firm. As for the fifty-five florins, the purchase-money of the ring, Tito had made up his mind what to do with some of them; he would carry out a pretty ingenious thought which would set him more at ease in accounting for the absence of his ring to Romola, and would also serve him as a means of guarding her mind from the recurrence of those monkish fancies which were especially repugnant to him; and with this thought in his mind, he went on to the Via Gualfonda to find Piero di Cosimo, the artist who at that time was pre-eminent in the fantastic mythological design which Tito's purpose required.

Entering the court on which Piero's dwelling opened, Tito found the heavy iron knocker on the door thickly bound round with wool and ingeniously fastened with cords. Remembering the painter's practice of stuffing his ears against obtrusive noises, Tito was not much surprised at this mode of defence against visitors' thunder, and betook himself first to rapping modestly with his knuckles, and then to a more importunate attempt to shake the door. In vain! Tito was moving away, blaming himself for wasting his time on this visit, instead of waiting till he saw the painter again at Nello's, when a little girl entered the court with a basket of eggs* on her arm, went up to the door, and standing on tip-toe, pushed up a small iron plate that ran in grooves, and putting her mouth to the aperture thus disclosed, called out in a piping voice, "Messer Piero!"

In a few moments Tito heard the sound of bolts, the door opened, and Piero presented himself in a red night-cap and a loose brown-serge tunic, with sleeves rolled up to the shoulder.

He darted a look of surprise at Tito, but without further notice of him stretched out his hand to take the basket from the child, re-entered the house, and presently returning with the empty basket, said, "How much to pay?"

"Two grossoni, Messer Piero; they are all ready boiled, my mother says."

Piero took the coin out of the leathern scarsella at his belt, and the little maiden trotted away, not without a few upward glances of awed admiration at the surprising young signor.

Piero's glance was much less complimentary as he said,

"What do you want at my door, Messer Greco? I saw you this morning at Nello's; if you had asked me then, I could have told you that I see no man in this house without knowing his business and agreeing with him beforehand."

"Pardon, Messer Piero," said Tito, with his imperturbable good humour; "I acted without sufficient reflection. I remembered nothing but your admirable skill in inventing pretty caprices, when a sudden desire for something of that sort prompted me to come to you."

The painter's manners were too notoriously odd to all the world for this reception to be held a special affront; but even if Tito had suspected any offensive intention, the impulse to resentment would have been less strong in him than the desire to conquer goodwill.

Piero made a grimace which was habitual with him when he was spoken to with flattering sauvity. He grinned, stretched out the corners of his mouth, and pressed down his brows, so as to defy any divination of his feelings under that kind of stroking.

"And what may that need be?" he said, after a moment's pause. In his heart he was tempted by the hinted opportunity of applying his invention.

"I want a very delicate miniature device taken from certain fables of the poets, which you will know how to combine for me. It must be painted on a wooden case—I will show you the size—in the form of a triptych. The inside may be simple gilding: it is on the outside I want the device. It is a favourite subject with you Florentines—the triumph of Bacchus and Ariadne; but I want it treated in a new way—a story in Ovid* will give you the necessary hints. The young Bacchus must be seated in a ship, his head bound with clusters of grapes, and a spear entwined with vine-leaves in his hand: dark-berried ivy must wind about the masts and sails, the oars must be thyrsi, and flowers must wreathe themselves about the poop; leopards and tigers must be crouching before him, and dolphins must be sporting round. But I want to have the fair-haired Ariadne with him, made immortal with her golden crown—that is not in Ovid's story, but no matter, you will conceive it all—and above there must be young loves, such as you know how to paint, shooting with roses at the points of their arrows—"

"Say no more!" said Piero. "I have Ovid in the vulgar tongue. Find me the passage. I love not to be choked with other men's thoughts. You may come in."

Piero led the way through the first room, where a basket of eggs was deposited on the open hearth, near a heap of broken egg-shells and a bank of ashes. In strange keeping with that sordid litter, there was a low bedstead of carved ebony, covered carelessly with a piece of rich oriental carpet, that looked as if it had served to cover the steps to a Madonna's throne; and a carved *cassone*, or large chest, with painted devices on its sides and lid. There was hardly any other furniture in the large room, except casts, wooden steps, easels and rough boxes, all festooned with cobwebs.

The next room was still larger, but it was also much more crowded. Apparently Piero was keeping the festa, for the double door underneath the window which admitted the painter's light from above, was thrown open, and showed a garden or rather thicket in which fig-trees and vines grew in tangled, trailing wildness among nettles and hemlocks, and a tall cypress lifted its dark head from a stifling mass of yellowing mulberry-leaves. It seemed as if that dank luxuriance had begun to penetrate even within the walls of the wide and lofty room; for in one corner, amidst a confused heap of carved marble fragments and rusty armour, tufts of long grass and dark feathery fennel had made their way, and a large stone vase, tilted on one side, seemed to be pouring out the ivy that streamed around. All about the walls hung pen and oil sketches of fantastic sea-monsters; dances of satyrs and mænads; Saint Margaret's resurrection out of the devouring dragon; Madonnas with the supernal light upon them;* studies of plants and grotesque heads; and on irregular rough shelves a few books were scattered among great drooping bunches of corn, bullock's horns, pieces of dried honeycomb, stones with patches of rare-coloured lichen, skulls and bones, peacocks' feathers, and large birds' wings. Rising from amongst the dirty litter of the floor were lay figures—one in the frock of a Vallombrosan monk, strangely surmounted by a helmet with barred visor, another smothered with brocade and skins hastily tossed over it. Amongst this heterogeneous still life, several speckled and white pigeons were perched or strutting, too tame to fly at the entrance of men; three corpulent toads were crawling in an intimate friendly way near the door-stone; and a white rabbit, apparently the model for that which was frightening Cupid in the picture of Mars and Venus,* placed on the central easel, was twitching its nose with much content on a box full of bran.

"And now, Messer Greco," said Piero, making a sign to Tito that he might sit down on a low stool near the door, and then standing over him with folded arms, "don't be trying to see everything at once, like Messer Domeneddio, but let me know how large you would have this same triptych."

Tito indicated the required dimensions, and Piero marked them on a piece of paper.

"And now for the book," said Piero, reaching down a manuscript volume.

"There's nothing about the Ariadne there," said Tito, giving him the passage; "but you will remember I want the crowned Ariadne by the side of the young Bacchus: she must have golden hair."

"Ha!" said Piero, abruptly, pursing up his lips again. "And you want them to be likenesses, eh?" he added, looking down into Tito's face.

Tito laughed and blushed. "I know you are great at portraits, Messer Piero; but I could not ask Ariadne to sit for you, because the painting is a secret."

"There it is! I want her to sit to me. Giovanni Vespucci wants me to paint him a picture of Œdipus and Antigone at Colonos,* as he has expounded it to me: I have a fancy for the subject, and I want Bardo and his daughter to sit for it. Now, you ask them; and then I'll put the likeness into Ariadne."

"Agreed, if I can prevail with them. And your price for the Bacchus and Ariadne?"

"*Baie!* If you get them to let me paint them, that will pay me. I'd rather not have your money: you may pay for the case."

"And when shall I sit for you?" said Tito, "for if we have one likeness, we must have two."

"I don't want *your* likeness—I've got it already," said Piero, "only I've made you look frightened. I must take the fright out of it for Bacchus."

As he was speaking, Piero laid down the book and went to look among some paintings, propped with their faces against the wall. He returned with an oil-sketch in his hand.

"I call this as good a bit of portrait as I ever did," he said, looking at it, as he advanced. "Yours is a face that expresses fear well, because it's naturally a bright one. I noticed it the first time I saw you. The rest of the picture is hardly sketched; but I've painted *you* in thoroughly."

Piero turned the sketch, and held it towards Tito's eyes. He saw himself with his right hand uplifted, holding a wine-cup, in the attitude of triumphant joy, but with his face turned away from the cup with an expression of such intense fear in the dilated eyes and pallid lips, that he felt a cold stream through his veins, as if he were being thrown into sympathy with his imaged self.

"You are beginning to look like it already," said Piero, with a short laugh, moving the picture away again. "He's seeing a ghost—that fine young man. I shall finish it some day, when I've settled what sort of ghost is the most terrible—whether it should look solid, like a dead man come to life, or half transparent, like a mist."

Tito, rather ashamed of himself for a sudden sensitiveness, strangely opposed to his usual easy self-command, said carelessly—

"That is a subject after your own heart, Messer Piero—a revel interrupted by a ghost. You seem to love the blending of the terrible with the gay. I suppose that is the reason your shelves are so well furnished with death's-heads, while you are painting those roguish loves who are running away with the armour of Mars. I begin to think you are a Cynic philosopher in the pleasant disguise of a cunning painter."

"Not I, Messer Greco; a philosopher is the last sort of animal I would choose to resemble. I find it enough to live, without spinning lies to account for life. Fowls cackle, asses bray, women chatter, and philosophers spin false reasons—that's the effect the sight of the world brings out of them. Well, I am an animal that paints instead of cackling, or braying, or spinning lies. And now, I think, our business is done; you'll keep to your side of the bargain about the Œdipus and Antigone?"

"I will do my best," said Tito—on this strong hint, immediately moving towards the door.

"And you'll let me know at Nello's. No need to come here again."

"I understand," said Tito, laughingly, lifting his hand in sign of friendly parting.

CHAPTER XIX.

The Old Man's Hope

MESSER BERNARDO DEL NERO was as inexorable as Romola had expected in his advice that the marriage should be deferred till Easter, and in this matter Bardo was entirely under the ascendancy of his sagacious and practical friend. Nevertheless, Bernardo himself, though he was as far as ever from any susceptibility to the personal fascination in Tito which was felt by others, could not altogether resist that argument of success which is always powerful with men of the world. Tito was making his way rapidly in high quarters. He was especially growing in favour with the young Cardinal Giovanni de' Medici, who had even spoken of Tito's forming part of his learned retinue on an approaching journey to Rome; and the bright young Greek, who had a tongue that was always ready without ever being quarrelsome, was more and more wished for at gay suppers in the Via Larga, and at Florentine games in which he had no pretension to excel, and could admire the incomparable skill of Piero de' Medici in the most graceful manner in the world. By an unfailing sequence, Tito's reputation as an agreeable companion in "magnificent" society made his learning and talent appear more lustrous; and he was really accomplished enough to prevent an exaggerated estimate from being hazardous to him. Messer Bernardo had old prejudices and attachments which now began to argue down the newer and feebler prejudice against the young Greek stranger who was rather too supple. To the old Florentine it was impossible to despise the recommendation of standing well with the best Florentine families, and since Tito began to be thoroughly received into that circle whose views were the unquestioned standard of social value, it seemed irrational not to admit that there was no longer any check to satisfaction in the prospect of such a son-in-law for Bardo, and such a husband for Romola. It was undeniable that Tito's coming had been the dawn of a new life for both father and daughter, and the first promise had even been surpassed. The blind old scholar—whose proud truthfulness would never enter into that commerce of feigned and preposterous admiration which, varied by a corresponding measurelessness in vituperation, made the woof of all learned intercourse—had fallen into neglect even among his fellow-citizens, and when he was alluded to at all, it had long been usual to say that though his blindness and the loss of his son were pitiable misfortunes, he was tiresome in contending for the value of his own labours; and that his discontent was a little inconsistent in a man who had been openly regardless of religious rites, and who in days past had refused offers made to him from various quarters on the slight condition that he would take orders, without which it was not easy for patrons to provide for every scholar. But since Tito's coming, there was no longer the same monotony in the thought that Bardo's name suggested; the old man, it was understood, had left off his plaints, and the fair daughter was no longer to be shut up in dowerless pride, waiting for a *parentado*. The winning manners and growing favour of the handsome Greek who was expected to enter into the double relation of son and husband helped to make the new interest a thoroughly friendly one, and it was no longer a rare occurrence when a visitor enlivened the quiet library. Elderly men came from that indefinite prompting to renew former intercourse which arises when an old acquaintance begins to be newly talked about; and young men whom Tito had asked leave to bring once, found it easy to go again when they overtook him on his way to the Via de' Bardi, and, resting their hands on his shoulder, fell into easy chat with him. For it was pleasant to look at Romola's beauty: to see her, like old Firenzuola's type of womanly majesty, "sitting with a certain grandeur, speaking with gravity, smiling with modesty, and casting around, as it were, an odour of queenliness;"* and she seemed to unfold like a strong white lily under this genial breath of admiration and homage; it was all one to her with her new bright life in Tito's love.

Tito had even been the means of strengthening the hope in

Bardo's mind that he might before his death receive the longed-for security concerning his library: that it should not be merged in another collection; that it should not be transferred to a body of monks, and be called by the name of a monastery; but that it should remain for ever the Bardi Library, for the use of Florentines. For the old habit of trusting in the Medici could not die out while their influence was still the strongest lever in the State; and Tito, once possessing the ear of the Cardinal Giovanni de' Medici, might do more even than Messer Bernardo towards winning the desired interest, for he could demonstrate to a learned audience the peculiar value of Bardo's collection. Tito himself talked sanguinely of such a result, willing to cheer the old man, and conscious that Romola repaid those gentle words to her father with a sort of adoration that no direct tribute to herself could have won from her.

This question of the library was the subject of more than one discussion with Bernardo del Nero when Christmas was turned and the prospect of the marriage was becoming near—but always out of Bardo's hearing. For Bardo nursed a vague belief, which they dared not disturb, that his property, apart from the library, was adequate to meet all demands. He would not even, except under a momentary pressure of angry despondency, admit to himself that the will by which he had disinherited Dino would leave Romola the heir of nothing but debts; or that he needed anything from patronage beyond the security that a separate locality should be assigned to his library, in return for a deed of gift by which he made it over to the Florentine Republic.

"My opinion is," said Bernardo to Romola, in a consultation they had under the loggia, "that since you are to be married, and Messer Tito will have a competent income, we should begin to wind up the affairs, and ascertain exactly the sum that would be necessary to save the library from being touched, instead of letting the debts accumulate any longer. Your father needs nothing but his shred of mutton and his macaroni every day, and I think Messer Tito may engage to supply that for the years that remain; he can let it be in place of the *morgen-cap*."

"Tito has always known that my life is bound up with my father's," said Romola; "and he is better to my father than I am: he delights in making him happy."

"Ah, he's not made of the same clay as other men, is he?"

said Bernardo, smiling. "Thy father has thought of shutting woman's folly out of thee by cramming thee with Greek and Latin; but thou hast been as ready to believe in the first pair of bright eyes and the first soft words that have come within reach of thee, as if thou couldst say nothing by heart but paternosters, like other Christian men's daughters."

"Now, godfather," said Romola, shaking her head playfully, "as if it were only bright eyes and soft words that made me love Tito! You know better. You know I love my father and you because you are both good; and I love Tito, too, because he is so good. I see it, I feel it, in everything he says and does. And if he is handsome, too, why should I not love him the better for that? It seems to me beauty is part of the finished language by which goodness speaks. You know *you* must have been a very handsome youth, godfather"—she looked up with one of her happy, loving smiles at the stately old man—"you were about as tall as Tito, and you had very fine eyes; only you looked a little sterner and prouder, and—"

"And Romola likes to have all the pride to herself?" said Bernardo, not inaccessible to this pretty coaxing. "However, it is well that in one way Tito's demands are more modest than those of any Florentine husband of fitting rank that we should have been likely to find for you; he wants no dowry."

So it was settled in that way between Messer Bernardo del Nero, Romola, and Tito. Bardo assented with a wave of the hand when Bernardo told him that he thought it would be well now to begin to sell property and clear off debts—being accustomed to think of debts and property as a sort of thick wood that his imagination never even penetrated, still less got beyond. And Tito set about winning Messer Bernardo's respect by inquiring, with his ready faculty, into Florentine money matters, the secrets of the *Monti* or public funds, the values of real property, and the profits of banking.

"You will soon forget that Tito is not a Florentine, godfather," said Romola. "See how he is learning everything about Florence!"

"It seems to me he is one of the *demoni*, who are of no particular country, child," said Bernardo, smiling. "His mind is a little too nimble to be weighted with all the stuff we men carry about in our hearts."

Romola smiled too, in happy confidence.

CHAPTER XX.

The Day of the Betrothal

It was the last week of the Carnival, and the streets of Florence were at their fullest and noisiest: there were the masqued processions, chanting songs, indispensable now they had once been introduced by Lorenzo the Magnificent; there was the favourite *rigoletto*, or round dance, footed "in piazza" under the blue frosty sky; there were practical jokes of all sorts, from throwing comfits to throwing stones—especially stones. For the boys and striplings, always a strong element in Florentine crowds, became at the height of Carnival time as loud and unmanageable as tree-crickets, and it was their immemorial privilege to bar the way with poles to all passengers, until a tribute had been paid towards furnishing these lovers of strong sensations with suppers and bonfires; to conclude with the standing entertainment of stone-throwing, which was not entirely monotonous, since the consequent maiming was various, and it was not always a single person who was killed. So that the pleasures of the Carnival were of a chequered kind, and if a painter were called upon to represent them truly, he would have to make a picture in which there would be so much grossness and barbarity that it must be turned with its face to the wall, except when it was taken down for the grave historical purpose of justifying a reforming zeal which, in ignorance of the facts, might be unfairly condemned for its narrowness. Still there was much of that more innocent picturesque merriment which is never wanting among a people with quick animal spirits and sensitive organs: there was not the heavy sottishness which belongs to the thicker northern blood, nor the stealthy fierceness which in the more southern regions of the peninsula makes the brawl lead to the dagger-thrust.

It was the high morning, but the merry spirits of the Carnival were still inclined to lounge and recapitulate the last night's jests, when Tito Melema was walking at a brisk pace on the way to the Via de' Bardi. Young Bernardo Dovizi, who now looks at us out of Raphael's portrait as the keen-eyed Cardinal da Bibbiena, was with him; and, as they went, they held animated talk about some subject that had evidently no relation to the sights and sounds through which they were pushing their way along the Por' Santa Maria. Nevertheless, as they discussed, smiled, and gesticulated, they both, from time to time, cast quick glances around them, and at the turning towards the Lung' Arno, leading to the Ponte Rubaconte, Tito had become aware, in one of these rapid surveys, that there was some one not far off him by whom he very much desired not to be recognized at that moment. His time and thoughts were thoroughly preoccupied, for he was looking forward to a unique occasion in his life—he was preparing for his betrothal, which was to take place on the evening of this very day. The ceremony had been resolved upon rather suddenly; for although preparations towards the marriage had been going forward for some time—chiefly in the application of Tito's florins to the fitting-up of rooms in Bardo's dwelling, which, the library excepted, had always been scantily furnished—it had been intended to defer both the betrothal and the marriage until after Easter, when Tito's year of probation, insisted on by Bernardo del Nero, would have been complete. But when an express proposition had come, that Tito should follow the Cardinal Giovanni to Rome to help Bernardo Dovizi with his superior knowledge of Greek in arranging a library, and there was no possibility of declining what lay so plainly on the road to advancement, he had become urgent in his entreaties that the betrothal might take place before his departure: there would be the less delay before the marriage, on his return, and it would be less painful to part if he and Romola were outwardly as well as inwardly pledged to each other—if he had a claim which defied Messer Bernardo or any one else to nullify it. For the betrothal, at which rings were exchanged and mutual contracts were signed, made more than half the legality of marriage, to be completed on a separate occasion by the nuptial benediction. Romola's feeling had met Tito's in this wish, and the consent of the elders had been won.

And now Tito was hastening, amidst arrangements for his departure the next day, to snatch a morning visit to Romola, to say and hear any last words that were needful to be said before their meeting for the betrothal in the evening. It was not a time when any recognition could be pleasant that was at all likely to detain him; still less a recognition by Tessa. And it was unmistakably Tessa whom he had caught sight of moving along, with a timid and forlorn look, towards that very turn of the Lung'

Arno which he was just rounding. As he continued his talk with the young Dovizi, he had an uncomfortable under-current of consciousness which told him that Tessa had seen him and would certainly follow him: there was no escaping her along this direct road by the Arno, and over the Ponte Rubaconte. But she would not dare to speak to him or approach him while he was not alone, and he would continue to keep Dovizi with him till they reached Bardo's door. He quickened his pace, and took up new threads of talk; but all the while the sense that Tessa was behind him, though he had no physical evidence of the fact, grew stronger and stronger; it was very irritating—perhaps all the more so because a certain tenderness and pity for the poor little thing made the determination to escape without any visible notice of her, a not altogether agreeable resource. Yet Tito persevered and carried his companion to the door, cleverly managing his "addio" without turning his face in a direction where it was possible for him to see an importunate pair of blue eyes; and as he went up the stone steps, he tried to get rid of unpleasant thoughts by saying to himself that after all Tessa might not have seen him, or, if she had, might not have followed him.

But—perhaps because that possibility could not be relied on strongly—when the visit was over, he came out of the doorway with a quick step and an air of unconsciousness as to anything that might be on his right hand or his left. Our eyes are so constructed, however, that they take in a wide angle without asking any leave of our will; and Tito knew that there was a little figure in a white hood standing near the doorway—knew it quite well, before he felt a hand laid on his arm. It was a real grasp, and not a light, timid touch; for poor Tessa, seeing his rapid step, had started forward with a desperate effort. But when he stopped and turned towards her, her face wore a frightened look, as if she dreaded the effect of her boldness.

"Tessa!" said Tito, with more sharpness in his voice than she had ever heard in it before. "Why are you here? You must not follow me—you must not stand about door-places waiting for me."

Her blue eyes widened with tears, and she said nothing. Tito was afraid of something worse than ridicule, if he were seen in the Via de' Bardi with a girlish contadina looking pathetically at him. It was a street of high silent-looking dwellings, not of traffic; but Bernardo del Nero, or some one almost as dangerous, might come up at any moment. Even if it had not been the day of his betrothal, the incident would have been awkward and annoying. Yet it would be brutal—it was impossible—to drive Tessa way with harsh words. That accursed folly of his with the *cerretano*—that it should have lain buried in a quiet way for months, and now start up before him as this unseasonable crop of vexation! He could not speak harshly, but he spoke hurriedly.

"Tessa, I cannot—must not talk to you here. I will go on to the bridge and wait for you there. Follow me slowly."

He turned and walked fast to the Ponte Rubaconte, and there leaned against the wall of one of the quaint little houses that rise at even distances on the bridge, looking towards the way by which Tessa would come. It would have softened a much harder heart than Tito's to see the little thing advancing with her round face much paled and saddened, since he had parted from it at the door of "the Nunziata." Happily it was the least frequented of the bridges, and there were scarcely any passengers on it at this moment. He lost no time in speaking as soon as she came near him.

"Now, Tessa, I have very little time. You must not cry. Why did you follow me this morning? You must not do so again."

"I thought," said Tessa, speaking in a whisper, and struggling against a sob that *would* rise immediately at this new voice of Tito's—"I thought you wouldn't be so long before you came to take care of me again. And the *patrigno* beats me, and I can't bear it any longer. And always when I come for a holiday I walk about to find you, and I can't. Oh, please don't send me away from you again! It has been so long, and I cry so now, because you never come to me. I can't help it, for the days are so long, and I don't mind about the goats and kids, or anything—and I can't—"

The sobs came fast now, and the great tears. Tito felt that he could not do otherwise than comfort her. Send her away—yes; that he *must* do, at once. But it was all the more impossible to tell her anything that would leave her in a state of hopeless grief. He saw new trouble in the background, but the difficulty of the moment was too pressing for him to weigh distant consequences.

"Tessa, my little one," he said, in his old caressing tones, "you must not cry. Bear with the cross *patrigno* a little longer. I will come back to you. But I'm going now to Rome—a long,

long way off. I shall come back in a few weeks, and then I promise you to come and see you. Promise me to be good and wait for me."

It was the well-remembered voice again, and the mere sound was half enough to soothe Tessa. She looked up at him with wide trusting eyes, that still glittered with tears, sobbing all the while, in spite of her utmost efforts to obey him. Again, he said, in a gentle voice:

"Promise me, my Tessa."

"Yes," she whispered. "But you won't be long?"

"No, not long. But I must go now. And remember what I told you, Tessa. Nobody must know that you ever see me, else you will lose me for ever. And now, when I have left you, go straight home, and never follow me again. Wait till I come to you. Good-by, my little Tessa: I *will* come."

There was no help for it; he must turn and leave her without looking behind him to see how she bore it, for he had no time to spare. When he did look round he was in the Via de' Benci, where there was no seeing what was happening on the bridge; but Tessa was too trusting and obedient not to do just what he had told her.

Yes, the difficulty was at an end for that day; yet this return of Tessa to him, at a moment when it was impossible for him to put an end to all difficulty with her by undeceiving her, was an unpleasant incident to carry in his memory. But Tito's mind was just now thoroughly penetrated with a hopeful first love, associated with all happy prospects flattering to his ambition; and that future necessity of grieving Tessa could be scarcely more to him than the far-off cry of some little suffering animal buried in the thicket, to a merry cavalcade in the sunny plain. When, for the second time that day, Tito was hastening across the Ponte Rubaconte, the thought of Tessa caused no perceptible diminution of his happiness. He was well muffled in his mantle, less, perhaps, to protect him from the cold than from the additional notice that would have been drawn upon him by his dainty apparel. He leaped up the stone steps by two at a time, and said hurriedly to Maso, who met him,

"Where is the damigella?"

"In the library; she is quite ready, and Monna Brigida and Messer Bernardo are already there with Ser Braccio, but none of the rest of the company."

"Ask her to give me a few minutes alone; I will await her in the *salotto*."

Tito entered a room which had been fitted up in the utmost contrast with the half-pallid, half-sombre tints of the library. The walls were brightly frescoed with "caprices" of nymphs and loves sporting under the blue among flowers and birds. The only furniture besides the red leather seats and the central table were two tall white vases, and a young faun playing the flute, modelled by a promising youth* named Michelangelo Buonarotti. It was a room that gave a sense of being in the sunny open air.

Tito kept his mantle round him, and looked towards the door. It was not long before Romola entered, all white and gold, more than ever like a tall lily. Her white silk garment was bound by a golden girdle, which fell with large tassels; and above that was the rippling gold of her hair, surmounted by the white mist of her long veil, which was fastened on her brow by a band of pearls, the gift of Bernardo del Nero, and was now parted off her face so that it all floated backward.

"*Regina mia!*" said Tito, as he took her hand and kissed it, still keeping his mantle round him. He could not help going backward to look at her again, while she stood in calm delight, with that exquisite self-consciousness which rises under the gaze of admiring love.

"Romola, will you show me the next room now?" said Tito, checking himself with the remembrance that the time might be short. "You said I should see it when you had arranged everything."

Without speaking, she led the way into a long narrow room, painted brightly like the other, but only with birds and flowers. The furniture in it was all old; there were old faded objects for feminine use or ornament, arranged in an open cabinet between the two narrow windows; above the cabinet was the portrait of Romola's mother; and below this, on the top of the cabinet, stood the crucifix which Romola had brought from San Marco.

"I have brought something under my mantle," said Tito, smiling; and throwing off the large loose garment, he showed the little tabernacle which had been painted by Piero di Cosimo. The painter had carried out Tito's intention charmingly, and so far had atoned for his long delay. "Do you know what this is for, my Romola?" added Tito, taking her by the hand, and leading her towards the cabinet. "It is a little shrine, which is to hide away from you for ever that remembrancer of sadness. You have done with sadness now; and we will bury all images of it—bury them in a tomb of joy. See!"

A slight quiver passed across Romola's face as Tito took hold of the crucifix. But she had no wish to prevent his purpose; on the contrary, she herself wished to subdue certain importunate memories and questionings which still flitted like unexplained shadows across her happier thought.

He opened the triptych and placed the crucifix within the central space; then closing it again, taking out the key, and setting the little tabernacle in the spot where the crucifix had stood, said,

"Now, Romola, look and see if you are satisfied with the portraits old Piero has made of us. Is it not a dainty device? and the credit of choosing it is mine."

"Ah, it is you—it is perfect!" said Romola, looking with moist joyful eyes at the miniature Bacchus, with his purple clusters. "And I am Ariadne, and you are crowning me! Yes, it is true, Tito; you have crowned my poor life."

They held each other's hands while she spoke, and both looked at their imaged selves. But the reality was far more beautiful; she all lily-white and golden, and he with his dark glowing beauty above the purple red-bordered tunic.

"And it was our good strange Piero who painted it?" said Romola. "Did you put it into his head to paint me as Antigone, that he might have my likeness for this?"

"No, it was he who made my getting leave for him to paint you and your father, a condition of his doing this for me."

"Ah, I see now what it was you gave up your precious ring for. I perceived you had some cunning plan to give me pleasure."

Tito did not blench. Romola's little illusions about himself had long ceased to cause him anything but satisfaction. He only smiled and said,

"I might have spared my ring; Piero will accept no money from me; he thinks himself paid by painting you. And now, while I am away, you will look every day at those pretty symbols of our life together—the ship on the calm sea, and the ivy that never withers, and those loves that have left off wounding us and shower soft petals that are like our kisses; and the leopards and tigers, they are the troubles of your life that are all quelled now;

and the strange sea-monsters, with their merry eyes—let us see—they are the dull passages in the heavy books, which have begun to be amusing since we have sat by each other."

"*Tito mio!*" said Romola, in a half laughing voice of love; "but you will give me the key?" she added, holding out her hand for it.

"Not at all!" said Tito, with playful decision, opening his scarsella and dropping in the little key. "I shall drown it in the Arno."

"But if I ever wanted to look at the crucifix again?"

"Ah! for that very reason it is hidden—hidden by these images of youth and joy."

He pressed a light kiss on her brow, and she said no more, ready to submit, like all strong souls, when she felt no valid reason for resistance.

And then they joined the waiting company, which made a dignified little procession as it passed along the Ponte Rubaconte towards Santa Croce. Slowly it passed, for Bardo, unaccustomed for years to leave his own house, walked with a more timid step than usual; and that slow pace suited well with the gouty dignity of Messer Bartolommeo Scala, who graced the occasion by his presence, along with his daughter Alessandra. It was customary to have very long troops of kindred and friends at the *sposalizio*, or betrothal, and it had even been found necessary in time past to limit the number by law to no more than *four hundred*—two hundred on each side; for since the guests were all feasted after this initial ceremony, as well as after the *nozze*, or marriage, the very first stage of matrimony had become a ruinous expense, as that scholarly Benedict, Leonardo Bruno,* complained in his own case. But Bardo, who in his poverty had kept himself proudly free from any appearance of claiming the advantages attached to a powerful family name, would have no invitations given on the strength of mere friendship; and the modest procession of twenty that followed the *sposi* were, with three or four exceptions, friends of Bardo's and Tito's, selected on personal grounds.

Bernardo del Nero walked as a vanguard before Bardo, who was led on the right by Tito, while Romola held her father's other hand. Bardo had himself been married at Santa Croce, and had insisted on Romola's being betrothed and married there, rather than in the little church of Santa Lucia close by their house, because he had a complete mental vision of the grand church where he hoped that a burial might be granted him among the Florentines who had deserved well. Happily, the way was short and direct, and lay aloof from the loudest riot of the Carnival, if only they could return before any dances or shows began in the great piazza of Santa Croce. The west was red as they passed the bridge, and shed a mellow light on the pretty procession, which had a touch of solemnity in the presence of the blind father. But when the ceremony was over, and Tito and Romola came out on to the broad steps of the church, with the golden links of destiny on their fingers, the evening had deepened into struggling starlight, and the servants had their torches lit.

While they came out a strange dreary chant, as of a *Miserere*,* met their ears, and they saw that at the extreme end of the piazza there seemed to be a stream of people impelled by something approaching from the Borgo de' Greci.

"It is one of their masked processions, I suppose," said Tito, who was now alone with Romola, while Bernardo took charge of Bardo.

And as he spoke there came slowly into view, at a height far above the heads of the on-lookers, a huge and ghastly image of Winged Time with his scythe and hour-glass, surrounded by his winged children, the Hours. He was mounted on a high car completely covered with black, and the bullocks that drew the car were also covered with black, their horns alone standing out white above the gloom; so that in the sombre shadow of the houses it seemed to those at a distance as if Time and his children were apparitions floating through the air. And behind them came what looked like a troop of the sheeted dead gliding above blackness. And as they glided slowly, they chanted in a wailing strain.

A cold horror seized on Romola, for at the first moment it seemed as if her brother's vision, which could never be effaced from her mind, was being half fulfilled. She clung to Tito, who, divining what was in her thoughts, said—

"What dismal fooling sometimes pleases your Florentines! Doubtless this is an invention of Piero di Cosimo,* who loves such grim merriment."

"Tito, I wish it had not happened. It will deepen the images of that vision which I would fain be rid of."

"Nay, Romola, you will look only at the images of our happiness now. I have locked all sadness away from you."

"But it is still there—it is only hidden," said Romola, in a low tone, hardly conscious that she spoke.

"See, they are all gone now!" said Tito. "You will forget this ghastly mummery when we are in the light, and can see each other's eyes. My Ariadne must never look backward now—only forward to Easter, when she will triumph with her Care-dispeller."*

END OF BOOK I

[*NOVEMBER 1862*]

BOOK II

CHAPTER XXI.

Florence Expects a Guest

IT was the seventeenth of November, 1494: more than eighteen months since Tito and Romola had been finally united in the joyous Easter time, and had had a rainbow-tinted shower of comfits thrown over them, after the ancient Greek fashion, in token that the heavens would shower sweets on them through all their double life.

Since that Easter a great change had come over the prospects of Florence; and as in the tree that bears a myriad of blossoms, each single bud with its fruit is dependent on the primary circulation of the sap, so the fortunes of Tito and Romola were dependent on certain grand political and social conditions which made an epoch in the history of Italy.

In this very November, little more than a week ago, the spirit of the old centuries seemed to have re-entered the breasts of Florentines. The great bell in the Palace tower had rung out the hammer-sound of alarm, and thc people had mustered with their rusty arms, their tools and impromptu cudgels, to drive out the Medici. The gate of San Gallo had been fairly shut on the arrogant, exasperating Piero, galloping away towards Bologna with his hired horsemen frightened behind him, and shut on his keener young brother, the cardinal, escaping in the disguise of a Franciscan monk: a price had been set on both their heads. After that, there had been some sacking of houses, according to old precedent; the ignominious images, painted on the public buildings, of the men who had conspired against the Medici in days gone by, were effaced; the exiled enemies of the Medici were invited home. The half-fledged tyrants were fairly out of their splendid nest in the Via Larga, and the Republic had recovered the use of its will again.

But now, a week later, the great palace in the Via Larga had been prepared for the reception of another tenant; and if drapery roofing the streets with unwonted colour, if banners and hangings pouring out from the windows, if carpets and tapestry stretched over all steps and pavement on which exceptional feet might tread, were an unquestionable proof of joy, Florence was very joyful in the expectation of its new guest. The stream of colour flowed from the Palace in the Via Larga round by the Cathedral, then by the great Piazza della Signoria, and across the Ponte Vecchio to the Porta San Frediano—the gate that looks towards Pisa. There, near the gate, a platform and canopy had been erected for the Signoria; and Messer Luca Corsini, doctor of law, felt his heart palpitating a little with the sense that he had a Latin oration to read; and every chief elder in Florence had to make himself ready, with smooth chin and well-lined silk *lucco*, to walk in procession; and the well-born youths were looking at their rich new tunics after the French mode, which was to impress the stranger as having a peculiar grace when worn by Florentines; and a large body of the clergy, from the archbishop in his effulgence to the train of monks, black, white, and grey, were consulting betimes in the morning how they should marshal themselves, with their burthen of relics, and sacred banners, and consecrated jewels, that their movements might be adjusted to the expected arrival of the illustrious visitor, at three o'clock in the afternoon.

An unexampled visitor! For he had come through the passes of the Alps with such an army as Italy had not seen before: with thousands of terrible Swiss, well used to fight for love and hatred as well as for hire; with a host of gallant cavaliers proud of a name; with an unprecedented infantry, in which every man in a hundred carried an harquebuss; nay, with cannon of bronze shooting not stones but iron balls, drawn not by bullocks but by horses, and capable of firing a second time before a city could mend the breach made by the first ball. Some compared the new comer to Charlemagne, reputed rebuilder of Florence, welcome conqueror of degenerate Kings, regulator and benefactor of the Church; some preferred the comparison to Cyrus, liberator of the chosen people, restorer of the Temple.* For he had come across the Alps with the most glorious projects: he was to march through Italy amidst the jubilees of a grateful and admiring people; he was to satisfy all conflicting complaints at Rome;

he was to take possession, by virtue of hereditary right and a little fighting, of the kingdom of Naples; and from that convenient starting-point he was to set out on the conquest of the Turks, who were partly to be cut to pieces and partly converted to the faith of Christ. It was a scheme that seemed to befit the Most Christian King,* head of a nation which, thanks to the devices of a subtle Louis the Eleventh, who had died in much fright as to his personal prospects ten years before, had become the strongest of Christian monarchies; and this antitype of Cyrus and Charlemagne was no other than the son of that subtle Louis—the young Charles the Eighth of France.

Surely, on a general statement, hardly anything could seem more grandiose, or fitter to revive in the breasts of men the memory of great dispensations by which new strata had been laid in the history of mankind. And there was a very widely spread conviction that the advent of the French King and his army into Italy was one of those events at which marble statues might well be believed to perspire, phantasmal fiery warriors to fight in the air, and quadrupeds to bring forth monstrous births*—that it did not belong to the usual order of Providence, but was in a peculiar sense the work of God. It was a conviction that rested less on the necessarily momentous character of a powerful foreign invasion than on certain moral emotions to which the aspect of the times gave the form of presentiments—emotions which had found a very remarkable utterance in the voice of a single man.

That man was Fra Girolamo Savonarola, Prior of the Dominican convent of San Marco in Florence. On a September morning, when men's ears were ringing with the news that the French army had entered Italy, he had preached in the Cathedral of Florence from the text, "Behold, I, even I, do bring a flood of waters upon the earth." He believed it was by supreme guidance that he had reached just so far in his exposition of Genesis the previous Lent; and he believed the "flood of waters"—emblem at once of avenging wrath and purifying mercy—to be the divinely indicated symbol of the French army. His audience, some of whom were held to be among the choicest spirits of the age—the most cultivated men in the most cultivated of Italian cities—believed it too, and listened with shuddering awe.* For this man had a power, rarely paralleled, of impressing his beliefs on others, and of swaying very various minds. And as long as four years ago he had proclaimed from the chief pulpit of Florence that a scourge was about to descend on Italy, and that by this scourge the Church was to be purified. Savonarola appeared to believe, and his hearers more or less waveringly believed, that he had a mission like that of the Hebrew prophets, and that the Florentines amongst whom his message was delivered were in some sense a second chosen people. The idea of prophetic gifts was not a remote one in that age: seers of visions, circumstantial heralds of things to be, were far from uncommon either outside or inside the cloister; but this very fact made Savonarola stand out the more conspicuously as a grand exception. While in others the gift of prophecy was very much like a farthing candle illuminating small corners of human destiny with prophetic gossip, in Savonarola it was like a mighty beacon shining far out for the warning and guidance of men. And to some of the soberest minds the supernatural character of his insight into the future gathered a strong attestation from the peculiar conditions of the age.

At the close of 1492, the year in which Lorenzo de' Medici died and Tito Melema came as a wanderer to Florence, Italy was enjoying a peace and prosperity unthreatened by any near and definite danger. There was no fear of famine, for the seasons had been plenteous in corn, and wine, and oil; new palaces had been rising in all fair cities, new villas on pleasant slopes and summits; and the men who had more than their share of these good things were in no fear of the larger number who had less. For the citizens' armour was getting rusty, and populations seemed to have become tame, licking the hands of masters who paid for a ready-made army when they wanted it, as they paid for goods of Smyrna. Even the fear of the Turk had ceased to be active, and the Pope found it more immediately profitable to accept bribes from him for a little prospective poisoning* than to form plans either for conquering or for converting him.

Altogether, this world, with its partitioned empire and its roomy universal Church, seemed to be a handsome establishment for the few who were lucky or wise enough to reap the advantages of human folly: a world in which lust and obscenity, lying and treachery, oppression and murder, were pleasant, useful, and, when properly managed, not dangerous. And as a sort of fringe or adornment to the substantial delights of tyranny, avarice, and lasciviousness, there was the patronage of polite learning and the fine arts, so that flattery could always be had in the choicest Latin to be commanded at that time, and sublime artists were at hand to paint the holy and the unclean with impartial skill. The Church, it was said, had never been so disgraced in its head, had never shown so few signs of renovating, vital belief in its lower members; nevertheless it was much more prosperous than in some past days. The heavens were fair and smiling above; and below there were no signs of earthquake.

Yet at that time, as we have seen, there was a man in Florence who for two years and more had been preaching that a scourge was at hand; that the world was certainly not framed for the lasting convenience of hypocrites, libertines, and oppressors. From the midst of those smiling heavens he had seen a sword hanging*—the sword of God's justice—which was speedily to descend with purifying punishment on the Church and the world. In brilliant Ferrara, seventeen years before, the contradiction between men's lives and their professed beliefs had pressed upon him with a force that had been enough to destroy his appetite for the world, and at the age of twenty-three had driven him into the cloister. He believed that God had committed to the Church the sacred lamp of truth for the guidance and salvation of men, and he saw that the Church, in its corruption, had become a sepulchre to hide the lamp. As the years went on scandals increased and multiplied, and hypocrisy seemed to have given place to impudence. Had the world then ceased to have a righteous Ruler? Was the Church finally forsaken? No, assuredly: in the Sacred Book there was a record of the past in which might be seen as in a glass what would be in the days to come, and the Book showed that when the wickedness of the chosen people, type of the Christian Church, had become crying, the judgments of God had descended on them. Nay, reason itself declared that vengeance was imminent, for what else would suffice to turn men from their obstinacy in evil? And unless the Church were reclaimed, how could the promises be fulfilled, that the heathens should be converted and the whole world become subject to the one true law? He had seen his belief reflected in visions—a mode of seeing which had been frequent with him from his youth up.

But the real force of demonstration for Girolamo Savonarola lay in his own burning indignation at the sight of wrong; in his fervent belief in an unseen Justice that would put an end to the wrong, and in an unseen Purity to which lying and uncleanness were an abomination. To his ardent, power-loving soul, believing in great ends, and longing to achieve those ends by the exertion of its own strong will, the faith in a supreme and righteous Ruler became one with the faith in a speedy divine interposition that would punish and reclaim.

Meanwhile, under that splendid masquerade of dignities sacred and secular which seemed to make the life of lucky churchmen and princely families so luxurious and amusing, there were certain conditions at work which slowly tended to disturb the general festivity. Ludovico Sforza*—copious in gallantry, splendid patron of an incomparable Lionardo da Vinci—holding the ducal crown of Milan in his grasp, and wanting to put it on his own head rather than let it rest on that of a feeble nephew who would take very little to poison him, was much afraid of the Spanish-born old King Ferdinand and the Crown Prince Alfonso of Naples, who, not liking cruelty and treachery which were useless to themselves, objected to the poisoning of a near relative for the advantage of a Lombard usurper; the royalties of Naples again were afraid of their suzerain, Pope Alexander Borgia; all three were anxiously watching Florence, lest with its midway territory it should determine the game by underhand backing; and all four, with every small state in Italy, were afraid of Venice—Venice the cautious, the stable, and the strong, that wanted to stretch its arms not only along both sides of the Adriatic but across to the ports of the western coast.

Lorenzo de' Medici, it was thought, did much to prevent the fatal outbreak of such jealousies, keeping up the old Florentine alliance with Naples and the Pope, and yet persuading Milan that the alliance was for the general advantage. But young Piero de' Medici's rash vanity had quickly nullified the effect of his father's wary policy, and Ludovico Sforza, roused to suspicion of a league against him, thought of a move which would checkmate his adversaries: he determined to invite the French King to march into Italy and, as heir of the house of Anjou, take possession of Naples. Ambassadors—"orators," as they were called in those haranguing times—went and came; a recusant Cardinal* determined not to acknowledge a Pope elected by bribery (and his own particular enemy), went and came also, and seconded the invitation with hot rhetoric; and the young King seemed to lend a willing ear. So that in 1493 the rumour spread and became louder and louder that Charles the Eighth of France was about to cross the Alps with a mighty army; and the Italian populations, accustomed, since Italy had ceased to be the heart of the Roman empire, to look for an arbitrator from afar, began vaguely to regard his coming as a means of avenging their wrongs and redressing their grievances.

And in that rumour Savonarola had heard the assurance that his prophecy was being verified. What was it that filled the ear of the prophets of old but the distant tread of foreign armies, coming to do the work of justice? He no longer looked vaguely to the horizon for the coming storm: he pointed to the rising cloud. The French army was that new deluge which was to purify the earth from iniquity; the French King, Charles VIII., was the instrument elected by God, as Cyrus had been of old, and all men who desired good rather than evil were to rejoice in his coming. For the scourge would fall destructively on the impenitent alone. Let any city of Italy, let Florence above all—Florence beloved of God, since to its ear the warning voice had been specially sent—repent and turn from its ways, like Nineveh* of old, and the storm-cloud would roll over it and leave only refreshing rain-drops.

Fra Girolamo's word was powerful; yet now that the new Cyrus had already been three months in Italy, and was not far from the gates of Florence, his presence was expected there with mixed feelings, in which fear and distrust certainly predominated. At present it was not understood that he had redressed any grievances; and the Florentines clearly had nothing to thank him for. He held their strong frontier fortresses, which Piero de' Medici had given up to him without securing any honourable terms in return; he had done nothing to quell the alarming revolt of Pisa, which had been encouraged by his presence to throw off the Florentine yoke; and "orators," even with a prophet at their head,* could win no assurance from him, except that he would settle everything when he was once within the walls of Florence. Still, there was the satisfaction of knowing that the exasperating Piero de' Medici had been fairly pelted out for the ignominious surrender of the fortresses, and in that act of energy the spirit of the Republic had recovered some of its old fire.

The preparations for the equivocal guest were not entirely those of a city resigned to submission. Behind the bright drapery and banners symbolical of joy, there were preparations of another sort made with common accord by government and people. Well hidden within walls there were hired soldiers of the Republic, hastily called in from the surrounding districts; there were old arms newly furbished, and sharp tools and heavy cudgels laid carefully at hand, to be snatched up on short notice; there were excellent boards and stakes to form barricades upon occasion, and a good supply of stones to make a surprising hail from the upper windows. Above all, there were people very strongly in the humour for fighting any personage who might be supposed to have designs of hectoring over them, they having lately tasted that new pleasure with much relish. This humour was not diminished by the sight of occasional parties of Frenchmen, coming beforehand to choose their quarters, with a hawk, perhaps, on their left wrist, and, metaphorically speaking, a piece of chalk in their right hand to mark Italian doors withal; especially as credible historians imply that many sons of France were at that time characterized by something approaching to a swagger, which must have whetted the Florentine appetite for a little stone-throwing.

And this was the temper of Florence on the morning of the seventeenth of November, 1494.

CHAPTER XXII.

The Prisoners

THE sky was grey, but that made little difference in the Piazza del Duomo, which was covered with its holiday sky of blue drapery, and its constellations of yellow lilies and coats of arms. The sheaves of banners were unfurled at the angles of the Baptistery, but there was no carpet yet on the steps of the Duomo, for the marble was being trodden by numerous feet that were not at all exceptional. It was the hour of the Advent sermons, and the very same reasons which had flushed the streets with holiday colour were reasons why the preaching in the Duomo could least of all be dispensed with.

But not all the feet in the piazza were hastening towards the steps. People of high and low degree were moving to and fro with the brisk pace of men who had errands before them;

groups of talkers were thickly scattered, some willing to be late for the sermon, others content not to hear it at all.

The expression on the faces of these apparent loungers was not that of men who are enjoying the pleasant laziness of an opening holiday. Some were in close and eager discussion; others were listening with keen interest to a single spokesman, and yet from time to time turned round with a scanning glance at any new passer-by. At the corner, looking towards the Via de' Cerretani—just where the artificial rainbow light of the piazza ceased, and the grey morning fell on the sombre stone houses—there was a remarkable cluster of the working people, most of them bearing on their dress or persons the signs of their daily labour, and almost all of them carrying some weapon, or some tool which might serve as a weapon upon occasion. Standing in the grey light of the street, with bare brawny arms and soiled garments, they made all the more striking the transition from the brightness of the piazza. They were listening to the thin notary, Ser Cioni, who had just paused on his way to the Duomo. His biting words could get only a contemptuous reception two years and a half before in the Mercato, but now he spoke with the more complacent humour of a man whose party is uppermost, and who is conscious of some influence with the people.

"Never talk to me," he was saying, in his incisive voice, "never talk to me of bloodthirsty Swiss or fierce French infantry: they might as well be in the narrow passes of the mountains as in our streets; and peasants have destroyed the finest armies of our condottieri in time past, when they had once got them between steep precipices. I tell you, Florentines need be afraid of no army in their own streets."

"That's true, Ser Cioni," said a man whose arms and hands were discoloured by crimson dye, which looked like bloodstains, and who had a small hatchet stuck in his belt; "and those French cavaliers, who came in squaring themselves in their smart doublets the other day, saw a sample of the dinner we could serve up for them. I was carrying my cloth in Ognissanti, when I saw my fine *Messeri* going by, looking round as if they thought the houses of the Vespucci and the Agli a poor pick of lodgings for them, and eying us Florentines, like topknotted cocks as they are, as if they pitied us because we didn't know how to strut. 'Yes, my fine *Galli*,'* says I, 'stick out your stomachs, I've got a meat-axe in my belt that will go inside you all the easier;' when presently the old cow lowed,* and I knew something had happened—no matter what. So I threw my cloth in at the first doorway, and took hold of my meat-axe and ran after my fine cavaliers towards the Vigna Nuova. And, 'What is it, Guccio?' said I, when he came up with me. 'I think it's the Medici coming back,' said Guccio. *Bembè!* I expected so! And up we reared a barricade, and the Frenchmen looked behind and saw themselves in a trap; and up comes a good swarm of our *Ciompi*,* and one of them with a big scythe he had in his hand mowed off one of the fine cavalier's feathers:—it's true! And the lasses peppered a few stones down to frighten them. However, Piero de' Medici wasn't come after all; and it was a pity; for we'd have left him neither legs nor wings to go away with again."

"Well spoken, Oddo," said a young butcher, with his knife at his belt, "and it's my belief Piero will be a good while before he wants to come back, for he looked as frightened as a hunted chicken, when we hustled and pelted him in the piazza. He's a coward, else he might have made a better stand when he'd got his horsemen. But we'll swallow no Medici any more, whatever else the French King wants to make us swallow."

"But I like not those French cannon they talk of," said Goro, none the less fat for two years' additional grievances. "San Giovanni defend us! If Messer Domeneddio means so well by us as your Frate says he does, Ser Cioni, why shouldn't he have sent the French another way to Naples?"

"Ay, Goro," said the dyer, "that's a question worth putting. Thou art not such a pumpkin-head as I took thee for. Why, they might have gone to Naples by Bologna, eh, Ser Cioni? or if they'd gone to Arezzo—we wouldn't have minded their going to Arezzo."

"Fools! It will be for the good and glory of Florence," Ser Cioni began. But he was interrupted by the exclamation, "Look there!" which burst from several voices at once, while the faces were all turned to a party who were advancing along the Via de' Cerretani.

"It's Lorenzo Tornabuoni,* and one of the French noblemen who are in his house," said Ser Cioni, in some contempt at this interruption. "He pretends to look well satisfied—that deep Tornabuoni—but he's a Medicean in his heart: mind that."

The advancing party was rather a brilliant one, for there was not only the distinguished presence of Lorenzo Tornabuoni, and the splendid costume of the Frenchman with his elaborately displayed white linen and gorgeous embroidery; there were two other Florentines of high birth in handsome dresses donned for the coming procession, and on the left hand of the Frenchman was a figure that was not to be eclipsed by any amount of intention or brocade—a figure we have often seen before. He wore nothing but black, for he was in mourning; but the black was presently to be covered by a red mantle, for he too was to walk in procession as Latin Secretary to the Ten. Tito Melema had become conspicuously serviceable in the intercourse with the French guests, from his familiarity with Southern Italy, and his readiness in the French tongue, which he had spoken in his early youth; and he had paid more than one visit to the French camp at Signa.* The lustre of good fortune was upon him; he was smiling, listening, and explaining, with his usual graceful unpretentious ease, and only a very keen eye bent on studying him could have marked a certain amount of change in him which was not to be accounted for by the lapse of eighteen months. It was that change which comes from the final departure of moral youthfulness—from the distinct self-conscious adoption of a part in life. The lines of the face were as soft as ever, the eyes as pellucid; but something was gone—something as indefinable as the changes in the morning twilight.

The Frenchman was gathering instructions concerning ceremonial before riding back to Signa, and now he was going to have a final survey of the Piazza del Duomo, where the royal procession was to pause for religious purposes. The distinguished party attracted the notice of all eyes as it entered the piazza, but the gaze was not entirely cordial and admiring; there were remarks not altogether allusive and mysterious to the Frenchman's hoof-shaped shoes—delicate flattery of royal superfluity in toes;* and there was no care that certain snarlings at "Mediceans" should be strictly inaudible. But Lorenzo Tornabuoni possessed that power of dissembling annoyance which is demanded in a man who courts popularity, and Tito, besides his natural disposition to overcome ill-will by good-humour, had the unimpassioned feeling of the alien towards names and details that move the deepest passions of the native. Arrived where they could get a good oblique view of the

Duomo, the party paused. The festoons and devices placed over the central doorway excited some demur, and Tornabuoni beckoned to Piero di Cosimo, who, as was usual with him at this hour, was lounging in front of Nello's shop. There was soon an animated discussion, and it became highly amusing from the Frenchman's astonishment at Piero's odd pungency of statement, which Tito translated literally. Even snarling on-lookers became curious, and their faces began to wear the half-smiling, half-humiliated expression of people who are not within hearing of the joke which is producing infectious laughter. It was a delightful moment for Tito, for he was the only one of the party who could have made so amusing an interpreter, and without any disposition to triumphant self-gratulation, he revelled in the sense that he was an object of liking—he basked in approving glances. The rainbow light fell about the laughing group, and the grave church-goers had all disappeared within the walls. It seemed as if the piazza had been decorated for a real Florentine holiday.

Meanwhile in the grey light of the unadorned streets there were on-comers who made no show of linen and brocade, and whose humour was far from merry. Here, too, the French dress and hoofed shoes were conspicuous, but they were being pressed upon by a larger and larger number of non-admiring Florentines. In the van of the crowd were three men in scanty clothing; each had his hands bound together by a cord, and a rope was fastened round his neck and body, in such a way that he who held the extremity of the rope might easily check any rebellious movement by the threat of throttling. The men who held the ropes were French soldiers, and by broken Italian phrases and strokes from the knotted end of the rope, they from time to time stimulated their prisoners to beg. Two of them were obedient, and to every Florentine they had encountered had held out their bound hands and said in piteous tones,

"For the love of God and the Holy Madonna, give us something towards our ransom! We are Tuscans: we were made prisoners in Lunigiana."*

But the third man remained obstinately silent under all the strokes from the knotted cord. He was very different in aspect from his two fellow-prisoners. They were young and hardy, and, in the scant clothing which the avarice of their captors had left them, looked like vulgar, sturdy mendicants. But he had passed the boundary of old age, and could hardly be less than four or five and sixty. His beard which had grown long in neglect, and the hair which fell thick and straight round his baldness, were nearly white. His thickset figure was still firm and upright, though emaciated, and seemed to express energy in spite of age—an expression that was partly carried out in the dark eyes and strong dark eyebrows, which had a strangely isolated intensity of colour in the midst of his yellow, bloodless, deep-wrinkled face with its lank grey hairs. And yet there was something fitful in the eyes which contradicted the occasional flash of energy: after looking round with quick fierceness at windows and faces, they fell again with a lost and wandering look. But his lips were motionless, and he held his hands resolutely down. He would not beg.

This sight had been witnessed by the Florentines with growing exasperation. Many standing at their doors or passing quietly along had at once given money—some in half automatic response to an appeal in the name of God, others in that unquestioning awe of the French soldiery which had been created by the reports of their cruel warfare, and on which the French themselves counted as a guarantee of immunity in their acts of insolence. But as the group had proceeded farther into the heart of the city, that compliance had gradually disappeared, and the soldiers found themselves escorted by a gathering troop of men and boys, who kept up a chorus of exclamations sufficiently intelligible to foreign ears without any interpreter. The soldiers themselves began to dislike their position, for with a strong inclination to use their weapons, they were checked by the necessity for keeping a secure hold on their prisoners, and they were now hurrying along in the hope of finding shelter in a hostelry.

"French dogs!" "Bullock-feet!" "Snatch their pikes from them!" "Cut the cords and make them run for their prisoners. They'll run as fast as geese—don't you see they're web-footed?" These were the cries which the soldiers vaguely understood to be jeers, and probably threats. But every one seemed disposed to give invitations of this spirited kind rather than to act upon them.

"*Santiddio!* here's a sight!" said the dyer, as soon as he had divined the meaning of the advancing tumult, "and the fools do nothing but hoot. Come along!" he added, snatching his axe from his belt, and running to join the crowd, followed by the butcher and all the rest of his companions, except Goro, who hastily retreated up a narrow passage.

The sight of the dyer, running forward with blood-red arms and axe uplifted, and with his cluster of rough companions behind him, had a stimulating effect on the crowd. Not that he did anything else than pass beyond the soldiers and thrust himself well among his fellow-citizens, flourishing his axe; but he served as a stirring symbol of street fighting, like the waving of a well-known gonfalon. And the first sign that fire was ready to burst out was something as rapid as a little leaping tongue of flame: it was an act of the conjuror's impish lad Lollo, who was dancing and jeering in front of the ingenuous boys that made the majority of the crowd. Lollo had no great compassion for the prisoners, but, being conscious of an excellent knife which was his unfailing companion, it had seemed to him from the first that to jump forward, cut a rope, and leap back again before the soldier who held it could use his weapon, would be an amusing and dexterous piece of mischief. And now, when the people began to hoot and jostle more vigorously, Lollo felt that his moment was come—he was close to the eldest prisoner: in an instant he had cut the cord.

"Run, old one!" he piped in the prisoner's ear, as soon as the cord was in two; and himself set the example of running as if he were helped along with wings, like a scared fowl.

The prisoner's sensations were not too slow for him to seize the opportunity: the idea of escape had been continually present with him, and he had gathered fresh hope from the temper of the crowd. He ran at once; but his speed would hardly have sufficed for him if the Florentines had not instantaneously rushed between him and his captor. He ran on into the piazza, but he quickly heard the tramp of feet behind him, for the other two prisoners had been released, and the soldiers were struggling and fighting their way after them, in such tardigrade fashion as their hoof-shaped shoes would allow— impeded, but not very resolutely attacked, by the people. One of the two younger prisoners turned up the Borgo di San Lorenzo, and thus made a partial diversion of the hubbub; but the main struggle was still towards the piazza, where all eyes were turned on it with alarmed curiosity. The cause could not be precisely guessed, for the French dress was screened by the impeding crowd.

"An escape of prisoners," said Lorenzo Tornabuoni, as he and his party turned round just against the steps of the Duomo, and saw a prisoner rushing by them. "The people are not content with having emptied the Bargello the other day. If there is no other authority in sight they must fall on the *sbirri* and secure freedom to thieves. Ah! there is a French soldier: that is more serious."

The soldier he saw was struggling along on the north side of the piazza, but the object of his pursuit had taken the other direction. That object was the eldest prisoner, who had wheeled round the Baptistery and was running towards the Duomo, determined to take refuge in that sanctuary rather than trust to his speed. But in mounting the steps, his foot received a shock; he was precipitated towards the group of Signori, whose backs were turned to him, and was only able to recover his balance as he clutched one of them by the arm.

It was Tito Melema who felt that clutch. He turned his head, and saw the face of his adoptive father, Baldassarre Calvo, close to his own.

The two men looked at each other, silent as death: Baldassarre, with dark fierceness and a tightening grip of the soiled worn hands on the velvet-clad arm; Tito, with cheeks and lips all bloodless, fascinated by terror. It seemed a long while to them—it was but a moment.

The first sound Tito heard was the short laugh of Piero di Cosimo, who stood close by him and was the only person that could see his face.

"Ha, ha! I know what a ghost should be now."

"This is another escaped prisoner," said Lorenzo Tornabuoni. "Who is he, I wonder?"

"*Some madman, surely*," said Tito.

He hardly knew how the words had come to his lips: there are moments when our passions speak and decide for us, and we seem to stand by and wonder. They carry in them an inspiration of crime, that in one instant does the work of long premeditation.

The two men had not taken their eyes off each other, and it seemed to Tito, when he had spoken, that some magical poison had darted from Baldassarre's eyes, and that he felt it rushing through his veins. But the next instant the grasp on his arm had relaxed, and Baldassarre had disappeared within the church.

CHAPTER XXIII.

After-thoughts

"YOU are easily frightened, though," said Piero, with another scornful laugh. "My portrait is not as good as the original. But the old fellow *had* a tiger look: I must go into the Duomo and see him again."

"It is not pleasant to be laid hold of by a madman, if madman he be", said Lorenzo Tornabuoni, in polite excuse of Tito, "but perhaps he is only a ruffian. We shall hear. I think we must see if we have authority enough to stop this disturbance between our people and your countrymen," he added, addressing the Frenchman.

They advanced towards the crowd with their swords drawn, all the quiet spectators making an escort for them. Tito went too: it was necessary that he should know what others knew about Baldassarre, and the first palsy of terror was being succeeded by the rapid devices to which mortal danger will stimulate the timid.

The rabble of men and boys, more inclined to hoot at the soldier and torment him than to receive or inflict any serious wounds, gave way at the approach of *signori* with drawn swords, and the French soldier was interrogated. He and his companions had simply brought their prisoners into the city that they might beg money for their ransom: two of the prisoners were Tuscan soldiers taken in Lunigiana; the other, an elderly man, was with a party of Genoese, with whom the French foragers had come to blows near Fivizzano.* He might be mad, but he was harmless. The soldier knew no more, being unable to understand a word the old man said. Tito heard so far, but he was deaf to everything else till he was specially addressed. It was Tornabuoni who spoke.

"Will you go back with us, Melema? Or, since Messere is going off to Signa now, will you wisely follow the fashion of the times and go to hear the Frate, who will be like the torrent at its height this morning? It's what we must all do, you know, if we are to save our Medicean skins. *I* should go if I had the leisure."

Tito's face had recovered its colour now, and he could make an effort to speak with gaiety.

"Of course I am among the admirers of the inspired orator," he said, smilingly; "but, unfortunately, I shall be occupied with the Segretario till the time of the procession."

"*I* am going into the Duomo to look at that savage old man again," said Piero.

"Then have the charity to show him to one of the hospitals for travellers, *Piero mio*," said Tornabuoni. "The monks may find out whether he wants putting into a cage."

The party separated, and Tito took his way to the Palazzo Vecchio, where he was to find Bartolommeo Scala. It was not a long walk, but, for Tito, it was stretched out like the minutes of our morning dreams: the short spaces of street and piazza held memories, and previsions, and torturing fears, that might have made the history of months. He felt as if a serpent had begun to coil round his limbs. Baldassarre living, and in Florence, was a living revenge, which would no more rest than a winding serpent would rest until it had crushed its prey. It was not in the nature of that man to let an injury pass unavenged: his love and his hatred were of that passionate fervour which subjugates all the rest of the being, and makes a man sacrifice himself to his passion as if it were a deity to be worshipped with self-destruction. Baldassarre had relaxed his hold, and had disappeared. Tito knew well how to interpret that: it meant that the vengeance was to be studied that it might be sure. If he had not uttered those decisive words—"He is a madman"—if he could have summoned up the state of mind, the courage, necessary for avowing his recognition of Baldassarre, would not the risk have been less? He might have declared himself to have had what he believed to be positive evidence of Baldassarre's death; and the only persons who could ever have had positive knowledge to contradict him were Fra Luca, who was dead, and the crew of the companion galley, who had brought him the news of the encounter with the pirates. The chances were infinite against Baldassarre's having met again with any one of that crew, and Tito thought with bitterness that a timely, well-devised falsehood might have saved him from any fatal consequences. But to have told that falsehood would have required perfect self-command in the moment of a convulsive shock: he seemed to have spoken without any preconception—the words had leaped forth like a sudden birth that has been begotten and nourished in the darkness.

Tito was experiencing that inexorable law of human souls, that we prepare ourselves for sudden deeds by the reiterated choice of good or evil which gradually determines character.

That was but one chance for him now: the chance of Baldassarre's failure in finding his revenge. And—Tito grasped at a thought more actively cruel than any he had ever encouraged before: might not his own unpremeditated words have some truth in them?—enough truth, at least, to bear him out in his denial of any declaration Baldassarre might make about him? The old man looked strange and wild: with his eager heart and brain, suffering was likely enough to have produced madness. If it were so, the vengeance that strove to inflict disgrace might be baffled.

But there was another form of vengeance not to be baffled by ingenious lying. Baldassarre belonged to a race to whom the thrust of the dagger seems almost as natural an impulse as the outleap of the tiger's talons. Tito shrank with shuddering dread from disgrace; but he had also that physical dread which is inseparable from a soft pleasure-loving nature, and which prevents a man from meeting wounds and death as a welcome relief from disgrace. His thoughts flew at once to some hidden defensive armour that might save him from a vengeance which no subtlety could parry.

He wondered at the power of the passionate fear that possessed him. It was as if he had been smitten with a blighting disease that had suddenly turned the joyous sense of young life into pain.

There was still one resource open to Tito. He might have turned back, sought Baldassarre again, confessed everything to him—to Romola—to all the world. But he never thought of that. The repentance which cuts off all moorings to evil, demands something more than selfish fear. He had no sense that there was strength and safety in truth; the only strength he trusted to lay in his ingenuity and his dissimulation. Now that the first shock, which had called up the traitorous signs of fear, was well past, he hoped to be prepared for all emergencies by cool deceit—and defensive armour.

It was a characteristic fact in Tito's experience at this crisis, that no direct measures for ridding himself of Baldassarre ever occurred to him. All other possibilities passed through his mind, even to his own flight from Florence; but he never thought of any scheme for removing his enemy. His dread generated no active malignity, and he would still have been glad not to give pain to any mortal. He had simply chosen to make life easy to himself—to carry his human lot, if possible, in such a way that it should pinch him nowhere; and the choice had, at various times, landed him in unexpected positions. The question now was, not whether he should divide the common pressure of destiny with his suffering fellow-men; it was whether all the resources of lying would save him from being crushed by the consequences of that habitual choice.

CHAPTER XXIV.

Inside the Duomo

WHEN Baldassarre, with his hands bound together, and the rope round his neck and body, pushed his way behind the curtain, and saw the interior of the Duomo before him, he gave a start of astonishment, and stood still against the doorway. He had expected to see a vast nave empty of everything but lifeless emblems—side altars with candles unlit, dim pictures, pale and rigid statues—with perhaps a few worshippers in the distant choir following a monotonous chant. That was the ordinary aspect of churches to a man who never went into them with any religious purpose.

And he saw, instead, a vast multitude of warm, living faces, upturned in breathless silence towards the pulpit, at the angle between the nave and the choir. The multitude was of all ranks, from magistrates and dames of gentle nurture to coarsely clad artisans and country people. In the pulpit was a Dominican friar, with strong features and dark hair, preaching with the crucifix in his hand. For the first few minutes Baldassarre noted nothing of his preaching. Silent as his entrance had been, some eyes near the doorway had been turned on him with surprise and suspicion. The rope indicated plainly enough that he was an escaped prisoner, but in that case the church was a sanctuary which he had a right to claim; his advanced years and look of wild misery were fitted to excite pity rather than alarm, and as he stood motionless, with eyes that soon wandered absently from the wide scene before him to the pavement at his feet, those who had observed his entrance presently ceased to regard him, and became absorbed again in the stronger interest of listening to the sermon. Among the eyes that had been turned towards him were Romola's: she had entered late through one of the side doors, and was so placed that she had a full view of the main entrance. She had looked long and attentively at Baldassarre, for grey hairs made a peculiar appeal to her, and the stamp of some unwonted suffering in the face, confirmed by the cord round the neck, stirred in her those sensibilities towards the sorrows of age, which her whole life had tended to develop. She fancied that his eyes had met hers in their first wandering gaze; but Baldassarre had not, in reality, noted her; he had only had a startled consciousness of the general scene, and the consciousness was a mere flash that made no perceptible break in the fierce tumult of emotion which the encounter with Tito had created. Images from the past kept urging themselves upon him like delirious visions strangely blended with thirst and anguish. No distinct thought for the future could shape itself in the midst of that fiery passion: the nearest approach to such thought was the bitter sense of enfeebled powers, and a vague determination to universal distrust and suspicion. Suddenly he felt himself vibrating to loud tones, which seemed like the thundering echo of his own passion. A voice that penetrated his very marrow with its accent of triumphant certitude was saying—"The day of vengeance is at hand!"

Baldassarre quivered and looked up. He was too distant to see more than the general aspect of the preacher standing with his right arm outstretched, lifting up the crucifix; but he panted for the threatening voice again as if it had been a promise of bliss. There was a pause before the preacher spoke again. He gradually lowered his arm. He deposited the crucifix on the edge of the pulpit, and crossed his arms over his breast, looking round at the multitude as if he would meet the glance of every individual face.

"All ye in Florence are my witnesses, for I spoke not in a corner. Ye are my witnesses, that four years ago, when there were yet no signs of war and tribulation, I preached the coming of the scourge. I lifted up my voice as a trumpet to the prelates and princes and people of Italy and said, The cup of your iniquity is full. Behold, the thunder of the Lord is gathering, and it shall fall and break the cup, and your iniquity, which seems to you as pleasant wine, shall be poured out upon you, and shall be as molten lead. And you, O priests, who say, Ha, ha! there is no Presence in the sanctuary—the Shechinah* is nought—the Mercy-seat is bare; we may sin behind the veil, and who shall punish us? To you, I said, the presence of God shall be revealed in his temple as a consuming fire, and your sacred garments shall become a winding-sheet of flame, and for sweet music there shall be shrieks and hissing, and for soft couches there shall be thorns, and for the breath of wantons shall come the pestilence. Trust not in your gold and silver, trust not in your high fortresses; for though the walls were of iron, and the fortresses of adamant, the Most High shall put terror into your hearts and weakness into your councils, so that you shall be confounded and flee like women. He shall break in pieces mighty men without number, and put others in their stead. For God will no longer endure the pollution of his sanctuary: he will thoroughly purge his Church.

"And forasmuch as it is written* that God will do nothing but he revealeth it to his servants the prophets, he has chosen me his unworthy servant, and made his purpose present to my soul in the living word of the Scriptures; and in the deeds of his Providence; and by the ministry of angels he has revealed it to me in visions. And his word possesses me so that I am but as the branch of the forest when the wind of heaven penetrates it, and it is not in me to keep silence, even though I may be a derision to the scorner. And for four years I have preached in obedience to the Divine will: in the face of scoffing I have preached three things, which the Lord has delivered to me: that *in these times God will regenerate His Church*, and that *before the regeneration must come the scourge over all Italy*, and that *these things will come quickly*. But hypocrites who cloak their hatred of the truth with a show of love have said to me 'Come now Frate, leave your prophesyings: it is enough to teach virtue.' To these I answer: 'Yes, you say in your hearts, God lives afar off, and his word is as a parchment written by dead men, and he deals not as in the days of old, rebuking the nations, and punishing the oppressors, and smiting the unholy priests as he smote the sons of Eli.* But I cry again in your ears: God is near and not afar off; his judgments change not. He is the God of armies; the strong men who go up to battle are his ministers, even as the storm, and fire, and pestilence. He drives them by the breath of his angels, and they come upon the chosen land which has forsaken the covenant. And thou, O Italy, art the chosen land: has not God placed his sanctuary within thee, and thou has polluted it? Behold! the ministers of his wrath are upon thee—they are at thy very doors!'"

Savonarola's voice had been rising in impassioned force up to this point, when he became suddenly silent, let his hands fall, and clasped them quietly before him. His silence, instead of being the signal for small movements amongst his audience, seemed to be as strong a spell to them as his voice. Through the vast area of the Cathedral men and women sat with faces upturned, like breathing statues, till the voice was heard again in clear low tones.

"Yet there is a pause—even as in the days when Jerusalem was destroyed there was a pause* that the children of God might flee from it. There is a stillness before the storm: lo, there is blackness above, but not a leaf quakes: the winds are stayed, that the voice of God's warning may be heard. Hear it now, O Florence, chosen city in the chosen land! Repent and forsake evil: do justice: love mercy: put away all uncleanness from among you, that the spirit of truth and holiness may fill your souls and breathe through all your streets and habitations, and then the pestilence shall not enter, and the sword shall pass over you and leave you unhurt.

"For the sword is hanging from the sky; it is quivering; it is about to fall! *The Sword of God upon the earth, swift and sudden!* Did I not tell you, years ago, that I had beheld the vision and heard the voice? And Behold, it is fulfilled! Is there not a King with his army at your gates? Does not the earth shake with the tread of horses and the wheels of swift cannon? Is there not a fierce multitude that can lay bare the land as with a sharp razor? I tell you the French King with his army is the minister of God: God shall guide him as the hand guides a sharp sickle, and the joints of the wicked shall melt before him, and they shall be mown down as stubble: he that fleeth of them shall not flee away, and he that escapeth of them shall not be delivered. And the tyrants who have made to themselves a throne out of the vices of the multitude, and the unbelieving priests who traffic in the souls of men and fill the very sanctuary with fornication, shall be hurled from their soft couches into burning hell;

and the pagans and they who sinned under the old covenant shall stand aloof and say: 'Lo! these men have brought the stench of a new wickedness into the everlasting fire.'

"But thou, O Florence, take the offered mercy. See! the Cross is held out to you: come and be healed. Which among the nations of Italy has had a token like unto yours? The tyrant is driven out from among you: the men who held a bribe in their left hand and a rod in their right are gone forth, and no blood has been spilled. And now put away every other abomination from among you, and you shall be strong in the strength of the living God. Wash yourselves from the black pitch of your vices, which have made you even as the heathens: put away the envy and hatred that have made your city as a nest of wolves. And there shall no harm happen to you: and the passage of armies shall be to you as the flight of birds, and rebellious Pisa shall be given to you again, and famine and pestilence shall be far from your gates, and you shall be as a beacon among the nations. But, mark! while you suffer the accursed thing to lie in the camp* you shall be afflicted and tormented, even though a remnant among you may be saved."

These admonitions and promises had been spoken in an incisive tone of authority; but in the next sentence the preacher's voice melted into a strain of entreaty.

"Listen, O people, over whom my heart yearns, as the heart of a mother over the children she has travailed for! God is my witness that but for your sakes I would willingly live as a turtle in the depths of the forest, singing low to my Beloved, who is mine and I am His. For you I toil, for you I languish, for you my nights are spent in watching, and my soul melteth away for very heaviness. O Lord, thou knowest I am willing—I am ready. Take me, stretch me on thy cross: let the wicked who delight in blood, and rob the poor, and defile the temple of their bodies, and harden themselves against thy mercy—let them wag their heads and shoot out the lip at me: let the thorns press upon my brow, and let my sweat be anguish—I desire to be made like thee in thy great love. But let me see of the fruit of my travail—let this people be saved! Let me see them clothed in purity: let me hear their voices rise in concord as the voices of the angels: let them see no wisdom but in thy eternal law, no beauty but in holiness. Then they shall lead the way before the nations, and the people from the four winds shall follow them, and be gathered into the fold of the blessed. For it is thy will, O God, that the earth shall be converted unto thy law: it is thy will that wickedness shall cease and love shall reign. Come, O blessed promise! and behold, I am willing—lay me on the altar: let my blood flow and the fire consume me; but let my witness be remembered among men, that iniquity shall not prosper for ever."*

During the last appeal, Savonarola had stretched out his arms and lifted up his eyes to heaven; his strong voice had alternately trembled with emotion and risen again in renewed energy; but the passion with which he offered himself as a victim became at last too strong to allow of further speech, and he ended in a sob. Every changing tone, vibrating through the audience, shook them into answering emotion. There were plenty among them who had very moderate faith in the Frate's prophetic mission, and who in their cooler moments loved him little; nevertheless, they too were carried along by the great wave of feeling which gathered its force from sympathies that lay deeper than all theory. A loud responding sob rose at once from the wide multitude, while Savonarola had fallen on his knees and buried his face in his mantle. He felt in that moment the rapture and glory of martyrdom without its agony.

In that great sob of the multitude Baldassarre's had mingled. Among all the human beings present, there was perhaps not one whose frame vibrated more strongly than his to the tones and words of the preacher; but it had vibrated like a harp of which all the strings had been wrenched away except one. That threat of a fiery inexorable vengeance—of a future into which the hated sinner might be pursued and held by the avenger in an eternal grapple, had come to him like the promise of an unquenchable fountain to unquenchable thirst. The doctrines of the sages, the old contempt for priestly superstitions, had fallen away from his soul like a forgotten language: if he could have remembered them, what answer could they have given to his great need like the answer given by this voice of energetic conviction? The thunder of denunciation fell on his passion-wrought nerves with all the force of self-evidence: his thought never went beyond it into questions—he was possessed by it as the war-horse is possessed by the clash of sounds. No word that was not a threat touched his consciousness; he had no fibre to be thrilled by it. But the fierce exultant delight to which he was moved by the idea of perpetual vengeance found at once a climax and a relieving outburst in the preacher's words of self-sacrifice. To Baldassarre those words only brought the vague triumphant sense that he too was devoting himself—signing with his own blood the deed by which he gave himself over to an unending fire, that would seem but coolness to his burning hatred.

"I rescued him—I cherished him—if I might clutch his heart-strings for ever! Come, O blessed promise! Let my blood flow; let the fire consume me!"

The one cord vibrated to its utmost. Baldassarre clutched his own palms, driving his long nails into them, and burst into a sob with the rest.

CHAPTER XXV.

Outside the Duomo

WHILE Baldassarre was possessed by the voice of Savonarola, he had not noticed that another man had entered through the doorway behind him, and stood not far off, observing him. It was Piero di Cosimo, who took no heed of the preaching, having come solely to look at the escaped prisoner. During the pause, in which the preacher and his audience had given themselves up to inarticulate emotion, the new comer advanced and touched Baldassarre on the arm. He looked round with the tears still slowly rolling down his face, but with a vigorous sigh, as if he had done with that outburst. The painter spoke to him in a low tone:—

"Shall I cut your cords for you? I have heard how you were made prisoner."

Baldassarre did not reply immediately: he glanced suspiciously at the officious stranger. At last he said, "If you will."

"Better come outside," said Piero.

Baldassarre again looked at him suspiciously; and Piero, partly guessing his thought, smiled, took out a knife, and cut the cords. He began to think that the idea of the prisoner's madness was not improbable, there was something so peculiar in the expression of his face. "Well," he thought, "if he does any mischief, he'll soon get tied up again. The poor devil shall have a chance, at least."

"You are afraid of me," he said again, in an under-tone; "you don't want to tell me anything about yourself."

Baldassarre was folding his arms in enjoyment of that long-absent muscular sensation. He answered Piero with a less suspicious look and a tone which had some quiet decision in it.

"No, I have nothing to tell."

"As you please," said Piero, "but perhaps you want shelter, and may not know how hospitable we Florentines are to visitors with torn doublets and empty stomachs. There's a hospital for poor travellers outside all our gates, and, if you liked, I could put you in the way to one. There's no danger from your French soldier. He has been sent off."

Baldassarre nodded, and turned in silent acceptance of the offer, and he and Piero left the church together.

"You wouldn't like to sit to me for your portrait, should you?" said Piero, as they went along the Via dell' Oriuolo, on the way to the gate of Santa Croce. "I am a painter: I would give you money to get your portrait."

The suspicion returned to Baldassarre's glance, as he looked at Piero, and said decidedly, "No."

"Ah!" said the painter, curtly. "Well, go straight on, and you'll find the Porta Santa Croce, and outside it there's a hospital for travellers. So you'll not accept any service from me?"

"I give you thanks for what you have done already. I need no more."

"It is well," said Piero, with a shrug, and they turned away from each other.

"A mysterious old tiger!" thought the artist, "well worth painting. Ugly—with deep lines—looking as if the plough and the harrow had gone over his heart. A fine contrast to my bland and smiling Messer Greco—my *Bacco trionfante*,* who has married the fair Antigone in contradiction to all history and fitness. Aha! his scholar's blood curdled uncomfortably at the old fellow's clutch."

When Piero re-entered the Piazza del Duomo the multitude who had been listening to Fra Girolamo were pouring out from all the doors, and the haste they made to go on their several ways was a proof how important they held the preaching which had detained them from the other occupations of the day. The artist leaned against an angle of the Baptistery and watched the departing crowd, delighting in the variety of the garb and of the keen characteristic faces—faces such as Masaccio had painted* more than fifty years before: such as Domenico Ghirlandajo had not yet quite left off painting.

This morning was a peculiar occasion, and the Frate's audience, always multifarious, had represented even more completely than usual the various classes and political parties of Florence. There were men of high birth, accustomed to public charges at home and abroad, who had become newly conspicuous not only as enemies of the Medici and friends of popular government, but as thorough Piagnoni, espousing to the utmost the doctrines and practical teaching of the Frate, and frequenting San Marco as the seat of another Samuel;* some of them men of authoritative and handsome presence, like Francesco Valori, and perhaps also of a hot and arrogant temper, very much gratified by an immediate divine authority for bringing about freedom in their own way; others, like Soderini,* with less of the ardent Piagnone, and more of the wise politician. There were men, also of family, like Piero Capponi*—simply brave undoctrinal lovers of a sober republican liberty, who preferred fighting to arguing, and had no particular reasons for thinking any ideas false that kept out the Medici and made room for public spirit. At their elbows were doctors of law whose studies of Accursius* and his brethren had not so entirely consumed their ardour as to prevent them from becoming enthusiastic Piagnoni—Messer Luca Corsini himself, for example, who on a memorable occasion yet to come was to raise his learned arms in street stone-throwing for the cause of religion, freedom, and the Frate.* And among these dignities who carried their black *lucco* or furred mantle with an air of habitual authority, there was an abundant sprinkling of men with more contemplative and sensitive faces; scholars inheriting such high names as Strozzi and Acciajoli, who were already minded to take the cowl and join the community of San Marco;* artists, wrought to a new and higher ambition by the teaching of Savonarola—like that young painter who had lately surpassed himself in his fresco of the Divine child on the wall of the Frate's bare cell—unconscious yet that he would one day himself wear the tonsure and the cowl, and be called Fra Bartolommeo.* There was the mystic poet Girolamo Benevieni hastening, perhaps, to carry tidings of the beloved Frate's speedy coming to his friend Pico della Mirandola, who was never to see the light of another morning.* There were well-born women attired with such scrupulous plainness that their more refined grace was the chief distinction between them and their less aristocratic sisters. There was a predominant proportion of the genuine *popolani* or middle class, belonging both to the Major and Minor Arts, conscious of purses threatened by war-taxes. And more striking and various, perhaps, than all the other classes of the Frate's disciples, there was the long stream of poorer tradesmen and artisans, whose faith and hope in his Divine message varied from the rude undiscriminating trust in him as the friend of the poor and the enemy of the luxurious oppressive rich, to that eager tasting of all the subtleties of biblical interpretation, which takes a peculiarly strong hold on the sedentary artisan, illuminating the long dim spaces beyond the board where he stitches, with a pale flame that seems to him the light of Divine science.

But among these various disciples of the Frate were scattered many who were not in the least his disciples. Some were Mediceans who had already, from motives of fear and policy, begun to show the presiding spirit of the popular party a feigned deference. Others were sincere advocates of a free government, but regarded Savonarola simply as an ambitious monk—half-sagacious, half-fanatical—who had made himself a powerful instrument with the people, and must be accepted as an important social fact. There were even some of his bitter enemies: members of the old aristocratic anti-Medicean party—determined to try and get the reins once more tight in the hands of certain chief families; or else licentious young men, who detested him as the kill-joy of Florence. For the sermons in the Duomo had already become political incidents, attracting the ears of curiosity and malice, as well as of faith. The men of ideas, like young Niccolò Macchiavelli, went to observe and write reports to friends away in country villas; the men of appetites, like Dolfo Spini,* bent on hunting down the Frate as a public nuisance who made game scarce, went to feed their hatred and lie in wait for grounds of accusation.

Perhaps, while no preacher ever had a more massive influence than Savonarola, no preacher ever had more heterogeneous materials to work upon. And one secret of the massive influence lay in the highly mixed character of his preaching. Baldassarre, wrought into an ecstasy of self-martyring revenge, was only an extreme case among the partial and narrow sympathies of that audience. In Savonarola's preaching there were strains that appealed to the very finest susceptibilities of men's natures, and there were elements that gratified low egoism, tickled gossiping curiosity, and fascinated timorous superstition. His need of personal predominance, his labyrinthine allegorical interpretations of the Scriptures, his enigmatic visions, and his false certitude about the Divine intentions, never ceased, in his own large soul, to be ennobled by that fervid piety, that passionate sense of the infinite, that active sympathy, that clear-sighted demand for the subjection of selfish interests to the general good, which he had in common with the greatest of mankind. But for the mass of his audience all the pregnancy of his preaching lay in his strong assertion of supernatural claims, in his denunciatory visions, in the false certitude which gave his sermons the interest of a political bulletin; and having once held that audience in his mastery, it was necessary to his nature—it was necessary for their welfare—that he should *keep* the mastery. The effect was inevitable. No man ever struggled to retain power over a mixed multitude without suffering vitiation: his standard must be their lower needs, and not his own best insight.

The mysteries of human character have seldom been presented in a way more fitted to check the judgments of facile knowingness than in Girolamo Savonarola; but we can give him a reverence that needs no shutting of the eyes to fact, if we regard his life as a drama in which there were great inward modifications accompanying the outward changes. And up to this period, when his more direct action on political affairs had only just begun, it is probable that his imperious need of ascendancy had burned undiscernibly in the strong flame of his zeal for God and man.

It was the fashion of old, when an ox was led out for sacrifice to Jupiter, to chalk the dark spots, and give the offering a false show of unblemished whiteness. Let us fling away the chalk, and boldly say,—the victim is spotted, but it is not therefore in vain that his mighty heart is laid on the altar of men's highest hopes.

CHAPTER XXVI.

The Garment of Fear

AT six o'clock that evening most people in Florence were glad the entrance of the new Charlemagne was fairly over. Doubtless when the roll of drums, the blast of trumpets, and the tramp of horses along the Pisan road began to mingle with the pealing of the excited bells, it was a grand moment for those who were stationed on turreted roofs, and could see the long-winding terrible pomp on the background of the green hills and valley. There was no sunshine to light up the splendour of banners, and spears, and plumes, and silken surcoats, but there was no thick cloud of dust to hide it, and as the picked troops advanced into close view they could be seen all the more distinctly for the absence of dancing glitter. Tall and tough Scotch archers, Swiss halberdiers fierce and ponderous, nimble Gascons ready to wheel and climb, cavalry in which each man looked like a knight-errant with his indomitable spear and charger—it was satisfactory to be assured that they would injure nobody but the enemies of God! With that confidence at heart it was a less dubious pleasure to look at the array of strength and splendour in nobles and knights, and youthful pages of choice lineage—at the bossed and jewelled sword hilts, at the satin scarfs embroidered with strange symbolical devices of pious or gallant meaning, at the gold chains and jewelled aigrettes, at the gorgeous horse-trappings and brocaded mantles, and at the transcendent canopy carried by select youths above the head of the Most Christian King. To sum up with an old diarist, whose spelling and diction halted a little behind the wonders of this royal visit,—"*fù gran magnificenza.*"*

But for the Signoria, who had been waiting on their platform against the gates, and had to march out at the right moment, with their orator in front of them, to meet the mighty guest, the grandeur of the scene had been somewhat screened by unpleasant sensations. If Messer Luca Corsini could have had a brief Latin welcome depending from his mouth in legible characters, it would have been less confusing when the rain came on, and created an impatience in men and horses that broke off the delivery of his well-studied periods, and reduced the representatives of the scholarly city to offer a make-shift welcome in impromptu French. But that sudden confusion had created a great opportunity for Tito. As one of the secretaries he was among the officials who were stationed behind the Signoria, and with whom these highest dignities were promiscuously thrown when pressed upon by the horses.

"Somebody step forward and say a few words in French," said Soderini. But no one of high importance chose to risk a second failure. "You, Francesco Gaddi*—you can speak." But Gaddi, distrusting his own promptness, hung back, and, pushing Tito, said, "You, Melema."

Tito stepped forward in an instant, and with the air of profound deference that came as naturally to him as walking, said the few needful words in the name of the Signoria; then gave way gracefully, and let the King pass on. His presence of mind, which had failed him in the terrible crisis of the morning, had been a ready instrument this time. It was an excellent livery servant that never forsook him when danger was not visible. But when he was complimented on his opportune service, he laughed it off as a thing of no moment, and to those who had not witnessed it, let Gaddi have the credit of the improvised welcome. No wonder Tito was popular: the touchstone by which men try us is most often their own vanity.

Other things besides the oratorical welcome had turned out rather worse than had been expected. If everything had happened according to ingenious preconceptions, the Florentine procession of clergy and laity would not have found their way choked up and been obliged to take a make-shift course through the back streets, so as to meet the King at the Cathedral only. Also, if the young monarch under the canopy, seated on his charger with his lance upon his thigh, had looked more like a Charlemagne and less like a hastily modelled grotesque, the imagination of his admirers would have been much assisted. It might have been wished that the scourge of Italian wickedness and "Champion of the honour of women" had had a less miserable leg, and only the normal sum of toes; that his mouth had been of a less reptilian width of slit, his nose and head of a less exorbitant outline. But the thin leg rested on cloth of gold and pearls, and the face was only an interruption of a few square inches in the midst of black velvet and gold, and the blaze of rubies, and the brilliant tints of the embroidered and bepearled canopy—"*fù gran magnificenza.*"

And the people had cried *Francia! Francia!* with an enthusiasm proportioned to the splendour of the canopy which they had torn to pieces as their spoil, according to immemorial custom; royal lips had duly kissed the altar; and after all mischances the royal person and retinue were lodged in the Palace of the Via Larga, the rest of the nobles and gentry were dispersed among the great houses of Florence, and the terrible soldiery were encamped in the Prato and other open quarters. The business of the day was ended.

But the streets still presented a surprising aspect, such as Florentines had not seen before under the November stars. Instead of a gloom unbroken except by a lamp burning feebly here and there before a saintly image at the street corners, or by a stream of redder light from an open doorway, there were lamps suspended at the windows of all houses, so that men could walk along no less securely and commodiously than by day—"*fù gran magnificenza.*"

Along those illuminated streets Tito Melema was walking at about eight o'clock in the evening, on his way homeward. He had been exerting himself throughout the day under the pressure of hidden anxieties, and had at last made his escape unnoticed from the midst of after-supper gaiety. Once at leisure thoroughly to face and consider his circumstances, he hoped that he could so adjust himself to them and to all probabilities as to get rid of his childish fear. If he had only not been wanting in the presence of mind necessary to recognize Baldassarre under that surprise!—it would have been happier for him on all accounts; for he still winced under the sense that he was deliberately inflicting suffering on his father: he would very much have preferred that Baldassarre should be prosperous and happy. But he had left himself no second path now: there could be no conflict any longer: the only thing he had to do was to take care of himself.

While these thoughts were in his mind he was advancing from the Piazza di Santa Croce along the Via dei Benci, and as he neared the angle turning into the Borgo Santa Croce his ear was struck by a music which was not that of evening revelry, but of vigorous labour—the music of the anvil. Tito gave a slight start and quickened his pace, for the sounds had suggested a welcome thought. He knew that they came from the workshop of Niccolò Caparra, famous resort of all Florentines who cared for curious and beautiful iron-work.*

"What makes the giant at work so late?" thought Tito. "But so much the better for me. I can do that little bit of business to-night instead of to-morrow morning."

Preoccupied as he was, he could not help pausing a moment in admiration as he came in front of the workshop. The wide doorway, standing at the truncated angle of a great block or "isle" of houses,* was surmounted by a loggia roofed with fluted tiles, and supported by stone columns with roughly carved capitals. Against the red light framed in by the outline of the fluted tiles and columns stood in black relief the grand figure of Niccolò, with his huge arms in rhythmical rise and fall, first hiding and then disclosing the profile of his firm mouth and powerful brow. Two slighter ebony figures, one at the anvil, the other at the bellows, served to set off his superior massiveness.

Tito darkened the doorway with a very different outline, standing in silence, since it was useless to speak until Niccolò should deign to pause and notice him. That was not until the smith had beaten the head of an axe to the due sharpness of edge and dismissed it from his anvil. But in the meantime Tito had satisfied himself by a glance round the shop that the object of which he was in search had not disappeared.

Niccolò gave an unceremonious but good-humoured nod as he turned from the anvil and rested his hammer on his hip.

"What is it, Messer Tito? Business?"

"Assuredly, Niccolò; else I should not have ventured to interrupt you when you are working out of hours, since I take that as a sign that your work is pressing."

"I've been at the same work all day—making axes and spear-heads. And every fool that has passed my shop has put his pumpkin-head in to say, 'Niccolò, wilt thou not come and see the King of France and his soldiers?' and I've answered, 'No: I don't want to see their faces—I want to see their backs.'"

"Are you making arms for the citizens, then, Niccolò?—that they may have something better than rusty scythes and spits in case of an uproar?"

"We shall see. Arms are good, and Florence is likely to want them. The Frate tells us we shall get Pisa again, and I hold with the Frate; but I should be glad to know how the promise is to be fulfilled, if we don't get plenty of good weapons forged? The

Frate sees a long way before him; that I believe. But he doesn't see birds caught with winking at them, as some of our people try to make out. He sees sense, and not nonsense. But you're a bit of a Medicean, Messer Tito Melema. *Ebbene!* so I've been myself in my time, before the cask began to run sour. What's your business?"

"Simply to know the price of that fine coat of mail I saw hanging up here the other day. I want to buy it for a certain personage who needs a protection of that sort under his doublet."

"Let him come and buy it himself, then," said Niccolò, bluntly. "I'm rather nice about what I sell, and whom I sell to. I like to know who's my customer."

"I know your scruples, Niccolò. But that is only defensive armour: it can hurt nobody."

"True: but it may make the man who wears it feel himself all the safer if he should want to hurt somebody. No, no: it's not my own work; but it's fine work of Maso of Brescia:* I should be loth for it to cover the heart of a scoundrel. I must know who is to wear it."

"Well, then, to be plain with you, *Niccolò mio*, I want it myself," said Tito, knowing it was useless to try persuasion. "The fact is, I am likely to have a journey to take—and you know what journeying is in these times. You don't suspect *me* of treason against the Republic?"

"No, I know no harm of you," said Niccolò, in his blunt way again. "But have you the money to pay for the coat? For you've passed my shop often enough to know my sign: you've seen the burning account-books—I trust nobody. The price is twenty florins, and that's because it's second hand. You're not likely to have so much money with you. Let it be till to-morrow."

"I happen to have the money," said Tito, who had been winning at play the day before, and had not emptied his purse. "I'll carry the armour home with me."

Niccolò reached down the finely wrought coat, which fell together into little more than two handfuls.

"There, then," he said, when the florins had been told down on his palm. "Take the coat. It's made to cheat sword or poniard or arrow. But, for my part, I would never put such a thing on. It's like carrying fear about with one."

Niccolò's words had an unpleasant intensity of meaning for Tito. But he smiled and said,—

"Ah, Niccolò, we scholars are all cowards. Handling the pen doesn't thicken the arm as your hammer-wielding does. Addio!"

He folded the armour under his mantle, and hastened across the Ponte Rubaconte.

[*DECEMBER 1862*]

CHAPTER XXVII.

The Young Wife

WHILE Tito was hastening across the bridge with the new-bought armour under his mantle, Romola was pacing up and down the old library, thinking of him and longing for his return.

It was but a few fair faces that had not looked forth from windows that day to see the entrance of the French King and his nobles. One of the few was Romola's. She had been present at no festivities since her father had died—died quite suddenly in his chair, three months before.

"Is not Tito coming to write?" he had said, when the bell had long ago sounded the usual hour in the evening. He had not asked before, from dread of a negative; but Romola had seen by his listening face and restless movements that nothing else was in his mind.

"No, father, he had to go to a supper at the Cardinal's: you know he is wanted so much by every one," she answered, in a tone of gentle excuse.

"Ah! then perhaps he will bring some positive word about the library; the cardinal promised last week," said Bardo, apparently pacified by this hope.

He was silent a little while; then, suddenly flushing, he said,—

"I must go on without him, Romola. Get the pen. He has brought me no new text to comment on; but I must say what I want to say about the New Platonists. I shall die and nothing will have been done. Make haste, my Romola."

"I am ready, father," she said, the next minute, holding the pen in her hand.

But there was silence. Romola took no note of this for a little while, accustomed to pauses in dictation; and when at last she looked round inquiringly, there was no change of attitude.

"I am quite ready, father!"

Still Bardo was silent, and his silence was never again broken.

Romola looked back on that hour with some indignation against herself, because even with the first outburst of her sorrow there had mingled the irrepressible thought, "Perhaps my life with Tito will be more perfect now."

For the dream of a triple life with an undivided sum of happiness had not been quite fulfilled. The rainbow-tinted shower of sweets, to have been perfectly typical, should have had some invisible seeds of bitterness mingled with them; the crowned Ariadne, under the snowing roses, had felt more and more the presence of unexpected thorns. It was not Tito's fault, Romola had continually assured herself. He was still all gentleness to her, and to her father also. But it was in the nature of things—she saw it clearly now—it was in the nature of things that no one but herself could go on month after month, and year after year, fulfilling patiently all her father's monotonous exacting demands. Even she, whose sympathy with her father had made all the passion and religion of her young years, had not always been patient, had been inwardly very rebellious. It was true that before their marriage, and even for some time after, Tito had seemed more unwearying than herself; but then, of course, the effort had the ease of novelty. We assume a load with confident readiness, and up to a certain point the growing irksomeness of pressure is tolerable; but at last the desire for relief can no longer be resisted. Romola said to herself that she had been very foolish and ignorant in her girlish time: she was wiser now, and would make no unfair demands on the man to whom she had given her best woman's love and worship. The breath of sadness that still cleaved to her lot while she saw her father month after month sink from elation into new disappointment as Tito gave him less and less of his time, and made bland excuses for not continuing his own share of the joint work—that sadness was no fault of Tito's, she said, but rather of their inevitable destiny. If he stayed less and less with her, why, that was because they could hardly ever be alone. His caresses were no less tender: if she pleaded timidly on any one evening that he should stay with her father instead of going to another engagement which was not peremptory, he excused himself with such charming gaiety, he seemed to linger about her with such fond playfulness before he could quit her, that she could only feel a little heart-ache in the midst of her love, and then go to her father and try to soften his vexation and disappointment. But all the while inwardly her imagination was busy trying to see how Tito could be as good as she had thought he was, and yet find it impossible to sacrifice those pleasures of society which were necessarily more vivid to a bright creature like him than to the common run of men. She herself would have liked more gaiety, more admiration: it was true, she gave it up willingly for her father's sake—she would have given up much more than that for the sake even of a slight wish on Tito's part. It was clear that their natures differed widely; but perhaps it was no more than the inherent difference between man and woman, that made her affections more absorbing. If there were any other difference she tried to persuade herself that the inferiority was on her side. Tito was really kinder than she was, better-tempered, less proud and resentful; he had no angry retorts, he met all complaints with perfect sweetness; he only escaped as quietly as he could from things that were unpleasant.

It belongs to every large nature, when it is not under the immediate power of some strong unquestioning emotion, to suspect itself, and doubt the truth of its own impressions, conscious of possibilities beyond its own horizon. And Romola was urged to doubt herself the more by the necessity of interpreting her disappointment in her life with Tito so as to satisfy at once her love and her pride. Disappointment? Yes, there was no other milder word that would tell the truth. Perhaps all women had to suffer the disappointment of ignorant hopes, if she only knew their experience. Still, there had been something peculiar in her lot: her relation to her father had claimed unusual sacrifices from her husband. Tito had once thought that his love would make those sacrifices easy; his love had not been great enough for that. She was not justified in resenting a self-delusion. No! resentment must not rise: all endurance seemed easy to Romola rather than a state of mind in which she would admit to herself that Tito acted unworthily. If she had felt a new heart-ache, in the solitary hours with her father through the last months of his life, it had been by no inexcusable fault of her husband's; and now—it was a hope that would make its presence felt even in the first moments when her father's place was empty—there was no longer any importunate claim to divide her from Tito; their young lives would flow in one current, and their true marriage would begin.

But the sense of something like guilt towards her father, in a hope that grew out of his death, gave all the more force to the anxiety with which she dwelt on the means of fulfilling his supreme wish. That piety towards his memory was all the atonement she could make now for a thought that seemed akin to joy at his loss. The laborious simple life, pure from vulgar corrupting ambitions, embittered by the frustration of the dearest hopes, imprisoned at last in total darkness—a long seed-time without a harvest—was at an end now, and all that remained of it besides the tablet in Santa Croce and the unfinished commentary on Tito's text, was the collection of manuscripts and antiquities, fruit of half a century's toil and frugality. The fulfilment of her father's life-long ambition about this library was a sacramental obligation for Romola.

The precious relic was safe from creditors, for when the deficit towards their payment had been ascertained, Bernardo del Nero, though he was far from being among the wealthiest Florentines, had advanced the necessary sum of about a thousand florins—a large sum in those days—accepting a lien on the collection as a security.*

"The State will repay me," he had said to Romola, making light of the service which had really cost him some inconvenience. "If the Cardinal* finds a building, as he seems to say he will, our Signoria may consent to do the rest. I have no children, I can afford the risk."

But within the last ten days all hopes in the Medici had come to an end: and the famous Medicean collections in the Via Larga were themselves in danger of dispersion. French agents had already begun to see that such very fine antique gems as Lorenzo had collected belonged by right to the first nation in Europe; and the Florentine State, which had got possession of the Medicean library, was likely to be glad of a customer for it. With a war to recover Pisa hanging over it, and with the certainty of having to pay large subsidies to the French King, the State was likely to prefer money to manuscripts.

To Romola these grave political changes had gathered their chief interest from their bearing on the fulfilment of her father's wish. She had been brought up in learned seclusion from the interests of actual life, and had been accustomed to think of heroic deeds and great principles as something antithetic to the vulgar present, of the Pnyx and the Forum* as something more worthy of attention than the councils of living Florentine men.

And now the expulsion of the Medici meant little more for her than the extinction of her best hope about her father's library. The times, she knew, were unpleasant for friends of the Medici, like her godfather and Tito: superstitious shopkeepers, and the stupid rabble, were full of suspicions; but her new keen interest in public events, in the outbreak of war, in the issue of the French King's visit, in the changes that were likely to happen in the State, was kindled solely by the sense of love and duty to her father's memory. All Romola's ardour had been concentrated in her affections. Her share in her father's learned pursuits had been for her little more than a toil which was borne for his sake; and Tito's airy brilliant faculty had no attraction for her that was not merged in the deeper sympathies that belong to young love and trust. Romola had had contact with no mind that could stir the larger possibilities of her nature; they lay folded and crushed like embryonic wings, making no element in her consciousness beyond an occasional vague uneasiness.

But this new personal interest of hers in public affairs had made her care at last to understand precisely what influence Fra Girolamo's preaching was likely to have on the turn of events. Changes in the form of the State were talked of, and all she could learn from Tito, whose secretaryship and serviceable talents carried him into the heart of public business, made her only the more eager to fill out her lonely day by going to hear for herself what it was that was just now leading all Florence by the ears. This morning, for the first time, she had been to hear one of the Advent sermons in the Duomo. When Tito had left her, she had formed a sudden resolution, and after visiting the spot where her father was buried in Santa Croce, had walked on to the Duomo. The memory of that last scene with Dino was still vivid within her whenever she recalled it, but it had receded behind the experience and anxieties of her married life. The new sensibilities and questions which it had half awakened in her were quieted again by that subjection to her husband's mind which is felt by every wife who loves her husband with passionate devotedness and full reliance. She remembered the effect of Fra Girolamo's voice and presence on her as a ground for expecting that his sermon might move her in spite of his being a narrow-minded monk. But the sermon did no more than slightly deepen her previous impression, that this fanatical preacher of tribulations was after all a man towards whom it might be possible for her to feel personal regard and reverence. The denunciations and exhortations simply arrested her attention. She felt no terror, no pangs of conscience: it was the roll of distant thunder, that seemed grand, but could not shake her. But when she heard Savonarola invoke martyrdom, she sobbed with the rest: she felt herself penetrated with a new sensation—a strange sympathy with something apart from all the definable interests of her life. It was not altogether unlike the thrill which had accompanied certain rare heroic touches in history and poetry; but the resemblance was as that between the memory of music, and the sense of being possessed by actual vibrating harmonies.

But that transient emotion, strong as it was, seemed to lie quite outside the inner chamber and sanctuary of her life. She was not thinking of Fra Girolamo now; she was listening anxiously for the step of her husband. During these three months of their double solitude she had thought of each day as an epoch in which their union might begin to be more perfect. She was conscious of being sometimes a little too sad or too urgent about what concerned her father's memory—a little too critical or coldly silent when Tito narrated the things that were said and done in the world he frequented—a little too hasty in suggesting that by living quite simply as her father had done, they might become rich enough to pay Bernardo del Nero, and reduce the difficulties about the library. It was not possible that Tito could feel so strongly on this last point as she did, and it was asking a great deal from him to give up luxuries for which he really laboured. The next time Tito came home she would be careful to suppress all those promptings that seemed to isolate her from him. Romola was labouring, as a loving woman must, to subdue her nature to her husband's. The great need of her heart compelled her to strangle, with desperate resolution, every rising impulse of suspicion, pride, and resentment; she felt equal to any self-infliction that would save her from ceasing to love. That would have been like the hideous nightmare in which the world had seemed to break away all round her, and leave her feet overhanging the darkness. Romola had never distinctly imagined such a future for herself; she was only beginning to feel the presence of effort in that clinging trust which had once been mere repose.

She waited and listened long, for Tito had not come straight home after leaving Niccolò Caparra, and it was more than two hours after the time when he was crossing the Ponte Rubaconte that Romola heard the great door of the court turning on its hinges, and hastened to the head of the stone steps. There was a lamp hanging over the stairs, and they could see each other distinctly as he ascended. The eighteen months had produced a more definable change in Romola's face than in Tito's: the expression was more subdued, less cold, and more beseeching, and, as the pink flush overspread her face now, in her joy that the long waiting was at an end, she was much lovelier than on the day when Tito had first seen her. On that day, any onlooker would have said that Romola's nature was made to command, and Tito's to bend; yet now Romola's mouth was quivering a little, and there was some timidity in her glance.

He made an effort to smile, as she said,

"My Tito, you are tired; it has been a fatiguing day: is it not true?"

Maso was there, and no more was said until they had crossed the antechamber and closed the door of the library behind them. The wood was burning brightly on the great dogs; that was one welcome for Tito, late as he was, and Romola's gentle voice was another.

He just turned and kissed her when she took off his mantle; then he went towards a high-backed chair placed for him near the fire, threw himself into it, and flung away his cap, saying, not peevishly, but in a fatigued tone of remonstrance, as he gave a slight shudder,

"Romola, I wish you would give up sitting in this library. Surely our own rooms are pleasanter in this chill weather."

Romola felt hurt. She had never seen Tito so indifferent in his manner; he was usually full of lively solicitous attention. And she had thought so much of his return to her after the long day's absence! He must be very weary.

"I wonder you have forgotten, Tito," she answered, looking at him anxiously, as if she wanted to read an excuse for him in the signs of bodily fatigue. "You know I am making the catalogue on the new plan that my father wished for; you have not time to help me, so I must work at it closely."

Tito, instead of meeting Romola's glance, closed his eyes and rubbed his hands over his face and hair. He felt he was behaving unlike himself, but he would make amends to-morrow. The terrible resurrection of secret fears, which, if Romola had known them, would have alienated her from him for ever, caused him to feel an alienation already begun between them—caused him to feel a certain repulsion towards a woman from whose mind he was in danger. The feeling had taken hold of him unawares, and he was vexed with himself for behaving in this new cold way to her. He could not suddenly command any affectionate looks or words; he could only exert himself to say what might serve as an excuse.

"I am not well, Romola; you must not be surprised if I am peevish."

"Ah, you have had so much to tire you to-day," said Romola, kneeling down close to him, and laying her arm on his chest while she put his hair back caressingly.

Suddenly she drew her arm away with a start, and a gaze of alarmed inquiry.

"What have you got on under your tunic, Tito? Something as hard as iron."

"It *is* iron—it is chain armour," he said at once. He was prepared for the surprise and the question, and he spoke quietly, as of something that he was not hurried to explain.

"There was some unexpected danger to-day, then?" said Romola, in a tone of conjecture. "You had it lent to you for the procession?"

"No; it is my own. I shall be obliged to wear it constantly, for some time."

"What is it that threatens you, my Tito?" said Romola, looking terrified, and clinging to him again.

"Every one is threatened in these times, who is not a rabid enemy of the Medici. Don't look distressed, my Romola—this armour will make me safe against covert attacks."

Tito put his hand on her neck and smiled. This little dialogue abut the armour had broken through the new crust, and made a channel for the sweet habit of kindness.

"But my godfather, then," said Romola; "is not he, too, in danger? And he takes no precautions—ought he not? since he must surely be in more danger than you, who have so little influence compared with him."

"It is just because I am less important that I am in more danger," said Tito, readily. "I am suspected constantly of being an envoy. And men like Messer Bernardo are protected by their position and their extended family connections, which spread among all parties, while I am a Greek that nobody would avenge."

"But, Tito, is it a fear of some particular person, or only a vague sense of danger that has made you think of wearing this?" Romola was unable to repel the idea of a degrading fear in Tito, which mingled itself with her anxiety.

"I have had special threats," said Tito, "but I must beg you to be silent on the subject, my Romola. I shall consider that you have broken my confidence, if you mention it to your godfather."

"Assuredly I will not mention it," said Romola, blushing, "if you wish it to be a secret. But, dearest Tito," she added, after a moment's pause, in a tone of loving anxiety, "it will make you very wretched."

"What will make me wretched?" he said, with a scarcely perceptible movement across his face, as from some darting sensation.

"This fear—this heavy armour. I can't help shuddering as I feel it under my arm. I could fancy it a story of enchantment—that some malignant fiend had changed your sensitive human skin into a hard shell. It seems so unlike my bright, light-hearted Tito!"

"Then you would rather have your husband exposed to danger, when he leaves you?" said Tito, smiling. "If you don't mind my being poniarded or shot, why need I mind? I will give up the armour—shall I?"

"No, Tito, no. I am fanciful. Do not heed what I have said. But such crimes are surely not common in Florence? I have always heard my father and godfather say so. Have they become frequent lately?"

"It is not unlikely they will become frequent, with the bitter hatreds that are being bred continually."

Romola was silent a few moments. She shrank from insisting further on the subject of the armour. She tried to shake it off.

"Tell me what has happened to-day," she said, in a cheerful tone. "Has all gone off well?"

"Excellently well. First of all, the rain came and put an end to Luca Corsini's oration, which nobody wanted to hear, and a ready-tongued personage—some say it was Gaddi, some say it was Melema, but really it was done so quickly no one knows who it was—had the honour of giving the Cristianissimo the briefest possible welcome in bad French."

"Tito, it was you, I know," said Romola, smiling brightly, and kissing him. "How is it you never care about claiming anything? And after that?"

"Oh! after that, there was a show of armour, and jewels, and trappings, such as you saw at the last Florentine *giostra*, only a great deal more of them. There was strutting, and prancing, and confusion, and scrambling, and the people shouted, and the Cristianissimo smiled from ear to ear. And after that there was a great deal of flattery, and eating, and play. I was at Tornabuoni's. I will tell you about it to-morrow."

"Yes, dearest—never mind now. But is there any more hope that things will end peaceably for Florence—that the Republic will not get into fresh troubles?"

Tito gave a shrug. "Florence will have no peace but what it pays well for—that is clear."

Romola's face saddened, but she checked herself, and said, cheerfully, "You would not guess where I went to-day, Tito. I went to the Duomo, to hear Fra Girolamo."

Tito looked startled; he had immediately thought of Baldassarre's entrance into the Duomo: but Romola gave his look another meaning.

"You are surprised, are you not? It was a sudden thought. I want to know all about the public affairs now, and I determined to hear for myself what the Frate promised the people about this French invasion."

"Well, and what did you think of the prophet?"

"He certainly has a very mysterious power, that man. A great deal of his sermon what was I expected; but once I was strangely moved—I sobbed with the rest."

"Take care, Romola," said Tito, playfully, feeling relieved that she had said nothing about Baldassarre; "you have a touch of fanaticism in you. I shall have you seeing visions, like your brother."

"No; it was the same with every one else. He carried them all with him; unless it were that gross Dolfo Spini, whom I saw there making grimaces. There was even a wretched-looking man, with a rope round his neck—an escaped prisoner, I should think, who had run in for shelter—a very wild-eyed old man: I saw him with great tears rolling down his cheeks, as he looked and listened quite eagerly."

There was a slight pause before Tito spoke.

"I saw the man," he said, "the prisoner. I was outside the Duomo with Lorenzo Tornabuoni when he ran in. He had escaped from a French soldier. Did you see him when you came out?"

"No, he went out with our good old Piero di Cosimo. I saw Piero come in and cut off his rope, and take him out of the church. But you want rest, Tito? You feel ill?"

"Yes," said Tito, rising. The horrible sense that he must live in continual dread of what Baldassarre had said or done pressed upon him like cold weight.

CHAPTER XXVIII.

The Painted Record

FOUR days later, Romola was on her way to the house of Piero di Cosimo, in the Via Gualfonda. Some of the streets through which she had to pass were lined with Frenchmen who were gazing at Florence, and with Florentines who were gazing at the French, and the gaze was not on either side entirely friendly and admiring. The first nation in Europe, of necessity finding itself, when out of its own country, in the presence of general inferiority, naturally assumed an air of conscious pre-eminence; and the Florentines, who had taken such pains to play the host amiably, were getting into the worst humour with their too superior guests.

For after the first smiling compliments and festivities were over—after wondrous Mysteries* with unrivalled machinery of floating clouds and angels had been presented in churches—after the royal guest had honoured Florentine dames with much of his Most Christian ogling at balls and suppers, and business had begun to be talked of—it appeared that the new Charlemagne regarded Florence as a conquered city, inasmuch as he had entered it with his lance in rest,* talked of leaving his viceroy behind him, and had thoughts of bringing back the Medici.

Singular logic this appeared to be on the part of an elect instrument of God! since the policy of Piero de' Medici, disowned by the people, had been the only offence of Florence against the Majesty of France. And Florence was determined not to submit. The determination was being expressed very strongly in consultations of citizens inside the Old Palace, and it was beginning to show itself on the broad flags of the streets and piazze wherever there was an opportunity of flouting an insolent Frenchman. Under these circumstances the streets were not altogether a pleasant promenade for well-born women; but Romola, shrouded in her black veil and mantle, and with old Maso by her side, felt secure enough from impertinent observation.

And she was impatient to visit Piero di Cosimo. A copy of her father's portrait as Œdipus, which he had long ago undertaken to make for her, was not yet finished; and Piero was so uncertain in his work—sometimes, when the demand was not peremptory, laying aside a picture for months; sometimes thrusting it into a corner or coffer, where it was likely to be utterly forgotten—that she felt it necessary to watch over his progress. She was a favourite with the painter, and he was inclined to fulfil any wish of hers, but no general inclination could be trusted as a safeguard against his sudden whims. He had told her the week before that the picture would perhaps be finished by this time; and Romola was nervously anxious to have in her possession a copy of the only portrait existing of her father in the days of his blindness, lest his image should grow dim in her mind. The sense of defect in her devotedness to him made her cling with all the force of compunction as well as affection to the duties of memory. Love does not aim simply at the conscious good of the beloved object: it is not satisfied without perfect loyalty of heart; it aims at its own completeness.

Romola, by special favour, was allowed to intrude upon the painter without previous notice. She lifted the iron slide and called Piero in a flute-like tone, as the little maiden with the eggs had done in Tito's presence. Piero was quick in answering, but when he opened the door he accounted for his quickness in a manner that was not complimentary.

"Ah, Madonna Romola, is it you? I thought my eggs were come; I wanted them."

"I have brought you something better than hard eggs, Piero. Maso has got a little basket full of cakes and *confetti* for you," said Romola, smiling, as she put back her veil. She took the basket from Maso, and stepping into the house, said,

"I know you like these things when you can have them without trouble. Confess you do."

"Yes, when they come to me as easily as the light does," said Piero, folding his arms and looking down at the sweetmeats as Romola uncovered them and glanced at him archly. "And they are come along with the light now," he added, lifting his eyes to her face and hair with a painter's admiration, as her hood, dragged by the weight of her veil, fell backward.

"But I know what the sweetmeats are for," he went on; "they are to stop my mouth while you scold me. Well, go on into the next room, and you will see I've done something to the picture since you saw it, though it's not finished yet. But I didn't promise, you know: I take care not to promise:

'Chi promette e non mantiene
L'anima sua non va mai bene.'"*

The door opening on the wild garden was closed now, and the painter was at work. Not at Romola's picture, however. That was standing on the floor, propped against the wall, and Piero stooped to lift it, that he might carry it into the proper light. But in lifting away this picture, he had disclosed another—the oil-sketch of Tito, to which he had made an important addition within the last few days. It was so much smaller than the other picture that it stood far within it, and Piero, apt to forget where he had placed anything, was not aware of what he had revealed as, peering at some detail in the painting which he held in his hands, he went to place it on an easel. But Romola exclaimed, flushing with astonishment,

"That is Tito!"

Piero looked round, and gave a silent shrug. He was vexed at his own forgetfulness.

She was still looking at the sketch in astonishment; but presently she turned towards the painter, and said with puzzled alarm,

"What a strange picture! When did you paint it? What does it mean?"

"A mere fancy of mine," said Piero, lifting off his skull-cap, scratching his head, and making the usual grimace by which he avoided the betrayal of any feeling. "I wanted a handsome young face for it, and your husband's was just the thing."

He went forward, stooped down to the picture, and lifting it away with its back to Romola, pretended to be giving it a passing examination, before putting it aside as a thing not good enough to show.

But Romola, who had the fact of the armour in her mind, and was penetrated by this strange coincidence of things which associated Tito with the idea of Fear, went to his elbow and said,—

"Don't put it away; let me look again. That man with the rope round his neck—I saw him—I saw you come to him in the Duomo. What was it that made you put him into a picture with Tito?"

Piero saw no better resource than to tell part of the truth.

"It was a mere accident. The man was running away—running up the steps, and caught hold of your husband: I suppose he had stumbled. I happened to be there, and saw it, and I thought the savage-looking old fellow was a good subject. But it's worth nothing—it's only a freakish daub of mine," Piero ended, contemptuously, moving the sketch away with an air of decision, and putting it on a high shelf. "Come and look at the Œdipus."

He had shown a little too much anxiety in putting the sketch out of her sight, and had produced the very impression he had sought to prevent—that there was really something unpleasant, something disadvantageous to Tito, in the circumstances out of which the picture arose. But this impression silenced her: her pride and delicacy shrank from questioning farther, where questions might seem to imply that she could entertain even a slight suspicion against her husband. She merely said, in as quiet a tone as she could,

"He was a strange piteous-looking man, that prisoner. Do you know anything more of him?"

"No more: I showed him the way to the hospital, that's all. See now, the face of Œdipus is pretty nearly finished; tell me what you think of it."

Romola now gave her whole attention to her father's portrait, standing in long silence before it.

"Ah!" she said at last, "you have done what I wanted. You have given it more of the listening look. My good Piero"—she turned towards him with bright moist eyes—"I am very grateful to you."

"Now, that's what I can't bear in you women," said Piero, turning impatiently, and kicking aside the objects that littered the floor—"you are always pouring out feelings where there's no call for them. Why should you be grateful to me for a picture you pay me for, especially when I make you wait for it? And if I paint a picture, I suppose it's for my own pleasure and credit to paint it well, eh? Are you to thank a man for not being a rogue or a noodle? It's enough if he himself thanks Messer Domeneddio, who has made him neither the one nor the other. But women think walls are held together with honey."

"You crusty Piero! I forgot how snappish you are. Here, put this nice sweetmeat in your mouth," said Romola, smiling through her tears, and taking something very crisp and sweet from the little basket.

Piero accepted it very much as that proverbial bear that dreams of pears might accept an exceedingly mellow "swan-egg"*—really liking the gift, but accustomed to have his pleasures and pains concealed under a shaggy coat.

"It's good, Madonna Antigone," said Piero, putting his fingers in the basket for another. He had eaten nothing but hard eggs for a fortnight. Romola stood opposite him, feeling her new anxiety suspended for a little while by the sight of this naïve enjoyment.

"Good-by, Piero," she said, presently, setting down the basket. "I promise not to thank you if you finish the portrait soon and well. I will tell you, you were bound to do it for your own credit."

"Good," said Piero, curtly, helping her with much deftness to fold her mantle and veil round her.

"I'm glad she asked no more questions about that sketch," he thought, when he had closed the door behind her. "I should be sorry for her to guess that I thought her fine husband a good model for a coward. But I made light of it; she'll not think of it again."

Piero was too sanguine, as open-hearted men are apt to be when they attempt a little clever simulation. The thought of the picture pressed more and more on Romola as she walked homeward. She could not help putting together the two facts of the chain armour and the encounter mentioned by Piero, between her husband and the prisoner, which had happened on the morning of the day when the armour was adopted. That look of terror which the painter had given Tito, had he seen it? What could it all mean?

"It means nothing," she tried to assure herself. "It was a mere coincidence. Shall I ask Tito about it?" Her mind said at last, "No: I will not question him about anything he did not tell me spontaneously. It is an offence against the trust I owe him." Her heart said, "I dare not ask him." There was a terrible flaw in the trust: she was afraid of any hasty movement, as men are who hold something precious and want to believe that it is not broken.

CHAPTER XXIX.

A Moment of Triumph

"THE old fellow has vanished; went on towards Arezzo the next morning; not liking the smell of the French, I suppose, after being their prisoner. I went to the hospital to inquire after him; I wanted to know if those broth-making monks had found out whether he was in his right mind or not. However, they said he showed no signs of madness—only took no notice of questions, and seemed to be planting a vine* twenty miles off. He was a mysterious old tiger. I should have liked to know something more about him."

It was in Nello's shop that Piero di Cosimo was speaking, on the twenty-fourth of November, just a week after the entrance of the French. There was a party of six or seven assembled at the rather unusual hour of three in the afternoon; for it was a day on which all Florence was excited by the prospect of some decisive political event. Every lounging-place was full, and every shopkeeper who had no wife or deputy to leave in charge stood at his door with his thumbs in his belt; while the streets were constantly sprinkled with artisans pausing or passing lazily like floating splinters, ready to rush forward impetuously if any object attracted them.

Nello had been thrumming the lute as he half sat on the board against the shop window, and kept an outlook towards the piazza.

"Ah," he said, laying down the lute, with emphasis, "I would not for a gold florin have missed that sight of the French soldiers waddling in their broad shoes after their runaway prisoners! That comes of leaving my shop to shave magnificent chins. It is always so: if ever I quit this navel of the earth something takes the opportunity of happening in my piazza."

"Yes, you ought to have been there," said Piero, in his biting way, "just to see your favourite Greek look as frightened as if Satanasso had laid hold of him. I like to see your ready-smiling *Messeri* caught in a sudden wind and obliged to show their lining in spite of themselves. What colour do you think a man's liver is, who looks like a bleached deer as soon as a chance stranger lays hold of him suddenly?"

"Piero, keep that vinegar of thine as sauce to thine own eggs! What is it against my *bel erudito* that he looked startled when he felt a pair of claws upon him and saw an unchained madman at his elbow? Your scholar is not like those beastly Swiss and Germans, whose heads are only fit for battering-rams, and who have such large appetites that they think nothing of taking a cannon-ball before breakfast. We Florentines count some other qualities in a man besides that vulgar stuff called bravery, which is to be got by hiring dunderheads at so much per dozen. I tell you, as soon as men found out that they had more brains than oxen they set the oxen to draw for them, and when we Florentines found out that we had more brains than other men we set them to fight for us."

"Treason, Nello!" a voice called out from the inner sanctum, "that is not the doctrine of the State. Florence is grinding its weapons; and the last well-authenticated vision announced by the Frate was Mars standing on the Palazzo Vecchio with his arm on the shoulder of San Giovanni Battista, who was offering him a piece of honeycomb."*

"It is well, Francesco," said Nello. "Florence has a few thicker skulls that may do to bombard Pisa with; there will still be the finer spirits left at home to do the thinking and the shaving. And, as for our Piero here, if he makes such a point of valour, let him carry his biggest brush for a weapon and his palette for a shield, and challenge the widest-mouthed Swiss he can see in the Prato to a single combat."

"*Va*, Nello," growled Piero, "thy tongue runs on as usual, like a mill when the Arno's full—whether there's grist or not."

"Excellent grist, I tell thee. For it would be as reasonable to expect a grizzled painter like thee to be fond of getting a javelin inside thee as to expect a man whose wits have been sharpened on the classics to like having his handsome face clawed by a wild beast."

"There you go, supposing you'll get people to put their legs into a sack because you call it a pair of hosen," said Piero. "Who said anything about a wild beast, or about an unarmed man rushing on battle? Fighting is a trade, and it's not my trade. I should be a fool to run after danger, but I could face it if it came to me."

"How is it you're so afraid of the thunder then, my Piero?" said Nello, determined to chase down the accuser. "You ought to be able to understand why one man is shaken by a thing that seems a trifle to others—you who hide yourself with the rats as soon as a storm comes on."*

"That is because I have a particular sensibility to loud sounds; it has nothing to do with my courage or my conscience."

"Well, and Tito Melema may have a peculiar sensibility to being laid hold of unexpectedly by prisoners who have run away from French soldiers. Men are born with antipathies; I myself can't abide the smell of mint. Tito was born with an antipathy to old prisoners who stumble and clutch. Ecco!"

There was a general laugh at Nello's defence, and it was clear that Piero's disinclination towards Tito was not shared by the company. The painter, with his undecipherable grimace, took the tow from his scarsella and stuffed his ears in indignant contempt, while Nello went on triumphantly,

"No, my Piero, I can't afford to have my *bel erudito* decried; and Florence can't afford it either, with her scholars moulting off her at the early age of forty. Our Phœnix Pico just gone straight to Paradise, as the Frate has informed us; and the incomparable Poliziano, not two months since,* gone—well, well, let us hope he is not gone to the eminent scholars in the Malebolge."

"By the way," said Francesco Cei, "have you heard that Camilla Rucellai* has outdone the Frate in her prophecies? She prophesied two years ago that Pico would die in the time of lilies. He has died in November. 'Not at all the time of lilies,' said the scorners. 'Go to!' says Camilla; 'it is the lilies of France I meant, and it seems to me they are close enough under your nostrils.' I say, 'Euge,* Camilla!' If the Frate can prove that any one of his visions has been as well fulfilled, I'll declare myself a Piagnone to-morrow."

"You are something too flippant about the Frate, Francesco," said Pietro Cennini, the scholarly. "We are all indebted to him in these weeks for preaching peace and quietness, and the laying aside of party quarrels. They are men of small discernment who would be glad to see the people slipping the Frate's leash just now. And if the Most Christian King is obstinate about the treaty to-day, and will not sign what is fair and honourable to Florence, Fra Girolamo is the man we must trust in to bring him to reason."

"You speak truth, Messer Pietro," said Nello, "the Frate is one of the firmest nails Florence has to hang on—at least, that is the opinion of the most respectable chins I have the honour of shaving. But young Messer Niccolò was saying here the other morning—and, doubtless, Francesco means the same thing—there is as wonderful a power of stretching in the meaning of visions as in Dido's bull's hide.* It seems to me a dream may mean whatever comes after it. As our Franco Sacchetti says,* a woman dreams over night of a serpent biting her, breaks a drinking-cup the next day, and cries out, 'Look you, I thought something would happen—it's plain now what the serpent meant.'"

"But the Frate's visions are not of that sort," said Cronaca. "He not only says what will happen—that the Church will be scourged and renovated, and the heathens converted—he says it shall happen quickly. He is no slippery pretender who provides loopholes for himself, he is—"

"What is this? what is this?" exclaimed Nello, jumping off the board, and putting his head out at the door. "Here are people streaming into the piazza, and shouting. Something must have happened in the Via Larga. Aha!" he burst forth with delighted astonishment, stepping out, laughing, and waving his cap.

All the rest of the company hastened to the door. News from the Via Larga was just what they had been waiting for. But if the news had come into the piazza, they were not a little surprised at the form of its advent. Carried above the shoulders of the people, on a bench apparently snatched up in the street, sat Tito Melema, in smiling amusement at the compulsion he was under. His cap had slipped off his head, and hung by the *becchetto* which was wound loosely round his neck; and as he saw the group at Nello's door he lifted up his fingers in beckoning recognition. The next minute he had leaped from the bench on to a cart filled with bales, that stood in the broad space between the Baptistery and the steps of the Duomo, while the people swarmed round him with the noisy eagerness of poultry expecting to be fed. But there was silence when he began to speak, in his clear mellow voice—

"Citizens of Florence! I have no warrant to tell the news except your will. But the news is good, and will harm no man in the telling. The Most Christian King is signing a treaty that is honourable to Florence. But you owe it to one of your citizens, who spoke a word worthy of the ancient Romans—you owe it to Piero Capponi!"

Immediately there was a roar of voices.

"Capponi! Capponi! What said our Piero?" "Ah! he wouldn't stand being sent from Herod to Pilate!"* "We knew Piero!" "*Orsù!* Tell us, what did he say?"

When the roar of insistance had subsided a little, Tito began again—

"The Most Christian King demanded a little too much—was obstinate—said at last, 'I shall order my trumpets to sound.' Then, Florentine citizens! your Piero Capponi, speaking with the voice of a free city, said, 'If you sound your trumpets, we will ring our bells!' He snatched the copy of the dishonouring conditions from the hands of the secretary, tore it in pieces, and turned to leave the royal presence."

Again there were loud shouts—and again impatient demands for more.

"Then, Florentines, the high majesty of France felt, perhaps for the first time, all the majesty of a free city. And the Most Christian King himself hastened from his place to call Piero Capponi back. The great spirit of your Florentine city did its work by a great word, without need of the great actions that lay ready behind it. And the King has consented to sign the treaty, which preserves the honour, as well as the safety, of Florence. The banner of France will float over every Florentine galley in sign of amity and common privilege, but above that banner will be written the word 'Liberty!'

"That is all the news I have to tell; is it not enough?—since it is for the glory of every one of you, citizens of Florence, that you have a fellow-citizen who knows how to speak your Will."

As the shouts rose again, Tito looked round with inward amusement at the variouis crowd, each of whom was elated with the notion that Piero Capponi had somehow represented him—that he was the mind of which Capponi was the mouthpiece. He enjoyed the humour of the incident, which had suddenly transformed him, an alien and a friend of the Medici, into an orator who tickled the ears of the people blatant for some unknown good which they called liberty. He felt quite glad that he had been laid hold of and hurried along by the crowd as he was coming out of the palace in the Via Larga with a commission to the Signoria. It was very easy, very pleasant, this exercise of speaking to the general satisfaction: a man who knew how to persuade need never be in danger from any party; he could convince each that he was feigning with all the others. The gestures and faces of weavers and dyers were certainly amusing when looked at from above in this way. Tito was beginning to get easier in his armour, and at this moment was quite unconscious of it. He stood with one hand holding his recovered cap, and with the other at his belt, the light of a complacent smile in his long lustrous eyes, as he made a parting reverence to his audience, before springing down from the bales—when suddenly his glance met that of a man who had not at all the amusing aspect of the exulting weavers, dyers, and wool-carders. The face of this man was clean-shaven, his hair close-clipped, and he wore a decent felt hat. A single glance would hardly have sufficed to assure any one but Tito that this was the face of the escaped prisoner who had laid hold of him on the steps. But to Tito it came not simply as the face of the escaped prisoner, but as a face with which he had been familiar long, long years before.

It seemed all compressed into a second—the sight of Baldassarre looking at him, the sensation shooting through him like a fiery arrow, and the act of leaping from the cart. He would have leaped down in the same instant, whether he had seen Baldassarre or not, for he was in a hurry to be gone to the Palazzo Vecchio: this time he had not betrayed himself by look or movement, and he said inwardly that he should not be taken by surprise again; he should be prepared to see this face rise up continually like the intermittent blotch that comes in diseased vision. But this reappearance of Baldassarre so much more in his own likeness, tightened the pressure of dread: the idea of his madness lost its likelihood now he was shaven and clad like a decent though poor citizen. Certainly, there was a great change in his face; but how could it be otherwise? And yet, if he were perfectly sane—in possession of all his powers and all his learning—why was he lingering in this way before making known his identity? It must be for the sake of making his scheme of vengeance more complete. But he did linger: that at least gave an opportunity for flight. And Tito began to think that flight was his only resource.

But while he, with his back turned on the Piazza del Duomo, had lost the recollection of the new part he had been playing, and was no longer thinking of the many things which a ready brain and tongue made easy, but of a few things which destiny had somehow made very difficult, the enthusiasm which he had fed contemptuously was creating a scene in that piazza in grand contrast with the inward drama of self-centred fear which he had carried away from it.

The crowd, on Tito's disappearance, had begun to turn their faces towards the outlets of the piazza in the direction of the Via Larga, when the sight of *mazzieri*, or mace-bearers, entering from the Via de' Martelli, announced the approach of dignitaries. They must be the syndics, or commissioners charged with the effecting of the Treaty; the Treaty must be already signed, and they had come away from the royal presence. Piero Capponi was coming—the brave heart that had known how to speak for Florence. The effect on the crowd was remarkable; they parted with softening, dropping voices, subsiding into silence,—and the silence became so perfect that the tread of the syndics on the broad pavement, and the rustle of their black silk garments, could be heard, like rain in the night. There were four of them; but it was not the two learned doctors of law, Messer Guidantonio Vespucci and Messer Domenico Bonsi, that the crowd waited for; it was not Francesco Valori, popular as he had become in these late days. The moment belonged to another man, of firm presence, as little inclined to humour the people as to humour any other unreasonable claimants—loving order, like one who by force of fortune had been made a merchant, and by force of nature had become a soldier. It was not till he was seen at the entrance of the piazza that the silence was broken, and then one loud shout of "Capponi, Capponi! Well done, Capponi!" rang through the piazza.

The simple, resolute man looked round him with grave joy. His fellow-citizens gave him a great funeral two years later, when he had died in fight: there were torches carried by all the magistracy, and torches again, and trains of banners. But it is not known that he felt any joy in the oration that was delivered in his praise, as the banners waved over his bier. Let us be glad that he got some thanks and praise while he lived.

CHAPTER XXX.

The Avenger's Secret

IT was the first time that Baldassarre had been in the Piazza del Duomo since his escape. He had a strong desire to hear the remarkable monk preach again, but he had shrunk from reappearing in the same spot where he had been seen half naked, with neglected hair, with a rope round his neck—in the same spot where he had been called a madman. The feeling, in its freshness, was too strong to be overcome by any trust he had in the change he had made in his appearance; for when the words "*some madman, surely*," had fallen from Tito's lips, it was not their baseness and cruelty only that had made their viper sting—it was Baldassarre's instantaneous bitter consciousness that he might be unable to prove the words false. Along with the passionate desire for vengeance which possessed him had arisen the keen sense that his power of achieving the vengeance was doubtful. It was as if Tito had been helped by some diabolical prompter, who had whispered Baldassarre's saddest secret in the traitor's ear. He was not mad; for he carried within him that piteous stamp of sanity—the clear consciousness of shattered faculties: he measured his own feebleness. With the first movements of vindictive rage awoke a vague caution, like that of a wild beast that is fierce but feeble—or like that of an insect whose little fragment of earth has given way, and made it pause in a palsy of distrust. It was this distrust, this determination to take no step which might betray anything concerning himself, that had made Baldassarre reject Piero di Cosimo's friendly advances.

He had been equally cautious at the hospital, only telling, in answer to the questions of the brethren there, that he had been made a prisoner by the French on his way from Genoa. But his age, and the indications in his speech and manner that he was of a different class from the ordinary mendicants and poor travellers who were entertained in the hospital, had induced the monks to offer him extra charity—a coarse woollen tunic to protect him from the cold, a pair of peasant's shoes, and a few *danari*, smallest of Florentine coins, to help him on his way. He had gone on the road to Arezzo early in the morning; but he had paused at the first little town, and had used a couple of his *danari* to get himself shaved, and to have his circle of hair clipped short, in his former fashion. The barber there had a little hand-mirror of bright steel: it was a long while, it was years, since Baldassarre had looked at himself, and now, as his eyes fell on that hand-mirror, a new thought shot through his mind. "Was he so changed that Tito really did not know him?" The thought was such a sudden arrest of impetuous currents, that it was a painful shock to him: his hand shook like a leaf, as he put away the barber's arm and asked for the mirror. He wished to see himself before he was shaved. The barber, noticing his tremulousness, held the mirror for him.

No, he was not so changed as that. He himself had known the wrinkles as they had been three years ago; they were only deeper now: there was the same rough, clumsy skin, making little superficial bosses on the brow, like so many cipher marks; the skin was only yellower, only looked more like a lifeless rind. That shaggy white beard—it was no disguise to eyes that had looked closely at him for sixteen years—to eyes that ought to have searched for him with the expectation of finding him changed, as men search for the beloved among the bodies cast up by the waters. There was something different in his glance, but it was a difference that should only have made the recognition of him the more startling; for is not a known voice all the more thrilling when it is heard as a cry? But the doubt was folly: he had felt that Tito knew him. He put out his hand and pushed the mirror away. The strong currents were rushing on again, and the energies of hatred and vengeance were active once more.

He went back on the way towards Florence again, but he did not wish to enter the city till dusk; so he turned aside from the high-road, and sat down by a little pool shadowed on one side by alder-bushes still sprinkled with yellow leaves. It was a calm November day, and he no sooner saw the pool than he thought its still surface might be a mirror for him. He wanted to contemplate himself slowly, as he had not dared to do in the presence of the barber. He sat down on the edge of the pool, and bent forward to look earnestly at the image of himself.

Was there something wandering and imbecile in his face—something like what he felt in his mind?

Not now; not when he was examining himself with a look of eager inquiry: on the contrary, there was an intense purpose in his eyes. But at other times? Yes, it must be so: in the long hours when he had the vague aching of an unremembered past within him—when he seemed to sit in dark loneliness, visited by whispers which died out mockingly as he strained his ear after them, and by forms that seemed to approach him and float away as he thrust out his hand to grasp them—in those hours, doubtless, there must be continual frustration and amazement in his glance. And, more horrible still, when the thick cloud parted for a moment, and, as he sprang forward with hope, rolled together again, and left him helpless as before; doubtless, there was then a blank confusion in his face, as of a man suddenly smitten with blindness.

Could he prove anything? Could he even begin to allege anything, with the confidence that the links of thought would not break away? Would any believe that he had ever had a mind filled with rare knowledge, busy with close thoughts, ready with various speech? It had all slipped away from him—that laboriously gathered store. Was it utterly and for ever gone from him, like the waters from an urn lost in the wide ocean? Or, was it still within him, imprisoned by some obstruction that might one day break asunder?

It might be so; he tried to keep his grasp on that hope. For, since the day when he had first walked feebly from his couch of straw, and had felt a new darkness within him under the sunlight, his mind had undergone changes, partly gradual and persistent, partly sudden and fleeting. As he had recovered his strength of body, he had recovered his self-command and the energy of his will; he had recovered the memory of all that part of his life which was closely inwrought with his emotions; and he had felt more and more constantly and painfully the uneasy sense of lost knowledge. But more than that—once or twice, when he had been strongly excited, he had seemed momentarily to be in entire possession of his past self, as old men doze for an instant, and get back the consciousness of their youth: he seemed again to see Greek pages and understand them, again to feel his mind moving unbenumbed among familiar ideas. It had been but a flash, and the darkness closing in again seemed the more horrible; but might not the same thing happen again for longer periods? If it would only come and stay long enough for him to achieve a revenge—devise an exquisite suffering, such as a mere right arm could never inflict!

He raised himself from his stooping attitude, and, folding his arms, attempted to concentrate all his mental force on the plan he must immediately pursue. He had to wait for knowledge and opportunity, and while he waited he must have the means of living without beggary. What he dreaded of all things now was, that any one should think him a foolish, helpless old man. No one must know that half his memory was gone: the lost strength might come again; and if it were only for a little while, *that* might be enough.

He knew how to begin to get the information he wanted about Tito. He had repeated the words "Bratti Ferravecchi" so constantly after they had been uttered to him, that they never slipped from him for long together. A man at Genoa, on whose finger he had seen Tito's ring, had told him that he bought that ring at Florence, of a young Greek, well drest, and with a handsome dark face, in the shop of a *rigattiere* called Bratti Ferravecchi, in the street also called Ferravecchi. This discovery had caused a violent agitation in Baldassarre. Until then he had clung with all the tenacity of his fervid nature to his faith in Tito, and had not for a moment believed himself to be wilfully forsaken. At first he had said, "My bit of parchment has never reached him; that is why I am still toiling at Antioch. But he is searching: he knows where I was lost; he will trace me out, and find me at last." Then, when he was taken to Corinth, he induced his owners, by the assurance that he should be sought out and ransomed, to provide securely against the failure of any inquiries that might be made about him at Antioch; and at Corinth he thought joyfully, "Here, at last, he must find me. Here he is sure to touch, whichever way he goes." But before another year had passed the illness had come from which he had risen with body and mind so shattered that he was worse than worthless to his owners except for the sake of the ransom that did not come. Then, as he sat helpless in the morning sunlight, he began to think, "Tito has been drowned, or they have made *him* a prisoner too. I shall see him no more. He set out after me, but misfortune overtook him. I shall see his face no more." Sitting in his new feebleness and despair, supporting his head between his hands, with blank eyes and lips that moved uncertainly, he looked so much like a hopelessly imbecile old man, that his owners were contented to be rid of him, and allowed a Genoese merchant, who had compassion on him as an Italian, to take him on board his galley. In a voyage of many months in the Archipelago, and along the sea-board of Asia Minor, Baldassarre had recovered his bodily strength, but on landing at Genoa he had so weary a sense of his desolateness that he almost wished he had died of that illness at Corinth. There was just one possibility that hindered the wish from being decided: it was that Tito might not be dead, but living in a state of imprisonment or destitution; and if he lived, there was still a hope for Baldassarre—faint, perhaps, and likely to be long deferred, but still a hope, that he might find his child, his cherished son again; might yet again clasp hands and meet face to face with the one who remembered him as he had been before his mind was broken.

In this state of feeling he had chanced to meet the stranger who wore Tito's onyx ring, and though Baldassarre would have been unable to describe the ring beforehand, the sight of it stirred the dormant fibres, and he recognized it. That Tito nearly a year after his father had been parted from him should have been living in apparent prosperity at Florence, selling the gem which he ought not to have sold till the last extremity, was a fact that Baldassarre shrank from trying to account for: he was glad to be stunned and bewildered by it, rather than to have any distinct thought; he tried to feel nothing but joy that he should behold Tito again. Perhaps Tito had thought that his father was dead; somehow the mystery would be explained. "But at least I shall meet eyes that will remember me. I am not alone in the world."

And now again Baldassarre said, "I am not alone in the world; I shall never be alone, for my revenge is with me."

It was as the instrument of that revenge, as something merely external and subservient to his true life, that he bent down again to examine himself with hard curiosity—not, he thought, because he had any care for a withered, forsaken old man, whom nobody loved, whose soul was like a deserted home, where the ashes were cold upon the hearth, and the walls were bare of all but the marks of what had been. It is in the nature of all human passion, the lowest as well as the highest, that there is a point where it ceases to be properly egoistic, and is like a fire kindled within our being to which everything else in us is mere fuel.

He looked at the pale black-browed image in the water till he identified it with that self from which his revenge seemed to be a thing apart; and he felt as if the image too heard the silent language of his thought.

"I was a loving fool—I worshipped a woman once, and believed she could care for me; and then I took a helpless child and fostered him; and I watched him as he grew, to see if he would care for me only a little—care for *me* over and above the good he got from me. I would have torn open my breast to warm him with my life-blood if I could only have seen him care a little for the pain of my wound. I have laboured, I have strained to crush out of this hard life one drop of unselfish love. Fool! men love their own delights*—there is no delight to be had in me. And yet I watched till I believed I saw what I watched for. When he was a child he lifted soft eyes towards me, and held my hand willingly: I thought, this boy will surely love me a little: because I give my life to him and strive that he shall know no sorrow, he will care a little when I am thirsty—the drop he lays on my parched lips will be a joy to him. . . . Curses on him! I wish I may see him lie with those red lips white and dry as ashes, and when he looks for pity I wish he may see my face rejoicing in his pain. It is all a lie—this world is a lie—there is no goodness but in hate. Fool! not one drop of love came with all your striving—life has not given you one drop. But there are deep draughts in this world for hatred and revenge. I have memory left for that, and there is strength in my arm—there is strength in my will—and if I can do nothing but kill him—"

But Baldassarre's mind rejected the thought of that brief punishment. His whole soul had been thrilled into immediate unreasoning belief in that eternity of vengeance where he, an undying hate, might clutch for ever an undying traitor, and hear that fair smiling hardness cry and moan with anguish. But the primary need and hope was to see a slow revenge under the same sky and on the same earth where he himself had been forsaken and had fainted with despair. And as soon as he tried to concentrate his mind on the means of attaining his end, the sense of his weakness pressed upon him like a frosty ache. This despised body, which was to be the instrument of a sublime vengeance, must be nourished and decently clad. If he had to wait he must labour, and his labour must be of a humble sort, for he had no skill. He wondered whether the sight of written characters would so stimulate his faculties that he might venture to try and find work as a copyist: *that* might win him some credence for his past scholarship. But no! he dared trust neither hand nor brain. He must be content to do the work that was most like that of a beast of burthen: in this mercantile city many porters must be wanted, and he could at least carry weights. Thanks to the justice that struggled in this confused world in behalf of vengeance, his limbs had got back some of their old sturdiness. He was stripped of all else that men would give coin for.

But the new urgency of this habitual thought brought a new suggestion. There was something hanging by a cord round his bare neck; something apparently so paltry that the piety of Turks and Frenchmen had spared it—a tiny parchment bag blackened with age. It had hung round his neck as a precious charm when he was a boy, and he had kept it carefully on his breast, not believing that it contained anything but a tiny scroll of parchment rolled up hard. He might long ago have thrown it away as a relic of his dead mother's superstition; but he had thought of it as a relic of her love, and had kept it. It was part of the piety associated with such *Brevi*, that they should never be opened, and at any previous moment in his life Baldassarre would have said that no sort of thirst would prevail upon him to open this little bag for the chance of finding that it contained, not parchment, but an engraved amulet which would be worth money. But now a thirst had come like that which makes men open their own veins to satisfy it, and the thought of the possible amulet no sooner crossed Baldassarre's mind than with nervous fingers he snatched the *Breve* from his neck. It all rushed through his mind—the long years he had worn it, the far-off sunny balcony at Naples looking towards the blue waters, where he had leaned against his mother's knee; but it made no moment of hesitation: all piety now was transmuted into a just revenge. He bit and tore till the doubles of parchment were laid open, and then—it was a sight that made him pant—there *was* an amulet. It was very small, but it was as blue as those far-off waters; it was an engraved sapphire, which must be worth some gold ducats. Baldassarre no sooner saw those possible ducats than he saw some of them exchanged for a poniard. He did not want to use the poniard yet, but he longed to possess it. If he could grasp its handle and try its edge, that blank in his mind—that past which fell away continually—would not make him feel so cruelly helpless: the sharp steel that despised talents and eluded strength would be at his side, as the unfailing friend of feeble justice. There was a sparkling triumph under Baldassarre's black eyebrows as he replaced the little sapphire inside the bits of parchment and wound the string tightly round them.

It was nearly dusk now, and he rose to walk back towards Florence. With his *danari* to buy him some bread, he felt rich: he could lie out in the open air, as he found plenty more doing in all corners of Florence. And in the next few days he had sold his sapphire, had added to his clothing, had bought a bright dagger, and had still a pair of gold florins left. But he meant to hoard that treasure carefully: his lodging was an outhouse with a heap of straw in it, in a thinly inhabited part of Oltrarno, and he thought of looking about for work as a porter.

He had bought his dagger at Bratti's. Paying his meditated visit there one evening at dusk, he had found that singular rag-merchant just returned from one of his rounds, emptying out his basketful of broken glass and old iron amongst his handsome show of miscellaneous second-hand goods. As Baldassarre entered the shop, and looked towards the smart pieces of apparel, the musical instruments, and weapons, which were displayed in the broadest light of the window, his eye at once singled out a dagger hanging up high against a red scarf. By buying that dagger he could not only satisfy a strong desire; he could open his original errand in a more indirect manner than by speaking of the onyx ring. In the course of bargaining for the weapon he let drop, with cautious carelessness, that he came from Genoa, and had been directed to Bratti's shop by an acquaintance in that city who had bought a very valuable ring here. Had the respectable trader any more such rings?

Whereupon Bratti had much to say as to the unlikelihood of such rings being within reach of many people, with much vaunting of his own rare connections, due to his known wisdom and honesty. It might be true that he was a pedlar—he chose to be a pedlar; though he was rich enough to kick his heels in his shop all day. But those who thought they had said all there was to be said about Bratti when they had called him a pedlar, were a good deal further off the truth than the other side of Pisa. How was it that he could put that ring in a stranger's way? It was, because he had a very particular knowledge of a handsome young Signor, who did not look quite so fine a feathered bird when Bratti first set eyes on him as he did at the present time. And by a question or two Baldassarre extracted, without any trouble, such a rough and rambling account of Tito's life as the pedlar could give, since the time when he had found him sleeping under the Loggia de' Cerchi. It never occurred to Bratti that the decent man (who was rather deaf, apparently, asking him to say many things twice over) had any curiosity about Tito; the curiosity was doubtless about himself, as a truly remarkable pedlar.

And Baldassarre left Bratti's shop, not only with the dagger at his side, but also with a general knowledge of Tito's conduct and position—of his early sale of the jewels, his immediate quiet settlement of himself at Florence, his marriage, and his great prosperity.

"What story had he told about his previous life—about his father?"

It would be difficult for Baldassarre to discover the answer to that question. Meanwhile, he wanted to learn all he could about Florence. But he found, to his acute distress, that of the new details he learned he could only retain a few, and those only by continual repetition; and he began to be afraid of listening to any new discourse, lest it should obliterate what he was already striving to remember.

The day he was discerned by Tito in the Piazza del Duomo, he had the fresh anguish of this consciousness in his mind, and Tito's ready speech fell upon him like the mockery of a glib, defying demon.

As he went home to his heap of straw, and passed by the

booksellers' shops in the Via del Garbo, he paused to look at the volumes spread open. Could he by long gazing at one of those books lay hold of the slippery threads of memory? Could he by striving get a firm grasp somewhere, and lift himself above these waters that flowed over him?

He was tempted, and bought the cheapest Greek book he could see. He carried it home and sat on his heap of straw, looking at the characters by the light of the small window; but no inward light arose on them. Soon the evening darkness came; but it made little difference to Baldassarre. His strained eyes seemed still to see the white pages with the unintelligible black marks upon them.

CHAPTER XXXI.

Fruit is Seed

"My Romola," said Tito, the second morning after he had made his speech in the Piazza del Duomo, "I am to receive grand visitors to-day; the Milanese Count is coming again, and the Seneschal de Beaucaire,* the great favourite of the Cristianissimo. I know you don't care to go through smiling ceremonies with these rustling magnates, whom we are not likely to see again; and as they will want to look at the antiquities and the library, perhaps you had better give up your work to-day, and go to see your cousin Brigida."

Romola discerned a wish in this intimation, and immediately assented. But presently, coming back in her hood and mantle, she said, "Oh, what a long breath Florence will take when the gates are flung open, and the last Frenchman is walking out of them! Even you are getting tired, with all your patience, my Tito; confess it. Ah, your head is hot."

He was leaning over his desk, writing, and she had laid her hand on his head, meaning to give a parting caress. The attitude had been a frequent one, and Tito was accustomed, when he felt her hand there, to raise his head, throw himself a little backward, and look up at her. But he felt now as unable to raise his head as if her hand had been a leaden cowl. He spoke instead, in a light tone, as his pen still ran along.

"The French are as ready to go from Florence as the wasps to leave a ripe pear when they have just fastened on it."

Romola, keenly sensitive to the absence of the usual response, took away her hand and said, "I am going, Tito."

"Farewell, my sweet one. I must wait at home. Take Maso with you."

Still Tito did not look up, and Romola went out without saying any more. Very slight things make epochs in married life, and this morning for the first time she admitted to herself not only that Tito had changed, but that he had changed towards her. Did the reason lie in herself? She might perhaps have thought so, if there had not been the facts of the armour and the picture to suggest some external event which was an entire mystery to her.

But Tito no sooner believed that Romola was out of the house than he laid down his pen and looked up, in delightful security from seeing anything else than parchment and broken marble. He was rather disgusted with himself that he had not been able to look up at Romola and behave to her just as usual. He would have chosen, if he could, to be even more than usually kind; but he could not, on a sudden, master an involuntary shrinking from her, which, by a subtle relation, depended on those very characteristics in him that made him desire not to fail in his marks of affection. He was about to take a step which he knew would arouse her deep indignation: he would have to encounter much that was unpleasant before he could win her forgiveness. And Tito could never find it easy to face displeasure and anger; his nature was one of those most remote from defiance or impudence, and all his inclinations leaned towards preserving Romola's tenderness. He was not tormented by sentimental scruples which, as he had demonstrated to himself by a very rapid course of argument, had no relation to solid utility; but his freedom from scruples did not release him from the dread of what was disagreeable. Unscrupulousness gets rid of much, but not of toothache, or wounded vanity, or the sense of loneliness, against which, as the world at present stands, there is no security but a thoroughly healthy jaw, and a just, loving soul. And Tito was feeling intensely at this moment that no devices could save him from pain in the impending collision with Romola; no persuasive blandness could cushion him against the shock towards which he was being driven like a timid animal urged to a desperate leap by the terror of the tooth and the claw that are close behind it.

The secret feeling he had previously had that the tenacious adherence to Bardo's wishes about the library had become under existing difficulties a piece of sentimental folly, which deprived himself and Romola of substantial advantages, might perhaps never have wrought itself into action but for the events of the past week, which had brought at once the pressure of a new motive and the outlet of a rare opportunity. Nay, it was not till his dread had been aggravated by the sight of Baldassarre looking more like his sane self, not until he had begun to feel that he might be compelled to flee from Florence, that he had brought himself to resolve on using his legal right to sell the library before the great opportunity offered by French and Milanese bidders slipped through his fingers. For if he had to leave Florence he did not want to leave it as a destitute wanderer. He had been used to an agreeable existence, and he wished to carry with him all the means at hand for retaining the same agreeable conditions. He wished among other things to carry Romola with him, and *not*, if possible, to carry any infamy. Success had given him a growing appetite for all the pleasures that depend on an advantageous social position, and at no moment could it look like a temptation to him, but only like a hideous alternative, to decamp under dishonour, even with a bag of diamonds, and incur the life of an adventurer. It was not possible for him to make himself independent even of those Florentines who only greeted him with regard; still less was it possible for him to make himself independent of Romola. She was the wife of his first love—he loved her still; she belonged to that furniture of life which he shrank from parting with. He winced under her judgment, he felt uncertain how far the revulsion of her feeling towards him might go; and all that sense of power over a wife which makes a husband risk betrayals that a lover never ventures on, would not suffice to counteract Tito's uneasiness. This was the leaden weight which had been too strong for his will, and kept him from raising his head to meet her eyes. Their pure light brought too near him the prospect of a coming struggle. But it was not to be helped: if they had to leave Florence, they must have money; indeed, Tito could not arrange life at all to his mind without a considerable sum of money. And that problem of arranging life to his mind had been the source of all his misdoing. He would have been equal to any sacrifice that was not unpleasant.

The rustling magnates came and went, the bargains had been concluded, and Romola returned home; but nothing grave was said that night. Tito was only gay and chatty, pouring forth to her, as he had not done before, stories and descriptions of what he had witnessed during the French visit. Romola thought she discerned an effort in his liveliness, and, attributing it to the consciousness in him that she had been wounded in the morning, accepted the effort as an act of penitence, inwardly aching a little at that sign of growing distance between them—that there was an offence about which neither of them dared to speak.

The next day Tito remained away from home until late at night. It was a marked day to Romola, for Piero di Cosimo, stimulated to greater industry on her behalf by the fear that he might have been the cause of pain to her in the past week, had sent home her father's portrait. She had propped it against the back of his old chair, and had been looking at it for some time, when the door opened behind her, and Bernardo del Nero came in.

"It is you, godfather! How I wish you had come sooner: it is getting a little dusk," said Romola, going towards him.

"I have just looked in to tell you the good news, for I know Tito is not come yet," said Bernardo. "The French King moves off to-morrow; not before it is high time. There has been another tussle between our people and his soldiers this morning. But there's a chance now of the city getting into order once more and trade going on."

"That is joyful," said Romola. "But it is sudden, is it not? Tito seemed to think yesterday that there was little prospect of the King's going soon."

"He has been well barked at, that's the reason," said Bernardo, smiling. "His own generals opened their throats pretty well, and at last our Signoria sent the mastiff of the city,* Fra Girolamo. The Cristianissimo was frightened at that thunder, and has given the order to move. I'm afraid there'll be small agreement among us when he's gone, but, at any rate, all parties are agreed in being glad not to have Florence stifled with soldiery any longer, and the Frate has barked this time to some purpose. Ah, what is this?" he added, as Romola, clasping him by the arm, led him in front of the picture. "Let us see."

He began to unwind his long scarf while she placed a seat for him.

"Don't you want your spectacles, godfather?" said Romola, in anxiety that he should see just what she saw.

"No, child, no," said Bernardo, uncovering his grey head, as he seated himself with firm erectness. "For seeing at this distance, my old eyes are perhaps better than your young ones. Old men's eyes are like old men's memories; they are strongest for things a long way off."

"It is better than having no portrait," said Romola, apologetically, after Bernardo had been silent a little while. "It is less like him now than the image I have in my mind, but then that might fade with the years." She rested her arm on the old man's shoulder as she spoke, drawn towards him strongly by their common interest in the dead.

"I don't know," said Bernardo. "I almost think I see Bardo as he was when he was young, better than that picture shows him to me as he was when he was old. Your father had a great deal of fire in his eyes when he was young. It was what I could never understand, that he, with his fiery spirit, which seemed much more impatient than mine, could hang over the books and live with shadows all his life. However, he had put his heart into that."

Bernardo gave a slight shrug as he spoke the last words, but Romola discerned in his voice a feeling that accorded with her own.

"And he was disappointed to the last," she said, involuntarily. But immediately fearing lest her words should be taken to imply an accusation against Tito, she went on almost hurriedly, "If we could only see his longest, dearest wish fulfilled just to his mind!"

"Well, so we may," said Bernardo, kindly, rising and putting on his cap. "The times are cloudy now, but fish are caught by waiting. Who knows? When the wheel has turned often enough, I may be Gonfaloniere yet before I die; and no creditor can touch these things." He looked round as he spoke. Then, turning to her, and patting her cheek, said, "And you need not be afraid of my dying; my ghost will claim nothing. I've taken care of that in my will."

Romola seized the hand that was against her cheek, and put it to her lips in silence.

"Haven't you been scolding your husband for keeping away from home so much lately? I see him everywhere but here," said Bernardo, willing to change the subject.

She felt the flush spread over her neck and face as she said, "He has been very much wanted; you know he speaks so well. I am glad to know that his value is understood."

"You are contented, then, Madonna Orgogliosa?" said Bernardo, smiling as he moved to the door.

"Assuredly."

Poor Romola! There was one thing that would have made the pang of disappointment in her husband harder to bear: it was, that any one should know he gave her cause for disappointment. This might be a woman's weakness, but it is closely allied to a woman's nobleness. She who willingly lifts up the veil of her married life has profaned it from a sanctuary into a vulgar place.

CHAPTER XXXII.

A Revelation

THE next day Romola, like every other Florentine, was excited about the departure of the French. Besides her other reasons for gladness, she had a dim hope, which she was conscious was half superstitious, that those new anxieties about Tito, having come with the burthensome guests, might perhaps vanish with them. The French had been in Florence hardly eleven days, but in that space she had felt more acute unhappiness than she had known in her life before. Tito had adopted the hateful armour on the day of their arrival, and though she could frame no distinct notion why their departure should remove the cause of his fear—though, when she thought of that cause, the image of the prisoner grasping him, as she had seen it in Piero's sketch, urged itself before her and excluded every other—still, when the French were gone, she would be rid of something that was strongly associated with her pain.

Wrapped in her mantle she waited under the loggia at the top of the house, and watched for the glimpses of the troops and the royal retinue passing the bridges on their way to the Porta San Piero, that looks towards Siena and Rome. She even returned to her station when the gates had been closed, that she might feel herself vibrating with the great peal of the bells. It was dusk then, and when at last she descended into the library, she lit her lamp, with the resolution that she would overcome the agitation which had made her idle all day, and sit down to work at her copying of the catalogue. Tito had left home early in the morning, and she did not expect him yet. Before he came she intended to leave the library, and sit in the pretty saloon, with the dancing nymphs and the birds. She had done so every evening since he had objected to the library as chill and gloomy.

To her great surprise, she had not been at work long before Tito entered. Her first thought was, how cheerless he would feel the wide darkness of this great room, with one little oil-lamp burning at the farther end, and the fire nearly out. She almost ran towards him.

"Tito, dearest, I did not know you would come so soon," she said, nervously, putting up her white arms to unwind his *becchetto*.

"I am not welcome then?" he said, with one of his brightest smiles, clasping her, but playfully holding his head back from her.

"Tito!" She uttered the word in a tone of pretty, loving reproach, and then he kissed her fondly, stroked her hair, as his manner was, and seemed not to mind about taking off his mantle yet. Romola quivered with delight. All the emotions of the day had been preparing in her a keener sensitiveness to the return of this habitual manner. "It will come back," she was saying to herself, "the old happiness will perhaps come back. He is like himself again."

Tito was taking great pains to be like himself; his heart was palpitating with anxiety.

"If I had expected you so soon," said Romola, as she at last helped him to take off his wrappings, "I would have had a little festival prepared to this joyful ringing of the bells. I did not mean to be here in the library when you came home."

"Never mind, sweet," he said, carelessly. "Do not think about the fire. Come—come and sit down."

There was a low stool against Tito's chair, and that was Romola's habitual seat when they were talking together. She rested her arm on his knee, as she used to do on her father's, and looked up at him while he spoke. He had never yet noticed the presence of the portrait, and she had not mentioned it—thinking of it all the more.

"I have been enjoying the clang of the bells for the first time, Tito," she began. "I liked being shaken and deafened by them: I fancied I was something like a Bacchante* possessed by a divine rage. Are not the people looking very joyful to-night?"

"Joyful after a sour and pious fashion," said Tito, with a shrug. "But, in truth, those who are left behind in Florence have little cause to be joyful; it seems to me, the most reasonable ground of gladness would be to have got out of Florence."

Tito had sounded the desired key-note without any trouble, or appearance of premeditation. He spoke with no emphasis, but he looked grave enough to make Romola ask rather anxiously,

"Why, Tito? Are there fresh troubles?"

"No need of fresh ones, my Romola. There are three strong parties in the city, all ready to fly at each other's throats. And if the Frate's party is strong enough to frighten the other two into silence, as seems most likely, life will be as pleasant and amusing as a funeral. They have the plan of a great Council simmering already; and if they get it, the man who sings sacred lauds the loudest will be the most eligible for office. And besides that, the city will be so drained by the payment of this great subsidy* to the French King, and by the war to get back Pisa, that the prospect would be dismal enough without the rule of fanatics. On the whole, Florence will be a delightful place for those worthies who entertain themselves in the evening by going into crypts and lashing themselves; but for everything else, the exiles have the best of it. For my own part, I have been thinking seriously that we should be wise to quit Florence, my Romola."

She started. "Tito, how could we leave Florence? Surely you do not think I could leave it—at least, not yet—not for a long while." She had turned cold and trembling, and did not find it quite easy to speak. Tito must know the reasons she had in her mind.

"That is all a fabric of your own imagination, my sweet one. Your secluded life has made you lay such false stress on a few things. You know I used to tell you, before we were married, that I wished we were somewhere else than in Florence. If you had seen more places and more people, you would know what I mean when I say that there is something in the Florentines that reminds me of their cutting spring winds. I like people who take life less eagerly; and it would be good for my Romola, too, to see a new life. I should like to dip her a little in the soft waters of forgetfulness."

He leaned forward and kissed her brow, and laid his hand on her fair hair again; but she felt his caress no more than if he had kissed a mask. She was too much agitated by the sense of the distance between their minds to be conscious that his lips touched her.

"Tito, it is not because I suppose Florence is the pleasantest place in the world that I desire not to quit it. It is because I—because we have to see my father's wish fulfilled. My godfather is old—he is seventy-one—we could not leave it to him."

"It is precisely those superstitions which hang about your mind like bedimming clouds, my Romola, that make one great reason why I could wish we were two hundred leagues from Florence. I am obliged to take care of you in opposition to your own will: if those dear eyes, that look so tender, see falsely, I must see for them, and save my wife from wasting her life in disappointing herself by impracticable dreams."

Romola sat silent and motionless: she could not blind herself to the direction in which Tito's words pointed: he wanted to persuade her that they might get the library deposited in some monastery, or take some other ready means to rid themselves of a task, and of a tie to Florence; and she was determined never to submit her mind to his judgment on this question of duty to her father; she was inwardly prepared to encounter any sort of pain in resistance. But the determination was kept latent in these first moments by the heart-crushing sense that now at last she and Tito must be confessedly divided in their wishes. He was glad of her silence; for, much as he had feared the strength of her feeling, it was impossible for him, shut up in the narrowness that hedges in all merely clever, unimpassioned men, not to over-estimate the persuasiveness of his own arguments. His conduct did not look ugly to himself, and his imagination did not suffice to show him exactly how it would look to Romola. He went on in the same gentle, remonstrating tone.

"You know, dearest—your own clear judgment always showed you—that the notion of isolating a collection of books and antiquities, and attaching a single name to them for ever, was one that had no valid, substantial good for its object: and yet more, one that was liable to be defeated in a thousand ways.

See what has become of the Medici collections!* And, for my part, I consider it even blameworthy to entertain those petty views of appropriation: why should any one be reasonably glad that Florence should possess the benefits of learned research and taste more than any other city? I understand your feeling about the wishes of the dead; but wisdom puts a limit to these sentiments, else lives might be continually wasted in that sort of futile devotion—like praising deaf gods for ever. You gave your life to your father while he lived; why should you demand more of yourself?"

"Because it was a trust," said Romola, in a low but distinct voice. "He trusted me, he trusted you, Tito. I did not expect you to feel anything else about it—to feel as I do—but I did expect you to feel that."

"Yes, dearest, of course I should feel it on a point where your father's real welfare or happiness was concerned; but there is no question of that now. If we believed in Purgatory, I should be as anxious as you to have masses said; and if I believed it could now pain your father to see his library preserved and used in a rather different way from what he had set his mind on, I should share the strictness of your views. But a little philosophy should teach us to rid ourselves of those air-woven fetters that mortals hang round themselves, spending their lives in misery under the mere imagination of weight. Your mind, which seizes ideas so readily, my Romola, is able to discriminate between substantial good and these brain-wrought fantasies. Ask yourself, dearest, what possible good can these books and antiquities do stowed together under your father's name in Florence, more than they would do if they were divided or carried elsewhere? Nay, is not the very dispersion of such things in hands that know how to value them, one means of extending their usefulness? This rivalry of Italian cities is very petty and illiberal. The loss of Constantinople was the gain of the whole civilized world."

Romola was still too thoroughly under the painful pressure of the new revelation Tito was making of himself, for her resistance to find any strong vent. As that fluent talk fell on her ears there was a rising contempt within her, which only made her more conscious of her bruised despairing love, her love for the Tito she had married and believed in. Her nature, possessed with the energies of strong emotion, recoiled from this hopelessly shallow readiness which professed to appropriate the widest sympathies and had no pulse for the nearest. She still spoke like one who was restrained from showing all she felt. She had only drawn away her arm from his knee and sat with her hands clasped before her, cold and motionless as locked waters.

"You talk of substantial good, Tito! Are faithfulness, and love, and sweet grateful memories, no good? Is it no good that we should keep our silent promises on which others build because they believe in our love and truth? Is it no good that a just life should be justly honoured? Or, is it good that we should harden our hearts against all the wants and hopes of those who have depended on us? What good can belong to men who have such souls? To talk cleverly, perhaps, and find soft couches for themselves, and live and die with their base selves as their best companions."

Her voice had gradually risen till there was a ring of scorn in the last words; she made a slight pause, but he saw there were other words quivering on her lips, and he chose to let them come.

"I know of no good for cities or the world if they are to be made up of such beings. But I am not thinking of other Italian cities and the whole civilized world—I am thinking of my father, and of my love and sorrow for him, and of his just claims on us. I would give up anything else, Tito,—I would leave Florence,—what else did I live for but for him and you? But I will not give up that duty. What have I to do with your arguments? It was a yearning of *his* heart, and therefore it is a yearning of mine."

Her voice, from having been tremulous, had become full and firm. She felt that she had been urged on to say all that it was needful for her to say. She thought, poor thing, there was nothing harder to come than this struggle against Tito's suggestions as against the meaner part of herself.

He had begun to see clearly that he could not persuade her into assent: he must take another course, and show her that the time for resistance was past. That, at least, would put an end to further struggle; and if the disclosure were not made by himself to-night, to-morrow it must be made in another way. This necessity nerved his courage; and his experience of her affectionateness and unexpected submissiveness, ever since their marriage until now, encouraged him to hope that, at last, she would accommodate herself to what had been his will.

"I am sorry to hear you speak in that spirit of blind persistence, my Romola," he said, quietly, "because it obliges me to give you pain. But I partly foresaw your opposition, and as a prompt decision was necessary, I avoided that obstacle, and decided without consulting you. The very care of a husband for his wife's interest compels him to that separate action sometimes—even when he has such a wife as you, my Romola."

She turned her eyes on him in breathless inquiry.

"I mean," he said, answering her look, "that I have arranged for the transfer, both of the books and of the antiquities, where they will find the highest use and value. The books have been bought for the Duke of Milan, the marbles and bronzes and the rest are going to France: and both will be protected by the stability of a great Power, instead of remaining in a city which is exposed to ruin."

Before he had finished speaking, Romola had started from her seat, and stood up looking down at him, with tightened hands falling before her, and, for the first time in her life, with a flash of fierceness in her scorn and anger.

"You have *sold* them?" she asked, as if she distrusted her ears.

"I have," said Tito, quailing a little. The scene was unpleasant—the descending scorn already scorched him.

"You are a treacherous man!" she said, with something grating in her voice, as she looked down at him.

She was silent for a minute, and he sat still, feeling that ingenuity was powerless just now. Suddenly she turned away, and said, in an agitated tone, "It may be hindered—I am going to my godfather."

In an instant Tito started up, went to the door, locked it, and took out the key. It was time for all the masculine predominance that was latent in him to show itself. But he was not angry; he only felt that the moment was eminently unpleasant, and that when this scene was at an end he should be glad to keep away from Romola for a little while. But it was absolutely necessary first that she should be reduced to passiveness.

"Try to calm yourself a little, Romola," he said, leaning in the easiest attitude possible against a pedestal under the bust of a grim old Roman. Not that he was inwardly easy: his heart palpitated with a moral dread, against which no chain armour could be found. He had locked-in his wife's anger and scorn, but he had been obliged to lock himself in with it; and his blood did not rise with contest—his olive cheek was perceptibly paled.

Romola had paused and turned her eyes on him as she saw him take his stand and lodge the key in his scarsella. Her eyes were flashing, and her whole frame seemed to be possessed by impetuous force that wanted to leap out in some deed. All the crushing pain of disappointment in her husband, which had made the strongest part of her consciousness a few minutes before, was annihilated by the vehemence of her indignation. She could not care in this moment that the man she was despising as he leaned there in his loathsome beauty—she could not care that he was her husband; she could only feel that she despised him. The pride and fierceness of the old Bardi blood had been thoroughly awaked in her for the first time.

"Try at least to understand the facts," said Tito, "and do not seek to take futile steps which may be fatal. It is of no use for you to go to your godfather. Messer Bernardo cannot reverse what I have done. Only sit down. You would hardly wish, if you were quite yourself, to make known to any third person what passes between us in private."

Tito knew that he had touched the right fibre there. But she did not sit down; she was too unconscious of her body voluntarily to change her attitude.

"Why can it not be reversed?" she said, after a pause. "Nothing is moved yet."

"Simply because the sale has been concluded by written agreement; the purchasers have left Florence, and I hold the bonds for the purchase-money."

"If my father had suspected you of being a faithless man," said Romola, in a tone of bitter scorn, which insisted on darting out before she could say anything else, "he would have placed the library safely out of your power. But death overtook him too soon, and when you were sure his ear was deaf, and his hand stiff, you robbed him." She paused an instant, and then said, with gathered passion, "Have you robbed somebody else, who is *not* dead? Is that the reason you wear armour?"

Romola had been driven to utter the words as men are driven to use the lash of the horsewhip. At first, Tito felt horribly cowed; it seemed to him that the disgrace he had been dreading would be worse than he had imagined it. But soon there was a reaction: such power of dislike and resistance as there was within him was beginning to rise against a wife whose voice seemed like the herald of a retributive fate. Her, at least, his quick mind told him that he might master.

"It is useless," he said, coolly, "to answer the words of madness, Romola. Your peculiar feeling about your father has made you mad at this moment. Any rational person looking at the case from a due distance will see that I have taken the wisest course. Apart from the influence of your exaggerated feelings on him, I am convinced that Messer Bernardo would be of that opinion."

"He would not!" said Romola. "He lives in the hope of seeing my father's wish exactly fulfilled. We spoke of it together only yesterday. He will help me yet. Who are these men to whom you have sold my father's property?"

"There is no reason why you should not be told, except that it signifies little. The Count di San Severino and the Seneschal de Beaucaire are now on their way with the King to Siena."

"They may be overtaken and persuaded to give up their purchase," said Romola, eagerly, her anger beginning to be surmounted by anxious thought.

"No, they may not," said Tito, with cool decision.

"Why?"

"Because I do not choose that they should."

"But if you were paid the money?—we will pay you the money," said Romola. No words could have disclosed more fully her sense of alienation from Tito; but they were spoken with less of bitterness than of anxious pleading. And he felt stronger, for he saw that the first impulse of fury was past.

"No, my Romola. Understand that such thoughts as these are impracticable. You would not, in a reasonable moment, ask your godfather to bury three thousand florins in addition to what he has already paid on the library. I think your pride and delicacy would shrink from that."

She began to tremble and turn cold again with discouragement, and sank down on the carved chest near which she was standing. He went on in a clear voice, under which she shuddered, as if it had been a narrow cold stream coursing over a hot cheek.

"Moreover, it is not my will that Messer Bernardo should advance the money, even if the project were not an utterly wild one. And I beg you to consider, before you take any step or utter any word on the subject, what will be the consequences of your placing yourself in opposition to me, and trying to exhibit your husband in the odious light which your own distempered feelings cast over him. What object will you serve by injuring me with Messer Bernardo? The event is irrevocable, the library is sold, and you are my wife."

Every word was spoken for the sake of a calculated effect, for his intellect was urged into the utmost activity by the danger of the crisis. He knew that Romola's mind would take in rapidly enough all the wide meaning of his speech. He waited and watched her in silence.

She had turned her eyes from him and was looking on the ground, and in that way she sat for several minutes. When she spoke, her voice was quite altered,—it was quiet and cold.

"I have one thing to ask."

"Ask anything that I can do without injuring us both, Romola."

"That you will give me that portion of the money which belongs to my godfather, and let me pay him."

"I must have some assurance from you, first, of the attitude you intend to take towards me."

"Do you believe in assurances, Tito?" she said, with a tinge of returning bitterness.

"From you, I do."

"I will do you no harm. I shall disclose nothing. I will say nothing to pain him or you. You say truly, the event is irrevocable."

"Then I will do what you desire to-morrow morning."

"To-night, if possible," said Romola, "that we may not speak of it again."

"It is possible," he said, moving towards the lamp, while she sat still, looking away from him with absent eyes.

Presently he came and bent down over her, to put a piece of paper into her hand. "You will receive something in return, you are aware, my Romola?" he said, gently, not minding so much what had passed, now he was secure; and feeling able to try and propitiate her.

"Yes," she said, taking the paper, without looking at him, "I understand."

"And you will forgive me, my Romola, when you have had time to reflect." He just touched her brow with his lips, but she took no notice, and seemed really unconscious of the act.

She was aware that he unlocked the door and went out. She moved her head and listened. The great door of the court opened and shut again. She started up as if some sudden freedom had come, and going to her father's chair where his picture was propped, fell on her knees before it, and burst into sobs.

[*JANUARY 1863*]

CHAPTER XXXIII.

Baldassarre Makes an Acquaintance

WHEN Baldassarre was wandering about Florence in search of a spare outhouse where he might have the cheapest of sheltered beds, his steps had been attracted towards that sole portion of ground within the walls of the city which is not perfectly level, and where the spectator, lifted above the roofs of the houses, can see beyond the city to the protecting hills and far-stretching valley, otherwise shut out from his view except along the welcome opening made by the course of the Arno. Part of that ground has been already seen by us as the Hill of Bogoli, at that time a great stone quarry; but the side towards which Baldassarre directed his steps was the one that sloped down behind the Via de' Bardi, and was most commonly called the Hill of San Giorgio. Bratti had told him that Tito's dwelling was in the Via de' Bardi; and, after surveying that street, he turned up the slope of the hill which he had observed as he was crossing the bridge. If he could find a sheltering outhouse on that hill, he would be glad: he had now for some years been accustomed to live with a broad sky about him; and, moreover, the narrow passes of the streets, with their strip of sky above, and the unknown labyrinth around them, seemed to intensify his sense of loneliness and feeble memory.

The hill was sparsely inhabited, and covered chiefly by gardens; but in one spot was a piece of rough ground jagged with great stones, which had never been cultivated since a landslip had ruined some houses there towards the end of the thirteenth century. Just above the edge of this broken ground stood a queer little square building, looking like a truncated tower roofed in with fluted tiles, and close by was a small outhouse, apparently built up against a piece of ruined stone wall. Under a large half-dead mulberry-tree that was now sending its last fluttering leaves in at the open doorways, a shrivelled, hardy old woman was untying a goat with two kids, and Baldassarre could see that part of the outbuilding was occupied by live stock; but the door of the other part was open, and it was empty of everything but some tools and straw. It was just the sort of place he wanted. He spoke to the old woman; but it was not till he got close to her and shouted in her ear, that he succeeded in making her understand his want of a lodging, and his readiness to pay for it. At first, he could get no answer beyond shakes of the head and the words, "No—no lodging," uttered in the muffled tone of the deaf. But, by dint of persistence, he made clear to her that he was a poor stranger from a long way over seas, and could not afford to go to hostelries; that he only wanted to lie on the straw in the outhouse, and would pay her a quattrino or two a week for that shelter. She still looked at him dubiously, shaking her head and talking low to herself; but presently, as if a new thought occurred to her, she fetched a hatchet from the house, and, showing him a chump that lay half covered with litter in a corner, asked him if he would chop that up for her: if he would, he might lie in the outhouse for one night. He agreed, and Monna Lisa stood with her arms akimbo to watch him, with a smile of gratified cunning, saying low to herself,

"It's lain there ever since my old man died. What then? I might as well have put a stone on the fire. He chops very well, though he does speak with a foreign tongue, and looks odd. I couldn't have got it done cheaper. And if he only wants a bit of straw to lie on, I might make him do an errand or two up and down the hill. Who need know? And sin that's hidden's half forgiven.* He's a stranger: he'll take no notice of *her*. And I'll tell her to keep her tongue still."

The antecedent to these feminine pronouns had a pair of blue eyes, which at that moment were applied to a large round hole in the shutter of the upper window. The shutter was closed, not for any penal reasons, but because only the opposite window had the luxury of glass in it: the weather was not warm, and a round hole four inches in diameter served all the purposes of observation. The hole was unfortunately a little too high, and obliged the small observer to stand on a low stool of a rickety character; but Tessa would have stood a long while in a much more inconvenient position for the sake of seeing a little variety in her life. She had been drawn to the opening at the first loud tones of the strange voice speaking to Monna Lisa; and darting gently across her room every now and then to peep at something, she continued to stand there until the wood had been chopped, and she saw Baldassarre enter the outhouse, as the dusk was gathering, and seat himself on the straw.

A great temptation had laid hold of Tessa's mind; she would go and take that old man part of her supper, and talk to him a little. He was not deaf like Monna Lisa, and besides she could say a great many things to him that it was no use to shout at Monna Lisa who knew them already. And he was a stranger—strangers came from a long way off and went away again, and lived nowhere in particular. It was naughty, she knew, for obedience made the largest part in Tessa's idea of duty; but it would be something to confess to the *padre* next Pasqua, and there was nothing else to confess except going to sleep sometimes over her beads, and being a little cross with Monna Lisa because she was so deaf; for she had as much idleness as she liked now, and was never frightened into telling white lies. She turned away from her shutter with rather an excited expression in her childish face, which was as pretty and pouting as ever. Her garb was still that of a simple contadina, but of a contadina prepared for a Festa: her gown of dark green serge, with its red girdle, was very clean and neat, she had the string of red glass beads round her neck, and her brown hair, rough from curliness, was duly knotted up and fastened with the silver pin. She had but one new ornament, and she was very proud of it, for it was a fine gold ring.

Tessa sat on the low stool, nursing her knees, for a minute or two, with her little soul poised in fluttering excitement on the edge of this pleasant transgression. It was quite irresistible. She had been commanded to make no acquaintances, and warned that if she did, all her new happy lot would vanish away, and be like a hidden treasure that turned to lead as soon as it was brought to the daylight; and she had been so obedient that when she had to go to church she had kept her face shaded by her hood and had pursed up her lips quite tightly. It was true her obedience had been a little helped by her own dread lest the alarming step-father Nofri should turn up even in this quarter, so far from the Por' del Prato, and beat her at least, if he did not drag her back to work for him. But this old man was not an aquaintance; he was a poor stranger going to sleep in the outhouse, and he probably knew nothing of step-father Nofri; and, besides, if she took him some supper, he would like her, and not want to tell anything about her. Monna Lisa would say she must not go and talk to him, therefore Monna Lisa must not be consulted. It did not signify what she found out after it had been done.

Supper was being prepared, she knew—a mountain of macaroni flavoured with cheese—fragrant enough to tame any stranger. So she tripped downstairs with a mind full of deep designs, and first asking with an innocent look what that noise of talking had been, without waiting for an answer, knit her brow with a peremptory air, something like a kitten trying to be formidable, and sent the old woman upstairs; saying, she chose to eat her supper down below. In three minutes Tessa, with her lantern in one hand and a wooden bowl of macaroni in the other, was kicking gently at the door of the outhouse, and Baldassarre, roused from sad reverie, doubted in the first moment whether he were awake as he opened the door and saw this surprising little handmaid, with delight in her wide eyes, breaking in on his dismal loneliness.

"I've brought you some supper," she said, lifting her mouth towards his ear and shouting, as if he had been deaf like Monna Lisa. "Sit down and eat it, while I stay with you."

Surprise and distrust surmounted every other feeling in Baldassarre, but, though he had no smile or word of gratitude ready, there could not be any impulse to push away this visitant, and he sank down passively on his straw again, while Tessa placed herself close to him, put the wooden bowl on his lap, and set down the lantern in front of them, crossing her hands before her, and nodding at the bowl with a significant smile, as much as to say, "Yes, you may really eat it." For, in the excitement of carrying out her deed, she had forgotten her previous thought that the stranger would not be deaf, and had fallen into her habitual alternative of dumb show and shouting.

The invitation was not a disagreeable one, for he had been gnawing a remnant of dried bread, which had left plenty of appetite for anything warm and relishing. Tessa watched the disappearance of two or three mouthfuls without speaking, for she had thought his eyes rather fierce at first; but now she ventured to put her mouth to his ear again and cry—

"I like my supper, don't you?"

It was not a smile, but rather the milder look of a dog touched by kindness but unable to smile, that Baldassarre turned on this round blue-eyed thing that was caring about him.

"Yes," he said; "but I can hear well—I'm not deaf."

"It is true; I forgot," said Tessa, lifting her hands and clasping them. "But Monna Lisa is deaf, and I live with her. She's a kind old woman, and I'm not frightened at her. And we live very well: we have plenty of nice things. I can have nuts if I like. And I'm not obliged to work now. I used to have to work, and I didn't like it; but I liked feeding the mules, and I should like to see poor Giannetta, the little mule, again. We've only got a goat and two kids, and I used to talk to the goat a good deal, because there was nobody else but Monna Lisa. But now I've got something else—can you guess what it is?"

She drew her head back, and looked with a challenging smile at Baldassarre, as if she had proposed a difficult riddle to him.

"No," said he, putting aside his bowl, and looking at her dreamily. It seemed as if this young prattling thing were some memory come back out of his own youth.

"You like me to talk to you, don't you?" said Tessa, "but you must not tell anybody. Shall I fetch you a bit of cold sausage?"

He shook his head, but he looked so mild now that Tessa felt quite at her ease.

"Well, then, I've got a little baby. Such a pretty *bambinetto*, with little fingers and nails! Not old yet; it was born at the Natività,* Monna Lisa says. I was married one Natività, a long, long while ago, and nobody knew. O Santa Madonna! I didn't mean to tell you that!"

Tessa set up her shoulders and bit her lip, looking at Baldassarre as if this betrayal of secrets must have an exciting effect on him too. But he seemed not to care much; and perhaps that was in the nature of strangers.

"Yes," she said, carrying on her thought aloud, "you are a stranger; you don't live anywhere or know anybody, do you?"

"No," said Baldassarre, also thinking aloud, rather than consciously answering, "I only know one man."

"His name is not Nofri, is it?" said Tessa, anxiously.

"No," said Baldassarre, noticing her look of fear. "Is that your husband's name?"

That mistaken supposition was very amusing to Tessa. She laughed and clapped her hands as she said,—

"No, indeed! But I must not tell you anything about my husband. You would never think what he is—not at all like Nofri!"

She laughed again at the delightful incongruity between the

name of Nofri—which was not separable from the idea of the cross-grained step-father—and the idea of her husband.

"But I don't see him very often," she went on, more gravely. "And sometimes I pray to the Holy Madonna to send him oftener, and once she did. But I must go back to my bimbo now. I'll bring it to show you to-morrow. You would like to see it. Sometimes it cries and makes a face, but only when it's hungry, Monna Lisa says. You wouldn't think it, but Monna Lisa had babies once, and they are all dead old men. My husband says she will never die now, because she's so well dried. I'm glad of that, for I'm fond of her. You would like to stay here to-morrow, shouldn't you?"

"I should like to have this place to come and rest in, that's all," said Baldassarre. "I would pay for it, and harm nobody."

"No, indeed; I think you are not a bad old man. But you look sorry about something. Tell me, is there anything you shall cry about when I leave you by yourself? *I* used to cry once."

"No, child; I think I shall cry no more."

"That's right; and I'll bring you some breakfast, and show you the bimbo. Good-night."

Tessa took up her bowl and lantern, and closed the door behind her. The pretty loving apparition had been no more to Baldassarre than a faint rainbow on the blackness to the man who is wrestling in deep waters. He hardly thought of her again till his dreamy waking passed into the more vivid images of disturbed sleep.

But Tessa thought much of him. She had no sooner entered the house than she told Monna Lisa what she had done, and insisted that the stranger should be allowed to come and rest in the outhouse when he liked. The old woman, who had had her notions of making him a useful tenant, made a great show of reluctance, shook her head, and urged that Messer Naldo would be angry if she let any one come about the house. Tessa did not believe that. Naldo had said nothing against strangers who lived nowhere; and this old man knew nobody except one person, who was not Nofri.

"Well," conceded Monna Lisa, at last, "if I let him stay for awhile and carry things up the hill for me, thou must keep thy counsel and tell nobody."

"No," said Tessa, "I'll only tell the bimbo."

"And then," Monna Lisa went on, in her thick under-tone,

"God may love us well enough not to let Messer Naldo find out anything about it. For he never comes near but at dark; and as he was here two days ago, it's likely he'll never come at all till the old man's gone away again."

"Oh, me! Monna," said Tessa, clasping her hands, "I wish Naldo had not to go such a long, long way sometimes before he comes back again."

"Ah, child, the world's big, they say. There are places behind the mountains, and if people go night and day, night and day, they get to Rome, and see the Holy Father."

Tessa looked submissive in the presence of this mystery, and began to rock her baby, and sing syllables of vague loving meaning, in tones that imitated a triple chime.

The next morning she was unusually industrious in the prospect of more dialogue and of the pleasure she should give the poor old stranger by showing him her baby. But before she could get ready to take Baldassarre his breakfast, she found that Monna Lisa had been employing him as a drawer of water. She deferred her paternosters, and hurried down to insist that Baldassarre should sit on his straw, so that she might come and sit by him again while he ate his breakfast. That attitude made the new companionship all the more delightful to Tessa, for she had been used to sitting on straw in old days along with her goats and mules.

"I will not let Monna Lisa give you too much work to do," she said, bringing him some steaming broth and soft bread. "I don't like much work, and I dare say you don't. I like sitting in the sunshine and feeding things. Monna Lisa says work is good, but she does it all herself, so I don't mind. She's not a cross old woman—you needn't be afraid of her being cross. And now, you eat that, and I'll go and fetch my baby and show it you."

Presently she came back with the small mummy case in her arms. The mummy looked very lively, having unusually large dark eyes, though no more than the usual indication of a future nose.

"This is my baby," said Tessa, seating herself close to Baldassarre. "You didn't think it was so pretty, did you? It is like the little Gesù, and I should think the Santa Madonna would be kinder to me now, is it not true? But I have not much to ask for, because I have every thing now—only that I should see my husband oftener. You may hold the *bambino* a little if you like, but I think you must not kiss him, because you might hurt him."

She spoke this prohibition in a tone of soothing excuse, and Baldassarre could not refuse to hold the small package. "Poor thing! poor thing!" he said, in a deep voice which had something strangely threatening in its apparent pity. It did not seem to him as if this guileless loving little woman could reconcile him to the world at all, but rather that she was with him against the world, that she was a creature who would need to be avenged.

"Oh, don't you be sorry for me," she said; "for though I don't see him often, he is more beautiful and good than anybody else in the world. I say prayers to him when he's away. You couldn't think what he is!"

She looked at Baldassarre with a wide glance of mysterious meaning, taking the baby from him again, and almost wishing he would question her as if he wanted very much to know more.

"Yes, I could," said Baldassarre, rather bitterly.

"No, I'm sure you never could," said Tessa, earnestly. "You thought he might be Nofri," she added with a triumphant air of conclusiveness. "But never mind; you couldn't know. What is your name?"

He rubbed his hand over his knitted brow, then looked at her blankly and said, "Ah, child, what is it?"

It was not that he did not often remember his name well enough; and if he had had presence of mind now to remember it, he would have chosen not to tell it. But a sudden question appealing to his memory, had a paralyzing effect, and in that moment he was conscious of nothing but helplessness.

Ignorant as Tessa was, the pity stirred in her by his blank look taught her to say,

"Never mind: you are a stranger, it is no matter about your having a name. Good-by now, because I want my breakfast. You will come here and rest when you like; Monna Lisa says you may. And don't you be unhappy, for we'll be good to you."

"Poor thing!" said Baldassarre again.

CHAPTER XXXIV.

No Place For Repentance

MESSER NALDO came again sooner than was expected: he came on the evening of the twenty-eighth of November, only eleven days after his previous visit, proving that he had not gone far beyond the mountains; and a scene which we have witnessed as it took place that evening in the Via de' Bardi may help to explain the impulse which turned his steps towards the Hill of San Giorgio.

When Tito had first found this home for Tessa, on his return from Rome, more than a year and a half ago, he had acted, he persuaded himself, simply under the constraint imposed on him by his own kindliness after the unlucky incident which had made foolish little Tessa imagine him to be her husband. It was true that the kindness was manifested towards a pretty trusting thing whom it was impossible to be near without feeling inclined to caress and pet her; but it was not less true that Tito had movements of kindness towards her apart from any contemplated gain to himself. Otherwise, charming as her prettiness and prattle were in a lazy moment, he might have preferred to be free from her; for he was not in love with Tessa—he was in love for the first time in his life with an entirely different woman, whom he was not simply inclined to shower caresses on, but whose presence possessed him so that the simple sweep of her long tresses across his cheek seemed to vibrate through the hours. All the young ideal passion he had in him had been stirred by Romola, and his fibre was too fine, his intellect too bright, for him to be tempted into the habits of a gross pleasure-seeker. But he had spun a web about himself and Tessa, which he felt incapable of breaking: in the first moments after the mimic marriage he had been prompted to leave her under an illusion by a distinct calculation of his own possible need, but since that critical moment it seemed to him that the web had gone on spinning itself in spite of him, like a growth over which he had no power. The elements of kindness and self-indulgence are hard to distinguish in a soft nature like Tito's; and the annoyance he had felt under Tessa's pursuit of him on the day of his betrothal, the thorough intention of revealing the truth to her with which he set out to fulfil his promise of seeing her again, were a sufficiently strong argument to him that in ultimately leaving Tessa under her illusion, and providing a home for her, he had been overcome by his own kindness. And in those days of his first devotion to Romola he needed a self-justifying argument. He had learned to be glad that she was deceived about some things. But every strong feeling makes to itself a conscience of its own—has it own piety; just as much as that feeling of the son towards the mother which will sometimes survive amid the worst fumes of depravation; and Tito could not yet be easy in committing a secret offence against his wedded love.

But he was all the more careful in taking precautions to preserve the secrecy of the offence. Monna Lisa, who, like many of her class, never left her habitation except to go to one or two particular shops, and to confession once a year, knew nothing of his real name and whereabout: she only knew that he paid her so as to make her very comfortable, and minded little about the rest, save that she got fond of Tessa, and found pleasure in the cares for which she was paid. There was some mystery behind, clearly, since Tessa was a contadina, and Messer Naldo was a signor; but, for aught Monna Lisa knew, he might be a real husband. For Tito had thoroughly frightened Tessa into silence about the circumstances of their marriage, by telling her that if she broke that silence she would never see him again; and Monna Lisa's deafness, which made it impossible to say anything to her without some premeditation, had saved Tessa from any incautious revelation to her, such as had run off her tongue in talking with Baldassarre. For a long while Tito's visits were so rare, that it seemed likely enough he took journeys between them. They were prompted chiefly by the desire to see that all things were going on well with Tessa; and though he always found his visit pleasanter than the prospect of it—always felt anew the charm of that pretty ignorant lovingness and trust—he had not yet any real need of it. But he was determined, if possible, to preserve the simplicity on which the charm depended; to keep Tessa a genuine contadina, and not place the small field-flower among conditions that would rob it of its grace. He would have been shocked to see her in the dress of any other rank than her own; the piquancy of her talk would be all gone if things began to have new relations for her, if her world became wider, her pleasures less childish; and the squirrel-like enjoyment of nuts at discretion marked the standard of the luxuries he provided for her. By this means, Tito saved Tessa's charm from being sullied; and he also, by a convenient coincidence, saved himself from aggravating expenses that were already rather importunate to a man whose money was all required for his avowed habits of life.

This, in brief, had been the history of Tito's relation to Tessa up to a very recent date. It is true that once or twice before Bardo's death, the sense that there was Tessa up the hill, with whom it was possible to pass an hour agreeably, had been an inducement to him to escape from a little weariness of the old man, when, for lack of any positive engagement, he might otherwise have borne the weariness patiently and shared Romola's burthen. But the moment when he had first felt a real hunger for Tessa's ignorant lovingness and belief in him had not come till quite lately, and it was distinctly marked out by circumstances as little to be forgotten as the oncoming of a malady that has permanently vitiated the sight and hearing. It was the day when he had first seen Baldassarre, and had bought the armour. Returning across the bridge that night, with the coat of mail in his hands, he had felt an unconquerable shrinking from an immediate encounter with Romola. She, too, knew little of the actual world; she, too, trusted him; but he had an uneasy consciousness that behind her frank eyes there was a nature that could judge him, and that any ill-founded trust of hers sprang not from pretty brute-like incapacity, but from a nobleness which might prove an alarming touchstone. He wanted a little ease, a little repose from self-control, after the agitation and exertions of the day; he wanted to be where he could adjust his mind to the morrow, without caring how he behaved at the present moment. And there was a sweet adoring creature within reach whose presence was as safe and unconstraining as that of her own kids,—who would believe any fable, and remain quite unimpressed by public opinion. And so on that evening when Romola was waiting and listening for him, he turned his steps up the hill.

No wonder, then, that the steps took the same course on this evening, eleven days later, when he had had to recoil under Romola's first outburst of scorn. He could not wish Tessa in his wife's place, or refrain from wishing that his wife should be thoroughly reconciled to him; for it was Romola, and not Tessa, that belonged to the world where all the larger desires of a man who had ambition and effective faculties must necessarily lie. But he wanted a refuge from a standard disagreeably rigorous, of which he could not make himself independent simply by thinking it folly; and Tessa's little soul was that inviting refuge.

It was not much more than eight o'clock when he went up the stone steps to the door of Tessa's room. Usually she heard his entrance into the house, and ran to meet him, but not to-night; and when he opened the door he saw the reason. A single dim light was burning above the dying fire, and showed Tessa in a kneeling attitude by the head of the bed where the baby lay. Her head had fallen aside on the pillow, and her brown rosary, which usually hung above the pillow over the picture of the Madonna and the golden palm branches, lay in the loose grasp of her right hand. She had gone fast asleep over her beads. Tito stepped lightly across the little room, and sat down close to her. She had probably heard the opening of the door as part of her dream, for he had not been looking at her two moments before she opened her eyes. She opened them without any start, and remained quite motionless looking at him, as if the sense that he was there smiling at her shut out any impulse which could disturb that happy passiveness. But when he put his hand under her chin, and stooped to kiss her, she said:—

"I dreamed it, and then I said it was dreaming—and then I awoke, and it was true."

"Little sinner!" said Tito, pinching her chin, "you have not said half your prayers. I will punish you by not looking at your baby; it is ugly."

Tessa did not like those words, even though Tito was smiling. She had some pouting distress in her face, as she said, bending anxiously over the baby,

"Ah, it is not true! He is prettier than anything. You do not think he is ugly. You *will* look at him. He is even prettier than when you saw him before—only he's asleep, and you can't see his eyes or his tongue, and I can't show you his hair—and it grows—isn't that wonderful? Look at him! It's true his face is very much all alike when he's asleep, there is not so much to see as when he's awake. If you kiss him very gently, he won't wake: you want to kiss him, is it not true?"

He satisfied her by giving the small mummy a butterfly kiss, and then putting his hand on her shoulder and turning her face towards him, said, "You like looking at the baby better than looking at your husband, you false one!"

She was still kneeling, and now rested her hands on his knee, looking up at him like one of Fra Lippo Lippi's round-cheeked adoring angels.*

"No," she said, shaking her head; "I love you always best, only I want you to look at the *bambino* and love him; I used only to want you to love me."

"And did you expect me to come again so soon?" said Tito, inclined to make her prattle. He still felt the effects of the agitation he had undergone, still felt like a man who has been violently jarred, and this was the easiest relief from silence and solitude.

"Ah, no," said Tessa, "I have counted the days—to-day I began at my right thumb again—since you put on the beautiful chain coat, that Messer San Michele gave you to take care of you on your journey. And you have got it on now," she said, peeping through the opening in the breast of his tunic. "Perhaps it made you come back sooner."

"Perhaps it did, Tessa," he said. "But don't mind the coat now. Tell me what has happened since I was here. Did you see the tents in the Prato, and the soldiers and horsemen when they passed the bridges—did you hear the drums and trumpets?"

"Yes, and I was rather frightened, because I thought the soldiers might come up here. And Monna Lisa was a little afraid too, for she said they might carry our kids off; she said it was their business to do mischief. But the Holy Madonna took care of us, for we never saw one of them up here. But something has happened, only I hardly dare tell you, and that is what I was saying more *aves* for."

"What do you mean, Tessa?" said Tito, rather anxiously. "Make haste and tell me."

"Yes, but will you let me sit on your knee? because then I think I shall not be so frightened."

He took her on his knee, and put his arm round her, but looked grave: it seemed that something unpleasant must pursue him even here.

"At first, I didn't mean to tell you," said Tessa, speaking almost in a whisper, as if that would mitigate the offence; "because we thought the old man would be gone away before you came again, and it would be as if it had not been. But now he is there, and you are come, and I never did anything you told me not to do before. And I want to tell you, and then you will perhaps forgive me, for it is a long while before I go to confession."

"Yes, tell me everything, my Tessa." He began to hope it was after all a trivial matter.

"Oh, you will be sorry for him: I'm afraid he cries about something when I don't see him. But that was not the reason I went to him first; it was because I wanted to talk to him and show him my baby, and he was a stranger that lived nowhere, and I thought you wouldn't care so much about my talking to him. And I think he is not a bad old man, and he wanted to come and sleep on the straw next to the goats, and I made Monna Lisa say, 'Yes, he might,' and he's away all the day almost, but when he comes back I talk to him, and take him something to eat."

"Some beggar, I suppose. It was naughty of you, Tessa, and I am angry with Monna Lisa. I must have him sent away."

"No, I think he is not a beggar, for he wanted to pay Monna Lisa, only she asked him to do work for her instead. And he gets himself shaved, and his clothes are tidy: Monna Lisa says he is a decent man. But sometimes I think he is not in his right mind. Lupo, at Peretola, was not in his right mind: and he looks a little like Lupo sometimes, as if he didn't know where he was."

"What sort of face has he?" said Tito, his heart beginning to beat strangely. He was so haunted by the thought of Baldassarre, that it was already he whom he saw in imagination sitting on the straw not many yards from him. "Fetch your stool, my Tessa, and sit on it."

"Shall you not forgive me?" she said, timidly, moving from his knee.

"Yes, I will not be angry—only sit down, and tell me what sort of old man this is."

"I can't think how to tell you: he is not like my step-father, Nofri, nor anybody. His face is yellow, and he has deep marks in it; and his hair is white, but there is none on the top of his head: and his eyebrows are black, and he looks from under them at me, and says, 'Poor thing!' to me, as if he thought I was beaten as I used to be; and that seems as if he couldn't be in his right mind, doesn't it? And I asked him his name once, but he couldn't tell it me: yet everybody has a name,—is it not true? And he has a book now, and keeps looking at it ever so long, as if he were a Padre. But I think he is not saying prayers, for his lips never move;—ah, you are angry with me, or is it because you are sorry for the old man?"

Tito's eyes were still fixed on Tessa; but he had ceased to see her, and was only seeing the objects her words suggested. It was this absent glance which frightened her, and she could not help going to kneel at his side again. But he did not heed her, and she dared not touch him, or speak to him: she knelt, trembling and wondering; and this state of mind suggesting her beads to her, she took them from the floor, and began to tell them again, her pretty lips moving silently, and her blue eyes wide with anxiety and struggling tears.

Tito was quite unconscious of her movements—unconscious of his own attitude: he was in that wrapt state in which a man will grasp painful roughness, and press, and press it closer, and never feel it. A new possibility had risen before him, which might dissolve at once the wretched conditions of fear and suppression that were marring his life. Destiny had brought within his reach an opportunity of retrieving that moment on the steps of the Duomo, when the Past had grasped him with living quivering hands, and he had disowned it. A few steps, and he might be face to face with his father, with no witness by; he might seek forgiveness and reconciliation; and there was money now, from the sale of the library, to enable them to leave Florence without disclosures, and go into Southern Italy, where, under the probable French rule, he had already laid a foundation for patronage. Romola need never know the whole truth, for she could have no certain means of identifying that prisoner in the Duomo with Baldassarre, or of learning what had taken place on the steps, except from Baldassarre himself; and if his father forgave, he would also consent to bury, that offence. But with this possibility of relief, by an easy spring, from present evil, there rose the other possibility, that the fierce-hearted man might refuse to be propitiated. Well—and if he did, things would only be as they had been before; for there would be *no witness by*. It was not repentance with a white sheet round it and taper in hand, confessing its hated sin in the eyes of men, that Tito was preparing for: it was a repentance that would make all things pleasant again, and keep all past unpleasant things secret. And Tito's soft-heartedness, his indisposition to feel himself in harsh relations with any creature, was in strong activity towards his father, now his father was brought near to him. It would be a state of ease that his nature could not but desire, if the poisonous hatred in Baldassarre's glance could be replaced by something of the old affection and complacency. Tito longed to have his world once again completely cushioned with good-will, and longed for it the more eagerly because of what he had just suffered from the collision with Romola. It was not difficult to him to smile pleadingly on those whom he had injured, and offer to do them much kindness: and no quickness of intellect could tell him exactly the taste of that honey on the lips of the injured. The opportunity was there, and it raised an inclination which hemmed in the calculating activity of his thought. He started up, and stepped towards the door; but Tessa's cry, as she dropped her beads, roused him from his absorption. He turned and said,

"My Tessa, get me a lantern; and don't cry, little pigeon, I am not angry."

They went down the stairs, and Tessa was going to shout the need of the lantern in Monna Lisa's ear, when Tito, who had opened the door, said, "Stay, Tessa—no, I want no lantern: go upstairs again, and keep quiet, and say nothing to Monna Lisa."

In half a minute he stood before the closed door of the outhouse, where the moon was shining white on the old paintless wood.

In this last decisive moment, Tito felt a tremor upon him—a sudden instinctive shrinking from a possible tiger glance, a possible tiger leap. Yet why should he, a young man, be afraid of an old one? a young man with armour on, of an old man without a weapon? It was but a moment's hesitation, and Tito laid his hand on the door. Was his father asleep? Was there nothing else but the door that screened him from the voice and the glance which no magic could turn into ease?

Baldassarre was not asleep. There was a square opening high in the wall of the hovel, through which the moonbeams sent in a stream of pale light; and if Tito could have looked through the opening, he would have seen his father seated on the straw, with something that shone like a white star in his hand. Baldassarre was feeling the edge of his poniard, taking refuge in that sensation from a hopeless blank of thought that seemed to lie like a great gulf between his passion and its aim. He was in one of his most wretched moments of conscious helplessness: he had been poring, while it was light, over the book that lay open beside him; then he had been trying to recall the names of his jewels, and the symbols engraved on them; and though at certain other times he had recovered some of those names and symbols, to-night they were all gone into darkness. And this effort at inward seeing had seemed to end in utter paralysis of memory. He was reduced to a sort of mad consciousness that he was a solitary pulse of just rage in a world filled with defiant baseness. He had clutched and unsheathed his dagger, and for a long while had been feeling its edge, his mind narrowed to one image, and the dream of one sensation—the sensation of plunging that dagger into a base heart, which he was unable to pierce in any other way.

Tito had his hand on the door and was pulling it: it dragged against the ground as such old doors often do, and Baldassarre, startled out of his dream-like state, rose from his sitting posture in vague amazement, not knowing where he was. He had not yet risen to his feet, and was still kneeling on one knee, when the door came wide open and he saw, dark against the moonlight, with the rays falling on one bright mass of curls and one rounded olive cheek, the image of his reverie—not shadowy—close and real like water at the lips after the thirsty dream of it. No thought could come athwart that eager thirst. In one moment, before Tito could start back, the old man, with the preternatural force of rage in his limbs, had sprung forward and the dagger had flashed out. In the next moment the dagger had snapped in two, and Baldassarre, under the parrying force of Tito's arm, had fallen back on the straw, clutching the hilt with its bit of broken blade. The pointed end lay shining against Tito's feet.

Tito had felt one great heart-leap of terror as he had staggered under the weight of the thrust: he felt now the triumph of deliverance and safety. His armour had been proved, and vengeance lay helpless before him. But the triumph raised no devilish impulse; on the contrary the sight of his father close to him and unable to injure him, made the effort at reconciliation easier. He was free from fear, but he had only the more unmixed and direct want to be free from the sense that he was hated. After they had looked at each other a little while, Baldassarre lying motionless in despairing rage, Tito said in his soft tones, just as they had sounded before the last parting on the shores of Greece,

"*Padre mio!*" There was a pause after those words, but no movement or sound till he said,—

"I came to ask your forgiveness!"

Again he paused, that the healing balm of those words might have time to work. But there was no sign of change in Baldassarre: he lay as he had fallen, leaning on one arm: he was trembling, but it was from the shock that had thrown him down.

"I was taken by surprise that morning. I wish now to be a son to you again. I wish to make the rest of your life happy, that you may forget what you have suffered."

He paused again. He had used the clearest and strongest words he could think of. It was useless to say more, until he had some sign that Baldassarre understood him. Perhaps his mind was too distempered or too imbecile even for that: perhaps the shock of his fall and his disappointed rage might have quite suspended the use of his faculties.

Presently Baldassarre began to move. He threw away the broken dagger, and slowly and gradually, still trembling, began to raise himself from the ground. Tito put out his hand to help him, and so strangely quick are men's souls that in this moment when he began to feel his atonement was accepted, he had a darting thought of the irksome efforts it entailed. Baldassarre clutched the hand that was held out, raised himself and clutched it still, going close up to Tito till their faces were not a foot off each other. Then he began to speak, in a deep trembling voice,

"I saved you—I nurtured you—I loved you. You forsook me—you robbed me—you denied me. What can you give me? You have made the world bitterness to me; but there is one draught of sweetness left—*that you shall know agony*."

He let fall Tito's hand, and going backward a little, first rested his arm on a projecting stone in the wall, and then sank again in a sitting posture on the straw. The outleap of fury in the dagger-thrust had evidently exhausted him.

Tito stood silent. If it had been a deep, yearning emotion which had brought him to ask his father's forgiveness, the denial of it might have caused him a pang which would have excluded the rushing train of thoughts that followed those decisive words. As it was, though the sentence of unchangeable hatred grated on him and jarred him terribly, his mind glanced round with a self-preserving instinct to see how far those words could have the force of a substantial threat. When he had come down to speak to Baldassarre, he had said to himself that if his effort at reconciliation failed, things would only be as they had been before. The first glance of his mind was backward to that thought again, but the future possibilities of danger that were conjured up along with it brought the perception that things were *not* as they had been before, and the perception came as a triumphant relief. There was not only the broken dagger, there was the certainty from what Tessa had told him, that Baldassarre's mind was broken too, and had no edge that could reach him. Tito felt he had no choice now: he must defy Baldassarre as a mad, imbecile old man; and the chances were so strongly on his side that there was hardly room for fear. No, except the fear of having to do many unpleasant things in order to save himself from what was yet more unpleasant. And one of those unpleasant things must be done immediately: it was very difficult.

"Do you mean to stay here?" he said.

"No," said Baldassarre, bitterly, "you mean to turn me out."

"Not so," said Tito. "I only ask."

"I tell you, you have turned me out. If it is your straw, you turned me off it three years ago."

"Then you mean to leave this place?" said Tito, more anxious about this certainty than the ground of it.

"I have spoken," said Baldassarre.

Tito turned and re-entered the house. Monna Lisa was nodding: he went up to Tessa, and found her crying by the side of her baby.

"Tessa," he said, sitting down, and taking her head between his hands. "Leave off crying, little goose, and listen to me."

He lifted her chin upward, that she might look at him, while he spoke very distinctly and emphatically.

"You must never speak to that old man again. He is a mad old man, and he wants to kill me. Never speak to him or listen to him again."

Tessa's tears had ceased, and her lips were pale with fright.

"Is he gone away?" she whispered.

"He will go away. Remember what I have said to you."

"Yes; I will never speak to a stranger any more," said Tessa, with a sense of guilt.

He told her, to comfort her, that he would come again tomorrow; and then went down to Monna Lisa to rebuke her severely for letting a dangerous man come about the house.

Tito felt that these were odious tasks; they were very evil-tasted morsels, but they were forced upon him. He heard Monna Lisa fasten the door behind him, and turned away, without looking towards the open door of the hovel. He felt secure that Baldassarre would go, and he could not wait to see him go. Even *his* young frame and elastic spirit were shattered by the agitations that had been crowded into this single evening.

Baldassarre was still sitting on the straw when the shadow of Tito passed by. Before him lay the fragments of the broken dagger; beside him lay the open book, over which he had pored in vain. They looked like mocking symbols of his utter helplessness; and his body was still too trembling for him to rise and walk away.

But the next morning very early, when Tessa peeped anxiously through the hole in her shutter, the door of the hovel was open, and the strange old man was gone.

CHAPTER XXXV.

What Florence was Thinking Of

For several days Tito saw little of Romola. He told her gently, the next morning, that it would be better for her to remove any small articles of her own from the library, as there would be agents coming to pack up the antiquities. Then, leaning to kiss her on the brow, he suggested that she should keep in her own room where the little painted tabernacle was, and where she was then sitting, so that she might be away from the noise of strange footsteps. Romola assented quietly, making no sign of emotion: the night had been one long waking to her, and, in spite of her healthy frame, sensation had become a dull continuous pain, as if she had been stunned and bruised. Tito divined that she felt ill, but he dared say no more; he only dared, perceiving that her hand and brow were stone cold, to fetch a furred mantle and throw it lightly round her. And in every brief interval that he returned to her, the scene was nearly the same: he tried to propitiate her by some unobtrusive act or word of tenderness, and she seemed to have lost the power of speaking to him, or of looking at him. "Patience!" he said to himself. "She will recover it, and forgive at last. The tie to me must still remain the strongest." When the stricken person is slow to recover and look as if nothing had happened, the striker easily glides into the position of the aggrieved party; he feels no bruise himself, and is strongly conscious of his own amiable behaviour since he inflicted the blow. But Tito was not naturally disposed to feel himself aggrieved; the constant bent of his mind was towards propitiation, and he would have submitted to much for the sake of feeling Romola's hand resting on his head again, as it did that morning when he first shrank from looking at her.

But he found it the less difficult to wait patiently for the return of his home happiness, because his life out of doors was more and more interesting to him. A course of action which is in strictness a slowly-prepared outgrowth of the entire character, is yet almost always traceable to a single impression as its point of apparent origin; and since that moment in the Piazza del Duomo, when Tito, mounted on the bales, had tasted a keen pleasure in the consciousness of his ability to tickle the ears of men with any phrases that pleased them, his imagination had glanced continually towards a sort of political activity which the troubled public life of Florence was likely enough to find occasion for. But the fresh dread of Baldassarre, waked in the same moment, had lain like an immovable rocky obstruction across that path, and had urged him into the sale of the library, as a preparation for the possible necessity of leaving Florence, at the very time when he was beginning to feel that it had a new attraction for him. That dread was nearly removed now: he must wear his armour still, he must prepare himself for possible demands on his coolness and ingenuity, but he did not feel obliged to take the inconvenient step of leaving Florence and seeking new fortunes. His father had refused the offered atonement—had forced him into defiance; and an old man in a strange place, with his memory gone, was weak enough to be defied.

Tito's implicit desires were working themselves out now in

very explicit thoughts. As the freshness of young passion faded, life was taking more and more decidedly for him the aspect of a game in which there was an agreeable mingling of skill and chance.

And the game that might be played in Florence promised to be rapid and exciting; it was a game of revolutionary and party struggle, sure to include plenty of that unavowed action in which brilliant ingenuity, able to get rid of all inconvenient beliefs except that "ginger is hot in the mouth,"* is apt to see the path of superior wisdom.

No sooner were the French guests gone than Florence was as agitated as a colony of ants when an alarming shadow has been removed, and the camp has to be repaired. "How are we to raise the money for the French King? How are we to manage the war with those obstinate Pisan rebels? Above all, how are we to mend our plan of government, so as to hit on the best way of getting our magistrates chosen and our laws voted?" Till those questions were well answered trade was in danger of standing still, and that large body of the working men who were not counted as citizens and had not so much as a vote to serve as an anodyne to their stomachs were likely to get impatient. Something must be done.

And first the great bell was sounded, to call the citizens to a parliament in the Piazza de' Signori; and when the crowd was wedged close, and hemmed in by armed men at all the outlets, the Signoria (or Gonfaloniere and eight Priors for the time being) came out and stood by the stone lion on the platform in front of the Old Palace, and proposed that twenty chief men of the city should have dictatorial authority given them, by force of which they should for one year choose all magistrates, and set the frame of government in order. And the people shouted their assent, and felt themselves the electors of the Twenty. This kind of "parliament" was a very old Florentine fashion, by which the will of the few was made to seem the choice of the many.

The shouting in the Piazza was soon at an end, but not so the debating inside the Palace: was Florence to have a Great Council after the Venetian mode, where all the officers of government might be elected, and all laws voted by a wide number of citizens of a certain age and of ascertained qualifications, without question of rank or party; or, was it to be governed on a narrower and less popular scheme, in which the hereditary influence of good families would be less adulterated with the votes of shopkeepers? Doctors of law disputed day after day, and far on into the night; Messer Pagolantonio Soderini alleged excellent reasons on the side of the popular scheme; Messer Guidantonio Vespucci alleged reasons equally excellent on the side of a more aristocratic form. It was a question of boiled or roast, which had been prejudged by the palates of the disputants, and the excellent arguing might have been protracted a long while without any other result than that of deferring the cooking. The majority of the men inside the Palace, having power already in their hands, agreed with Vespucci, and thought change should be moderate; the majority outside the palace, conscious of little power and many grievances, were less afraid of change.

And there was a force outside the Palace which was gradually tending to give the vague desires of that majority the character of a determinate will. That force was the preaching of Savonarola. Impelled partly by the spiritual necessity that was laid upon him to guide the people, and partly by the prompting of public men who could get no measures carried without his aid, he was rapidly passing in his daily sermons from the general to the special—from telling his hearers that they must postpone their private passions and interests to the public good, to telling them precisely what sort of government they must have in order to promote that good—from "Choose whatever is best for all" to "Choose the Great Council," and "the Great Council is the will of God."

To Savonarola these were as good as identical propositions. The Great Council was the only practicable plan for giving an expression to the public will large enough to counteract the vitiating influence of party interests; it was a plan that would make honest impartial public action at least possible. And the purer the government of Florence could become—the more secure from the designs of men who saw their own advantage in the moral debasement of their fellows—the nearer would the Florentine people approach the character of a pure community, worthy to lead the way in the renovation of the Church and the world. And Fra Girolamo's mind never stopped short of that sublimest end: the objects towards which he felt himself working had always the same moral magnificence. He had no private malice, he sought no petty gratification. Even in the last terrible days, when ignominy, torture, and the fear of torture, had laid bare every hidden weakness of his soul, he could say to his importunate judges, "Do not wonder if it seems to you that I have told but few things; for my purposes were few and great."*

CHAPTER XXXVI.

Ariadne Discrowns Herself

It was more than three weeks before the contents of the library were all packed and carried away. And Romola, instead of shutting her eyes and ears, had watched the process. The exhaustion consequent on violent emotion is apt to bring a dreamy disbelief in the reality of its cause; and in the evening, when the workmen were gone, Romola took her hand-lamp, and walked slowly round amongst the confusion of straw and wooden cases, pausing at every vacant pedestal, every well-known object laid prostrate, with a sort of bitter desire to assure herself that there was a sufficient reason why her love was gone and the world was barren for her. And still, as the evenings came, she went and went again; no longer to assure herself, but because this vivifying of pain and despair about her father's memory was the strongest life left to her affections. On the 23rd of December, she knew that the last packages were going. She ran to the loggia at the top of the house that she might not lose the last pang of seeing the slow wheels move across the bridge.

It was a cloudy day, and nearing dusk. Arno ran dark and shivering; the hills were mournful; and Florence with its girdling stone towers had that silent, tomblike look, which unbroken shadow gives to a city seen from above. Santa Croce, where her father lay, was dark amidst that darkness, and slowly crawling over the bridge, and slowly vanishing up the narrow street, was the white load, like a cruel, deliberate fate carrying away her father's life-long hope to bury it in an unmarked grave. Romola felt less that she was seeing this herself than that her father was conscious of it as he lay helpless under the imprisoning stones, where her hand could not reach his to tell him that he was not alone.

She stood still even after the load had disappeared, heedless of the cold, and soothed by the gloom which seemed to cover her like a mourning garment and shut out the discord of joy. When suddenly the great bell in the palace tower rang out a mighty peal: not the hammer-sound of alarm, but an agitated peal of triumph; and one after another every other bell in every other tower seemed to catch the vibration and join the chorus. And as the chorus swelled and swelled till the air seemed made of sound, little flames, vibrating too, as if the sound had caught fire, burst out between the turrets of the palace and on the girdling towers.

That sudden clang, that leaping light, fell on Romola like sharp wounds. They were the triumph of demons at the success of her husband's treachery, and the desolation of her life. Little more than three weeks ago she had been intoxicated with the sound of these very bells; and in the gladness of Florence she had heard a prophecy of her own gladness. But now the general joy seemed cruel to her; she stood aloof from that common life—that Florence which was flinging out its loud exultation to stun the ears of sorrow and loneliness. She could never join hands with gladness again, but only with those whom it was in the hard nature of gladness to forget. And in her bitterness she felt that all rejoicing was mockery. Men shouted pæans with their souls full of heaviness, and then looked in their neighbours' faces to see if there was really such a thing as joy. Romola had lost her belief in the happiness she had once thirsted for: it was a hateful, smiling, soft-handed thing, with a narrow, selfish heart.

She ran down from the loggia, with her hands pressed against her ears, and was hurrying across the ante-chamber, when she was startled by unexpectedly meeting her husband, who was coming to seek her.

His step was elastic, and there was a radiance of satisfaction about him not quite usual.

"What! the noise was a little too much for you?" he said; for Romola, as she started at the sight of him, had pressed her hands all the closer against her ears. He took her gently by the wrist, and drew her arm within his, leading her into the saloon surrounded with the dancing nymphs and fauns, and then went on speaking: "Florence is gone quite mad at getting its Great Council, which is to put an end to all the evils under the sun—

especially to the vice of merriment. You may well look stunned, my Romola, and you are cold. You must not stay so late under that windy loggia without wrappings. I was coming to tell you that I am suddenly called to Rome—about some learned business for Bernardo Rucellai. I am going away immediately, for I am to join my party at San Gaggio* to-night, that we may start early in the morning. I need give you no trouble; I have had my packages made already. It will not be very long before I am back again."

He knew he had nothing to expect from her but quiet endurance of what he said and did. He could not even venture to kiss her brow this evening, but just pressed her hand to his lips, and left her. Tito felt that Romola was a more unforgiving woman than he had imagined; her love was not that sweet clinging instinct, stronger than all judgments, which, he began to see now, made the great charm of a wife. Still, this petrified coldness was better than a passionate, futile opposition. Her pride and capability of seeing where resistance was useless had their convenience.

But when the door had closed on Tito, Romola lost the look of cold immobility which came over her like an inevitable frost whenever he approached her. Inwardly she was very far from being in a state of quiet endurance, and the days that had passed since the scene which had divided her from Tito had been days of active planning and preparation for the fulfilment of a purpose.

The first thing she did now was to call old Maso to her.

"Maso," she said, in a decided tone, "we take our journey to-morrow morning. We shall be able now to overtake that first convoy of cloth, while they are waiting at San Piero.* See about the two mules to-night, and be ready to set off with them at break of day, and wait for me at Trespiano."*

She meant to take Maso with her as far as Bologna, and then send him back with letters to her godfather and Tito, telling them that she was gone and never meant to return. She had planned her departure so that its secresy might be perfect, and her broken love and life might be hidden away unscanned by vulgar eyes. Bernardo del Nero had been absent at his villa, willing to escape from political suspicions to his favourite occupation of attending to his land, and she had paid him the debt without a personal interview. He did not even know that the library was sold, and was left to conjecture that some sudden piece of good fortune had enabled Tito to raise this sum of money. Maso had been taken into her confidence only so far that he knew her intended journey was a secret; and to do just what she told him was the thing he cared most for in his withered wintry age.

Romola did not mean to go to bed that night. When she had fastened the door she took her taper to the carved and painted chest which contained her wedding-clothes. The white silk and gold lay there, the long white veil and the circlet of pearls. A great sob rose as she looked at them: they seemed the shroud of her dead happiness. In a tiny gold loop of the circlet a sugar-plum had lodged—a pink hailstone from the shower of sweets: Tito had detected it first, and had said that it should always remain there. At certain moments—and this was one of them—Romola was carried, by a sudden wave of memory, back again into the time of perfect trust, and felt again the presence of the husband whose love made the world as fresh and wonderful to her as to a little child that sits in stillness among the sunny flowers: heard the gentle tones and saw the soft eyes without any lie in them, and breathed again that large freedom of the soul which comes from the faith that the being who is nearest to us is greater than ourselves. And in those brief moments the tears always rose: the woman's lovingness felt something akin to what the bereaved mother feels when the tiny fingers seem to lie warm on her bosom, and yet are marble to her lips as she bends over the silent bed.

But there was something else lying in the chest besides the wedding-clothes: it was something dark and coarse, rolled up in a close bundle. She turned away her eyes from the white and gold to the dark bundle, and as her hands touched the serge, her tears began to be checked. That coarse roughness recalled her fully to the present, from which love and delight were gone. She unfastened the thick white cord and spread the bundle out on the table. It was the grey serge dress of a Sister belonging to the Third order of St. Francis, living in the world but specially devoted to deeds of piety—a personage whom the Florentines were accustomed to call a Pinzochera. Romola was going to put on this dress as a disguise, and she determined to put it on at once, so that, if she needed sleep before the morning, she might wake up in perfect readiness to be gone. She put off her black garment, and as she thrust her soft white arms into the harsh sleeves of the serge mantle and felt the hard girdle of rope hurt her fingers as she tied it, she courted those rude sensations: they were in keeping with her new scorn of that thing called pleasure which made men base—that dexterous contrivance for selfish ease, that shrinking from endurance and strain, when others were bowing beneath burthens too heavy for them, which now made one image with her husband.

Then she gathered her long hair together, drew it away tight from her face, bound it in a great hard knot at the back of her head, and taking a square piece of black silk, tied it in the fashion of a kerchief close across her head and under her chin; and over that she drew the cowl. She lifted the candle to the mirror. Surely her disguise would be complete to any one who had not lived very near to her. To herself she looked strangely like her brother Dino: the full oval of the check had only to be wasted; the eyes, already sad, had only to become a little sunken. Was she getting more like him in anything else? Only in this, that she understood now how men could be prompted to rush away for ever from earthly delights, how they could be prompted to dwell on images of sorrow rather than of beauty and joy.

But she did not linger at the mirror: she set about collecting and packing all the relics of her father and mother that were too large to be carried in her small travelling wallet. They were all to be put in the chest along with her wedding-clothes, and the chest was to be committed to her godfather when she was safely gone. First she laid in the portraits; then one by one every little thing that had a sacred memory clinging to it was put into her wallet or into the chest.

She paused. There was still something else to be stript away from her, belonging to that past on which she was going to turn her back for ever. She put her thumb and forefinger to her betrothal ring; but they rested there, without drawing it off. Romola's mind had been rushing with an impetuous current towards this act for which she was preparing: the act of quitting a husband who had disappointed all her trust, the act of breaking an outward tie that no longer represented the inward bond of love. But that force of outward symbols by which our active life is knit together so as to make an inexorable external identity for us, not to be shaken by our wavering consciousness, gave a strange effect to this simple movement towards taking off her ring—a movement which was but a small sequence of her energetic resolution. It brought a vague but arresting sense that she was somehow violently rending her life in two: a presentiment that the strong impulse which had seemed to exclude doubt and make her path clear might after all be blindness, and that there was something in human bonds which must prevent them from being broken with the breaking of illusions.

If that beloved Tito who had placed the betrothal ring on her finger was not in any valid sense the same Tito whom she had ceased to love, why should she return to him the sign of their union, and not rather retain it as a memorial? And this act, which came as a palpable demonstration of her own and his identity, had a power, unexplained to herself, of shaking Romola. It is the way with half the truth amidst which we live, that it only haunts us and makes dull pulsations that are never born into sound. But there was a passionate voice speaking within her that presently nullified all such muffled murmurs.

"It cannot be! I cannot be subject to him. He is false. I shrink from him. I despise him!"

She snatched the ring from her finger and laid it on the table against the pen with which she meant to write. Again she felt that there could be no law for her but the law of her affections. That tenderness and keen fellow-feeling for the near and the loved which are the main outgrowth of the affections, had made the religion of her life: they had made her patient in spite of natural impetuosity; they would have sufficed to make her heroic. But now all that strength was gone, or, rather, it was converted into the strength of repulsion. She had recoiled from Tito in proportion to the energy of that young belief and love which he had disappointed, of that life-long devotion to her father against which he had committed an irredeemable offence. And now it seemed as if all motive had slipped away from her, except the indignation and scorn that made her tear herself asunder from him. She was not acting after any precedent, or obeying any adopted maxims. The grand severity of the Stoical philosophy in which her father had taken care to instruct her, was familiar enough to her ears and lips, and its lofty spirit had raised certain echoes within her; but she had never used it, never needed it as a rule of life. She had endured and forborne* because she loved: maxims which told her to feel less, and not to cling close lest the onward course of great Nature should jar her, had been as powerless on her tenderness as they had been on her father's yearning for just fame. She had appropriated no theories: she had simply felt strong in the strength of affection, and life without that energy came to her as an entirely new problem.

She was going to solve the problem in a way that seemed to her very simple. Her mind had never yet bowed to any obligation apart from personal love and reverence; she had no keen sense of any other human relations, and all she had to obey now was the instinct to sever herself from the man she loved no longer.

Yet the unswerving resolution was accompanied with continually varying phases of anguish. And now that the active preparation for her departure was almost finished, she lingered: she deferred writing the irrevocable words of parting from all her little world. The emotions of the past weeks seemed to rush in again with cruel hurry, and take possession even of her limbs. She was going to write and her hand fell. Bitter tears came now at the delusion which had blighted her young years: tears very different from the sob of remembered happiness with which she had looked at the circlet of pearls and the pink hailstone. And now she felt a tingling shame at the words of ignominy she had cast at Tito—"Have you robbed some one else who is *not* dead?' To have had such words wrung from her—to have uttered them to her husband seemed a degradation of her whole life. Hard speech between those who have loved is hideous in the memory, like the sight of greatness and beauty sunk into vice and rags.

That heart-cutting comparison of the present with the past urged itself upon Romola till it even transformed itself into wretched sensations: she seemed benumbed to everything but inward throbbings, and began to feel the need of some hard contact. She drew her hands tight along the harsh knotted cord that hung from her waist. She started to her feet and seized the rough lid of the chest: there was nothing else to go in? No. She closed the lid, pressing her hand upon the rough carving, and locked it.

Then she remembered that she had still to complete her equipment as a Pinzochera. The large leather purse or scarsella, with small coin in it, had to be hung on the cord at her waist (her florins and small jewels, presents from her godfather and cousin Brigida, were safely fastened within her serge mantle)—and on the other side must hang the rosary. It did not occur to Romola as she hung that rosary by her side that something else besides the mere garb would perhaps be necessary to enable her to pass as a Pinzochera, and that her whole air and expression were as little as possible like those of a sister whose eyelids were used to be bent and whose lips were used to move in silent iteration. Her inexperience prevented her from picturing distant details, and it helped her proud courage in shutting out any foreboding of danger and insult. She did not know that any Florentine woman had ever done exactly what she was going to do: unhappy wives often took refuge with their friends, or in the cloister, she knew, but both those courses were impossible to her; she had invented a lot for herself—to go to the most learned woman in the world, Cassandra Fedele, at Venice, and ask her how an instructed woman could support herself in a lonely life there. She was not daunted by the practical difficulties in the way or the dark uncertainty at the end. Her life could never be happy any more, but it must not, could not be ignoble. And by a pathetic mixture of childish romance with her woman's trials, the philosophy which had nothing to do with this great decisive deed of hers had its place in her imagination of the future: so far as she conceived her solitary loveless life at all, she saw it animated by a proud stoical heroism, and by an indistinct but strong purpose of labour, that she might be wise enough to write something which would rescue her father's name from oblivion. After all, she was only a young girl—this poor Romola, who had found herself at the end of her joys.

There were other things yet to be done. There was a small key in a casket on the table—but now Romola perceived that her taper was dying out, and she had forgotten to provide herself with any other light. In a few moments the room was in total darkness. Feeling her way to the nearest chair, she sat down to wait for the morning.

Her purpose in seeking the key had called up certain memories which had come back upon her during the past week with the new vividness that remembered words always have for us when we have learned to give them a new meaning. Since the shock of the revelation which had seemed to divide her for ever from Tito, that last interview with Dino had never been for many hours together out of her mind. And it solicited her all the more, because while its remembered images pressed upon her almost with the imperious force of sensations, they raised struggling thoughts which resisted their influence. She could not prevent herself from hearing inwardly the dying prophetic voice saying again and again,—"The man whose face was a blank loosed thy hand and departed; and as he went, I could see his face, and it was the face of the Great Tempter. . . . And thou, Romola, didst wring thy hands and seek for water, and there was none. . . . and the plain was bare and stony again, and thou wast alone in the midst of it. . . . and then it seemed that the night fell, and I saw no more." She could not prevent herself from dwelling with a sort of agonized fascination on the wasted face; on the straining gaze at the crucifix; on the awe which had compelled her to kneel; on the last broken words and then the unbroken silence—on all the details of the death-scene, which had seemed like a sudden opening into a world apart from that of her life-long knowledge.

But her mind was roused to resistance of impressions that, from being obvious phantoms, seemed to be getting solid in the daylight. As a strong body struggles against fumes with the more violence when they begin to be stifling, a strong soul struggles against phantasies with all the more alarmed energy when they threaten to govern in the place of thought. What had the words of that vision to do with her real sorrows? That fitting of certain words was a mere chance; the rest was all vague—nay, those words themselves were vague; they were determined by nothing but her brother's memories and beliefs. He believed there was something fatal in pagan learning; he believed that celibacy was more holy than marriage; he remembered their home, and all the objects in the library; and of these threads the vision was woven. What reasonable warrant could she have had for believing in such a vision and acting on it? None. True as the voice of foreboding had proved, Romola saw with unshaken conviction that to have renounced Tito in obedience to a warning like that, would have been meagre-hearted folly. Her trust had been delusive, but she would have chosen over again to have acted on it rather than be a creature led by phantoms and disjointed whispers in a world where there was the large music of reasonable speech, and the warm grasp of living hands.

But the persistent presence of these memories, linking themselves in her imagination with her actual lot, gave her a glimpse of understanding into the lives which had before lain utterly aloof from her sympathy—the lives of the men and women who were led by such inward images and voices.

"If they were only a little stronger in me," she said to herself, "I should lose the sense of what that vision really was, and take it for a prophetic light. I might in time get to be a seer of visions myself, like the Suora Maddalena,* and Camilla Rucellai, and the rest."

Romola shuddered at the possibility. All the instruction, all the main influences of her life had gone to fortify her scorn of that sickly superstition which led men and women, with eyes too weak for the daylight, to sit in dark swamps and try to read human destiny by the chance flame of wandering vapours.

And yet she was conscious of something deeper than that coincidence of words which made the parting contact with her dying brother live anew in her mind, and gave her a new sisterhood to the wasted face. If there were much more of such experience as his in the world, she would like to understand it—would even like to learn the thoughts of men who sank in ecstasy before the pictured agonies of martyrdom. There seemed to be something more than madness in that supreme fellowship with suffering. The springs were all dried up around her: she wondered what other waters there were at which men drank and found strength in the desert. And those moments in the Duomo when she had sobbed with a mysterious mingling of rapture and pain, while Fra Girolamo offered himself a willing sacrifice for the people, came back to her as if they had been a transient taste of some such far-off fountain. But again she shrank from impressions that were alluring her within the sphere of visions and narrow fears which compelled men to outrage natural affections as Dino had done.

This was the tangled web that Romola had in her mind as she sat weary in the darkness. No radiant angel came across the gloom with a clear message for her. In those times, as now, there were human beings who never saw angels or heard perfectly clear messages. Such truth as came to them was brought confusedly in the voices and deeds of men not at all like the seraphs of unfailing wing and piercing vision—men who believed falsities as well as truths, and did the wrong as well as the right. The helping hands stretched out to them were the hands of men who stumbled and often saw dimly, so that these beings unvisited by angels had no other choice than to grasp that stumbling guidance along the path of reliance and action which is the path of life, or else to pause in loneliness and disbelief, which is no path, but the arrest of inaction and death.

And so Romola, seeing no ray across the darkness, and heavy with conflict that changed nothing, sank at last to sleep.

CHAPTER XXXVII.

The Tabernacle Unlocked

ROMOLA was waked by a tap at the door. The cold light of early morning was in the room, and Maso was come for the travelling wallet. The old man could not help starting when she opened the door, and showed him, instead of the graceful outline he had been used to, crowned with the brightness of her hair, the thick folds of the grey mantle and the pale face shadowed by the dark cowl.

"It is well, Maso," said Romola, trying to speak in the calmest voice, and make the old man easy. "Here is the wallet quite ready. You will go on quietly, and I shall not be far behind you. When you get out of the gates, you may go more slowly, for I shall perhaps join you before you get to Trespiano."

She closed the door behind him, and then put her hand on the key which she had taken from the casket the last thing in the night. It was the original key of the little painted tabernacle: Tito had forgotten to drown it in the Arno, and it had lodged, as such small things will, in the corner of the embroidered scarsella which he wore with the purple tunic. One day, long after their marriage, Romola had found it there, and had put it by, without using it, but with a sense of satisfaction that the key was within reach. The cabinet on which the tabernacle stood had been moved to the side of the room, close to one of the windows, where the pale morning light fell upon it so as to make the painted forms discernible enough to Romola, who knew them well,—the triumphant Bacchus, with his clusters and his vine-clad spear, clasping the crowned Ariadne; the Loves showering roses, the wreathed vessel, the cunning-eyed dolphins, and the rippled sea; all encircled by a flowery border, like a bower of paradise. Romola looked at the familiar images with new bitterness and repulsion: they seemed a more pitiable mockery than ever on this chill morning, when she had waked up to wander in loneliness. They had been no tomb of sorrow, but a lying screen. Foolish Ariadne! with her gaze of love, as if that bright face, with its hyacinthine curls like tendrils among the vines, held the deep secret of her life!

"Ariadne is wonderfully transformed," thought Romola. "She would look strange among the vines and the roses now."

She took up the mirror, and looked at herself once more. But the sight was so startling in this morning light that she laid it down again, with a sense of shrinking almost as strong as that with which she had turned from the joyous Ariadne. The recognition of her own face, with the cowl about it, brought back the dread lest she should be drawn at last into fellowship with some wretched superstition—into the company of the howling fanatics and weeping nuns who had been her contempt from childhood till now. She thrust the key into the tabernacle hurriedly: hurriedly she opened it, and took out the crucifix, without looking at it; then, with trembling fingers, she passed a cord through the little ring, hung the crucifix round her neck, and hid it in the bosom of her mantle. "For Dino's sake," she said to herself.

Still there were the letters to be written which Maso was to carry back from Bologna. They were very brief. The first said,

"Tito, my love for you is dead; and therefore, so far as I was yours, I too am dead. Do not try to put in force any laws for the sake of fetching me back: that would bring you no happiness. The Romola you married can never return. I need explain nothing to you after the words I uttered to you the last time we spoke long together. If you supposed them to be words of transient anger, you will know now that they were the sign of an irreversible change.

"I think you will fulfil my wish that my bridal chest should be sent to my godfather, who gave it me. It contains my wedding clothes and the portraits and other relics of my father and mother."

She folded the ring inside the letter, and wrote Tito's name outside. The next letter was to Bernardo del Nero:—

"Dearest Godfather,—If I could have been any good to your life by staying, I would not have gone away to a distance. But now I am gone. Do not ask the reason; and if you loved my father, try to prevent any one from seeking me. I could not bear my life at Florence. I cannot bear to tell any one why. Help to cover my lot in silence. I have asked that my bridal chest should be sent to you: when you open it, you will know the reason. Please to give all the things that were my mother's to my cousin Brigida, and ask her to forgive me for not saying any words of parting to her.

"Farewell, my second father. The best thing I have in life is still to remember your goodness and be grateful to you.

ROMOLA.'

Romola put the letters, along with the crucifix, within the bosom of her mantle, and then felt that everything was done. She was ready now to depart.

No one was stirring in the house, and she went almost as quietly as a grey phantom down the stairs and into the silent street. Her heart was palpitating violently, yet she enjoyed the sense of her firm tread on the broad flags—of the swift movement, which was like a chained-up resolution set free at last. The anxiety to carry out her act, and the dread of any obstacle, averted sorrow; and as she reached the Ponte Rubaconte, she felt less that Santa Croce was in her sight than that the yellow streak of morning which parted the grey was getting broader and broader, and that, unless she hastened her steps, she should have to encounter faces. Her simplest road was to go right on to the Borgo Pinti, and then along by the walls to the Porta San Gallo, from which she must leave the city; and this road carried her by the Piazza di Santa Croce. But she walked as steadily and rapidly as ever though the piazza, not trusting herself to look towards the church. The thought that any eyes might be turned on her with a look of curiosity and recognition, and that indifferent minds might be set speculating on her private sorrows, made Romola shrink physically as from the imagination of torture. She felt degraded even by that act of her husband from which she was helplessly suffering. But there was no sign that any eyes looked forth from windows to notice this tall grey sister, with the firm step, and proud attitude of the cowled head. Her road lay aloof from the stir of early traffic, and when she reached the Porta San Gallo, it was easy to pass while a dispute was going forward about the toll for panniers of eggs and market produce which were just entering.

Out! Once past the houses of the *Borgo* and she would be beyond the last fringe of Florence, the sky would be broad above her, and she would have entered on her new life—a life of loneliness and endurance, but of freedom. She had been strong enough to snap asunder the bonds she had accepted in blind faith: whatever befel her, she would no more feel the breath of soft, hated lips warm upon her cheek, no longer feel the breath of an odious mind stifling her own. The bare wintry morning, the chill air, were welcome in their severity: the leafless trees, the sombre hills, were not haunted by the gods of beauty and joy, whose worship she had forsaken for ever.

But presently the light burst forth with sudden strength, and shadows were thrown across the road. It seemed that the sun was going to chase away the greyness. The light is perhaps never felt more strongly as a divine presence stirring all those inarticulate sensibilities which are our deepest life, than in these moments when it instantaneously awakens the shadows. A certain awe which inevitably accompanied this most momentous act of her life became a more conscious element in Romola's feeling as she found herself in the sudden presence of the impalpable golden glory and the long shadow of herself that was not to be escaped. Hitherto she had met no one but an occasional contadino with mules, and the many turnings of the road on the level prevented her from seeing that Maso was not very far ahead of her. But when she had passed Pietra* and was on rising ground, she lifted up the hanging roof of her cowl and looked eagerly before her.

The cowl was dropped again immediately. She had seen, not Maso, but—two monks, who were approaching within a few yards of her. The edge of her cowl making a penthouse on her brow had shut out the objects above the level of her eyes, and for the last few moments she had been looking at nothing but the brightness on the path and at her own shadow, tall and shrouded like a dread spectre. She wished now that she had not looked up. Her disguise made her especially dislike to encounter monks: they might expect some pious passwords of which she knew nothing, and she walked along with a careful appearance of unconsciousness till she had seen the skirts of the black mantles pass by her. The encounter had made her heart beat disagreeably, for Romola had an uneasiness in her religious disguise, a shame at this studied concealment, which was made more distinct by a special effort to appear unconscious under actual glances.

But the black skirts would be gone the faster because they were going down hill; and seeing a great flat stone against a cypress that rose from a projecting green bank, she yielded to the desire which the slight shock had given her, to sit down and rest.

She turned her back on Florence, not meaning to look at it till the monks were quite out of sight; and raising the edge of her cowl again when she had seated herself, she discerned Maso and the mules at a distance where it was not hopeless for her to overtake them, as the old man would probably linger in expectation of her.

Meanwhile she might pause a little. She was free and alone.

[*FEBRUARY 1863*]

CHAPTER XXXVIII.

The Black Marks Become Magical

THAT journey of Tito's to Rome, which had removed many difficulties from Romola's departure, had been resolved on quite suddenly, at a supper, only the evening before.

Tito had set out towards that supper with agreeable expectations. The meats were likely to be delicate, the wines choice, the company distinguished; for the place of entertainment was the Selva, or Orto de' Rucellai, or, as we should say, the Rucellai Gardens; and the host, Bernardo Rucellai, was quite a typical Florentine grandee. Even his family name has a significance which is prettily symbolic: properly understood, it may bring before us a little lichen, popularly named *orcella* or *roccella*, which grows on the rocks of Greek isles and in the Canaries; and having drunk a great deal of light into its little stems and button-heads, will, under certain circumstances,* give it out again as a reddish purple dye, very grateful to the eyes of men. By bringing the excellent secret of this dye, called *oricello*, from the Levant to Florence, a certain merchant, who lived nearly a hundred years before our Bernardo's time, won for himself and his descendants much wealth, and the pleasantly suggestive surname of Oricellari, or Roccellari, which on Tuscan tongues speedily became Rucellai. And our Bernardo,* who stands out more prominently than the rest on this purple background, had added all sorts of distinction to the family name: he had married the sister of Lorenzo de' Medici, and had had the most splendid wedding in the memory of Florentine upholstery; and for these and other virtues he had been sent on embassies to France and Venice, and had been chosen Gonfaloniere; he had not only built himself a fine palace, but had finished putting the black and white marble façade to the church of Santa Maria Novella; he had planted a garden with rare trees, and had made it classic ground by receiving within it the meetings of the Platonic Academy, orphaned by the death of Lorenzo; he had written an excellent, learned book, of a new topographical sort, about ancient Rome; he had collected antiquities; he had a pure Latinity. The simplest account of him, one sees, reads like a laudatory epitaph, at the end of which the Greek and Ausonian Muses might be confidently requested to tear their hair,* and Nature to desist from any second attempt to combine so many virtues with one set of viscera.

His invitation had been conveyed to Tito through Lorenzo Tornabuoni, with an emphasis which would have suggested that the object of the gathering was political, even if the public questions of the time had been less absorbing. As it was, Tito felt sure that some party purposes were to be furthered by the excellent flavours of stewed fish and old Greek wine; for Bernardo Rucellai was not simply an influential personage, but he was one of the elect Twenty who for three weeks had held the reins of Florence. This assurance put Tito in the best spirits as he made his way to the Via della Scala, where the classic garden was to be found: without it, he might have had some uneasy speculation as to whether the high company he would have the honour of meeting was likely to be dull as well as distinguished; for he had had experience of various dull suppers even in the Rucellai gardens, and especially of the dull-philosophic sort, wherein he had not only been called upon to accept an entire scheme of the universe (which would have been easy to him), but to listen to an exposition of the same, from the origin of things to their complete ripeness in the tractate of the philosopher then speaking.

It was a dark evening, and it was only when Tito crossed the occasional light of a lamp suspended before an image of the Virgin, that the outline of his figure was discernible enough for recognition. At such moments any one caring to watch his passage from one of these lights to another might have observed that the tall and graceful personage with the mantle folded round him was followed constantly by a very different form, thick-set and elderly, in a serge tunic and felt hat. The conjunction might have been taken for mere chance, since there were many passengers along the streets at this hour. But when Tito stopped at the gate of the Rucellai gardens, the figure behind stopped too. The *sportello*, or smaller door of the gate, was already being held open by the servant, who, in the distraction of attending to some question, had not yet closed it since the last arrival, and Tito turned in rapidly, giving his name to the servant, and passing on between the evergreen bushes that shone like metal in the torchlight. The follower turned in too.

"Your name?" said the servant.

"Baldassarre Calvo," was the immediate answer.

"You are not a guest; the guests have all passed."

"I belong to Tito Melema, who has just gone in. I am to wait in the gardens."

The servant hesitated. "I had orders to admit only guests. Are you a servant of Messer Tito?"

"No, friend, I am not a servant; I am a scholar."

There are men to whom you need only say, "I am a buffalo," in a certain tone of quiet confidence, and they will let you pass. The porter gave way at once, Baldassarre entered, and heard the door closed and chained behind him, as he too disappeared among the shining bushes.

Those ready and firm answers argued a great change in Baldassarre since the last meeting face to face with Tito, when the dagger broke in two. The change had declared itself in a startling way.

At the moment when the shadow of Tito passed in front of the hovel as he departed homeward, Baldassarre was sitting in that state of after-tremor known to every one who is liable to great outbursts of passion: a state in which physical powerlessness is sometimes accompanied by an exceptional lucidity of thought, as if that disengagement of excited passion had carried away a fire-mist and left clearness behind it. He felt unable to rise and walk away just yet; his limbs seemed benumbed; he was cold, and his hand shook. But in that bodily helplessness he sat surrounded, not by the habitual dimness and vanishing shadows, but by the clear images of the past: he was living again in an unbroken course through that life which seemed a long preparation for the taste of bitterness. For some minutes he was too thoroughly absorbed by the images to reflect on the fact that he saw them, and note the fact as a change. But when that sudden clearness had travelled through the distance, and came at last to rest on the scene just gone by, he felt fully where he was: he remembered Monna Lisa and Tessa. Ah! *he* then was the mysterious husband; he who had another wife in the Via de' Bardi. It was time to pick up the broken dagger and go—go and leave no trace of himself; for to hide his feebleness seemed the thing most like power that was left to him. He leaned to take up the fragments of the dagger; then he turned towards the book which lay open at his side. It was a fine large manuscript, an odd volume of Pausanias. The moonlight was upon it, and he could see the large letters at the head of the page:

ΜΕΣΣΗΝΙΚΑ. ΚΒ'*

In old days he had known Pausanias familiarly; yet an hour or two ago he had been looking hopelessly at that page, and it had suggested no more meaning to him than if the letters had been black weather-marks on a wall; but at this moment they were once more the magic signs that conjure up a world. That moonbeam falling on the letters had raised Messenia before him, and its struggle against the Spartan oppression. He snatched up the book, but the light was too pale for him to read further by. No matter; he knew that chapter; he read inwardly. He saw the stoning of the traitor Aristocrates*—stoned by a whole people, who cast him out from their borders to lie unburied, and set up a pillar with verses upon it, telling how Time had brought home justice to the unjust. The words arose within him, and stirred innumerable vibrations of memory. He forgot that he was old: he could almost have shouted. The light was come again, mother of knowledge and joy! In that exultation his limbs recovered their strength: he started up with his broken dagger and book, and went out under the broad moonlight. It was a nipping frosty air, but Baldassarre could feel no chill—he only felt the glow of conscious power. He walked about and paused on all the open spots of that high ground, and looked down on the domed and towered city, sleeping darkly under its sleeping guardians, the mountains; on the pale gleam of the river; on the valley vanishing towards the peaks of snow; and felt himself master of them all. That sense of mental empire which belongs to us all in moments of exceptional clearness was intensified for him by the long days and nights in which memory had been little more than the consciousness of something gone. That city, which had been a weary labyrinth, was material that he could subdue to his purposes now: his mind glanced through its affairs with flashing conjecture; he was once more a man who knew cities, whose sense of vision was instructed with large experience, and who felt the keen delight of holding all things in the grasp of language. Names! Images!—his mind rushed through its wealth without pausing, like one who enters on a great inheritance.

But admist all that rushing eagerness there was one End presiding in Baldassarre's consciousness,—a dark deity in the inmost cell, who only seemed forgotten while his hecatomb* was being prepared. And when the first triumph in the certainty of recovered power had had its way, his thoughts centred themselves on Tito. That fair slippery viper could not escape him now: thanks to struggling justice, the heart that never quivered with tenderness for another had its sensitive selfish fibres that could be reached by the sharp point of anguish. The soul that bowed to no right, bowed to the great lord of mortals, Pain.

He could search into every secret of Tito's life now: he knew some of the secrets already, and the failure of the broken dagger, which seemed like frustration, had been the beginning of achievement. Doubtless that sudden rage had shaken away the obstruction which stifled his soul. Twice before, when his memory had partially returned, it had been in consequence of sudden excitation: once when he had had to defend himself from an enraged dog; once when he had been overtaken by the waves and had had to scramble up a rock to save himself.

Yes, but if this time, as then, the light were to die out, and the dreary conscious blank come back again! This time the light was stronger and steadier; but what security was there that before the morrow the dark fog would not be round him again? Even the fear seemed like the beginning of feebleness: he thought with alarm that he might sink the faster for this excited vigil of his on the hill, which was expending his force; and after seeking anxiously for a sheltered corner where he might lie down, he nestled at last against a heap of warm garden straw, and so fell asleep.

When he opened his eyes again it was daylight. The first moments were filled with strange bewilderment: he was a man with a double identity; to which had he awaked?—to the life of dim-sighted sensibilities, like the sad heirship of some fallen greatness, or to the life of recovered power? Surely the last, for the events of the night all came back to him: the recognition of the page in Pausanias, the crowding resurgence of facts and names, the sudden wide prospect which had given him such a moment as that of the Mænad in the glorious amaze of her morning waking on the mountain top.* He took up the book again, he read, he remembered without reading. He saw a name, and the images of deeds rose with it; he saw the mention of a deed, and he linked it with a name. There were stories of inexpiable crimes, but stories also of guilt that seemed successful. There were sanctuaries for swift-footed miscreants; baseness had its armour, and the weapons of justice sometimes broke against it. What then? If baseness triumphed everywhere else, if it could heap to itself all the goods of the world, and even hold the keys of hell, it would never triumph over the hatred which it had itself awakened. It could devise no torture that would seem greater than the torture of submitting to its smile. Baldassarre felt the indestructible independent force of a supreme emotion, which knows no terror, and asks for no motive—which is itself an ever-burning motive, consuming all other desire. And now, in this morning light, when the assurance came again that the fine fibres of association were active still, and that his recovered self had not departed, all his gladness was but the hope of vengeance.

From that time till the evening on which we have seen him enter the Rucellai gardens, he had been incessantly, but cautiously, inquiring into Tito's position and all his circumstances, and there was hardly a day on which he did not contrive to follow his movements. But he wished not to arouse any alarm in Tito: he wished to secure a moment when the hated favourite of blind fortune was at the summit of confident ease, surrounded by chief men on whose favour he depended. It was not any retributive payment or recognition of himself for his own behoof, on which Baldassarre's whole soul was bent: it was to find the sharpest edge of disgrace and shame by which a selfish smiler could be pierced; it was to send through his marrow the most sudden shock of dread. He was content to lie hard, and live stintedly—he had spent the greater part of his remaining money in buying another poniard: his hunger and his thirst were after nothing exquisite but an exquisite vengeance. He had avoided addressing himself to any one whom he suspected of intimacy with Tito, lest an alarm raised in Tito's mind should urge him either to flight, or to some other counteracting measure which hard-pressed ingenuity might devise. For this reason he had never entered Nello's shop, which he observed that Tito frequented, and he had turned aside to avoid meeting Piero di Cosimo.

The possibility of frustration gave added eagerness to his desire that the great opportunity he sought should not be deferred. The desire was eager in him on another ground: he trembled lest his memory should go again. Whether from the agitating presence of that fear, or from some other causes, he had twice felt a sort of mental dizziness, in which the inward sense or imagination seemed to be losing the distinct forms of things. Once he had attempted to enter the Palazzo Vecchio and make his way into a council-chamber where Tito was, and had failed. But now on this evening, he felt that his occasion was come.

CHAPTER XXXIX.

A Supper in the Rucellai Gardens

ON entering the handsome pavilion, Tito's quick glance soon discerned in the selection of the guests the confirmation of his conjecture that the object of the gathering was political, though, perhaps, nothing more distinct than that strengthening of party which comes from good fellowship. Good dishes and good wine were at that time believed to heighten the consciousness of political preferences, and in the inspired ease of after-supper talk it was supposed that people ascertained their own opinions with a clearness quite inaccessible to uninvited stomachs. The Florentines were a sober and frugal people; but wherever men have gathered wealth, Madonna della Gozzoviglia and San Buonvino* have had their worshippers; and the Rucellai were among the few Florentine families who kept a great table and lived splendidly. It was not probable that on this evening there would be any attempt to apply high philosophic theories; and there could be no objection to the bust of Plato looking on, or even to the modest presence of the cardinal virtues in fresco on the walls.

That bust of Plato had been long used to look down on conviviality of a more transcendental sort, for it had been brought from Lorenzo's villa after his death, when the meetings of the Platonic Academy* had been transferred to these gardens. Especially on every thirteenth of November, reputed anniversary of Plato's death, it had looked down from under laurel leaves on a picked company of scholars and philosophers, who met to eat and drink with moderation, and to discuss and admire, perhaps with less moderation, the doctrines of the great master:—on Pico della Mirandola, once a Quixotic young genius with long curls, astonished at his own powers, and astonishing Rome with heterodox theses;* afterwards a more humble student, with a consuming passion for inward perfection, having come to find the universe more astonishing than his own cleverness:—on innocent, laborious Marsilio Ficino, picked out young to be reared as a Platonic philosopher, and fed on Platonism in all its stages till his mind was perhaps a little pulpy from that too exclusive diet:—on Angelo Poliziano, chief literary genius of that age, a born poet, and a scholar without dulness, whose phrases had blood in them and are alive still:—or, farther back, on Leon Battista Alberti,* a reverend senior when those three were young, and of a much grander type than they, a robust, universal mind, at once practical and theoretic, artist, man of science, inventor, poet:—and on many more valiant workers whose names are not registered where every day we turn the leaf to read them, but whose labours make a part, though an unrecognized part, of our inheritance, like the ploughing and sowing of past generations.

Bernardo Rucellai was a man to hold a distinguished place in that Academy even before he became its host and patron. He was still in the prime of life, not more than four and forty, with a somewhat haughty, cautiously dignified presence; conscious of an amazingly pure Latinity, but, says Erasmus,* not to be caught speaking Latin—no word of Latin to be sheared off him by the sharpest of Teutons. He welcomed Tito with more marked favour than usual, and gave him a place between Lorenzo Tornabuoni and Giannozzo Pucci, both of them accomplished young members of the Medicean party.

Of course the talk was the lightest in the world while the brass bowl filled with scented water was passing round, that the company might wash their hands, and rings flashed on white fingers under the wax-lights, and there was the pleasant fragrance of fresh white damask newly come from France. The tone of remark was a very common one in those times. Some one asked what Dante's pattern old Florentine* would think if the life could come into him again under his leathern belt and bone clasp, and he could see the silver forks on the table? And it was agreed on all hands that the habits of posterity would be very surprising to ancestors, if ancestors could only know them. And while the silver forks were just dallying with the appetizing delicacies that introduced the more serious business of the supper—such as morsels of liver, cooked to that exquisite point that they would melt in the mouth—there was time to admire the designs on the enamelled silver centres of the brass service, and to say something, as usual, about the silver dish for *confetti*, a masterpiece of Antonio Pollajuolo, whom patronizing Popes had seduced from his native Florence to more gorgeous Rome.*

"Ah, I remember," said Niccolò Ridolfi, a middle-aged man, with that negligent ease of manner which, seeming to claim nothing, is really based on the life-long consciousness of commanding rank—"I remember our Antonio getting bitter about his chiselling and enamelling of these metal things, and taking in a fury to painting, because, said he, 'the artist who puts his work into gold and silver, puts his brains into the melting-pot.'"*

"And that is not unlikely to be a true foreboding of Antonio's," said Giannozzo Pucci. "If this pretty war with Pisa goes on, and the revolt only spreads a little to our other towns, it is not only our silver dishes that are likely to go; I doubt whether Antonio's silver saints round the altar of San Giovanni will not some day vanish from the eyes of the faithful to be worshipped more devoutly in the form of coin."

"The Frate is preparing us for that already," said Tornabuoni. "He is telling the people that God will not have silver crucifixes and starving stomachs; and that the church is best adorned with the gems of holiness and the fine gold of brotherly love."

"A very useful doctrine of war-finance, as many a Condottiere has found," said Bernardo Rucellai, drily. "But politics come on after the *confetti*, Lorenzo, when we can drink wine enough to wash them down; they are too solid to be taken with roast and boiled."

"Yes, indeed," said Niccolò Ridolfi. "Our Luigi Pulci would have said this delicate boiled kid must be eaten with an impartial mind. I remember one day at Careggi, when Luigi was in his rattling vein, he was maintaining that nothing perverted the palate like opinion. 'Opinion,' said he, 'corrupts the saliva—that's why men took to pepper. Scepticism is the only philosophy that doesn't bring a taste in the mouth.' 'Nay,' says poor

Lorenzo de' Medici, 'you must be out there, Luigi. Here is this untainted sceptic, Matteo Franco,* who wants hotter sauce than any of us.' 'Because he has a strong opinion of *himself*,' flashes out Luigi, 'which is the original egg of all other opinion. *He* a sceptic? He believes in the immortality of his own verses. He is such a logician as that preaching friar who described the pavement of the bottomless pit.' Poor Luigi! his mind was like sharpest steel that can touch nothing without cutting."

"And yet a very gentle-hearted creature," said Giannozzo Pucci. "It seemed to me his talk was a mere blowing of soap bubbles.* What dithyrambs* he went into about eating and drinking! and yet he was as temperate as a butterfly."

The light talk and the solid eatables were not soon at an end, for after the roast and boiled meats came the indispensable capon and game, and, crowning glory of a well-spread table, a peacock cooked according to the receipt of Apicius* for cooking partridges, namely, with the feathers on, but not plucked afterwards, as that great authority ordered concerning his partridges; on the contrary, so disposed on the dish that it might look as much as possible like a live peacock taking its unboiled repose. Great was the skill required in that confidential servant who was the official carver, respectfully to turn the classical though insipid bird on its back, and expose the plucked breast from which he was to dispense a delicate slice to each of the honourable company, unless any one should be of so independent a mind as to decline that expensive toughness and prefer the vulgar digestibility of capon.

Hardly any one was so bold. Tito quoted Horace,* and dispersed his slice in small particles over his plate; Bernardo Rucellai made a learned observation about the ancient price of peacocks' eggs, but did not pretend to eat his slice; and Niccolò Ridolfi held a mouthful on his fork while he told a favourite story of Luigi Pulci's,* about a man of Siena, who, wanting to give a splendid entertainment at moderate expense, bought a wild goose, cut off its beak and webbed feet, and boiled it in its feathers, to pass for a pea-hen.

In fact, very little peacock was eaten; but there was the satisfaction of sitting at a table where peacock was served up in a remarkable manner, and of knowing that such caprices were not within reach of any but those who supped with the very wealthiest men. And it would have been rashness to speak slightingly of peacock's flesh, or any other venerable institution, at a time when Fra Girolamo was teaching the disturbing doctrine that it was not the duty of the rich to be luxurious for the sake of the poor.

Meanwhile, in the chill obscurity that surrounded this centre of warmth, and light, and savoury odours, the lonely disowned man was walking in gradually narrowing circuits. He paused among the trees, and looked in at the windows, which made brilliant pictures against the gloom. He could hear the laughter; he could see Tito gesticulating with careless grace, and hear his voice, now alone, now mingling in the merry confusion of interlacing speeches. Baldassarre's mind was highly strung. He was preparing himself for the moment when he could win his entrance into this brilliant company; and he had a savage satisfaction in the sight of Tito's easy gaiety, which seemed to be preparing the unconscious victim for more effective torture.

But the men seated among the branching tapers and the flashing cups could know nothing of the pale fierce face that watched them from without. The light can be a curtain as well as the darkness.

And the talk went on with more eagerness as it became less disconnected and trivial. The sense of citizenship was just then strongly forced even on the most indifferent minds. What the over-mastering Fra Girolamo was saying and prompting was really uppermost in the thoughts of every one at table; and before the stewed fish was removed, and while the favourite sweets were yet to come, his name rose to the surface of the conversation, and, in spite of Rucellai's previous prohibition, the talk again became political. At first, while the servants remained present, it was mere gossip: what had been done in the Palazzo on the first day's voting for the Great Council; how hot-tempered and domineering Francesco Valori was, as if he were to have everything his own way by right of his austere virtue; and how it was clear to everybody who heard Soderini's speeches in favour of the Great Council, and also heard the Frate's sermons, that they were both kneaded in the same trough.*

"My opinion is," said Niccolò Ridolfi, "that the Frate has a longer head for public matters than Soderini or any Piagnone among them: you may depend on it that Soderini is his mouthpiece more than he is Soderini's."

"No, Niccolò; there I differ from you," said Bernardo

Rucellai: "the Frate has an acute mind, and readily sees what will serve his own ends; but it is not likely that Pagolantonio Soderini, who has had long experience of affairs, and has specially studied the Venetian Council, should be much indebted to a monk* for ideas on that subject. No, no: Soderini loads the cannon; though, I grant you, Fra Girolamo brings the powder and lights the match. He is master of the people, and the people are getting master of us. Ecco!"

"Well," said Lorenzo Tornabuoni, presently, when the room was clear of servants, and nothing but wine was passing round, "whether Soderini is indebted or not, *we* are indebted to the Frate for the general amnesty* which has gone along with the scheme of the Council. We might have done without the fear of God and the reform of morals being passed by a majority of black beans; but that excellent proposition, that our Medicean heads should be allowed to remain comfortably on our shoulders, and that we should not be obliged to hand over our property in fines, has my warm approval, and it is my belief that nothing but the Frate's predominance could have procured that for us. And you may rely on it that Fra Girolamo is as firm as a rock on that point of promoting peace. I have had an interview with him."

There was a murmur of surprise and curiosity at the further end of the table; but Bernardo Rucellai simply nodded, as if he knew what Tornabuoni had to say, and wished him to go on.

"Yes," proceeded Tornabuoni, "I have been favoured with an interview in the Frate's own cell, which, let me tell you, is not a common favour; for I have reason to believe that even Francesco Valori very seldom sees him in private. However, I think he saw me the more willingly because I was not a ready-made follower, but had to be converted. And, for my part, I see clearly enough that the only safe and wise policy for us Mediceans to pursue is to throw our strength into the scale of the Frate's party. We are not strong enough to make head on our own behalf; and if the Frate and the popular party were upset, every one who hears me knows perfectly well what other party would be uppermost just now: Nerli, Alberti, Pazzi, and the rest—*Arrabbiati*,* as somebody christened them the other day—who, instead of giving us an amnesty, would be inclined to fly at our throats like mad dogs, and not be satisfied till they had banished half of us."

There were strong interjections of assent to this last sentence of Tornabuoni's, as he paused and looked round a moment.

"A wise dissimulation," he went on, "is the only course for moderate rational men in times of violent party feeling. I need hardly tell this company what are my real political attachments: I am not the only man here who has strong personal ties to the banished family; but, apart from any such ties, I agree with my more experienced friends, who are allowing me to speak for them in their presence, that the only lasting and peaceful state of things for Florence is the predominance of some single family interest. This theory of the Frate's, that we are to have a popular government, in which every man is to strive only for the general good, and know no party names, is a theory that may do for some isle of Cristoforo Colombo's finding, but will never do for our fine old quarrelsome Florence. A change must come before long, and with patience and caution we have every chance of determining the change in our favour. Meanwhile, the best thing we can do will be to keep the Frate's flag flying, for if any other were to be hoisted just now it would be a black flag for us."

"It's true," said Niccolò Ridolfi, in a curt decisive way. "What you say is true, Lorenzo. For my own part, I am too old for anybody to believe that I've changed my feathers. And there are certain of us—our old Bernardo del Nero for one—whom you would never persuade to borrow another man's shield. But we can lie still, like sleepy old dogs; and it's clear enough that barking would be of no use just now. As for this psalm-singing party, who vote for nothing but the glory of God, and want to make believe we can all love each other, and talk as if vice could be swept out with a besom by the Magnificent Eight, their day will not be a long one. After all the talk of scholars, there are but two sorts of government: one where men show their teeth at each other, and one where men show their tongues and lick the feet of the strongest. They'll get their Great Council finally voted to-morrow—that's certain enough—and they'll think they've found out a new plan of government; but as sure as there's a human skin under every *lucco* in the Council, their new plan will end like every other, in snarling or in licking. That's my view of things as a plain man. Not that I consider it becoming in men of family and following, who have got others depending on their constancy and on their sticking to their colours, to go a hunting with a fine net to catch reasons in the air,* like doctors of law. I say frankly that, as the head of my family, I shall be true to my old alliances; and I have never yet seen any chalk-mark on political reasons to tell me which is true and which is false. My friend Bernardo Rucellai here is a man of reasons, I know, and I've no objection to anybody's finding fine-spun reasons for me, so that they don't interfere with my actions as a man of family who has faith to keep with his connections."

"If that is an appeal to me, Niccolò," said Bernardo Rucellai, with a formal dignity, in amusing contrast with Ridolfi's curt and pithy ease, "I may take this opportunity of saying, that while my wishes are partly determined by long-standing personal relations, I cannot enter into any positive schemes with persons over whose actions I have no control. I myself might be content with a restoration of the old order of things; but with modifications—with important modifications. And the one point on which I wish to declare my concurrence with Lorenzo Tornabuoni is, that the best policy to be pursued by our friends is, to throw the weight of their interest into the scale of the popular party. For myself, I condescend to no dissimulation; nor do I at present see the party or the scheme that commands my full assent. In all alike there is crudity and confusion of ideas, and of all the twenty men who are my colleagues in the present crisis, there is not one with whom I do not find myself in wide disagreement."

Niccolò Ridolfi shrugged his shoulders, and left it to some one else to take up the ball. As the wine went round the talk became more and more frank and lively, and the desire of several at once to be the chief speaker, as usual caused the company to break up into small knots of two and three. It was a result which had been foreseen by Lorenzo Tornabuoni and Giannozzo Pucci, and they were among the first to turn aside from the high-road of general talk and enter into a special conversation with Tito, who sat between them; gradually pushing away their seats, and turning their backs on the table and wine.

"In truth, Melema," Tournabuoni was saying at this stage, laying one hose-clad leg across the knee of the other, and caressing his ancle, "I know of no man in Florence who can serve our party better than you. You see what most of our friends are: men who can no more hide their prejudices than a dog can hide the natural tone of his bark, or else men whose political ties are so notorious, that they must always be objects of suspicion. Giannozzo here, and I, I flatter myself, are able to overcome that suspicion; we have that power of concealment and finesse, without which a rational cultivated man, instead of having any prerogative, is really at a disadvantage compared with a wild bull or a savage. But, except yourself, I know of no one else on whom we could rely for the necessary discretion."

"Yes," said Giannozzo Pucci, laying his hand on Tito's shoulder, "the fact is, *Tito mio*, you can help us better than if you were Ulysses himself, for I am convinced that Ulysses often made himself disagreeable.* To manage men one ought to have a sharp mind in a velvet sheath. And there is not a soul in Florence who could undertake a business like this journey to Rome, for example, with the same safety that you can. There is your scholarship, which may always be a pretext for such journeys; and what is better, there is your talent, which it would be harder to match than your scholarship. Niccolò Macchiavelli might have done for us if he had been on our side, but hardly so well. He is too much bitten with notions, and has not your powers of fascination. All the worse for him. He has lost a great chance in life, and you have got it."

"Yes," said Tournabuoni, lowering his voice in a significant manner, "you have only to play your game well, Melema, and the future belongs to you. For the Medici, you may rely upon it, will keep a foot in Rome as well as in Florence, and the time may not be far off when they will be able to make a finer career for their adherents even than they did in old days. Why shouldn't you take orders some day? There's a cardinal's hat at the end of that road, and you would not be the first Greek who has worn that ornament."

Tito laughed gaily. He was too acute not to measure Tornabuoni's exaggerated flattery, but still the flattery had a pleasant flavour.

"My joints are not so stiff yet," he said, "that I can't be induced to run without such a high prize as that. I think the income of an abbey or two held 'in commendam,'* without the trouble of getting my head shaved, would satisfy me at present."

"I was not joking," said Tournabuoni, with grave suavity; "I think a scholar would always be the better off for taking orders. But we'll talk of that another time. One of the objects to be first borne in mind, is that you should win the confidence of the men who hang about San Marco; that is what Giannozzo and I shall do, but you may carry it farther than we can, because you are less observed. In that way you can get a thorough knowledge of their doings, and you will make a broader screen for your agency on our side. Nothing of course can be done before you start for Rome, because this bit of business between Piero de' Medici and the French nobles must be effected at once. I mean when you come back, of course; I need say no more. I believe you could make yourself the pet votary of San Marco, if you liked; but you are wise enough to know that effective dissimulation is never immoderate."

"If it were not that an adhesion to the popular side is necessary to your safety as an agent of our party, *Tito mio*," said Giannozzo Pucci, who was more fraternal and less patronizing in his manners than Tornabuoni, "I could have wished your skill to have been employed in another way, for which it is still better fitted. But now we must look out for some other man among us who will manage to get into the confidence of our sworn enemies, the Arrabbiati; we need to know their movements more than those of the Frate's party, who are strong enough to play above board. Still, it would have been a difficult thing for you, from your known relations with the Medici a little while back, and that sort of kinship your wife has with Bernardo del Nero. We must find a man who has no distinguished connexions, and who has not yet taken any side."

Tito was pushing his hair backward automatically, as his manner was, and looking straight at Pucci with a scarcely perceptible smile on his lip.

"No need to look out for any one else," he said promptly. "I can manage the whole business with perfect ease. I will engage to make myself the special confidant of that thick-headed Dolfo Spini, and know his projects before he knows them himself."

Tito seldom spoke so confidently of his own powers, but he was in a state of exaltation at the sudden opening of a new path before him, where Fortune seemed to have hung higher prizes than any he had thought of hitherto. Hitherto he had seen success only in the form of favour; it now flashed on him in the shape of power—of such power as is possible to talent without traditional ties, and without beliefs. Each party that thought of him as a tool might become dependent on him. His position as an alien, his indifference to the ideas or prejudices of the men amongst whom he moved, were suddenly transformed into advantages; he became newly conscious of his own adroitness in the presence of a game that he was called on to play. And all the motives which might have made Tito shrink from the triple deceit that came before him as a tempting game, had been slowly strangled in him by the successive falsities of his life.

Our lives make a moral tradition for our individual selves, as the life of mankind at large makes a moral tradition for the race; and to have once acted nobly seems a reason why we should always be noble. But Tito was feeling the effect of an opposite tradition: he had won no memories of self-conquest and perfect faithfulness from which he could have a sense of falling.

The triple colloquy went on with growing spirit till it was interrupted by a call from the table. Probably the movement came from the listeners in the party, who were afraid lest the talkers should tire themselves. At all events it was agreed that there had been enough of gravity, and Rucellai had just ordered new flasks of Montepulciano.*

"How many minstrels are there among us?" he said, when there had been a general rallying round the table. "Melema, I think you are the chief: Matteo will give you the lute."

"Ah, yes!" said Giannozzo Pucci; "lead the last chorus from Poliziano's *Orfeo*, that you have found such an excellent measure for, and we will all fall in:

Ciascun segua, o Bacco, te:*
Bacco, Bacco, evoè, evoè!"

The servant put the lute into Tito's hands, and then said something in an under-tone to his master. A little subdued questioning and answering went on between them, while Tito touched the lute in a preluding way to the strain of the chorus, and there was a confusion of speech and musical humming all round the table. Bernardo Rucellai had said, "Wait a moment, Melema;" but the words had been unheard by Tito, who was leaning towards Pucci, and singing low to him the phrases of the Mænad-chorus. He noticed nothing until the buzz round the table suddenly ceased, and the notes of his own voice, with its soft low-toned triumph, "Evoè, evoè!" fell in startling isolation.

It was a strange moment. Baldassarre had moved round the

table till he was opposite Tito, and as the hum ceased there might be seen for an instant Baldassarre's fierce dark eyes bent on Tito's bright smiling unconsciousness, while the low notes of triumph dropped from his lips into the silence.

Tito looked up with a slight start, and his lips turned pale, but he seemed hardly more moved than Giannozzo Pucci, who had looked up at the same moment—or even than several others round the table; for that sallow deep-lined face with the hatred in its eyes seemed a terrible apparition across the wax-lit ease and gaiety. And Tito quickly recovered some self-command. "A mad old man—he looks like it—he *is* mad!" was the instantaneous thought that brought some courage with it; for he could conjecture no inward change in Baldassarre since they had met before. He just let his eyes fall and laid the lute on the table with apparent ease; but his fingers pinched the neck of the lute hard while he governed his head and his glance sufficiently to look with an air of quiet appeal towards Bernardo Rucellai, who said at once,—

"Good man, what is your business? What is the important declaration that you have to make?"

"Messer Bernardo Rucellai, I wish you and your honourable friends to know in what sort of company you are sitting. There is a traitor among you."

There was a general movement of alarm. Every one present, except Tito, thought of political danger, and not of private injury.

Baldassarre began to speak as if he were thoroughly assured of what he had to say; but, in spite of his long preparation for this moment, there was the tremor of overmastering excitement in his voice. His passion shook him. He went on, but he did not say what he had meant to say. As he fixed his eyes on Tito again the passionate words were like blows—they defied premeditation.

"There is a man among you who is a scoundrel, a liar, a robber. I was a father to him. I took him from beggary when he was a child. I reared him, I cherished him, I taught him, I made him a scholar. My head has lain hard that his might have a pillow. And he left me in slavery; he sold the gems that were mine, and when I came again, he denied me."

The last words had been uttered with almost convulsed agitation, and Baldassarre paused, trembling. All glances were turned on Tito, who was now looking straight at Baldassarre. It was a moment of desperation that annihilated all feeling in him, except the determination to risk anything for the chance of escape. And he gathered confidence from the agitation by which Baldassarre was evidently shaken. He had ceased to pinch the neck of the lute, and had thrust his thumbs into his belt, while his lips had begun to assume a slight curl. He had never yet done an act of murderous cruelty even to the smallest animal that could utter a cry, but at that moment he would have been capable of treading the breath from a smiling child for the sake of his own safety.

"What does this mean, Melema?" said Bernardo Rucellai, in a tone of cautious surprise. He, as well as the rest of the company, felt relieved that the tenor of the accusation was not political.

"Messer Bernardo," said Tito, "I believe this man is mad. I did not recognize him the first time he encountered me in Florence, but I know now that he is the servant who years ago accompanied me and my adoptive father to Greece, and was dismissed on account of misdemeanours. His name is Jacopo di Nola. Even at that time I believe his mind was unhinged, for, without any reason, he had conceived a strange hatred towards me; and now I am convinced that he is labouring under a mania which causes him to mistake his identity. He has already attempted my life since he has been in Florence; and I am in constant danger from him. But he is an object of pity rather than of indignation. It is too certain that my father is dead. You have only my word for it; but I must leave it to your judgment how far it is probable that a man of intellect and learning would have been lurking about in dark corners for the last month with the purpose of assassinating me; or how far it is probable that, if this man were my second father, I could have any motive for denying him. That story about my being rescued from beggary, is the vision of a diseased brain. But it will be a satisfaction to me at least if you will demand from him proofs of his identity, lest any malignant person should choose to make this mad impeachment a reproach to me."

Tito had felt more and more confidence as he went on: the lie was not so difficult when it was once begun; and as the words fell easily from his lips, they gave him a sense of power such as men feel when they have begun a muscular feat successfully. In this way he acquired boldness enough to end with a challenge for proofs.

Baldassarre, while he had been walking in the gardens, and afterwards waiting in an outer room of the pavilion with the servants, had been making anew the digest of the evidence he would bring to prove his identity and Tito's baseness, recalling the description and history of his gems, and assuring himself by rapid mental glances that he could attest his learning and his travels. It might be partly owing to this nervous strain that the new shock of rage he felt as Tito's lie fell on his ears brought a strange bodily effect with it: a cold stream seemed to rush over him, and the last words of the speech seemed to be drowned by ringing chimes. Thought gave way to a dizzy horror, as if the earth were slipping away from under him. Every one in the room was looking at him as Tito ended, and saw that the eyes which had had such fierce intensity only a few minutes before had now a vague fear in them. He clutched the back of a seat, and was silent.

Hardly any evidence could have been more in favour of Tito's assertion.

"Surely I have seen this man before, somewhere," said Tornabuoni.

"Certainly you have," said Tito, readily, in a low tone. "He is the escaped prisoner who clutched me on the steps of the Duomo. I did not recognize him then; he looks now more as he used to do, except that he has a more unmistakable air of mad imbecility."

"I cast no doubt on your word, Melema," said Bernardo Rucellai, with cautious gravity, "but you are right to desire some positive test of the fact." Then turning to Baldassarre, he said, "If you are the person you claim to be, you can doubtless give some description of the gems which were your property. I myself was the purchaser of more than one gem from Messer Tito—the chief rings, I believe, in his collection. One of them is a fine sard,* engraved with a subject from Homer. If, as you allege, you are a scholar, and the rightful owner of that ring, you can doubtless turn to the noted passage in Homer from which that subject is taken. Do you accept this test, Melema? or have you anything to allege against its validity? The Jacopo you speak of, was he a scholar?"

It was a fearful crisis for Tito. If he said, "Yes," his quick mind told him that he would shake the credibility of his story: if he said, "No," he risked everything on the uncertain extent of Baldassarre's imbecility. But there was no noticeable pause before he said, "No. I accept the test."

There was a dead silence while Rucellai moved towards the recess where the books were, and came back with the fine Florentine Homer in his hand. Baldassarre, when he was addressed, had turned his head towards the speaker, and Rucellai believed that he had understood him. But he chose to repeat what he had said, that there might be no mistake as to the test.

"The ring I possess," he said, "is a fine sard, engraved with a subject from Homer. There was no other at all resembling it in Messer Tito's collection. Will you turn to the passage in Homer from which that subject is taken? Seat yourself here," he added, laying the book on the table, and pointing to his own seat while he stood beside it.

Baldassarre had so far recovered from the first confused horror produced by the sensation of rushing coldness and chiming din in the ears as to be partly aware of what was said to him; he was aware that something was being demanded from him to prove his identity, but he formed no distinct idea of the details. The sight of the book recalled the habitual longing and faint hope that he could read and understand, and he moved towards the chair immediately. The book was open before him, and he bent his head a little towards it, while everybody watched him eagerly. He turned no leaf. His eyes wandered over the pages that lay before him, and then fixed on them with a straining gaze. His lasted for two or three minutes in dead silence. Then he lifted his hands to each side of his head, and said, in a low tone of despair, "Lost, lost!"

There was something so piteous in the wandering look and the low cry, that while they confirmed the belief in his madness they raised compassion. Nay, so distinct sometimes is the working of a double consciousness within us, that Tito himself, while he triumphed in the apparent verification of his lie, wished that he had never made the lie necessary to himself—wished he had recognized his father on the steps—wished he had gone to seek him—wished everything had been different. But he had borrowed from the terrible usurer Falsehood, and the loan had mounted and mounted with the years, until he belonged to the usurer, body and soul.

The compassion excited in all the witnesses was not without its danger to Tito; for conjecture is constantly guided by feeling, and more than one person suddenly conceived that this man might have been a scholar and have lost his faculties. On the other hand, they had not present to their minds the motives which could have led Tito to the denial of his benefactor, and having no ill-will towards him, it would have been difficult to them to believe that he had been uttering the basest of lies. And the originally common type of Baldassarre's person, coarsened by years of hardship, told as a confirmation of Tito's lie. If Baldassarre, to begin with, could have uttered precisely the words he had premeditated, there might have been something in the form of his accusation which would have given it the stamp not only of true experience but of mental refinement. But there had been no such testimony in his impulsive agitated words; and there seemed the very opposite testimony in the rugged face and the coarse hands that trembled beside it, standing out in strong contrast in the midst of that velvet-clad, fair-handed company. His next movement, while he was being watched in silence, told against him too. He took his hands from his head, and felt for something under his tunic. Every one guessed what that movement meant—guessed that there was a weapon at his side. Glances were interchanged; and Bernardo Rucellai said, in a quiet tone, touching Baldassarre's shoulder:—

"My friend, this is an important business of yours. You shall have all justice. Follow me into a private room."

Baldassarre was still in that half-stunned state in which he was susceptible to any prompting, in the same way as an insect that forms no conception of what the prompting leads to. He rose from his seat, and followed Rucellai out of the room.

In two or three minutes Rucellai came back again, and said,—

"He is safe under lock and key. Piero Pitti, you are one of the Magnificent Eight, what do you think of our sending Matteo to the palace for a couple of *sbirri*, who may escort him to the Stinche?* If there is any danger in him, as I think there is, he will be safe there; and we can inquire about him to-morrow."

Pitti assented, and the order was given.

"He is certainly an ill-looking fellow," said Tournabuoni. "And you say he has attempted your life already, Melema?"

And the talk turned on the various forms of madness, and the fierceness of the Southern blood. If the seeds of conjecture unfavourable to Tito had been planted in the mind of any one present, they were hardly strong enough to grow without the aid of much daylight and ill-will. The common-looking, wild-eyed old man, clad in serge, might have won belief without very strong evidence, if he had accused a man who was envied and disliked. As it was, the only congruous and probable view of the case seemed to be the one that sent the unpleasant accuser safely out of sight, and left the pleasant serviceable Tito just where he was before.

The subject gradually floated away, and gave place to others, till a heavy tramp, and something like the struggling of a man who was being dragged away, were heard outside. The sounds soon died out, and the interruption seemed to make the last hour's conviviality more resolute and vigorous. Every one was willing to forget a disagreeable incident.

Tito's heart was palpitating, and the wine tasted no better to him than if it had been blood.

To-night he had paid a heavier price than ever to make himself safe. He did not like the price, and yet it was inevitable that he should be glad of the purchase.

And after all he led the chorus. He was in a state of excitement in which oppressive sensations, and the wretched consciousness of something hateful but irrevocable, were mingled with a feeling of triumph which seemed to assert itself as the feeling that would subsist and be master of the morrow.

And it *was* master. For on the morrow, as we saw, when he was about to start on his mission to Rome, he had the air of a man well satisfied with the world.

CHAPTER XL.

An Arresting Voice

WHEN Romola sat down on the stone under the cypress, all things conspired to give her the sense of freedom and solitude: her escape from the accustomed walls and streets; the widening distance from her husband, who was by this time riding towards Siena, while every hour would take her farther on the opposite way; the morning stillness; the great dip of ground on the roadside making a gulf between her and the sombre calm of the mountains. For the first time in her life she felt alone in the presence of the earth and sky, with no human presence interposing and making a law for her.

Suddenly a voice close to her said,—

"You are Romola de' Bardi, the wife of Tito Melema."

She knew the voice: it had vibrated through her more than once before; and because she knew it, she did not turn round or look up. She sat shaken by awe, and yet inwardly rebelling against the awe. It was one of those black-skirted monks who was daring to speak to her, and interfere with her privacy: that was all. And yet she was shaken, as if that destiny which men thought of as a sceptred deity had come to her, and grasped her with fingers of flesh.

"You are fleeing from Florence in disguise. I have a command from God to stop you. You are not permitted to flee."

Romola's anger at the intrusion mounted higher at these imperative words. She would not turn round to look at the speaker, whose examining gaze she resented. Sitting quite motionless, she said,—

"What right have you to speak to me, or to hinder me?"

"The right of a messenger. You have put on a religious garb, and you have no religious purpose. You have sought the garb as a disguise. But you were not suffered to pass me without being discerned. It was declared to me who you were: it is declared to me that you are seeking to escape from the lot God has laid upon you. You wish your true name and your true place in life to be hidden, that you may choose for yourself a new name and a new place, and have no rule but your own will. And I have a command to call you back. My daughter, you must return to your place."

Romola's mind rose in stronger rebellion with every sentence. She was the more determined not to show any sign of submission, because the consciousness of being inwardly shaken made her dread lest she should fall into irresolution. She spoke with more irritation than before.

"I will not return. I acknowledge no right of priests and monks to interfere with my actions. You have no power over me."

"I know—I know you have been brought up in scorn of obedience. But it is not the poor monk who claims to interfere with you: it is the truth that commands you. And you cannot escape it. Either you must obey it, and it will lead you; or you must disobey it, and it will hang on you with the weight of a chain which you will drag for ever. But you will obey it, my daughter. Your old servant will return to you with the mules: my companion is gone to fetch him; and you will go back to Florence."

She started up with anger in her eyes, and faced the speaker. It was Fra Girolamo: she knew that well enough before. She was nearly as tall as he was, and their faces were almost on a level. She had started up with defiant words ready to burst from her lips, but they fell back again without utterance. She had met Fra Girolamo's calm glance, and the impression from it was so new to her, that her anger sank ashamed as something irrelevant.

There was nothing transcendent in Savonarola's face. It was not beautiful. It was strong-featured, and owed all its refinement to habits of mind and rigid discipline of the body. The source of the impression his glance produced on Romola was the sense it conveyed to her of interest in her and care for her apart from any personal feeling. It was the first time she had encountered a gaze in which simple human fellowship expressed itself as a strongly-felt bond. Such a glance is half the vocation of the priest or spiritual guide of men, and Romola felt it impossible again to question his authority to speak to her. She stood silent, looking at him. And he spoke again.

"You assert your freedom proudly, my daughter. But who is so base as the debtor that thinks himself free?"

There was a sting in those words, and Romola's countenance changed as if a subtle pale flash had gone over it.

"And you are flying from your debts: the debt of a Florentine woman; the debt of a wife. You are turning your back on the lot that has been appointed for you—you are going to choose another. But can man or woman choose duties? No more than they can choose their birthplace or their father and mother. My daughter, you are fleeing from the presence of God into the wilderness."

As the anger melted from Romola's mind, it had given place to a new presentiment of the strength there might be in submission, if this man, at whom she was beginning to look with a vague reverence, had some valid law to show her. But no—it was impossible; he could not know what determined her. Yet she could not again simply refuse to be guided; she was constrained to plead; and in her new need to be reverent while she resisted, the title which she had never given him before came to her lips without forethought.

"My father, you cannot know the reasons which compel me to go. None can know them but myself. None can judge for me. I have been driven by great sorrow. I am resolved to go."

"I know enough, my daughter: my mind has been so far illuminated concerning you, that I know enough. You are not happy in your married life; but I am not a confessor, and I seek to know nothing that should be reserved for the seal of confession. I have a divine warrant to stop you, which does not depend on such knowledge. You were warned by a message from heaven, delivered in my presence—you were warned before marriage, when you might still have lawfully chosen to be free from the marriage bond. But you chose the bond; and in wilfully breaking it—I speak to you as a pagan, if the holy mystery of matrimony is not sacred to you—you are breaking a pledge. Of what wrongs will you complain, my daughter, when you yourself are committing one of the greatest wrongs a woman and a citizen can be guilty of—withdrawing in secrecy and disguise from a pledge which you have given in the face of God and your fellow-men? Of what wrongs will you complain, when you yourself are breaking the simplest law that lies at the foundation of the trust which binds man to man—faithfulness to the spoken word? This, then, is the wisdom you have gained by scorning the mysteries of the Church?—not to see the bare duty of integrity, where the Church would have taught you to see, not integrity only, but religion."

The blood had rushed to Romola's face, and she shrank as if she had been stricken. "I would not have put on a disguise," she began; but she could not go on,—she was too much shaken by the suggestion in the Frate's words of a possible affinity between her own conduct and Tito's.

"And to break that pledge you fly from Florence: Florence, where there are the only men and women in the world to whom you owe the debt of a fellow-citizen."

"I should never have quitted Florence," said Romola, tremulously, "as long as there was any hope of my fulfilling a duty to my father there."

"And do you owe no tie but that of a child to her father in the flesh? Your life has been spent in blindness, my daughter. You have lived with those who sit on a hill aloof, and look down on the life of their fellow-men.* I know their vain discourse. It is of what has been in the times which they fill with their own fancied wisdom, while they scorn God's work in the present. And doubtless you were taught how there were pagan women who felt what it was to live for the Republic; yet you have never felt that you, a Florentine woman, should live for Florence. If your own people are wearing a yoke, will you slip from under it, instead of struggling with them to lighten it? There is hunger and misery in our streets, yet you say, 'I care not; I have my own sorrows; I will go away, if peradventure I can ease them.' The servants of God are struggling after a law of justice, peace, and charity, that the hundred thousand citizens among whom you were born may be governed righteously; but you think no more of this than if you were a bird, that may spread its wings and fly whither it will in search of food to its liking. And yet you have scorned the teaching of the Church, my daughter. As if you, a wilful wanderer, following your own blind choice, were not below the humblest Florentine woman who stretches forth her hands with her own people, and craves a blessing for them; and feels a close sisterhood with the neighbour who kneels beside her and is not of her own blood; and thinks of the mighty purpose that God has for Florence; and waits and endures because the promised work is great, and she feels herself little."

"I was not going away to ease and self-indulgence," said Romola, raising her head again, with a prompting to vindicate herself. "I was going away to hardship. I expect no joy: it is gone from my life."

"You are seeking your own will, my daughter. You are seeking some good other than the law you are bound to obey. But how will you find good? It is not a thing of choice: it is a river that flows from the foot of the Invisible Throne, and flows by the path of obedience. I say again, man cannot choose his duties. You may choose to forsake your duties, and choose not to have the sorrow they bring. But you will go forth; and what will you find, my daughter? Sorrow without duty—bitter herbs, and no bread with them."

"But if you knew," said Romola, clasping her hands and

pressing them tight, as she looked pleadingly at Fra Girolamo; "if you knew what it was to me—how impossible it seemed to me to bear it."

"My daughter," he said, pointing to the cord round Romola's neck, "you carry something within your mantle; draw it forth, and look at it."

Romola gave a slight start, but her impulse now was to do just what Savonarola told her. Her self-doubt was grappled by a stronger will and a stronger conviction than her own. She drew forth the crucifix. Still pointing towards it, he said,

"There, my daughter, is the image of a Supreme Offering, made by Supreme Love, because the need of man was great."

He paused, and she held the crucifix trembling—trembling under a sudden impression of the wide distance between her present and her past self. What a length of road she had travelled through since she first took that crucifix from the Frate's hands! Had life as many secrets before her still as it had for her then, in her young blindness? It was a thought that helped all other subduing influences; and at the sound of Fra Girolamo's voice again, Romola, with a quick involuntary movement, pressed the crucifix against her mantle, and looked at him with more submission than before.

"Conform your life to that image, my daughter; make your sorrow an offering: and when the fire of divine charity burns within you, and you behold the need of your fellow-men by the light of that flame, you will not call your offering great. You have carried yourself proudly, as one who held herself not of common blood or of common thoughts; but you have been as one unborn to the true life of man. What! you say your love for your father no longer tells you to stay in Florence? Then, since that tie is snapped, you are without a law, without religion: you are no better than a beast of the field when she is robbed of her young. If the yearning of a fleshly love is gone, you are without love, without obligation. See, then, my daughter, how you are below the life of the believer who worships that image of the Supreme Offering, and feels the glow of a common life with the lost multitude for whom that offering was made, and beholds the history of the world as the history of a great redemption in which he is himself a fellow-worker, in his own place and among his own people! If you held that faith, my beloved daughter, you would not be a wanderer flying from suffering, and blindly seeking the good of a freedom which is lawlessness. You would feel that Florence was the home of your soul as well as your birthplace, because you would see the work that was given you to do there. If you forsake your place, who will fill it? You ought to be in your place now, helping in the great work by which God will purify Florence, and raise it to be the guide of the nations. What! the earth is full of iniquity—full of groans—the light is still struggling with a mighty darkness, and you say, 'I cannot bear my bonds; I will burst them asunder; I will go where no man claims me'? My daughter, every bond of your life is a debt: the right lies in the payment of that debt; it can lie nowhere else. In vain will you wander over the earth; you will be wandering forever away from the right."

Romola was inwardly struggling with strong forces: that immense personal influence of Savonarola, which came from the energy of his emotions and beliefs; and her consciousness, surmounting all prejudice, that his words implied a higher law than any she had yet obeyed. But the resisting thoughts were not yet overborne.

"How then could Dino be right? He broke ties. He forsook his place."

"That was a special vocation. He was constrained to depart, else he could not have attained the higher life. It would have been stifled within him."

"And I too"—said Romola, raising her hands to her brow, and speaking in a tone of anguish, as if she were being dragged to some torture. "Father, you may be wrong."

"Ask your conscience, my daughter. You have no vocation such as your brother had. You are a wife. You seek to break your ties in self-will and anger, not because the higher life calls upon you to renounce them. The higher life begins for us, my daughter, when we renounce our own will to bow before a divine law. That seems hard to you. It is the portal of wisdom, and freedom, and blessedness. And the symbol of it hangs before you. That wisdom is the religion of the cross. And you stand aloof from it: you are a pagan; you have been taught to say, 'I am as the wise men who lived before the time when the Jew of Nazareth was crucified.' And that is your wisdom! To be as the dead whose eyes are closed, and whose ear is deaf to the work of God that has been since their time. What has your dead wisdom done for you, my daughter? It has left you without a heart for the neighbours among whom you dwell, without care for the great work by which Florence is to be regenerated and the world made holy; it has left you without a share in the divine life which quenches the sense of suffering Self in the ardours of an ever-growing love. And now, when the sword has pierced your soul, you say, 'I will go away; I cannot bear my sorrow.' And you think nothing of the sorrow and the wrong that are within the walls of the city where you dwell: you would leave your place empty, when it ought to be filled with your pity and your labour. If there is wickedness in the streets, your steps should shine with the light of purity: if there is a cry of anguish, you, my daughter, because you know the meaning of the cry, should be there to still it. My beloved daughter, sorrow has come to teach you a new worship: the sign of it hangs before you."

Romola's mind was still torn by conflict. She foresaw that she should obey Savonarola and go back: his words had come to her as if they were an interpretation of that revulsion from self-satisfied ease, and of that new fellowship with suffering, which had already been awakened in her. His arresting voice had brought a new condition into her life, which made it seem impossible to her that she could go on her way as if she had not heard it; yet she shrank as one who sees the path she must take, but sees, too, that the hot lava lies there. And the instinctive shrinking from a return to her husband brought doubts. She turned away her eyes from Fra Girolamo, and stood for a minute or two with her hands hanging clasped before her, like a statue. At last she spoke, as if the words were being wrung from her, still looking on the ground,

"My husband. . . . he is not. . . . my love is gone!"

"My daughter, there is a bond of a higher love. Marriage is not carnal only, made for selfish delight. See what that thought leads you to! It leads you to wander away in a false garb from all the obligations of your place and name. That would not have been, if you had learned that it is a sacramental vow, from which none but God can release you. My daughter, your life is not as a grain of sand, to be blown by the winds; it is a thing of flesh and blood, that dies if it be sundered. Your husband is not a malefactor?"

Romola started. "Heaven forbid! No; I accuse him of nothing."

"I did not suppose he was a malefactor. I meant, that if he were a malefactor, your place would be in the prison beside him. My daughter, if the cross comes to you as a wife, you must carry it as a wife. You may say, 'I will forsake my husband,' but you cannot cease to be a wife."

"Yet if—oh, how could I bear—" Romola had involuntarily begun to say something which she sought to banish from her mind again.

"Make your marriage-sorrows an offering too, my daughter: an offering to the great work by which sin and sorrow are being made to cease. The end is sure, and is already beginning. Here in Florence it is beginning, and the eyes of faith behold it. And it may be our blessedness to die for it: to die daily by the crucifixion of our selfish will—to die at last by laying our bodies on the altar. My daughter, you are a child of Florence; fulfil the duties of that great inheritance. Live for Florence—for your own people, whom God is preparing to bless the earth. Bear the anguish and the smart. The iron is sharp—I know, I know—it rends the tender flesh. The draught is bitterness on the lips. But there is rapture in the cup—there is the vision which makes all life below it dross for ever. Come, my daughter, come back to your place!"

While Savonarola spoke with growing intensity, his arms tightly folded before him still, as they had been from the first, but his face alight as from an inward flame, Romola felt herself surrounded and possessed by the glow of his passionate faith. The chill doubts all melted away; she was subdued by the sense of something unspeakably great to which she was being called by a strong being who roused a new strength within herself. In a voice that was like a low, prayerful cry, she said—

"Father, I will be guided. Teach me! I will go back."

Almost unconsciously she sank on her kness. Savonarola stretched out his hand over her; but feeling would no longer pass through the channel of speech, and he was silent.

CHAPTER XLI.

Coming Back

"RISE, my daughter," said Fra Girolamo at last. "Your servant is waiting not far off with the mules. It is time that I should go onward to Florence."

Romola arose from her knees. That silent attitude had been a sort of sacrament to her, confirming the state of yearning passivity on which she had newly entered. By the one act of renouncing her resolve to quit her husband, her will seemed so utterly bruised that she felt the need of direction even in small things. She lifted up the edge of her cowl, and saw Maso and the second Dominican standing with their backs towards her on the edge of the hill about ten yards from her; but she looked at Savonarola again without speaking, as if the order to Maso to turn back must come from him and not from her.

"I will go and call them," he said, answering her glance of appeal; "and I will recommend you, my daughter, to the Brother who is with me. You desire to put yourself under guidance, and to learn that wisdom which has been hitherto as foolishness to you. A chief gate of that wisdom is the Sacrament of Confession. You will need a confessor, my daughter, and I desire to put you under the care of Fra Salvestro, one of the brethren of San Marco in whom I most confide."

"I would rather have no guidance but yours, father," said Romola, looking anxious.

"My daughter, I do not act as a confessor. The vocation I have withdraws me from offices that would force me into frequent contact with the laity, and interfere with my special duties."

"Then shall I not be able to speak to you in private? if I waver. . . . if—" Romola broke off from rising agitation. She felt a sudden alarm lest her new strength in renunciation should vanish if the immediate personal influence of Savonarola vanished.

"My daughter, if your soul has need of the word in private from my lips, you will let me know it through Fra Salvestro, and I will see you in the sacristy or in the choir of San Marco. And I will not cease to watch over you. I will instruct my brother concerning you, that he may guide you into that path of labour for the suffering and the hungry to which you are called as a daughter of Florence in these times of hard need. I desire to behold you among the feebler and more ignorant sisters as the apple-tree among the trees of the forest, so that your fairness and all natural gifts may be but as a lamp through which the divine light shines the more purely. I will go now and call your servant."

When Maso had been sent a little way in advance, Fra Salvestro came forward, and Savonarola led Romola towards him. She had beforehand felt an inward shrinking from a new guide who was a total stranger to her; but to have resisted Savonarola's advice would have been to assume an attitude of independence at a moment when all her strength must be drawn from the renunciation of independence. And the whole bent of her mind now was towards doing what was painful rather than what was easy. She bowed reverently to Fra Salvestro before looking directly at him; but when she raised her head and saw him fully, her reluctance became a palpitating doubt. There are men whose presence infuses trust and reverence; there are others to whom we have need to carry our trust and reverence ready made; and that difference flashed on Romola as she ceased to have Savonarola before her, and saw in his stead Fra Salvestro Maruffi. It was not that there was anything manifestly repulsive in Fra Salvestro's face and manner, any air of hypocrisy, any tinge of coarseness; his face was handsomer than Fra Girolamo's, his person a little taller. He was the long-accepted confessor of many among the chief personages in Florence, and had therefore had large experience as a spiritual director. But his face had the vacillating expression of a mind unable to concentrate itself strongly in the channel of one great emotion or belief, an expression which is fatal to influence over an ardent nature like Romola's. Such an expression is not the stamp of insincerity; it is the stamp simply of a shallow soul, which will often be found sincerely striving to fill a high vocation, sincerely composing its countenance to the utterance of sublime formulas, but finding the muscles twitch or relax in spite of belief, as prose insists on coming instead of poetry to the man who has not the divine frenzy. Fra Salvestro had a peculiar liability to visions, dependent apparently on a constitution given to somnambulism.* Savonarola believed in the supernatural character of these visions, while Fra Salvestro himself had originally resisted such an interpretation of them, and had even rebuked Savonarola for his prophetic preaching. Another proof, if one were wanted, that the relative greatness of men is not to be gauged by their tendency to disbelieve the superstitions of their age. For of these two there can be no question which was the great man and which the small.

The difference between them was measured very accurately by the change in Romola's feeling as Fra Salvestro began to address her in words of exhortation and encouragement. After her first angry resistance of Savonarola had passed away, she had lost all remembrance of the old dread lest any influence should drag her within the circle of fanaticism and sour monkish piety. But now again, the chill breath of that dread stole over her. It could have no decisive effect against the impetus her mind had just received; it was only like the closing of the grey clouds over the sunrise, which made her returning path monotonous and sombre.

And perhaps of all sombre paths that on which we go back after treading it with a strong resolution is the one that most severely tests the fervour of renunciation. As they re-entered the city gates the light snow-flakes fell about them, and as the grey sister walked hastily homeward from the Piazza di San Marco, and trod the bridge again, and turned in at the large door in the Via de' Bardi, her footsteps were marked darkly on the thin carpet of snow, and her cowl fell laden and damp about her face.

She went up to her room, threw off her serge, destroyed the parting letters, replaced all her precious trifles, unbound her hair, and put on her usual black dress. Instead of taking a long exciting journey, she was to sit down in her usual place. The snow fell against the windows, and she was alone.

She felt the dreariness, yet her courage was high, like that of a seeker who has come on new signs of gold. She was going to thread life by a fresh clue. She had thrown all the energy of her will into renunciation. The empty tabernacle remained locked, and she placed Dino's crucifix outside it.

Nothing broke the outward monotony of her solitary home, till the night came like a white ghost at the windows. Yet it was the most memorable Christmas-eve in her life to Romola, this of 1494.

END OF BOOK II

[*MARCH 1863*]

BOOK III

CHAPTER XLII.

Romola in her Place

IT was the thirtieth of October, 1496. The sky that morning was clear enough, and there was a pleasant autumnal breeze. But the Florentines just then thought very little about the land breezes: they were thinking of the gales at sea, which seemed to be uniting with all other powers to disprove the Frate's declaration that Heaven took special care of Florence.

For those terrible gales had driven away from the coast of Leghorn certain ships from Marseilles, freighted with soldiery and corn; and Forence was in the direst need, first of food, and secondly of fighting men. Pale Famine was in her streets, and her territory was threatened on all its borders.

For the French King, that new Charlemagne, who had entered Italy in anticipatory triumph, and had conquered Naples without the least trouble, had gone away again fifteen months ago, and was even, it was feared, in his grief for the loss of a new-born son,* losing the languid intention of coming back again to redress grievances and set the Church in order. A league had been formed* against him—a Holy League, with Pope Borgia at its head, to "drive out the barbarians," who still garrisoned the fortresses of Naples. That had a patriotic sound; but, looked at more closely, the Holy League seemed very much like an agreement among certain wolves to drive away all other wolves and then to see which among themselves could snatch the largest share of the prey. And there was a general disposition to regard Florence not as a fellow wolf, but rather as a desirable carcase. Florence, therefore, of all the chief Italian States, had alone declined to join the League, adhering still to the French alliance.

She had declined at her peril. At this moment Pisa, still

fighting savagely for liberty, was being encouraged not only by strong forces from Venice and Milan, but by the presence of the German Emperor Maximilian, who had been invited by the League, and was joining the Pisans with such troops as he had in the attempt to get possession of Leghorn, while the coast was invested by Venetian and Genoese ships. And if Leghorn should fall into the hands of the enemy, woe to Florence! For if that one outlet towards the sea were closed, hedged in as she was on the land by the bitter ill-will of the Pope and the jealousy of smaller Sates, how could succours reach her?

The government of Florence had shown a great heart in this urgent need, meeting losses and defeats with vigorous effort, raising fresh money, raising fresh soldiers, but not neglecting the good old method of Italian defence—conciliatory embassies. And while the scarcity of food was every day becoming greater, they had resolved, in opposition to old precedent, not to shut out the starving country people, and the mendicants driven from the gates of other cities, who came flocking to Florence like birds from a land of snow. These acts of a government in which the disciples of Savonarola made the strongest element were not allowed to pass without criticism. The disaffected were plentiful, and they saw clearly that the government took the worst course for the public welfare. Florence ought to join the League and make common cause with the other great Italian States, instead of drawing down their hostility by a futile adherence to a foreign ally. Florence ought to take care of her own citizens, instead of opening her gates to famine and pestilence in the shape of starving contadini and alien mendicants.

Every day the distress became sharper: every day the murmurs became louder. And, to crown the difficulties of the government, for a month and more—in obedience to a mandate from Rome—Fra Girolamo had ceased to preach. But on the arrival of the terrible news that the ships from Marseilles had been driven back, and that no corn was coming, the need for the voice that could infuse faith and patience into the people became too imperative to be resisted. In defiance of the Papal mandate the Signoria requested Savonarola to preach. And two days ago he had mounted again the pulpit of the Duomo, and had told the people only to wait and be steadfast, and the divine help would certainly come. It was a bold sermon: he consented to have his frock stripped off him if, when Florence persevered in fulfilling the duties of piety and citizenship, God did not come to her rescue.

Yet at present, on this morning of the thirtieth, there were no signs of rescue. Perhaps if the precious Tabernacle of the Madonna dell' Impruneta were brought into Florence and carried in devout procession to the Duomo, that Mother, rich in sorrows and therefore in mercy, would plead for the suffering city? For a century and a half there were records of how the Florentines, suffering from drought, or flood, or famine, or pestilence, or the threat of wars, had fetched the potent image within their walls, and had found deliverance. And grateful honour had been done to her and her ancient church of L'Impruneta; the high house of Buondelmonti, patrons of the church, had to guard her hidden Image with bare sword; wealth had been poured out for prayers at her shrine, for chantings, and chapels, and ever-burning lights; and lands had been added, till there was much quarrelling for the privilege of serving her. The Florentines were deeply convinced of her graciousness to them, so that the sight of her Tabernacle within their walls was like the parting of the cloud, and the proverb ran, that the Florentines had a Madonna who would do what they pleased. When were they in more need of her pleading pity than now? And already, the evening before, the Tabernacle containing the miraculous hidden image had been brought with high and reverend escort from L'Impruneta, the privileged spot six miles beyond the gate of San Piero that looks towards Rome, and had been deposited in the church of San Gaggio, outside the gate, whence it was to be fetched in solemn procession by all the fraternities, trades, and authorities of Florence.

But the Pitying Mother had not yet entered within the walls, and the morning arose on unchanged misery and despondency. Pestilence was hovering in the track of famine. Not only the hospitals were full, but the courtyards of private houses had been turned into refuges and infirmaries; and still there was unsheltered want. And early this morning, as usual, members of the various fraternities who made it part of their duty to bury the unfriended dead, were bearing away the corpses that had sunk by the wayside. As usual, sweet womanly forms, with the refined air and carriage of the well-born, but in the plainest garb, were moving about the streets on their daily errands of tending the sick and relieving the hungry.

One of these forms was easily distinguishable as Romola de' Bardi. Clad in the simplest garment of black serge, with a plain piece of black drapery drawn over her head, so as to hide all her hair, except the bands of gold that rippled apart on her brow, she was advancing from the Ponte Vecchio towards the Por' Santa Maria—the street in a direct line with the bridge—when she found her way obstructed by the pausing of a bier, which was being carried by members of the company of San Jacopo del Popolo,* in search for the unburied dead. The brethren at the head of the bier were stooping to examine something, while a group of idle workmen, with features paled and sharpened by hunger, were clustering round and all talking at once.

"He's dead, I tell you! Messer Domeneddio has loved him well enough to take him."

"Ah, and it would be well for us all if we could have our legs stretched out and go with our heads two or three *bracci* foremost!* It's ill standing upright with hunger to prop you."

"Well, well, he's an old fellow. Death has got a poor bargain. Life's had the best of him."

"And no Florentine, ten to one! A beggar turned out of Siena. San Giovanni defend us! They've no need of soldiers to fight us. They send us an army of starving men."

"No, no! This man is one of the prisoners turned out of the Stinche. I know by the grey patch where the prison badge was."

"Keep quiet! Lend a hand! Don't you see the brethren are going to lift him on the bier?"

"It's likely he's alive enough if he could only look it. The soul may be inside him if it had only a drop of *vernaccia* to warm it."

"In truth, I think he is not dead," said one of the brethren, when they had lifted him on the bier. "He has perhaps only sunk down for want of food."

"Let me try to give him some wine," said Romola, coming forward. She loosened the small flask which she carried at her belt, and, leaning towards the prostrate body, with a deft hand she applied a small ivory implement between the teeth, and poured into the mouth a few drops of wine. The stimulus acted: the wine was evidently swallowed. She poured more, till the head was moved a little towards her, and the eyes of the old man opened full upon her with the vague look of returning consciousness. Then for the first time a sense of complete recognition came over Romola. Those wild dark eyes opening in the sallow deep-lined face, with the white beard, which was now long again, were like an unmistakable signature to a remembered handwriting. The light of two summers had not made that image any fainter in Romola's memory: the image of the escaped prisoner, whom she had seen in the Duomo the day when Tito first wore the armour—at whose grasp Tito was paled with terror in the strange sketch she had seen in Piero's studio. A wretched tremor and palpitation seized her. Now at last, perhaps, she was going to know some secret which might be more bitter than all that had gone before. She felt an impulse to dart away as from a sight of horror; and again, a more imperious need to keep close by the side of this old man whom, the divination of keen feeling told her, her husband had injured. In the very instant of this conflict she still leaned towards him and kept her right hand ready to administer more wine, while her left was passed under his neck. Her hands trembled, but their habit of soothing helpfulness would have served to guide them without the direction of her thought.

Baldassarre was looking at *her* for the first time. The close seclusion in which Romola's trouble had kept her in the weeks preceding her flight and his arrest, had denied him the opportunity he had sought of seeing the Wife who lived in the Via de' Bardi: and at this moment the descriptions he had heard of the fair golden-haired woman were all gone, like yesterday's waves.

"Will it not be well to carry him to the steps of San Stefano?" said Romola. "We shall cease then to stop up the street, and you can go on your way with your bier."

They had only to move onward for about thirty yards before reaching the steps of San Stefano, and by this time Baldassarre was able himself to make some efforts towards getting off the bier, and propping himself on the steps against the church doorway. The charitable brethren passed on, but the group of interested spectators, who had nothing to do and much to say, had considerably increased. The feeling towards the old man was not so entirely friendly now it was quite certain that he was alive, but the respect inspired by Romola's presence caused the passing remarks to be made in a rather more subdued tone than before.

"Ah, they gave him his morsel every day in the Stinche—that's why he can't do so well without it. You and I, Cecco, know better what it is to go to bed fasting."

"*Gnaffè!* that's why the Magnificent Eight have turned out some of the prisoners, that they may shelter honest people instead. But if every thief is to be brought to life with good wine and wheaten bread, we Ciompi had better go and fill ourselves in Arno while the water's plenty."

Romola had seated herself on the steps by Baldassarre, and was saying, "Can you eat a little bread now? perhaps by and by you will be able, if I leave it with you. I must go on, because I have promised to be at the hospital. But I will come back, if you will wait here, and then I will take you to some shelter. Do you understand? Will you wait? I will come back."

He looked dreamily at her, and repeated her words, "come back." It was no wonder that his mind was enfeebled by his bodily exhaustion, but she hoped that he apprehended her meaning. She opened her basket, which was filled with pieces of soft bread, and put one of the pieces into his hand.

"Do you keep your bread for those that can't swallow, madonna?" said a rough-looking fellow, in a red night-cap, who had elbowed his way into the inmost circle of spectators—a circle that was pressing rather closely on Romola.

"If anybody isn't hungry," said another, "I say, let him alone. He's better off than people who've got craving stomachs and no breakfast."

"Yes, indeed; if a man's a mind to die, it's a time to encourage him, instead of making him come back to life against his will. Dead men want no trencher."

"Oh, you don't understand the Frate's charity," said a young man in an excellent cloth tunic, whose face showed no signs of want. "The Frate has been preaching to the birds, like Saint Anthony,* and he's been telling the hawks they were made to feed the sparrows, as every good Florentine citizen was made to feed six starving beggarmen from Arezzo or Bologna. Madonna, there, is a pious Piagnone: she's not going to throw away her good bread on honest citizens who've got all the Frate's prophecies to swallow."

"Come, madonna," said he of the red cap, "the old thief doesn't eat the bread, you see: you'd better try *us*. We fast so much, we're half saints already."

The circle had narrowed till the coarse men—most of them gaunt from privation—had left hardly any margin round Romola. She had been taking from her basket a small horn cup, into which she put the piece of bread and just moistened it with wine; and hitherto she had not appeared to heed them. But now she rose to her feet, and looked round at them. Instinctively the men who were nearest to her pushed backward a little, as if their rude nearness were the fault of those behind. Romola held out the basket of bread to the man in the night-cap, looking at him without any reproach in her glance, as she said,—

"Hunger is hard to bear, I know, and you have the power to take this bread if you will. It was saved for sick women and children. You are strong men; but if you do not choose to suffer because you are strong, you have the power to take everything from the weak. You can take the bread from this basket; but I shall watch by this old man; I shall resist your taking the bread from *him.*"

For a few moments there was perfect silence, while Romola looked at the faces before her, and held out the basket of bread. Her own pale face had the slightly pinched look and the deepening of the eye-socket which indicate unusual fasting in the habitually temperate, and the large direct gaze of her hazel eyes was all the more impressive. The man in the night-cap looked rather silly, and backed, thrusting his elbow into his neighbour's ribs with an air of moral rebuke. The backing was general, every one wishing to imply that he had been pushed forward against his will; and the young man in the fine cloth tunic had disappeared.

But at this moment the armed servitors of the Signoria, who had begun to patrol the line of streets through which the procession was to pass, came up to disperse the group which was obstructing the narrow street. The man addressed as Cecco retreated from a threatening mace up the church steps, and said to Romola, in a respectful tone,—

"Madonna, if you want to go on your errands, I'll take care of the old man."

Cecco was a wild-looking figure: a very ragged tunic, made shaggy and variegated by cloth-dust and clinging fragments of wool, gave relief to a pair of bony arms and a long sinewy neck; his square jaw shaded by a bristly black beard, his bridgeless nose and low forehead, made his face look as if it had been crushed down for purposes of packing, and a narrow piece of red rag tied over his ears seemed to assist in the compression. Romola looked at him with some hesitation.

"Don't mistrust me, madonna," said Cecco, who understood her look perfectly; "I'm not so pretty as you, but I've got an old mother who eats my porridge for me. What! there's a heart inside me, and I've bought a candle for the Most Holy Virgin before now. Besides, see there, the old fellow is eating his sop. He's hale enough: he'll be on his legs as well as the best of us by and by."

"Thank you for offering to take care of him, friend," said Romola, rather penitent for her doubting glance. Then leaning to Baldassarre, she said, "Pray wait for me till I come again."

He assented with a slight movement of the head and hand, and Romola went on her way towards the hospital of San Matteo, in the Piazza di San Marco.

CHAPTER XLIII.

The Unseen Madonna

In returning from the hospital, more than an hour later, Romola took a different road, making a wider circuit towards the river, which she reached at some distance from the Ponte Vecchio. She turned her steps towards that bridge, intending to hasten to San Stefano in search of Baldassarre. She dreaded to know more about him, yet she felt as if, in forsaking him, she would be forsaking some near claim upon her.

But when she approached the meeting of the roads where the Por' Santa Maria would be on her right hand and the Ponte Vecchio on her left, she found herself involved in a crowd who suddenly fell on their knees; and she immediately knelt with them. The Cross was passing—the Great Cross of the Duomo—which headed the procession. Romola was later than she had expected to be, and now she must wait till the procession had passed. As she rose from her knees, when the Cross had disappeared, the return to a standing posture, with nothing to do but gaze, made her more conscious of her fatigue than she had been while she had been walking and occupied. A shopkeeper by her side said,—

"Madonna Romola, you will be weary of standing: Gian Fantoni will be glad to give you a seat in his house. Here is his door close at hand. Let me open it for you. What! he loves God and the Frate as we do. His house is yours."

Romola was accustomed now to be addressed in this fraternal way by ordinary citizens, whose faces were familiar to her from her having seen them constantly in the Duomo. The idea of home had come to be identified for her less with the house in the Via de' Bardi, where she sat in frequent loneliness, than with the towered circuit of Florence, where there was hardly a turn of the streets at which she was not greeted with looks of appeal or of friendliness. She was glad enough to pass through the opened door on her right hand and be led by the fraternal hose-vendor to an upstairs window, where a stout woman with three children, all in the plain garb of Piagnoni, made a place for her with much reverence above the bright hanging draperies. From this corner station she could see, not only the procession pouring in solemn slowness between the lines of houses on the Ponte Vecchio, but also the river and the Lung' Arno on towards the bridge of the Santa Trinità.

In sadness and in stillness came the slow procession. Not even a wailing chant broke the silent appeal for mercy: there was only the tramp of footsteps, and the faint sweep of woollen garments. They were young footsteps that were passing when Romola first looked from the window—a long train of the Florentine youth, bearing high in the midst of them the white image of the youthful Jesus, with a golden glory above his head, standing by the tall cross where the thorns and the nails lay ready.

After that train of fresh beardless faces came the mysterious-looking Companies of Discipline,* bound by secret rules to self-chastisement, and devout praise, and special acts of piety; all wearing a garb which concealed the whole head and face except the eyes. Every one knew that these mysterious forms were Florentine citizens of various ranks, who might be seen at ordinary times going about the business of the shop, the counting-house, or the State; but no member now was discernible as son, husband, or father. They had dropped their personality, and walked as symbols of a common vow. Each company had its colour and its badge, but the garb of all was a complete shroud, and left no expression but that of fellowship.

In comparison with them, the multitude of monks seemed to be strongly distinguished individuals, in spite of the common tonsure and the common frock. First came a white stream of reformed Benedictines; and then a much longer stream of the Frati Minori, or Franciscans, in that age all clad in grey, with the knotted cord round their waists, and some of them with the *zoccoli*, or wooden sandals, below their bare feet;—perhaps the most numerous order in Florence, and owning many zealous members who loved mankind and hated the Dominicans. And after the grey came the black of the Augustinians of San Spirito, with more cultured human faces above it—men who had inherited the library of Boccaccio, and had made the most learned company in Florence when learning was rarer; then the white over dark of the Carmelites; and then again the unmixed black of the Servites, that famous Florentine order founded by seven merchants who forsook their gains to adore the Divine Mother.*

And now the hearts of all on-lookers began to beat a little faster, either with hatred or with love, for there was a stream of black and white coming over the bridge—of black mantles over white scapularies; and every one knew that the Dominicans were coming. Those of Fiesole passed first. One black mantle parted by white after another, one tonsured head after another, and still expectation was suspended. They were very coarse mantles, all of them, and many were threadbare, if not ragged; for the Prior of San Marco had reduced the fraternities under his rule to the strictest poverty and discipline. But in the long line of black and white there was at last singled out a mantle only a little more worn than the rest, with a tonsured head above it which might not have appeared supremely remarkable to a stranger who had not seen it on bronze medals, with the sword of God as its obverse; or surrounded by an armed guard on the way to the Duomo; or transfigured by the inward flame of the orator as it looked round on a rapt multitude.

As the approach of Savonarola was discerned, none dared conspicuously to break the stillness by a sound which would rise above the solemn tramp of footsteps and the faint sweep of garments; nevertheless his ear, as well as other ears, caught a mingled sound of low hissing that longed to be curses, and murmurs that longed to be blessings. Perhaps it was the sense that the hissing predominated which made two or three of his disciples in the foreground of the crowd, at the meeting of the roads, fall on their knees as if something divine were passing. The movement of silent homage spread: it went along the sides of the streets like a subtle shock, leaving some unmoved, while it made the most bend the knee and bow the head. But the hatred, too, gathered a more intense expression; and as Savonarola passed up the Por' Santa Maria, Romola could see that some one at an upper window spat upon him.

Monks again—Frati Umiliati, or Humbled Brethren, from Ognissanti, with a glorious tradition of being the earliest workers in the wool trade; and again more monks—Vallombrosan* and other varieties of Benedictines, reminding the instructed eye by niceties of form and colour that in ages of abuse, long ago, reformers had arisen who had marked a change of spirit by a change of garb; till at last the shaven crowns were at an end, and there came the train of untonsured secular priests.

Then followed the twenty-one incorporated Arts of Florence* in long array, with their banners floating above them in proud declaration that the bearers had their distinct functions, from the bakers of bread to the judges and notaries. And then all the secondary officers of state, beginning with the less and going on to the greater, till the line of secularities was broken by the Canons of the Duomo, carrying a sacred relic—the very head, enclosed in silver, of San Zenobio,* immortal bishop of Florence, whose virtues were held to have saved the city perhaps a thousand years before.

Here was the nucleus of the procession. Behind the relic came the Archbishop in gorgeous cope, with canopy held above him; and after him the mysterious hidden Image—hidden first by rich curtains of brocade enclosing an outer painted tabernacle, but within this, by the more ancient tabernacle which had never been opened in the memory of living men, or the fathers of living men. In that inner shrine was the image of the Pitying Mother,* found ages ago in the soil of L'Impruneta, uttering a cry as the spade struck it. Hitherto the unseen Image had hardly ever been carried to the Duomo without having rich gifts borne before it. There was no reciting the list of precious offerings made by emulous men and communities, especially of veils and curtains and mantles. But the richest of all these, it was said, had been given by a poor abbess and her nuns, who, having no money to buy materials, wove a mantle of gold brocade with their prayers, embroidered it and adorned it with their prayers, and, finally, saw their work presented to the Blessed Virgin in the great Piazza by two beautiful youths who spread out white wings and vanished in the blue.

But to-day there were no gifts carried before the Tabernacle: no donations were to be given to-day except to the poor. That had been the advice of Fra Girolamo, whose preaching never insisted on gifts to the invisible powers, but only on help to visible need; and altars had been raised at various points in front of the churches, on which the oblations for the poor were deposited. Not even a torch was carried. Surely the hidden Mother cared less for torches and brocade than for the wail of the hungry people. Florence was in extremity: she had done her utmost, and could only wait for something divine that was not in her own power.

The Frate in the torn mantle had said that help would certainly come, and many of the faint-hearted were clinging more to their faith in the Frate's word, than to their faith in the virtues of the unseen Image. But there were not a few of the fierce-hearted who thought with secret rejoicing that the Frate's word might be proved false.

Slowly the Tabernacle moved forward, and knees were bent. There was profound stillness; for the train of priests and chaplains from L'Impruneta stirred no passion in the on-lookers. The procession was about to close with the Priors and the Gonfaloniere; the long train of companies and symbols, which have their silent music and stir the mind as a chorus stirs it, was passing out of sight, and now a faint yearning hope was all that struggled with the accustomed despondency.

Romola, whose heart had been swelling, half with foreboding, half with that enthusiasm of fellowship which the life of the last two years had made as habitual to her as the consciousness of costume to a vain and idle woman, gave a deep sigh, as at the end of some long mental tension, and remained on her knees for very languor; when suddenly there flashed from between the houses on to the distant bridge something bright-coloured. In the instant, Romola started up and stretched out her arms, leaning from the window, while the black drapery fell from her head, and the golden gleam of her hair and the flush in her face seemed the effect of one illumination. A shout arose in the same instant; the last troops of the procession paused, and all faces were turned towards the distant bridge.

But the bridge was passed now; the horseman was pressing at full gallop along by the Arno; the sides of his bay horse, just streaked with foam, looked all white from swiftness; his cap was flying loose by his red *becchetto*, and he waved an olive branch in his hand. It was a messenger—a messenger of good tidings! The blessed olive branch spoke afar off. But the impatient people could not wait. They rushed to meet the on-comer, and seized his horse's rein, pushing and trampling.

And now Romola could see that the horseman was her husband, who had been sent to Pisa a few days before on a private embassy. The recognition brought no new flash of joy into her eyes. She had checked her first impulsive attitude of expectation; but her governing anxiety was still to know what news of relief had come for Florence.

"Good news!" "Best news!" "News to be paid with hose (*novelle da calze*)!" were the vague answers with which Tito met the importunities of the crowd, until he had succeeded in pushing on his horse to the spot at the meeting of the ways where the Gonfaloniere and the Priors were awaiting him. There he paused, and, bowing low, said:—

"Magnificent Signori! I have to deliver to you the joyful news that the galleys from France, laden with corn and men, have arrived safely in the port of Leghorn, by favour of a strong wind, which kept the enemy's fleet at a distance."

The words had no sooner left Tito's lips than they seemed to vibrate up the streets. A great shout rang through the air, and rushed along the river; and then another, and another; and the shouts were heard spreading along the line of the procession towards the Duomo; and then there were fainter answering shouts, like the intermediate plash of distant waves in a great lake whose waters obey one impulse.

For some minutes there was no attempt to speak further: the Signoria themselves lifted up their caps, and stood bare-headed in the presence of a rescue which had come from outside the limit of their own power—from that region of trust and resignation which has been in all ages called divine.

At last, as the signal was given to move forward, Tito said, with a smile—

"I ought to say, that any hose to be bestowed by the Magnificent Signoria in reward of these tidings, are due, not to me, but to another man who had ridden hard to bring them, and would have been here in my place if his horse had not broken down just before he reached Signa. Meo di Sasso will doubtless be here in an hour or two, and may all the more justly claim the glory of the messenger, because he has had the chief labour and has lost the chief delight."

It was a graceful way of putting a necessary statement, and after a word of reply from the *Proposto*, or spokesman of the Signoria, this dignified extremity of the procession passed on, and Tito turned his horse's head to follow in its train, while the great bell of the Palazzo Vecchio was already beginning to swing, and give a louder voice to the people's joy.

In that moment, when Tito's attention has ceased to be imperatively directed, it might have been expected that he would look round and recognize Romola; but he was apparently engaged with his cap, which, now the eager people were leading his horse, he was able to seize and place on his head, while his right hand was still encumbered with the olive branch. He had a becoming air of lassitude after his exertions; and Romola, instead of making any effort to be recognized by him, threw her black drapery over her head again, and remained perfectly quiet. Yet she felt almost sure that Tito had seen her; he had the power of seeing everything without seeming to see it.

CHAPTER XLIV.

The Visible Madonna

THE crowd had no sooner passed onward than Romola descended to the street, and hastened to the steps of San Stefano. Cecco had been attracted with the rest towards the Piazza, and she found Baldassarre standing alone against the church door, with the horn cup in his hand, waiting for her. There was a striking change in him: the blank, dreamy glance of a half-returned consciousness had given place to a fierceness which, as she advanced and spoke to him, flashed upon her as if she had been its object. It was the glance of caged fury that sees its prey passing safe beyond the bars.

Romola started as the glance was turned on her, but her immediate thought was that he had seen Tito. And as she felt the look of hatred grating on her, something like a hope arose that this man might be the criminal, and that her husband might not have been guilty towards him. If she could learn that now, by bringing Tito face to face with him, and have her mind set at rest!

"If you will come with me," she said, "I can give you shelter and food until you are quite rested and strong. Will you come?"

"Yes," said Baldassarre, "I shall be glad to get my strength. I want to get my strength," he repeated, as if he were muttering to himself, rather than speaking to her.

"Come!" she said, inviting him to walk by her side, and taking the way by the Arno towards the Ponte Rubaconte as the more private road.

"I think you are not a Florentine," she said, presently, as they turned on to the bridge.

He looked round at her without speaking. His suspicious caution was more strongly upon him than usual, just now that the fog of confusion and oblivion was made denser by bodily feebleness. But she was looking at him too, and there was something in her gentle eyes which at last compelled him to answer her. But he answered cautiously,—

"No, I am no Florentine; I am a lonely man."

She observed his reluctance to speak to her, and dared not question him further, lest he should desire to quit her. As she glanced at him from time to time, her mind was busy with thoughts which quenched the faint hope that there was nothing painful to be revealed about her husband. If this old man had been in the wrong, where was the cause for dread and secrecy? They walked on in silence till they reached the entrance into the Via de' Bardi, and Romola noticed that he turned and looked at her with a sudden movement as if some shock had passed through him. A few moments after, she paused at the half-open door of the court and turned towards him.

"Ah!" he said, not waiting for her to speak, "you are his wife."

"Whose wife?" said Romola.

It would have been impossible for Baldassarre to recall any name at that moment. The very force with which the image of Tito pressed upon him seemed to expel any verbal sign. He made no answer, but looked at her with strange fixedness.

She opened the door wide and showed the court covered with straw, on which lay four or five sick people, while some little children crawled or sat on it at their ease—tiny pale creatures, biting straws and gurgling.

"If you will come in," said Romola, tremulously. "I will find you a comfortable place, and bring you some more food."

"No, I will not come in," said Baldassarre. But he stood still, arrested by the burthen of impressions under which his mind was too confused to choose a course.

"Can I do nothing for you?" said Romola. "Let me give you some money that you may buy food. It will be more plentiful soon."

She had put her hand into her scarsella as she spoke, and held out her palm with several grossi in it. She purposely offered him more than she would have given to any other man in the same circumstances. He looked at the coins a little while, and then said,—

"Yes, I will take them."

She poured the coins into his palm, and he grasped them tightly.

"Tell me," said Romola, almost beseechingly. "What shall you—"

But Baldassarre had turned away from her, and was walking again towards the bridge. Passing from it, straight on up the Via del Fosso, he came upon the shop of Niccolò Caparra, and turned towards it without a pause, as if it had been the very object of his search. Niccolò was at that moment in procession with the Armourers of Florence, and there was only one apprentice in the shop. But there were all sorts of weapons in abundance hanging there, and Baldassarre's eyes discerned what he was more hungry for than for bread. Niccolò himself would probably have refused to sell anything that might serve as a weapon to this man with signs of the prison on him, but the apprentice, less observant and scrupulous, took three grossi for a sharp hunting-knife without any hesitation. It was a conveniently small weapon, which Baldassarre could easily thrust within the breast of his tunic, and he walked on, feeling stronger. That sharp edge might give deadliness to the thrust of an aged arm: at least it was a companion, it was a power in league with him, even if it failed. It would break against armour, but was the armour sure to be always there? In those long months while vengeance had lain in prison, baseness had perhaps become forgetful and secure. The knife had been bought with the traitor's own money. That was just. Before he took the money, he had felt what he should do with it—buy a weapon. Yes, and if possible, food too: food to nourish the arm that would grasp the weapon, food to nourish the body which was the temple of vengeance. When he had had enough bread, he would be able to think and act—to think first how he could hide himself, lest Tito should have him dragged away again. With that idea of hiding in his mind, Baldassarre turned up the narrowest streets, bought himself some meat and bread, and sat down under the first loggia to eat. The bells that swung out louder and louder peals of joy, laying hold of him and making him vibrate along with all the air, seemed to him simply part of that strong world which was against him.

Romola had watched Baldassarre until he had disappeared round the turning into the Piazza de' Mozzi, half feeling that his departure was a relief, half reproaching herself for not seeking with more decision to know the truth about him, for not assuring herself whether there were any guiltless misery in his lot which she was not helpless to relieve. Yet what could she have done if the truth had proved to be the burthen of some painful secret about her husband, in addition to the anxieties that already weighed upon her? Surely a wife was permitted to desire ignorance of a husband's wrong-doing, since she alone must not protest and warn men against him. But that thought stirred too many intricate fibres of feeling to be pursued now in her weariness. It was a time to rejoice, since help had come to Florence; and she turned into the court to tell the good news to her patients on their straw beds. She closed the door after her, lest the bells should drown her voice, and then throwing the black drapery from her head, that the women might see her better, she stood in the midst and told them that corn was coming, and that the bells were ringing for gladness at the news. They all sat up to listen, while the children trotted or crawled towards her, and pulled her black skirts, as if they were impatient at being all that long way off her face. She yielded to them, weary as she was, and sat down on the straw, while the little pale things peeped into her basket and pulled her hair down, and the feeble voices around her said, "The Holy Virgin be praised!" "It was the procession!" "The Mother of God has had pity on us!"

At last Romola rose from the heap of straw, too tired to try and smile any longer, saying as she turned up the stone steps,—

"I will come by and by, to bring you your dinner."

"Bless you, madonna! bless you!" said the faint chorus, in

much the same tone as that in which they had a few minutes before praised and thanked the unseen Madonna.

Romola cared a great deal for that music. She had no innate taste for tending the sick and clothing the ragged, like some women to whom the details of such work are welcome in themselves, simply as an occupation. Her early training had kept her aloof from such womanly labours; and if she had not brought to them the inspiration of her deepest feelings, they would have been irksome to her. But they had come to be the one unshaken resting-place of her mind, the one narrow pathway on which the light fell clear. If the gulf between herself and Tito which only gathered a more perceptible wideness from her attempts to bridge it by submission, brought a doubt whether, after all, the bond to which she had laboured to be true might not itself be false—if she came away from her confessor, Fra Salvestro, or from some contact with the disciples of Savonarola amongst whom she worshipped, with a sickening sense that these people were miserably narrow, and with an almost impetuous reaction towards her old contempt for their superstition—she found herself recovering a firm footing in her works of womanly sympathy. Whatever else made her doubt, the help she gave to her fellow-citizens made her sure that Fra Girolamo had been right to call her back. According to his unforgotten words, her place had not been empty: it had been filled with her love and her labour. Florence had had need of her, and the more her own sorrow pressed upon her, the more gladness she felt in the memories, stretching through the two long years, of hours and moments in which she had lightened the burthen of life to others. All that ardour of her nature which could no longer spend itself in the woman's tenderness for father and husband, had transformed itself into an enthusiasm of sympathy with the general life. She had ceased to think that her own lot could be happy—had ceased to think of happiness at all: the one end of her life seemed to her to be the diminishing of sorrow.

Her enthusiasm was continually stirred to fresh vigour by the influence of Savonarola. In spite of the wearisome visions and allegories from which she recoiled in disgust when they came as stale repetitions from other lips than his, her strong affinity for his passionate sympathy and the splendour of his aims had lost none of its power. His burning indignation against the abuses and oppression that made the daily story of the Church and of

States had kindled the ready fire in her too. His special care for liberty and purity of government in Florence, with his constant reference of this immediate object to the wider end of a universal regeneration, had created in her a new consciousness of the great drama of human existence in which her life was a part; and through her daily helpful contact with the less fortunate of her fellow-citizens this new consciousness became something stronger than a vague sentiment; it grew into a more and more definite motive of self-denying practice. She thought little about dogmas, and shrank from reflecting closely on the Frate's prophecies of the immediate scourge and closely following regeneration. She had submitted her mind to his and had entered into communion with the Church, because in this way she had found an immediate satisfaction for moral needs which all the previous culture and experience of her life had left hungering. Fra Girolamo's voice had waked in her mind a reason for living, apart from personal enjoyment and personal affection; but it was a reason that seemed to need feeding with greater forces than she possessed within herself, and her submissive use of all offices of the Church was simply a watching and waiting if by any means fresh strength might come. The pressing problem for Romola just then was not to settle questions of controversy, but to keep alive that flame of unselfish emotion by which a life of sadness might still be a life of active love.

Her trust in Savonarola's nature as greater than her own made a large part of the strength she had found. And the trust was not to be lightly shaken. It is not force of intellect which causes ready repulsion from the aberrations and eccentricities of greatness, any more than it is force of vision that causes the eye to explore the warts on a face bright with human expression; it is simply the negation of high sensibilities. Romola was so deeply moved by the grand energies of Savonarola's nature, that she found herself listening patiently to all dogmas and prophecies, when they came in the vehicle of his ardent faith and believing utterance.*

No soul is desolate as long as there is a human being for whom it can feel trust and reverence. Romola's trust in Savonarola was something like a rope suspended securely by her path, making her step elastic while she grasped it; if it were suddenly removed, no firmness of the ground she trod could save her from staggering, or perhaps from falling.

CHAPTER XLV.

At the Barber's Shop

AFTER that welcome appearance as the messenger with the olive branch, which was an unpromised favour of Fortune, Tito had other commissions to fulfil of a more premeditated character. He paused at the Palazzo Vecchio, and awaited there the return of the Ten, who managed external and war affairs, that he might duly deliver to them the results of his private mission to Pisa, intended as a preliminary to an avowed embassy of which Bernardo Rucellai was to be the head, with the object of coming, if possible, to a pacific understanding with the Emperor Maximilian and the League.*

Tito's talents for diplomatic work had been well ascertained, and as he gave with fullness and precision the results of his inquiries and interviews, Bernardo del Nero, who was at that time one of the Ten, could not withhold his admiration. He would have withheld it if he could; for his original dislike of Tito had returned, and become stronger, since the sale of the library. Romola had never uttered a word to her godfather on the circumstances of the sale, and Bernardo had understood her silence as a prohibition to him to enter on the subject, but he felt sure that the breach of her father's wish had been a blighting grief to her, and the old man's observant eyes discerned other indications that her married life was not happy.

"Ah," he said, inwardly, "that doubtless is the reason she has taken to listening to Fra Girolamo, and going amongst the Piagnoni, which I never expected from her. These women, if they are not happy, and have no children, must either take to folly or to some overstrained religion that makes them think they've got all heaven's work on their shoulders. And as for my poor child Romola, it is as I always said—the cramming with Latin and Greek has left her as much a woman as if she had done nothing all day but prick her fingers with the needle. And this husband of hers, who gets employed everywhere, because he's a tool with a smooth handle, I wish Tornabuoni and the rest may not find their fingers cut. Well, well, *solco torto*, *sacco dritto*—many a full sack comes from a crooked furrow; and he who will be captain of none but honest men will have small hire to pay."

With this long-established conviction that there could be no moral sifting of political agents, the old Florentine abstained from all interference in Tito's disfavour. Apart from what must be kept sacred and private for Romola's sake, Bernardo had nothing distinct to allege against the useful Greek, except that he was a Greek, and that he, Bernardo, did not like him; for the doubleness of feigning attachment to the popular government, while at heart a Medicean, was common to Tito with more than half the Medicean party. He only feigned with more skill than the rest: that was all. So Bernardo was simply cold to Tito, who returned the coldness with a scrupulous, distant respect. And it was still the notion in Florence that the old tie between Bernardo and Bardo made any service done to Romola's husband an acceptable homage to her godfather.

After delivering himself of his charge at the Old Palace, Tito felt that the avowed official work of the day was done. He was tired and adust with long riding; but he did not go home. There were certain things in his scarsella and on his mind from which he wished to free himself as soon as possible, but the opportunities must be found so skilfully that they must not seem to be sought. He walked from the Palazzo in a sauntering fashion towards the Piazza del Duomo. The procession was at an end now, but the bells were still ringing, and the people were moving about the streets restlessly, longing for some more definite vent to their joy. If the Frate could have stood up in the great Piazza and preached to them, they might have been satisfied, but now, in spite of the new discipline which declared Christ to be the special King of the Florentines and required all pleasures to be of a Christian sort, there was a secret longing in many of the youngsters who shouted "Viva Gesù!" for a little vigorous stone-throwing in sign of thankfulness.

Tito as he passed along could not escape being recognized by some as the welcome bearer of the olive branch, and could only rid himself of an inconvenient ovation, chiefly in the form of eager questions, by telling those who pressed on him that Meo di Sasso, the true messenger from Leghorn, must now be entering, and might certainly be met towards the Porta San Frediano. He could tell much more than Tito knew.

Freeing himself from importunities in this adroit manner, he made his way to the Piazza del Duomo, casting his long eyes round the space with an air of the utmost carelessness, but really seeking to detect some presence which might furnish him with one of his desired opportunities. The fact of the procession having terminated at the Duomo made it probable that there would be more than the usual concentration of loungers and talkers in the Piazza and round Nello's shop. It was as he expected. There was a group leaning against the rails near the north gates of the Baptistery, so exactly what he sought, that he looked more indifferent than ever, and seemed to recognize the tallest member of the group entirely by chance as he had half passed him, just turning his head to give him a slight greeting, while he tossed the end of his *becchetto* over his left shoulder.

Yet the tall, broad-shouldered personage greeted in that slight way looked like one who had considerable claims. He wore a richly embroidered tunic, with a great show of linen, after the newest French mode, and at his belt there hung a sword and poniard of fine workmanship. His hat, with a red plume in it, seemed a scornful protest against the gravity of Florentine costume, which had been exaggerated to the utmost under the influence of the Piagnoni. Certain undefinable indications of youth made the breadth of his face and the large diameter of his waist appear the more emphatically a stamp of coarseness, and his eyes had that rude desecrating stare at all men and things which to a refined mind is as intolerable as a bad odour or a flaring light.

He and his companions, also young men dressed expensively and wearing arms, were exchanging jokes with that sort of ostentatious laughter which implies a desire to prove that the laugher is not mortified though some people might suspect it. There were good reasons for such a suspicion; for this broad-shouldered man with the red feather was Dolfo Spini, leader of the *Compagnacci*,* or Evil Companions—that is to say, of all the dissolute young men belonging to the old aristocratic party, enemies of the Mediceans, enemies of the popular government, but still more bitter enemies of Savonarola. Dolfo Spini, heir of the great house with the loggia, over the bridge of the Santa Trinità,* had organized these young men into an armed band, as sworn champions of extravagant suppers and all the pleasant sins of the flesh, against reforming pietists who threatened to make the world chaste and temperate to so intolerable a degree that there would soon be no reason for living, except the extreme unpleasantness of the alternative. Up to this very morning he had been loudly declaring that Florence was given up to famine and ruin entirely through its blind adherence to the advice of the Frate, and that there could be no salvation for Florence but in joining the League and driving the Frate out of the city—sending him to Rome, in fact, whither he ought to have gone long ago in obedience to the summons of the Pope. It was suspected, therefore, that Messer Dolfo Spini's heart was not aglow with pure joy at the unexpected succours which had come in apparent fulfilment of the Frate's prediction, and the laughter, which was ringing out afresh as Tito joined the group at Nello's door, did not serve to dissipate the suspicion. For leaning against the door-post in the centre of the group was a close-shaven, keen-eyed personage, named Niccolò Macchiavelli, who, young as he was, had penetrated all the small secrets of egoism.

"Messer Dolfo's head," he was saying, "is more of a pumpkin than I thought. I measure men's dulness by the devices they trust in for deceiving others. Your dullest animal of all is he who grins and says he doesn't mind just after he has had his shins kicked. If I were a trifle duller now," he went on, smiling as the circle opened to admit Tito, "I should pretend to be fond of this Melema, who has got a Secretaryship that would exactly suit me—as if Latin ill-paid could love better Latin that's better paid! Melema, you are a pestiferously clever fellow, very much in my way, and I'm sorry to hear you've had another piece of good luck to-day."

"Questionable luck, Niccolò," said Tito, touching him on the shoulder in a friendly way; "I have got nothing by it yet but being laid hold of and breathed upon by wool-beaters, when I am as soiled and battered with riding as a *tabellario* (letter-carrier) from Bologna."

"Ah! you want a touch of my art, Messer Oratore," said Nello, who had come forward at the sound of Tito's voice; "your chin, I perceive, has yesterday's crop upon it. Come, come—consign yourself to the priest of all the Muses. Sandro, quick with the lather!"

"In truth, Nello, that is just what I most desire at this moment," said Tito, seating himself; "and that was why I turned my steps towards thy shop, instead of going home at once, when I had done my business at the Palazzo."

"Yes, indeed, it is not fitting that you should present yourself to Madonna Romola with a rusty chin and a tangled *zazzera*.

Nothing that is not dainty ought to approach the Florentine lily; though I see her constantly going about like a sunbeam amongst the rags that line our corners—if indeed she is not more like a moonbeam now, for I thought yesterday, when I met her, that she looked as pale and worn as that fainting Madonna of Fra Giovanni's.* You must see to it, my *bel erudito*: she keeps too many fasts and vigils in your absence."

Tito gave a melancholy shrug. "It is too true, Nello. She has been depriving herself of half her proper food every day during this famine. But what can I do? Her mind has been set all aflame. A husband's influence is powerless against the Frate's."

"As every other influence is likely to be, that of the Holy Father included," said Domenico Cennini, one of the group at the door, who had turned in with Tito. "I don't know whether you have gathered anything at Pisa about the way the wind sits at Rome, Melema?"

"Secrets of the council chamber, Messer Domenico!" said Tito, smiling and opening his palms in a deprecatory manner. "An envoy must be as dumb as a father confessor."

"Certainly, certainly," said Cennini. "I ask for no breach of that rule. Well, my belief is, that if his Holiness were to drive Fra Girolamo to extremity, the Frate would move heaven and earth to get a General Council of the Church—ay, and would get it too; and I, for one, should not be sorry, though I'm no Piagnone."

"With leave of your greater experience, Messer Domenico," said Macchiavelli, "I must differ from you—not in your wish to see a General Council which might reform the Church, but in your belief that the Frate will checkmate his Holiness. The Frate's game is an impossible one. If he had contented himself with preaching against the vices of Rome, and with prophesying that in some way, not mentioned, Italy would be scourged, depend upon it Pope Alexander would have allowed him to spend his breath in that way as long as he could find hearers. Such spiritual blasts as those knock no walls down. But the Frate wants to be something more than a spiritual trumpet: he wants to be a lever, and what is more, he *is* a lever. He wants to spread the doctrine of Christ by maintaining a popular government in Florence, and the Pope, as I know, on the best authority, has private views to the contrary."

"Then Florence will stand by the Frate," Cennini broke in,

with some fervour. "I myself should prefer that he would let his prophesying alone, but if our freedom to choose our own government is to be attacked—I am an obedient son of the Church, but I would vote for resisting Pope Alexander the Sixth, as our forefathers resisted Pope Gregory the Eleventh."*

"But pardon me, Messer Domenico," said Macchiavelli, sticking his thumbs into his belt, and speaking with that cool enjoyment of exposition which surmounts every other force in discussion. "Have you correctly seized the Frate's position? How is it that he has become a lever, and made himself worth attacking by an acute man like his Holiness? Because he has got the ear of the people: because he gives them threats and promises, which they believe come straight from God, not only about hell, purgatory, and paradise, but about Pisa and our Great Council. But let events go against him, so as to shake the people's faith, and the cause of his power will be the cause of his fall. He is accumulating three sorts of hatred on his head—the hatred of average mankind against every one who wants to lay on them a strict yoke of virtue; the hatred of the stronger powers in Italy, who want to farm Florence for their own purposes; and the hatred of the people, to whom he has ventured to promise good in this world, instead of confining his promises to the next. If a prophet is to keep his power, he must be a prophet like Mahomet, with an army at his back, that when the people's faith is fainting it may be frightened into life again."

"Rather sum up the three sorts of hatred in one," said Francesco Cei, impetuously, "and say he has won the hatred of all men who have sense and honesty, by inventing hypocritical lies. His proper place is among the false prophets in the Inferno,* who walk with their heads turned hind foremost."

"You are too angry, my Francesco," said Macchiavelli, smiling; "you poets are apt to cut the clouds in your wrath. I am no votary of the Frate's, and would not lay down my little finger for his veracity. But veracity is a plant of paradise, and the seeds have never flourished beyond the walls. You yourself, my Francesco, tell poetical lies only; partly compelled by the poet's fervour, partly to please your audience; but you object to lies in prose. Well, the Frate differs from you as to the boundary of poetry, that's all. When he gets into the pulpit of the Duomo, he has the fervour within him, and without him he has the audience to please. Ecco!"

"You are somewhat lax there, Niccolò," said Cennini, gravely. "I myself believe in the Frate's integrity, though I don't believe in his prophecies, and as long as his integrity is not disproved, we have a popular party strong enough to protect him and resist foreign interference."

"A party that seems strong enough," said Macchiavelli, with a shrug, and an almost imperceptible glance towards Tito, who was abandoning himself with much enjoyment to Nello's combing and scenting. "But how many Mediceans are there among you? How many who will not be turned round by a private grudge?"

"As to the Mediceans," said Cennini, "I believe there is very little genuine feeling left on behalf of the Medici. Who would risk much for Piero de' Medici? A few old staunch friends, perhaps, like Bernardo del Nero; but even some of those most connected with the family are hearty friends of the popular government, and would exert themselves for the Frate; I was talking to Giannozzo Pucci only a little while ago, and I'm convinced there's nothing he would set his face against more than against any attempt to alter the new order of things."

"You are right there, Messer Domenico," said Tito, with a laughing meaning in his eyes, as he rose from the shaving-chair; "and I fancy the tender passion came in aid of hard theory there. I am persuaded there was some jealousy at the bottom of Giannozzo's alienation from Piero de' Medici; else so amiable a creature as he would never feel the bitterness he sometimes allows to escape him in that quarter. He was in the procession with you, I suppose?"

"No," said Cennini; "he is at his villa—went there three days ago."

Tito was settling his cap and glancing down at his splashed hose as if he hardly heeded the answer. In reality he had obtained a much-desired piece of information. He had at that moment in his scarsella a crushed gold ring which he had engaged to deliver to Giannozzo Pucci. He had received it from an envoy of Piero de' Medici, whom he had ridden out of his way to meet at Certaldo on the Siena road. Since Pucci was not in the town, he would send the ring by Fra Michele, a Carthusian lay brother in the service of the Mediceans, and the receipt of that sign would bring Pucci back to hear the verbal part of Tito's mission.

"Behold him!" said Nello, flourishing his comb and pointing it at Tito, "the handsomest scholar in the world or in the wolds,* now he has passed through my hands! A trifle thinner in the face, though, than when he came in his first bloom to Florence—eh? and, I vow, there are some lines just faintly hinting themselves about your mouth, Messer Oratore! Ah, mind is an enemy to beauty! I myself was thought beautiful by the women at one time—when I was in my swaddling-bands. But now—*oimè*! I carry my unwritten poems in cipher on my face!"

Tito, laughing with the rest as Nello looked at himself tragically in the hand-mirror, made a sign of farewell to the company generally, and took his departure.

"I'm of our old Piero di Cosimo's mind," said Francesco Cei. "I don't half like Melema. That trick of smiling gets stronger than ever—no wonder he has lines about the mouth."

"He's too successful," said Macchiavelli, playfully. "I'm sure there's something wrong about him, else he wouldn't have that Secretaryship."

"He's an able man," said Cennini, in a tone of judicial fairness. "I and my brother have always found him useful with our Greek sheets, and he gives great satisfaction to the Ten. I like to see a young man work his way upward by merit. And the Secretary Scala, who befriended him from the first, thinks highly of him still, I know."

"Doubtless," said a notary in the background. "He writes Scala's official letters for him, or corrects them, and gets well paid for it too."

"I wish Messer Bartolommeo would pay *me* to doctor his gouty Latin," said Macchiavelli, with a shrug. "Did *he* tell you about the pay, Ser Ceccone, or was it Melema himself?" he added, looking at the notary with a face ironically innocent.

"Melema? no, indeed," answered Ser Ceccone. "He is as close as a nut. He never brags. That's why he's employed everywhere. They say he's getting rich with doing all sorts of underhand work."

"It *is* a little too bad," said Macchiavelli, "and so many able notaries out of employment!"

"Well, I must say I thought that was a nasty story a year or two ago about the man who said he had stolen jewels," said Cei. "It got hushed up somehow; but I remember Piero di Cosimo said, at the time, he believed there was something in it, for he saw Melema's face when the man laid hold of him, and he never saw a visage so 'painted with fear,' as our sour old Dante says."*

"Come, spit no more of that venom, Francesco," said Nello, getting indignant, "else I shall consider it a public duty to cut your hair awry the next time I get you under my scissors. That story of the stolen jewels was a lie. Bernardo Rucellai and the Magnificent Eight knew all about it. The man was a dangerous madman, and he was very properly kept out of mischief in prison. As for our Piero di Cosimo, his wits are running after the wind of Mongibello: he has such an extravagant fancy that he would take a lizard for a crocodile. No: that story has been dead and buried too long—our noses object to it."

"It is true," said Macchiavelli. "You forget the danger of the precedent, Francesco. The next mad beggarman may accuse you of stealing his verses, or me, God help me! of stealing his coppers. Ah!" he went on, turning towards the door, "Dolfo Spini has carried his red feather out of the Piazza. That captain of swaggerers would like the republic to lose Pisa just for the chance of seeing the people tear the frock off the Frate's back. With your pardon, Francesco—I know he is a friend of yours—there are few things I should like better than to see him play the part of Capo d'Oca, who went out to the tournament blowing his trumpets and returned with them in a bag."*

CHAPTER XLVI.

By a Street Lamp

THAT evening, when it was dark and threatening rain, Romola, returning with Maso and the lantern by her side, from the hospital of San Matteo, which she had visited after vespers, encountered her husband just issuing from the monastery of San Marco. Tito, who had gone out again shortly after his arrival in the Via de' Bardi, and had seen little of Romola during the day, immediately proposed to accompany her home, dismissing Maso, whose short steps annoyed him. It was only usual for him to pay her such an official attention when it was obviously demanded from him. Tito and Romola never jarred, never remonstrated with each other. They were too hopelessly alienated in their inner life ever to have that contest which is an effort towards agreement. They talked of all affairs, public and private, with careful adherence to an adopted course. If Tito wanted a supper prepared in the old library, now pleasantly furnished as a banqueting-room, Romola assented, and saw that everything needful was done; and Tito, on his side, left her entirely uncontrolled in her daily habits, accepting the help she offered him in transcribing or making digests, and in return meeting her conjectured want of supplies for her charities. Yet he constantly, as on this very morning, avoided exchanging glances with her: affected to believe that she was out of the house, in order to avoid seeking her in her own room; and playfully attributed to her a perpetual preference of solitude to his society.

In the first ardour of her self-conquest, after she had renounced her resolution of flight, Romola had made many timid efforts towards the return of a frank relation between them. But to her such a relation could only come by open speech about their differences, and the attempt to arrive at a moral understanding; while Tito could only be saved from alienation from her by such a recovery of her effusive tenderness as would have presupposed oblivion of their differences. He cared for no explanation between them; he felt any thorough explanation impossible: he would have cared to have Romola fond again, and to her, fondness was impossible. She could be submissive and gentle, she could repress any sign of repulsion; but tenderness was not to be feigned. She was helplessly conscious of the result: her husband was alienated from her.

It was an additional reason why she should be carefully kept outside of secrets which he would in no case have chosen to communicate to her. With regard to his political action he sought to convince her that he considered the cause of the Medici hopeless; and that on that practical ground, as well as in theory, he heartily served the popular government, in which she had now a warm interest. But impressions subtle as odours made her uneasy about his relations with San Marco. She was painfully divided between the dread of seeing any evidence to arouse her suspicions, and the impulse to watch lest any harm should come that she might have arrested.

As they walked together this evening, Tito said:—"The business of the day is not yet quite ended for me. I shall conduct you to our door, my Romola, and then I must fulfil another commission, which will take me an hour, perhaps, before I can return and rest, as I very much need to do."

And then he talked amusingly of what he had seen at Pisa, until they were close upon a loggia, near which there hung a lamp before a picture of the Virgin. The street was a quiet one, and hitherto they had passed few people; but now there was a sound of many approaching footsteps and confused voices.

"We shall not get home without a wetting, unless we take shelter under this convenient loggia," Tito said, hastily, hurrying Romola, with a slightly startled movement, up the step of the loggia.

"Surely it is useless to wait for this small drivelling rain," said Romola, in surprise.

"No; I felt it becoming heavier. Let us wait a little." With that wakefulness to the faintest indications which belongs to a mind habitually in a state of caution, Tito had detected by the glimmer of the lamp that the leader of the advancing group wore a red feather and a glittering sword-hilt—in fact, was almost the last person in the world he would have chosen to meet at this hour with Romola by his side. He had already during the day had one momentous interview with Dolfo Spini, and the business he had spoken of to Romola as yet to be done was a second interview with that personage, a sequence of the visit he had paid at San Marco. Tito, by a long preconcerted plan, had been the bearer of letters to Savonarola—carefully forged letters, one of them, by a strategem, bearing the very signature and seal of the Cardinal of Naples, who of all the Sacred College had most exerted his influence at Rome in favour of the Frate. The purport of the letters was to state that the Cardinal was on his progress from Pisa, and, unwilling for strong reasons to enter Florence, yet desirous of taking counsel with Savonarola at this difficult juncture, intended to pause this very day at San Casciano, about ten miles from the city, whence he would ride out the next morning in the plain garb of a priest, and meet Savonarola, as if casually, five miles on the Florence road, two hours after sunrise. The plot, of which these forged letters were the initial step, was that Dolfo Spini with a band of his Compagnacci was to be posted in ambush on the road, at a lonely spot about five miles from the gates; that he was to seize Savonarola with the Dominican Brother who would accompany him according to rule, and deliver him over to a small detachment of Milanese horse in readiness near San Casciano, by whom he was to be carried into the Roman territory.

There was a strong chance that the penetrating Frate would suspect a trap, and decline to incur the risk, which he had for some time avoided, of going beyond the city walls. Even when he preached, his friends held it necessary that he should be attended by an armed guard; and here he was called on to commit himself to a solitary road, with no other attendant than a fellow monk. On this ground the minimum of time had been given him for decision, and the chance in favour of his acting on the letters was, that the eagerness with which his mind was set on the combining of interests within and without the Church towards the procuring of a General Council, and also the expectation of immediate service from the Cardinal in the actual juncture of his contest with the Pope, would triumph over his shrewdness and caution in the brief space allowed for deliberation.

Tito had had an audience of Savonarola, having declined to put the letters into any hands but his, and with consummate art had admitted that incidentally, and by inference, he was able so far to conjecture their purport as to believe they referred to a rendezvous outside the gates, in which case he urged that the Frate should seek an armed guard from the Signoria, and offered his services in carrying the request with the utmost privacy. Savonarola had replied briefly that this was impossible: an armed guard was incompatible with privacy. He spoke with a flashing eye, and Tito felt convinced that he meant to incur the risk.

Tito himself did not much care for the result. He managed his affairs so cleverly, that all results, he considered, must turn to his advantage. Whichever party came uppermost, he was secure of favour and money. That is an indecorously naked statement; the fact, clothed as Tito habitually clothed it, was that his acute mind, discerning the equal hollowness of all parties, took the only rational course in making them subservient to his own interest.

If Savonarola fell into the snare, there were diamonds in question and papal patronage; if not, Tito's adroit agency had strengthened his position with Savonarola and with Spini, while any confidence he obtained from them made him the more valuable as an agent of the Mediceans.

But Spini was an inconvenient colleague. He had cunning

enough to delight in plots, but not the ability or self-command necessary to so complex an effect as secrecy. He frequently got excited with drinking, for even sober Florence had its "Beoni,"* or topers, both lay and clerical, who became loud at taverns and private banquets; and in spite of the agreement between him and Tito, that their public recognition of each other should invariably be of the coolest sort, there was always the possibility that on an evening encounter he would be suddenly blurting and affectionate. The delicate sign of casting the *becchetto* over the left shoulder was understood in the morning, but the strongest hint short of a threat might not suffice to keep off a fraternal grasp of the shoulder in the evening.

Tito's chief hope now was that Dolfo Spini had not caught sight of him, and the hope would have been well-founded if Spini had had no clearer view of him than he had caught of Spini. But, himself in shadow, he had seen Tito illuminated for an instant by the direct rays of the lamp, and Tito in his way was as strongly-marked a personage as the Captain of the Compagnacci. Romola's black-shrouded figure had escaped notice, and she now stood behind her husband's shoulder in the corner of the loggia. Tito was not left to hope long.

"Ha! my carrier-pigeon!" grated Spini's harsh voice, in what he meant to be an under-tone, while his hand grasped Tito's shoulder; "what did you run into hiding for? You didn't know it was comrades who were coming. It's well I caught sight of you; it saves time. What of the chase to-morrow morning? Will the bald-headed game rise? Are the falcons to be got ready?"

If it had been in Tito's nature to feel an access of rage, he would have felt it against this bull-faced accomplice, unfit either for a leader or a tool. His lips turned white, but his excitement came from the pressing difficulty of choosing a safe device. If he attempted to hush Spini, that would only deepen Romola's suspicion, and he knew her well enough to know that if some strong alarm were roused in her, she was neither to be silenced nor hoodwinked; on the other hand, if he repelled Spini angrily the wine-breathing Compagnaccio might become savage, being more ready at resentment than at the divination of motives. He adopted a third course, which proved that Romola retained one sort of power over him—the power of dread.

He pressed her hand, as if intending a hint to her, and said in a good-humoured tone of comradeship,—

"Yes, my Dolfo, you may prepare in all security. But take no trumpets with you."

"Don't be afraid," said Spini, a little piqued. "No need to play Ser Saccente* with me. I know where the devil keeps his tail* as well as you do. What! he swallowed the bait whole? The prophetic nose didn't scent the hook at all?" he went on, lowering his tone a little, with a blundering sense of secrecy.

"The brute will not be satisfied till he has emptied the bag," thought Tito; but aloud he said,—"Swallowed all as easily as you swallow a cup of Trebbiano.* Ha! I see torches: there must be a dead body coming. The pestilence has been spreading, I hear."

"Santiddio! I hate the sight of those biers. Good night," said Spini, hastily moving off.

The torches were really coming, but they preceded a church dignitary, who was returning homeward; the suggestion of the dead body and the pestilence was Tito's device for getting rid of Spini without telling him to go. The moment he had moved away, Tito turned to Romola and said, quietly,—

"Do not be alarmed by anything that *bestia* has said, my Romola. We will go on now: I think the rain has not increased."

She was quivering with indignant resolution: it was of no use for Tito to speak in that unconcerned way. She distrusted every word he could utter.

"I will not go on," she said. "I will not move nearer home until I have some security against this treachery being perpetrated."

"Wait, at least, until these torches have passed," said Tito, with perfect self-command, but with a new rising of dislike to a wife who this time, he foresaw, might have the power of thwarting him in spite of the husband's predominance.

The torches passed, with the Vicario dell' Arcivescovo,* and due reverence was done by Tito, but Romola saw nothing outward. If for the defeat of this treachery, in which she believed with all the force of long presentiment, it had been necessary at that moment for her to spring on her husband and hurl herself with him down a precipice, she felt as if she could have done it. Union with this man! At that moment the self-quelling discipline of two years seemed to be nullified: she felt nothing but that they were divided.

They were nearly in darkness again, and could only see each other's faces dimly.

"Tell me the truth, Tito—this time tell me the truth," said Romola, in a low quivering voice. "It will be safer for you."

"Why should I desire to tell you anything else, my angry saint?" said Tito, with a slight touch of contempt, which was the vent of his annoyance; "since the truth is precisely that over which you have most reason to rejoice—namely, that my knowing a plot of Spini's enables me to secure the Frate from falling a victim to it."

"What is the plot?"

"That I decline to tell," said Tito. "It is enough that the Frate's safety will be secured."

"It is a plot for drawing him outside the gates that Spini may murder him."

"There has been no intention of murder. It is simply a plot for compelling him to obey the Pope's summons to Rome. But as I serve the popular government, and think the Frate's presence here is a necessary means of maintaining it at present, I choose to prevent his departure. You may go to sleep with entire ease of mind to-night."

For a moment Romola was silent. Then she said, in a voice of anguish, "Tito, it is of no use: I have no belief in you."

She could just discern his action as he shrugged his shoulders, and spread out his palms in silence. That cold dislike which is the anger of unimpassioned beings was hardening within him.

"If the Frate leaves the city—if any harm happens to him," said Romola, after a slight pause, in a new tone of indignant resolution,—"I will declare what I have heard to the Signoria, and you will be disgraced. What if I am your wife?" she went on, impetuously; "I will be digraced with you. If we are united, I am that part of you that will save you from crime. Others shall not be betrayed."

"I am quite aware of what you would be likely to do, *anima mia*," said Tito, in the coolest of his liquid tones; "therefore if you have a small amount of reasoning at your disposal just now, consider that if you believe me in nothing else, you may believe me when I say I will take care of myself, and not put it in your power to ruin me."

"Then you assure me that the Frate is warned—he will not go beyond the gates?"

"He shall not go beyond the gates."

There was a moment's pause, but distrust was not to be expelled.

"I will go back to San Marco now and find out," Romola said, making a movement forward.

"You shall not!" said Tito, in a bitter whisper, seizing her wrists with all his masculine force. "I am master of you. You shall not set yourself in opposition to me."

There were passers-by approaching. Tito had heard them, and that was why he spoke in a whisper. Romola was too conscious of being mastered to have struggled, even if she had remained unconscious that witnesses were at hand. But she was aware now of footsteps and voices, and her habitual sense of personal dignity made her at once yield to Tito's movement towards leading her from the loggia.

They walked on in silence for some time, under the small drizzling rain. The first rush of indignation and alarm in Romola had begun to give way to more complicated feelings, which rendered speech and action difficult. In that simpler state of vehemence, open opposition to the husband from whom she felt her soul revolting, had had the aspect of a temptation for her; it seemed the easiest of all courses. But now, habits of self-questioning, memories of impulse subdued, and that proud reserve which all discipline had left unmodified, began to emerge from the flood of passion. The grasp of her wrists, which asserted her husband's physical predominance, instead of arousing a new fierceness in her, as it might have done if her impetuosity had been of a more vulgar kind, had given her a momentary shuddering horror at this form of contest with him. It was the first time they had been in declared hostility to each other since her flight and return, and the check given to her ardent resolution then, retained the power to arrest her now. In this altered condition her mind began to dwell on the probabilities that would save her from any desperate course: Tito would not risk betrayal by her; whatever had been his original intention, he must be determined now by the fact that she knew of the plot. She was not bound now to do anything else than to hang over him that certainty that if he deceived her, her lips would not be closed. And then, it was possible—yes, she must cling to that possibility till it was disproved—that Tito had never meant to aid in the betrayal of the Frate.

Tito, on his side, was busy with thoughts, and did not speak again till they were near home. Then he said—

"Well, Romola, have you now had time to recover calmness? If so, you can supply your want of belief in me by a little rational inference: you can see, I presume, that if I had had any intention of furthering Spini's plot I should now be aware that the possession of a fair Piagnone for my wife, who knows the secret of the plot, would be a serious obstacle in my way."

Tito assumed the tone which was just then the easiest to him, conjecturing that in Romola's present mood persuasive deprecation would be lost upon her.

"Yes, Tito," she said, in a low voice, "I think you believe that I would guard the Republic from further treachery. You are right to believe it: if the Frate is betrayed, I will denounce you." She paused a moment, and then said with an effort, "But it was not so. I have perhaps spoken too hastily—you never meant it. Only, why will you seem to be that man's comrade?"

"Such relations are inevitable to practical men, my Romola," said Tito, gratified by discerning the struggle within her. "You fair creatures live in the clouds. Pray go to rest with an easy heart," he added, opening the door for her.

[*APRIL 1863*]

CHAPTER XLVII.

Check

TITO'S clever arrangements had been unpleasantly frustrated by trivial incidents which could not enter into a clever man's calculations. It was very seldom that he walked with Romola in the evening, yet he had happened to be walking with her precisely on this evening when her presence was supremely inconvenient. Life was so complicated a game that the devices of skill were liable to be defeated at every turn by air-blown chances, incalculable as the descent of thistle-down.

It was not that he minded about the failure of Spini's plot, but he felt an awkward difficulty in so adjusting his warning to Savonarola on the one hand, and to Spini on the other, as not to incur suspicion. Suspicion roused in the popular party might be fatal to his reputation and ostensible position in Florence: suspicion roused in Dolfo Spini might be as disagreeable in its effects as the hatred of a fierce dog not to be chained.

If Tito went forthwith to the monastery to warn Savonarola before the monks went to rest, his warning would follow so closely on his delivery of the forged letters that he could not escape unfavourable surmises. He could not warn Spini at once without telling him the true reason, since he could not immediately allege the discovery that Savonarola had changed his purpose; and he knew Spini well enough to know that his understanding would discern nothing but that Tito had "turned round" and frustrated the plot. On the other hand, by deferring his warning to Savonarola until the early morning, he would be almost sure to lose the opportunity of warning Spini that the Frate had changed his mind; and the band of Compagnacci would come back in all the rage of disappointment. This last, however, was the risk he chose, trusting to his power of soothing Spini by assuring him that the failure was due only to the Frate's caution.

Tito was annoyed. If he had had to smile it would have been an unusual effort to him. He was determined not to encounter Romola again, and he did not go home that night.

She watched through the night, and never took off her clothes. She heard the rain become heavier and heavier. She liked to hear the rain: the stormy heavens seemed a safeguard against men's devices, compelling them to inaction. And Romola's mind was again assailed, not only by the utmost doubt of her husband, but by doubt as to her own conduct. What lie might he not have told her? What project might he not have, of which she was still ignorant? Every one who trusted Tito was in danger; it was useless to try and persuade herself of the contrary. And was not she selfishly listening to the promptings of her own pride, when she shrank from warning men against him? "If her husband was a malefactor, her place was in the prison by his side"—that might be; she was contented to fulfil that claim. But was she, a wife, to allow a husband to inflict the injuries that would make him a malefactor, when it might be in her power to prevent them? Prayer seemed impossible to her. The activity of her thought excluded a mental state of which the essence is expectant passivity.

The excitement became stronger and stronger. Her imagination, in a state of morbid activity, conjured up possible schemes by which, after all, Tito would have eluded her threat; and towards daybreak the rain became less violent, till at last it ceased, the breeze rose again and dispersed the clouds, and the morning fell clear on all the objects around her. It made her uneasiness all the less endurable. She wrapped her mantle round her, and ran up to the loggia, as if there could be anything in the wide landscape that might determine her action; as if there could be anything but roofs hiding the line of street along which Savonarola might be walking towards betrayal.

If she went to her godfather, might she not induce him, without any specific revelation, to take measures for preventing Fra Girolamo from passing the gates? But that might be too late. Romola thought, with new distress, that she had failed to learn any guiding details from Tito, and it was already long past seven. She must go to San Marco: there was nothing else to be done.

She hurried down the stairs, she went out into the street without looking at her sick people, and walked at a swift pace along the Via de' Bardi towards the Ponte Vecchio. She would go through the heart of the city; it was the most direct road, and, besides, in the great Piazza there was a chance of encountering her husband, who, by some possibility to which she still clung might satisfy her of the Frate's safety, and leave no need for her to go to San Marco. When she arrived in front of the Palazzo Vecchio, she looked eagerly into the pillared court; then her eyes swept the Piazza; but the well-known figure, once painted in her heart by young love, and now branded there by eating pain, was nowhere to be seen. She hurried straight on to the Piazza del Duomo. It was already full of movement: there were worshippers passing up and down the marble steps, there were men pausing for chat, and there were market people carrying their burthens. Between these moving figures Romola caught a glimpse of her husband. On his way from San Marco he had turned into Nello's shop, and was now leaning against the doorpost. As Romola approached she could see that he was standing and talking, with the easiest air in the world, holding his cap in his hand, and shaking back his freshly-combed hair. The contrast of this ease with the bitter anxieties he had created convulsed her with indignation: the new vision of his hardness heightened her dread. She recognized Cronaca and two other frequenters of San Marco standing near her husband. It flashed through her mind—"I will compel him to speak before those men." And her light step brought her close upon him before he had time to move, while Cronaca was saying, "Here comes Madonna Romola."

A slight shock passed through Tito's frame as he felt himself face to face with his wife. She was haggard with her anxious watching, but there was a flash of something else than anxiety in her eyes as she said,—

"Is the Frate gone beyond the gates?"

"No," said Tito, feeling completely helpless before this woman, and needing all the self-command he possessed to preserve a countenance in which there should seem to be nothing stronger than surprise.

"And you are certain that he is not going?" she insisted.

"I am certain that he is not going."

"That is enough," said Romola, and she turned up the steps, to take refuge in the Duomo, till she could recover from her agitation.

Tito never had a feeling so near hatred as that with which his eyes followed Romola retreating up the steps.

There were present not only genuine followers of the Frate,

but Ser Ceccone,* the notary, who at that time, like Tito himself, was secretly an agent of the Mediceans. Ser Francesco di Ser Barone, more briefly known to infamy as Ser Ceccone, was not learned, not handsome, not successful, and the reverse of generous. He was a traitor without charm. It followed that he was not fond of Tito Melema.

CHAPTER XLVIII.

Counter Check

It was late in the afternoon when Tito returned home. Romola, seated opposite the cabinet in her narrow room, copying documents, was about to desist from her work because the light was getting dim, when her husband entered. He had come straight to this room to seek her, with a thoroughly defined intention, and there was something new to Romola in his manner and expression as he looked at her silently on entering, and, without taking off his cap and mantle, leaned one elbow on the cabinet, and stood directly in front of her.

Romola, fully assured during the day of the Frate's safety, was feeling the reaction of some penitence for the access of distrust and indignation which had impelled her to address her husband publicly on a matter that she knew he wished to be private. She told herself that she had probably been wrong. The scheming duplicity which she had heard even her godfather allude to as inseparable from party tactics might be sufficient to account for the connexion with Spini, without the supposition that Tito had ever meant to further the plot. She wanted to atone for her impetuosity by confessing that she had been too hasty, and for some hours her mind had been dwelling on the possibility that this confession of hers might lead to other frank words breaking the two years' silence of their hearts. The silence had been so complete, that Tito was ignorant of her having fled from him and come back again; they had never approached an avowal of that past which, both in its young love and in the shock that shattered the love, lay locked away from them like a banquet-room where death had once broken the feast.

She looked up at him with that submission in her glance

which belonged to her state of self-reproof; but the subtle change in his face and manner arrested her speech. For a few moments they remained silent, looking at each other.

Tito himself felt that a crisis was come in his married life. The husband's determination to mastery, which lay deep below all blandness and beseechingness, had risen permanently to the surface now, and seemed to alter his face, as a face is altered by a hidden muscular tension with which a man is secretly throttling or stamping out the life from something feeble, yet dangerous.

"Romola," he began, in the cool liquid tone that made her shiver, "it is time that we should understand each other." He paused.

"That is what I most desire, Tito," she said, faintly. Her sweet pale face, with all its anger gone and nothing but the timidity of self-doubt in it, seemed to give a marked predominance to her husband's dark strength.

"You took a step this morning," Tito went on, "which you must now yourself perceive to have been useless—which exposed you to remark and may involve me in serious practical difficulties."

"I acknowledge that I was too hasty; I am sorry for any injustice I may have done you." Romola spoke these words in a fuller and firmer tone; Tito, she hoped, would look less hard when she had expressed her regret, and then she could say other things.

"I wish you once for all to understand," he said, without any change of voice, "that such collisions are incompatible with our position as husband and wife. I wish you to reflect on the mode in which you were led to that step, that the process may not be repeated."

"That depends chiefly on you, Tito," said Romola, taking fire slightly. It was not what she had at all thought of saying, but we see a very little way before us in mutual speech.

"You would say, I suppose," answered Tito, "that nothing is to occur in future which can excite your unreasonable suspicions. You were frank enough to say last night that you have no belief in me. I am not surprised at any exaggerated conclusion you may draw from slight premisses, but I wish to point out to you what is likely to be the fruit of your making such exaggerated conclusions a ground for interfering in affairs of which you are ignorant. Your attention is thoroughly awake to what I am saying?"

He paused for a reply.

"Yes," said Romola, flushing in irrepressible resentment at this cold tone of superiority.

"Well, then, it may possibly not be very long before some other chance words or incidents set your imagination at work devising crimes for me, and you may perhaps rush to the Palazzo Vecchio to alarm the Signoria and set the city in an uproar. Shall I tell you what may be the result? Not simply the disgrace of your husband, to which you look forward with so much courage, but the arrest and ruin of many among the chief men in Florence, including Messer Bernardo del Nero."

Tito had meditated a decisive move, and he had made it. The flush died out of Romola's face, and her very lips were pale—an unusual effect with her, for she was little subject to fear. Tito perceived his success.

"You would perhaps flatter yourself," he went on, "that you were performing a heroic deed of deliverance; you might as well try to turn locks with fine words as apply such notions to the politics of Florence. The question now is, not whether you can have any belief in me, but whether, now you have been warned, you will dare to rush, like a blind man with a torch in his hand, amongst intricate affairs of which you know nothing."

Romola felt as if her mind were held in a vice by Tito's: the possibilities he had indicated were rising before her with terrible clearness.

"I am too rash," she said. "I will try not to be rash."

"Remember," said Tito, with unsparing insistance, "that your act of distrust towards me this morning might, for aught you knew, have had more fatal effects than that sacrifice of your husband which you have learned to contemplate without flinching."

"Tito, it is not so," Romola burst forth in a pleading tone, rising and going nearer to him, with a desperate resolution to speak out. "It is false that I would willingly sacrifice you. It has been the greatest effort of my life to cling to you. I went away in my anger two years ago, and I came back again because I was more bound to you than to anything else on earth. But it is useless. You shut me out from your mind. You affect to think of me as a being too unreasonable to share in the knowledge of your affairs. You will be open with me about nothing."

She looked like his good angel pleading with him, as she bent her face towards him with dilated eyes, and laid her hand upon his arm. But Romola's touch and glance no longer stirred any fibre of tenderness in her husband. The good-humoured, tolerant Tito, incapable of hatred, incapable almost of impatience, disposed always to be gentle towards the rest of the world, felt himself becoming strangely hard towards this wife whose presence had once been the strongest influence he had known. With all his softness of disposition, he had a masculine effectiveness of intellect and purpose which, like sharpness of edge, is itself an energy, working its way without any strong momentum. Romola had an energy of her own which thwarted his, and no man, who is not exceptionally feeble, will endure being thwarted by his wife. Marriage must be a relation either of sympathy or of conquest.

No emotion darted across his face as he heard Romola for the first time speak of having gone away from him. His lips only looked a little harder as he smiled slightly and said—

"My Romola, when certain conditions are ascertained we must make up our minds to them. No amount of wishing will fill the Arno, as your people say, or turn a plum into an orange.* I have not observed even that prayers have much efficacy that way. You are so constituted as to have certain strong impressions inaccessible to reason: I cannot share those impressions, and you have withdrawn all trust from me in consequence. You have changed towards me; it has followed that I have changed towards you. It is useless to take any retrospect. We have simply to adapt ourselves to altered conditions."

"Tito, it would not be useless for us to speak openly," said Romola, with the sort of exasperation that comes from using living muscle against some lifeless insurmountable resistance. "It was the sense of deception in you that changed me, and that has kept us apart. And it is not true that I changed first. You changed towards me the night you first wore that chain armour. You had some secret from me—it was about that old man—and I saw him again yesterday. Tito," she went on, in a tone of agonized entreaty, "if you would once tell me every thing, let it be what it may—I would not mind pain—that there might be no wall between us! Is it not possible that we could begin a new life?"

This time there was a flash of emotion across Tito's face. He stood perfectly still; but the flash seemed to have whitened him. He took no notice of Romola's appeal, but after a moment's pause said, quietly,

"Your impetuosity about trifles, Romola, has a freezing influence that would cool the baths of Nero."* At these cutting words Romola shrank and drew herself up into her usual self-sustained attitude. Tito went on. "If by 'that old man' you mean the mad Jacopo di Nola who attempted my life and made a strange accusation against me, of which I told you nothing because it would have alarmed you to no purpose, he, poor wretch, has died in prison. I saw his name in the list of dead."

"I know nothing about his accusation," said Romola. "But I know he is the man whom I saw with the rope round his neck in the Duomo—the man whose portrait Piero di Cosimo painted, grasping your arm as he saw him grasp it the day the French entered, the day you first wore the armour."

"And where is he now, pray?" said Tito, still pale, but governing himself.

"He was lying lifeless in the street from starvation," said Romola. "I revived him with bread and wine. I brought him to our door, but he refused to come in. Then I gave him some money, and he went away without telling me anything. But he had found out that I was your wife. *Who* is he?"

"A man, half mad, half imbecile, who was once my father's servant in Greece, and who has a rancorous hatred towards me because I got him dismissed for theft. Now you have the whole mystery, and the further satisfaction of knowing that I am again in danger of assassination. The fact of my wearing the armour, about which you seem to have thought so much, must have led you to infer that I was in danger from this man. Was that the reason you chose to cultivate his acquaintance and invite him into the house?"

Romola was mute. To speak was only like rushing with bare breast against a shield.

Tito moved from his leaning posture, slowly took off his cap and mantle, and pushed back his hair. He was collecting himself for some final words. And Romola stood upright looking at him as she might have looked at some on-coming deadly force, to be met only by silent endurance.

"We need not refer to these matters again, Romola," he said, precisely in the same tone as that in which he had spoken at first. "It is enough if you will remember that the next time your generous ardour leads you to interfere in political affairs, you are likely, not to save any one from danger, but to be raising scaffolds and setting houses on fire. You are not yet a sufficiently ardent Piagnone to believe that Messer Bernardo del Nero is the prince of darkness, and Messer Francesco Valori the archangel Michael. I think I need demand no promise from you?"

"I have understood you too well, Tito."

"It is enough," he said, leaving the room.

Romola turned round with despair in her face and sank into her seat. "Oh, God, I have tried—I cannot help it. We shall always be divided." Those words passed silently through her mind. "Unless", she said aloud, as if some sudden vision had startled her into speech—"unless misery should come and join us!"

Tito, too, had a new thought in his mind after he had closed the door behind him. With the project of leaving Florence as soon as his life there had become a high enough stepping-stone to a life elsewhere, perhaps at Rome or Milan, there was now for the first time associated a desire to be free from Romola, and to leave her behind him. She had ceased to belong to the desirable furniture of his life: there was no possibility of an easy relation between them without genuineness on his part. Genuineness implied confession of the past, and confession involved a change of purpose. But Tito had as little bent that way as a leopard has to lap milk when its teeth are grown. From all relations that were not easy and agreeable, we know that Tito shrank: why should he cling to them?

And Romola had made his relations difficult with others besides herself. He had had a troublesome interview with Dolfo Spini, who had come back in a rage after an ineffectual soaking with rain and long waiting in ambush, and that scene between Romola and himself at Nello's door, once reported in Spini's ear, might be a seed of something more unmanageable than suspicion. But now, at least, he believed that he had mastered Romola by a terror which appealed to the strongest forces of her nature. He had alarmed her affection and her conscience by the shadowy image of consequences; he had arrested her intellect by hanging before it the idea of a hopeless complexity in affairs, which defied any moral judgment.

Yet Tito was not at ease. The world was not yet quite cushioned with velvet, and, if it had been, he could not have abandoned himself to that softness with thorough enjoyment; for before he went out again this evening he put on his coat of chain armour.

CHAPTER XLIX.

The Pyramid of Vanities

THE wintry days passed for Romola as the white ships pass one who is standing lonely on the shore—passing in silence and sameness, yet each bearing a hidden burthen of coming change. Tito's hint had mingled so much dread with her interest in the progress of public affairs that she had begun to court ignorance rather than knowledge. The threatening German Emperor* was gone again; and, in other ways besides, the position of Florence was alleviated; but so much distress remained that Romola's active duties were hardly diminished, and in these, as usual, her mind found a refuge from its doubt.

She dared not rejoice that the relief which had come in extremity and had appeared to justify the policy of the Frate's party was making that party so triumphant, that Francesco Valori, hot-tempered chieftain of the Piagnoni, had been elected Gonfaloniere at the beginning of the year, and was making haste to have as much of his own liberal way as possible during his two months of power. That seemed for the moment like a strengthening of the party most attached to freedom, and a reinforcement of protection to Savonarola; but Romola was now alive to every suggestion likely to deepen her foreboding, that whatever the present might be, it was only an unconscious brooding over the mixed germs of Change which might any day become tragic. And already by Carnival time, a little after mid-February, her presentiment was confirmed by the signs of a very decided change: the Mediceans had ceased to be passive, and were openly exerting themselves to procure the election of Bernardo del Nero as the new Gonfaloniere.

On the last day of the Carnival, between ten and eleven in the morning, Romola walked out, according to promise, towards the Corso degli Albizzi, to fetch her cousin Brigida, that they might both be ready to start from the Via de' Bardi early in the afternoon, and take their places at a window which Tito had had reserved for them in the Piazza della Signoria, where there was to be a scene of so new and striking a sort, that all Florentine eyes must desire to see it. For the Piagnoni were having their own way thoroughly about the mode of keeping the Carnival. In vain Dolfo Spini and his companions had struggled to get up the dear old masques and practical jokes, well spiced with indecency. Such things were not to be in a city where Christ had been declared King.*

Romola set out in that languid state of mind with which every one enters on a long day of sight-seeing, purely for the sake of gratifying a child, or some dear childish friend. The day was certainly an epoch in Carnival-keeping; but this phase of reform had not touched her enthusiasm: and she did not know that it was an epoch in her own life, when *another* lot would begin to be no longer secretly but visibly entwined with her own.

She chose to go through the great Piazza that she might take a first survey of the unparalleled sight there while she was still alone. Entering it from the south, she saw something monstrous and many-coloured in the shape of a pyramid, or, rather, like a huge fir-tree, sixty feet high, with shelves on the branches, widening and widening towards the base till they reached a circumference of eighty yards. The Piazza was full of life: slight young figures, in white garments, with olive wreaths on their heads, were moving to and fro about the base of the pyramidal tree, carrying baskets full of bright-coloured things; and maturer forms, some in the monastic frock, some in the loose tunics and dark-red caps of artists, were helping and examining, or else retreating to various points in the distance to survey the wondrous whole; while a considerable group, amongst whom Romola recognized Piero di Cosimo, standing on the marble steps of Orgagna's Loggia, seemed to be keeping aloof in discontent and scorn.

Approaching nearer, she paused to look at the multifarious objects ranged in gradation from the base to the summit of the pyramid. There were tapestries and brocades of immodest design, pictures and sculptures held too likely to incite to vice; there were boards and tables for all sorts of games, playing-cards along with the blocks for printing them, dice, and other apparatus for gambling; there were worldly music-books, and musical instruments in all the pretty varieties of lute, drum, cymbal, and trumpet; there were masks and masquerading dresses used in the old carnival shows; there were handsome copies of Ovid, Boccaccio, Petrarca, Pulci, and other books of a vain or impure sort; there were all the implements of feminine vanity—rouge-pots, false hair, mirrors, perfumes, powders, and transparent veils intended to provoke inquisitive glances: lastly, at the very summit, there was the unflattering effigy of a probably mythical Venetian merchant, who was understood to have offered a heavy sum for this collection of marketable abominations, and, soaring above him in surpassing ugliness, the symbolic figure of the old debauched Carnival.

This was the preparation for a new sort of bonfire—the Burning of Vanities. Hidden in the interior of the pyramid was a plentiful store of dry fuel and gunpowder; and on this last day of the festival, at evening, the pile of vanities was to be set ablaze to the sound of trumpets, and the ugly old Carnival was to tumble into the flames amid the songs of reforming triumph.

This crowning act of the new festivities could hardly have been prepared but for a peculiar organization which had been started by Savonarola two years before. The mass of the Florentine boyhood and youth was no longer left to its own genial promptings towards street mischief and crude dissoluteness. Under the training of Fra Domenico, a sort of lieutenant to Savonarola, lads and striplings, the hope of Florence, were to have none but pure words on their lips, were to have a zeal for Unseen Good that should put to shame the lukewarmness of their elders, and were to know no pleasures save of an angelic sort—singing divine praises and walking in white robes. It was for them that the ranges of seats had been raised high against the walls of the Duomo; and they had been used to hear Savonarola appeal to them as the future glory of a city specially appointed to do the work of God.

These fresh-cheeked troops were the chief agents in the regenerated merriment of the new Carnival, which was a sort of sacred parody of the old. Had there been bonfires in the old time? There was to be a bonfire now, consuming impurity from off the earth. Had there been symbolic processions? There were to be processions now, but the symbols were to be white robes and red crosses and olive wreaths—emblems of peace and innocent gladness—and the banners and images held aloft were to tell the triumphs of goodness. Had there been dancing in a ring under the open sky of the Piazza, to the sound of choral voices chanting loose songs? There was to be dancing in a ring now, but dancing of monks and laity in fraternal love and divine joy, and the music was to be the music of hymns. As for the collections from street passengers, they were to be greater than ever—not for gross and superfluous suppers, but—for the benefit of the hungry and needy; and, besides, there was the collecting of the *Anathema*, or the Vanities to be laid on the great pyramidal bonfire.

Troops of young inquisitors went from house to house on this exciting business of asking that the *Anathema* should be given up to them. Perhaps after the more avowed vanities had been surrendered, Madonna, at the head of the household, had still certain little reddened balls brought from the Levant, intended to produce on a sallow cheek a sudden bloom of the most ingenuous falsity? If so, let her bring them down and cast them into the basket of doom. Or, perhaps, she had ringlets and coils of "dead hair"?*—if so, let her bring them to the street-door, not on her head, but in her hands, and publicly renounce the *Anathema* which hid the respectable signs of age under a ghastly mockery of youth. And, in reward, she would hear fresh young voices pronounce a blessing on her and her house.

The beardless inquisitors, organized into little regiments, doubtless took to their work very willingly. To coerce people by shame, or other spiritual pelting, into the giving up of things it will probably vex them to part with, is a form of piety to which the boyish mind is most readily converted; and if some obstinately wicked men got enraged and threatened the whip or the cudgel, this also was exciting. Savonarola himself evidently felt about the training of these boys the difficulty weighing on all minds with noble yearnings towards great ends, yet with that imperfect perception of means which forces a resort to some supernatural constraining influence as the only sure hope. The Florentine youth had had very evil habits and foul tongues: it seemed at first an unmixed blessing when they were got to shout "*Viva Gesù!*" but Savonarola was forced at last to say from the pulpit, "There is a little too much shouting of '*Viva Gesù!*' This constant utterance of sacred words brings them into contempt. Let me have no more of that shouting till the next Festa."

Nevertheless, as the long stream of white-robed youthfulness, with its little red crosses and olive wreaths, had gone to the Duomo at dawn this morning to receive the communion from the hands of Savonarola, it was a sight of beauty; and, doubtless, many of those young souls were laying up memories of hope and awe that might save them from ever resting in a merely vulgar view of their work as men and citizens. There is no kind of conscious obedience that is not an advance on lawlessness, and these boys became the generation of men who fought greatly and endured greatly in the last struggle of their Republic.* Now, in the intermediate hours between the early communion and dinner-time, they were making their last perambulations to collect alms and vanities, and this was why Romola saw the slim white figures moving to and fro about the base of the great pyramid.

"What think you of this folly, Madonna Romola?" said a brusque voice close to her ear. "Your Piagnoni will make *Ninferno** a pleasant prospect to us, if they are to carry things their own way on earth. It's enough to fetch a cudgel over the mountains to see painters, like Lorenzo di Credi and young Baccio* there, helping to burn colour out of life in this fashion."

"My good Piero," said Romola, looking up and smiling at the grim man, "even you must be glad to see some of these things burnt. Look at those gew-gaws and wigs and rouge-pots: I have heard you talk as indignantly against those things as Fra Girolamo himself."

"What then?" said Piero, turning round on her sharply. "I never said a woman should make a black patch of herself against the background. *Va!* Madonna Antigone, it's a shame for a woman with your hair and shoulders to run into such nonsense—leave it to women who are not worth painting. What! the most holy Virgin herself has always been dressed well; that's the doctrine of the Church:—talk of heresy, indeed! And I should like to know what the excellent Messer Bardo would have said to the burning of the divine poets by these Frati, who are no better an imitation of men than if they were onions with the bulbs uppermost. Look at that Petrarca sticking up beside a rouge-pot: do the idiots pretend that the heavenly Laura* was a painted harridan? And Boccaccio, now: do you mean to say, Madonna Romola—you who are fit to be a model for a wise

Saint Catherine of Egypt*—do you mean to say you have never read the stories of the immortal Messer Giovanni?"

"It is true I have read them, Piero," said Romola. "Some of them a great many times over, when I was a little girl. I used to get the book down when my father was asleep, so that I could read to myself."

"*Ebbene?*" said Piero, in a fiercely challenging tone.

"There are some things in them I do not want ever to forget," said Romola, "but you must confess, Piero, that a great many of those stories are only about low deceit for the lowest ends. Men do not want books to make them think lightly of vice, as if life were a vulgar joke. And I cannot blame Fra Girolamo for teaching that we owe our time to something better."

"Yes, yes, it's very well to say so now you've read them," said Piero, bitterly, turning on his heel and walking away from her.

Romola too walked on, smiling at Piero's innuendo, with a sort of tenderness towards the odd painter's anger, because she knew that her father would have felt something like it. For herself, she was conscious of no inward collision with the strict and sombre view of pleasure which tended to repress poetry in the attempt to repress vice. Sorrow and joy have each their peculiar narrowness; and a religious enthusiasm like Savonarola's, which ultimately blesses mankind by giving the soul a strong propulsion towards sympathy with pain, indignation against wrong, and the subjugation of sensual desire, must always incur the reproach of a great negation. Romola's life had given her an affinity for sadness which inevitably made her unjust towards merriment. That subtle result of culture which we call Taste was subdued by the need for deeper motive; just as the nicer demands of the palate are annihilated by urgent hunger. Moving habitually among scenes of suffering, and carrying woman's heaviest disappointment in her heart, the severity which allied itself with self-renouncing beneficent strength had no dissonance for her.

CHAPTER L.

Tessa Abroad and at Home

ANOTHER figure easily recognized by us—a figure not clad in black, but in the old red, green, and white—was approaching the Piazza that morning to see the Carnival. She came from an opposite point, for Tessa no longer lived on the Hill of San Giorgio. After what had happened there with Baldassarre, Tito had thought it best for that and other reasons to find her a new home, but still in a quiet airy quarter, in a house bordering on the wide garden grounds north of the Porta Santa Croce.

Tessa was not come out sight-seeing without special leave. Tito had been with her the evening before, and she had kept back the entreaty which she felt to be swelling her heart and throat until she saw him in a state of radiant ease, with one arm round the sturdy Lillo, and the other resting gently on her own shoulder as she tried to make the tiny Ninna steady on her legs. She was sure then that the weariness with which he had come in and flung himself into his chair had quite melted away from his brow and lips. Tessa had not been slow at learning a few small stratagems by which she might avoid vexing Naldo and yet have a little of her own way. She could read nothing else, but she had learned to read a good deal in her husband's face.

And certainly the charm of that bright, gentle-humoured Tito who woke up under the Loggia de' Cerchi on a Lenten morning five years before, not having yet given any hostages to deceit, never returned so nearly as in the person of Naldo, seated in that straight-backed, carved arm-chair which he had provided for his comfort when he came to see Tessa and the children. Tito himself was surprised at the growing sense of relief which he felt in these moments. No guile was needed towards Tessa: she was too ignorant and too innocent to suspect him of anything. And the little voices calling him "Babbo" were very sweet in his ears for the short while that he heard them. When he thought of leaving Florence, he never thought of leaving Tessa and the little ones behind. He was very fond of these round-cheeked, wide-eyed human things that clung about him and knew no evil of him. And wherever affection can spring, it is like the green leaf and the blossom—pure, and breathing purity, whatever soil it may grow in. Poor Romola, with all her self-sacrificing effort, was really helping to harden Tito's nature by chilling it with a positive dislike which had beforehand seemed impossible in him; but Tessa kept open the fountains of kindness.

"Ninna is very good without me now," began Tessa, feeling her request rising very high in her throat, and letting Ninna seat herself on the floor. "I can leave her with Monna Lisa any time, and if she is in the cradle and cries, Lillo is as sensible as can be—he goes and thumps Monna Lisa."

Lillo, whose great dark eyes looked all the darker because his curls were of a light brown like his mother's, jumped off Babbo's knee, and went forthwith to attest his intelligence by thumping Monna Lisa, who was shaking her head slowly over her spinning at the other end of the room.

"A wonderful boy!" said Tito, laughing.

"Isn't he?" said Tessa, eagerly, getting a little closer to him, "and I might go and see the Carnival to-morrow, just for an hour or two, mightn't I?"

"Oh, you wicked pigeon!" said Tito, pinching her cheek; "those are your longings, are they? What have you to do with Carnivals now you are an old woman with two children?"

"But old women like to see things," said Tessa, her lower lip hanging a little. "Monna Lisa said she should like to go, only she's so deaf she can't hear what is behind her, and she thinks we couldn't take care of both the children."

"No, indeed, Tessa," said Tito, looking rather grave, "you must not think of taking the children into the crowded streets, else I shall be angry."

"But I have never been into the Piazza without leave," said Tessa, in a frightened, pleading tone, "since the Holy Saturday, and Nofri I think is dead, for you know the poor madre died; and I shall never forget the carnival I saw once; it was so pretty—all roses and a king and queen under them—and singing. I liked it better than the San Giovanni."

"But there's nothing like that now, my Tessa. They are going to make a bonfire in the piazza—that's all. But I cannot let you go out by yourself in the evening."

"Oh, no, no! I don't want to go in the evening. I only want to go and see the procession by daylight. There *will* be a procession—is it not true?"

"Yes, after a sort," said Tito, "as lively as a flight of cranes. You must not expect roses and glittering kings and queens, my Tessa. However, I suppose any string of people to be called a procession will please your blue eyes. And there's a thing they have raised in the Piazza de' Signori for the bonfire. You may like to see that. But come home early, and look like a grave little old woman; and if you see any men with feathers and swords, keep out of their way: they are very fierce, and like to cut old women's heads off."

"Santa Madonna! where do they come from? Ah! you are laughing; it is not so bad. But I will keep away from them. Only," Tessa went on in a whisper, putting her lips near Naldo's ear, "if I might take Lillo with me! He is very sensible."

"But who will thump Monna Lisa then, if she doesn't hear?" said Tito, finding it difficult not to laugh, but thinking it necessary to look serious. "No, Tessa, you could not take care of Lillo if you got into a crowd, and he's too heavy for you to carry him."

"It is true," said Tessa, rather sadly, "and he likes to run away. I forgot that. Then I will go alone. But now look at Ninna—you have not looked at her enough."

Ninna was a blue-eyed thing, at the tottering, tumbling age—a fair solid, which, like a loaded die, found its base with a constancy that warranted prediction. Tessa went to snatch her up, and when Babbo was paying due attention to the recent teeth and other marvels, she said, in a whisper, "And shall I buy some *confetti* for the children?"

Tito drew some small coins from his scarsella, and poured them into her palm.

"That will buy no end," said Tessa, delighted at this abundance. "I shall not mind going without Lillo so much, if I bring him something."

So Tessa set out in the morning towards the great Piazza where the bonfire was to be. She did not think the February breeze cold enough to demand further covering than her green woollen dress. A mantle would have been oppressive, for it would have hidden a new necklace and a new clasp, mounted with silver, the only ornamental presents Tito had ever made her. Tessa did not think at all of showing her figure, for no one had ever told her it was pretty; but she was quite sure that her necklace and clasp were of the prettiest sort ever worn by the richest contadina, and she arranged her white hood over her head so that the front of her necklace might be well displayed. These ornaments, she considered, must inspire respect for her as the wife of some one who could afford to buy them.

She tripped along very cheerily in the February sunshine, thinking much of the purchases for the little ones, with which she was to fill her small basket, and not thinking at all of any one who might be observing her. Yet her descent from her upper story into the street had been watched, and she was being kept in sight as she walked by a person who had often waited in vain to see if it were not Tessa who lived in that house to which he had more than once dogged Tito. Baldassarre was carrying a package of yarn: he was constantly employed in that way, as a means of earning his scanty bread, and keeping the sacred fire of vengeance alive; and he had come out of his way this morning, as he had often done before, that he might pass by the house to which he had followed Tito in the evening. His long imprisonment had so intensified his timid suspicion and his belief in some diabolic fortune favouring Tito, that he had not dared to pursue him, except under cover of a crowd or of the darkness; he felt with instinctive horror, that if Tito's eyes fell upon him, he should again be held up to obloquy, again be dragged away; his weapon would be taken from him, and he should be cast helpless into a prison-cell. His fierce purpose had become as stealthy as a serpent's, which depends for its prey on one dart of the fang. Justice was weak and unfriended; and he could not hear again the voice that pealed the promise of vengeance in the Duomo: he had been there again and again, but that voice, too, had apparently been stifled by cunning strong-armed wickedness. For a long while, Baldassarre's ruling thought was to ascertain whether Tito still wore the armour, for now at last his fainting hope would have been contented with a successful stab on this side the grave; but he would never risk his precious knife again. It was a weary time he had had to wait for the chance of answering this question by touching Tito's back in the press of the street. Since then, the knowledge that the sharp steel was useless, and that he had no hope but in some new device, had fallen with leaden weight on his enfeebled mind. A dim vision of winning one of those two wives to aid him came before him continually, and continually slid away. The wife who had lived on the hill was no longer there. If he could find her again, he might grasp some thread of a project, and work his way to more clearness.

And this morning he had succeeded. He was quite certain now where this wife lived, and as he walked bent a little under his burthen of yarn, yet keeping the green and white figure in sight, his mind was dwelling upon her and her circumstances as feeble eyes dwell on lines and colours, trying to interpret them into consistent significance.

Tessa had to pass through various long streets without seeing any other sign of the Carnival than unusual groups of the country people in their best garments, and that disposition in everybody to chat and loiter which marks the early hours of a holiday, before the spectacle has begun. Presently, in her disappointed search for remarkable objects, her eyes fell on a man with a pedlar's basket before him, who seemed to be selling nothing but little red crosses to all the passengers. A little red cross would be pretty to hang up over the bed; it would also help to keep off harm, and would perhaps make Ninna stronger. Tessa went to the other side of the street that she might ask the pedlar the price of the crosses, fearing that they would cost a little too much for her to spare from her purchase of sweets. The pedlar's back had been turned towards her hitherto, but when she came near him she recognized an old acquaintance of the Mercato, Bratti Ferravecchi, and accustomed to feel that she was to avoid old acquaintances, she turned away again and passed to the other side of the street. But Bratti's eye was too well practised in looking out at the corner after possible customers, for her movement to have escaped him, and she was presently arrested by a tap on the arm from one of the red crosses.

"Young woman," said Bratti, as she unwillingly turned her head, "you come from some castello a good way off, it seems to me, else you'd never think of walking about, this blessed Carnival, without a red cross in your hand. Santa Madonna! Four white quattrini is a small price to pay for your soul—prices rise in purgatory, let me tell you."

"Oh, I should like one," said Tessa, hastily, "but I couldn't spare four white quattrini."

Bratti had at first regarded Tessa too abstractedly as a mere customer to look at her with any scrutiny, but when she began to speak he exclaimed, "By the head of San Giovanni, it must be the little Tessa, and looking as fresh as a ripe apple! What, you've done none the worse, then, for running away from father Nofri? You were in the right of it, for he goes on crutches now, and a crabbed fellow with crutches is dangerous; he can reach across the house and beat a woman as he sits."

"I'm married," said Tessa, rather demurely, remembering Naldo's command that she should behave with gravity; "and my husband takes great care of me."

"Ah, then you've fallen on your feet! Nofri said you were good-for-nothing vermin; but what then? An ass may bray a good while before he shakes the stars down.* I always said you did well to run away, and it isn't often Bratti's in the wrong. Well, and so you've got a husband and plenty of money? Then you'll never think much of giving four white quattrini for a red cross. I get no profit; but what with the famine and the new religion, all other merchandise is gone down. You live in the country where the chestnuts are plenty, eh? You've never wanted for polenta, I can see."

"No, I've never wanted anything," said Tessa, still on her guard.

"Then you can afford to buy a cross. I got a *padre* to bless them, and you get blessing and all for four quattrini. It isn't for the profit; I hardly get a danaro by the whole lot. But then they're holy wares, and it's getting harder and harder work to see your way to Paradise: the very Carnival is like Holy Week, and the least you can do to keep the devil from getting the upper hand is to buy a cross. God guard you! think what the devil's tooth is! You've seen him biting the man in San Giovanni,* I should hope?"

Tessa felt much teased and frightened. "Oh, Bratti, she said, with a discomposed face, "I want to buy a great many *confetti*: I've got little Lillo and Ninna at home. And nice coloured sweet things cost a great deal. And they will not like the cross so well, though I know it would be good to have it."

"Come, then," said Bratti, fond of laying up a store of merits by imagining possible extortions and then heroically renouncing them, "Since you're an old aquaintance, you shall have it for two quattrini. It's making you a present of the cross, to say nothing of the blessing."

Tessa was reaching out her two quattrini with trembling hesitation, when Bratti said, abruptly, "Stop a bit! Where do you live?"

"Oh, a long way off," she answered, almost automatically, being preoccupied with her quattrini; "beyond San Ambrogio, in the Via Piccola, at the top of the house where the wood is stacked below."

"Very good," said Bratti, in a patronizing tone; "then I'll let you have the cross on trust, and call for the money. So you live inside the gates? Well, well, I shall be passing."

"No, no!" said Tessa, frightened lest Naldo should be angry at this revival of an old aquaintance. "I can spare the money. Take it now."

"No," said Bratti, resolutely; "I'm not a hard-hearted pedlar. I'll call and see if you've got any rags, and you shall make a bargain. See, here's the cross; and there's Pippo's shop, not far behind you: you can go and fill your basket, and I must go and get mine empty. *Addio, piccina.*"

Bratti went on his way, and Tessa, stimulated to change her money into *confetti* before further accidents, went into Pippo's shop, a little fluttered by the thought that she had let Bratti know more about her than her husband would approve. There were certainly more dangers in coming to see the Carnival than in staying at home; and she would have felt this more strongly if she had known that the wicked old man, who had wanted to kill her husband on the hill, was still keeping her in sight. But she had not noticed the man with the burthen on his back.

The consciousness of having a small basketful of things to make the children glad, dispersed her anxiety, and as she entered the Via de' Libraj her face had its usual expression of child-like content. And now she thought there was really a procession coming, for she saw white robes and a banner, and her heart began to palpitate with expectation. She stood a little aside, but in that narrow street there was the pleasure of being obliged to look very close. The banner was pretty: it was the Holy Mother with the Babe, whose love for her Tessa had believed in more and more since she had had her babies; and the figures in white had not only green wreaths on their heads, but little red crosses by their side, which caused her some satisfaction that she also had her red cross. Certainly, they looked as beautiful as the angels on the clouds, and to Tessa's mind they too had a background of cloud, like everything else that came to her in life. How and whence did they come? She did not mind much about knowing. But one thing surprised her as newer than wreaths and crosses; it was that some of the white figures carried baskets between them. What could the baskets be for?

But now they were very near, and, to her astonishment, they wheeled aside and came straight up to her. She trembled as she would have done if St. Michael in the picture had shaken his head at her, and was conscious of nothing but terrified wonder till she saw close to her a round boyish face, lower than her own, and heard a treble voice saying, "Sister, you carry the *Anathema* about you. Yield it up to the blessed Gesù, and he will adorn you with the gems of his grace."

Tessa was only more frightened, understanding nothing. Her first conjecture settled on her basket of sweets. They wanted that, these alarming angels. Oh, dear, dear! She looked down at it.

"No, sister," said a taller youth, pointing to her necklace and the clasp of her belt, "it is those vanities that are the *Anathema*. Take off that necklace and unclasp that belt, that they may be burned in the holy Bonfire of Vanities, and save *you* from burning."

"It is the truth, my sister," said a still taller youth, evidently the archangel of this band. "Listen to these voices speaking the divine message. You already carry a red cross: let that be your only adornment. Yield up your necklace and belt, and you shall obtain grace."

This was too much. Tessa, overcome with awe, dared not say "no," but she was equally unable to render up her beloved necklace and clasp. Her pouting lips were quivering, the tears rushed to her eyes, and a great drop fell. For a moment she ceased to see anything; she felt nothing but confused terror and misery. Suddenly a gentle hand was laid on her arm, and a soft, wonderful voice, as if the Holy Madonna were speaking, said, "Do not be afraid; no one shall harm you."

Tessa looked up and saw a lady in black, with a young heavenly face and loving hazel eyes. She had never seen any one like this lady before, and under other circumstances might have had awe-struck thoughts about her; but now everything else was overcome by the sense that loving protection was near her. The tears only fell the faster, relieving her swelling heart, as she looked up at the heavenly face, and, putting her hand to her necklace, said sobbingly,

"I can't give them to be burnt. My husband—he bought

them for me—and they are so pretty—and Ninna—Oh, I wish I'd never come!"

"Do not ask her for them," said Romola, speaking to the white-robed boys in a tone of mild authority. "It answers no good end for people to give up such things against their will. That is not what Fra Girolamo approves: he would have such things given up freely."

Madonna Romola's word was not to be resisted, and the white train moved on. They even moved with haste, as if some new object had caught their eyes; and Tessa felt with bliss that they were gone, and that her necklace and clasp were still with her.

"Oh, I will go back to the house," she said, still agitated; "I will go nowhere else. But if I should meet them again, and you not be there?" she added, expecting everything from this heavenly lady.

"Stay a little," said Romola. "Come with me under this doorway, and we will hide the necklace and clasp, and then you will be in no danger."

She led Tessa under the archway, and said, "Now, can we find room for your necklace and belt in your basket? Ah! your basket is full of crisp things that will break: let us be careful, and lay the heavy necklace under them."

It was like a change in a dream to Tessa—the escape from nightmare into floating safety and joy—to find herself taken care of by this lady, so lovely, and powerful, and gentle. She let Romola unfasten her necklace and clasp, while she herself did nothing but look up at the face that bent over her.

"They are sweets for Lillo and Ninna," she said, as Romola carefully lifted up the light parcels in the basket, and placed the ornaments below them.

"Those are your children?" said Romola, smiling. "And you would rather go home to them than see any more of the Carnival? Else you have not far to go to the Piazza de' Signori, and there you would see the pile for the great bonfire."

"No; oh, no!" said Tessa, eagerly; "I shall never like bonfires again. I will go back."

"You live at some castello, doubtless," said Romola, not waiting for an answer. "Towards which gate do you go?"

"Towards Por' Santa Croce."

"Come, then," said Romola, taking her by the hand and leading her to the corner of a street nearly opposite. "If you go down there," she said, pausing, "you will soon be in a straight road. And I must leave you now, because some one else expects me. You will not be frightened. Your pretty things are quite safe now. Addio."

"Addio, Madonna," said Tessa, almost in a whisper, not knowing what else it would be right to say; and in an instant the heavenly lady was gone. Tessa turned to catch a last glimpse, but she only saw the tall gliding figure vanish round the projecting stonework. So she went on her way in wonder, longing to be once more safely housed with Monna Lisa, undesirous of Carnivals for ever more.

Baldassarre had kept Tessa in sight till the moment of her parting with Romola: then he went away with his bundle of yarn. It seemed to him that he had discerned a clue which might guide him if he could only grasp the necessary details firmly enough. He had seen the two wives together, and the sight had brought to his conceptions that vividness which had been wanting before. His power of imagining facts needed to be reinforced continually by the senses. The tall wife was the noble and rightful wife; she had the blood in her that would be readily kindled to resentment; she would know what scholarship was, and how it might lie locked in by the obstructions of the stricken body, like a treasure buried by earthquake. She could believe him: she would be *inclined* to believe him, if he proved to her that her husband was unfaithful. Women cared about that: they would take Vengeance for that. If this wife of Tito's loved him, she would have a sense of injury which Baldassarre's mind dwelt on with keen longing, as if it would be the strength of another will added to his own, the strength of another mind to form devices.

Both these wives had been kind to Baldassarre, and their acts towards him, being bound up with the very image of them, had not vanished from his memory; yet the thought of their pain could not present itself to him as a check. To him it seemed that pain was the order of the world for all except the hard and base. If any were innocent, if any were noble, where could the utmost gladness lie for them? Where it lay for him—in unconquerable hatred and triumphant vengeance. But he must be cautious: he must watch this wife in the Via de' Bardi, and learn more of her; for even here frustration was possible. There was no power for him now but in patience.

CHAPTER LI.

Monna Brigida's Conversion

WHEN Romola said that some one else expected her, she meant her cousin Brigida, but she was far from suspecting how much that good kinswoman was in need of her. Returning together towards the Piazza, they had descried the company of youths coming to a stand before Tessa, and when Romola, having approached near enough to see the simple little contadina's distress, said, "Wait for me a moment, cousin," Monna Brigida said hastily, "Ah, I will not go on: come for me to Boni's shop,—I shall go back there."

The truth was, Monna Brigida had a consciousness on the one hand of certain "vanities" carried on her person, and on the other of a growing alarm lest the Piagnoni should be right in holding that rouge, and false hair, and pearl embroidery, endamaged the soul. Their serious view of things filled the air like an odour; nothing seemed to have exactly the same flavour as it used to have; and there was the dear child Romola, in her youth and beauty, leading a life that was uncomfortably suggestive of rigorous demands on woman. A widow at fifty-five whose satisfaction has been largely drawn from what she thinks of her own person, and what she believes others think of it, requires a great fund of imagination to keep her spirits buoyant. And Monna Brigida had begun to have frequent struggles at her toilet. If her soul would prosper better without them, was it really worth while to put on the rouge and the braids? But when she lifted up the hand-mirror and saw a sallow face with baggy cheeks, and crows' feet that were not to be dissimulated by any simpering of the lips—when she parted her grey hair, and let it lie in simple Piagnone fashion round her face, her courage failed. Monna Berta would certainly burst out laughing at her, and call her an old hag, and as Monna Berta was really only fifty-two, she had a superiority which would make the observation cutting. Every woman who was not a Piagnone would give a shrug at the sight of her, and the men would accost her as if she were their grandmother. Whereas, at fifty-five a woman was not so very old—she only required making up a little. So the rouge and the braids and the embroidered berretta went on again, and Monna Brigida was satisfied with the accustomed effect; as for her neck, if she covered it up, people might suppose it was too old to show, and on the contrary, with the necklaces round it, it looked better than Monna Berta's. This very day, when she was preparing for the Piagnone Carnival, such a struggle had occurred, and the conflicting fears and longings which caused the struggle, caused her to turn back and seek refuge in the druggist's shop rather than encounter the collectors of the *Anathema* when Romola was not by her side.

But Monna Brigida was not quite rapid enough in her retreat. She had been descried, even before she turned away, by the white-robed boys in the rear of those who wheeled round towards Tessa, and the willingness with which Tessa was given up was, perhaps, slightly due to the fact that part of the troop had already accosted a personage carrying more markedly upon her the dangerous weight of the *Anathema*. It happened that several of this troop were at the youngest age taken into peculiar training; and a small fellow of ten, his olive wreath resting above cherubic cheeks and wide brown eyes, his imagination really possessed with a hovering awe at existence as something in which great consequences impended on being good or bad, his longings nevertheless running in the direction of mastery and mischief, was the first to reach Monna Brigida and place himself across her path. She felt angry, and looked for an open door, but there was not one at hand, and by attempting to escape now, she would only make things worse. But it was not the cherubic-faced young one who first addressed her; it was a youth of fifteen, who held one handle of a wide basket.

"Venerable mother!" he began, "the blessed Jesus commands you to give up the *Anathema* which you carry upon you. That cap embroidered with pearls, those jewels that fasten up your false hair—let them be given up and sold for the poor; and cast the hair itself away from you, as a lie that is only fit for burning. Doubtless, too, you have other jewels under your silk mantle."

"Yes, lady," said the youth at the other handle, who had many of Fra Girolamo's phrases by heart, "they are too heavy for you: they are heavier than a millstone, and are weighting you for perdition. Will you adorn yourself with the hunger of the poor, and be proud to carry God's curse upon your head?"

"In truth you are old, buona madre," said the cherubic boy, in a sweet soprano. "You look very ugly with the red on your cheeks and that black glistening hair, and those fine things. It is only Satan who can like to see you. Your Angel is sorry. He wants you to rub away the red."

The little fellow snatched a soft silk scarf from the basket, and held it towards Monna Brigida, that she might use it as her guardian angel desired. Her anger and mortification were fast giving way to spiritual alarm. Monna Berta, and that cloud of witnesses, highly-drest society in general, were not looking at her, and she was surrounded by young monitors, whose white robes, and wreaths, and red crosses, and dreadful candour, had something awful in their unusualness. Her Franciscan confessor, Fra Cristoforo, of Santa Croce, was not at hand to reinforce her distrust of Dominican teaching, and she was helplessly possessed and shaken by a vague sense that a supreme warning was come to her. Unvisited by the least suggestion of any other course that was open to her, she took the scarf that was held out, and rubbed her cheeks, with trembling submissiveness.

"It is well, Madonna," said the second youth. "It is a holy beginning. And when you have taken those vanities from your head, the dew of heavenly grace will descend on it." The infusion of mischief was getting stronger, and putting his hand to one of the jewelled pins that fastened her braids to the berretta, he drew it out. The heavy black plait fell down over Monna Brigida's face, and dragged the rest of the head-gear forward. It was a new reason for not hesitating: she put up her hands hastily, undid the other fastenings, and flung down into the basket of doom her beloved crimson-velvet berretta,* with all its unsurpassed embroidery of seed-pearls, and stood an unrouged woman, with grey hair pushed backward from a face where certain deep lines of age had triumphed over embonpoint.*

But the berretta was not allowed to lie in the basket. With impish zeal, the youngsters lifted it, and held it up pitilessly, with the false hair dangling.

"See, venerable mother," said the taller youth, "what ugly lies you have delivered yourself from! And now you look like the blessed Saint Anna, the mother of the Holy Virgin."

Thoughts of going into a convent forthwith, and never showing herself in the world again, were rushing through Monna Brigida's mind. There was nothing possible for her but to take care of her soul. Of course, there were spectators laughing: she had no need to look round to assure herself of that. Well! it would, perhaps, be better to be forced to think more of paradise. But at the thought that the dear accustomed world was no longer in her choice, there gathered some of those hard tears which just moisten elderly eyes, and she could see but dimly a large rough hand holding a red cross, which was suddenly thrust before her over the shoulders of the boys, while a strong guttural voice said, "Only four quattrini, Madonna, blessing and all! Buy it. You'll find a comfort in it now your wig's gone. Deh! what are we sinners doing all our lives? Making soup in a basket, and getting nothing but the scum for our stomachs. Better buy a blessing, Madonna! Only four quattrino; the profit is not so much as the smell of a danaro, and it goes to the poor."

Monna Brigida, in dim-eyed confusion, was proceeding to the further submission of reaching money from her embroidered scarsella, at present hidden by her silk mantle, when the group round her, which she had not yet entertained the idea of escaping, opened before a figure as welcome as an angel loosing prison bolts.*

"Romola, look at me!" said Monna Brigida, in a piteous tone, putting out both her hands.

The white troop was already moving away, with a slight consciousness that its zeal about the head-gear had been superabundant enough to afford a dispensation from any further demand for penitential offerings.

"Dear cousin, don't be distressed," said Romola, smitten with pity, yet hardly able to help smiling at the sudden apparition of her kinswoman in a genuine, natural guise, strangely contrasted with all memories of her. She took the black drapery from her own head, and threw it over Monna Brigida's. "There," she went on, soothingly, "no one will remark you now. We will turn down the Via del Palagio and go straight to our house."

They hastened away, Monna Brigida grasping Romola's hand tightly as if to get a stronger assurance of her being actually there.

"Ah, my Romola, my dear child," said the short fat woman, hurrying with frequent steps to keep pace with the majestic young figure beside her. "What an old scarecrow I am! I must be good—I mean to be good!"

"Yes, yes; buy a cross!" said the guttural voice, while the rough hand was thrust once more before Monna Brigida; for Bratti was not to be abashed by Romola's presence into renouncing a probable customer, and had quietly followed up their retreat. "Only four quattrini, blessing and all—and if there was any profit, it would all go to the poor."

Monna Brigida would have been compelled to pause, even if she had been in a less submissive mood. She put up one hand deprecatingly to arrest Romola's remonstrance, and with the other reached out a grosso, worth many white quattrini, saying, in an entreating tone—

"Take it, good man, and begone."

"You're in the right, Madonna," said Bratti, taking the coin quickly, and thrusting the cross into her hand, "I'll not offer you change, for I might as well rob you of a mass. What! we must all be scorched a little, but you'll come off the easier; better fall from the window than the roof.* A good Easter and a good year to you!"

"Well, Romola," cried Monna Brigida, pathetically, as Bratti left them, "if I'm to be a Piagnone, it's no matter how I look!"

"Dear cousin", said Romola, smiling at her affectionately, "you don't know how much better you look than you ever did before. I see now how good-natured your face is, like yourself. That red and finery seemed to thrust themselves forward and hide expression. Ask our Piero or any other painter if he would not rather paint your portrait now than before. I think all lines of the human face have something either touching or grand, unless they seem to come from low passions. How fine old men are, like my godfather! Why should not old women look grand and simple?"

"Yes, when one gets to be sixty, my Romola," said Brigida, relapsing a little; "but I'm only fifty-five, and Monna Berta and everybody—but it's no use: I will be good, like you. Your mother, if she'd been alive, would have been as old as I am—we were cousins together. One *must* either die or get old. But it doesn't matter about being old, if one's a Piagnone."

[*MAY 1863*]

CHAPTER LII.

A Prophetess

THE incidents of that Carnival day seemed to Romola to carry no other personal consequences to her than the new care of supporting poor cousin Brigida in her fluctuating resignation to age and grey hairs; but they introduced a Lenten time in which she was kept at a high pitch of mental excitement and active effort.

Bernardo del Nero had been elected Gonfaloniere. By great exertions the Medicean party had so far triumphed, and that triumph had deepened Romola's presentiment of some secretly prepared scheme likely to ripen either into success or betrayal during these two months of her godfather's authority. Every morning the dim daybreak as it peered into her room seemed to be that haunting fear coming back to her. Every morning the fear went with her as she passed through the streets on her way to the early sermon in the Duomo: but there she gradually lost the sense of its chill presence, as men lose the dread of death in the clash of battle.

In the Duomo she felt herself sharing in a passionate conflict which had wider relations than any enclosed within the walls of Florence. For Savonarola was preaching—preaching the last course of Lenten sermons he was ever allowed to finish in the Duomo: he knew that excommunication was imminent, and he had reached the point of defying it. He held up the condition of the Church in the terrible mirror of his unflinching speech, which called things by their right names and dealt in no polite periphrases; he proclaimed with heightening confidence the advent of renovation—of a moment when there would be a general revolt against corruption. As to his own destiny, he seemed to have a double and alternating prevision: sometimes he saw himself taking a glorious part in that revolt, sending forth a voice that would be heard through all Christendom, and making the dead body of the Church tremble into new life, as the body of Lazarus trembled when the divine voice pierced the sepulchre;* sometimes he saw no prospect for himself but persecution and martyrdom:—this life for him was only a vigil, and only after death would come the dawn.

The position was one which must have had its impressiveness for all minds that were not of the dullest order, even if they were inclined, as Macchiavelli was, to interpret the Frate's character by a key that presupposed no loftiness. To Romola, whose kindred ardour gave her a firm belief in Savonarola's genuine greatness of purpose, the crisis was as stirring as if it had been part of her personal lot. It blent itself as an exalting memory with all her daily labours; and those labours were calling not only for difficult perseverance, but for new courage. Famine had never yet taken its flight from Florence, and all distress, by its long continuance, was getting harder to bear; disease was spreading in the crowded city, and the Plague was expected. As Romola walked, often in weariness, among the sick, the hungry, and the murmuring, she felt it good to be inspired by something more than her pity—by the belief in a heroism struggling for sublime ends, towards which the daily action of her pity could only tend feebly, as the dews that freshen the weedy ground to-day tend to prepare an unseen harvest in the years to come.

But that mighty music which stirred her in the Duomo was not without its jarring notes. Since those first days of glowing hope when the Frate, seeing the near triumph of good in the reform of the Republic and the coming of the French deliverer, had preached peace, charity, and oblivion of political differences, there had been a marked change of conditions: political intrigue had been too obstinate to allow of the desired oblivion; the belief in the French deliverer, who had turned his back on his high mission, seemed to have wrought harm; and hostility, both on a petty and on a grand scale, was attacking the Prophet with new weapons and new determination. It followed that the spirit of contention and self-vindication pierced more and more conspicuously in his sermons; that he was urged to meet the popular demands not only by increased insistance and detail concerning visions and private revelations, but by a tone of defiant confidence against objectors; and from having denounced the desire for the miraculous, and declared that miracles had no relation to true faith, he had come to assert that at the right moment the divine power would attest the truth of his prophetic preaching by a miracle. And continually, in the rapid transitions of excited feeling, as the vision of triumphant good receded behind the actual predominance of evil, the threats of coming vengeance against vicious tyrants and corrupt priests gathered some impetus from personal exasperation, as well as from indignant zeal. In the career of a great public orator who yields himself to the inspiration of the moment, that conflict of selfish and unselfish emotion which in most men is hidden in the chamber of the soul, is brought into terrible evidence: the language of the inner voices is written out in letters of fire.

But if the tones of exasperation jarred on Romola, there was often another member of Fra Girolamo's audience to whom they were the only thrilling tones, like the vibration of deep bass notes to the deaf. Baldassarre had found out that the wonderful Frate was preaching again, and as often as he could, he went to hear the Lenten sermon, that he might drink in the threats of a voice which seemed like a power on the side of justice. He went the more because he had seen that Romola went too; for he was waiting and watching for a time when not only outward circumstance, but his own varying mental state, would mark the right moment for seeking an interview with her. Twice Romola had caught sight of his face in the Duomo—once when its dark glance was fixed on hers. She wished not to see it again, and yet she looked for it, as men look for the reappearance of a portent. But any revelation that might be yet to come about this old man was a subordinate fear now: it referred, she thought, only to the past, and her anxiety was almost absorbed by the present.

Yet the stirring Lent passed by; April, the second and final month of her godfather's supreme authority, was near its close; and nothing had occurred to fulfil her presentiment. In the public mind, too, there had been fears, and rumours had spread from Rome of a menacing activity on the part of Piero de' Medici; but in a few days the suspected Bernardo would go out of power.

Romola was trying to gather some courage from the review of her futile fears, when on the twenty-seventh, as she was walking out on her usual errands of mercy in the afternoon, she was met by a messenger from Camilla Rucellai, chief among the feminine seers of Florence, desiring her presence forthwith on matters of the highest moment. Romola, who shrank with unconquerable repulsion from the shrill volubility of those illuminated women, and had just now a special repugnance towards Camilla because of a report that she had announced revelations hostile to Bernardo del Nero, was at first inclined to send back a flat refusal. Camilla's message might refer to public affairs, and Romola's immediate prompting was to close her ears against knowledge that might only make her mental burthen heavier. But it had become so thoroughly her habit to reject her impulsive choice, and to obey passively the guidance of outward claims, that, reproving herself for allowing her presentiments to make her cowardly and selfish, she ended by compliance, and went straight to Camilla. She found the nervous grey-haired woman in a chamber arranged as much as possible like a convent cell. The thin fingers clutching Romola as she sat, and the eager voice addressing her at first in a loud whisper, caused her a physical shrinking that made it difficult for her to keep her seat.

Camilla had a vision to communicate—a vision in which it had been revealed to her by Romola's Angel, that Romola knew certain secrets concerning her godfather, Bernardo del Nero, which, if disclosed, might save the Republic from peril. Camilla's voice rose louder and higher as she narrated her vision, and ended by exhorting Romola to obey the command of her Angel, and separate herself from the enemy of God.

Romola's impetuosity was that of a massive nature, and, except in moments when she was deeply stirred, her manner was calm and self-controlled. She had a constitutional disgust for the shallow excitability of women like Camilla, whose faculties seemed all wrought up into fantasies, leaving nothing for emotion and thought. The exhortation was not yet ended when she started up and attempted to wrench her arm from Camilla's tightening grasp. It was of no use. The prophetess kept her hold like a crab, and, only incited to more eager exhortation by Romola's resistance, was carried beyond her own intention into a shrill statement of other visions which were to corroborate this. Christ himself had appeared to her and ordered her to send his commands to certain citizens in office that they should throw Bernardo del Nero from the window of the Palazzo Vecchio. Fra Girolamo himself knew of it, and had not dared this time to say that the vision was not of divine authority.

"And since then," said Camilla, in her excited treble, straining upward with wild eyes towards Romola's face, "the Blessed

Infant has come to me and laid a wafer of sweetness on my tongue in token of his pleasure that I had done his will."

"Let me go!" said Romola, in a deep voice of anger. "God grant you are mad! else you are detestably wicked!"

The violence of her effort to be free was too strong for Camilla now. She wrenched away her arm and rushed out of the room, not pausing till she had hurriedly gone far along the street, and found herself close to the church of the Badia. She had but to pass behind the curtain under the old stone arch, and she would find a sanctuary shut in from the noise and hurry of the street, where all objects and all uses suggested the thought of an eternal peace subsisting in the midst of turmoil. She turned in, and sinking down on the step of the altar in front of Filippino Lippi's serene Virgin appearing to St. Bernard,* she waited in hope that the inward tumult which agitated her would by and by subside.

The thought which pressed on her the most acutely, was that Camilla could allege Savonarola's countenance of her wicked folly. Romola did not for a moment believe that he had sanctioned the throwing of Bernardo del Nero from the window as a divine suggestion; she felt certain that there was falsehood or mistake in that allegation. Savonarola had become more and more severe in his views of resistance to malcontents; but the ideas of strict law and order were fundamental to all his political teaching. Still, since he knew the possibly fatal effects of visions like Camilla's, since he had a marked distrust of such spirit-seeing women, and kept aloof from them as much as possible, why, with his readiness to denounce wrong from the pulpit, did he not publicly denounce these pretended revelations which brought new darkness instead of light across the conception of a Supreme Will? Why? The answer came with painful clearness: he was fettered inwardly by the consciousness that such revelations were not, in their basis, distinctly separable from his own visions; he was fettered outwardly by the foreseen consequence of raising a cry against himself even among members of his own party, as one who would suppress all divine inspiration of which he himself was not the vehicle—he or his confidential and supplementary seer of visions, Fra Salvestro.

Romola, kneeling with buried face on the altar step, was enduring one of those sickening moments, when the enthusiasm which had come to her as the only energy strong enough to make life worthy, seemed to be inevitably bound up with vain dreams and wilful eye-shutting. Her mind rushed back with a new attraction towards the strong worldly sense, the dignified prudence, the untheoretic virtues of her godfather, who was to be treated as a sort of Agag* because he held that a more restricted form of government was better than the Great Council, and because he would not pretend to forget old ties to the banished family. But with this last thought rose the presentiment of some plot to restore the Medici; and then again she felt that the popular party was half justified in its fierce suspicion. Again she felt that to keep the Government of Florence pure, and to keep out a vicious rule, was a sacred cause; the Frate was right there, and had carried her understanding irrevocably with him. But at this moment the assent of her understanding went alone; it was given unwillingly. Her heart was recoiling from a right allied to so much narrowness; a right apparently entailing that hard systematic judgment of men which measures them by assents and denials quite superficial to the manhood within them. Her affection and respect were clinging with new tenacity to her godfather, and with him to those memories of her father which were in the same opposition to the division of men into sheep and goats by the easy mark of some political or religious symbol.

After all has been said that can be said about the widening influence of ideas, it remains true that they would hardly be such strong agents unless they were taken in a solvent of feeling. The great world-struggle of developing thought is continually foreshadowed in the struggle of the affections, seeking a justification for love and hope. If Romola's intellect had been less capable of discerning the complexities in human things, all the early loving associations of her life would have forbidden her to accept implicitly the denunciatory exclusiveness of Savonarola. She had simply felt that his mind had suggested deeper and more efficacious truth to her than any other, and the large breathing-room which she found in his grand view of human duties had made her patient towards that part of his teaching which she could not absorb, so long as its practical effect came into collision with no strong force in her. But now a sudden insurrection of feeling had brought about that collision. Her indignation, once roused by Camilla's visions, could not pause there, but ran like an illuminating fire over all the kindred facts in Savonarola's teaching, and for the moment she felt what was true in the scornful sarcasms she heard continually flung against him, more keenly than she felt what was false.

But it was an illumination that made all life look ghastly to her. Where were the beings to whom she could cling, with whom she could work and endure, with the belief that she was working for the right? On the side from which moral energy came lay a fanaticism from which she was shrinking with newly startled repulsion; on the side to which she was drawn by affection and memory, there was the presentiment of some secret plotting, which her judgment told her would not be unfairly called crime. And still surmounting every other thought was the dread inspired by Tito's hints, lest that presentiment should be converted into knowledge, in such a way that she would be torn by irreconcilable claims.

Calmness would not come even on the altar step; it would not come from looking at the serene picture where the saint, writing in the rocky solitude, was being visited by faces with celestial peace in them. Romola was in the hard press of human difficulties, and that rocky solitude was too far off. She rose from her knees that she might hasten to her sick people in the courtyard, and, by some immediate beneficent action, revive that sense of worth in life which at this moment was unfed by any wider faith. But when she turned round, she found herself face to face with a man who was standing only two yards off her. The man was Baldassarre.

CHAPTER LIII.

On San Miniato

"I WOULD speak with you," said Baldassarre, as Romola looked at him in silent expectation. It was plain that he had followed her, and had been waiting for her. She was going at last to know the secret about him.

"Yes," she said, with the same sort of submission that she might have shown under an imposed penance. "But you wish to go where no one can hear us."

"Where *he* will not come upon us," said Baldassarre, turning and glancing behind him timidly. "Out—in the air—away from the streets."

"I sometimes go to San Miniato at this hour," said Romola. "If you like, I will go now, and you can follow me. It is far, but we can be solitary there."

He nodded assent, and Romola set out. To some women it might have seemed an alarming risk to go to a comparatively solitary spot with a man who had some of the outward signs of that madness which Tito attributed to him. But Romola was not given to personal fears, and she was glad of the distance that interposed some delay before another blow fell on her. The afternoon was far advanced, and the sun was already low in the west, when she paused on some rough ground in the shadow of the cypress trunks, and looked round for Baldassarre. He was not far off, but when he reached her, he was glad to sink down on an edge of stony earth. His thick-set frame had no longer the sturdy vigour which belonged to it when he first appeared with the rope round him in the Duomo; and under the transient tremor caused by the exertion of walking up the hill, his eyes seemed to have a more helpless vagueness.

"The hill is steep," said Romola, with compassionate gentleness, seating herself by him. "And I fear you have been weakened by want."

He turned his head and fixed his eyes on her in silence, unable, now the moment for speech was come, to seize the words that would convey the thought he wanted to utter: and she remained as motionless as she could, lest he should suppose her impatient. He looked like nothing higher than a common-bred, neglected old man; but she was used now to be very near to such people, and to think a great deal about their troubles. Gradually his glance gathered a more definite expression, and at last he said with abrupt emphasis—

"Ah! you would have been my daughter!"

The swift flush came in Romola's face and went back again as swiftly, leaving her with white lips a little apart, like a marble image of horror. For her mind, this revelation was made. She divined the facts that lay behind that single word, and in the first moment there could be no check to the impulsive belief which sprang from her keen experience of Tito's nature. The sensitive response of her face was a stimulus to Baldassarre; for the first time his words had wrought their right effect. He went on with gathering eagerness and firmness, laying his hand on her arm.

"You are a woman of proud blood—is it not true? You go to hear the preacher; you hate baseness—baseness that smiles and triumphs. You hate your husband?"

"Oh, God! were you really his father?" said Romola, in a low voice, too entirely possessed by the images of the past to take any note of Baldassarre's question. "Or was it as he said? Did you take him when he was little?"

"Ah, you believe me—you know what he is!" said Baldassarre, exultingly, tightening the pressure on her arm, as if the contact gave him power. "You will help me."

"Yes," said Romola, not interpreting the words as he meant them. She laid her palm gently on the rough hand that grasped her arm, and the tears came to her eyes as she looked at him. "Oh! it is piteous! Tell me—why, you were a great scholar; you taught him. *How* is it?"

She broke off. Tito's allegation of this man's madness had come across her; and where were the signs even of past refinement? But she had the self-command not to move her hand. She sat perfectly still, waiting to listen with new caution.

"It is gone!—it is all gone!" said Baldassarre; "and they would not believe me, because he lied, and said I was mad; and they had me dragged to prison. And I am old—my mind will not come back. And the world is against me."

He paused a moment, and his eyes sank as if he were under a wave of despondency. Then he looked up at her again, and said with renewed eagerness—

"But *you* are not against me. He made you love him, and he has been false to you; and you hate him. Yes, he made *me* love him: he was beautiful and gentle, and I was a lonely man. I took him when they were beating him. He slept in my bosom when he was little, and I watched him as he grew, and gave him all my knowledge, and everything that was mine I meant to be his. I had many things: money, and books, and gems. He had my gems—he sold them; and he left me in slavery. He never came to seek me, and when I came back poor and in misery, he denied me. He said I was a madman."

"He told us his father was dead—was drowned," said Romola, faintly. "Surely he must have believed it then. Oh! he could not have been so base *then!*"

A vision had risen of what Tito was to her in those first days when she thought no more of wrong in him than a child thinks of poison in flowers. The yearning regret that lay in that memory brought some relief from the tension of horror. With one great sob the tears rushed forth.

"Ah, you are young, and the tears come easily," said Baldassarre, with some impatience. "But tears are no good; they only put out the fire within, and it is the fire that works. Tears will hinder us. Listen to me."

Romola turned towards him with a slight start. Again the possibility of his madness had darted through her mind, and checked the rush of belief. If, after all, this man were only a mad assassin? But her deep belief in his story still lay behind, and it was more in sympathy than in fear that she avoided the risk of paining him by any show of doubt.

"Tell me," she said, as gently as she could, "how did you lose your memory—your scholarship?"

"I was ill. I can't tell how long—it was a blank. I remember nothing, only at last I was sitting in the sun among the stones, and everything else was darkness. And slowly, and by degrees, I felt something besides that: a longing for something—I did not know what—that never came. And when I was in the ship on the waters I began to know what I longed for; it was for the Boy to come back—it was to find all my thoughts again, for I was locked away outside them all. And I am outside now. I feel nothing but a wall and darkness."

Baldassarre had become dreamy again, and sank into silence, resting his head between his hands; and again Romola's belief in him had submerged all cautioning doubts. The pity with which she dwelt on his words seemed like the revival of an old pang. Had she not daily seen how her father missed Dino and all the future he had dreamed of in that son?

"It all came back once," Baldassarre went on presently. "I was master of everything. I saw all the world again, and my gems, and my books; and I thought I had him in my power, and I went to expose him where—where the lights were and the trees; and he lied again, and said I was mad, and they dragged me away to prison. . . . Wickedness is strong, and he wears armour."

The fierceness had flamed up again. He spoke with his former intensity, and again he grasped Romola's arm.

"But you will help me. He has been false to you too. He has another wife, and she has children. He makes her believe he is her husband, and she is a foolish, helpless thing. I will show you where she lives."

The first shock that passed through Romola was visibly one of anger. The woman's sense of indignity was inevitably foremost. Baldassarre instinctively felt her in sympathy with him.

"You hate him," he went on. "Is it not true? There is no love between you; I know that. I know women can hate; and you have proud blood. You hate falseness, and you can love revenge."

Romola sat paralysed by the shock of conflicting feelings. She was not conscious of the grasp that was bruising her tender arm.

"You shall contrive it,' said Baldassarre, presently, in an eager whisper. "I have learned by heart that you are his rightful wife. You are a noble woman. You go to hear the preacher of vengeance; you will help justice. But you will think for me. My mind goes—everything goes sometimes—all but the fire. The fire is God: it is justice: it will not die. You believe that—is it not true? If they will not hang him for robbing me, you will take away his armour—you will make him go without it, and I will stab him. I have a knife, and my arm is still strong enough."

He put his hand under his tunic, and reached out the hidden knife, feeling the edge abstractedly, as if he needed the sensation to keep alive his ideas.

It seemed to Romola as if every fresh hour of her life were to become more difficult than the last. Her judgment was too vigorous and rapid for her to fall into the mistake of using futile deprecatory words to a man in Baldassarre's state of mind. She chose not to answer his last speech. She would win time for his excitement to allay itself by asking something else that she cared to know. She spoke rather tremulously—

"You say she is foolish and helpless—that other wife—and believes him to be her real husband. Perhaps he is: perhaps he married her before he married me."

"I cannot tell," said Baldassarre, pausing in that action of feeling the knife, and looking bewildered. "I can remember no more. I only know where she lives. You shall see her. I will take you; but not now," he added, hurriedly, "*he* may be there. The night is coming on."

"It is true," said Romola, starting up with a sudden consciousness that the sun had set, and the hills were darkening; "but you will come and take me—when?"

"In the morning," said Baldassarre, dreaming that she, too, wanted to hurry to her vengeance.

"Come to me, then, where you came to me to-day, in the church. I will be there at ten; and if you are not there, I will go again towards midday. Can you remember?"

"Midday," said Baldassarre—"only midday. The same place, and midday. And, after that," he added, rising, and grasping her arm again with his left hand, while he held the knife in his right; "we will have our revenge. He shall feel the sharp edge of justice. The world is against me, but you will help me."

"I would help you in other ways," said Romola, making a first, timid effort to dispel his illusion about her. "I fear you are in want; you have to labour, and get little. I should like to bring you comforts, and make you feel again that there is some one who cares for you."

"Talk no more about that," said Baldassarre, fiercely. "I will have nothing else. Help me to wring one drop of vengeance on this side of the grave. I have nothing but my knife. It is sharp; but there is a moment after the thrust when men see the face of death,—and it shall be *my* face that he will see."

He loosed his hold, and sank down again in a sitting posture. Romola felt helpless: she must defer all intentions till the morrow.

"Midday, then," she said, in a distinct voice.

"Yes," he answered, with an air of exhaustion. "Go; I will rest here."

She hastened away. Turning at the last spot whence he was likely to be in sight, she saw him seated still.

CHAPTER LIV.

The Evening and the Morning

ROMOLA had a purpose in her mind as she was hastening away; a purpose which had been growing through the afternoon hours like a side-stream, rising higher and higher along with the main current. It was less a resolve than a necessity of her feeling. Heedless of the darkening streets, and not caring to call for Maso's slow escort, she hurried across the bridge where the river showed itself black before the distant dying red, and took the most direct way to the Old Palace. She might encounter her husband there. No matter. She could not weigh probabilities; she must discharge her heart. She did not know what she passed in the pillared court or up the wide stairs; she only knew that she asked an usher for the Gonfaloniere, giving her name, and begging to be shown into a private room.

She was not left long alone with the frescoed figures and the newly-lit tapers. Soon the door opened, and Bernardo del Nero entered, still carrying his white head erect above his silk *lucco*.

"Romola, my child, what is this?" he said, in a tone of anxious surprise as he closed the door.

She had uncovered her head and went towards him without speaking. He laid his hand on her shoulder, and held her a little way from him that he might see her better. Her face was haggard from fatigue and long agitation, her hair had rolled down in disorder; but there was an excitement in her eyes that seemed to have triumphed over the bodily consciousness.

"What has he done?" said Bernardo, abruptly. "Tell me everything, child; throw away pride. I am your father."

"It is not about myself—nothing about myself," said Romola, hastily. "Dearest godfather, it is about you. I have heard things—some I cannot tell you. But you are in danger in the palace; you are in danger everywhere. There are fanatical men who would harm you, and—and there are traitors. Trust nobody. If you trust, you will be betrayed."

Bernardo smiled.

"Have you worked yourself up into this agitation, my poor child," he said, raising his hand to her head, and patting it gently, "to tell such old truths as that to an old man like me?"

"Oh, no, no! they are not old truths I mean," said Romola, pressing her clasped hands painfully together, as if that action would help her to suppress what must not be told. "They are fresh things that I know, but cannot tell. Dearest godfather, you know I am not foolish. I would not come to you without reason. Is it too late to warn you against any one, *every* one who seems to be working on your side? Is it too late to say, Go to your villa and keep away in the country when these three more days of office are over? Oh, God! perhaps it is too late! and if any harm comes to you, it will be as if I had done it!"

The last words had burst from Romola involuntarily: a long-stifled feeling had found spasmodic utterance. But she herself was startled and arrested.

"I mean," she added, hesitatingly, "I know nothing positive. I only know what fills me with fears."

"Poor child!" said Bernardo, looking at her with quiet penetration for a moment or two. Then he said—"Go, Romola, go home and rest. These fears may be only big ugly shadows of something very little and harmless. Even traitors must see their interest in betraying; the rats will run where they smell the cheese, and there is no knowing yet which way the scent will come."

He paused, and turned away his eyes from her with an air of abstraction, till, with a slow shrug, he added—

"As for warnings, they are of no use to me, child. I enter into no plots, but I never forsake my colours. If I march abreast with obstinate men, who will rush on guns and pikes, I must share the consequences. Let us say no more about that. I have not many years left at the bottom of my sack for them to rob me of. Go, child; go home and rest."

He put his hand on her head again caressingly, and she could not help clinging to his arm, and pressing her brow against his shoulder. Her godfather's caress seemed the last thing that was left to her out of that young filial life, which now looked so happy to her even in its troubles, for they were troubles untainted by anything hateful.

"Is silence best, my Romola?" said the old man.

"Yes, now; but I cannot tell whether it always will be," she answered, hesitatingly, raising her head with an appealing look.

"Well, you have a father's ear while I am above ground"—he lifted the black drapery and folded it round her head, adding—"and a father's home; remember that." Then opening the door, he said: "There, hasten away. You are like a black ghost; you will be safe enough."

When Romola fell asleep that night, she slept deep. Agitation had reached its limits; she must gather strength before she could suffer more; and, in spite of rigid habit, she slept on far beyond sunrise.

When she awoke, it was to the sound of guns. Piero de'

Medici, with thirteen hundred men* at his back, was before the gate that looks towards Rome.

So much Romola learned from Maso, with many circumstantial additions of dubious quality. A countryman had come in and alarmed the Signoria before it was light, else the city would have been taken by surprise. His master was not in the house, having been summoned to the Palazzo long ago. She sent out the old man again, that he might gather news, while she went up to the loggia from time to time to try and discern any signs of the dreaded entrance having been made, or of its having been effectively repelled. Maso brought her word that the great Piazza was full of armed men, and that many of the chief citizens suspected as friends of the Medici had been summoned to the Palace and detained there. Some of the people seemed not to mind whether Piero got in or not, and some said the Signoria itself had invited him; but however that might be, they were giving him an ugly welcome; and the soldiers from Pisa were coming against him.

In her memory of those morning hours, there were not many things that Romola could distinguish as actual external experiences standing markedly out above the tumultuous waves of retrospect and anticipation. She knew that she had really walked to the Badia by the appointed time in spite of street alarms; she knew that she had waited there in vain. And the scene she had witnessed when she came out of the church, and stood watching on the steps while the doors were being closed behind her for the afternoon interval, always came back to her like a remembered waking.

There was a change in the faces and tones of the people, armed and unarmed, who were pausing or hurrying along the streets. The guns were firing again, but the sound only provoked laughter. She soon knew the cause of the change. Piero de' Medici and his horsemen had turned their backs on Florence, and were galloping as fast as they could along the Siena road. She learned this from a substantial shopkeeping Piagnone, who had not yet laid down his pike.

"It is true," he ended, with a certain bitterness in his emphasis. "Piero is gone, but there are those left behind who were in the secret of his coming—we all know that; and if the new Signoria does its duty we shall soon know *who* they are."

The words darted through Romola like a sharp spasm; but

the evil they foreshadowed was not yet close upon her, and as she entered her home again, her most pressing anxiety was the possibility that she had lost sight for a long while of Baldassarre.

CHAPTER LV.

Waiting

THE lengthening sunny days went on without bringing either what Romola most desired or what she most dreaded. They brought no sign from Baldassarre, and, in spite of special watch on the part of the Government, no revelation of the suspected conspiracy. But they brought other things which touched her closely, and bridged the phantom-crowded space of anxiety with active sympathy in immediate trial. They brought the spreading Plague and the Excommunication of Savonarola.

Both those events tended to arrest her incipient alienation from the Frate, and to rivet again her attachment to the man who had opened to her the new life of duty, and who seemed now to be worsted in the fight for principle against profligacy. For Romola could not carry from day to day into the abodes of pestilence and misery the sublime excitement of a gladness that, since such anguish existed, she too existed to make some of the anguish less bitter, without remembering that she owed this transcendent moral life to Fra Girolamo. She could not witness the silencing and excommunication of a man whose distinction from the great mass of the clergy lay, not in any heretical belief, not in his superstitions, but in the energy with which he sought to make the Christian life a reality, without feeling herself drawn strongly to his side.

Far on in the hot days of June the Excommunication, for some weeks arrived from Rome, was solemnly published in the Duomo. Romola went to witness the scene, that the resistance it inspired might invigorate that sympathy with Savonarola which was one source of her strength. It was in memorable contrast with the scene she had been accustomed to witness there. Instead of upturned citizen-faces filling the vast area under the morning light, the youngest rising amphitheatre-wise towards the walls and making a garland of hope around the memories of age—

instead of the mighty voice thrilling all hearts with the sense of great things, visible and invisible, to be struggled for—there were the bare walls at evening made more sombre by the glimmer of tapers, there was the black and grey flock of monks and secular clergy with bent unexpectant faces, there was the occasional tinkling of little bells in the pauses of a monotonous voice reading a sentence which had already been long hanging up in the churches, and at last there was the extinction of the tapers, and the slow shuffling tread of monkish feet departing in the dim silence.

Romola's ardour on the side of the Frate was doubly strengthened, by the gleeful triumph she saw in hard and coarse faces, and by the fear-stricken confusion in the faces and speech of many among his strongly attached friends. The question where the duty of obedience ends, and the duty of resistance begins, could in no case be an easy one; but it was made overwhelmingly difficult by the belief that the Church was—not a compromise of parties to secure a more or less approximate justice in the appropriation of funds, but—a living organism instinct with divine power to bless and to curse. To most of the pious Florentines, who had hitherto felt no doubt in their adherence to the Frate, that belief in the Divine potency of the Church was not an embraced opinion, it was an inalienable impression, like the concavity of the blue firmament; and the boldness of Savonarola's written arguments that the Excommunication was unjust, and that, being unjust, it was not valid, only made them tremble the more, as a defiance cast at a mystic image, against whose subtle immeasurable power there was neither weapon nor defence.

But Romola, whose mind had not been allowed to draw its early nourishment from the traditional associations of the Christian community, in which her father had lived a life apart, felt her relation to the Church only through Savonarola; his moral force had been the only authority to which she had bowed; and in his excommunication she only saw the menace of hostile vice: on one side she saw a man whose life was devoted to the ends of public virtue and spiritual purity, and on the other the assault of alarmed selfishness, headed by a lustful, greedy, lying, and murderous old man, once called Rodrigo Borgia, and now lifted to the pinnacle of infamy as Pope Alexander the Sixth. The finer shades of fact which soften the edge of such antitheses are not apt to be seen except by neutrals, who are not distressed to discern some folly in martyrs and some judiciousness in the men who burn them. But Romola required a strength that neutrality could not give; and this Excommunication, which simplified and ennobled the resistant position of Savonarola by bringing into prominence its wider relations, seemed to come to her like a rescue from the threatening isolation of criticism and doubt. The Frate was now withdrawn from that smaller antagonism against Florentine enemies into which he continually fell in the unchecked excitement of the pulpit, and presented himself simply as appealing to the Christian world against a vicious exercise of ecclesiastical power. He was a standard-bearer leaping into the breach. Life never seems so clear and easy as when the heart is beating faster at the sight of some generous self-risking deed. We feel no doubt then what is the highest prize the soul can win; we almost believe in our own power to attain it. By a new current of such enthusiasm Romola was helped through these difficult summer days.

She had ventured on no words to Tito that would apprise him of her late interview with Baldassarre, and the revelation he had made to her. What would such agitating, difficult words win from him? No admission of the truth; nothing, probably, but a cool sarcasm about her sympathy with his assassin. Baldassarre was evidently helpless: the thing to be feared was, not that he should injure Tito, but that Tito, coming upon his traces, should carry out some new scheme for ridding himself of the injured man who was a haunting dread to him. Romola felt that she could do nothing decisive until she had seen Baldassarre again, and learned the full truth about that "other wife"—learned whether she were the wife to whom Tito was first bound.

The possibilities about that other wife, which involved the worst wound to her hereditary pride, mingled themselves as a newly embittering suspicion with the earliest memories of her illusory love, eating away the lingering associations of tenderness with the past image of her husband; and her irresistible belief in the rest of Baldassarre's revelation made her shrink from Tito with a horror which would perhaps have urged some passionate speech in spite of herself if he had not been more than usually absent from home. Like many of the wealthier citizens in that time of pestilence, he spent the intervals of business chiefly in the country: the agreeable Melema was welcome at many villas, and since Romola had refused to leave the city, he had no need to provide a country residence of his own.

But at last, in the later days of July, the alleviation of those public troubles which had absorbed her activity and much of her thought, left Romola to a less counteracted sense of her personal lot. The plague had almost disappeared, and the position of Savonarola was made more hopeful by a favourable magistracy, who were writing urgent vindicatory letters to Rome on his behalf, entreating the withdrawal of the Excommunication.

Romola's healthy and vigorous frame was undergoing the reaction of languor inevitable after continuous excitement and over-exertion; but her mental restlessness would not allow her to remain at home without peremptory occupation, except during the sultry hours. In the cool of the morning and evening she walked out constantly, varying her direction as much as possible, with the vague hope that if Baldassarre were still alive she might encounter him. Perhaps some illness had brought a new paralysis of memory, and he had forgotten where she lived—forgotten even her existence. That was her most sanguine explanation of his non-appearance. The explanation she felt to be most probable was, that he had died of the Plague.

CHAPTER LVI.

The Other Wife

THE morning warmth was already beginning to be rather oppressive to Romola, when, after a walk along by the walls on her way from San Marco, she turned towards the intersecting streets again at the Gate of Santa Croce.

The Borgo La Croce was so still, that she listened to her own footsteps on the pavement in the sunny silence, until, on approaching a bend in the street, she saw, a few yards before her, a little child not more than three years old, with no other clothing than his white shirt, pause from a waddling run and look around him. In the first moment of coming nearer she could only see his back—a boy's back, square and sturdy, with a cloud of reddish-brown curls above it; but in the next he turned towards her, and she could see his dark eyes wide with tears, and his lower lip pushed up and trembling, while his fat brown fists clutched his shirt helplessly. The glimpse of a tall black figure sending a shadow over him brought his bewildered fear to a climax, and a loud crying sob sent the big tears rolling.

Romola, with the ready maternal instinct which was one hidden source of her passionate tenderness, instantly uncovered her head, and, stooping down on the pavement, put her arms round him, and her cheek against his, while she spoke to him in caressing tones. At first his sobs were only the louder, but he made no effort to get away, and presently the outburst ceased with that strange abruptness which belongs to childish joys and griefs: his face lost its distortion, and was fixed in an open-mouthed gaze at Romola.

"You have lost yourself, little one," she said, kissing him. "Never mind! we will find the house again. Perhaps Mamma will meet us."

She divined that he had made his escape at a moment when the mother's eyes were turned away from him, and thought it likely that he would soon be followed.

"Oh, what a heavy, heavy boy!" she said, trying to lift him. "I cannot carry you. Come, then, you must toddle back by my side."

The parted lips remained motionless in awed silence, and one brown fist still clutched the shirt with as much tenacity as ever; but the other yielded itself quite willingly to the wonderful white hand, strong but soft.

"You *have* a Mamma?" said Romola, as they set out, looking down at the boy with a certain yearning. But he was mute. A girl under those circumstances might perhaps have chirped abundantly; not so this square-shouldered little man with the big cloud of curls.

He was awake to the first sign of his whereabout, however. At the turning by the front of San Ambrogio he dragged Romola towards it, looking up at her.

"Ah, that is the way home, is it?" she said, smiling at him. He only thrust his head forward and pulled, as an admonition that they should go faster.

There was still another turning that he had a decided opinion about, and then Romola found herself in a short street leading to open garden ground. It was in front of a house at the end of this street that the little fellow paused, pulling her towards some stone stairs. He had evidently no wish for her to loose his hand, and she would not have been willing to leave him without being sure that she was delivering him to his friends. They mounted the stairs, seeing but dimly in that sudden withdrawal from the sunlight, till, at the final landing place, an extra stream of light came from an open doorway. Passing through a small lobby they came to another open door, and there Romola paused. Her approach had not been heard.

On a low chair at the farther end of the room, opposite the light, sat Tessa, with one hand on the edge of the cradle, and her head hanging a little on one side, fast asleep. Near one of the windows, with her back turned towards the door, sat Monna Lisa at her work of preparing salad, in deaf unconsciousness. There was only an instant for Romola's eyes to take in that still scene; for Lillo snatched his hand away from her and ran up to his mother's side, not making any direct effort to wake her, but only leaning his head back against her arm, and surveying Romola seriously from that distance.

As Lillo pushed against her Tessa opened her eyes, and looked up in bewilderment; but her glance had no sooner rested on the figure at the opposite doorway than she started up, blushed deeply, and began to tremble a little, neither speaking nor moving forward.

"Ah! we have seen each other before," said Romola, smiling, and coming forward. "I am glad it was *your* little boy. He was crying in the street; I suppose he had run away. So we walked together a little way, and then he knew where he was, and brought me here. But you had not missed him? That is well, else you would have been frightened."

The shock of finding that Lillo had run away overcame every other feeling in Tessa for the moment. Her colour went again, and, seizing Lillo's arm, she ran with him to Monna Lisa, saying, with a half sob, loud in the old woman's ear—

"Oh, Lisa, you are wicked! Why will you stand with your back to the door? Lillo ran away ever so far into the street."

"Holy Mother!" said Monna Lisa, in her meek, thick tone, letting the spoon fall from her hands. "Where were *you*, then? I thought you were there, and had your eye on him."

"But you *know* I go to sleep when I am rocking," said Tessa, in pettish remonstrance.

"Well, well, we must keep the outer door shut, or else tie him up," said Monna Lisa, "for he'll be as cunning as Satan before long, and that's the holy truth. But how came he back, then?"

This question recalled Tessa to the consciousness of Romola's presence. Without answering, she turned towards her, blushing and timid again, and Monna Lisa's eyes followed her movement. The old woman made a low reverence, and said—

"Doubtless the most noble lady brought him back." Then, advancing a little nearer to Romola, she added, "It's my shame for him to have been found with only his shirt on; but he kicked, and wouldn't have his other clothes on this morning, and the mother, poor thing, will never hear of his being beaten. But what's an old woman to do without a stick when the lad's legs get so strong? Let your nobleness look at his legs."

Lillo, conscious that his legs were in question, pulled his shirt up a little higher, and looked down at their olive roundness with a dispassionate and curious air. Romola laughed, and stooped to give him a caressing shake and a kiss, and this action helped the reassurance that Tessa had already gathered from Monna Lisa's address to Romola. For when Naldo had been told about the adventure at the Carnival, and Tessa had asked him who the heavenly lady that had come just when she was wanted, and had vanished so soon, was likely to be—whether she could be the Holy Madonna herself?—he had answered, "Not exactly, my Tessa; only one of the saints," and had not chosen to say more. So that in the dream-like combination of small experience which made up Tessa's thought, Romola had remained confusedly associated with the pictures in the churches, and when she reappeared, the grateful remembrance of her protection was slightly tinctured with religious awe—not deeply, for Tessa's dread was chiefly of ugly and evil things. It seemed unlikely that good beings would be angry and punish her, as it was the nature of Nofri and the devil to do. And now that Monna Lisa had spoken freely about Lillo's legs and Romola had laughed, Tessa was more at her ease.

"Ninna's in the cradle," she said. "*She's* pretty too."

Romola went to look at the sleeping Ninna, and Monna Lisa, one of the exceptionally meek deaf, who never expect to be spoken to, returned to her salad.

"Ah! she is waking: she has opened her blue eyes," said

Romola. "You must take her up, and I will sit down in this chair—may I?—and nurse Lillo. Come, Lillo!"

She had sat down in Tito's chair, and put out her arms towards the lad, whose eyes had followed her. He hesitated, and, pointing his small fingers at her with a half-puzzled, half-angry feeling, said, "That's Babbo's chair," not seeing his way out of the difficulty if Babbo came and found Romola in his place.

"But Babbo is not here, and I shall go soon. Come, let me nurse you as he does," said Romola, wondering to herself for the first time what sort of Babbo he was whose wife was dressed in contadina fashion, but had a certain daintiness about her person that indicated idleness and plenty. Lillo consented to be lifted up, and, finding the lap exceedingly comfortable, began to explore her dress and hands, to see if there were any ornaments besides her rosary.

Tessa, who had hitherto been occupied in coaxing Ninna out of her waking peevishness, now sat down in her low chair, near Romola's knee, arranging Ninna's tiny person to advantage, jealous that the strange lady too seemed to notice the boy most, as Naldo did.

"Lillo was going to be angry with me because I sat in Babbo's chair," said Romola, as she bent forward to kiss Ninna's little foot. "Will he come soon and want it?"

"Ah, no!" said Tessa; "you can sit in it a long while. I shall be sorry when you go. When you first came to take care of me at the Carnival, I thought it was wonderful; you came and went away again so fast. And Naldo said, perhaps you were a saint, and that made me tremble a little, though the saints are very good, I know; and you were good to me, and now you have taken care of Lillo. Perhaps you will always come and take care of me. That was how Naldo did a long while ago; he came and took care of me when I was frightened, one San Giovanni. I couldn't think where he came from—he was so beautiful and good. And so are you," ended Tessa, looking up at Romola with devout admiration.

"Naldo is your husband. His eyes are like Lillo's," said Romola, looking at the boy's darkly-pencilled eyebrows, unusual at his age. She did not speak interrogatively, but with a quiet certainty of inference which was necessarily mysterious to Tessa.

"Ah! you know him!" she said, pausing a little in wonder. "Perhaps you know Nofri and Peretola, and our house on the hill, and everything. Yes, like Lillo's; but not his hair. His hair is dark and long—" she went on, getting rather excited. "Ah! if you know it, ecco!"

She had put her hand to a thin red silk cord that hung round her neck, and drew from her bosom the tiny old parchment *Breve*, the horn of red coral, and a long dark curl carefully tied at one end and suspended with those mystic treasures. She held them towards Romola, away from Ninna's snatching hand.

"It is a fresh one. I cut it lately. See how bright it is!" she said, laying it against the white background of Romola's fingers. "They get dim, and then he lets me cut another when his hair is grown; and I put it with the *Breve*, because sometimes he is away a long while, and then I think it helps to take care of me."

A slight shiver passed through Romola as the curl was laid across her fingers. At Tessa's first mention of her husband as having come mysteriously she knew not whence, a possibility had risen before Romola that made her heart beat faster; for to one who is anxiously in search of a certain object, the faintest suggestions have a peculiar significance. And when the curl was held towards her, it seemed for an instant like a mocking phantasm of the lock she herself had cut to wind with one of her own five years ago. But she preserved her outward calmness, bent not only on knowing the truth, but also on coming to that knowledge in a way that would not pain this poor, trusting, ignorant thing, with the child's mind in the woman's body. "Foolish and helpless:" yes; so far she corresponded to Baldassarre's account.

"It is a beautiful curl," she said, resisting the impulse to withdraw her hand. "Lillo's curls will be like it, perhaps, for *his* cheek, too, is dark. And you never know where your husband goes to when he leaves you?"

"No," said Tessa, putting back her treasures out of the children's way. "But I know Messer San Michele takes care of him, for he gave him a beautiful coat, all made of little chains; and if he puts that on, nobody can kill him. And, perhaps, if—" Tessa hesitated a little, under a recurrence of that original dreamy wonder about Romola which had been expelled by chatting contact—"if you *were* a saint, you would take care of him, too, because you have taken care of me and Lillo."

An agitated flush came over Romola's face in the first

moment of certainty, but she had bent her cheek against Lillo's head. The feeling that leaped out in that flush was something like exultation at the thought that the wife's burthen might be about to slip from her overladen shoulders; that this little ignorant creature might prove to be Tito's lawful wife. A strange exultation for a proud and high-born woman to have been brought to! But it seemed to Romola as if that were the only issue that would make duty anything else for her than an unsolvable problem. Yet she was not deaf to Tessa's last appealing words; she raised her head, and said, in her clearest tones,—

"I will always take care of you, if I see you need me. But that beautiful coat? your husband did not wear it when you were first married? Perhaps he used not to be so long away from you then?"

"Ah, yes! he was. Much—much longer. So long, I thought he would never come back. I used to cry. Oh, me! I was beaten then; a long, long while ago at Peretola, where we had the goats and mules."

"And how long had you been married before your husband had that chain-coat?" said Romola, her heat beating faster and faster.

Tessa looked meditative, and began to count on her fingers, and Romola watched the fingers as if they would tell the secret of her destiny.

"The chestnuts were ripe when we were married," said Tessa, marking off her thumb and fingers again as she spoke; "and then again they were ripe at Peretola before he came back, and then again, after that, on the hill. And soon the soldiers came and we heard the trumpets, and then Naldo had the coat."

"You had been married more than two years. In which church were you married?" said Romola, too entirely absorbed by one thought to put any question that was less direct. Perhaps before the next morning she might go to her godfather and say that she was not Tito Melema's lawful wife—that the vows which had bound her to strive after an impossible union had been made void beforehand.

Tessa gave a slight start at Romola's new tone of inquiry, and looked up at her with a hesitating expression. Hitherto she had prattled on without consciousness that she was making revelations, any more than when she said old things over and over again to Monna Lisa.

"Naldo said I was never to tell about that," she said, doubtfully. "Do you think he would not be angry if I told you?"

"It is right that you should tell me. Tell me everything," said Romola, looking at her with mild authority.

If the impression from Naldo's command had been much more recent than it was, the constraining effect of Romola's mysterious authority would have overcome it. But the sense that she was telling what she had never told before made her begin with a lowered voice.

"It was not in a church—it was at the Natività, when there was the fair, and all the people went overnight to see the Madonna in the Nunziata, and my mother was ill and couldn't go, and I took the bunch of cocoons for her; and then he came to me in the church and I heard him say, 'Tessa!' I knew him because he had taken care of me at the San Giovanni, and then we went into the Piazza where the fair was, and I had some *berlingozzi*, for I was hungry and he was very good to me; and at the end of the Piazza there was a holy father and an altar like what they have at the processions outside the churches. So he married us, and then Naldo took me back into the church and left me; and I went home, and my mother died, and Nofri began to beat me more, and Naldo never came back. And I used to cry, and once at the Carnival I saw him and followed him, and he was angry, and said he would come some time, I must wait. So I went and waited; but, oh! it was a long while before he came; but he would have come if he could, for he was good; and then he took me away, because I cried and said I could not bear to stay with Nofri. And, oh! I was so glad, and since then I have been always happy, for I don't mind about the goats and mules, because I have Lillo and Ninna now; and Naldo is never angry, only I think he doesn't love Ninna so well as Lillo, and she *is* pretty."

Quite forgetting that she had thought her speech rather momentous at the beginning, Tessa fell to devouring Ninna with kisses, while Romola sat in silence with absent eyes. It was inevitable that in this moment she should think of the three beings before her chiefly in their relation to her own lot, and she was feeling the chill of disappointment that her difficulties were not to be solved by external law. She had relaxed her hold of Lillo, and was leaning her cheek against her hand, seeing nothing of the scene around her. Lillo was quick in perceiving a change that was not agreeable to him; he had not yet made any return to her caresses, but he objected to their withdrawal, and putting up both his brown arms to pull her head towards him, he said, "Play with me again!"

Romola, roused from her self-absorption, clasped the lad anew, and looked from him to Tessa, who had now paused from her shower of kisses, and seemed to have returned to the more placid delight of contemplating the heavenly lady's face. That face was undergoing a subtle change, like the gradual oncoming of a warmer, softer light. Presently Romola took her scissors from her scarsella, and cut off one of her long wavy locks, while the three pair of wide eyes followed her movements with kitten-like observation.

"I must go away from you now," she said, "but I will leave this lock of hair that it may remind you of me, because if you are ever in trouble you can think that perhaps God will send me to take care of you again. I cannot tell you where to find me, but if I ever know that you want me, I will come to you. Addio!"

She had set down Lillo hurriedly, and held out her hand to Tessa, who kissed it with a mixture of awe and sorrow at this parting. Romola's mind was oppressed with thoughts; she needed to be alone as soon as possible, but with her habitual care for the least fortunate, she turned aside to put her hand in a friendly way on Monna Lisa's shoulder and make her a farewell sign. Before the old woman had finished her deep reverence, Romola had disappeared.

Monna Lisa and Tessa moved towards each other by simultaneous impulses, while the two children stood clinging to their mother's skirts as if they, too, felt the atmosphere of awe.

"Do you think she *was* a saint?" said Tessa, in Lisa's ear, showing her the lock.

Lisa rejected that notion very decidedly by a backward movement of her fingers, and then stroking the rippled gold, said,—

"She's a great and noble lady. I saw such in my youth."

Romola went home and sat alone through the sultry hours of the day with the heavy certainty that her lot was unchanged. She was thrown back again on the conflict between the demands of an outward law which she recognized as a widely ramifying obligation, and the demands of inner moral facts which were becoming more and more peremptory. She had drunk in deeply the spirit of that teaching by which Savonarola had urged her to return to her place. She felt that the sanctity attached to all close relations, and, therefore, pre-eminently to the closest, was but the expression in outward law of that result towards which all human goodness and nobleness must spontaneously tend; that the light abandonment of ties, whether inherited or voluntary, because they had ceased to be pleasant, was the uprooting of social and personal virtue. What else had Tito's crime towards Baldassarre been but that abandonment working itself out to the most hideous extreme of falsity and ingratitude?

And the inspiring consciousness breathed into her by Savonarola's influence that her lot was vitally united with the general lot had exalted even the minor details of obligation into religion. She was marching with a great army; she was feeling the stress of a common life. If victims were needed, and it was uncertain on whom the lot might fall, she would stand ready to answer to her name. She had stood long; she had striven hard to fulfil the bond; but she had seen all the conditions which made the fulfilment possible gradually forsaking her. The one effect of her marriage-tie seemed to be the stifling predominance over her of a nature that she despised. All her efforts at union had only made its impossibility more palpable, and the relation had become for her simply a degrading servitude. The law was sacred. Yes, but rebellion might be sacred too. It flashed upon her mind that the problem before her was essentially the same as that which had lain before Savonarola—the problem where the sacredness of obedience ended and where the sacredness of rebellion began. To her, as to him, there had come one of those moments in life when the soul must dare to act on its own warrant, not only without external law to appeal to, but in the face of a law which is not unarmed with divine lightnings—lightnings that may yet fall if the warrant has been false.

Before the sun had gone down she had adopted a resolve. She would ask no counsel of her godfather or of Savonarola until she had made one determined effort to speak freely with Tito and obtain his consent that she should live apart from him. She desired not to leave him clandestinely again, or to forsake Florence. She would tell him that if he ever felt a real need of her, she would come back to him. Was not that the utmost faithfulness to her bond that could be required of her? A shuddering anticipation came over her that he would clothe a refusal in a sneering suggestion that she should enter a convent as the only mode of quitting him that would not be scandalous. He knew well that her mind revolted from that means of escape, not only because of her own repugnance to a narrow rule, but because all the cherished memories of her father forbade that she should adopt a mode of life which was associated with his deepest griefs and his bitterest dislike.

Tito had announced his intention of coming home this evening. She would wait for him, and say what she had to say at once, for it was difficult to get his ear during the day. If he had the slightest suspicion that personal words were coming, he slipped away with an appearance of unpremeditated ease. When she sent for Maso to tell him that she would wait for his master, she observed that the old man looked at her and lingered with a mixture of hesitation and wondering anxiety; but finding that she asked him no question, he slowly turned away. Why should she ask questions? Perhaps Maso only knew or guessed something of what she knew already.

It was late before Tito came. Romola had been pacing up and down the long room which had once been the library, with the windows open and a loose white linen robe on instead of her usual black garment. She was glad of that change after the long hours of heat and motionless meditation; but the coolness and exercise made her more intensely wakeful, and as she went with the lamp in her hand to open the door for Tito he might well have been startled by the vividness of her eyes and the expression of painful resolution which was in contrast with her usual self-restrained quiescence before him. But it seemed that this excitement was just what he expected.

"Ah! it is you, Romola. Maso is gone to bed," he said, in a grave, quiet tone, interposing to close the door for her. Then, turning round, he said, looking at her more fully than he was wont, "You have heard it all, I see."

Romola quivered. *He*, then, was inclined to take the initiative. He had been to Tessa. She led the way through the nearest door, set down her lamp, and turned towards him again.

"You must not think despairingly of the consequences," said Tito, in a tone of soothing encouragement, at which Romola stood wondering, until he added, "The accused have too many family ties with all parties not to escape; and Messer Bernardo del Nero has other things in his favour besides his age."

Romola started, and gave a cry as if she had been suddenly stricken by a sharp weapon.

"What! you did not know it?" said Tito, putting his hand under her arm that he might lead her to a seat; but she seemed to be unaware of his touch.

"Tell me," she said, hastily—"tell me what it is."

"A man, whose name you may forget—Lamberto dell' Antella—who was banished, has been seized within the territory: a letter has been found on him of very dangerous import to the chief Mediceans, and the scoundrel, who was once a favourite hound of Piero de' Medici, is ready now to swear what any one pleases against him or his friends.* Some have made their escape, but five are now in prison."

"My godfather?" said Romola, scarcely above a whisper, as Tito made a slight pause.

"Yes; I grieve to say it. But along with him there are three, at least, whose names have a commanding interest even among the popular party—Niccolò Ridolfi, Lorenzo Tornabuoni, and Giannozzo Pucci."

The tide of Romola's feeling had been violently turned into a new channel. In the tumult of that moment there could be no check to the words which came as the impulsive utterance of her long-accumulating horror. When Tito had named the men of whom she felt certain he was the confederate, she said, with a recoiling gesture and low-toned bitterness—

"And *you*—you are safe?"

"You are certainly an amiable wife, my Romola," said Tito, with the coolest irony. "Yes; I am safe."

They turned away from each other in silence.

[*JUNE 1863*]

CHAPTER LVII.

Why Tito was Safe

TITO had good reasons for saying that he was safe. In the last three months, during which he had foreseen the discovery of the Medicean conspirators as a probable event, he had had plenty of time to provide himself with resources. He had been strengthening his influence at Rome and at Milan, by being the medium of secret information and indirect measures against the Frate and the popular party; he had cultivated more assiduously than ever the regard of this party by showing subtle evidence that his political convictions were entirely on their side; and all the while, instead of withdrawing his agency from the Mediceans, he had sought to be more actively employed and exclusively trusted by them. It was easy to him to keep up this triple game. The principle of duplicity admitted by the Mediceans on their own behalf deprived them of any standard by which they could measure the trustworthiness of a colleague who had not, like themselves, hereditary interests, alliances, and prejudices, which were intensely Medicean. In their minds to deceive the opposite party was fair stratagem, to deceive their own party was a baseness to which they felt no temptation; and in using Tito's facile ability they were not keenly awake to the fact that the absence of traditional attachments which made him a convenient agent was also the absence of what among themselves was the chief guarantee of mutual honour. Again, the Roman and Milanese friends of the aristocratic party, or Arrabbiati, who were the bitterest enemies of Savonarola, carried on a system of underhand correspondence and espionage, in which the deepest hypocrisy was the best service, and demanded the heaviest pay; so that to suspect an agent because he played a part strongly would have been an absurd want of logic. On the other hand, the Piagnoni of the popular party, who had the directness that belongs to energetic conviction, were the more inclined to credit Tito with sincerity in his political adhesion to them, because he affected no religious sympathies.

By virtue of these conditions the last three months had been a time of flattering success to Tito. The result he most cared for was the securing of a future position for himself at Rome or at Milan, for he had a growing determination, when the favourable moment should come, to quit Florence for one of those great capitals where life was easier, and the rewards of talent and learning were more splendid. At present, the scale dipped in favour of Milan; and if within the year he could render certain services to Duke Ludovico Sforza, he had the prospect of a place at the Milanese court, which outweighed the advantages of Rome.

The revelation of the Medicean conspiracy, then, had been a subject of forethought to Tito; but he had not been able to foresee the mode in which it would be brought about. The arrest of Lamberto dell' Antella with a tell-tale letter on his person, and a bitter rancour against the Medici in his heart, was an incalculable event. It was not possible, in spite of the careful pretexts with which his agency had been guarded, that Tito should escape implication: he had never expected this in case of any wide discovery concerning the Medicean plots. But his quick mind had soon traced out the course that would secure his own safety with the fewest unpleasant concomitants. It is agreeable to keep a whole skin; but the skin still remains an organ sensitive to the atmosphere.

His reckoning had not deceived him. That night before he returned home, he had secured the three results for which he most cared: he was to be freed from all proceedings against him on account of complicity with the Mediceans; he was to retain his Secretaryship for another year, unless he previously resigned it; and, lastly, the price by which he had obtained these guarantees was to be kept as a State secret. The price would have been thought heavy by most men; and Tito himself would rather not have paid it.

He had applied himself first to win the mind of Francesco Valori, who was not only one of the Ten under whom he immediately held his Secretaryship, but one of the special council appointed to investigate the evidence of the plot. Francesco Valori, as we have seen, was the head of the Piagnoni, a man with certain fine qualities that were not incompatible with violent partisanship, with an arrogant temper that alienated his friends, nor with bitter personal animosities—one of the bitterest being directed against Bernardo del Nero. To him, in a brief private interview, after obtaining a pledge of secrecy, Tito avowed his own agency for the Mediceans—an agency induced by motives about which he was very frank, declaring at the same time that he had always believed their efforts futile, and that he sincerely preferred the maintenance of the popular government; affected to confide to Valori, as a secret, his own personal dislike for Bernardo del Nero; and after this preparation, came to the important statement that there was another Medicean plot, of which, if he obtained certain conditions from the government, he could, by a journey to Siena, and into Romagna where Piero de' Medici was again trying to gather forces, obtain documentary evidence to lay before the council. To this end it was essential that his character as a Medicean agent should be unshaken for all Mediceans, and hence the fact that he had been a source of information to the authorities must be wrapped in profound secrecy. Still, some odour of the facts might escape in spite of precaution, and before Tito could incur the unpleasant consequences of acting against his friends, he must be assured of immunity from any prosecution as a Medicean, and from deprivation of office for a year to come.

These propositions did not sound in the ear of Francesco Valori precisely as they sound to us. Valori's mind was not intensely bent on the estimation of Tito's conduct; and it *was* intensely bent on procuring an extreme sentence against the five prisoners. There were sure to be immense efforts to save them; and it was to be wished (on public grounds) that the evidence against them should be of the strongest, so as to alarm all well-affected men at the dangers of clemency. The character of legal proceedings at that time implied that evidence was one of those desirable things which could only be come at by foul means. To catch a few people and torture them into confessing everybody's guilt was one step towards justice; and it was not always easy to see the next unless a traitor turned up. Lamberto dell' Antella had been tortured in aid of his previous willingness to tell more than he knew; nevertheless, additional and stronger facts were desirable, especially against Bernardo del Nero, who, so far as appeared hitherto, had simply refrained from betraying the late plot after having tried in vain to discourage it; for the welfare of Florence demanded that the guilt of Bernardo del Nero should be put in the strongest light. So Francesco Valori zealously believed; and perhaps he was not himself aware that the strength of his zeal was determined by his hatred. He decided that Tito's proposition ought to be accepted, laid it before his colleagues without disclosing Tito's name, and won them over to his opinion. Late in the day Tito was admitted to an audience of the special council, and produced a deep sensation among them by revealing another plot* for insuring the mastery of Florence to Piero de' Medici, which was to have been carried into execution in the middle of this very month of August. Documentary evidence on this subject would do more than anything else to make the right course clear. He received a commission to start for Siena by break of day; and, besides this, he carried away with him from the council-chamber a written guarantee of his immunity and of his retention of office.

Among the twenty Florentines who bent their grave eyes on Tito, as he stood gracefully before them, speaking of startling things with easy periphrasis, and with that apparently unaffected admission of being actuated by motives short of the highest which is often the intensest affectation, there were several whose minds were not too entirely preoccupied for them to pass a new judgment on him in these new circumstances; they silently concluded that this ingenious and serviceable Greek was in future rather to be used for public needs than for private intimacy. Unprincipled men were useful, enabling those who had more scruples to keep their hands tolerably clean in a world where there was much dirty work to be done. Indeed, it was not clear to respectable Florentine brains, unless they held the Frate's extravagant belief in a possible purity and loftiness to be striven for on this earth, how life was to be carried on in any department without human instruments whom it would not be unbecoming to kick or to spit upon in the act of handing them their wages. Some of these very men who passed a tacit judgment on Tito were shortly to be engaged in a memorable transaction that could by no means have been carried through without the use of an unscrupulousness* as decided as his; but, as their own bright poet Pulci had said for them, it is one thing to love the fruits of treachery, and another thing to love traitors.

"Il tradimento a molti piace assai,
Ma il traditore a gnun non piacque mai."*

The same society has had a gibbet for the murderer and a gibbet for the martyr, an execrating hiss for a dastardly act, and as loud a hiss for many a word of generous truthfulness or just insight: a mixed condition of things which is the sign, not of hopeless confusion, but of struggling order.

For Tito himself, he was not unaware that he had sunk a little in the estimate of the men who had accepted his services. He had that degree of self-contemplation which necessarily accompanies the habit of acting on well-considered reasons, of whatever quality; and if he could have chosen, he would have declined to see himself disapproved by men of the world. He had never meant to be disapproved; he had meant always to conduct himself so ably that if he acted in opposition to the standard of other men they should not be aware of it; and the barrier between himself and Romola had been raised by the impossibility of such concealment with her. He shrank from condemnatory judgments as from a climate to which he could not adapt himself. But things were not so plastic in the hands of cleverness as could be wished, and events had turned out inconveniently. He had really no rancour against Messer Bernardo del Nero; he had a personal liking for Lorenzo Tornabuoni and Giannozzo Pucci. He had served them very ably, and in such a way that if their party had been winners he would have merited high reward; but was he to relinquish all the agreeable fruits of life because their party had failed? His proffer of a little additional proof against them would probably have no influence on their fate; in fact, he felt convinced they would escape any extreme consequences; but if he had not given it, his own fortunes, which made a promising fabric, would have been utterly ruined. And what motive could any man really have, except his own interest? Florentines whose passions were engaged in their petty and precarious political schemes might have no self-interest separable from family pride and tenacity in old hatred and attachments; a modern simpleton who swallowed whole one of the old systems of philosophy, and took the indigestion it occasioned for the signs of a divine afflux or the voice of an inward monitor, might see his interest in a form of self-conceit which he called self-rewarding virtue; fanatics who believed in the coming Scourge and Renovation might see their own interest in a future palm branch and white robe: but no man of clear intellect allowed his course to be determined by such puerile impulses or questionable inward fumes. Did not Pontanus, poet and philosopher of unrivalled Latinity, make the finest possible oration at Naples to welcome the French King, who had come to dethrone the learned orator's royal friend and patron? and still Pontanus held up his head and prospered. Men did not really care about these things, except when their personal spleen was touched. It was weakness only that was despised; power of any sort carried its immunity; and no man, unless by very rare good fortune, could mount high in the world without incurring a few unpleasant necessities which laid him open to enmity, and perhaps to a little hissing, when enmity wanted a pretext.

It was a faint prognostic of that hissing, gathered by Tito from certain indications when he was before the council, which gave his present conduct the character of an epoch to him, and made him dwell on it with argumentative vindication. It was not that he was taking a deeper step in wrong-doing, for it was not possible that he should feel any tie to the Mediceans to be stronger than the tie to his father; but his conduct to his father had been hidden by successful lying: his present act did not admit of total concealment—in its very nature it was a revelation. And Tito winced under his new liability to disesteem.

Well! a little patience, and in another year, or perhaps in half a year, he might turn his back on these hard, eager Florentines, with their futile quarrels and sinking fortunes. His brilliant success at Florence had had some ugly flaws in it: he had fallen in love with the wrong woman, and Baldassarre had come back under incalculable circumstances. But as Tito galloped with a loose rein towards Siena, he saw a future before him in which he would no longer be haunted by those mistakes. He had much money safe out of Florence already; he was in the fresh ripeness of eight-and-twenty; he was conscious of well-tried skill. Could he not strip himself of the past, as of rehearsal clothing, and throw away the old bundle, to robe himself for the real scene?

It did not enter into Tito's meditations on the future, that, on issuing from the council chamber and descending the stairs, he had brushed against a man whose face he had not stayed to recognize in the lamplight. The man was Ser Ceccone—also willing to serve the State by giving information against unsuccessful employers.

CHAPTER LVIII.

A Final Understanding

TITO soon returned from Siena, but almost immediately set out on another journey, from which he did not return till the seventeenth of August. Nearly a fortnight had passed since the arrest of the accused, and still they were in prison, still their fate was uncertain. Romola had felt during this interval as if all cares were suspended for her, other than watching the fluctuating probabilities concerning that fate. Sometimes they seemed strongly in favour of the prisoners; for the chances of effective interest on their behalf were heightened by delay, and an indefinite prospect of delay was opened by the reluctance of all persons in authority to incur the odium attendant on any decision. On the one side there was a loud cry that the Republic was in danger, and that lenity to the prisoners would be the signal of attack for all its enemies; on the other, there was the certainty that a sentence of death and confiscation of property passed on five citizens of distinguished name, would entail the rancorous hatred of their relatives on all who were conspicuously instrumental to such a sentence.

The final judgment properly lay with the Eight, who presided over the administration of criminal justice; and the sentence depended on a majority of six votes. But the Eight shrank from their onerous responsibility, and asked in this exceptional case to have it shared by the Signoria (or the Gonfaloniere and the eight Priors). The Signoria in its turn shrugged its shoulders, and proposed the Appeal to the Great Council. For, according to a law passed by the earnest persuasion of Savonarola nearly three years before, whenever a citizen was condemned to death by the fatal six votes (called the *sei fave* or *six beans*, beans being in more senses than one the political pulse of Florence), he had the right of appealing from that sentence to the Great Council.

But in this stage of the business, the friends of the accused resisted the Appeal, determined chiefly by the wish to gain delay; and, in fact, strict legality required that sentence should have been passed prior to the Appeal. Their resistance prevailed, and a middle course was taken: the sentence was referred to a large assembly convened on the seventeenth, consisting of all the higher magistracies, the smaller council or senate of eighty,* and a select number of citizens.

On this day Romola, with anxiety heightened by the possibility that before its close her godfather's fate might be decided, had obtained leave to see him for the second time, but only in the presence of witnesses. She had returned to the Via de' Bardi in company with her cousin Brigida, still ignorant whether the council had come to any decisive issue; and Monna Brigida had gone out again to await the momentous news at the house of a friend belonging to one of the magistracies, that she might bring back authentic tidings as soon as they were to be had.

Romola had sunk on the first seat in the bright saloon, too much agitated, too sick at heart to care about her place, or be conscious of discordance in the objects that surrounded her. She sat with her back to the door, resting her head on her hands. It seemed a long while since Monna Brigida had gone, and Romola was expecting her return. But when the door opened she knew it was not Monna Brigida who entered.

Since she had parted from Tito on that memorable night, she had had no external proof to warrant her belief that he had won his safety by treachery; on the contrary, she had had evidence that he was still trusted by the Mediceans and was believed by them to be accomplishing certain errands of theirs in Romagna, under cover of fulfilling a commission of the government. For the obscurity in which the evidence concerning the conspirators was shrouded allowed it to be understood that Tito had escaped any implication.

But Romola's suspicion was not to be dissipated: her horror of his conduct towards Baldassarre projected itself over every conception of his acts; it was as if she had seen him committing a murder and had had a diseased impression ever after that his hands were covered with fresh blood.

As she heard his step on the stone floor, a chill shudder passed through her; she could not turn round, she could not rise to give any greeting. He did not speak, but after an instant's pause took a seat on the other side of the table just opposite to her. Then she raised her eyes and looked at him; but she was mute. He did not show any irritation, but said, coolly—

"This meeting corresponds with our parting, Romola. But I understand that it is a moment of terrible suspense. I am come, however, if you will listen to me, to bring you the relief of hope."

She started, and altered her position, but looked at him dubiously.

"It will not be unwelcome to you to hear—even though it is I who tell it—that the council is prorogued till the twenty-first. The Eight have been frightened at last into passing a sentence of condemnation, but the demand has now been made on behalf of the condemned for the Appeal to the Great Council."

Romola's face lost its dubious expression; she asked eagerly—

"And when is it to be made?"

"It has not yet been granted; but it *may* be granted. The Special Council is to meet again on the twenty-first to deliberate whether the Appeal shall be allowed or not. In the meantime there is an interval of three days in which chances may occur in favour of the prisoners—in which interest may be used on their behalf."

Romola started from her seat. The colour had risen to her face like a visible thought, and her hands trembled. In that moment her feeling towards Tito was forgotten.

"Possibly," said Tito, also rising, "your own intention may have anticipated what I was going to say. You are thinking of the Frate."

"I am," said Romola, looking at him with surprise. "Has he done anything? Is there anything to tell me?"

"Only this. It was Messer Francesco Valori's bitterness and violence which chiefly determined the course of things in the council to-day. Half the men who gave in their opinion against the prisoners were frightened into it, and there are numerous friends of Fra Girolamo both in this Special Council and out of it who are strongly opposed to the sentence of death—Piero Guicciardini, for example, who is one member of the Signoria that made the stoutest resistance; and there is Giovan Battista Ridolfi,* who, Piagnone as he is, will not lightly forgive the death of his brother Niccolò."

"But how can the Appeal be denied," said Romola, indignantly, "when it is the law—when it was one of the chief glories of the popular government to have passed the law?"

"They call this an exceptional case. Of course there are ingenious arguments, but there is much more of loud bluster about the danger of the republic. But, you see, no opposition could prevent the assembly from being prorogued, and a certain powerful influence rightly applied during the next three days might determine the wavering courage of those who desire that the Appeal should be granted, and might even give a check to the headlong enmity of Francesco Valori. It happens to have come to my knowledge that the Frate has so far interfered as to send a message to him in favour of Lorenzo Tornabuoni. I know you can sometimes have access to the Frate: it might at all events be worth while to use your privilege now."

"It is true," said Romola, with an air of abstraction. "I cannot believe that the Frate would approve denying the Appeal."

"I heard it said by more than one person in the court of the Palazzo, before I came away, that it would be to the everlasting discredit of Fra Girolamo if he allowed a government which is almost entirely made up of his party, to deny the Appeal, without entering his protest, when he has been boasting in his books and sermons that it was he who got the law passed.* But, between ourselves, with all respect for your Frate's ability, my Romola, he has got into the practice of preaching that form of human sacrifices called killing tyrants and wicked malcontents which some of his followers are likely to think inconsistent with lenity in the present case."

"I know, I know," said Romola, with a look and tone of pain. "But he is driven into those excesses of speech. It used to be different. I *will* ask for an interview. I cannot rest without it. I trust in the greatness of his heart."

She was not looking at Tito; her eyes were bent with a vague gaze towards the ground, and she had no distinct consciousness that the words she heard came from her husband.

"Better lose no time, then," said Tito, with unmixed suavity, moving his cap round in his hands as if he were about to put it on and depart. "And now, Romola, you will perhaps be able to see, in spite of prejudice, that my wishes go with yours in this matter. You will not regard the misfortune of my safety as an offence."

Something like an electric shock passed through Romola: it was the full consciousness of her husband's presence returning to her. She looked at him without speaking.

"At least," he added, in a slightly harder tone, "you will endeavour to base our intercourse on some other reasoning than that because an evil deed is possible, *I* have done it. Am I alone to be beyond the pale of your extensive charity?"

The feelings which had been driven back from Romola's lips

a fortnight before rose again with the gathered force of a tidal wave. She spoke with a decision which told him that she was careless of consequences.

"It is too late, Tito. There is no killing the suspicion that deceit has once begotten. And now I know everything. I know who that old man was: he was your father, to whom you owe everything—to whom you owe more than if you had been his own child. By the side of that, it is a small thing that you broke my trust and my father's. As long as you deny the truth about that old man, there is a horror rising between us: the law that should make us one can never be obeyed. I too am a human being. I have a soul of my own that abhors your actions. Our union is a pretence—as if a perpetual lie could be a sacred marriage."

Tito did not answer immediately. When he did speak it was with a calculated caution, that was stimulated by alarm.

"And you mean to carry out that independence by quitting me, I presume?"

"I desire to quit you," said Romola, impetuously.

"And supposing I do not submit to part with what the law gives me some security for retaining? You will then, of course, proclaim your reasons in the ear of all Florence. You will bring forward your mad assassin, who is doubtless ready to obey your call, and you will tell the world that you believe his testimony because he is so rational as to desire to assassinate me. You will first inform the Signoria that I am a Medicean conspirator, and then you will inform the Mediceans that I have betrayed them, and in both cases you will offer the excellent proof that you believe me capable in general of everything bad. It will certainly be a striking position for a wife to adopt. And if, on such evidence, you succeed in holding me up to infamy, you will have surpassed all the heroines of the Greek drama."

He paused a moment, but she stood mute. He went on with the sense of mastery.

"I believe you have no other grievance against me—except that I have failed in fulfilling some lofty indefinite conditions on which you gave me your wifely affection, so that, by withdrawing it, you have gradually reduced me to the careful supply of your wants as a fair Piagnone of high condition and liberal charities. I think your success in gibbeting me is not certain. But doubtless you would begin by winning the ear of Messer Bernardo del Nero?"

"Why do I speak of anything?" cried Romola, in anguish, sinking on her chair again. "It is hateful in me to be thinking of myself!"

She did not notice when Tito left the room, or know how long it was before the door opened to admit Monna Brigida. But in that instant she started up and said—

"Cousin, we must go to San Marco directly. I must see my confessor, Fra Salvestro."

CHAPTER LIX.

Pleading

THE morning was in its early brightness when Romola was again on her way to San Marco, having obtained through Fra Salvestro, the evening before, the promise of an interview with Fra Girolamo in the chapter-house of the convent. The rigidity with which Savonarola guarded his life from all the pretexts of calumny made such interviews very rare, and whenever they were granted, they were kept free from any appearance of mystery. For this reason the hour chosen was one at which there were likely to be other visitors in the outer cloisters of San Marco.

She chose to pass through the heart of the city that she might notice the signs of public feeling. Every loggia, every convenient corner of the piazza, every shop that made a rendezvous for gossips, was astir with the excitement of gratuitous debate; a languishing trade tending to make political discussion all the more vigorous. It was clear that the parties for and against the death of the conspirators were bent on making the fullest use of the three days' interval in order to determine the popular mood. Already handbills were in circulation; some presenting, in large print, the alternative of Justice on the Conspirators or Ruin to the Republic, others in equally large print urging the observance of the Law and the granting of the Appeal. Round these jutting islets of black capitals there were lakes of smaller characters setting forth arguments less necessary to be read; for it was an opinion entertained at that time (in the first flush of triumph at the discovery of printing), that there was no argument more widely convincing than question-begging phrases in large type.

Romola, however, cared especially to become acquainted with the arguments in smaller type, and though obliged to hasten forward she looked round anxiously as she went that she might miss no opportunity of securing copies. For a long way she saw none but such as were in the hands of eager readers, or else fixed on the walls, from which in some places the *sbirri* were tearing them down. But at last, passing behind San Giovanni with a quickened pace that she might avoid the many acquaintances who frequented the piazza, she saw Bratti with a stock of handbills which he appeared to be exchanging for small coin with the passers-by. She was too familiar with the humble life of Florence for Bratti to be any stranger to her, and turning towards him she said, "Have you two sorts of handbills, Bratti? Let me have them quickly."

"Two sorts," said Bratti, separating the wet sheets with a slowness that tried Romola's patience. "There's 'Law,' and there's 'Justice.'"

"Which sort do you sell most of?"

"'Justice'—'Justice' goes the quickest,—so I raised the price and made it two danari. But then I bethought me the 'Law' was good ware too, and had as good a right to be charged for as 'Justice;' for people set no store by cheap things, and if I sold the 'Law' at one danaro, I should be doing it a wrong. And I'm a fair trader. 'Law,' or 'Justice,' it's all one to me; they're good wares. I get 'em both for nothing, and I sell 'em at a fair profit. But you'll want more than one of a sort?"

"No, no: here's a white quattrino for the two," said Romola, folding up the bills and hurrying away.

She was soon in the outer cloisters of San Marco, where Fra Salvestro was awaiting her under the cloister, but did not notice the approach of her light step. He was chatting, according to his habit, with lay visitors; for under the auspices of a government friendly to the Frate, the timidity about frequenting San Marco, which had followed on the first shock of the excommunication, had been gradually giving way. In one of these lay visitors she recognized a well-known satellite of Francesco Valori, named Andrea Cambini,* who was narrating or expounding with emphatic gesticulation, while Fra Salvestro was listening with that air of trivial curiosity which tells that the listener cares very much about news and very little about its quality. This characteristic of her confessor, which was always repulsive to

Romola, was made exasperating to her at this moment by the certainty she gathered, from the disjointed words which reached her ear, that Cambini was narrating something relative to the fate of the conspirators. She chose not to approach the group, but as soon as she saw that she had arrested Fra Salvestro's attention, she turned towards the door of the chapter-house, while he, making a sign of approval, disappeared within the inner cloister. A lay Brother stood ready to open the door of the chapter-house for her, and closed it behind her as she entered.

Once more looked at by those sad frescoed figures* which had seemed to be mourning with her at the death of her brother Dino, it was inevitable that something of that scene should come back to her; but the intense occupation of her mind with the present made the remembrance less a retrospect than an indistinct recurrence of impressions which blended themselves with her agitating fears, as if her actual anxiety were a revival of the strong yearning she had once before brought to this spot—to be repelled by marble rigidity. She gave no space for the remembrance to become more definite, for she at once opened the handbills, thinking she should perhaps be able to read them in the interval before Fra Girolamo appeared. But by the time she had read to the end of the one that recommended the observance of the law, the door was opening, and doubling up the papers she stood expectant.

When the Frate had entered she knelt, according to the usual practice of those who saw him in private; but as soon as he had uttered a benedictory greeting she rose and stood opposite to him at a few yards' distance. Owing to his seclusion since he had been excommunicated, it had been an unusually long while since she had seen him, and the late months had visibly deepened in his face the marks of overtaxed mental activity and bodily severities; and yet Romola was not so conscious of this change as of another, which was less definable. Was it that the expression of serene elevation and pure human fellowship which had once moved her was no longer present in the same force, or was it that the sense of his being divided from her in her feeling about her godfather roused the slumbering sources of alienation, and marred her own vision? Perhaps both causes were at work. Our relations with our fellow-men are most often determined by coincident currents of that sort; the inexcusable word or deed seldom comes until after affection or reverence has been already enfeebled by the strain of repeated excuses.

It was true that Savonarola's glance at Romola had some of that hardness which is caused by an egoistic prepossession. He divined that the interview she had sought was to turn on the fate of the conspirators, a subject on which he had already had to quell inner voices that might become loud again when encouraged from without. Seated in his cell, correcting the sheets of his "Triumph of the Cross,"* it was easier to repose on a resolution of neutrality.

"It is a question of moment, doubtless, on which you wished to see me, my daughter," he began, in a tone which was gentle rather from self-control than from immediate inclination. "I know you are not wont to lay stress on small matters."

"Father, you know what it is before I tell you," said Romola, forgetting everything else as soon as she began to pour forth her plea. "You know what I am caring for—it is for the life of the old man I love best in the world. The thought of him has gone together with the thought of my father as long as I remember the daylight. That is my warrant for coming to you, even if my coming should have been needless. Perhaps it is: perhaps you have already determined that your power over the hearts of men shall be used to prevent them from denying to Florentines a right which you yourself helped to earn for them."

"I meddle not with the functions of the State, my daughter," said Fra Girolamo, strongly disinclined to reopen externally a debate which he had already gone through inwardly. "I have preached and laboured that Florence should have a good government, for a good government is needful to the perfecting of the Christian life; but I keep away my hands from particular affairs, which it is the office of experienced citizens to administer."

"Surely, father—" Romola broke off. She had uttered this first word almost impetuously, but she was checked by the counter agitation of feeling herself in an attitude of remonstrance towards the man who had been the source of guidance and strength to her. In the act of rebelling she was bruising her own reverence.

Savonarola was too keen not to divine something of the conflict that was arresting her—too noble, deliberately to assume in calm speech that self-justifying evasiveness into which he was often hurried in public by the crowding impulses of the orator.

"Say what is in your heart; speak on, my daughter," he said, standing with his arms laid one upon the other, and looking at her with quiet expectation.

"I was going to say, father, that this matter is surely of higher moment than many about which I have heard you preach and exhort fervidly. If it belonged to you to urge that men condemned for offences against the State should have the right to appeal to the Great Council—if—" Romola was getting eager again—"if you count it a glory to have won that right for them, can it less belong to you to declare yourself against the right being denied to almost the first men who need it? Surely that touches the Christian life more closely than whether you knew beforehand* that the Dauphin would die, or whether Pisa will be conquered."

There was a subtle movement, like a subdued sign of pain, in Savonarola's strong lips, before he began to speak.

"My daughter, I speak as it is given me to speak—I am not master of the times when I may become the vehicle of knowledge beyond the common lights of men. In this case I have no illumination beyond what wisdom may give to those who are charged with the safety of the State. As to the Law of Appeal against the Six Votes, I laboured to have it passed in order that no Florentine should be subject to loss of life and goods through the private hatred of a few who might happen to be in power; but these five men, who have desired to overthrow a free government and restore a corrupt tyrant, have been condemned with the assent of a large assembly of their fellow-citizens. They refused at first to have their cause brought before the Great Council. They have lost the right to the Appeal."

"How can they have lost it?" said Romola. "It is the right to appeal against condemnation, and they have never been condemned till now; and, forgive me, father, it *is* private hatred that would deny them the Appeal; it *is* the violence of the few that frightens others; else why was the assembly divided again directly, after it had seemed to agree? And if anything weighs against the observance of the Law, let this weigh *for* it—this, that you used to preach more earnestly than all else, that there should be no place given to hatred and bloodshed because of these party strifes, so that private ill-will should not find its opportunities in public acts. Father, you *know* that there is private hatred concerned here: will it not dishonour you not to have interposed on the side of mercy, when there are many who hold that it is also the side of law and justice?"

"My daughter," said Fra Girolamo, with more visible emotion than before, "there is a mercy which is weakness, and even treason against the common good. The safety of Florence, which means even more than the welfare of Florentines, now demands severity, as it once demanded mercy. It is not only for a past plot that these men are condemned, but also for a plot which has not yet been executed; and the devices that were leading to its execution are not put an end to: the tyrant is still gathering his forces in Romagna, and the enemies of Florence, that sit in the highest places of Italy, are ready to hurl any stone that will crush her."

"What plot?" said Romola, reddening, and trembling with alarmed surprise.

"You carry papers in your hand, I see," said Fra Girolamo, pointing to the handbills. "One of them will, perhaps, tell you that the government has had new information."

Romola hastily opened the handbill she had not yet read, and saw that the government had now positive evidence of a second plot, which was to have been carried out in this August time. To her mind it was like reading a confirmation that Tito had won his safety by foul means; his pretence of wishing that the Frate should exert himself on behalf of the condemned only helped the wretched conviction. She crushed up the paper in her hand, and, turning to Savonarola, she said, with new passion, "Father, what safety can there be for Florence when the worst man can always escape? And," she went on, a sudden flash of remembrance coming from the thought about her husband, "have not you yourself encouraged this deception which corrupts the life of Florence, by wanting more favour to be shown to Lorenzo Tornabuoni, who has worn two faces, and flattered you with a show of affection, when my godfather has always been honest? Ask all Florence who of those five men has the truest heart, and there will not be many who will name any other name than Bernardo del Nero. You did interpose with Francesco Valori for the sake of one prisoner: you have *not* then been neutral; and you know that your word will be powerful."

"I do not desire the death of Bernardo," said Savonarola, colouring deeply. "It would be enough if he were sent out of the city."

"Then why do you not speak to save an old man of seventy-five from dying a death of ignominy—to give him at least the fair chances of the law?" burst out Romola, the impetuosity of her nature so roused that she forgot everything but her indignation. "It is not that you feel bound to be neutral; else why did you speak for Lorenzo Tornabuoni? You spoke for him because he is more friendly to San Marco; my godfather feigns no friendship. It is not then as a Medicean that my godfather is to die; it is as a man you have no love for!"

When Romola paused, with cheeks glowing, and with quivering lips, there was dead silence. As she saw Fra Girolamo standing motionless before her, she seemed to herself to be hearing her own words over again; words that in this echo of consciousness were in strange, painful dissonance with the memories that made part of his presence to her. The moments of silence were expanded by gathering compunction and self-doubt. She had committed sacrilege in her passion. And even the sense that she could retract nothing of her plea, that her mind could not submit itself to Savonarola's negative, made it the more needful to her to satisfy those reverential memories. With a sudden movement towards him, she said,

"Forgive me, father; it is pain to me to have spoken those words—yet I cannot help speaking. I am little and feeble compared with you; you brought me light and strength. But I submitted because I felt the proffered strength—because I saw the light. *Now* I cannot see it. Father, you yourself declare that there comes a moment when the soul must have no guide but the voice within it, to tell whether the consecrated thing has sacred virtue. And therefore I must speak."

Savonarola had that readily roused resentment towards opposition, hardly separable from a power-loving and powerful nature, accustomed to seek great ends that cast a reflected grandeur on the means by which they are sought. His sermons have much of that red flame in them. And if he had been a meaner man his susceptibility might have shown itself in irritation at Romola's accusatory freedom, which was in strong contrast with the deference he habitually received from his disciples. But at this moment such feelings were nullified by that hard struggle which made half the tragedy of his life—the struggle of a mind possessed by a never-silent hunger after purity and simplicity, yet caught in a tangle of egoistic demands, false ideas, and difficult outward conditions, that made simplicity impossible. Keenly alive to all the suggestions of Romola's remonstrating words, he was rapidly surveying, as he had done before, the courses of action that were open to him, and their probable results. But it was a question on which arguments could seem decisive only in proportion as they were charged with feeling, and he had received no impulse that could alter his bias. He looked at Romola and said—

"You have full pardon for your frankness, my daughter. You speak, I know, out of the fullness of your family affections. But these affections must give way to the needs of the Republic. If those men who have a close acquaintance with the affairs of the State believe, as I understand they do, that the public safety requires the extreme punishment of the law to fall on the five conspirators, I cannot control their opinion, seeing that I stand aloof from such affairs."

"Then you desire that they should die? You desire that the Appeal should be denied them?" said Romola, feeling anew repelled by a vindication which seemed to her to have the nature of a subterfuge.

"I have said that I do not desire their death."

"Then," said Romola, her indignation rising again, "you can be indifferent that Florentines should inflict death which you do not desire, when you might have protested against it—when you might have helped to hinder it, by urging the observance of a law which you held it good to get passed. Father, you used not to stand aloof: you used not to shrink from protesting. Do not say you cannot protest where the lives of men are concerned; say rather, you desire their death. Say rather, you hold it good for Florence that there shall be more blood and more hatred. Will the death of five Mediceans put an end to parties in Florence? Will the death of a noble old man like Bernardo del Nero save a city that holds such men as Dolfo Spini?"

"My daughter, it is enough. The cause of freedom, which is the cause of God's kingdom upon earth, is often most injured by the enemies who carry within them the power of certain human virtues. The wickedest man is often not the most insurmountable obstacle to the triumph of Good."

"Then why do you say again, that you do not desire my godfather's death?" said Romola, in mingled anger and despair. "Rather, you hold it the more needful he should die because he is the better man. I cannot unravel your thoughts, father; I cannot hear the real voice of your judgment and conscience."

There was a moment's pause. Then Savonarola said, with keener emotion than he had yet shown,

"Be thankful, my daughter, if your own soul has been spared perplexity; and judge not those to whom a harder lot has been given. *You* see one ground of action in this matter. I see many. I have to choose that which will further the work entrusted to me. The end I seek is one to which minor respects must be sacrificed. The death of five men—were they less guilty than these—is a light matter weighed against the withstanding of the vicious tyrannies which stifle the life of Italy, and foster the corruption of the Church; a light matter weighed against the furthering of God's Kingdom upon earth, the end for which I live and am willing myself to die."

Under any other circumstances, Romola would have been sensitive to the appeal at the beginning of Savonarola's speech; but at this moment she was so utterly in antagonism with him, that what he called perplexity seemed to her sophistry and doubleness; and as he went on, his words only fed that flame of indignation, which now again, more fully than ever before, lit up the memory of all his mistakes, and made her trust in him seem to have been a purblind delusion. She spoke almost with bitterness.

"Do you then know so well what will further the coming of God's Kingdom, father, that you will dare to despise the plea of mercy—of justice—of faithfulness to your own teaching? Has the French King then brought renovation to Italy? Take care, father, lest your enemies have some reason when they say, that in your visions of what will further God's Kingdom you see only what will strengthen your own party."

"And that is true!" said Savonarola, with flashing eyes. Romola's voice had seemed to him in that moment the voice of his enemies. "The cause of my party *is* the cause of God's Kingdom."

"I do not believe it!" said Romola, her whole frame shaken with passionate repugnance. "God's Kingdom is something wider—else, let me stand outside it with the beings that I love."

The two faces were lit up, each with an opposite emotion, each with an opposite certitude. Further words were impossible. Romola hastily covered her head and went out in silence.

CHAPTER LX.

The Scaffold

THREE days later the moon that was just surmounting the buildings of the piazza in front of the Old Palace within the hour of midnight, did not make the usual broad lights and shadows on the pavement. Not a hand's breadth of pavement was to be seen, but only the heads of an eager struggling multitude. And instead of that background of silence on which the pattering footsteps and buzzing voices, the lute-thrumming or rapid scampering of the many night-wanderers of Florence stood out in obtrusive distinctness, there was the background of a roar from mingled shouts and imprecations, tramplings and pushings, and accidental clashing of weapons, across which nothing was distinguishable but a darting shriek or the heavy dropping toll of a bell.

Almost all who could call themselves the public of Florence were awake at that hour, and either enclosed within the limits of that piazza, or struggling to enter it. Within the palace were still assembled in the council chamber all the chief magistracies, the eighty members of the senate, and the other select citizens who had been in hot debate through long hours of daylight and torchlight whether the Appeal should be granted or whether the sentence of death should be executed on the prisoners forthwith, to forestal the dangerous chances of delay. And the debate had been so much like fierce quarrel that the noise from the council chamber had reached the crowd outside. Only within the last hour had the question been decided: the Signoria had remained divided, four of them standing out resolutely for the Appeal in spite of the strong argument that if they did not give way their houses should be sacked, until Francesco Valori, in brief and furious speech, made the determination of his party more ominously distinct by declaring that if the Signoria would not defend the liberties of the Florentine people by executing those five perfidious citizens, there would not be wanting others who would take that cause in hand to the peril of all who opposed it. The Florentine Cato* triumphed. When the votes were counted again, the four obstinate white beans no longer appeared; the whole nine were of the fatal affirmative black, deciding the death of the five prisoners without delay—deciding also, only tacitly and with much more delay, the death of Francesco Valori.

And now, while the judicial Eight were gone to the Bargello to prepare for the execution, the five condemned men were being led barefoot and in irons through the midst of the council. It was their friends who had contrived this: would not Florentines be moved by the visible association of such cruel ignominy with two venerable men like Bernardo del Nero and Niccolò Rodolfi, who had taken their bias long before the new order of things had come to make Mediceanism retrograde—with two brilliant popular young men like Tornabuoni and Pucci, whose absence would be felt as a haunting vacancy wherever there was a meeting of chief Florentines? It was useless: such pity as could be awakened now was of that hopeless sort which leads not to rescue, but to the tardier action of revenge.

While this scene was passing upstairs Romola stood below against one of the massive pillars in the court of the palace, expecting the moment when her godfather would appear, on his way to execution. By the use of strong interest she had gained permission to visit him in the evening of this day, and remain with him until the result of the council should be determined. And now she was waiting with his confessor to follow the guard that would lead him to the Bargello. Her heart was bent on clinging to the presence of the childless old man to the last moment, as her father would have done, and she had overpowered all remonstrances. Giovan Battista Ridolfi, a disciple of Savonarola, who was going in bitterness to behold the death of his elder brother Niccolò, had promised that she should be guarded, and now stood by her side.

Tito, too, was in the palace; but Romola had not seen him. Since the evening of the seventeenth they had avoided each other, and Tito only knew by inference from the report of the Frate's neutrality that her pleading had failed. He was now surrounded with official and other personages, both Florentine and foreign, who had been awaiting the issue of the long-protracted council, maintaining, except when he was directly addressed, the subdued air and grave silence of a man whom actual events are placing in a painful state of strife between public and private feeling. When an allusion was made to his wife in relation to those events, he implied that, owing to the violent excitement of her mind, the mere fact of his continuing to hold office under a government concerned in her godfather's condemnation, roused in her a diseased hostility towards him; so that for her sake he felt it best not to approach her.

"Ah, the old Bardi blood!" said Cennini, with a shrug. "I shall not be surprised if this business shakes *her* loose from the Frate, as well as some others I could name."

"It is excusable in a woman, who is doubtless beautiful, since she is the wife of Messer Tito," said a young French envoy, smiling and bowing to Tito, "to think that her affections must overrule the good of the State, and that nobody is to be beheaded who is anybody's cousin; but such a view is not to be encouraged in the male population. It seems to me your Florentine polity is much weakened by it."

"That is true," said Niccolò Macchiavelli; "but where personal ties are strong, the hostilities they raise must be taken due account of. Many of these halfway severities are mere hot-headed blundering. The only safe blows to be inflicted on men and parties are the blows that are too heavy to be avenged."*

"Niccolò," said Cennini, "there is a clever wickedness in thy talk sometimes that makes me mistrust thy pleasant young face as if it were a mask of Satan."

"Not at all, my good Domenico," said Macchiavelli, smiling, and laying his hand on the elder's shoulder. "Satan was a blunderer, an introducer of *novità*, who made a stupendous failure. If he had succeeded, we should all have been worshipping him, and his portrait would have been more flattered."

"Well, well," said Cennini, "I say not thy doctrine is not too clever for Satan: I only say it is wicked enough for him."

"I tell you," said Macchiavelli, "my doctrine is the doctrine of all men who seek an end a little farther off than their own noses. Ask our Frate, our Prophet, how his universal renovation is to be brought about: he will tell you, first, by getting a free and pure government; and since it appears that cannot be done by making all Florentines love each other, it must be done by cutting off every head that happens to be obstinately in the way. Only if a man incurs odium by sanctioning a severity that is not thorough enough to be final, he commits a blunder. And something like that blunder, I suspect, the Frate has committed. It was an occasion on which he might have won some lustre by exerting himself to maintain the Appeal; instead of that, he has lost lustre, and has gained no strength."

Before any one else could speak, there came the expected announcement that the prisoners were about to leave the council chamber; and the majority of those who were present hurried towards the door, intent on securing the freest passage to the Bargello in the rear of the prisoners' guard; for the scene of the execution was one that drew alike those who were moved by the deepest passions and those who were moved by the coldest curiosity.

Tito was one of those who remained behind. He had a native repugnance to sights of death and pain, and five days ago whenever he had thought of this execution as a possibility he had hoped that it would not take place, and that the utmost sentence would be exile: his own safety demanded no more. But now he felt that it would be a welcome guarantee of his security when he had learned that Bernardo del Nero's head was off the shoulders. The new knowledge and new attitude towards him disclosed by Romola on the day of his return, had given him a new dread of the power she possessed to make his position insecure. If any act of hers only succeeded in making him an object of suspicion and odium, he foresaw not only frustration, but frustration under unpleasant circumstances. Her belief in Baldassarre had clearly determined her wavering feelings against further submission, and if her godfather lived she would win him to share her belief without much trouble. Romola seemed more than ever an unmanageable fact in his destiny. But if Bernardo del Nero were dead, the difficulties that would beset her in placing herself in opposition to her husband would probably be insurmountable to her shrinking pride. Therefore Tito had felt easier when he knew that the Eight had gone to the Bargello to order the instant erection of the scaffold. Four other men—his intimates and confederates—were to die, besides Bernardo del Nero. But a man's own safety is a god that sometimes makes very grim demands. Tito felt them to be grim: even in the pursuit of what was agreeable, this paradoxical life forced upon him the desire for what was disagreeable. But he had had other experience of this sort, and as he heard through the open doorway the shuffle of many feet and the clanking of metal on the stairs, he was able to answer the questions of the young French envoy without showing signs of any other feeling than that of sad resignation to State necessities.

Those sounds fell on Romola as if her power of hearing had been exalted along with every other sensibility of her nature.

She needed no arm to support her; she shed no tears. She felt that intensity of life which seems to transcend both grief and joy—in which the mind seems to itself akin to elder forces that wrought out existence before the birth of pleasure and pain. Since her godfather's fate had been decided, the previous struggle of feeling in her had given way to an identification of herself with him in these supreme moments: she was inwardly asserting for him that, if he suffered the punishment of treason, he did not deserve the name of traitor; he was the victim to a collision between two kinds of faithfulness. It was not given to him to die for the noblest cause, and yet he died because of his nobleness. He might have been a meaner man and found it easier not to incur this guilt. Romola was feeling the full force of that sympathy with the individual lot that is continually opposing itself to the formulæ by which actions and parties are judged. She was treading the way with her second father to the scaffold, and nerving herself to defy ignominy by the consciousness that it was not deserved.

The way was fenced in by three hundred armed men, who had been placed as a guard by the orders of Francesco Valori, for among the apparent contradictions that belonged to this event, not the least striking was the alleged alarm on the one hand at the popular rage against the conspirators, and the alleged alarm on the other lest there should be an attempt to rescue them in the midst of a hostile crowd. When they had arrived within the court of the Bargello, Romola was allowed to approach Bernardo with his confessor for a moment of farewell. Many eyes were bent on them even in that struggle of an agitated throng, as the aged man, forgetting that his hands were bound with irons, lifted them towards the golden head that was bent towards him, and then, checking that movement, leaned to kiss her. She seized the fettered hands that were hung down again, and kissed them as if they had been sacred things.

"My poor Romola," said Bernardo, in a low voice, "I have only to die, but thou hast to live—and I shall not be there to help thee."

"Yes," said Romola, hurriedly, "you *will* help me—always—because I shall remember you."

She was taken away and conducted up the flight of steps that led to the loggia surrounding the grand old court. She took her place there, determined to look till the moment when her godfather laid his head on the block. Now while the prisoners were allowed a brief interval with their confessors, the spectators were pressing into the court until the crowd became dense around the black scaffold, and the torches fixed in iron rings against the pillars threw a varying startling light at one moment on passionless stone carvings, at another on some pale face agitated with suppressed rage or suppressed grief—the face of one among the many near relatives of the condemned, who were presently to receive their dead and carry them home.

Romola's face looked like a marble image against the dark arch as she stood watching for the moment when her godfather would appear at the foot of the scaffold. He was to suffer first, and Battista Ridolfi, who was by her side, had promised to take her away through a door behind them when she should have seen the last look of the man who alone in all the world had shared her pitying love for her father. And still, in the background of her thought, there was the possibility striving to be a hope, that some rescue might yet come, something that would keep that scaffold unstained by blood.

For a long while there was constant movement, lights flickering, heads swaying to and fro, confused voices within the court, rushing waves of sound through the entrance from without. It seemed to Romola as if she were in the midst of a storm-troubled sea, caring nothing about the storm, caring only to hold out a signal till the eyes that looked for it could seek it no more.

Suddenly there was stillness, and the very tapers seemed to tremble into quiet. The executioner was ready on the scaffold, and Bernardo del Nero was seen ascending it with a slow firm step. Romola made no visible movement, uttered not even a suppressed sound: she stood more firmly, caring for *his* firmness. She saw him pause, saw the white head kept erect, while he said in a voice distinctly audible,

"It is but a short space of life that my fellow-citizens have taken from me."

She perceived that he was gazing slowly round him as he spoke. She felt that his eyes were resting on her, and that she was stretching out her arms towards him. Then she saw no more till—a long while after as it seemed—a voice said, "My daughter, all is peace now. I can conduct you to your house."

She uncovered her head and saw her godfather's confessor

standing by her, in a room where there were other grave men talking in subdued tones.

"I am ready," she said, starting up. "Let us lose no time."

She thought all clinging was at an end for her: all her strength now should be given to escape from a grasp under which she shuddered.

CHAPTER LXI.

Drifting Away

On the eighth day from that memorable night Romola was standing on the brink of the Mediterranean, watching the gentle summer pulse of the sea just above what was then the little fishing village of Viareggio.*

Again she had fled from Florence, and this time no arresting voice had called her back. Again she wore the grey religious dress; and this time, in her heart-sickness, she did not care that it was a disguise. A new rebellion had risen within her, a new despair. Why should she care about wearing one badge more than another, or about being called by her own name? She despaired of finding any consistent duty belonging to that name. What force was there to create for her that supremely hallowed motive which men call duty, but which can have no inward constraining existence save through some form of believing love? The bonds of all strong affection were snapped. In her marriage, the highest bond of all, she had ceased to see the mystic union which is its own guarantee of indissolubleness, had ceased even to see the obligation of a voluntary pledge: had she not proved that the things to which she had pledged herself were impossible? The impulse to set herself free had risen again with overmastering force; yet the freedom could only be an exchange of calamity. There is no compensation for the woman who feels that the chief relation of her life has been no more than a mistake. She has lost her crown. The deepest secret of human blessedness has half whispered itself to her, and then for ever passed her by.

And now Romola's best support under that supreme woman's sorrow had slipped away from her. The vision of any great purpose, any end of existence which could ennoble endurance and exalt the common deeds of a dusty life with divine ardours, was utterly eclipsed for her now by the sense of a confusion in human things which made all efforts a mere dragging at tangled threads; all fellowship, either for resistance or advocacy, mere unfairness and exclusiveness. What, after all, was the man who had represented for her the highest heroism: the heroism not of hard self-contained endurance, but of willing, self-offering love? What was the cause he was struggling for? Romola had lost her trust in Savonarola, had lost that fervour of admiration which had made her unmindful of his aberrations, and attentive only to the grand curve of his orbit. And now that her keen feeling for her godfather had thrown her into antagonism with the Frate, she saw all the repulsive and inconsistent details in his teaching with a painful lucidity which exaggerated their proportions. In the bitterness of her disappointment she said that his striving after the renovation of the Church and the world was a striving after a mere name which told no more than the title of a book: a name that had come to mean practically the measures that would strengthen his own position in Florence; nay, often questionable deeds and words, for the sake of saving his influence from suffering by his own errors. And that political reform which had once made a new interest in her life seemed now to reduce itself to narrow devices for the safety of Florence, in contemptible contradiction with the alternating professions of blind trust in the Divine care.

It was inevitable that she should judge the Frate unfairly on a question of individual suffering, at which *she* looked with the eyes of personal tenderness, and *he* with the eyes of theoretic conviction. In that declaration of his, that the Cause of his party was the Cause of God's kingdom, she heard only the ring of egoism. Perhaps such words have rarely been uttered without that meaner ring in them; yet they are the implicit formula of all energetic belief. And if such energetic belief, pursuing a grand and remote end, is often in danger of becoming a demon-worship, in which the votary lets his son and daughter pass through the fire with a readiness that hardly looks like sacrifice; tender fellow-feeling for the nearest has its danger too, and is apt to be timid and sceptical towards the larger aims without which life cannot rise into religion. In this way poor Romola was being blinded by her tears.

No one who has ever known what it is thus to lose faith in a fellow man whom he has profoundly loved and reverenced, will lightly say that the shock can leave the faith in the invisible goodness unshaken. With the sinking of high human trust, the dignity of life sinks too; we cease to believe in our own better self, since that also is part of the common nature which is degraded in our thought; and all the finer impulses of the soul are dulled. Romola felt even the springs of her once active pity drying up, and leaving her to barren egoistic complaining. Had not *she* had her sorrows too? And few had cared for her, while she had cared for many. She had done enough; she had striven after the impossible, and was weary of this stifling crowded life. She longed for that repose in mere sensation which she had sometimes dreamed of in the sultry afternoons of her early girlhood, when she had fancied herself floating naiad-like* in the waters.

The clear waves seemed to invite her: she wished she could lie down to sleep on them and pass from sleep into death. But Romola could not directly seek death; the fulness of young life in her forbade that. She could only wish that death would come.

At the spot where she had paused there was a deep bend in the shore and a small boat with a sail was moored there. In her longing to glide over the waters that were getting golden with the level sun-rays, she thought of a story which had been one of the things she had loved to dwell on in Boccaccio, when her father fell asleep and she glided from her stool to sit on the floor and read the *Decamerone*. It was the story of that fair Gostanza* who in her love-lornness desired to live no longer, but not having the courage to attack her young life, had put herself into a boat and pushed off to sea; then, lying down in the boat, had wrapt her mantle round her head, hoping to be wrecked, so that her fear would be helpless to flee from death. The memory had remained a mere thought in Romola's mind, without budding into any distinct wish; but now, as she paused again in her walking to and fro, she saw gliding black against the red gold another boat with one man in it, making towards the bend where the first and smaller boat was moored. Walking on again, she at length saw the man land, pull his boat ashore, and begin to unlade something from it. He was perhaps the owner of the smaller boat also: he would be going away soon, and her opportunity would be gone with him—her opportunity of buying that smaller boat. She had not yet admitted to herself that she meant to use it, but she felt a sudden eagerness to secure the possibility of using it, which disclosed the half-unconscious growth of a thought into a desire.

"Is that little boat yours also?" she said to the fisherman, who had looked up, a little startled by the tall grey figure, and had made a reverence to this holy sister wandering thus mysteriously in the evening solitude.

It *was* his boat; an old one, hardly sea-worthy, yet worth repairing to any man who would buy it. By the blessing of San Antonio, whose chapel was in the village yonder, his fishing had prospered, and he had now a better boat, which had once been Gianni's who died. But he had not yet sold the old one. Romola asked him how much it was worth, and then, while he was busy, thrust the price into a little satchel lying on the ground and containing the remnant of his dinner. After that, she watched him furling his sail and asked him how he should set it if he wanted to go out to sea, and then, pacing up and down again, waited to see him depart.

The imagination of herself gliding away in that boat on the darkening waters was growing more and more into a longing, as the thought of a cool brook in sultriness becomes a painful thirst. To be freed from the burthen of choice when all motive was bruised, to commit herself, sleeping, to destiny which would either bring death or else new necessities that might rouse a new life in her!—it was a thought that beckoned her the more because the soft evening air made her long to rest in the still solitude, instead of going back to the noise and heat of the village.

At last the slow fisherman had gathered up all his moveables and was walking away. Soon the gold was shrinking and getting duskier in sea and sky, and there was no living thing in sight, no sound but the lulling monotony of the lapping waves. In this sea there was no tide that would help to carry her away if she waited for its ebb; but Romola thought the breeze from the land was rising a little. She got into the boat, unfurled the sail, and fastened it as she had learned in that first brief lesson. She saw that it caught the light breeze, and this was all she cared for. Then she loosed the boat from its moorings, and tried to urge it with an oar, till she was far out from the land, till the sea was dark even to the west, and the stars were disclosing themselves like a palpitating life over the wide heavens. Resting at last, she threw back her cowl, and, taking off the kerchief underneath, which confined her hair, she doubled them both under her head for a pillow on one of the boat's ribs. The fair head was still very young and could bear a hard pillow.

And so she lay, with the soft night air breathing on her while she glided on the waters and watched the deepening quiet of the sky. She was alone now: she had freed herself from all claims, she had freed herself even from that burthen of choice which presses with heavier and heavier weight when claims have loosed their guiding hold.

Had she found anything like the dream of her girlhood? No. Memories hung upon her like the weight of broken wings that could never be lifted—memories of human sympathy which even in its pains leaves a thirst that the Great Mother has no milk to still. Romola felt orphaned in those wide spaces of sea and sky. She read no message of love for her in that far-off symbolic writing of the heavens, and with a great sob she wished that she might be gliding into death.

She drew the cowl over her head again and covered her face, choosing darkness rather than the light of the stars, which seemed to her like the hard light of eyes that looked at her without seeing her. Presently she felt that she was in the grave, but not resting there: she was touching the hands of the beloved dead beside her, and trying to wake them.

[*JULY 1863*]

CHAPTER LXII.

The Benediction

ABOUT ten o'clock on the morning of the twenty-seventh of February the current of passengers along the Florentine streets set decidedly towards San Marco. It was the last morning of the Carnival, and every one knew there was a second Bonfire of Vanities being prepared in front of the Old Palace; but at this hour it was evident that the centre of popular interest lay elsewhere.

The Piazza di San Marco was filled by a multitude who showed no other movement than that which proceeded from the pressure of new comers trying to force their way forward from all the openings; but the front ranks were already close-serried and resisted the pressure. Those ranks were ranged around a semicircular barrier in front of the church, and within this barrier were already assembling the Dominican Brethren of San Marco.

But the temporary wooden pulpit erected over the church door was still empty. It was presently to be entered by the man whom the Pope's command had banished from the pulpit of the Duomo, whom the other ecclesiastics of Florence had been forbidden to consort with, whom the citizens had been forbidden to hear on pain of excommunication. This man had said,* "A wicked, unbelieving Pope who has gained the pontifical chair by bribery is not Christ's Vicar. His curses are broken swords: he grasps a hilt without a blade. His commands are contrary to the Christian life: it is lawful to disobey them—nay, *it is not lawful to obey them.*" And the people still flocked to hear him as he preached in his own church of San Marco, though the Pope was hanging terrible threats over Florence if it did not renounce the pestilential schismatic and send him to Rome to be "converted"—still, as on this very morning, accepted the communion from his excommunicated hands. For how if this Frate had really more command over the divine lightnings than that official successor of Saint Peter? It was a momentous question, which for the mass of citizens could never be decided by the Frate's ultimate test, namely, what was and what was not accordant with the highest spiritual law. No: in such a case as this, if God had chosen the Frate as his Prophet to rebuke the High Priest who carried the mystic raiment unworthily, he would attest his choice by some unmistakable sign. As long as the belief in the Prophet carried no threat of outward calamity, but rather the confident hope of exceptional safety, no sign was needed: his preaching was a music to which the people felt themselves marching along the way they wished to go; but now that belief meant an immediate blow to their commerce, the shaking of their position among the Italian States, and an interdict on their city, there inevitably came the question, "What miracle showest thou?" Slowly at first, then faster and faster, that fatal demand had been swelling in Savonarola's ear, provoking a response, outwardly in the declaration that at the fitting time the miracle would come; inwardly in the faith—not unwavering, for what faith is so?—that if the need for miracle became urgent, the work he had before him was too great for the divine power to leave it halting. His faith wavered, but not his speech: it is the lot of every man who has to speak for the satisfaction of the crowd, that he must often speak in virtue of yesterday's faith, hoping it will come back to-morrow.

It was in preparation for a scene which was really a response to the popular impatience for some supernatural guarantee of the Prophet's mission that the wooden pulpit had been erected above the church door. But while the ordinary Frati in black mantles were entering and arranging themselves, the faces of the multitude were not yet eagerly directed towards the pulpit: it was felt that Savonarola would not appear just yet, and there was some interest in singling out the various monks, some of them belonging to high Florentine families, many of them having fathers, brothers, or cousins among the artisans and shopkeepers who made the majority of the crowd. It was not till the tale of monks was complete, not till they had fluttered their books and had begun to chant, that people said to each other, "Fra Girolamo must be coming now."

That expectation rather than any spell from the accustomed wail of psalmody was what made silence and expectation seem to spread like a paling solemn light over the multitude of upturned faces, all now directed towards the empty pulpit.

The next instant the pulpit was no longer empty. A figure covered from head to foot in black cowl and mantle had entered it, and was kneeling with bent head and with face turned away. It seemed a weary time to the eager people while the black figure knelt and the monks chanted. But the stillness was not broken, for the Frate's audiences with heaven were yet charged with electric awe for that mixed multitude, so that those who had already the will to stone him felt their arms unnerved.

At last there was a vibration among the multitude, each seeming to give his neighbour a momentary aspen-like touch, as when men who have been watching for something in the heavens see the expected presence silently disclosing itself. The Frate had risen, turned towards the people, and partly pushed back his cowl. The monotonous wail of psalmody had ceased, and to those who stood near the pulpit, it was as if the sounds which had just been filling their ears had suddenly merged themselves in the force of Savonarola's flashing glance, as he looked round him in the silence. Then he stretched out his hands, which, in their exquisite delicacy, seemed transfigured from an animal organ for grasping into vehicles of sensibility too acute to need any gross contact: hands that came like an appealing speech from that part of his soul which was masked by his strong passionate face, written on now with deeper lines about the mouth and brow than are made by forty-four years of ordinary life.

At the first stretching out of the hands some of the crowd in the front ranks fell on their knees, and here and there a devout disciple farther off; but the great majority stood firm, some resisting the impulse to kneel before this excommunicated man (might not a great judgment fall upon him even in this act of blessing?)—others jarred with scorn and hatred of the ambitious deceiver who was getting up this new comedy, before which, nevertheless, they felt themselves impotent, as before the triumph of a fashion.

But then came the voice, clear and low at first, uttering the words of absolution—"*Misereatur vestri*"—and more fell on their knees; and as it rose higher and yet clearer, the erect heads became fewer and fewer, till, at the words "*Benedicat vos omnipotens Deus*,"* it rose to a masculine cry, as if protesting its power to bless under the clutch of a demon that wanted to stifle it: it rang like a trumpet to the extremities of the Piazza, and under it every head was bowed.

After the utterance of that blessing Savonarola himself fell on his knees and hid his face in temporary exhaustion. Those great jets of emotion were a necessary part of his life: he himself had said to the people long ago, "Without preaching I cannot live."* But it was a life that shattered him.

In a few minutes more, some had risen to their feet, but a larger number remained kneeling, and all faces were intently watching him. He had taken into his hands a crystal vessel, containing the consecrated Host, and was about to address the people.

"You remember, my children, three days ago I besought you, when I should hold this Sacrament in my hand in the face of you all, to pray fervently to the Most High that if this work of mine does not come from Him, He will send a fire and consume me,* that I may vanish into the eternal darkness away from His light which I have hidden with my falsity. Again I beseech you to make that prayer, and to make it *now*."

It was a breathless moment: perhaps no man really prayed, if some in a spirit of devout obedience made the effort to pray. Every consciousness was chiefly possessed by the sense that Savonarola was praying, in a voice not loud but distinctly audible in the wide stillness.

"Lord, if I have not wrought in sincerity of soul, if my word cometh not from Thee, strike me in this moment with Thy thunder, and let the fires of Thy wrath enclose me."

He ceased to speak, and stood motionless, with the consecrated Mystery in his hand, with eyes uplifted and a quivering excitement in his whole aspect. Every one else was motionless and silent too, while the sunlight, which for the last quarter of an hour had here and there been piercing the greyness, made fitful streaks across the convent wall, causing some awe-stricken spectators to start timidly. But soon there was a wider parting, and with a gentle quickness, like a smile, a stream of brightness poured itself on the crystal vase, and then spread itself over Savonarola's face with mild glorification.

An instantaneous shout rang through the Piazza, "Behold the answer!"

The warm radiance thrilled through Savonarola's frame, and so did the shout. It was his last moment of troubled triumph, and in its rapturous confidence he felt carried to a grander scene yet to come, before an audience that would represent all

Christendom, in whose presence he should again be sealed as the messenger of the supreme righteousness, and feel himself full charged with divine strength. It was but a moment that expanded itself in that prevision. While the shout was still ringing in his ears he turned away within the church, feeling the strain too great for him to bear it longer.

But when the Frate had disappeared, and the sunlight seemed no longer to have anything special in its illumination, but was spreading itself impartially over all things clean and unclean, there began, along with the general movement of the crowd, a confusion of voices in which certain strong discords and varying scales of laughter made it evident that, in the previous silence and universal kneeling, hostility and scorn had only submitted unwillingly to a momentary spell.

"It seems to me the plaudits are giving way to criticism," said Tito, who had been watching the scene attentively from an upper loggia in one of the houses opposite the church. "Nevertheless it was a striking moment, eh, Messer Pietro? Fra Girolamo is a man to make one understand that there was a time when the monk's frock was a symbol of power over men's minds rather than over the keys of women's cupboards."

"Assuredly," said Pietro Cennini. "And until I have seen proof that Fra Girolamo has much less faith in God's judgments than the common run of men, instead of having considerably more, I shall not believe that he would brave heaven in this way if his soul were laden with a conscious lie."

CHAPTER LXIII.

Ripening Schemes

A MONTH after that Carnival, one morning near the end of March, Tito descended the marble steps of the Old Palace, bound on a pregnant errand to San Marco. For some reason, he did not choose to take the direct road, which was but a slightly bent line from the Old Palace; he chose rather to make a circuit by the Piazza di Santa Croce, where the people would be pouring out of the church after the early sermon.

It was in the grand church of Santa Croce that the daily

Lenten sermon had of late had the largest audience. For Savonarola's voice had ceased to be heard even in his own church of San Marco, a hostile Signoria having imposed silence on him in obedience to a new letter from the Pope, threatening the city with an immediate interdict if this "wretched worm" and "monstrous idol"* were not forbidden to preach, and sent to demand pardon at Rome. And next to hearing Fra Girolamo himself, the most exciting Lenten occupation was to hear him argued against and vilified. This excitement was to be had in Santa Croce, where the Franciscan appointed to preach the Quaresimal sermons had offered to clench his arguments by walking through the fire with Fra Girolamo. Had not that schismatical Dominican said, that his prophetic doctrine would be proved by a miracle at the fitting time? Here, then, was the fitting time. Let Savonarola walk through the fire, and if he came out unhurt, the divine origin of his doctrine would be demonstrated; but if the fire consumed him, his falsity would be manifest; and that he might have no excuse for evading the test, the Franciscan declared himself willing to be a victim to this high logic, and to be burned for the sake of securing the necessary minor premiss.

Savonarola, according to his habit, had taken no notice of these pulpit attacks. But it happened that the zealous preacher of Santa Croce was no other than the Fra Francesco di Puglia, who at Prato the year before had been engaged in a like challenge with Savonarola's fervent follower Fra Domenico, but had been called home by his superiors while the heat was simply oratorical. Honest Fra Domenico, then, who was preaching Lenten sermons to the women in the Via del Cocomero, no sooner heard of this new challenge, than he took up the gauntlet for his master and declared himself ready to walk through the fire with Fra Francesco. Already the people were beginning to take a strong interest in what seemed to them a short and easy method of argument (for those who were to be convinced), when Savonarola, keenly alive to the dangers that lay in the mere discussion of the case, commanded Fra Domenico to withdraw his acceptance of the challenge and secede from the affair. The Franciscan declared himself content: he had not directed his challenge to any subaltern, but to Fra Girolamo himself.

After that, the popular interest in the Lenten sermons had flagged a little. But this morning, when Tito entered the Piazza di Santa Croce, he found, as he expected, that the people were pouring from the church in large numbers. Instead of dispersing, many of them concentrated themselves towards a particular spot near the entrance of the Franciscan monastery, and Tito took the same direction, threading the crowd with a careless and leisurely air, but keeping careful watch on that monastic entrance, as if he expected some object of interest to issue from it.

It was no such expectation that occupied the crowd. The object they were caring about was already visible to them in the shape of a large placard, affixed by order of the Signoria, and covered with very legible official handwriting. But curiosity was somewhat baulked by the fact that the manuscript was chiefly in Latin; and though nearly every man knew beforehand approximately what the placard contained, he had an appetite for more exact knowledge, which gave him an irritating sense of his neighbour's ignorance in not being able to interpret the learned tongue. For that aural acquaintance with Latin phrases which the unlearned might pick up from pulpit quotations constantly interpreted by the preacher could help them little when they saw written Latin; the spelling even of the modern language being in an unorganized and scrambling condition for the mass of people who could read and write,* while the majority of those assembled nearest to the placard were not in the dangerous predicament of possessing that little knowledge.

"It's the Frate's doctrines that he's to prove by being burned," said that large public character Goro, who happened to be among the foremost gazers. "The Signoria has taken it in hand, and the writing is to let us know. It's what the Padre has been telling us about in his sermon."

"Nay, Goro," said a sleek shopkeeper, compassionately, "thou hast got thy legs into twisted hose there. The Frate has to prove his doctrines by *not* being burned: he is to walk through the fire, and come out on the other side sound and whole."

"Yes, yes," said a young sculptor, who wore his white-streaked cap and tunic with a jaunty air. "But Fra Girolamo objects to walking through the fire. Being sound and whole already, he sees no reason why he should walk through the fire to come out in just the same condition. He leaves such odds and ends of work to Fra Domenico."

"Then I say he flinches like a coward," said Goro, in a wheezy treble. "Suffocation! that was what he did at the

Carnival. He had us all in the piazza to see the lightning strike him, and nothing came of it."

"Stop that bleating," said a tall shoemaker, who had stepped in to hear part of the sermon, with bunches of slippers hanging over his shoulders. "It seems to me, friend, that you are about as wise as a calf with water on its brain. The Frate will flinch from nothing: he'll say nothing beforehand, perhaps, but when the moment comes he'll walk through the fire without asking any grey-frock to keep him company. But I would give a shoestring to know what this Latin all is."

"There's so much of it," said the shopkeeper, "else I'm pretty good at guessing. Is there no scholar to be seen?" he added, with a slight expression of disgust.

There was a general turning of heads, which caused the talkers to descry Tito approaching in their rear.

"Here is one," said the young sculptor, smiling and raising his cap.

"It is the secretary of the Ten: he is going to the convent, doubtless; make way for him," said the shopkeeper, also doffing, though that mark of respect was rarely shown by Florentines except to the highest officials. The exceptional reverence was really exacted by the splendour and grace of Tito's appearance, which made his black mantle, with its gold fibula,* look like a regal robe, and his ordinary black velvet cap like an entirely exceptional head-dress. The hardening of his cheeks and mouth, which was the chief change in his face since he came to Florence, seemed to a superficial glance only to give his beauty a more masculine character. He raised his own cap immediately and said,

"Thanks, my friend, I merely wished, as you did, to see what is at the foot of this placard—ah, it is as I expected. I had been informed that the government permits any one who will to subscribe his name as a candidate to enter the fire—which is an act of liberality worthy of the magnificent Signoria—reserving of course the right to make a selection. And doubtless many believers will be eager to subscribe their names. For what is it to enter the fire, to one whose faith is firm? A man is afraid of the fire, because he believes it will burn him; but if he believes the contrary?"—here Tito lifted his shoulders and made an oratorical pause— "for which reason I have never been one to disbelieve the Frate, when he has said that he would enter the fire to prove his doctrine. For in his place, if you believed the fire would not burn you, which of you, my friends, would not enter it as readily as you would walk along the dry bed of the Mugnone?"*

As Tito looked round him during this appeal, there was a change in some of his audience very much like the change in an eager dog when he is invited to smell something pungent. Since the question of burning was becoming practical, it was not every one who would rashly commit himself to any general view of the relation between faith and fire. The scene might have been too much for a gravity less under command than Tito's.

"Then, Messer Segretario," said the young sculptor, "it seems to me Fra Francesco is the greater hero, for he offers to enter the fire for the truth, though he is sure the fire will burn him."

"I do not deny it," said Tito, blandly. "But if it turns out that Fra Francesco is mistaken, he will have been burned for the wrong side, and the Church has never reckoned such victims to be martyrs. We must suspend our judgment until the trial has really taken place."

"It is true, Messer Segretario," said the shopkeeper, with subdued impatience. "But will you favour us by interpreting the Latin?"

"Assuredly," said Tito. "It does but express the conclusions or doctrines which the Frate specially teaches, and which the Trial by Fire is to prove true or false. They are doubtless familiar to you. First, that Florence—"

"Let us have the Latin bit by bit, and then tell us what it means," said the shoemaker, who had been a frequent hearer of Fra Girolamo.

"Willingly," said Tito, smiling. "You will then judge if I give you the right meaning."

"Yes, yes; that's fair," said Goro.

"*Ecclesia Dei indiget renovatione*, that is, the Church of God needs purifying or regenerating."

"It is true," said several voices at once.

"That means, the priests ought to lead better lives; there needs no miracle to prove that. That's what the Frate has always been saying," said the shoemaker.

"*Flagellabitur*," Tito went on. "That is, it will be scourged. *Renovabitur:* it will be purified. *Florentia quoque post flagella ren-*

ovabitur et prosperabitur: Florence also, after the scouring, shall be purified and shall prosper."

"That means, we are to get Pisa again," said the shopkeeper.

"And get the wool from England as we used to do,* I should hope," said an elderly man, in an old fashioned berretta, who had been silent till now. "There's been scourging enough with the sinking of the trade."

At this moment, a tall personage, surmounted by a red feather, issued from the door of the convent, and exchanged an indifferent glance with Tito; who, tossing his becchetto carelessly over his left shoulder, turned to his reading again, while the bystanders, with more timidity than respect, shrank to make a passage for Messer Dolfo Spini.

"*Infideles convertentur ad Christum,*" Tito went on. "That is, the Infidels shall be converted to Christ."

"Those are the Turks and the Moors. Well, I've nothing to say against that," said the shopkeeper, dispassionately.

"*Hæc autem omnia erunt temporibus nostris:* and all these things shall happen in our times."

"Why, what use would they be, else?" said Goro.

"*Excommunicatio nuper lata contra Reverendum Patrem nostrum Fratrem Hieronymum nulla est:* the excommunication lately pronounced against our Reverend Father, Fra Girolamo, is null. *Non observantes eam non peccant:* those who disregard it are not committing a sin."

"I shall know better what to say to that when we have had the Trial by Fire," said the shopkeeper.

"Which doubtless will clear up everything," said Tito. "That is all the Latin—all the conclusions that are to be proved true or false by the trial. The rest you can perceive is simply a proclamation of the Signoria in good Tuscan, calling on such as are eager to walk through the fire, to come to the Palazzo and subscribe their names. Can I serve you further? If not—"

Tito, as he turned away, raised his cap and bent slightly, with so easy an air that the movement seemed a natural prompting of deference.

He quickened his pace as he left the Piazza, and after two or three turnings he paused in a quiet street before a door at which he gave a light and peculiar knock. It was opened by a young woman whom he chucked under the chin as he asked her if the Padrone was within, and he then passed, without further ceremony, through another door which stood ajar on his right hand. It admitted him into a handsome but untidy room, where Dolfo Spini sat playing with a fine stag-hound which alternately snuffed at a basket of pups and licked his hands with that affectionate disregard of her master's morals sometimes held to be one of the most agreeable attributes of her sex. He just looked up as Tito entered, but continued his play, simply from that disposition to persistence in some irrelevant action, by which slow-witted sensual people seem to be continually counteracting their own purposes. Tito was patient.

"A handsome *bracca* that," he said quietly, standing with his thumbs in his belt. Presently he added, in that cool liquid tone which seemed mild, but compelled attention, "When you have finished such caresses as cannot possibly be deferred, my Dolfo, we will talk of business, if you please. My time, which I could wish to be eternity at your service, is not entirely my own this morning."

"Down, Mischief, down!" said Spini, with sudden roughness. "Malediction!" he added, still more gruffly, pushing the dog aside; then, starting from his seat, he stood close to Tito, and put a hand on his shoulder as he spoke.

"I hope your sharp wits see all the ins and outs of this business, my fine necromancer, for it seems to me no clearer than the bottom of a sack."

"What is your difficulty, my cavaliere?"

"These accursed Frati Minori at Santa Croce. They are drawing back now. Fra Francesco himself seems afraid of sticking to his challenge; talk of the Prophet being likely to use magic to get up a false miracle—thinks he himself might be dragged into the fire and burned, and the Prophet might come out whole by magic, and the Church be none the better. And then, after all our talking, there's not so much as a blessed lay brother who will offer himself to pair with that pious sheep Fra Domenico."

"It is the peculiar stupidity of the tonsured skull that prevents them from seeing of how little consequence it is whether they are burned or not," said Tito. "Have you sworn well to them that they shall be in no danger of entering the fire?"

"No," said Spini, looking puzzled; "because one of them will be obliged to go in with Fra Domenico, who thinks it a thousand years till the faggots are ready."

"Not at all. Fra Domenico himself is not likely to go in. I have told you before, my Dolfo, only your powerful mind is not to be impressed without more repetition than suffices for the vulgar—I have told you that now you have got the Signoria to take up this affair and prevent it from being hushed up by Fra Girolamo, nothing is necessary but that on a given day the fuel should be prepared in the Piazza, and the people got together with the expectation of seeing something prodigious. If, after that, the Prophet quits the Piazza without any appearance of a miracle on his side, he is ruined with the people: they will be ready to pelt him out of the city, the Signoria will find it easy to banish him from the territory, and his Holiness may do as he likes with him. Therefore, my Alcibiades,* swear to the Franciscans that their grey frocks shall not come within singeing distance of the fire."

Spini rubbed the back of his head with one hand, and tapped his sword against his leg with the other, to stimulate his power of seeing these intangible combinations.

"But," he said presently, looking up again, "unless we fall on him in the Piazza, when the people are in a rage, and make an end of him and his lies then and there, Valori and the Salviati and the Albizzi* will take up arms and raise a fight for him. I know that was talked of when there was the hubbub on Ascension Sunday. And the people may turn round again: there may be a story raised of the French King coming again, or some other cursed chance in the hypocrite's favour. The city will never be safe till he's out of it."

"He *will* be out of it before long, without your giving yourself any further trouble than this little comedy of the Trial by Fire. The wine and the sun will make vinegar without any shouting to help them, as your Florentine sages would say. You will have the satisfaction of delivering your city from an incubus* by an able strategem, instead of risking blunders with sword-thrusts."

"But suppose he *did* get magic and the devil to help him, and walk through the fire after all?" said Spini, with a grimace intended to hide a certain shyness in trenching on this speculative ground. "How do you know there's nothing in those things? Plenty of scholars believe in them, and this Frate is bad enough for anything."

"Oh, of course there are such things," said Tito, with a

shrug; "but I have particular reasons for knowing that the Frate is not on such terms with the devil as can give him any confidence in this affair. The only magic he relies on is his own ability."

"Ability!" said Spini. "Do you call it ability to be setting Florence at loggerheads with the Pope and all the powers of Italy—all to keep beckoning at the French King who never comes? You may call him able, but I call him a hypocrite, who wants to be master of everybody, and get himself made Pope."

"You judge with your usual penetration, my captain, but our opinions do not clash. The Frate, wanting to be master, and to carry out his projects against the Pope, requires the lever of a foreign power, and requires Florence as a fulcrum. I used to think him a narrow-minded bigot, but now I think him a shrewd ambitious man who knows what he is aiming at, and directs his aim as skilfully as you direct a ball when you are playing at *maglio*."*

"Yes, yes," said Spini, cordially, "I can aim a ball."

"It is true," said Tito, with bland gravity; "and I should not have troubled you with my trivial remark on the Frate's ability, but that you may see how this will heighten the credit of your success against him at Rome and at Milan, which is sure to serve you in good stead when the city comes to change its policy."

"Well, thou art a good little demon, and shalt have good pay," said Spini, patronizingly; whereupon he thought it only natural that the useful Greek adventurer should smile with gratification as he said,—

"Of course, any advantage to me depends entirely on your—"

"We shall have our supper at my palace to-night," interrupted Spini, with a significant nod and an affectionate pat on Tito's shoulder, "and I shall expound the new scheme to them all."

"Pardon, my magnificent patron," said Tito; "the scheme has been the same from the first—it has never varied except in your memory. Are you sure you have fast hold of it now?"

Spini rehearsed.

"One thing more," he said, as Tito was hastening away. "There is that sharp-nosed notary, Ser Ceccone; he has been handy of late. Tell me, you who can see a man wink when you're behind him, do you think I may go on making use of him?"

Tito dared not say "no." He knew his companion too well to

trust him with advice when all Spini's vanity and self-interest were not engaged in concealing the adviser.

"Doubtless," he answered, promptly. "I have nothing to say against Ceccone."

That suggestion of the notary's intimate access to Spini caused Tito a passing twinge, interrupting his amused satisfaction in the success with which he made a tool of the man who fancied himself a patron. For he had been rather afraid of Ser Ceccone. Tito's nature made him peculiarly alive to circumstances that might be turned to his disadvantage; his memory was much haunted by such possibilities, stimulating him to contrivances by which he might ward them off. And it was not likely that he should forget that October morning more than a year ago, when Romola had appeared suddenly before him at the door of Nello's shop, and had compelled him to declare his certainty that Fra Girolamo was not going outside the gates. The fact that Ser Ceccone had been a witness of that scene, together with Tito's perception that for some reason or other he was an object of dislike to the notary, had received a new importance from the recent turn of events. For after having been implicated in the Medicean plots, and having found it advisable in consequence to retire into the country for some time, Ser Ceccone had of late, since his reappearance in the city, attached himself to the Arrabbiati, and cultivated the patronage of Dolfo Spini. Now that captain of the Compagnacci was much given, when in the company of intimates, to confidential narrative about his own doings, and if Ser Ceccone's powers of combination were sharpened by enmity, he might gather some knowledge which he could use against Tito with very unpleasant results.

It would be pitiable to be baulked in well-conducted schemes by an insignificant notary; to be lamed by the sting of an insect whom he had offended unawares. "But," Tito said to himself, "the man's dislike to me can be nothing deeper than the ill-humour of a dinnerless dog; I shall conquer it if I can make him prosperous." And he had been very glad of an opportunity which had presented itself to providing the notary with a temporary post as an extra *cancelliere* or registering secretary under the Ten, believing that with this sop and the expectation of more, the waspish cur must be quite cured of the disposition to bite him.

But perfect scheming demands omniscience, and the notary's envy had been stimulated into hatred by causes of which Tito knew nothing. That evening when Tito, returning from his critical audience with the Special Council, had brushed by Ser Ceccone on the stairs, the notary, who had only just returned from Pistoja, and learned the arrest of the conspirators, was bound on an errand which bore a humble resemblance to Tito's. He also, without giving up a show of popular zeal, had been putting in the Medicean lottery. He also had been privy to the unexecuted plot, and was willing to tell what he knew, but knew much less to tell. He also would have been willing to go on treacherous errands, but a more eligible agent had forestalled him. His propositions were received coldly; the council, he was told, was already in possession of the needed information, and since he had been thus busy in sedition, it would be well for him to retire out of the way of mischief, otherwise the government might be obliged to take note of him. Ser Ceccone wanted no evidence to make him attribute his failure to Tito, and his spite was the more bitter because the nature of the case compelled him to hold his peace about it. Nor was this the whole of his grudge against the flourishing Melema. On issuing from his hiding-place, and attaching himself to the Arrabbiati, he had earned some pay as one of the spies who reported information on Florentine affairs to the Milanese court, but his pay had been small, notwithstanding his pains to write full letters, and he had lately been apprised that his news was seldom more than a late and imperfect edition of what was known already. Now Ser Ceccone had no positive knowledge that Tito had an underhand connection with the Arrabbiati and the Court of Milan, but he had a suspicion of which he chewed the cud with as strong a sense of flavour as if it had been a certainty.

This fine-grown vigorous hatred could swallow the feeble opiate of Tito's favours, and be as lively as ever after it. Why should Ser Ceccone like Melema any the better for doing him favours? Doubtless the suave secretary had his own ends to serve; and what right had he to the superior position which made it possible for him to show favour? But since he had tuned his voice to flattery, Ser Ceccone would pitch his in the same key, and it remained to be seen who would win at the game of outwitting.

To have a mind well oiled with that sort of argument which

prevents any claim from grasping it, seems eminently convenient sometimes; only the oil becomes objectionable when we find it anointing other minds on which we want to establish a hold.

Tito, however, not being quite omniscient, felt now no more than a passing twinge of uneasiness at the suggestion of Ser Ceccone's power to hurt him. It was only for a little while that he cared greatly about keeping clear of suspicions and hostility. He was now playing his final game in Florence, and the skill he was conscious of applying gave him a pleasure in it even apart from the expected winnings. The errand on which he was bent to San Marco was a stroke in which he felt so much confidence that he had already given notice to the Ten of his desire to resign his office at an indefinite period within the next month or two, and had obtained permission to make that resignation suddenly, if his affairs needed it, with the understanding that Niccolò Macchiavelli was to be his provisional substitute,* if not his successor. He was acting on hypothetic grounds, but this was the sort of action that had the keenest interest for his diplomatic mind. From a combination of general knowledge concerning Savonarola's purposes with diligently observed details he had framed a conjecture which he was about to verify by this visit to San Marco. If he proved to be right, his game would be won, and he might soon turn his back on Florence. He looked eagerly towards that consummation, for many circumstances besides his own weariness of the place told him that it was time for him to be gone.

CHAPTER LXIV.

The Prophet in his Cell

TITO'S visit to San Marco had been announced beforehand, and he was at once conducted by Fra Niccolò, Savonarola's secretary, up the spiral staircase into the long corridors lined with cells—corridors where Fra Angelico's frescoes, delicate as the rainbow on the melting cloud, startled the unaccustomed eye here and there, as if they had been sudden reflections cast from an etherial world, where the Madonna sat crowned in her radiant glory, and the divine Infant looked forth with perpetual promise.

It was an hour of relaxation in the monastery, and most of the cells were empty. The light through the narrow windows looked in on nothing but bare walls, and the hard pallet, and the crucifix. And even behind that door at the end of a long corridor, in the inner cell opening from an ante-chamber where the Prior usually sat at his desk or received private visitors, the high jet of light fell on only one object more that looked quite as common a monastic sight as the bare walls and hard pallet. It was but the back of a figure in the long white Dominican tunic and scapulary, kneeling with bowed head before a crucifix. It might have been any ordinary Fra Girolamo, who had nothing worse to confess than thinking of wrong things when he was singing *in coro*, or feeling a spiteful joy when Fra Benedetto* dropped the ink over his own miniatures in the breviary he was illuminating—who had no higher thought than that of climbing safely into paradise up the narrow ladder of prayer, fasting, and obedience. But under this particular white tunic there was a heart beating with a consciousness inconceivable to the average monk, and perhaps hard to be conceived by any man who has not arrived at self-knowledge through a tumultuous inner life: a consciousness in which irrevocable errors and lapses from veracity were so entwined with noble purposes and sincere beliefs, in which self-justifying expediency was so inwoven with the tissue of a great work which the whole being seemed as unable to abandon as the body was unable to abandon glowing and trembling before the objects of hope and fear, that it was perhaps impossible, whatever course might be adopted, for the conscience to find perfect repose.

Savonarola was not only in the attitude of prayer, there were Latin words of prayer on his lips; and yet he was not praying. He had entered his cell, had fallen on his knees, and burst into words of supplication, seeking in this way for an influx of calmness which would be a warrant to him that the resolutions urged on him by crowding thoughts and passions were not wresting him away from the divine support; but the previsions and impulses which had been at work within him for the last hour were too imperious; and while he pressed his hands against his face, and while his lips were uttering audibly, "*Cor mundum crea in me*,"* his mind was still filled with the images of the snare his enemies had prepared for him, was still busy with the arguments by which he could justify himself against their taunts and accusations.

And it was not only against his opponents that Savonarola had to defend himself. This morning he had had new proof that his friends and followers were as much inclined to urge on the Trial by Fire as his enemies; desiring and tacitly expecting that he himself would at last accept the challenge and evoke the long-expected miracle which was to dissipate doubt and triumph over malignity. Had he not said that God would declare Himself at the fitting time? And to the understanding of plain Florentines, eager to get party questions settled, it seemed that no time could be more fitting than this. Certainly, if Fra Domenico walked through the fire unhurt, *that* would be a miracle, and the faith and ardour of that good brother were felt to be a cheering augury; but Savonarola was acutely conscious that the secret longing of his followers to see him accept the challenge had not been dissipated by any reasons he had given for his refusal.

Yet it was impossible to him to satisfy them; and with bitter distress he saw now that it was impossible for him any longer to resist the prosecution of the trial in Fra Domenico's case. Not that Savonarola had uttered and written a falsity when he declared his belief in a future supernatural attestation of his work; but his mind was so constituted that while it was easy for him to believe in a miracle which, being distant and undefined, was screened behind the strong reasons he saw for its occurrence, and yet easier for him to have a belief in inward miracles such as his own prophetic inspiration and divinely wrought intuitions; it was at the same time insurmountably difficult to him to believe in the probability of a miracle which, like this of being carried unhurt through the fire, pressed in all its details on his imagination and involved a demand not only for belief but for exceptional action.

Savonarola's nature was one of those in which opposing tendencies co-exist in almost equal strength: the passionate sensibility which, impatient of definite thought, floods every idea with emotion and tends towards contemplative ecstasy, alternated in him with a keen perception of outward facts and a vigorous practical judgment of men and things. And in this case of the Trial by Fire, the latter characteristics were stimulated into unusual activity by an acute physical sensitiveness which gives overpowering force to the conception of pain and destruction as a necessary sequence of facts which have already been causes of pain in our experience. The promptitude with which men will consent to touch red-hot iron with a wet finger is not to be measured by their theoretic acceptance of the impossibility that the iron will burn them: practical belief depends on what is most strongly represented in the mind at a given moment. And with the Frate's constitution, when the Trial by Fire was urged on his imagination as an immediate demand, it was impossible for him to believe that he or any other man could walk through the flames unhurt—impossible for him to believe that even if he resolved to offer himself, he would not shrink at the last moment.

But the Florentines were not likely to make these fine distinctions. To the common run of mankind it has always seemed a proof of mental vigour to find moral questions easy, and judge conduct according to concise alternatives. And nothing was likely to seem plainer than that a man who at one time declared that God would not leave him without the guarantee of a miracle, and yet drew back when it was proposed to test his declaration, had said what he did not believe. Were not Fra Domenico and Fra Mariano, and scores of Piagnoni besides, ready to enter the fire? What was the cause of their superior courage, if it was not their superior faith? Savonarola could not have explained his conduct satisfactorily to his friends, even if he had been able to explain it thoroughly to himself. And he was not. Our naked feelings make haste to clothe themselves in propositions which lie at hand among our store of opinions, and to give a true account of what passes within us something else is necessary besides sincerity, even when sincerity is unmixed. In these very moments, when Savonarola was kneeling in audible prayer, he had ceased to hear the words on his lips. They were drowned by argumentative voices within him that shaped their reasons more and more for an outward audience.

"To appeal to heaven for a miracle bv a rash acceptance of a challenge, which is a mere snare prepared for me by ignoble foes, would be a tempting of God, and the appeal would not be responded to. Let the Pope's Legate come, let the ambassadors of all the great Powers come and promise that the calling of a General Council and the reform of the Church shall hang on the miracle, and I will enter the flames, trusting that God will not withhold His seal from that great work. Until then I reserve myself for higher duties which are directly laid upon me: it is not permitted to me to leap from the chariot for the sake of wrestling with every loud vaunter. But Fra Domenico's invincible zeal to enter into the trial may be the sign of a Divine vocation, may be a pledge that the miracle—"

But no! when Savonarola brought his mind close to the threatened scene in the Piazza, and imagined a human body entering the fire, his belief recoiled again. It was not an event that his imagination could simply see: he felt it with shuddering vibrations to the extremities of his sensitive fingers. The miracle could not be. Nay, the trial itself was not to happen: he was warranted in doing all in his power to hinder it. The fuel might be got ready in the Piazza, the people might be assembled, the preparatory formalities might be gone through: all this was perhaps inevitable now, and he could no longer resist it without bringing dishonour on—himself? Yes, and therefore on the cause of God. But it was not really intended that the Franciscan should enter the fire, and while *he* hung back there would be the means of preventing Fra Domenico's entrance. At the very worst, if Fra Domenico were compelled to enter, he should carry the consecrated Host with him, and with that Mystery in his hand, there might be a warrant for expecting that the ordinary effects of fire would be stayed; or, more probably, this demand would be resisted, and might thus be a final obstacle to the trial.

But these intentions could not be avowed: he must appear frankly to await the trial, and to trust in its issue. That dissidence between inward reality and outward seeming was not the Christian simplicity after which he had striven through years of his youth and prime, and which he had preached as a chief fruit of the divine life. In the stress and heat of the day, with cheeks burning, with shouts ringing in the ears, who is so blest as to remember the yearnings he had in the cool and silent morning and know that he has not belied them?

"O God, it is for the sake of the people—because they are blind—because their faith depends on me. If I put on sackcloth and cast myself among the ashes, who will take up the standard and head the battle? Have I not been led by a way which I knew not to the work that lies before me?"

The conflict was one that could not end, and in the effort at prayerful pleading the uneasy mind laved its smart continually in thoughts of the greatness of that task which there was no man else to fulfil if he forsook it. It was not a thing of every day that a man should be inspired with the vision and the daring that made a sacred rebel.

Even the words of prayer had died away. He continued to kneel, but his mind was filled with the images of results to be felt through all Europe; and the sense of immediate difficulties was being lost in the glow of that vision, when the knocking at the door announced the expected visit.

Savonarola drew on his mantle before he left his cell, as was his custom when he received visitors; and with that immediate response to any appeal from without which belongs to a power-loving nature accustomed to make its power felt by speech, he met Tito with a glance as self-possessed and strong as if he had risen from resolution instead of conflict.

Tito did not kneel, but simply made a greeting of profound deference, which Savonarola received quietly without any sacerdotal words, and then desiring him to be seated, said at once,

"Your business is something of weight, my son, that could not be conveyed through others?"

"Assuredly, father, else I should not have presumed to ask it. I will not trespass on your time by any proem. I gathered from a remark of Messer Domenico Mazzinghi that you might be glad to make use of the next special courier who is sent to France with despatches from the Ten. I must intreat you to pardon me if I have been too officious; but inasmuch as Messer Domenico is at this moment away at his villa, I wished to apprise you that a courier carrying important letters is about to depart for Lyons at daybreak to-morrow."

The muscles of Fra Girolamo's face were eminently under command, as must be the case with all men whose personality is powerful, and in deliberate speech he was habitually cautious, confiding his intentions to none without necessity. But under any strong mental stimulus, his eyes were liable to a dilation and added brilliancy that no strength of will could control. He looked steadily at Tito, and did not answer immediately, as if he had to consider whether the information he had just heard met any purpose of his.

Tito, whose glance never seemed observant, but rarely let anything escape it, had expected precisely that dilation and flash of Savonarola's eyes which he had noted on other occasions. He saw it, and then immediately busied himself in adjusting his gold fibula, which had got wrong; seeming to imply that he awaited an answer patiently.

The fact was that Savonarola had expected to receive this intimation from Domenico Mazzinghi, one of the Ten, an ardent disciple of his whom he had already employed to write a private letter to the Florentine ambassador in France, to prepare the way for a letter to the French King himself in Savonarola's handwriting, which now lay ready in the desk at his side. It was a letter calling on the King to assist in summoning a General Council, that might reform the abuses of the Church, and begin by deposing Pope Alexander, who was not rightfully Pope, being a vicious unbeliever, elected by corruption, and governing by simony.

This fact was not what Tito knew, but what his constructive talent, guided by subtle indications, had led him to guess and hope.

"It is true, my son," said Savonarola, quietly, "It is true I have letters which I would gladly send by safe conveyance under cover to our ambassador. Our community of San Marco, as you know, has affairs in France, being, amongst other things, responsible for a debt to that singularly wise and experienced Frenchman, Signor Philippe de Comines,* on the library of the Medici, which we purchased;* but I apprehend that Domenico Mazzinghi himself may return to the city before evening, and I should gain more time for preparation of the letters if I waited to deposit them in his hands."

"Assuredly, reverend father, that might be better on all grounds except one, namely, that if anything occurred to hinder Messer Domenico's return, the despatch of the letters would require either that I should come to San Marco again at a late hour, or that you should send them to me by your secretary; and I am aware that you wish to guard against the false inferences which might be drawn from a too frequent communication between yourself and any officer of the government." In throwing out this difficulty Tito felt that the more unwillingness the Frate showed to trust him, the more certain he would be of his conjecture.

Savonarola was silent; but while he kept his mouth firm, a slight glow rose in his face with the suppressed excitement that was growing within him. It would be a critical moment—that in which he delivered the letter out of his own hands.

"It is most probable that Messer Domenico will return in time," said Tito, affecting to consider the Frate's determination settled, and rising from his chair as he spoke. "With your permission, I will take my leave, father, not to trespass on your time when my errand is done; but as I may not be favoured with another interview, I venture to confide to you what is not yet known to others except to the magnificent Ten, that I contemplate resigning my secretaryship, and leaving Florence shortly. Am I presuming too much on your interest in stating what relates chiefly to myself?"

"Speak on, my son," said the Frate; "I desire to know your prospects."

"I find, then, that I have mistaken my real vocation in forsaking the career of pure letters, for which I was brought up. The politics of Florence, father, are worthy to occupy the greatest mind—to occupy yours—when a man is in a position to execute his own ideas; but when, like me, he can only hope to be the mere instrument of changing schemes, he requires to be animated by the minor attachments of a born Florentine: also, my wife's unhappy alienation from a Florentine residence since the painful events of August naturally influences me. I wish to join her."

Savonarola inclined his head approvingly.

"I intend, then, soon to leave Florence, to visit the chief courts of Europe, and to widen my acquaintance with the men of letters in the various universities. I shall go first to the court of Hungary, where scholars are eminently welcome;* and I shall probably start in a week or ten days. I have not concealed from you, father, that I am no religious enthusiast; I have not my wife's ardour; but religious enthusiasm, as I conceive, is not necessary in order to appreciate the grandeur and justice of your views concerning the government of nations and the Church. And if you condescend to intrust me with any commission that will further the relations you wish to establish, I shall feel honoured. May I now take my leave?"

"Stay, my son. When you depart from Florence I will send a letter to your wife, of whose spiritual welfare I would fain be assured, for she left me in anger. As for the letters to France, such as I have ready—"

Savonarola rose and turned to his desk as he spoke. He took from it a letter on which Tito could see, but not read, an address in the Frate's own minute and exquisite handwriting, still to be seen* covering the margins of his Bibles. He took a large sheet of paper, enclosed the letter, and sealed it.

"Pardon me, father," said Tito, before Savonarola had time to speak, "unless it were your decided wish, I would rather not incur the responsibility of carrying away the letter. Messer Domenico Mazzinghi will doubtless return, or, if not, Fra Niccolò can convey it to me at the second hour of the evening, when I shall place the other despatches in the courier's hands."

"At present, my son," said the Frate, waiving that point, "I wish you to address this packet to our ambassador in your own handwriting, which is preferable to my secretary's."

Tito sat down to write the address while the Frate stood by him with folded arms, the glow mounting in his cheek, and his lip at last quivering. Tito rose and was about to move away, when Savonarola said abruptly,

"Take it, my son. There is no use in waiting. It does not please me that Fra Niccolò should have needless errands to the Palazzo."

As Tito took the letter, Savonarola stood in suppressed excitement that forbade further speech. There seems to be a subtle emanation from passionate natures like his, making their mental states tell immediately on others; when they are absent-minded and inwardly excited there is silence in the air.

Tito made a deep reverence and went out with the letter under his mantle.

The letter was duly delivered to the courier and carried out of Florence. But before that happened another messenger, privately employed by Tito, had conveyed information in cipher, which was carried by a series of relays to armed agents of Ludovico Sforza, Duke of Milan, on the watch for the very purpose of intercepting despatches on the borders of the Milanese territory.

CHAPTER LXV.

The Trial by Fire

LITTLE more than a week after, on the seventh of April, the great Piazza della Signoria presented a stranger spectacle even than the famous Bonfire of Vanities. And a greater multitude had assembled to see it than had ever before tried to find place for themselves in the wide Piazza, even on the day of San Giovanni.

It was near midday, and since the early morning there had been a gradual swarming of the people at every coign of vantage or disadvantage* offered by the façades and roofs of the houses, and such spaces of the pavement as were free to the public. Men were seated on iron rods that made a sharp angle with the rising wall, were clutching slim pillars with arms and legs, were astride on the necks of the rough statuary that here and there surmounted the entrances of the grander houses, were finding a palm's breadth of seat on a bit of architrave, and a footing on the rough projections of the rustic stone-work,* while they clutched the strong iron rings or staples driven into the walls beside them.

For they were come to see a miracle: cramped limbs and abraded flesh seemed slight inconveniences with that prospect close at hand. It is the ordinary lot of mankind to hear of miracles, and more or less believe in them; but now the Florentines were going to see one. At the very least they would see half a miracle; for if the monk did not come whole out of the fire, they would see him enter it, and infer that he was burned in the middle.

There could be no reasonable doubt, it seemed, that the fire would be kindled, and that the monks would enter it. For there, before their eyes, was the long platform, eight feet broad, and twenty yards long, with a grove of fuel heaped up terribly, great branches of dry oak as a foundation, crackling thorns above, and well-anointed tow and rags, known to make fine flames in Florentine illuminations. The platform began at the corner of the marble terrace in front of the Old Palace, close to Marzocco, the stone lion, whose aged visage looked frowningly along the grove of fuel that stretched obliquely across the Piazza.

Besides that, there were three large bodies of armed men: five hundred hired soldiers of the Signoria stationed before the Palace; five hundred Compagnacci under Dolfo Spini, far off on the opposite side of the Piazza; and three hundred armed citizens of another sort, under Marco Salviati, Savonarola's friend, in front of Orgagna's Loggia, where the Franciscans and Dominicans were to be placed with their champions.

Here had been much expense of money and labour, and high dignities were concerned. There could be no reasonable doubt that something great was about to happen; and it would certainly be a great thing if the two monks were simply burned, for in that case too God would have spoken, and said very plainly that Fra Girolamo was not his prophet.

And there was not much longer to wait, for it was now near midday. Half the monks were already at their post, and that half of the Loggia that lies towards the Palace was already filled with grey mantles; but the other half, divided off by boards, was still empty of everything except a small altar. The Franciscans had entered and taken their places in silence. But now, at the other side of the Piazza, was heard loud chanting from two hundred voices, and there was general satisfaction, if not in the chanting, at least in the evidence that the Dominicans were come. That loud chanting repetition of the prayer, "Let God arise, and let his enemies be scattered,"* was unpleasantly suggestive to some impartial ears of a desire to vaunt confidence and excite dismay; and so was the flame-coloured velvet cope in which Fra Domenico was arrayed as he headed the procession, cross in hand, his simple mind really exalted with faith, and with the genuine intention to enter the flames for the glory of God and Fra Girolamo. Behind him came Savonarola in the white vestment of a priest, carrying in his hands a vessel containing the consecrated Host. He too was chanting loudly, he too looked firm and confident, and as all eyes were turned eagerly on him either in anxiety, curiosity or malignity, from the moment when he entered the Piazza till he mounted the steps of the loggia and deposited the Sacrament on the altar, there was an intensifying flash and energy in his countenance responding to that scrutiny.

We are so made, almost all of us, that the false seeming which we have thought of with painful shrinking when beforehand in our solitude it has urged itself on us as a necessity, will possess our muscles and move our lips as if nothing but that were easy when once we have come under the stimulus of expectant eyes and ears. And the strength of that stimulus to Savonarola can hardly be measured by the experience of ordinary lives. Perhaps no man has ever had a mighty influence over his fellows without having the innate need to dominate, and this need usually becomes the more imperious in proportion as the complications of life make self inseparable from a purpose which is not selfish. In this way it came to pass that on the day of the Trial by Fire, the doubleness which is the pressing temptation in every public career, whether of priest, orator, or statesman, was more strongly defined in Savonarola's consciousness as the acting of a part, than at any other period in his life. He was struggling not against impending martyrdom, but against impending ruin.

Therefore he looked and acted as if he were thoroughly confident, when all the while foreboding was pressing with leaden weight on his heart, not only because of the probable issues of this trial, but because of another event already past—an event which was spreading a sunny satisfaction through the mind of a man who was looking down at the passion-worn prophet from a window of the Old Palace. It was a common turning-point towards which those widely sundered lives had been converging, that two evenings ago the news had come that the Florentine courier of the Ten had been arrested and robbed of all his despatches, so that Savonarola's letter was already in the hands of the Duke of Milan, and would soon be in the hands of the Pope, not only heightening rage but giving a new justification to extreme measures. There was no malignity in Tito Melema's satisfaction: it was the mild self-gratulation of a man who has won a game that has employed hypothetic skill, not a game that has stirred the muscles and heated the blood. Of course that bundle of desires and contrivances called human nature, when moulded into the form of a plain-featured Frate Predicatore, more or less of an impostor, could not be a pathetic object to a brilliant-minded scholar who understood everything. Yet this tonsured Girolamo with the high nose and large under lip was an immensely clever Frate, mixing with his absurd superstitions or fabrications very remarkable notions about government: no babbler, but a man who could keep his secrets. Tito had no more spite against him than against Saint Dominic. On the contrary, Fra Girolamo's existence had been highly convenient to Tito Melema, furnishing him with that round of the ladder from which he was about to leap on to a new and smooth footing very much to his heart's content. And everything now was in forward preparation for that leap: let one more sun rise and set, and Tito hoped to quit Florence. He had been so industrious that he felt at full leisure to amuse himself with today's comedy, which the thick-headed Dolfo Spini could never have brought about but for him.

Not yet did the loud chanting cease, but rather swelled to a deafening roar, being taken up in all parts of the Piazza by the Piagnoni, who carried their little red crosses as a badge and, most of them, chanted the prayer for the confusion of God's enemies with the expectation of an answer to be given through the medium of a more signal personage than Fra Domenico. This good Frate in his flame-coloured cope was now kneeling before the little altar on which the Sacrament was deposited, awaiting his summons.

On the Franciscan side of the Loggia there was no chanting and no flame-colour: only silence and greyness. But there was this counterbalancing difference, that the Franciscans had two champions: a certain Fra Giuliano was to pair with Fra Domenico, while the original champion, Fra Francesco, confined his challenge to Savonarola.

"Surely," thought the men perched uneasily on rods and pillars, "all must be ready now. This chanting might stop, and we should see better when the Frati are moving towards the platform."

But the Frati were not to be seen moving yet. Pale Franciscan faces were looking uneasily over the boarding at that flame-coloured cope. It had an evil look and might be enchanted, so that a false miracle would be wrought by magic. Your monk may come whole out of the fire, and yet it may be the work of the devil.

And now there was passing to and fro between the Loggia and the marble terrace of the Palazzo, and the roar of chanting became a little quieter, for every one at a distance was beginning to watch more eagerly. But it soon appeared that the new movement was not a beginning, but an obstacle to beginning. The dignified Florentines appointed to preside over this affair as moderators on each side, went in and out of the Palace, and there was much debate with the Franciscans. But at last it was clear that Fra Domenico, conspicuous in his flame-colour, was being fetched towards the Palace. Probably the fire had already been kindled—it was difficult to see at a distance—and the miracle was going to begin.

Not at all. The flame-coloured cope disappeared within the Palace; then another Dominican was fetched away; and for a long while everything went on as before—the tiresome chanting, which was not miraculous, and Fra Girolamo in his white vestment standing just in the same place. But at last something happened: Fra Domenico was seen coming out of the Palace again, and returning to his brethren. He had changed all his clothes with a brother monk, but he was guarded on each flank by a Franciscan, lest coming into the vicinity of Savonarola he should be enchanted again.

"Ah, then," thought the distant spectators, a little less conscious of cramped limbs and hunger, "Fra Domenico is not going to enter the fire. It is Fra Girolamo who offers himself after all. We shall see him move presently, and if he comes out of the flames we shall have a fine view of him!"

But Fra Girolamo did not move, except with the ordinary action accompanying speech. The speech was bold and firm, perhaps somewhat ironically remonstrant, like that of Elijah to the priests of Baal,* demanding the cessation of these trivial delays. But speech is the most irritating kind of argument for those who are out of hearing, cramped in the limbs, and empty in the stomach. And what need was there for speech? If the miracle did not begin, it could be no one's fault but Fra Girolamo's, who might put an end to all difficulties by offering himself now the fire was ready, as he had been forward enough to do when there was no fuel in sight.

More movement to and fro, more discussion; and the afternoon seemed to be slipping away all the faster because the clouds had gathered, and changed the light on everything, and sent a chill through the spectators, hungry in mind and body.

Now it was the crucifix which Fra Domenico wanted to carry into the fire and must not be allowed to profane in that manner. After some little resistance Savonarola gave way to this objection, and thus had the advantage of making one more concession; but he immediately placed in Fra Domenico's hands the vessel containing the consecrated Host. The idea that the presence of the sacred mystery might in the worst extremity avert the ordinary effects of fire hovered in his mind as a possibility; but the issue on which he counted was of a more positive kind. In taking up the Host he said quietly, as if he were only doing what had been presupposed from the first,

"Since they are not willing that you should enter with the crucifix, my Brother, enter simply with the Sacrament."

New horror in the Franciscans; new firmness in Savonarola. "It was impious presumption to carry the Sacrament into the fire: if it were burned the scandal would be great in the minds of the weak and ignorant." "Not at all: even if it were burned, the Accidents only would be consumed, the Substance* would remain." Here was a question that might be argued till set of sun and remain as elastic as ever; and no one could propose settling it by proceeding to the trial, since it was essentially a preliminary question. It was only necessary that both sides should remain firm—that the Franciscans should persist in not permitting the Host to be carried into the fire, and that Fra Domenico should persist in refusing to enter without it.

Meanwhile the clouds were getting darker, the air chiller. Even the chanting was missed now it had given way to inaudible argument; and the confused sounds of talk from all points of the Piazza, showing that expectation was everywhere relaxing, contributed to the irritating presentiment that nothing decisive would be done. Here and there a dropping shout was heard; then, more frequent shouts in a rising scale of scorn.

"Light the fire and drive them in!" "Let us have a smell of roast—we want our dinner!" "Come, Prophet, let us know whether anything is to happen before the twenty-four hours are over!" "Yes, yes, what's your last vision?" "Oh, he's got a dozen in his inside; they're the small change for a miracle!" "Olà, Frate, where are you? Never mind wasting the fuel!"

Still the same movement to and fro between the Loggia and the Palace; still the same debate, slow and unintelligible to the multitude as the colloquies of insects that touch antennæ to no other apparent effect than that of going and coming. But an interpretation was not long wanting to unheard debates in which Fra Girolamo was constantly a speaker: it was he who was hindering the trial; everybody was appealing to him now, and he was hanging back.

Soon the shouts ceased to be distinguishable, and were lost in an uproar not simply of voices, but of clashing metal and trampling feet. The suggestions of the irritated people had stimulated old impulses in Dolfo Spini and his band of Compagnacci; it seemed an opportunity not to be lost for putting an end to Florentine difficulties by getting possession of the arch-hypocrite's person; and there was a vigorous rush of the armed men towards the Loggia, thrusting the people aside, or driving them on to the file of soldiery stationed in front of the Palace. At this movement, everything was suspended both with monks and embarrassed magistrates except the palpitating watch to see what would come of the struggle.

But the Loggia was well guarded by the band under the brave Salviati; the soldiers of the Signoria assisted in the repulse; and the trampling and rushing were all backward again towards the Tetto de' Pisani,* when the blackness of the heavens seemed to intensify in this moment of utter confusion, and the rain, which had already been felt in scattered drops, began to fall with rapidly growing violence, wetting the fuel, and running in streams off the platform, wetting the weary, hungry people to the skin, and driving every man's disgust and rage inwards to ferment there in the damp darkness.

Everybody knew now that the Trial by Fire was not to happen. The Signoria was doubtless glad of the rain, as an obvious reason, better than any pretext, for declaring that both parties might go home. It was the issue which Savonarola had expected and desired; yet it would be an ill description of what he felt to say that he was glad. As that rain fell, and plashed on the edge of the Loggia, and sent spray over the altar and all garments and faces, the Frate knew that the demand for him or his to enter the fire was at an end. But he knew too, with a certainty as irresistible as the damp chill that had taken possession of his frame, that the design of his enemies was fulfilled, and that his honour was not saved. He knew that he should have to make his way to San Marco again through the enraged crowd, and that the hearts of many friends who would once have defended him with their lives would now be turned against him.

When the rain had ceased he asked for a guard from the Signoria, and it was given him. Had he said that he was willing to die for the work of his life? Yes, and he had not spoken falsely. But to die in dishonour—held up to scorn as a hypocrite and a false prophet? "O God! *that* is not martyrdom! It is the blotting out of a life that has been a protest against wrong. Let me die because of the worth that is in me, not because of my weakness."

The rain had ceased, and the light from the breaking clouds fell on Savonarola as he left the Loggia in the midst of his guard, walking, as he had come, with the Sacrament in his hand. But there seemed no glory in the light that fell on him now, no smile of heaven: it was only that light which shines on, patiently and impartially, justifying or condemning by simply showing all things in the slow history of their ripening. He heard no blessing, no tones of pity, but only taunts and threats. He knew this was but a foretaste of coming bitterness; yet his courage mounted under all moral attack, and he showed no sign of dismay.

"Well parried, Frate!" said Tito, as Savonarola descended the steps of the Loggia. "But I fear your career at Florence is ended. What say you, my Niccolò?"

"It is a pity his falsehoods were not all of a wise sort," said Macchiavelli, with a melancholy shrug. "With the times so much on his side as they are about Church affairs, he might have done something great."

CHAPTER LXVI.

A Masque of the Furies

THE next day was Palm Sunday, or Olive Sunday, as it was chiefly called in the olive-growing Valdarno; and the morning sun shone with a more delicious clearness for the yesterday's rain. Once more Savonarola mounted the pulpit in San Marco, and saw a flock around him whose faith in him was still unshaken; and this morning in calm and sad sincerity he declared himself ready to die: in the front of all visions he saw his own doom. Once more he uttered the benediction, and saw the faces of men and women lifted towards him in venerating love. Then he descended the steps of the pulpit and turned away from that sight for ever.

For before the sun had set Florence was in an uproar. The passions which had been roused the day before had been smouldering through that quiet morning, and had now burst out again with a fury not unassisted by design, and not without official connivance. The uproar had begun at the Duomo in an attempt of some Compagnacci to hinder the evening sermon, which the Piagnoni had assembled to hear. But no sooner had men's blood mounted and the disturbance had become an affray than the cry arose, "To San Marco! the fire to San Marco!"

And long before the daylight had died, both the church and convent were being besieged by an enraged and continually increasing multitude. Not without resistance. For the monks, long conscious of growing hostility without, had arms within their walls, and some of them fought as vigorously in their long white tunics as if they had been Knights Templars.* Even the command of Savonarola could not prevail against the impulse to self-defence in arms that were still muscular under the Dominican serge. There were laymen too who had not chosen to depart, and some of them fought fiercely: there was firing from the high altar close by the great Crucifix, there was pouring of stones and hot embers from the convent roof, there was close fighting with swords in the cloisters. Notwithstanding the force of the assailants the attack lasted till deep night.

The demonstrations of the Government had all been against the convent; early in the attack guards had been sent for, not to disperse the assailants, but to command all within the convent to lay down their arms, all laymen to depart from it, and Savonarola himself to quit the Florentine territory within twelve hours. Had Savonarola quitted the convent then, he could hardly have escaped being torn to pieces; he was willing to go, but his friends hindered him. It was felt to be a great risk even for some laymen of high name to depart by the garden wall, but among those who had chosen to do so was Francesco Valori, who hoped to raise rescue from without.

And now when it was deep night—when the struggle could hardly have lasted much longer, and the Compagnacci might soon have carried their swords into the library, where Savonarola was praying with the Brethren who had either not taken up arms or had laid them down at his command—there came a second body of guards, commissioned by the Signoria to demand the persons of Fra Girolamo and his two coadjutors, Fra Domenico and Fra Salvestro.

Loud was the roar of triumphant hate when the light of lanterns showed the Frate issuing from the door of the convent with a guard who promised him no other safety than that of the prison. The struggle now was, who should get first in the stream that rushed up the narrow street to see the Prophet carried back in ignominy to the Piazza where he had braved it yesterday—who should be in the best place for reaching his ear with insult, nay, if possible, for smiting him and kicking him. This was not difficult for some of the armed Compagnacci who were not prevented from mixing themselves with the guards.

When Savonarola felt himself dragged and pushed along in the midst of that hooting multitude; when lanterns were lifted to show him deriding faces; when he felt himself spat upon, smitten and kicked with grossest words of insult, it seemed to him that the worst bitterness of life was past. If men judged him guilty, and were bent on having his blood, it was only death that awaited him. But the worst drop of bitterness can never be wrung on to our lips from without: the lowest depth of resignation is not to be found in martyrdom; it is only to be found when we have covered our heads in silence and felt, "I am not worthy to be a martyr: the Truth shall prosper, but not by me."

But that brief imperfect triumph of insulting the Frate, who had soon disappeared under the doorway of the Old Palace, was only like the taste of blood to the tiger. Were there not the houses of the hypocrite's friends to be sacked? Already one half of the armed multitude, too much in the rear to share greatly in the siege of the convent, had been employed in the more profitable work of attacking rich houses, not with planless desire for plunder, but with that discriminating selection of such as belonged to chief Piagnoni, which showed that the riot was under guidance, and that the rabble with clubs and staves was well officered by sword-girt Compagnacci. Was there not—next criminal after the Frate—the ambitious Francesco Valori, suspected of wanting with the Frate's help to make himself a Doge or Gonfaloniere for life? And the grey-haired man who, eight months ago, had lifted his arm and his voice in such ferocious demand for justice on five of his fellow-citizens, only escaped from San Marco to experience what *others* called justice—to see his house surrounded by an angry, greedy multitude, to see his wife shot dead with an arrow, and to be himself murdered, as he was on his way to answer a summons to the Palazzo, by the swords of men named Ridolfi and Tornabuoni.*

In this way that Masque of the Furies, called Riot, was played on in Florence through the hours of night and early morning.

But the chief director was not visible: he had his reasons for issuing his orders from a private retreat, being of rather too high a name to let his red feather be seen waving amongst all the work that was to be done before the dawn. The retreat was the same house and the same room in a quiet street between Santa Croce and San Marco, where we have seen Tito paying a secret visit to Dolfo Spini. Here the Captain of the Compagnacci sat through his memorable night, receiving visitors who came and went, and went and came, some of them in the guise of armed Compagnacci, others dressed obscurely and without visible arms. There was abundant wine on the table, with drinking cups for chance comers; and though Spini was on his guard against excessive drinking, he took enough from time to time to heighten the excitement produced by the news that was being brought to him continually.

Among the obscurely dressed visitors Ser Ceccone was one of the most frequent, and as the hours advanced towards the morning twilight he had remained as Spini's constant companion, together with Francesco Cei, who was then in rather careless hiding in Florence, expecting to have his banishment revoked when the Frate's fall had been accomplished.

The tapers had burnt themselves into low shapeless masses, and holes in the shutters were just marked by a sombre outward light, when Spini, who had started from his seat and walked up and down with an angry flush on his face at some talk that had been going forward with those two unmilitary companions, burst out—

"The devil spit him! he shall pay for it, though. Ha, ha! the claws shall be down on him when he little thinks of them. So *he* was to be the great man after all! He's been pretending to chuck everything towards my cap, as if I were a blind beggarman, and all the while he's been winking and filling his own scarsella. I should like to hang skins about him and set my hounds on him! And he's got that fine ruby of mine, I was fool enough to give him yesterday. Malediction! And he was laughing at me in his sleeve two years ago, and spoiling the best plan that ever was laid. I was a fool for trusting myself with a rascal who had long-twisted contrivances that nobody could see to the end of but himself."

"A Greek, too, who dropped into Florence with gems packed about him," said Francesco Cei, who had a slight smile of amusement on his face at Spini's fuming. "You did *not* choose your confidant very wisely, my Dolfo."

"He's a cursed deal cleverer than you, Francesco, and handsomer too," said Spini, turning on his associate with a general desire to worry anything that presented itself.

"I humbly conceive," said Ser Ceccone, "that Messer Francesco's poetic genius will outweigh— "

"Yes, yes, rub your hands! I hate that notary's trick of yours," interrupted Spini, whose patronage consisted largely in this sort of frankness. "But there comes Taddeo, or somebody: now's the time! What news, eh?" he went on, as two Compagnacci entered with heated looks.

"Bad!" said one. "The people had made up their minds they were going to have the sacking of Soderini's house, and now they've been baulked we shall have them turning on us, if we don't take care. I suspect there are some Mediceans buzzing about among them, and we may see them attacking your palace over the bridge before long, unless we can find a bait for them another way."

"I have it," said Spini, and seizing Taddeo by the belt he drew him aside to give him directions, while the other went on telling Cei how the Signoria had interfered about Soderini's house.

"Ecco!" exclaimed Spini, presently, giving Taddeo a slight push towards the door. "Go and make quick work."

CHAPTER LXVII.

Waiting by the River

About the time when the two Compagnacci went on their errand, there was another man who, on the opposite side of the Arno, was also going out into the chill grey twilight. His errand, apparently, could have no relation to theirs; he was making his way to the brink of the river at a spot which, though within the city walls, was overlooked by no dwellings, and which only seemed the more shrouded and lonely for the warehouses and granaries which at some little distance backward turned their shoulders to the river. There was a sloping width of long grass and rushes made all the more dank by broad gutters which here and there emptied themselves into the Arno.

The gutters and the loneliness were the attraction that drew this man to come and sit down among the grass, and bend over the waters that ran swiftly in the channelled slope at his side. For he had once had a large piece of bread brought to him by one of those friendly runlets, and more than once a raw carrot and apple parings. It was worth while to wait for such chances in a place where there was no one to see, and often in his restless wakefulness he came to watch here before daybreak; it might save him for one day the need of that silent begging which consisted in sitting on a church step or by the wayside out beyond the Porta San Frediano.

For Baldassarre hated begging so much that he would have perhaps chosen to die rather than make even that silent appeal, but for one reason that made him desire to live. It was no longer a hope; it was only that possibility which clings to every idea that has taken complete possession of the mind: the sort of possibility that makes a woman watch on a headland for the ship which held something dear, though all her neighbours are certain that the ship was a wreck long years ago. After he had come out of the convent hospital, where the monks of San Miniato* had taken care of him as long as he was helpless; after he had watched in vain for the Wife who was to help him, and had begun to think that she was dead of the pestilence that seemed to fill all the space since the night he parted from her, he had been unable to conceive any way in which sacred vengeance could satisfy itself through his arm. His knife was gone, and he was too feeble in body to win another by work, too feeble in mind, even if he had had the knife, to contrive that it should serve its one purpose. He was a shattered, bewildered, lonely old man; yet he desired to live: he waited for something of which he had no distinct vision—something dim, formless—that startled him, and made strong pulsations within him, like that unknown thing which we look for when we start from sleep, though no voice or touch has waked us. Baldassarre desired to live; and therefore he crept out in the grey light and seated himself in the long grass and watched the waters that had a faint promise in them.

Meanwhile the Compagnacci were busy at their work. The formidable bands of armed men, left to do their will, with very little interference from an embarrassed if not conniving Signoria, had parted into two masses, but both were soon making their way by different roads towards the Arno. The smaller mass was making for the Ponte Rubaconte, the larger for the Ponte Vecchio; but in both the same words had passed from mouth to mouth as a signal, and almost every man of the multitude knew that he was going to the Via de' Bardi to sack a house there. If he knew no other reason, could he demand a better?

The armed Compagnacci knew something more, for a brief word of command flies quickly, and the leaders of the two streams of rabble had a perfect understanding that they would meet before a certain house a little towards the eastern end of the Via de' Bardi, where the master would probably be in bed, and be surprised in his morning sleep.

But the master of that house was neither sleeping nor in bed: he had not been in bed that night. For Tito's anxiety to quit Florence had been stimulated by the events of the previous day: investigations would follow in which appeals might be made to him delaying his departure; and in all delay he had an uneasy sense that there was danger. Falsehood had prospered and waxed strong; but it had nourished the twin life, Fear. He no longer wore his armour, he was no longer afraid of Baldassarre; but from the corpse of that dead fear a spirit had risen—the undying *habit* of fear. He felt he should not be safe till he was out of this fierce, turbid Florence; and now he was ready to go. Maso was to deliver up his house to the new tenant; his horses and mules were awaiting him in San Gallo; Tessa and the children had been lodged for the night in the Borgo outside the gate, and would be dressed in readiness to mount the mules and join him. He descended the stone steps into the courtyard, he passed through the great doorway, not the same Tito, but nearly as brilliant as on the day when he had first entered that house and made the mistake of falling in love with Romola. The mistake was remedied now, the old life was cast off, and was soon to be far behind him.

He turned with rapid steps towards the Piazza dei Mozzi, intending to pass over the Ponte Rubaconte; but as he went along certain sounds came upon his ears that made him turn round and walk yet more quickly in the opposite direction. Was the mob coming into Oltrarno? It was a vexation, for he would have preferred the more private road. He must now go by the Ponte Vecchio; and unpleasant sensations made him draw his mantle close round him, and walk at his utmost speed. There was no one to see him in that grey twilight. But before he reached the end of the Via de' Bardi like sounds fell on his ear again, and this time they were much louder and nearer. Could he have been deceived before? The mob must be coming over the Ponte Vecchio. Again he turned, from an impulse of fear that was stronger than reflection; but it was only to be assured that the mob was actually entering the street from the opposite end. He chose not to go back to his house: after all, they would not attack *him*. Still, he had some valuables about him; and all things except reason and order are possible with a mob. But necessity does the work of courage. He went on towards the Ponte Vecchio, the rush and the trampling and the confused voices getting so loud before him that he had ceased to hear them behind.

For he had reached the end of the street, and the crowd pouring from the bridge met him at the turning and hemmed in his way. He had not time to wonder at a sudden shout before he felt himself surrounded, not, in the first instance, by an unarmed rabble, but by armed Compagnacci; the next sensation was that his cap fell off, and that he was thrust violently forward amongst the rabble, along the narrow passage of the bridge. Then he distinguished the shouts, "Piagnone! Medicean! Piagnone! Throw him over the bridge!"

His mantle was being torn off him with strong pulls that would have throttled him if the fibula had not given way. Then his scarsella was snatched at; but all the while he was being hustled and dragged; and the snatch failed—his scarsella still hung at his side. Shouting, yelling, half-motiveless execration rang stunningly in his ears, spreading even amongst those who had not yet seen him, and only knew there was a man to be reviled. Tito's horrible dread was that he should be struck down or trampled on before he reached the open arches that surmount the centre of the bridge. There was one hope for him—that they might throw him over before they had wounded him or beaten the strength out of him; and his whole soul was absorbed in that one hope and its obverse terror.

Yes—they *were* at the arches. In that moment Tito, with

bloodless face and eyes dilated, had one of the self-preserving inspirations that come in extremity. With a sudden desperate effort he mastered the clasp of his belt, and flung belt and scarsella forward towards a yard of clear space against the parapet, crying in a ringing voice,—

"There are diamonds! there is gold!"

In the instant the hold on him was relaxed, and there was a rush towards the scarsella. He threw himself on the parapet with a desperate leap, and the next moment plunged—plunged with a great plash into the dark river far below.

It was his chance of salvation; and it was a good chance. His life had been saved once before by his fine swimming, and as he rose to the surface again after his long dive he had a sense of deliverance. He struck out with all the energy of his strong prime, and the current helped him. If he could only swim beyond the Ponte alla Carraja he might land in a remote part of the city, and even yet reach San Gallo. Life was still before him. And the idiot mob, shouting and bellowing on the bridge there, would think he was drowned.

They did think so. Peering over the parapet along the dark stream, they could not see afar off the moving blackness of the floating hair, and the velvet tunic-sleeves.

It was only from the other way that a pale olive face could be seen looking white above the dark water: a face not easy even for the indifferent to forget, with its square forehead, the long low arch of the eyebrows, and the long lustrous agate-like eyes. Onward the face went on the dark current, with inflated quivering nostrils, with the blue veins distended on the temples. One bridge was passed—the bridge of Santa Trinità. Should he risk landing now rather than trust to his strength? No. He heard, or fancied he heard, yells and cries pursuing him. Terror pressed him most from the side of his fellow-men: he was less afraid of indefinite chances, and he swam on, panting and straining. He was not so fresh as he would have been if he had passed the night in sleep.

Yet the next bridge—the last bridge*—was passed. He was conscious of it; but in that tumult of his blood, he could only feel vaguely that he was safe and might land. But where? The current was having its way with him: he hardly knew where he was: exhaustion was bringing on the dreamy state that precedes unconsciousness.

But now there were eyes that discerned him—aged eyes, strong for the distance. Baldassarre, looking up blankly from the search in the runlet that brought him nothing, had seen a white object coming along the broader stream. Could that be any fortunate chance for *him*? He looked and looked till the object gathered form: then he leaned forward with a start as he sat among the rank green stems, and his eyes seemed to be filled with a new light. Yet he only watched—motionless. Something was being brought to him.

The next instant a man's body was cast violently on the grass two yards from him, and he started forward like a panther, clutching the velvet tunic as he fell forward on the body and flashed a look in the man's face.

Dead—was he dead? The eyes were rigid. But no, it could not be—Justice had brought him. Men looked dead sometimes, and yet the life came back into them. Baldassarre did not feel feeble in that moment. He knew just what he could do. He got his large fingers within the neck of the tunic and held them there, kneeling on one knee beside the body and watching the face. There was a fierce hope in his heart, but it was mixed with trembling. In his eyes there was only fierceness: all the slow-burning remnant of life within him seemed to have leaped into flame.

Rigid—rigid still. Those eyes with the half-fallen lids were locked against vengeance. *Could* it be that he was dead? There was nothing to measure the time: it seemed long enough for hope to freeze into despair.

Surely at last the eyelids were quivering: the eyes were no longer rigid. There was a vibrating light in them: they opened wide.

"Ah, yes! You see me—you know me!"

Tito knew him; but he did not know whether it was life or death that had brought him into the presence of his injured father. It might be death—and death might mean this chill gloom with the face of the hideous past hanging over him for ever.

But now Baldassarre's only dread was, lest the young limbs should escape him. He pressed his knuckles against the round throat and knelt upon the chest with all the force of his aged frame. Let death come now!

Again he kept his watch on the face. And when the eyes were rigid again, he dared not trust them. He would never loose his hold till some one came and found them. Justice would send some witness, and then, he, Baldassarre, would declare that he had killed this traitor, to whom he had once been a father. They would perhaps believe him now, and then he would be content with the struggle of justice on earth—then he would desire to die with his hold on this body, and follow the traitor to hell that he might clutch him there.

And so he knelt, and so he pressed his knuckles against the round throat, without trusting to the seeming death, till the light got strong and he could kneel no longer. Then he sat on the body, still clutching the neck of the tunic. But the hours went on, and no witness came. No eyes descried afar off the two human bodies among the tall grass by the river side. Florence was busy with greater affairs, and the preparation of a deeper tragedy.

Not long after those two bodies were lying in the grass, Savonarola was being tortured and crying out in his agony, "I will confess!"

It was not until the sun was westward that a waggon drawn by a mild grey ox came to the edge of the grassy margin, and as the man who led it was leaning to gather up the round stones that lay heaped in readiness to be carried away, he detected some startling object in the grass. The aged man had fallen forward, and his dead clutch was on the garment of the other. It was not possible to separate them: nay, it was better to put them into the waggon and carry them as they were into the great Piazza, that notice might be given to the Eight.

As the waggon entered the frequented streets there was a growing crowd escorting it with its strange burthen. No one knew the bodies for a long while, for the aged face had fallen forward, half hiding the younger. But before they had been moved out of sight, they had been recognized.

"I know that old man," Piero di Cosimo had testified. "I painted his likeness once. He is the prisoner who clutched Melema on the steps of the Duomo."

"He is perhaps the same old man who appeared at supper in my gardens," said Bernardo Rucellai, one of the Eight. "I had forgotten him. I thought he had died in prison. But there is no knowing the truth now."

Who shall put his finger on the work of Justice, and say, "It is there"? Justice is like the Kingdom of God—it is not without us as a fact, it is within us as a great yearning.

[*AUGUST 1863*]

CHAPTER LXVIII.

Romola's Waking

ROMOLA in her boat passed from dreaming into long deep sleep, and then again from deep sleep into busy dreaming, till at last she felt herself stretching out her arms in the court of the Bargello, where the flickering flames of the tapers seemed to get stronger and stronger till the dark scene was blotted out with light. Her eyes opened, and she saw it was the light of morning. Her boat was lying still in a little creek: on her right hand lay the speckless sapphire-blue of the Mediterranean; on her left one of those scenes which were and still are repeated again and again, like a sweet rhythm, on the shores of that loveliest sea.

In a deep curve of the mountains lay a breadth of green land, curtained by gentle tree-shadowed slopes leaning towards the rocky heights. Up these slopes might be seen here and there, gleaming between the tree-tops, a pathway leading to a little irregular mass of building that seemed to have clambered in a hasty way up the mountain side, and taken a difficult stand there for the sake of showing the tall belfry as a sight of beauty to the scattered and clustered houses of the village below. The rays of the newly-risen sun fell obliquely on the westward horn of this crescent-shaped nook: all else lay in dewy shadow. No sound came across the stillness; the very waters seemed to have curved themselves there for rest.

The delicious sun-rays fell on Romola and thrilled her gently like a caress. She lay motionless, hardly watching the scene; rather, feeling simply the presence of peace and beauty. While we are still in our youth there can always come, in our early waking, moments when mere passive existence is itself a Lethe,* when the exquisiteness of subtle indefinite sensation creates a bliss which is without memory and without desire. As the soft warmth penetrated Romola's young limbs, as her eyes rested on this sequestered luxuriance, it seemed that the agitating past had glided away like that dark scene in the Bargello, and that the afternoon dreams of her girlhood had really come back to her.

For a minute or two the oblivion was untroubled; she did not even think that she could rest here for ever, she only felt that she rested. Then she became distinctly conscious that she was lying in the boat which had been bearing her over the waters all through the night. Instead of bringing her to death, it had been the gently lulling cradle of a new life. And in spite of her evening despair she was glad that the morning had come to her again—glad to think that she was resting in the familiar sunlight rather than in the unknown regions of death. *Could* she not rest here? No sound from Florence would reach her. Already oblivion was troubled; from behind the golden haze were piercing domes and towers and walls, parted by a river and enclosed by the green hills.

She rose from her reclining posture and sat up in the boat, willing, if she could, to resist the rush of thoughts that urged themselves along with the conjecture how far the boat had carried her. Why need she mind? This was a sheltered nook where there were simple villagers who would not harm her. For a little while, at least, she might rest and resolve on nothing. Presently she would go and get some bread and milk, and then she would nestle in the green quiet, and feel that there was a pause in her life. She turned to watch the crescent-shaped valley, that she might get back the soothing sense of peace and beauty which she had felt in her first waking.

She had not been in this attitude of contemplation more than a few minutes when across the stillness there came a piercing cry; not a brief cry, but continuous and more and more intense. Romola felt sure it was the cry of a little child in distress that no one came to help. She started up and put one foot on the side of the boat ready to leap on to the beach; but she paused there and listened—the mother of the child must be near, the cry must soon cease. But it went on, and drew Romola so irresistibly, seeming the more piteous to her for the sense of peace which had preceded it, that she jumped on to the beach and walked many paces before she knew what direction she would take. The cry, she thought, came from some rough garden growth many yards on her right hand, where she saw a half-ruined hovel. She climbed over a low broken stone fence, and made her way across patches of weedy green crops and ripe but neglected corn. The cry grew plainer, and, convinced that she was right she hastened towards the hovel; but even in that hurried walk she felt an oppressive change in the air as she left the sea behind. Was there some taint lurking amongst the green luxuriance that had seemed such an inviting shelter from the heat of the coming day? She could see the opening into the hovel now, and the cry was darting through her like a pain. The next moment her foot was within the doorway, but the sight she beheld in the sombre light arrested her with a shock of awe and horror. On the straw, with which the floor was scattered, lay three dead bodies, one of a tall man, one of a girl about eight years old, and one of a young woman whose long black hair was being clutched and pulled by a living child—the child that was sending forth the piercing cry. Romola's experience in the haunts of death and disease made thought and action prompt: she lifted the little living child, and in trying to soothe it on her bosom, still bent to look at the bodies and see if they were really dead. The strongly marked type of race in their features and their peculiar garb made her conjecture that they were Spanish or Portuguese Jews, who had perhaps been put ashore and abandoned there by rapacious sailors, to whom their property remained as a prey. Such things were happening continually to Jews compelled to abandon their homes by the Inquisition:* the cruelty of greed thrust them from the sea, and the cruelty of superstition thrust them back to it.

"But surely," thought Romola, "I shall find some woman in the village whose mother's heart will not let her refuse to tend this helpless child—if the real mother is indeed dead."

This doubt remained, because while the man and girl looked emaciated and also showed signs of having been long dead, the woman seemed to have been hardier, and had not quite lost the robustness of her form. Romola, kneeling, was about to lay her hand on the heart; but as she lifted the piece of yellow woollen drapery that lay across the bosom, she saw the purple spots which marked the familiar pestilence. Then it struck her that if the villagers knew of this, she might have more difficulty than she had expected in getting help from them; they would perhaps shrink from her with that child in her arms. But she had money to offer them, and they would not refuse to give her some goats' milk in exchange for it.

She set out at once towards the village, her mind filled now with the effort to soothe the little dark creature, and with wondering how she should win some woman to be good to it. She could not help hoping a little in a certain awe she had observed herself to inspire, when she appeared, unknown and unexpected, in her religious dress. As she passed across a breadth of cultivated ground, she noticed, with wonder, that little patches of corn mingled with the other crops had been left to over-ripeness untouched by the sickle, and that golden apples and dark figs lay rotting on the weedy earth. There were grassy spaces within sight, but no cow, or sheep, or goat. The stillness began to have something fearful in it to Romola; she hurried along towards the thickest cluster of houses, where there would be the most life to appeal to on behalf of the helpless life she carried in her arms. But she had picked up two figs, and bit little pieces from the sweet pulp to still the child with.

She entered between two lines of dwellings. It was time that villagers should have been stirring long ago, but not a soul was in sight. The air was becoming more and more oppressive, laden, it seemed, with some horrible impurity. There was a door open; she looked in, and saw grim emptiness. Another open door; and through that she saw a man lying dead with all his garments on, his head lying athwart a spade handle, and an earthenware cruise in his hand, as if he had fallen suddenly.

Romola felt horror taking possession of her. Was she in a village of the unburied dead? She wanted to listen if there were any faint sound, but the child cried out afresh when she ceased to feed it, and the cry filled her ears. At last she saw a figure crawling slowly out of a house, and soon sinking back in a sitting posture against the wall. She hastened towards the figure; it was a young woman in fevered anguish, and she, too, held a pitcher in her hand. As Romola approached her she did not start; the one need was too absorbing for any other idea to impress itself on her.

"Water! get me water!" she said, with a moaning utterance.

Romola stooped to take the pitcher, and said gently in her ear, "You shall have water; can you point towards the well?"

The hand was lifted towards the more distant end of the little street, and Romola set off at once with as much speed as she could use under the difficulty of carrying the pitcher as well as feeding the child. But the little one was getting more content as the morsels of sweet pulp were repeated, and ceased to distress her with its cry, so that she could give a less distracted attention to the objects around her.

The well lay twenty yards or more beyond the end of the street, and as Romola was approaching it her eyes were directed to the opposite green slope immediately below the church. High up, on a patch of grass between the trees, she had descried a cow and a couple of goats, and she tried to trace a line of path that would lead her close to that cheering sight, when once she had done her errand to the well. Occupied in this way, she was not aware that she was very near the well, and that some one approaching it on the other side had fixed a pair of astonished eyes upon her.

Romola certainly presented a sight which, at that moment and in that place, could hardly have been seen without some pausing and palpitation. With her gaze fixed intently on the distant slope, the long lines of her thick grey garment giving a gliding character to her rapid walk, her hair rolling backward and illuminated on the left side by the sun-rays, the little olive baby on her right arm now looking out with jet-black eyes, she might well startle that youth of fifteen, accustomed to swing the censer in the presence of a Madonna less fair and marvellous than this.

"She carries a pitcher in her hand—to fetch water for the sick. It is the Holy Mother, come to take care of the people who have the pestilence."

It was a sight of awe: she would, perhaps, be angry with those who fetched water for themselves only. The youth flung down his vessel in terror, and Romola, aware now of some one near her, saw the black and white figure fly as if for dear life towards the slope she had just been contemplating. But remembering the parched sufferer, she half filled her pitcher quickly and hastened back.

Entering the house to look for a small cup, she saw salt meat and meal: there were not signs of want in the dwelling. With nimble movements she seated baby on the ground, and lifted a cup of water to the sufferer, who drank eagerly and then closed her eyes and leaned her head backward, seeming to give herself up to the sense of relief. Presently she opened her eyes, and, looking at Romola, said launguidly,—

"Who are you?"

"I came over the sea," said Romola. "I only came this morning. Are all the people dead in these houses?"

"I think they are all ill now—all that are not dead. My father and my sister lie dead upstairs, and there is no one to bury them: and soon I shall die."

"Not so, I hope," said Romola. "I am come to take care of you. I am used to the pestilence; I am not afraid. But there must be some left who are not ill. I saw a youth running towards the mountain when I went to the well."

"I cannot tell. When the pestilence came, a great many people went away, and drove off the cows and goats. Give me more water!"

Romola, suspecting that if she followed the direction of the youth's flight, she should find some men and women who were still healthy and able, determined to seek them out at once, that she might at least win them to take care of the child, and leave her free to come back and see how many living needed help, and how many dead needed burial. She trusted to her powers of persuasion to conquer the aid of the timorous, when once she knew what was to be done.

Promising the sick woman to come back to her, she lifted the dark bantling again, and set off towards the slope. She felt no burthen of choice on her now, no longing for death. She was thinking how she would go to the other sufferers, as she had gone to that fevered woman.

But, with the child on her arm, it was not so easy to her as usual to walk up a slope, and it seemed a long while before the winding path took her near the cow and the goats. She was beginning herself to feel faint from heat, hunger, and thirst, and as she reached a double turning, she paused to consider whether she would not wait near the cow, which some one was likely to come and milk soon, rather than toil up to the church before she had taken any rest. Raising her eyes to measure the steep distance, she saw peeping between the boughs, not more than five yards off, a broad round face, watching her attentively, and lower down the black skirt of a priest's garment, and a hand grasping a bucket. She stood mutely observing, and the face, too, remained motionless. Romola had often witnessed the overpowering force of dread in cases of pestilence, and she was cautious.

Raising her voice in a tone of gentle pleading, she said, "I came over the sea. I am hungry, and so is the child. Will you not give us some milk?"

Romola had divined part of the truth, but she had not divined that preoccupation of the priest's mind which charged her words with a strange significance. Only a little while ago, the young acolyte had brought word to the Padre that he had seen the Holy Mother with the Babe, fetching water for the sick: she was as tall as the cypresses, and had a light about her head, and she looked up at the church. The *pievano** had not listened with entire belief: he had been more than fifty years in the world without having any vision of the Madonna, and he thought the boy might have misinterpreted the unexpected appearance of a villager. But he had been made uneasy, and before venturing to come down and milk his cow, he had repeated many Aves. The pievano's conscience tormented him a little: he trembled at the pestilence, but he also trembled at the thought of the mild-faced Mother, conscious that that Invisible Mercy might demand something more of him than prayers and "Hails." In this state of mind—unable to banish the image the boy had raised of the Mother with the glory about her tending the sick—the pievano had come down to milk his cow, and had suddenly caught sight of Romola pausing at the parted way. Her pleading words, with their strange refinement of tone and accent, instead of being explanatory, had a preternatural sound for him. Yet he did not quite believe he saw the Holy Mother: he was in a state of alarmed hesitation. If anything miraculous were happening, he felt there was no strong presumption that the miracle would be in his favour. He dared not run away; he dared not advance.

"Come down," said Romola, after a pause. "Do not fear. Fear rather to deny food to the hungry when they ask you."

A moment after, the boughs were parted, and the complete figure of a thick-set priest with a broad, harmless face, his black frock much worn and soiled, stood, bucket in hand, looking at her timidly, and still keeping aloof as he took the path towards the cow in silence.

Romola followed him and watched him without speaking again, as he seated himself against the tethered cow, and, when he had nervously drawn some milk, gave it to her in a brass cup he carried with him in the bucket. As Romola put the cup to the lips of the eager child, and afterwards drank some milk herself, the Padre observed her from his wooden stool with a timidity that changed its character a little. He recognized the Hebrew baby, he was certain that he had a substantial woman before him; but there was still something strange and unaccountable in Romola's presence in this spot, and the Padre had a presentiment that things were going to change with him. Moreover, that Hebrew baby was terribly associated with the dread of pestilence.

Nevertheless, when Romola smiled at the little one sucking its own milky lips, and stretched out the brass cup again, saying, "Give us more, good father," he obeyed less nervously than before.

Romola, on her side, was not unobservant; and when the second supply of milk had been drunk, she looked down at the round-headed man, and said with mild decision,

"And now tell me, father, how this pestilence came, and why you let your people die without the Sacraments, and lie unburied. For I am come over the sea to help those who are left alive—and you, too, will help them now."

He told her the story of the pestilence: and while he was telling it, the youth, who had fled before, had come peeping and advancing gradually, till at last he stood and watched the scene from behind a neighbouring bush.

Three families of Jews, twenty souls in all, had been put ashore many weeks ago, some of them already ill of the pestilence. The villagers, said the priest, had of course refused to give shelter to the miscreants, otherwise than in a distant hovel, and under heaps of straw. But when the strangers had died of the plague, and some of the people had thrown the bodies into the sea, the sea had brought them back again in a great storm, and everybody was smitten with terror. A grave was dug, and the bodies were buried; but then the pestilence attacked the Christians, and the greater number of the villagers went away over the mountain, driving away their few cattle, and carrying provisions. The priest had not fled; he had stayed and prayed for the people, and he had prevailed on the youth Jacopo to stay with him; but he confessed that a mortal terror of the plague had taken hold of him, and he had not dared to go down into the valley.

"You will fear no longer, father," said Romola, in a tone of encouraging authority; "you will come down with me, and we will see who is living, and we will look for the dead to bury them. I have walked about for months where the pestilence was, and see, I am strong. Jacopo will come with us," she added, motioning to the peeping lad, who came slowly from behind his defensive bush, as if invisible threads were dragging him.

"Come, Jacopo," said Romola again, smiling at him, "you will carry the child for me. See! your arms are strong, and I am tired."

That was a dreadful proposal to Jacopo, and to the priest also; but they were both under a peculiar influence forcing them to obey. The suspicion that Romola was a supernatural form was dissipated, but their minds were filled instead with the more effective sense that she was a human being whom God had sent over the sea to command them.

"Now we will carry down the milk," said Romola, "and see if any one wants it."

So they went all together down the slope, and that morning the sufferers saw help come to them in their despair. There were hardly more than a score alive in the whole valley; but all of these were comforted, most were saved, and the dead were buried.

In this way, days, weeks, and months passed with Romola, till the men were digging and sowing again, till the women smiled at her as they carried their great vases on their heads to the well, and the Hebrew baby was a tottering tumbling Christian, Benedetto by name, having been baptized in the church on the mountain side. But by that time she herself was suffering from the fatigue and languor that must come after a continuous strain on mind and body. She had taken for her dwelling one of the houses abandoned by their owners, standing a little aloof from the village street, and here on a thick heap of clean straw—a delicious bed for those who do not dream of down—she felt glad to lie still through most of the daylight hours, taken care of along with the little Benedetto by a woman whom the pestilence had widowed.

Every day the Padre and Jacopo and the small flock of surviving villagers paid their visit to this cottage to see the Blessed Lady, and to bring her of their best as an offering—honey, fresh cakes, eggs, and polenta. It was a sight they could none of them forget, a sight they all told of in their old age—how the sweet and sainted Lady with her fair face, her golden hair, and her brown eyes that had a blessing in them, lay weary with her labours after she had been sent over the sea to help them in their extremity, and how the queer little black Benedetto used to crawl about the straw by her side and want everything that was brought to her, and she always gave him a bit of what she took, and told them if they loved her they must be good to Benedetto.

Many legends were afterwards told in that valley about the blessed Lady who came over the sea, but they were legends by which all who heard might know that in times gone by a woman had done beautiful loving deeds there, rescuing those who were ready to perish.

CHAPTER LXIX.

Homeward

In those silent wintry hours when Romola lay resting from her weariness, her mind, travelling back over the past, and gazing across the undefined distance of the future, saw all objects from a new position. Her experience since the moment of her waking in the boat had come to her with as strong an effect as that of the fresh seal on the dissolving wax. She had felt herself without bonds, without motive; sinking in mere egoistic complaining that life could bring her no content; feeling a right to say, "I am tired of life; I want to die." That thought had sobbed within her as she fell asleep, but from the moment after her waking when the cry had drawn her, she had not even reflected, as she used to do in Florence, that she was glad to live because she could lighten sorrow—she had simply lived, with so energetic an impulse to share the life around her, to answer the call of need and do the work which cried aloud to be done, that the reasons for living, enduring, labouring, never took the form of argument.

The experience was like a new baptism to Romola. In Florence the simpler relations of the human being to his fellow-men had been complicated for her with all the special ties of marriage, the State, and religious discipleship, and when these had disappointed her trust the shock seemed to have shaken her aloof from life and stunned her sympathy. But now she said, "It was mere baseness in me to desire death. If everything else is doubtful, this suffering that I can help is certain; if the glory of the cross is an illusion, the sorrow is only the truer. While the strength is in my arm I will stretch it out to the fainting; while the light visits my eyes they shall seek the forsaken."

And then the past arose with a fresh appeal to her. Her work in this green valley was done, and the emotions that were disengaged from the people immediately around her rushed back into the old deep channels of use and affection. That rare possibility of self-contemplation which comes in any complete severance from our wonted life made her judge herself as she had never done before: the compunction which is inseparable from a sympathetic nature keenly alive to the possible experience of others, began to stir in her with growing force. She questioned the justness of her own conclusions, of her own deeds: she had been rash, arrogant, always dissatisfied that others were not good enough, while she herself had not been true to what her soul had once recognized as the best. She began to condemn her flight: after all, it had been cowardly self-care; the grounds on which Savonarola had once taken her back were truer, deeper than the grounds she had had for her second flight. How could she feel the needs of others and not feel above all the needs of the nearest?

But then came reaction against such self-reproach. The memory of her life with Tito, of the conditions which made their real union impossible, while their external union imposed a set of false duties on her which were essentially the concealment and sanctioning of what her mind revolted from, told her that flight had been her only resource. All minds, except such as are delivered from doubt by dulness of sensibility, must be subject to this recurring conflict where the many-twisted conditions of life have forbidden the fulfilment of a bond. For in strictness there is no replacing of relations: the presence of the new does not nullify the failure and breach of the old. Life has lost its perfection: it has been maimed; and until the wounds are quite scarred, conscience continually casts backward doubting glances.

Romola shrank with dread from the renewal of her proximity to Tito, and yet she was uneasy that she had put herself out of reach of knowing what was his fate—uneasy that the moment might yet come when he would be in misery and need her. There was still a thread of pain within her, testifying to those words of Fra Girolamo, that she could not cease to be a wife. Could anything utterly cease for her that had once mingled itself with the current of her heart's blood?

Florence, and all her life there, had come back to her like hunger; her feelings could not go wandering after the possible and the vague: their living fibre was fed with the memory of familiar things. And the thought that she had divided herself from them for ever became more and more importunate in these hours that were unfilled with action. What if Fra Girolamo had been wrong? What if the life of Florence was a web of inconsistencies? Was she, then, something higher, that she should shake the dust from off her feet, and say, "This world is not good enough for me"? If she had been really higher, she would not so easily have lost all her trust.

Her indignant grief for her godfather had no longer complete possession of her, and her sense of debt to Savonarola was recovering predominance. Nothing that had come, or was to come, could do away with the fact that there had been a great inspiration in him which had waked a new life in her. Who, in all her experience, could demand the same gratitude from her as he? His errors—might they not bring calamities?

She could not rest. She hardly knew whether it was her strength returning with the budding leaves that made her active again, or whether it was her eager longing to get nearer Florence. She did not imagine herself daring to enter Florence, but the desire to be near enough to learn what was happening there urged itself with a strength that excluded all other purposes.

And one March morning the people in the valley were gathered together to see the blessed Lady depart. Jacopo had fetched a mule for her, and was going with her over the mountains. The Padre, too, was going with her to the nearest town, that he might help her in learning the safest way by which she might get to Pistoja. Her store of trinkets and money, untouched in this valley, was abundant for her needs.

If Romola had been less drawn by the longing that was taking her away, it would have been a hard moment for her when she walked along the village street for the last time, while the Padre and Jacopo, with the mule, were awaiting her near the well. Her steps were hindered by the wailing people, who knelt and kissed her hands, then clung to her skirts and kissed the grey folds, crying, "Ah, why will you go, when the good season is beginning and the crops will be plentiful? Why will you go?"

"Do not be sorry," said Romola, "you are well now, and I shall remember you. I must go and see if my own people want me."

"Ah, yes, if they have the pestilence!"

"Look at us again, Madonna!"

"Yes, yes, we will be good to the little Benedetto!"

At last Romola mounted her mule, but a vigorous screaming from Benedetto as he saw her turn from him in this new position, was an excuse for all the people to follow her and insist that he must ride on the mule's neck to the foot of the slope.

The parting must come at last, but as Romola turned continually before she passed out of sight, she saw the little flock lingering to catch the last waving of her hand.

CHAPTER LXX.

Meeting Again

ON the fourteenth of April Romola was once more within the walls of Florence. Unable to rest at Pistoja, where contradictory reports reached her about the Trial by Fire, she had gone on to Prato; and was beginning to think that she should be drawn on to Florence in spite of dread, when she encountered that monk of San Spirito who had been her godfather's confessor. From him she learned the full story of Savonarola's arrest, and of her husband's death. This Augustinian monk had been in the stream of people who had followed the waggon with its awful burthen into the Piazza, and he could tell her what was generally known in Florence—that Tito had escaped from an assaulting mob by leaping into the Arno, but had been murdered on the bank by an old man who had long had an enmity against him. But Romola understood the catastrophe as no one else did. Of Savonarola the monk told her, in that tone of unfavourable prejudice which was usual in the Black Brethren (Frati Neri) towards the Brother who showed white under his black, that he had confessed himself a deceiver of the people.

Romola paused no longer. That evening she was in Florence, sitting in agitated silence under the exclamations of joy and wailing, mingled with exuberant narrative, which were poured into her ears by Monna Brigida, who had backslided into false hair in Romola's absence, but now drew it off again and declared she would not mind being grey, if her dear child would stay with her.

Romola was too deeply moved by the main events which she had known before coming to Florence, to be wrought upon by the doubtful gossiping details added in Brigida's narrative. The tragedy of her husband's death, of Fra Girolamo's confession of duplicity under the coercion of torture, left her hardly any power of apprehending minor circumstances. All the mental activity she could exert under that load of awe-stricken grief, was absorbed by two purposes which must supersede every other; to try and see Savonarola, and to learn what had become of Tessa and the children.

"Tell me, cousin," she said abruptly, when Monna Brigida's tongue had run quite away from troubles into projects of Romola's living with her, "has anything been seen or said since Tito's death of a young woman with two little children?"

Brigida started, rounded her eyes, and lifted up her hands.

"Cristo! no. What! was he so bad as that, my poor child? Ah, then, that was why you went away and left me word only that you went of your own free will. Well, well, if I'd known that, I shouldn't have thought you so strange and flighty. For I did say to myself, though I didn't tell anybody else, 'What was she to go away from her husband for, leaving him to mischief, only because they cut poor Bernardo's head off? She's got her father's temper,' I said, 'that's what it is.' Well, well, never scold me, child: Bardo *was* fierce, you can't deny it. But if you had only told me the truth, that there was a young hussey and children, I should have understood it all. Anything seen or said of her? No; and the less the better. They say enough of ill about him without that. But since that was the reason you went—"

"No, dear cousin," said Romola, interrupting her earnestly, "pray do not talk so. I wish above all things to find that young woman and her children, and to take care of them. They are quite helpless. Say nothing against it; that is the thing I shall do first of all."

"Well," said Monna Brigida, shrugging her shoulders and lowering her voice with an air of puzzled discomfiture, "if that's being a Piagnone, I've been taking peas for paternosters. Why, Fra Girolamo said as good as that widows ought not to marry again. Step in at the door and it's a sin and a shame, it seems; but come down the chimney and you're welcome. *Two* children—Santiddio!"

"Cousin, the poor thing has done no conscious wrong: she is ignorant of everything. I will tell you—but not now."

Early the next morning Romola's steps were directed to the house beyond San Ambrogio where she had once found Tessa; but it was as she had feared: Tessa was gone. Romola conjectured that Tito had sent her away beforehand to some spot where he had intended to join her, for she did not believe that he would willingly part with those children. It was a painful conjecture, because, if Tessa were out of Florence, there was hardly a chance of finding her, and Romola pictured the childish creature waiting and waiting at some wayside spot in wondering helpless misery. Those who lived near could tell her nothing except that old deaf Lisa had gone away a week ago with her goods, but no one knew where Tessa had gone. Romola saw no further active search open to her; for she had no knowledge that could serve as a starting-point for inquiry, and not only her innate reserve but a more noble sensitiveness made her shrink from assuming an attitude of generosity in the eyes of others by publishing Tessa's relation to Tito along with her own desire to find her. Many days passed in anxious inaction. Even under strong solicitation from other thoughts Romola found her heart palpitating if she caught sight of a pair of round brown legs, or of a short woman in the contadina dress.

She never for a moment told herself that it was heroism or exalted charity in her to seek these beings; she needed something that she was bound specially to care for; she yearned to clasp the children and to make them love her. This at least would be some sweet result, for others as well as herself, from all her past sorrow. It appeared there was much property of Tito's to which she had a claim; but she distrusted the cleanness of that money, and she had determined to make it all over to the State, except so much as was equal to the price of her father's library. This would be enough for the modest support of Tessa and the children. But Monna Brigida threw such planning into the background by clamorously insisting that Romola must live with her and never forsake her till she had seen her safe in Paradise—else why had she persuaded her to turn Piagnone?—and if Romola wanted to rear other people's children, she, Monna Brigida, must rear them too. Only they must be found first.

Romola felt the full force of that innuendo. But strong feeling unsatisfied is never without its superstition, either of hope or despair. Romola's was the superstition of hope: *somehow* she was to find that mother and the children. And at last another direction for active inquiry suggested itself. She learned that Tito had provided horses and mules to await him in San Gallo; he was therefore going to leave Florence by the gate of San Gallo, and she determined, though without much confidence in the issue, to try and ascertain from the gate-keepers if they had observed any one corresponding to the description of Tessa, with her children, to have passed the gates before the morning of the ninth of April. Walking along the Via San Gallo, and looking watchfully about her through her long widow's veil, lest she should miss any object that might aid her, she descried Bratti chaffering with a customer. That roaming man, she thought, might aid her: she would not mind talking of Tessa to *him*. But as she put aside her veil and crossed the street towards him, she saw something hanging from the corner of his basket which made her heart leap with a much stronger hope.

"Bratti, my friend," she said abruptly, "where did you get that necklace?"

"Your servant, Madonna," said Bratti, looking round at her very deliberately, his mind not being subject to surprise. "It's a necklace worth money, but I shall get little by it, for my heart's too tender for a trader's; I've promised to keep it in pledge."

"Pray tell me where you got it:—from a little woman named Tessa, is it not true?"

"Ah! if you know her," said Bratti, "and would redeem it of me at a small profit, and give it her again, you'd be doing a charity, for she cried at parting with it—you'd have thought she was running into a brook. It's a small profit I'll charge you. You shall have it for a florin, for I don't like to be hard-hearted."

"Where is she?" said Romola, giving him the money, and unclasping the necklace from the basket in joyful agitation.

"Outside the gate there, at the other end of the Borgo, at old Sibilla Manetti's: anybody will tell you which is the house."

Romola went along with winged feet, blessing that incident of the Carnival which had made her learn by heart the appearance of this necklace. Soon she was at the house she sought. The young woman and the children were in the inner room—were to have been fetched away a fortnight ago and more—had no money, only their clothes, to pay a poor widow with for their food and lodging. But since Madonna knew them—Romola waited to hear no more, but opened the door.

Tessa was seated on the low bed: her crying had passed into tearless sobs, and she was looking with sad blank eyes at the two children, who were playing in an opposite corner—Lillo covering his head with his skirt and roaring at Ninna to frighten her, then peeping out again to see how she bore it. The door was a little behind Tessa, and she did not turn round when it opened, thinking it was only the old woman: expectation was no longer alive. Romola had thrown aside her veil and paused a moment, holding the necklace in sight. Then she said, in that pure voice that used to cheer her father,—

"Tessa!"

Tessa started to her feet and looked round.

"See," said Romola, clasping the beads on Tessa's neck, "God has sent me to you again."

The poor thing screamed and sobbed, and clung to the arms that fastened the necklace. She could not speak. The two children came from their corner, laid hold of their mother's skirts, and looked up with wide eyes at Romola.

That day they all went home to Monna Brigida's, in the Borgo degli Albizzi. Romola had made known to Tessa by gentle degrees, that Naldo could never come to her again; not because he was cruel, but because he was dead.

"But be comforted, my Tessa," said Romola. "I am come to take care of you always. And we have got Lillo and Ninna."

Monna Brigida's mouth twitched in the struggle between her awe of Romola and the desire to speak unseasonably.

"Let be, for the present," she thought; "but it seems to me a thousand years till I tell this little contadina, who seems not to know how many fingers she's got on her hand, who Romola is. And I *will* tell her some day, else she'll never know her place. It's all very well for Romola; nobody will call their souls their own when she's by; but if I'm to have this puss-faced minx living in my house, she must be humble to me."

However, Monna Brigida wanted to give the children too many sweets for their supper, and confessed to Romola, the last thing before going to bed, that it would be a shame not to take care of such cherubs.

"But you must give up to me a little, Romola, about their

eating, and those things. For you have never had a baby, and I had twins, only they died as soon as they were born."

CHAPTER LXXI.

The Confession

WHEN Romola brought home Tessa and the children April was already near its close, and the other great anxiety on her mind had been wrought to its highest pitch by the publication in print of Fra Girolamo's Trial, or rather of the confessions drawn from him by the sixteen Florentine citizens commissioned to interrogate him. The appearance of this document, issued by order of the Signoria, had called forth such strong expressions of public suspicion and discontent, that severe measures were immediately taken for recalling it. Of course there were copies accidentally mislaid, and a second edition, *not* by order of the Signoria, was soon in the hands of eager readers.

Romola, who began to despair of ever speaking with Fra Girolamo, read this evidence again and again, desiring to judge it by some clearer light than the contradictory impressions that were taking the form of assertions in the mouths of both partisans and enemies.

In the more devout followers of Savonarola his want of constancy under torture, and his retractation of prophetic claims, had produced a consternation too profound to be at once displaced as it ultimately was by the suspicion, which soon grew into a positive datum, that any reported words of his which were in inexplicable contradiction to their faith in him, had not come from the lips of the Prophet, but from the falsifying pen of Ser Ceccone, that notary of evil repute, who had made the digest of the examination. But there were obvious facts that at once threw discredit on the printed document. Was not the list of sixteen examiners half made up of the Prophet's bitterest enemies? Was not the notorious Dolfo Spini one of the new Eight prematurely elected, in order to load the dice* against a man whose ruin had been determined on by the party in power? It was but a murder with slow formalities that was being transacted in the Old Palace. The Signoria had resolved to drive a good bargain with the Pope and the Duke of Milan, by extinguishing the man who was as great a molestation to vicious citizens and greedy foreign tyrants as to a corrupt clergy. The Frate had been doomed beforehand, and the only question that was pretended to exist now was, whether the Republic, in return for a permission to lay a tax on ecclesiastical property, should deliver him alive into the hands of the Pope, or whether the Pope should further concede to the Republic what its dignity demanded—the privilege of hanging and burning its own Prophet on its own Piazza.

Who, under such circumstances, would give full credit to this so-called confession? If the Frate had denied his prophetic gift, the denial had only been wrenched from him by the agony of torture—agony that, in his sensitive frame, must quickly produce raving. What if these wicked examiners declared that he had only had the torture of the rope and pulley thrice, and only on one day, and that his confessions had been made when he was under no bodily coercion—was that to be believed? He had been tortured much more; he had been tortured in proportion to the distress his confessions had created in the hearts of those who loved him.

Other friends of Savonarola, who were less ardent partisans, did not doubt the substantial genuineness of the confession, however it might have been coloured by the transpositions and additions of the notary; but they argued indignantly that there was nothing which could warrant a condemnation to death, or even to grave punishment. It must be clear to all impartial men that if this examination represented the only evidence against the Frate, he would die, not for any crime, but because he had made himself inconvenient to the Pope, to the rapacious Italian States that wanted to dismember their Tuscan neighbour, and to those unworthy citizens who sought to gratify their private ambition in opposition to the common weal.

Not a shadow of political crime had been proved against him. Not one stain had been detected on his private conduct: his fellow monks, including one who had formerly been his secretary* for several years, and who, with more than the average culture of his companions, had a disposition to criticize Fra Girolamo's rule as Prior, bore testimony, even after the shock of his retractation, to an unimpeachable purity and consistency in his life, which had commanded their unsuspecting veneration. The Pope himself had not been able to raise a charge of heresy against the Frate, except on the ground of disobedience to a mandate, and disregard of the sentence of excommunication. It was difficult to justify that breach of discipline by argument, but there was a moral insurgence in the minds of grave men against the court of Rome, which tended to confound the theoretic distinction between the Church and churchmen, and to lighten the scandal of disobedience.

Men of ordinary morality and public spirit felt that the triumph of the Frate's enemies was really the triumph of gross licence. And keen Florentines like Soderini and Piero Guicciardini may well have had an angry smile on their lips at a severity which dispensed with all law in order to hang and burn a man in whom the seductions of a public career had warped the strictness of his veracity; may well have remarked that if the Frate had mixed a much deeper fraud with a zeal and ability less inconvenient to high personages, the fraud would have been regarded as an excellent oil for ecclesiastical and political wheels.

Nevertheless such shrewd men were forced to admit that, however poor a figure the Florentine government made in its clumsy pretence of a judicial warrant for what had in fact been predetermined as an act of policy, the measures of the Pope against Savonarola were necessary measures of self-defence. Not to try and rid himself of a man who wanted to stir up the powers of Europe to summon a General Council and depose him, would have been adding ineptitude to iniquity. There was no denying that towards Alexander the Sixth Savonarola was a rebel, and what was much more, a dangerous rebel. Florence had heard him say, and had well understood what he meant, that he would not *obey the devil.** It was inevitably a life and death struggle between the Frate and the Pope; but it was less inevitable that Florence should make itself the Pope's executioner.

Romola's ears were filled in this way with the suggestions of a faith still ardent under its wounds, and the suggestions of worldly discernment, judging things according to a very moderate standard of what is possible to human nature. She could be satisfied with neither. She brought to her long meditations over that printed document many painful observations, registered more or less consciously through the years of her discipleship, which whispered a presentiment that Savonarola's retractation of his prophetic claims was not merely a spasmodic effort to escape from torture. But, on the other hand, her soul cried out for some explanation of his lapses which would make it still possible for her to believe that the main striving of his life had been pure and grand. The recent memory of the selfish discontent which had come over her like a blighting wind along with the loss of her trust in the man who had been for her an incarnation of the highest motives, had produced a reaction which is known to many as a sort of faith that has sprung up to them out of the very depths of their despair. It was impossible, she said now, that the negative disbelieving thoughts which had made her soul arid of all good, could be founded in the truth of things: impossible that it had not been a living spirit, and no hollow pretence, which had once breathed in the Frate's words, and kindled a new life in her. Whatever falsehood there had been in him, had been a fall and not a purpose; a gradual entanglement in which he struggled, not a contrivance encouraged by success.

Looking at the printed confessions she saw many sentences which bore the stamp of bungling fabrication: they had that emphasis and repetition in self-accusation which none but very low hypocrites use to their fellow-men. But the fact that these sentences were in striking opposition, not only to the character of Savonarola, but also to the general tone of the confessions, strengthened the impression that the rest of the text represented in the main what had really fallen from his lips. Hardly a word was dishonourable to him except what turned on his prophetic annunciations. He was unvarying in his statement of the ends he had pursued for Florence, the Church, and the world; and, apart from the mixture of falsity in that claim to special inspiration by which he sought to gain hold of men's minds, there was no admission of having used unworthy means. Even in this confession, and without expurgation of the notary's malign phrases, Fra Girolamo shone forth as a man who had sought his own glory indeed, but sought it by labouring for the very highest end—the moral welfare of men—not by vague exhortations, but by striving to turn beliefs into energies that would work in all the details of life.

"Everything that I have done," said one memorable passage,* which may perhaps have had its erasures and interpolations, "I have done with the design of being for ever famous, in the present and in future ages; and that I might win credit in Florence;

and that nothing of great import should be done without my sanction. And when I had thus established my position in Florence, I had it in my mind to do great things in Italy and beyond Italy, by means of those chief personages with whom I had contracted friendship and consulted on high matters, such as this of the General Council. And in proportion as my first efforts succeeded, I should have adopted further measures. Above all, when the General Council had once been brought about, I intended to rouse the princes of Christendom, and especially those beyond the borders of Italy, to subdue the infidels. It was not much in my thoughts to get myself made a Cardinal or Pope; for when I should have achieved the work I had in view, I should, without being Pope, have been the first man in the world in the authority I should have possessed, and the reverence that would have been paid me. If I had been made Pope, I would not have refused the office: but it seemed to me that to be the head of that work was a greater thing than to be Pope; because a man without virtue may be Pope, but *such a work as I contemplated demanded a man of excellent virtues.*"

That blending of ambition with belief in the supremacy of goodness made no new tone to Romola, who had been used to hear it in the voice that rang through the Duomo. It was the habit of Savonarola's mind to conceive great things, and to feel that he was the man to do them. Iniquity should be brought low; the cause of justice, purity, and love should triumph; and it should triumph by his voice, by his work, by his blood. In moments of ecstatic contemplation, doubtless, the sense of self melted in the sense of the Unspeakable, and in that part of his experience lay the elements of genuine self-abasement; but in the presence of his fellow-men for whom he was to act, pre-eminence seemed a necessary condition of his life.

And perhaps this confession, even when it described a doubleness that was conscious and deliberate, really implied no more than that wavering of belief concerning his own impressions and motives which most human beings who have not a stupid inflexibility of self-confidence must be liable to under a marked change of external conditions? In a life where the experience was so tumultuously mixed as it must have been in the Frate's, what a possibility was opened for a change of self-judgment, when, instead of eyes that venerated and knees that knelt, instead of a great work on its way to accomplishment, and in its prosperity stamping the agent as a chosen instrument, there came the hooting and the spitting and the curses of the crowd; and then the hard faces of enemies made judges; and then the horrible torture, and with the torture the irrepressible cry, "It is true, what you would have me say: let me go, do not torture me again: yes, yes, I am guilty. O God! Thy stroke has reached me!"

As Romola thought of the anguish that must have followed the confession—whether, in the subsequent solitude of the prison, conscience retracted or confirmed the self-taxing words—that anguish seemed to be pressing on her own heart and urging the slow bitter tears. Every vulgar self-ignorant person in Florence was glibly pronouncing on this man's demerits, while *he* was knowing a depth of sorrow which can only be known to the soul that has loved and sought the most perfect thing, and beholds itself fallen.

She had not then seen—what she saw afterwards—the evidence of the Frate's mental state after he had had thus to lay his mouth in the dust. As the days went by, the reports of new unpublished examinations, eliciting no change of confessions, ceased; Savonarola was left alone in his prison and allowed pen and ink for a while, that, if he liked, he might use his poor bruised and strained right arm to write with. He wrote; but what he wrote was no vindication of his innocence, no protest against the proceedings used towards him: it was a continued colloquy with that divine purity with which he sought complete reunion; it was the outpouring of self-abasement; it was one long cry for inward renovation. No lingering echoes of the old vehement self-assertion, "Look at my work, for it is good, and those who set their faces against it are the children of the devil!" The voice of Sadness tells him, "God placed thee in the midst of the people even as if thou hadst been one of the excellent. In this way thou hast taught others, and hast failed to learn thyself. Thou hast cured others: and thou thyself hast been still diseased. Thy heart was lifted up at the beauty of thy own deeds, and through this thou hast lost thy wisdom and art become, and shalt be to all eternity, nothing. . . . After so many benefits with which God has honoured thee, thou art fallen into the depths of the sea; and after so many gifts bestowed on thee, thou, by thy pride and vainglory, hast scandalized all the world." And when Hope speaks and argues that the divine love has not forsaken him, it says nothing now of a great work to be done, but only says, "Thou art not forsaken, else why is thy heart bowed in penitence? That too is a gift."

There is no jot of worthy evidence that from the time of his imprisonment to the supreme moment, Savonarola thought or spoke of himself as a martyr. The idea of martyrdom had been to him a passion dividing the dream of the future with the triumph of beholding his work achieved. And now, in place of both, had come a resignation which he called by no glorifying name.

But therefore he may the more fitly be called a martyr by his fellow-men to all time. For power rose against him not because of his sins, but because of his greatness—not because he sought to deceive the world, but because he sought to make it noble. And through that greatness of his he endured a double agony: not only the reviling, and the torture, and the death-throe, but the agony of sinking from the vision of glorious achievement into that deep shadow where he could only say, "I count as nothing: darkness encompasses me: yet the light I saw was the true light."

CHAPTER LXXII.

The Last Silence

ROMOLA had seemed to hear, as if they had been a cry, the words repeated to her by many lips—the words uttered by Savonarola when he took leave of those Brethren of San Marco who had come to witness his signature of the Confession: "Pray for me, for God has withdrawn from me the spirit of prophecy."

Those words had shaken her with new doubts as to the mode in which he looked back at the past in moments of complete self-possession. And the doubts were strengthened by more piteous things still, which soon reached her ears.

The nineteenth of May had come, and by that day's sunshine there had entered into Florence the two Papal Commissaries, charged with the completion of Savonarola's trial. They entered amid the acclamations of the people, calling for the death of the

Frate. For now the popular cry was, "It is the Frate's deception that has brought on all our misfortunes; let him be burned, and all things right will be done, and our evils will cease."

The next day it is well certified that there was fresh and fresh torture of the shattered sensitive frame; and now, at the first threat and first sight of the horrible implements, Savonarola, in convulsed agitation, fell on his knees, and in brief, passionate words, *retracted his confession*, declared that he had spoken falsely in denying his prophetic gift, and that if he suffered, he would suffer for the truth—"The things that I have spoken, I had them from God."

But not the less the torture was laid upon him, and when he was under it he was asked why he had uttered those retracting words. Men were not demons in those days, and yet nothing but confessions of guilt were held a reason for release from torture. The answer came: "I said it that I might seem good; tear me no more, I will tell you the truth."*

There were Florentine assessors at this new trial, and those words of twofold retractation had soon spread. They filled Romola with dismayed uncertainty.

"But"—it flashed across her—"there will come a moment when he may speak. When there is no dread hanging over him but the dread of falsehood, when they have brought him into the presence of death, when he is lifted above the people, and looks on them for the last time, they cannot hinder him from speaking a last decisive word. I will be there."

Three days after, on the 23rd of May, 1498, there was again a long narrow platform stretching across the great Piazza, from the Palazzo Vecchio towards the Tetto de' Pisani. But there was no grove of fuel as before: instead of that, there was one great heap of fuel placed on the circular area which made the termination of the long narrow platform. And above this heap of fuel rose a gibbet with three halters on it; a gibbet which, having two arms, still looked so much like a cross as to make some beholders uncomfortable, though one arm had been truncated to avoid the resemblance.

On the marble terrace of the Palazzo were three tribunals; one near the door for the Bishop, who was to perform the ceremony of degradation on Fra Girolamo and the two Brethren who were to suffer as his followers and accomplices; another for the Papal Commissaries, who were to pronounce them heretics and schismatics, and deliver them over to the secular arm; and a third, close to Marzocco, at the corner of the terrace where the platform began, for the Gonfaloniere, and the Eight who were to pronounce the sentence of death.

Again the Piazza was thronged with expectant faces: again there was to be a great fire kindled. In the majority of the crowd that pressed around the gibbet the expectation was that of ferocious hatred, or of mere hard curiosity to behold a barbarous sight. But there were still many spectators on the wide pavement, on the roofs, and at the windows, who, in the midst of their bitter grief and their own endurance of insult as hypocritical Piagnoni, were not without a lingering hope, even at this eleventh hour, that God would interpose, by some sign, to manifest their beloved Prophet as His servant. And there were yet more who looked forward with trembling eagerness, as Romola did, to that final moment when Savonarola might say, "O people, I was innocent of deceit."

Romola was at a window on the north side of the Piazza, far away from the marble terrace where the tribunals stood; and near her, also looking on in painful doubt concerning the man who had won his early reverence, was a young Florentine of two-and-twenty, named Jacopo Nardi,* afterwards to deserve honour as one of the very few who, feeling Fra Girolamo's eminence, have written about him with the simple desire to be veracious. He had said to Romola, with respectful gentleness, when he saw the struggle in her between her shuddering horror of the scene and her yearning to witness what might happen in the last moment,

"Madonna, there is no need for you to look at these cruel things. I will tell you when he comes out of the Palazzo. Trust to me; I know what you would see."

Romola covered her face, but the hootings that seemed to make the hideous scene still visible could not be shut out. At last her arm was touched, and she heard the words, "He comes." She looked towards the Palace, and could see Savonarola led out in his Dominican garb; could see him standing before the Bishop, and being stripped of the black mantle, the white scapulary, and long white tunic, till he stood in a close woollen under-tunic, that told of no sacred office, no rank. He had been degraded, and cut off from the Church Militant.

The baser part of the multitude delight in degradations, apart from any hatred; it is the satire they best understand. There was a fresh hoot of triumph as the three degraded Brethren passed on to the tribunal of the Papal Commissaries, who were to pronounce them schismatics and heretics. Did not the Prophet look like a schismatic and heretic now? It is easy to believe in the damnable state of a man who stands stripped and degraded.

Then the third tribunal was passed—that of the Florentine officials who were to pronounce sentence, and amongst whom, even at her distance, Romola could discern the odious figure of Dolfo Spini, indued in the grave black *lucco*, as one of the Eight.

Then the three figures, in their close white raiment, trod their way along the platform, amidst yells and grating tones of insult.

"Cover your eyes, madonna," said Jacopo Nardi; "Fra Girolamo will be the last."

It was not long before she had to uncover them again. Savonarola was there. He was not far off her now. He had mounted the steps; she could see him look round on the multitude.

But in the same moment expectation died, and she only saw what he was seeing—torches waving to kindle the fuel beneath his dead body, faces glaring with a yet worse light; she only heard what *he* was hearing—gross jests, taunts, and curses.

The moment was past. Her face was covered again, and she only knew that Savonarola's voice had passed into eternal silence.

EPILOGUE

On the evening of the twenty-second of May, 1509, five persons, of whose history we have known something, were seated in a handsome upper room opening on to a loggia which, at its right-hand corner, looked all along the Borgo Pinti, and over the city gate towards Fiesole, and the solemn heights beyond it.

At one end of the room was an archway opening into a narrow inner room, hardly more than a recess, where the light fell from above on a small altar covered with fair white linen. Over the altar was a picture, discernible at the distance where the little party sat only as the small full-length portrait of a Dominican Brother. For it was shaded from the light above by overhanging branches and wreaths of flowers, and the fresh tapers below it were unlit. But it seemed that the decoration of the altar and its recess was not complete. For part of the floor was strown with a confusion of flowers and green boughs, and among them sat a delicate blue-eyed girl of thirteen, tossing her long light-brown hair out of her eyes, as she made selections for the wreaths she was weaving, or looked up at her mother's work in the same kind, and told her how to do it with a little air of instruction.

For that mother was not very clever at weaving flowers or at any other work. Tessa's fingers had not become more adroit with the years—only very much fatter. She got on slowly and turned her head about a good deal, and asked Ninna's opinion with much deference; for Tessa never ceased to be astonished at the wisdom of her children. She still wore her contadina gown: it was only broader than the old one; and there was the silver pin in her rough curly brown hair, and round her neck the memorable necklace, with a red cord under it, that ended mysteriously in her bosom. Her rounded face wore even a more perfect look of childish content than in her younger days: everybody was so good in the world, Tessa thought; even Monna Brigida never found fault with her now, and did little else than sleep, which was an amiable practice in everybody, and one that Tessa liked for herself.

Monna Brigida was asleep at this moment, in a straight-backed arm-chair, a couple of yards off. Her hair, parting backward under her black hood, had that soft whiteness which is not like snow or anything else, but is simply the lovely whiteness of aged hair. Her chin had sunk on her bosom, and her hands rested on the elbow of her chair. She had not been weaving flowers or doing anything else: she had only been looking on as usual, and as usual had fallen asleep.

The other two figures were seated farther off, at the wide doorway that opened on to the loggia. Lillo sat on the ground with his back against the angle of the door-post, and his long legs stretched out, while he held a large book open on his knee and occasionally made a dash with his hand at an inquisitive fly, with an air of interest stronger than that excited by the finely-printed copy of Petrarch which he kept open at one place, as if he were learning something by heart.

Romola sat nearly opposite Lillo, but she was not observing him. Her hands were crossed on her lap and her eyes were fixed absently on the distant mountains: she was evidently unconscious of anything around her. An eager life had left its marks upon her: the finely moulded cheek had sunk a little, the golden crown was less massive; but there was a placidity in Romola's face which had never belonged to it in youth. It is but once that we can know our worst sorrows, and Romola had known them while life was new.

Absorbed in this way, she was not at first aware that Lillo had ceased to look at his book, and was watching her with a slightly impatient air, which meant that he wanted to talk to her, but was not quite sure whether she would like that entertainment just now. But persevering looks make themselves felt at last. Romola did presently turn away her eyes from the distance and met Lillo's impatient dark gaze with a brighter and brighter smile. He shuffled along the floor, still keeping the book on his lap, till he got close to her and lodged his chin on her knee.

"What is it, Lillo?" said Romola, pulling his hair back from his brow. Lillo was a handsome lad, but his features were turning out to be more massive and less regular than his father's. The blood of the Tuscan peasant was in his veins.

"Mamma Romola, what am I to be?" he said, well contented that there was a prospect of talking till it would be too late to con "Spirto gentil"* any longer.

"What should you like to be, Lillo? You might be a scholar.

My father was a scholar, you know, and taught me a great deal. That is the reason why I can teach you."

"Yes," said Lillo, rather hesitatingly. "But he is old and blind in the picture. Did he get a great deal of glory?"

"Not much, Lillo. The world was not always very kind to him, and he saw meaner men than himself put into higher places, because they could flatter and say what was false. And then his dear son thought it right to leave him and become a monk; and after that, my father being blind and lonely, felt unable to do the things that would have made his learning of greater use to men, so that he might still have lived in his works after he was in his grave."

"I should not like that sort of life," said Lillo. "I should like to be something that would make me a great man, and very happy besides—something that would not hinder me from having a good deal of pleasure."

"That is not easy, my Lillo. It is only a poor sort of happiness that could ever come by caring very much about our own narrow pleasures. We can only have the highest happiness, such as goes along with being a great man, by having wide thoughts, and much feeling for the rest of the world, as well as ourselves; and this sort of happiness often brings so much pain with it, that we can only tell it from pain by its being what we would choose before everything else, because our souls see it is good. There are so many things wrong and difficult in the world, that no man can be great—he can hardly keep himself from wickedness—unless he gives up thinking much about pleasures or rewards, and gets strength to endure what is hard and painful. My father had the greatness that belongs to integrity; he chose poverty and obscurity rather than falsehood. And there was Fra Girolamo—you know why I keep to-morrow sacred: *he* had the greatness which belongs to a life spent in struggling against powerful wrong, and in trying to raise men to the highest deeds they are capable of. And so, my Lillo, if you mean to act nobly and seek to know the best things God has put within reach of men, you must learn to fix your mind on that end, and not on what will happen to you because of it. And remember, if you were to choose something lower, and make it the rule of your life to seek your own pleasure and escape from what is disagreeable, calamity might come just the same; and it would be calamity falling on a base mind, which is the one form of sorrow that has no balm in it, and that may well make a man say,—'It would have been better for me if I had never been born.' I will tell you something, Lillo."

Romola paused a moment. She had taken Lillo's cheeks between her hands, and his young eyes were meeting hers.

"There was a man to whom I was very near, so that I could see a great deal of his life, who made almost every one fond of him, for he was young, and clever, and beautiful, and his manners to all were gentle and kind. I believe, when I first knew him, he never thought of doing anything cruel or base. But because he tried to slip away from everything that was unpleasant, and cared for nothing else so much as his own safety, he came at last to commit some of the basest deeds—such as make men infamous. He denied his father, and left him to misery; he betrayed every trust that was reposed in him, that he might keep himself safe and get rich and prosperous. Yet calamity overtook him."

Again Romola paused. Her voice was unsteady, and Lillo was looking up at her with awed wonder.

"Another time, my Lillo—I will tell you another time. See, there are our old Piero di Cosimo and Nello coming up the Borgo Pinti, bringing us their flowers. Let us go and wave our hands to them, that they may know we see them."

"How queer old Piero is," said Lillo, as they stood at the corner of the loggia, watching the advancing figures. "He abuses you for dressing the altar, and thinking so much of Fra Girolamo, and yet he brings you the flowers."

"Never mind," said Romola. "There are many good people who did not love Fra Girolamo. Perhaps I should never have learned to love him if he had not helped me when I was in great need."

THE END.

EXPLANATORY NOTES

Even by the standards of Victorian fiction, *Romola* is a formidably learned book. GE spent fully six months of preparation in painstaking background research, and the novel abounds with all manner of recondite factual details. Readers wanting a more comprehensive account of GE's appropriation of documentary sources should refer to the Clarendon edition (ed. Andrew Brown, 1993). Here the notes concentrate on glossing the 100 or so actual historical persons referred to in the text, identifying the numerous quotations and literary, biblical, and mythological allusions, and explaining the most important historical and topographical references. Translations of Italian words and phrases are given in a separate glossary.

GE kept several notebooks during the period of her preparatory research for *Romola*. These are referred to in the notes by the following abbreviations:

Q Notebook, entitled 'Quarry for Romola', in Princeton University Library (AM 14959)

BL Notebook in the British Library (Add. MSS 40768)

Bod Notebook in the Bodleian Library at Oxford (MS. Don. g. 8)

WN Notebook in the Beinecke Library at Yale, published as *George Eliot: A Writer's Notebook 1854–1879*, ed. Joseph Wiesenfarth (1981)

Pf Notebook published as *Some George Eliot Notebooks: An Edition of the Carl H. Pforzheimer Library's George Eliot Holograph Notebooks* (volume ii—MSS 707–11), ed. William Baker (1984)

In the notes below, the autograph manuscript of *Romola* (in the British Library) is referred to by the abbreviation *MS*. GE herself supplied a number of footnotes to the novel. For convenience of layout these are interspersed in sequence with my own notes; they are given in inverted commas, followed by the designation [GE] in square brackets. Occasionally I interpolate explanatory remarks of my own within quotations in the notes; these are indicated by square brackets.

3 *from the Levant to the Pillars of Hercules*: i.e. from the Eastern Mediterranean to the straits of Gibraltar. The Pillars of Hercules are the rocks on either side of the straits, supposedly joined together until Hercules tore them apart, and in ancient times thought to mark the end of the habitable world. In the spring of 1492, however, when the action of the novel opens,

Columbus was about to explode this myth by sailing westwards from Spain and discovering the New World.

4 *Palos*: Columbus sailed from Palos in Andalucia on 3 August 1492.

revisit the glimpses: cf. 'What may this mean, | That thou, dead corse, again in complete steel | Revisits thus the glimpses of the moon' (*Hamlet*, I. iv. 51–3).

5 *Old Palace . . . great dome*: the Palazzo Vecchio, or Old Palace (also known as the Palace of the People), was built in the late 13th cent. and served as the town hall of Florence. The cupola of the Duomo, or Cathedral (1420–36), by Brunelleschi, was the highest and largest of its time, and the first dome designed so as not to require a wooden frame to support the vault during construction.

Giotto's . . . Badia: the bell tower of the Duomo was begun by Giotto (*c.*1266–1337) in 1334. Like the Duomo itself, it is built of coloured marbles. The Badia is the church of an ancient Benedictine abbey, rebuilt in the late 13th cent.

Santa Croce: the Franciscan church of Santa Croce was begun in 1294 by Arnolfo di Cambio (*c.*1245–1302) and soon became the fashionable place to be buried. By the 15th cent. the floor was entirely covered with tombstones of the Florentine nobility, and the walls lined with commemorative monuments and plaques. Romola's father is buried there in 1494 (see p. 234). The spired bell tower was not added until the 1840s. From its 1847 edition onward, *Murray's Handbook for Travellers in Northern Italy* described it as 'a monument of bad taste, and entirely out of keeping with the style of the church', an opinion with which GE's Florentine Spirit evidently concurred.

Frati Minori: 'The Franciscans.' [GE]

Brunelleschi or Michelozzo: Filippo Brunelleschi (1377–1446) was the architect of the churches of San Lorenzo and Santo Spirito, as well as of the cupola of the Duomo. Among the buildings of his pupil Michelozzo di Bartolommeo Michelozzi (1396–1472) were the convent of San Marco and the Medici Palace in the Via Larga.

Bogoli: 'Now Boboli.' [GE]

that great palace . . . Oltrarno: the Pitti Palace, begun in 1458, was intended by Luca Pitti to show off his wealth and importance. It was to be greater than all others in Florence, and in particular the first-floor windows were to be as large as the doors of the Medici Palace. In 1466, however, following an abortive conspiracy against the Medici, Pitti was disgraced and bankrupted; work on the palace ceased and it was still incomplete when he died in 1472. The hill from which the stone was quarried is now the site of the adjacent Boboli gardens, which date from the 16th cent. Oltrarno is the area of the city on the south bank of the River Arno.

6 *anxious voting with black and white beans . . . the Priori . . . Orgagna's Loggia*: the council known as the 'Magnificent Eight', which presided over the State's legal and judicial business, was empowered to pass sentence of confiscation of property, imprisonment, exile, or death on a citizen. Voting on such matters was carried out with black and white beans; six black beans were required for a verdict of guilty. Alternatively, GE may be referring to the *scrutinio* (see note below). The *Signoria*, or State executive, was made up of nine *Priori* (priors, chief officers), each holding office for just two months. The Loggia dei Lanzi or Loggia della Signoria, also known after its probable designer, Andrea Orcagna (or Orgagna, *fl.* 1344–68), was constructed (1376–82) beside the Palazzo Vecchio and used for State ceremonial. The 'significant banners' would be those of the nine priors then in office.

keep a hated name out of the borsa: from the early 14th cent. public officials in Florence were elected by lot. The names of those eligible for the various magistracies were selected by a complicated procedure, known as the *scrutinio*, and put into *borse* (leather bags or purses) from which the required number were then drawn. Voting in the *scrutinio* was carried out with black and white beans (black for, white against).

the "Ten" . . . Gonfaloniere: the committee of ten, the *Dieci di Guerra*, was elected only in time of war. The *Gonfaloniere di Giustizia* (standard-bearer of Justice) was the city's chief magistrate. Like the priors, he served for just two months. Government policy was largely determined by the party to which he belonged.

bloodless battles . . . casual falls and tramplings: in his *History of Florence* Machiavelli remarks that the 1440s were the least dangerous times ever for waging war. In his description of the Battle of Anghiari, he notes that only one man was killed and that even he perished 'non di ferite o d'altro virtuoso colpo, ma caduto da cavallo e calpesto' ('not from a blow dealt in combat or any other honourable wound, but from being trampled after falling off his horse').

7 *truncis naribus*: the phrase is taken from the 1st cent. AD Roman poet Martial (*Epigrams*, 2. 83. 3): 'trunci naribus auribusque voltus' ('a face shorn of nose and ears'). In *BL* GE records a contemporary remark about Niccolò Niccoli's (see p. 51) collection of antique busts—'some "truncis naribus" but others perfect'.

that fine Homer: the great edition of Homer by Demetrius Chalcondylas (see p. 335) was printed in 1488.

waxen image: see p. 139.

Lucretius . . . Luigi Pulci . . . dal tetto in su: the Roman poet Lucretius (1st cent. AD) contended in *De Rerum Natura* that the order of the world could be explained without recourse to divine intervention. Denouncing all forms of superstition, he thus sought to liberate men from the credulous awe of controlling deities. Luigi Pulci (1432–84) was a popular Florentine poet, considered a master of idiomatic vernacular expression. He is best known for his comic epic *Il morgante maggiore*, which is quoted on several occasions in *Romola*. His interest in magic and his religious scepticism, notably concerning the immortality of the soul, led to accusations of heresy, and he was denied burial in consecrated ground. *Morgante*'s mockery of orthodox Christian beliefs prompted Savonarola's supporters to burn all available copies of the book on the 'Pyramid of Vanities' (see Ch. 49). The supper-table referred to by the Spirit was probably that of Lorenzo de' Medici, of whose circle Pulci was a colourful member. GE may have come across the distinctive phrase *dal tetto in su* in the *Cedrus Libani* of the Dominican monk and poet Fra Benedetto (see n. to p. 492), where it is used to describe the lax morals and unbelieving temper of the 1490s during the Papacy of Rodrigo Borgia: 'La verità non se dicea più . . . Nè quasi si credea dal tetto in su' ('no one spoke the truth any more and people hardly believed anything from the roof upward').

Aristotle . . . was a thoroughly irreligious philosopher: following the publication in 1438 of a pamphlet by the Greek scholar Gemistos Plethon, *De Platonicae atque Aristoteliae Philosophia Differentia*, a debate sprang up in 15th-cent. Italy between the respective claims of the two philosophers. Florence became the seat of the Platonic school, while Aristotle was championed in the north of Italy. It proved harder, however, to make

Aristotle's doctrines accord with the Christian creed than those of Plato.

circling hours: in classical mythology the Horae—Eunomia, Dice, and Irene—were three sisters, daughters of Zeus and Themis, who presided over the seasons of spring, summer, and winter.

baptized in San Giovanni . . . coming judgment: peculiar to Florence, there were no baptismal fonts in the city's churches. All baptisms were carried out in the central Baptistery of San Giovanni, adjacent to the Duomo. The ceiling of the Baptistery is decorated with mosaics of Byzantine influence, one of which depicts the Last Judgement.

8 *Epicurean levity*: for the philosophy of Epicurus, see n. to p. 34. Here the adjective is used in its common English sense, referring to the mere pursuit of sensual enjoyment.

Pope Angelico . . . simony . . . Innocent the Eighth: that such a religious leader would emerge, heralding a new, spiritual age, was a common belief throughout medieval and Renaissance times. Savonarola's remarkable rise to power was held by many to be a vindication of the legend. Simony was the practice of selling religious offices or indulgences for money. Pope Innocent VIII reigned from 1484 to 1492.

Iddio non paga il Sabato: '"God does not pay on a Saturday."' [GE]

Frate Predicatore: a preaching friar—a Dominican.

9 *Lorenzo de' Medici . . . San Marco . . . Careggi*: Lorenzo de' Medici (1449–92), known as 'the Magnificent', became the effective ruler of Florence on his father's death in 1469. Lorenzo's grandfather, Cosimo, had commissioned Michelozzo to rebuild the Dominican convent of San Marco in the mid-15th cent. The Medici villa at Careggi, just to the north of Florence, was one of Lorenzo's favourite retreats, and the house in which he died.

his handsome son would play the part of Rehoboam: Lorenzo's eldest son Piero (1471–1503) inherited neither his father's charm nor his political acumen; he was banished from Florence in 1494 (see Ch. 21). Rehoboam was the son of Solomon, who, when he succeeded his father, rejected the advice of the elders and instead followed that of his young, reckless friends, saying to the people 'My father chastised you with whips, but I will chastise you with scorpions' (1 Kings 12: 14).

the Great Turk . . . rare animals . . . fugitive enemies: among Lorenzo's gifts from the Turkish Sultan Mahomet II were a lion and a giraffe; he was also sent the person of Bernardo Bandini, the murderer of his brother Giuliano, who had taken refuge at Constantinople.

famous scholar . . . Latin letters of the Republic . . . lecturing on Dante: the senior posts in the government of most 15th-cent. Italian States were held by classical scholars, for they alone were sufficiently fluent in the Latin used for all official documents and negotiations with other States. A chair for the explanation of Dante was established at Florence in the mid-14th cent., when it was first held by Boccaccio.

Regno: 'The name given to Naples by way of distinction among the Italian States.' [GE]

Marmi . . . Loggie: *Marmi* is the plural of *marmo* (marble), here referring to the city's marble pavements; a *loggia* (plural *loggie*) is a roofed arch or arcade.

trade in the Calimala: the Via de Calimala was a centre for the trade in foreign cloth.

11 *QUI NACQUE IL DIVINO POETA*: 'The Divine Poet [i.e. Dante] was born here'; the house GE refers to is in the Via Dante Alighieri.

12 *Bratti Ferravecchi*: *ferravecchio* is Italian for scrap (literally, 'old') iron dealer. Bratti is a colloquial contraction of *barattare* ('to exchange')—as in '*Chi abbaratta—baratta—b'ratta*' (see p. 13). The name, in other words, is derived from the street cry. The street of the *Ferravecchi*, which no longer exists, led into the Mercato Vecchio. In *BL* GE notes that 'a Ferravecchio . . . commonly called Bratti Ferravecchio, died very rich'.

San Giovanni: Midsummer Day: the Feast of St John the Baptist, patron saint of Florence.

Messer San Michele: the Archangel Michael.

can't tell a hook from a hanger: hooks and hangers were basic shapes practised by children learning to write.

13 *Rovezzano . . . Mercato Vecchio . . . an Ave*: Rovezzano is a village some 2½ miles to the east of the city. The Mercato Vecchio (Old Market) was demolished at the end of the 19th cent. to make way for the Piazza Vittorio Emanuele, now the Piazza della Repubblica. An *Ave* (*Maria*) is a 'Hail Mary'.

San Niccolò: as always, GE has attended to the smallest background detail: as well as being a patron of travellers and a protector against robbery, St Nicholas of Myra was patron saint of the city of Bari, Tito's birthplace.

"Chi abbaratta . . . vecchi?": '"Who wants to exchange rags, broken glass, or old iron?"' [GE]

a Ridolfi: the Ridolfi were one of the great Florentine families. Two of them, Niccolò and Giovan Battista, appear in the novel.

a paternoster: literally, an 'our father'; a rosary whose beads are fingered in sequence while the Lord's Prayer is recited.

a raven to . . . mind the stock: ravens were commonly kept in shops to deter thieves by the noise they would make if anyone entered while the owner was not there.

win no hose: the Florentine custom of rewarding the bringer of good tidings with hose (*novelle da calze*) is referred to again in Ch. 43.

14 *not born of a Sunday—the salt shops were open*: GE has taken this phrase, signifying that the person concerned is very shrewd, from Boccaccio's *Decameron* (8. 9).

as hot as Spain . . . all the profits of usury: for the persecution of Spanish Jews by the Inquisition in the 1490s (when Naples too was a Spanish dominion) see n. to p. 520. By an ordinance of 1437 only Jews were permitted to act as money-lenders and pawnbrokers in Florence.

grey cloth is against yellow cloth: the Franciscans were known as grey friars from the colour of their habit. Jews were obliged to wear a piece of yellow cloth as a distinguishing badge—men on their hats, women on their sleeves. For the Franciscans' enmity towards Jews see n. to p. 166.

hose for Saint Christopher . . . sight of him: St Christopher was a giant (hence the amount of cloth required to make hose for him). It was commonly believed that to see a picture of him would bring good luck for the rest of the day.

Fesulean ancestors: Florence was supposedly founded by merchants from the ancient hill city of Fiesole, some three miles distant, who erected buildings by the Arno to facilitate trade with the population of the valley.

15 *the old poet Antonio Pucci accounts a . . . dignità*: the popular poet Antonio Pucci (*c.*1310–88) was for most of his life the town crier of Florence. Much of his verse is on patriotic, civic,

and historic themes. GE alludes here to line 25 of his poem *La proprietà di Mercato Vecchio*. The butchers' stalls were located in a pavilion in the very centre of the market.

E vedesi . . . ingoffi: *La proprietà di Mercato Vecchio*, lines 91–3 ('You can see the losers panting heavily, cursing with hands to the jaw, and the exchanging of many blows').

castello: 'Walled village.' [GE]

16 *a venerable pillar . . . statue of Plenty*: the Colonna dell' Abbondanza, a granite Roman pillar, had been moved to the Mercato Vecchio from the Baptistery in the early 15th cent. The statue by Donatello (1384–1466), known as 'La Dovizia' (Abundance, Plenty) was probably executed in the early 1430s. The figure had a basket of fruit on her head and carried a cornucopia.

very sour crabs: possibly an allusion to Dante's description (*Inferno*, 15. 61–5) of the 'thankless and malignant people' who first made up the Florentine populace as 'lazzi sorbi' (bitter sorbs, or *crab-apples*).

excommunicated us again: a papal interdict had last been laid upon Florence by Sixtus IV in 1478.

17 *it seems a thousand years*: a translation of the Italian expression *parer mill'anni*.

A bad Easter and a bad year: the expression is almost certainly taken from Boccaccio. In both *Pf* and *Bod*, in sections of notes from the *Decameron*, GE jots down the phrase 'Che Dio ti dia il malanno e male pasqua' ('May God grant you a bad year and a bad Easter'), which appears to be a running together of lines from *Decameron* 7. 5 and 7. 7.

Palle: 'Arms of the Medici.' [GE] Six red balls (*palle*) on a gold background.

18 *Lantern of the Duomo struck . . . Lions tearing each other to pieces*: on 5 April 1492 the lions in the city menagerie had inexplicably turned on each other and killed one of their number. That night a thunderbolt struck the lantern of the Duomo out of a clear sky and split it almost in half. The vision of the hysterical woman in Santa Maria Novella, of a huge bull with fiery horns destroying the church, was widely reported by contemporary chroniclers. All such portents were believed to foretell an impending civic catastrophe.

Boto: 'A votive image of Lorenzo, in wax, hung up in the

church of the Annunziata, supposed to have fallen at the time of his death. *Boto* is popular Tuscan for *Voto*.' [GE]

Frati Serviti: the Santissima Annunziata was the church of the Servite order of friars (Servants of the Blessed Virgin Mary; see p. 358).

netto di specchio: 'The phrase used to express the absence of disqualification—*i.e.*, the not being entered as a debtor in the public book (*specchio*).' [GE] The *specchio* (literally 'mirror') was a register of citizens who had not paid their taxes and who were therefore disqualified from taking part in public life.

19 *raise a riot over your quattrini bianchi*: in 1490 the Government of Florence called in the small coins known as *quattrini neri* and issued new ones, the *quattrini bianchi*, in their place, of one fifth greater value. Then, while insisting on all payments to itself being made in the new coinage, it made its own payments in the old, which caused widespread dissatisfaction.

saddled and bridled Milan: on the death of the last Visconti Duke of Milan in 1447 a republic had been established, but it lasted only three years before the tyrannical Sforza family took control of the city.

Balaam's ass: for the story of Balaam's ass, who was miraculously given the power of speech by God, see Numbers 22: 21–34. In referring thus sarcastically to a 'pious notary' GE may also have in mind the term 'Balaamite'—i.e. someone who follows religion for personal gain. 'Ser' (i.e. 'Sir'), as in 'Ser Cioni', was a title commonly given to notaries.

20 *Fra Menico . . . running after the wind of Mongibello . . . the fate of certain swine*: the Franciscan monk Fra Domenico (diminutive Menico) da Ponzo was a prominent opponent of Savonarola and the Dominicans. Mongibello is an alternative name for the Sicilian volcano Mount Etna. The proverbial expression 'andare dietro al vento di Mongibello' signifies to indulge in a wild-goose chase. For the story of the Gadarene swine, which, possessed by devils, drowned themselves in the Sea of Galilee, see Matthew 8: 28–32; Mark 5: 1–13; Luke 8: 26–33.

Domenico Ghirlandajo . . . reflect the life of Florence: a reference to the frescoes by Ghirlandaio (1449–94) in Ognissanti, Santa Maria Novella, and the Sassetti Chapel in Santa Trinità, in which many of the figures are portraits of the artist's contemporaries. The character described here is the smith Niccolò Grosso who appears again in Ch. 26.

21 *San Gallo*: the area of parkland, on the north-east of the city, around the Augustinian convent of San Gallo, a favourite summer resort.

Marzocco: 'The stone Lion, emblem of the Republic.' [GE] There were numerous such statues in the city; the most famous, by Donatello, was in the Piazza della Signoria.

22 *the Abbot Joachim*: the Cistercian Abbot Joachim of Fiore (*c.*1135–1202) argued that the history of the world was divided into three ages. The first, the period of the Old Testament, was that of the Father, dominated by law and fear. The second, from the birth of Christ to the year 1260, was that of the Son, a period of grace and faith. The third age was that of the Holy Ghost, characterized by love and spirituality and led by monks. Though his following inevitably declined after the year 1260 had passed without (as he had announced) the conversion of the Jews and Saracens to Christianity, his influence remained considerable. Savonarola invoked him on a number of occasions, referring in particular to his prophecy of a coming scourge and renovation. For Savonarola's vision of 'the sword hanging from the sky' see p. 199.

the Magnifico sent for the Frate at the last: on his deathbed at Careggi, despite his previous antipathy to him, Lorenzo de' Medici sent for Savonarola hoping to receive absolution at his hands. Savonarola insisted that he could offer this only if Lorenzo would agree to restore to Florence the republican government of which he had despoiled it. Even *in extremis* Lorenzo could not bring himself to submit to such a condition, and Savonarola accordingly refused to grant him absolution; the 'Magnifico', in other words, did indeed die without the Frate's blessing.

23 *tell peas from paternosters*: GE found the expression 's'io non conosco il bacello da' paternostri!' ('if I don't know peas from paternosters') in no. 209 of Franco Sacchetti's *Trecentonovelle* (see n. to p. 120). The comparison is between a pea and a single rosary bead.

Midas: the legendary King of Phrygia to whom the gods gave the gift of turning everything he touched into gold.

Ognissanti: the area around the church of All Saints, where one of the main centres of the city's woollen industry was located.

24 *obolus*: an ancient Greek coin, worth half a drachma. Later, the word was used allusively for any coin of small value. Tito

presumably spoke to himself in the Italianate Greek of his native Apulia.

26 *a murrain to you*: 'a plague upon you'.

27 *the first and last requisite of eloquence*: Cicero records (*Brutus*, 38. 142) that when Demosthenes was asked to list the first, second, and third requisites of oratory, he replied 'action' to all three.

the excellent Demetrio: born in Athens, the scholar Demetrius Chalcondylas (1424–1511) was invited to Florence in 1479 by Lorenzo de' Medici and remained there as professor of Greek until 1492. Among his many achievements was the edition of Homer referred to in the Proem.

Bernardo Rucellai: see Ch. 38.

29 *carries his skin*: St Bartholomew was martyred by being flayed alive. He is often represented in pictures carrying his own skin over his arm.

the Muses are tearing their hair: see n. to p. 316.

Pericles: the statesman Pericles dominated Athenian politics from 460 BC to his death in 429. The parallel with Lorenzo de' Medici is an appropriate one, for though the city was nominally a democracy he, as its first citizen, became its effective ruler.

the accomplished Marullo . . . Alessandra Scala: Michael Marullus Tarchaniota came to Italy as a boy following the fall of Constantinople in 1453, and won fame there as both a poet and a soldier. His fortunes were assured when in 1487 he married the 'learned and lovely' Alessandra Scala (1475–1506), daughter of the Secretary of the Florentine Republic. He was drowned near Volterra in 1500. The broad parallels between Marullo and Tito and Alessandra and Romola are self-evident.

Greek stock . . . peaches are Persian: the Florentine silk trade began in the early 15th cent. and was subsequently encouraged by Lorenzo de' Medici, who planted mulberry trees (native to Asia) on his estate. The ancient and much-fought-over city of Bari, in Apulia in south-east Italy, had had a mixed Graeco-Roman population since classical times. The Latin name for peach is *persicum malum*—Persian apple. The line 'in fact, I am a Greek, very much as your peaches are Persian' was changed to this reading by GE on the proofs of the Cabinet Edition. All previous states of the text read 'in fact, may rather be called a

Græculus than a Greek'. The Latin word *Græculus* ('Greekling'), however, was often used in a pejorative or even contemptuous sense. The revised reading here is less derogatory: signifying, presumably, that Tito's pedigree is a familiar and well-established one—that he is an import fully acclimatized to Italy, with no hint of the fraudulent or meretricious about him.

30 *Minerva*: the Roman goddess of wisdom, equivalent to the Greek Athena; 'fallacious' here since the information given to Tito proves false. The underlying allusion is probably to the episode in the *Odyssey* in which Athena, in disguise, counsels Telemachus to fit out a ship and go in search of his father Odysseus.

Alamanno Rinuccini: the Rinuccini were one of the great Florentine mercantile families. Alamanno (1426–1504), a close friend of Lorenzo de' Medici, was a notable scholar and historian.

passed the Rubicon: i.e. taken an irrevocable step. The expression derives from Julius Caesar's crossing, in 49 BC, of the stream called Rubicon which marked the border between Italy and the province of Cisalpine Gaul. By taking this small step he technically became an invader, and thus made inevitable the war against Pompey and the Senate through which he rose to supreme power.

Messer Angelo: Angelo Poliziano, or Politian, 1454–94. The celebrated humanist, scholar, and poet was born in the Tuscan village of Montepulciano and went to study in Florence at the age of 10. As a teenager he wrote Greek poems, edited Catullus, and began to translate Homer into Latin. In 1473 Lorenzo de' Medici appointed him tutor to his son Piero, and in 1480 to a chair of Greek and Latin, in which post he lectured on a wide range of classical authors. He translated works by Epictetus, Hippocrates, Plutarch, and Plato, among others, and edited the *Pandects* of Justinian (see n. to p. 51). His compositions in Italian include the lyric pastoral *Orfeo* (see n. to p. 331).

Pietro Crinito: *c.*1465–1505. The transcriber of numerous classical texts and the author of a commentary on Cicero, his second name is the Latinized form of *riccio* ('curly-locks'), a nickname given to his father. Nello's unflattering portrait of him follows that of Paulus Jovius' unreliable *Elogia Virorum*

Literis Illustrium, which records that his fondness for wine, 'uncircumscribed by the reliable bounds of dignity and modesty, opened the way to insults and to ruin'. Jovius goes on to note, doubtless apocryphally, that he died as a result of 'the unaccustomed outrage' of a homosexual advance made towards him while drunk at a friend's country house.

31 *hyacinthine locks*: the phrase is from *Paradise Lost* (4. 301), describing the appearance of Adam. If GE is not being anachronistic, however, Nello must be referring to Homer's description of Ulysses (*Odyssey*, 6. 231), whose hair flowed 'like the hyacinth flower'.

Pico di Mirandola: Giovanni Pico, Prince of Mirandola (1463–94), was famous both for his learning and his beauty. According to Poliziano, he was a man 'on whom Nature had lavished all the endowments both of body and mind; erect and elegant in his person, there was something in his appearance almost divine'.

gates of storied bronze: the octagonal Baptistery of San Giovanni has three sets of bronze doors. The south doors are by Andrea Pisano and date from the mid-14th cent. Those on the north (1403–24) and the east (1425–52) are the work of Lorenzo Ghiberti; the latter are reported to have been described by Michelangelo as worthy of the gates of Paradise. The original marble façade of the Duomo, left uncompleted by Giotto, was removed in the 16th cent. Its replacement, the 'ignominious . . . stucco' seen by GE (and described by her in her journal as 'the wretched unfinished façade'), was itself removed in the 1870s, whence the present façade dates.

32 *rough with imagery*: in *MS* this phrase is followed by a quotation which indicates its origin: '*signis exstantibus asper*' (meaning 'rough with high-wrought figures'). The words, which GE deleted before sending the manuscript to the printer, are from Ovid, *Metamorphoses*, 12. 235.

half a century ago . . . hardly so many years as you do: Nello's remark is not strictly accurate. The last doors were indeed completed exactly 50 years previously, but by then Ghiberti, who died in 1455, was 74 years old. The north doors were begun when Ghiberti was 25.

Poliziano . . . in spite of his canonicate: Poliziano was appointed a canon of the Cathedral in 1486. The remark attributed to him by Nello about the gods awaking, though not taken from his own writings, is appropriately suggestive of the rediscovery of classical sources of inspiration. The 'quotation' that follows about the vulgar speaking Latin is equally in character, though it too is almost certainly made up.

33 *Burchiello*: the barber and vernacular poet Domenico di Giovanni (1404–49) was known as 'Il Burchiello' because he had the sign of a small barge [*burchio* = barge; *burchiello* = wherry] outside his shop in the Via Calimala, where many of the leading Florentine poets and artists of the day congregated. Nello is plainly modelled on Burchiello, details of whose character and works GE recorded at length in *BL*. One of Burchiello's sonnets, 'La Poesia contende col Rasajo' ('Poetry argues with the Razor'), in which he contrasts his high artistic vocation with his lowly tonsorial profession, probably prompted GE's choice of 'Apollo and the Razor' as the sign for Nello's shop. Nello's boast that his shop is 'the navel of the earth' is based on another of Burchiello's sonnets, which begins 'Nel bilicato centro della terra' [*bilicato* = umbilical, navel], and in which he maintains that *his* shop should be thus termed since it stood at the centre of Florence, which in turn was at the centre of Tuscany, and therefore at the centre of the world.

Triptolemus: according to Greek legend, it was Triptolemus who taught men the art of ploughing. By implication Nello suggests a similar, though anonymous, mythological patron of *reaping* ('the first reaper of beards, the sublime *Anonimo*').

adytum: the innermost part or sanctuary of a temple.

a fancy of Piero di Cosimo's: the sketch is in fact a fancy of GE's. It resembles no known work by the artist, who is to play an important role in the novel; neither do the portraits of Tito as Sinon (see p. 180) or of Bardo and Romola as Oedipus and Antigone (see p. 243). As for Piero's drawing inspiration from 'looking at a mouldy wall', GE's source is evidently Giorgio Vasari's 16th-cent. *Lives of the Most Eminent Painters*, which records that Piero 'would sometimes stand beside a wall, against which various impurities were cast, and from these he would image forth the most singular scenes'.

34 *the wise philosophy of Epicurus*: the Athenian philosopher Epicurus (341–270 BC) held that pleasure (defined as the absence of pain) is the only good, and that the highest pleasure consists of that perfect harmony of body and mind which is brought about by plain living and the pursuit of virtue.

the Graces: the classical goddesses of beauty and charm.

the sign of 'The Moor': there was a chemist's shop in Florence in the 1490s known from the painting on the board above it as *Il Moro* (the Moor). GE read about the custom of doctors waiting inside chemists' shops for patients, or even sitting on horseback outside the door, in nos. 155 and 168 of Franco Sacchetti's *Trecentonovelle*.

35 *the e hath the stronger following in Florence*: in 1488 Cristofero Landino (see p. 60) had pronounced that Virgil should in fact be spelled with an 'e', and the case had subsequently been taken up by Poliziano in his *Miscellanea*, 1489 (ch. 77: 'Quo argumento dicendum Vergilius non Virgilius').

to discern il pelo nell' uovo: the Italian expression *cercare il pelo nell' uovo* (literally, 'to look for the hair in the egg') is broadly equivalent to the English 'to split hairs'. Machiavelli, the Florentine political theorist and historian, was 22 years old in April 1492.

Venetian mirror from Murano, the true nosce teipsum: Murano, in the Venetian lagoon, became the centre of the Venetian glass industry in the late 13th cent. *Nosce teipsum* ('Know thyself') was a precept particularly associated with the Delphic oracle.

37 *the old Furies*: the Roman name (*Furiae*) for the Greek *Erinyes* (also known as *Eumenides* (see p. 112)), the merciless goddesses of vengeance who pursued and punished transgressors, especially those who neglected filial or familial duty.

leaven . . . Doxology: Nello is alluding to liturgical and theological differences between the Greek and Roman Churches. Leavened bread is used during the Mass in the Greek Church, unleavened in the Roman. The dispute over doxology—the form of offering of glory to God—specifically concerned the *Filioque* section of the Nicene Creed, the Roman Church holding that the Holy Ghost proceeds from the Father and the Son, the Greek that it proceeds from the Father alone. Both issues were debated by representatives of the two Churches at the Council of Florence in 1439.

Ingenium velox . . . torrentior: The quotation is from Juvenal (*fl.* c.98–128 AD), *Satires*, 3. 73–4: 'quick witted and of unbounded impudence, they are as ready of speech as Isaeus [an Assyrian rhetorician] and more garrulous'.

Giovanni Argiropulo, who ran full tilt against Cicero: Johannes

Argyropylus (1404–74) was a Greek scholar brought to Florence by Cosimo de' Medici in 1459. His supercilious criticism of Cicero is recorded by Poliziano, to whom he served as tutor.

38 *a fine Cleopatra cut in sardonyx . . . intaglios and cameos*: GE found information about just such a stone in Charles William King's *Antique Gems* (1860): 'a bust of Cleopatra, given in exact accordance with the prescribed type of the Queen . . . worked out with extreme delicacy in the black layer of Onyx in very flat relief'. An intaglio, like Tito's Cleopatra, is a precious stone with a design engraved on it. A cameo is a stone with two layers of contrasting colour; the design is carved in relief from the upper layer, while the lower serves as a background.

another sort of Cleopatra that he covets most: Nello is probably alluding to a mistress of Piero de' Medici, using the name Cleopatra to signify a woman of luxurious tastes and dubious morals.

'branny monster': on more than one occasion (see p. 76) Poliziano stigmatized Scala as *monstrum furfuraceum*. 'Furfur' is Latin for bran.

such a steed as Ser Benghi's: Ser Benghi was a corruption of or nickname for Ser Gherardo, a Florentine whose comic antics on an old hack under whose tail a thistle had been surreptitiously placed are recounted in no. 64 of Franco Sacchetti's *Trecentonovelle*.

the halving of a fennel seed: in *Bod* GE notes that 'Finocchio = fennel seed, is used in the same way as "mustard seed" to express the minimum.' The expression signifies that the person concerned will be scrupulous to a fault.

39 *Florentine lily . . . got quarrelsome, and turned red*: until the middle of the 13th cent. the Florentine banner consisted of a white lily on a red field. In the year 1251, at the height of the conflict between the Guelfs and the Ghibellines (see n. to p. 79), a group of the latter faction committed treason and joined forces with the city's enemies, but still flew the white lily at the head of their column, whereupon the government of Florence promptly changed its emblem to a *red* lily on a *white* field. In the *Paradiso* (16. 151–4) Dante speaks wistfully of the Florentine people 'so glorious and so just that the lily had never been reversed on the spear, nor by dissension changed to red'.

'raggia come stella per sereno': 'shines like a star in a clear sky' (Pulci, *Il morgante maggiore*, 3. 17).

as opportunely as cheese on macaroni: from the Italian expression *essere come il cacio sui maccheroni*, meaning to turn up at the right time.

Menico Cennini . . . Bernardo Cennini: Bernardo Cennini (1415–98) was a Florentine engraver and goldsmith (he assisted Lorenzo Ghiberti with one of the doors of the Baptistery of San Giovanni) who became interested in printing, built a press, and issued his first book in 1471. His son Domenico (1452–1504) carried on the family business. 'Grave' Domenico may have been, but in 1492, aged 40, he was scarcely 'elderly'. Later in the novel (p. 83) his brother Piero, a notary and copyist, appears; this is an odd slip by GE: Piero, Bernardo's eldest son, had died in 1484.

40 *Francesco Filelfo . . . Guarino*: Filelfo (1398–1481) was appointed to the chair of Rhetoric at Padua at the age of 18. He subsequently became professor of Eloquence at Venice, of Moral Philosophy at Bologna, and then of Rhetoric at Florence (1429–34). He frequently boasted that no other man alive had mastered the whole of ancient literature as he had. Guarino of Verona (1374–1460), sometime professor of Rhetoric at Florence, was a noted collector of ancient manuscripts. His hair is reputed to have turned white from grief following a shipwreck in which he lost all the treasures he had acquired on a trip to Greece.

man . . . about fifty: GE's source is presumably Vasari, who gives Piero di Cosimo's birthdate as 1441. (In *Pf* she writes that he died in 1521 aged 80.) In fact, he was born in 1462 (he did indeed die in 1521), which would have made him 30 years old at this point in the novel.

Sinon deceiving old Priam: it was Sinon who persuaded King Priam to bring the wooden horse into the city of Troy.

Saint Sebastian . . . troops of devout women: Sebastian was a Roman soldier martyred for his Christian belief by the Emperor Diocletian, who ordered him shot to death with arrows. The scene became a popular one with artists in the 15th cent., supposedly because it afforded the opportunity of displaying the almost naked body of a young man in an unimpeachably religious context.

Bacchus . . . Phœbus Apollo . . . a 'credo': Bacchus was the Roman god of wine and fertility, Phoebus Apollo the Greek sun god; 'in the space of a "credo"' signifies a mere moment—no longer than it takes to say 'I believe [in God]'.

41 *a curious and valuable ring . . . onyx, or rather nicolo . . . restore to him whatever he may have lost*: onyx consists of two layers of contrasting colours; the variety known as nicolo (*onicolo*: little onyx) has a blue layer over a black one. As one would expect, the device on Tito's ring has been carefully researched: in her notes from King's *Antique Gems* in *Bod* GE records that 'the figure of a big fish . . . cut on a stone with a large crested serpent with a long mane above it . . . gives good luck at sea, & restores lost things'. 'Sigils' are seals.

42 *horoscopes are all a nonsensical dream*: Pico della Mirandola's *De Astrologia* was one of the first books systematically to deny the power of astrological influences over men's lives. The term 'Phoenix', denoting a person of unique excellence or matchless beauty, was commonly applied to Pico by his contemporary admirers.

made his Judas as beautiful as St. John: Nello is presumably referring to Leonardo da Vinci's famous painting of the Last Supper, in Milan, which includes representations of both Judas and John. In fact, however, the painting was not commissioned until 1494 (i.e. two years after Nello's remark). GE's spelling of the painter's name as 'Lionardo' follows Vasari.

43 *old tutelar God Mars . . . his rival, the Baptist*: in ancient times Mars, the Roman god of war, was honoured as patron of Florence until, with the coming of Christianity, he was gradually replaced in this eminence by St John the Baptist. Dante describes medieval Florence as standing 'tra Marte e 'l Batista' ('between Mars and the Baptist': *Paradiso*, 16. 47).

44 *certain noteworthy circumstances . . . honest pages of Giovanni Villani*: as the 14th-cent. chronicler Giovanni Villani relates, in August 1343, a group of noble Florentine families, including the Bardi, sought to acquire power over the city by force of arms, but were roundly defeated in the ensuing struggle with the people. The Bardi, barricaded in their houses in the Via de' Bardi, between the Ponte Vecchio and the Ponte Rubaconte, held out longer than any of their allies, but were eventually overcome by an attack from the rear launched from the hill of San Giorgio. Villani reports the subsequent burning of their twenty-two 'palagi e case grandi e ricche' ('palaces and large wealthy houses').

kinship: 'A sign that such contrasts were peculiarly frequent in Florence, is the fact that Saint Antonine, Prior of San Marco, and afterwards Archbishop, in the first half of this fifteenth century, founded the society of Buonuomini di San Martino (Good Men of St. Martin) with the main object of succouring the *poveri vergognosi*—in other words, paupers of good family. In the records of the famous Panciatichi family we find a certain Girolamo in this century who was reduced to such a state of poverty that he was obliged to seek charity for the mere means of sustaining life, though other members of his family were extremely wealthy.' [GE]

45 *Scheldt . . . Euxine*: the Scheldt is the river on which both Ghent and Antwerp stand. Pontus Euxinus is the Latin name for the Black Sea.

46 *Magna Græcia*: the name given to the Greek colonies in southern Italy.

Politian's Miscellanea: a collection of occasional pieces, or 'miscellanies', published in 1489, consisting of observations on the writings of ancient authors. The translation of the passage quoted is GE's own.

47 *Nonnus, in the fifth book of the Dionysiaca*: the Greek poet Nonnus (5th cent. AD) was the author of a huge epic in 48 books on the legendary adventures of the god Dionysus, known as the *Dionysiaca*. The passage quoted by Politian from book 5 comprises verses 337–8 and 341–2.

48 *mens divinior*: 'the more god-like mind' (the phrase is from Horace, *Satires*, I. I. 43).

the very fountains of Parnassus: i.e. the source of literary inspiration. Parnassus was a mountain to the north of Delphi with twin peaks: one sacred to Apollo and the Muses, the other to Dionysus.

49 *Lamiæ*: according to legend, Lamia was a Libyan queen with whom Zeus fell in love. The jealous Hera, Zeus' consort, robbed her of her children, and in vengeful despair Lamia then stole and murdered the children of others. Her savage cruelty distorted her once beautiful face, and to mitigate this effect Zeus gave her the power of taking her eyes out of her head and putting them back again at will. Bardo is referring here to Poliziano's *Lamia*, the introductory essay to a course of lectures on Aristotle which he delivered in Florence in 1492–3. In it Poliziano defends himself against the malicious sniping of fellow scholars by arguing humorously that Florence too has its Lamiae, who put their eyes in when in public but remove them

at home. Thus they are quick to criticize others but blind to their own shortcomings.

saying with Petrarca . . . junguntur: Francesco Petrarca (Petrarch), 1304–74, was a leading humanist philosopher and the most celebrated poet of his time. The quotation, taken from one of his letters, may be translated: 'books delight our inmost being; they converse with us, advise us, and become living companions to us' (*Rerum Familiarium*, 3. 18).

the younger Crisolora: GE is presumably thinking of Johannes, the nephew of Emmanuel Chrysoloras (see n. to p. 58), who did indeed teach Greek in Florence. Johannes died in 1426, however, so for Bardo to have studied with him, even as a youth, would mean that Bardo must now be around 80 years old—as opposed simply to 'rather more than seventy', as he is described on p. 53.

50 *try to be a pentathlos*: Bardo is alluding to the *Encheiridion* of the Greek Stoic philosopher Epictetus (*c*.60–140 AD)—'do you wish to be a pentathlos, or a wrestler? Look to your arms, your thighs; see what your limbs are like.' The pentathlos, or pentathlete, took part in an athletic contest comprising five exercises: throwing the discus, running, jumping, wrestling, and throwing the javelin. The word *palaestra* means wrestling-place or wrestling-school.

energumen: someone possessed by a devil.

Panhormita . . . Poggio: the poet and classical scholar Antonio Beccadelli (1394–1471), known as Panhormita from his birthplace of Palermo (Latin: Panormus), was the first president of the Neapolitan literary academy. His poem *Hermaphroditus* (dedicated to Cosimo de' Medici and praising the pleasures of physical love between two young men) was publicly burned in several Italian cities on grounds of indecency; Pope Eugenius IV proscribed the reading of it under penalty of excommunication. The Florentine Poggio Bracciolini (1380–1459) was one of the most distinguished scholars of his day. While in the papal service he travelled widely in Europe, and discovered and edited manuscripts of several classical authors (hence, presumably, Bardo's admiration). He also published philosophical dialogues and a History of Florence. In 1453 he became Chancellor of the Florentine Republic. Bardo's disapproval is probably on account of his bawdy collection of stories, the *Facetiae*, widely considered to be an outrage against good taste and decorum.

51 *Thomas of Sarzana . . . the Pandects . . . Ficino*: Thommaso Parentucelli, from Sarzana near Spezia, became Pope Nicholas V in 1447 and died in 1455. An accomplished scholar and an enthusiastic collector of classical manuscripts, he was responsible for the founding of the Vatican library. Bardo's use of his secular name implies that the 'discussion' between them took place prior to his election to the papacy, probably when Parentucelli was in Florence, engaged by Cosimo de' Medici to catalogue his books. Poliziano was born in 1454. The 'Pandects', the *Digesta seu Pandectae*, was a compendium of writings on civil law by Roman jurists, ordered by the Emperor Justinian in the year 533. Poliziano's edition of the work was commissioned by Lorenzo de' Medici. The philosopher and scholar Marsilio Ficino (1433–99) was the son of Cosimo de' Medici's doctor. Himself a student of medicine, he started reading Plato in his twenties. He went on to translate most of his works into Latin, to teach him to Lorenzo de' Medici, and to become the central figure of the Florentine Platonic Academy. In his commentary on the *Symposium* he developed the concept of Platonic love. His major philosophical work, *Theologica Platonicae de Immortalitate Animarum*, was designed in part to reconcile the tenets of Platonism and Christianity (he became a priest in 1473). A believer also in astrology and the magic arts (the 'superstitious fancies' scorned by Bardo), he translated the occult *Corpus Hermeticum* of Hermes Trismegistus from Greek into Latin. His Latin style ('an offence' to the donnish Bardo) was fluent but inelegant; he wrote a number of his works in the Tuscan vernacular.

massive prophylactic rings: rings containing certain precious stones were believed to have the power of protecting the wearer against illness.

Niccolò Niccoli: like Bardo, Niccoli (1363–1437) was a member of a rich Florentine mercantile family who devoted his life to scholarship and to acquiring antiquities. He bequeathed his collection to the city, but left so many debts that there was insufficient money to found the library he had desired. In fact, Cosimo de' Medici paid off the debts (much as Bardo hoped that Lorenzo would do his) and gave the collection of antiquities to San Marco.

52 *Cassandra Fedele*: a Venetian, Cassandra Fedele (1465–1558) was renowned throughout Italy for her Greek and Latin learning. Poliziano hailed her as as much a prodigy among women as was Pico della Mirandola among men.

the divine Petrarca . . . the Aulularia of Plautus . . . the supreme Greek intellect: Bardo's quotation from Petrarch is from *Rerum Familiarium*, 4. 19. *Aulularia* is a comedy by the Roman playwright Plautus (254–184 BC). The passage in it referred to by Petrarch reads (lines 138–9) 'nam optimam nulla potest eligi: | alia alia peior, frater est' ('there is no such thing as picking out the best woman: it's only a question of comparative badness, brother'). The 'supreme Greek intellect' in this context is probably the poet Hesiod (*c.*8th cent. BC), whose poem 'Works and Days', as GE notes in *Bod*, is fiercely critical of women.

53 *the choice words of Quintilian*: the quotation is from the *Institutio Oratoria* (11. 3. 40) of Quintilian (1st cent. AD): 'sweet, enduring, resonant, clear, pure, carrying far and penetrating the ear'.

the great Boccaccio: Giovanni Boccaccio (?1313–75), best known for his narrative masterpiece the *Decameron*, was a noted collector of ancient manuscripts, which he bequeathed to the Augustinian monastery of Santo Spirito in Florence.

Aldo Manuzio: 1449–1515, an editor and printer of classical texts who set up a printing press in Venice in 1494.

54 *Hymettus*: a mountain to the east of Athens famous for its honey.

Pontanus or Merula: Giovanni Pontano (1429–1503) was a driving force behind the Neapolitan literary academy, within which he adopted the Latinized name of Jovianus Pontanus. Alfonso I of Naples made Pontano tutor to his children and then showered him with numerous gifts and honours, but when Charles VIII of France entered the city in 1494 to depose Alfonso's dynasty Pontano greeted him with a self-seeking panegyrical oration. The textual scholar Georgius Merula (*c.*1424–94) devoted his career primarily to the emendation of classical manuscripts. He spent much of his life at the Milanese court, and repaid the favour he was shown there by an unduly flattering account of the ruling house of Sforza in his history of the city.

from the client's basket: Bardo is alluding to the practice, common in Republican Rome, whereby a wealthy noble would have numerous 'clients' or dependants attached to his household, whom he would support and on whose allegiance he in turn could always count. In later, Imperial times, however, the institution of the *clientela* was so much abused that many so-called clients were mere hangers-on who presented themselves at stated times at their patron's house simply to receive food, which was dispensed to them in baskets.

a Promethean word: in Greek mythology Prometheus was a Titan who stole fire from the gods and gave it to mankind. The adjective 'Promethean' may be used to signify something vital, 'kindling', or inspiriting. Here, though, it may be that Bardo is more specifically alluding to the 'Promethean unguent', made from a herb on to which some drops of Prometheus' blood had fallen, given by Medea to Jason to render him safe against fire and weapons. Romola's 'Promethean word' makes Bardo feel proof against the '*shafts* of Fortune' and reminds him that he has the '*armour* . . . of a clear conscience'.

æs triplex: Horace, *Odes*, 1. 3. 9–10: 'illi robur et aes triplex | circa pectus erat' ('oak and triple bronze must have girt the breast').

says Epictetus: the quotations are from nos. 5 and 14 of the *Encheiridion*.

55 *Zeno . . . Epicurus . . . 'duabus sellis sedere'*: Zeno of Citium (4th cent. BC) was the founder of the Stoic school of philosophy, whose stern asceticism is embraced by Bardo in preference to the more self-indulgent principles of Epicureanism. 'Duabus sellis sedere' means to sit on two stools, to sit on the fence; it was famously employed by Seneca in his *Controversiae* when referring to Cicero's attempt to keep in with both Pompey and Caesar.

Sunt qui non habeant . . . habere: 'Some don't have these things, and there is someone who doesn't want to have them' (Horace, *Epistles*, 2. 2. 182).

'inanis': Bardo is probably alluding to Horace's phrase 'titulos inanis' ('empty glory'): *Satires*, 2. 3. 212.

parchment . . . in a sealed bag: see p. 258.

57 *panther-skin and . . . thyrsus*: the Roman god Bacchus (equivalent of the Greek Dionysus), with whom Tito is so often associated, was often represented wearing a panther skin. As god of wine he carried a *thyrsus*, a rod tipped with a pine-cone and wreathed with ivy or vine leaves.

58 *Manuelo Crisolora*: the Greek scholar Emmanuel Chrysoloras (*c.*1350–1415) was a pioneer in spreading the knowledge of

Greek literature in the West. He taught Greek in Florence for a while in the 1390s, translated Homer and Plato, and wrote a Greek grammar.

lippi: Latin: near-sighted, blear-eyed.

59 *Nauplia*: Nauplia (now Nauplion) was the port and chief town of Argolis, at the head of the Gulf of Argos.

60 *if there are two things not to be hidden—love and a cough*: Nello's remark is a quotation from Luigi Pulci's poem *Il morgante maggiore* (4. 88).

tonsor inequalis: 'the unskilful barber' (Horace, *Epistles*, 1. 1. 94).

Perdonimi . . . latino: 'May I be forgiven if I make a mistake: the person who hears me can understand my vulgar tongue with his Latin' (Pulci, *Il morgante maggiore*, 2. 57. 2–3).

grylli: the Latin word *gryllus*, meaning cricket or grasshopper, was used figuratively to signify a comic caricature.

Landino: Cristoforo Landino (1424–98), who held the chair of Poetry and Rhetoric at Florence from 1458, was the author of a notable commentary on Virgil's *Aeneid*.

the example of Lorenzo . . . an age worse than that of iron: Bardo is probably alluding to Lorenzo de' Medici's bawdy *Canti carnascialeschi*, or Carnival Songs. The period between the death of Charlemagne and the end of the Carolingian dynasty (814–987) was sometimes called the 'age of iron' because of its ceaseless wars. Bardo's contemptuous description of his own time as 'an age of tinsel and gossamer' may be in allusion to Marsilio Ficino's famous remark that 'this is an age of gold . . . at Florence', or to that of the contemporary historian Jacopo Nardi that 'from iron was born a golden age [at Florence]'.

61 *Aurispa . . . laden with manuscripts . . . erudite Greeks*: the scholar and collector Giovanni Aurispa (1370–1459), who spent some years teaching at Florence, is said to have brought back to Italy, in a single year, over 200 manuscripts of works—by Plato and other ancient writers—many of which were hitherto unknown. The 'days when erudite Greeks flocked to our shores' is a reference to the period immediately following the fall of Constantinople to the Turks in 1453, when many Greek scholars sought refuge in Italy and gave added impetus to the renascent interest in antiquity.

62 *Ciriaco*: born in Ancona, a seaport on the Adriatic coast of

central Italy, and largely self-educated (he began life as a shipping-clerk), Ciriaco de Filippo Pizzicolli (*c.*1391–*c.*1450) spent many years travelling in Greece, Asia Minor, and Egypt in search of classical inscriptions and antiquities. (It was from him, for example, that Florence received first-hand knowledge of the Pyramids.) When asked why he had devoted himself to these labours, he replied, 'I go to awake the dead.' He wrote various accounts of his travels; one of them took the form of a long letter to Pope Eugenius IV entitled *Itinerarium*, which is presumably the book referred to by Bardo (see p. 63).

plains of the Eurotas . . . the gigantic stones of Mycenæ and Tyrins: the Eurotas is the river on which Sparta stood. The ancient Greek cities of Mycenae and Tiryns, about nine miles apart, both have massive walls which were said to have been built by the Cyclopes.

63 *the Isolario of Cristofero Buondelmonte . . . Ambrogio Traversari*: a Florentine merchant turned priest, Buondelmonte (d. 1422) travelled widely among the Greek islands in search of manuscripts for Cosimo de' Medici. He described his voyages in *De Insulis Archipelago*, the book referred to by Bardo as the *Isolario* (*isola* = island). Ambrogio Traversari (1386–1439) was a Camaldolensian monk who had studied Greek at Constantinople. Later, as General of the Camaldolensian order, he made an extended inspection tour of monasteries throughout Italy, where he discovered a number of important ancient manuscripts. He wrote an account of his travels in the *Hodoeporicon*—the book referred to by Bardo as an *Itinerarium*.

hideous crimes: GE is probably thinking of the notorious feud in which Poggio branded his fellow scholar Filelfo the bastard son of a country priest and a tripe-seller and then accused him of 'fraud, ingratitude, theft, adultery, and yet more scandalous crimes'. Poggio also vilified Lorenzo Valla (see n. to p. 115) for once writing *illi* instead of *sibi*—the occasion, perhaps, of the reference here to Bardo being attacked 'for having shown error in a single preposition'.

64 *Setine*: a Turkish corruption of the name Athens.

conquered rival: Athens was named for Athena, who had successfully disputed with Poseidon for the honour of being the city's patron.

where St. Philip baptized the Ethiopian eunuch: as recorded in the Acts of the Apostles (8: 26–39), the baptism in fact took place on the road from Jerusalem to Gaza. The preposterous relocation of the event to Athens is borrowed from the account of an anonymous Greek traveller to Athens in 1460. This account, in a manuscript in the Imperial Library in Vienna, is quoted by the French historian Léon de Laborde in his *History of Athens* (1854), a book from which GE made copious notes.

65 *temple . . . now again perverted to the accursed ends of the Moslem*: the chief temple of Pallas Athena on the Acropolis, the Parthenon was originally associated with the cult of Athena Parthenos the Virgin. It was transformed into a church in the 5th cent. and dedicated to the Virgin Mary in 662. The Turks turned it into a mosque after the fall of Athens in 1458.

'old stones': the phrase is taken from Laborde, who notes that Western travellers in 15th-cent. Athens would have been thought to be Venetian spies if they tried to examine the ancient ruins which the Turks regarded simply as 'vieilles pierres' ('old stones').

Pausanias and Pliny described: Pausanias (2nd cent. AD) described the monuments of ancient Greece in his *Periegesis*; Pliny the Elder (1st cent. AD) touches on them in his *Historia Naturalis*.

Helicon . . . fountain Hippocrene: the fountain of Hippocrene was located on the higher slopes of Mount Helicon, in Boeotia, which was regarded as the seat of the Muses.

66 *girl of eighteen*: Bardo says that Romola was 6 when he went blind (p. 53), and that his sight was 'fast failing' in 1477 (p. 47), which suggests that in 1492 Romola should have been 20 or 21.

67 *Margites . . . 'abnormis sapiens'*: Margites—'the booby'—is the hero of a lost Greek comic poem that was widely believed to have been written by Homer. A ludicrous figure, he displayed conceit and ignorance in equal measure. 'Abnormis sapiens' (Horace, *Satires*, 2. 2. 3) means 'strangely wise', 'an unschooled scholar'.

68 *Con viso che tacendo dicea, Taci*: 'With a look that silently said, "Be silent"' (Dante, *Purgatorio*, 21. 104).

69 *sanctioned by Pliny*: in book 37 of the *Historia Naturalis*.

Camillo Leonardi: the author of *Speculum Lapidum* ('The Mirror of Stones'), a 15th-cent. book on the mystic properties of gems, which GE consulted in her preparations for the novel.

71 *'To wish ill or well . . . wrongs or kindness'*: in *Pf* GE jots down the original of this statement by Farinata degli Uberti, a prominent Florentine of the Ghibelline faction in the 13th cent.: 'Volere e disvolere, per oltraggi e grazie riceviste.'

73 *now known as the Casa Gherardesca . . . Gradatim*: in 1558 the Scala palace was sold to Cardinal Alessandro de' Medici, on whose death it descended to his sister Constanza, wife of Ugo della Gherardesca. Scala's Latin motto *Gradatim* means 'step by step'.

embassy to Rome . . . Gonfaloniere: Scala went to Rome in December 1484 to deliver the Florentine Republic's official oration in honour of the new Pope, Innocent VIII—as a result of which the Pope conferred on him the various dignities mentioned in the novel. As to the date of Scala's election to the office of Gonfaloniere, GE has made an uncharacteristic slip. As she records in *Q*, he was elected in 1486; however, 'eight years ago' from this point in the novel would be 1484.

a very typical and pretty quarrel: in fact, though Scala and Poliziano had crossed swords on previous occasions, the specific quarrel which GE goes on to describe in such detail took place early in 1494—some 18 months after this point in the action of the novel. The following two paragraphs comprise a close paraphrase of the published correspondence between Scala and Poliziano. GE has not reproduced the entire interchange, but the salient and representative details she has selected are taken directly from the letters.

74 *a lucky man*: when Scala had been elected Gonfaloniere in 1486, Poliziano had written an ode declaring that neither nobility of birth nor virtue, but the merest good fortune, had been responsible for his advancement. The insult was repeated by Poliziano in a letter of 1494 during the 'learned squabble' described in this chapter.

the terrible Joseph Scaliger: Joseph Justus Scaliger (1540–1609) was celebrated alike for his learning and his vituperative criticisms of fellow scholars. Of Scala he remarked, 'I shall say nothing about that man except that he didn't have the remotest clue about Latin.'

hendecasyllables: i.e. verse written in lines of eleven syllables each. A heavy-handed joke is made about a clumsy attempt to elide two syllables which has resulted in a line too long for the chosen form—not by as much as a (metrical) *foot*, but 'at least a *toe* too much'. 'Solecisms' are syntactical incongruities.

75 *Latin epigram . . . feminine gender . . . conceit about Venus, Cupid, and the culex*: the word *culex* is indeed almost always masculine, though it appears in the feminine gender in Plautus' play *Casina* and in one manuscript of the poem *Culex* (see below). Poliziano's Latin epigram, written as if from the culex itself, reads: 'I am not a woman, Scala, neither in Latin nor Greek, and therefore I like girls.' The 'conceit' in Poliziano's Greek epigram was about the gnat in the role of a lover, rising like Venus from breeding waters and flying like Cupid to suck the blood of sleeping women while singing, 'What man bears as many marks of love as the gnat?'

the doctrine of Thales: the philosopher Thales (6th cent. BC), one of the so-called 'Seven Wise Men' of ancient Greece, was credited by Aristotle with having suggested that all matter has its origin in water.

the gnat . . . "alumnus of the waters": until well into the 20th cent. the anonymous poem *Culex* was generally believed to be an early work of Virgil. Line 183 of the poem refers to the gnat as 'umoris alumnus' ('nursling of the damp').

nihil ad rem: Latin: not to the point, irrelevant.

76 *a Homeric sentiment*: Poliziano's quotation was from *Iliad*, 9. 312–13 (Achilles to Odysseus): 'hateful to me even as the gates of hell is he that hides one thing in his heart and says another'.

branny monster . . . dignissimus: Poliziano's letter reads: 'At ego monstru vocavi te furfuraceum. Monstrum quide, quod ex colluvione monstrorum compositus es. Furfuraceum vero, quod in pistrini sordibus natus, & quidem pistrino dignissimus.' ('I've called you a branny monster. A monster certainly, since created from the droppings of monsters. Branny indeed because born amid the filth of a mill, and entirely suited to a mill.')

77 *assuming to be a Hercules . . . destroy all the literary monstrosities*: Scala did indeed criticize Poliziano in these terms in one of the letters of their correspondence. He is alluding to the famous labours of the mythical Greek hero Hercules, several of which involved the killing of fabulous monsters.

thought they wrote like Cicero . . . "esse videtur": Cicero's preferred ending was in fact *esse videatur* ('it seems to be'); the hexameter verse ending *esse videtur* would have been inappropriate to a prose sentence. What I take to be GE's mistake here (though conceivably she intends it as a remarkably erudite joke at Scala's expense) is the stranger in that she appears to be alluding to Quintilian's *Institutio Oratoria*, 10. 2. 18 (as did Poliziano himself in a letter to another correspondent): 'I have known some who thought that they had produced a brilliant imitation of the style of that divine orator, by ending their periods with the phrase *esse videatur*.' Though they argued at length about Ciceronian style, and whose Latin was closest to it, neither Scala nor Poliziano invoked this comparison in their correspondence.

O wise young judge!: cf. *The Merchant of Venice*, IV. i. 222–3: 'A Daniel come to judgement! Yea, a Daniel! O wise young judge, how I do honour thee!'

lusus naturæ . . . Cupid riding on the lion . . . the "Jew's Stone," with the lion-headed serpent: a *lusus naturæ* is a 'freak of nature', here referring to a gemstone of particularly unusual markings—resembling Cupid astride a lion, the design on the signet ring of the 6th cent. BC Greek tyrant Polycrates, about which GE found information in King's *Antique Gems*. A frequent design on ancient Egyptian amulets was a serpent with a lion's head, representing the god Chneph. In Renaissance times such amulets were commonly thought to have a Jewish origin, and were thus called Jews' Stones.

78 *Theodolinda . . . Constantine the Great and Pope Sylvester*: Theodelinda was Queen of the Lombards in the late 6th cent. The Roman Emperor Constantine was supposedly cured of leprosy by being baptized by St Sylvester in the early 3rd cent. The story goes that as a result he bestowed upon Sylvester and his heirs as bishop of Rome (i.e. the Popes) the sovereignty of Rome, and himself founded a new capital in the east (Constantinople).

79 *the man-destroyer*: Ares, the Greek equivalent of Mars, is described by Homer as 'murderous' (*Odyssey*, 8. 115) and as 'blood-stained bane of mortals' (*Iliad*, 5. 31).

Guelf and Ghibelline . . . Black and White . . . heretic Paterini . . . hated Pisa: the Guelphs and Ghibellines were political factions whose most violent clashes occurred in the 13th cent. The Blacks and the Whites (*Bianchi e Neri*) were rival factions in the 14th cent. whose quarrel initially derived from a family feud. The common ancestor of the two houses concerned had had two wives; one was called Bianca, and the descendants of that branch were therefore known as *Bianchi* (whites), whereupon their rivals took the name of *Neri* (blacks). As the quarrel spread and became political, the *Bianchi* were associated with the Ghibellines and the *Neri* with the Guelphs. *Paterini* (from Pattaria, a poor quarter of Milan) was originally the name given to the followers of deacon Arialdi in 11th-cent. Milan, who opposed the marriage of priests; it was subsequently applied as a general term of religious opprobrium to any 'heretical' sect. After decades of bitter struggle Florence finally conquered Pisa in 1406, thus giving it direct access to the sea for the first time.

"the fifth element" . . . Madonna dell' Impruneta: on the occasion of the first Jubilee, or Plenary Indulgence, instituted by Pope Boniface VIII in the year 1300, no fewer than 12 European states sent Florentines to Rome as their ambassadors, leading the Pope to remark that Florentines were 'a fifth element of the world'. For the Madonna dell' Impruneta see n. to p. 359.

80 *Cecca . . . Perugino*: Francesco d'Angelo (1447–88), known as Cecca—a variant of Cecco, from Francesco—was a noted Florentine engineer, builder of siege engines, and improver of the city's defensive walls and towers. He was also responsible for designing the spectacular 'special effects' associated with the celebration of major religious festivals, such as that of San Giovanni. Those described by GE in this paragraph and on p. 82 are taken from Vasari's account in his 'Life of Cecca'. As for the saints which 'may be seen to this day in the pictures of Perugino' (Pietro Vannucci, 1445–1524, known as Perugino from his long residence in Perugia), GE is probably thinking of his *Assumption of the Virgin* with saints Giovanni Gualberto, Benedict, Bernardo degli Uberti, and Michael (*c.*1500: now in the Uffizi Gallery, though GE saw it in the Accademia delle Belle Arti, describing it in her journal as 'an assumption by Perugino which I like well for its cherubs and angels, and for some of the adoring figures below').

81 *says an old chronicler*: Goro Dati, of whose account, dating from the year 1400, the remainder of this sentence is a direct translation.

Pope Innocent was dying . . . set Italy by the ears: Innocent VIII died almost exactly a month after Midsummer Day 1492, on 25 July. Charles VIII of France was being encouraged by the ambitious Ludovico Sforza of Milan to invade Italy and claim the throne of Naples.

82 *the Bargello*: in 1492 the building, which had been begun in 1255, would in fact have been known as the Palazzo del Podestà (see n. to p. 88). It did not become the headquarters of the Bargello (Chief of Police) until the mid-16th cent.

the Church worshipped in the catacombs: a reference to the days when early Christians (most notably in Rome) were obliged to hold their services secretly in underground catacombs to avoid persecution.

83 *the Valdarno*: the valley of the River Arno in the countryside outside Florence.

'hound of the Lord': 'A play on the name of the Dominicans (*Domini Canes*) which was accepted by themselves, and which is pictorially represented in a fresco painted for them by Simone Memmi.' [GE] The fresco of the Church Militant, showing St Dominic sending forth the hounds of the Lord (*Domini Canes*), is in the Spanish Chapel of the Dominican church of Santa Maria Novella, and is in fact by Andrea di Bonaiuto (*fl.* 1343–77), who is also known as Andrea da Firenze. The fresco was formerly thought to be by the Sienese painter Simone Martini (*c.*1283–1344), who in the 19th cent. was sometimes confused with his brother-in-law Lippo Memmi (*fl.* 1317–47).

84 *Francesco Cei*: 1471–1505, a minor poet. Among the foremost of the *Compagnacci* (see n. to p. 370), he was instrumental in precipitating a riot in San Marco on the occasion of Savonarola's Ascension Day sermon there in 1497. Dissolute and irreverent, he wrote numerous poems against the Church in general and Savonarola in particular.

Cronaca . . . put the Frate's doctrines into stone: the architect Simone Masi (1455–1509), more generally known as Simone del Pollaiuolo from his being related to the sculptor Antonio Pollaiuolo, was also known as 'Il Cronaca' ('the chronicler') because of the vivid and detailed accounts he would give of the antiquities he had seen while living in Rome. Among his most important works are the Strozzi Palace, the sacristy of Santo Spirito, and the Salone dei Cinquecento in the Palazzo Vecchio. During the last years of his life, according to Vasari, 'he became possessed with such a frenzy for the discourses of Fra Girolamo Savonarola, and his head was so filled with them, that he would speak of nothing else'.

Orators: ambassadors (the usage is now obsolete; the first English use of the word recorded by *OED* is in 1494).

85 *Venetian . . . at ease on the back of a dolphin*: the speaker being Cennini, the printer, the allusion here is perhaps to Aldus Manutius' (see n. to p. 53) typographical device of an anchor and dolphin, which appeared as a logo on the title-pages of his books.

the Madonna Nunziata: Nello is referring to the 'miraculous fresco' (p. 139) of the Annunciation in the church of the Annunziata, popularly believed to have been painted by a friar under the guidance of an angel or, according to a variant of the legend, by the angels themselves.

Pisans false, Florentines blind: from the Tuscan proverb 'Fiorentini ciechi, Pisani traditori'.

Minerva with her peplos: the Greek counterpart of Minerva was Athena, who was patroness of Athens as San Giovanni was patron of Florence. A new robe (*peplos*) was woven each year for her statue in Athens.

86 *says the old chronicler*: again the chronicler concerned is Goro Dati, and again GE's description (from 'warriors on horseback' to '"all things that could delight the eye and the heart"') is a word-for-word translation of his account.

Mugello . . . Casentino . . . grotesque sketches: Vasari records that Leonardo da Vinci was so fascinated by 'faces of extraordinary character, or heads, beards or hair of unusual appearance' that he would follow their owners about the streets all day and then go home and draw them. He is also reported to have invited a number of peasants to supper on one occasion and then told them funny stories to make them laugh so that he could sketch their faces in extravagant contortions. Mugello and Casentino were rural districts of Tuscany.

Romagnole: from Romagna, the northern part of the Papal States, between the Apennines and the River Po.

Saint Anthony's swine: St Anthony (251–356), also known as St Anthony the Abbot, is commonly represented in paintings with a pig—a symbol of sensuality, which he subdued. This image gave rise to the superstition that the pig was under his special protection, and by association he became the patron saint of swineherds. The monks of the order of St Anthony kept herds of consecrated pigs, which were allowed to feed at the public cost and which it was sacrilege to kill.

car: really 'cart' or 'waggon'—from the Italian *carro*.

87 *St. John the Baptist . . . the Holy Family*: by the mid-15th cent. the figure of St John as a solitary hermit was well established in religious iconography. It was not until the very end of the cent. that the tendency arose to intensify the relationship between John and Jesus (as children, or infants), whereby John was introduced into the family group. The 'garment of tiger-skins' in which the mimic San Giovanni is clad was a vernacular tradition (the Bible relates that he wore a raiment of camel's hair) peculiar to the Midsummer Day procession in Florence.

"beautiful sheepfold": Dante, *Paradiso*, 25. 5.

eidolon: image, apparition.

corporation of Calimala: '"Arte di Calimala," "arte" being, in this use of it, equivalent to corporation.' [GE] A citizen could be matriculated, i.e. admitted to membership in a guild, only after giving evidence of suitable skills.

88 *harpies*: literally, 'snatchers'. Their representation on the car of the Zecca was as the ravenous birds of Greek mythology, whose beaks Francesco Cei here likens to the noses of money-changers.

Diogenes-fashion . . . the Feast of Fools: the Cynic philosopher Diogenes of Sinope (4th cent. BC) is reported to have lit a lamp in broad daylight and announced that he was going in search of an honest man. Four hundred candle-bearing members of the Calimala Guild traditionally accompanied the car of the Zecca in processions. The Feast of Fools was a form of clerical saturnalia or burlesque mass with indecent songs and obscene dances, common throughout the Middle Ages and usually held between 26 and 28 December.

Donatello's statue of Judith: in 1492 Maestro Vaiano's monkeys could not in fact have seen this statue by Donatello (1384–1466) unless they had access to the gardens of the Medici Palace. It was removed from there to a site outside the Palazzo Vecchio in 1495 following the expulsion of the Medici from Florence, and then placed in Orgagna's Loggia—where GE would have seen it—in 1506. The statue was cast in the late 1450s. For Maestro Vaiano, see Ch. 10.

ancients . . . gravity and jest: Cei may be alluding to Juvenal's account (*Satires*, 10. 28–30) of two Greek sages, one of whom laughed and one of whom wept each time they observed their fellow men.

foreign Podestà: the office of Podestà or chief magistrate, abolished in Florence by the Medici in the 1470s, was common to most Lombard and Tuscan cities from the early 13th cent. onwards. The Podestà was a non-Florentine, elected for a period of one year, as an impartial arbiter in both civil and criminal cases. He also acted as commander-in-chief of the army and as the city's representative in dealings with foreign powers. He received a fixed salary from the State and had his official residence in the building later known as the Bargello.

over-doctored by clever medici: Cennini is punning on the name Medici, the Italian word for doctors.

Proposto: 'Spokesman or Moderator.' [GE] The position rotated among the Priors, generally being changed twice a week, and sometimes every second day.

89 *dragon that guards . . . Bardo's gold*: in Greek mythology the golden apples received by Hera as a marriage-gift were guarded by a dragon in the Garden of the Hesperides.

Pactolus: the Pactolus is a river in Asia Minor believed to have gold in the sands beneath its waters after King Midas bathed in it to rid himself of his fatal gift of turning everything he touched to gold.

90 *singular good fortune*: Endymion was a shepherd with whom Selene, the moon goddess, fell in love.

Da quel giorno . . . cortese: 'From the very day when love enflamed me I have become through her both gentle and courteous' (Pulci, *Il morgante maggiore*, 2. 68. 7–8).

under our four eyes that I talk: a translation of the Italian expression 'parlare a quattr' occhi'.

he can see a buffalo in the snow: i.e. he can see something that is entirely obvious. The expression is taken from Sacchetti's *Trecentonovelle* (no. 209).

93 *forbidden by the Signory to wear the richest brocade*: like many other Italian cities in the 15th cent., Florence had regulations known as sumptuary laws designed to check extravagance among its citizens (particularly of the lower classes, and generally ignored by the nobility). Among the items of dress they proscribed was 'any brocade of silver or gold, or embroidery'. The scarcity of (gold and silver) plate in 15th-cent. Florence is commented on again on p. 120.

94 *morgen cap*: 'A sum given by the bridegroom to the bride the day after the marriage (*Morgengabe*).' [GE]

99 *hostelry of the Bertucce*: one of the most celebrated inns of 15th-cent. Florence, a favourite resort of Lorenzo de' Medici.

100 *she'll come back presently, as the toad said to the harrow*: GE has taken this expression, signifying that the person has absolutely no wish to return at all, from Machiavelli's comic drama *La mandragola* (3. 6).

father-in-law: GE uses the word in its archaic sense of 'step-father'.

San Pulinari: a church just off the Piazza della Signoria.

101 *Peretola*: a village some three-and-a-half miles to the north-west of the city.

102 *badge of the yellow veil*: prostitutes were obliged to wear this as a sign of their profession.

Lorenzo de' Medici's Nencia da Barberino . . . Theocritus: Lorenzo's poem tells the story of the wooing by a young peasant (Vallera) of a peasant girl (Nencia). Theocritus was a Greek poet of the 3rd cent. BC whose *Idylls* created the model for classical bucolic poetry, of which *Nencia* is an imitation.

105 *Breve . . . Prato*: a *breve* is a relic, or prayer written on a scrap of paper, in a bag worn round the neck as a charm. Prato is a town about seven miles north-west of Florence.

107 *bit of red coral . . . a 'buon fortuna'*: in her notes in *WN* from John Paris's *Pharmacologia; or the History of Medicinal Substances* (1820) GE writes: 'it was even supposed that coral would drive away devils & evil spirits; hence arose the custom of wearing coral amulets round the neck . . . In Sicily it is also commonly worn as an amulet by persons of all ranks as a security against an evil eye: a small twisted piece, resembling a horn, is worn at the watchchain, under the name of "Buon Fortuna," & is occasionally pointed at those who are supposed to have evil intentions.'

111 *nidus*: Latin: nest.

112 *sing the old Eumenides, in Æschylus*: *Eumenides*, 517–25.

114 *the poet has wisely said*: Horace, *Satires*, 1. 9. 59–60: 'life grants no reward to man without much toil'.

'palma sine pulvere': Horace, *Epistles*, 1. 1. 51: 'the prize without the effort' (literally, 'the palm without the dust').

115 *what says the Greek?*: Bardo's quotation is from an untitled fragment by Hesiod.

excursus: a dissertation appended to a scholarly work.

Calderino: Domizio Calderino (*c.*1447–78) was professor of Rhetoric at Rome and a celebrated editor of classical texts. In the preface to his *Miscellanea*, Poliziano attacks the widespread malpractices among contemporary scholars who 'ascribe to classical authorities words which are not theirs, quote non-existent classical authors, cite ancient manuscripts which are nowhere to be found, and fill their books with painstaking vanities'. Though Calderino is not referred to here by name, he is the most frequent target of Poliziano's invective in the ensuing chapters.

Lorenzo Valla: 1407–57, classical scholar, philologist, and moral philosopher. As Apostolic Secretary to Pope Nicholas V he translated Thucydides into Latin. His treatise *Elegentiae Linguae Latinae* sought to establish the correct usage of the ancient Romans on numerous points of grammar and style, and thus to restore the Latin language to its original purity—something which Bardo would clearly have applauded. Valla was certainly held 'in dubious fame' by the Church, by which he was branded a heretic and summoned to appear before the Inquisition. Neither was he a popular figure with many of his fellow-scholars, with whom he indulged in rancorous literary feuds (see p. 63). The epigram referred to by Bardo was anonymous; it read 'Dopo che morto il Valla giunse fra le ombre, Plutone non ardisce di parlare in latino' ('Since Valla died and arrived among the shades, Pluto has not dared to speak Latin').

117 *scholia*: scholarly notes.

Three rows of pearls . . . rose-coloured petticoat . . . seed pearl arabesques . . . coral rosary . . . clasp of silver wrought in niello: each item of Monna Ghita's elaborate costume is taken from a description of the trousseau of a certain Ginevra d'Ugolino di Niccolò Martelli, who married Cino di Filippo Rinuccini in Florence in 1461. Niello is a black alloy of silver, lead, copper, and sulphur, used to fill in engraved designs on silver and gold.

119 *as solemn as San Giuseppe*: neither St Joseph the husband of the Virgin nor St Joseph of Arimathea was generally represented in art as looking especially solemn (nor does the Bible describe either of them as such). GE may perhaps be thinking of the former in Gentile da Fabriano's *Adoration of the Magi*

which she saw in the Accademia di Belle Arti (now in the Uffizi Gallery), whose face might be described as 'solemn' in the sense of 'sad' or 'thoughtful'.

Piagnoni: 'Funereal mourners: properly, paid mourners.' [GE] The term, meaning 'weepers' or 'snivellers', was applied to members of the popular party because, like Savonarola himself, they continually bewailed the sins of the city.

Pinzochera: 'A Sister of the Third Order of St. Francis: an uncloistered nun.' [GE] The third order of Franciscans consisted of *lay* brothers and sisters. The word has since come to signify any kind of religious zealot—or bigot.

the Frate's book about widows: Savonarola's pamphlet 'Libro della Vita Viduale' was published in 1491. In it, though acknowledging that widows might remarry under certain circumstances, he declares that the most fitting life for them is to renounce the world, devote themselves entirely to God, and become 'even as the dove, which is a chaste creature, and therefore, having lost its mate, never couples with another, but spends the rest of its life in lonely lamentation'.

Francesco Valori: like many of the supporters of Savonarola and the popular party, Valori had been a close associate of Lorenzo de' Medici (whose palace was in the Via Larga). Like many of Lorenzo's adherents, however, he became thoroughly disaffected with the wilful and incompetent Piero de' Medici, and transferred his allegiance to Savonarola.

120 *Franco Sacchetti's book*: Sacchetti (?1332–1400) was a prolific poet and story-writer, whose prose masterpiece, the *Trecentonovelle*, modelled on Boccaccio's *Decameron*, consists of brief moral tales on all aspects of contemporary men and manners. The reference here is probably to novella 136, which tells of women's remarkable ability to disguise impurities in their faces by the skilful application of make-up.

121 *as comfortable as wet chickens*: from the Tuscan expression 'come un pulcin bagnato' ('like a soaked chicken').

last Quaresima in San Lorenzo: i.e. Savonarola's Lenten sermons of 1492, delivered in the church of San Lorenzo.

the Befana: 'The name given to the grotesque black-faced figures, supposed to represent the Magi, carried about or placed in the windows on Twelfth Night: a corruption of *Epifania*.' [GE] *the good men of St. Martin*: the charitable society devoted to relieving the poor of Florence, referred to in GE's footnote to p. 44.

the great preachers Fra Mariano and Fra Menico . . . the Pope's dream: the Augustinian Fra Mariano da Gennazzano was a fashionable preacher known for his ornately eloquent style of delivery. In 1491, alarmed at the growing influence of Savonarola's denunciations of State and Church corruption, Lorenzo de' Medici encouraged Fra Mariano to preach against him. He duly accused Savonarola of being a false prophet and a vain disseminator of scandal and disorder among the people. For Fra Menico see n. to p. 20. In 1210 Pope Innocent III is reported to have had a dream in which he saw Francis of Assisi propping up the wall of the Lateran church in Rome, which seemed about to fall down. He promptly sent for Francis and approved the *Regula Prima* which governed the newly formed Franciscan order. The dream became a favourite subject for artists.

125 *mora*: a game for *two* players: one holds up a random number of fingers while the other simultaneously guesses the number. Either Sandro is remarkably dim-witted, or GE has misunderstood the nature of the game.

126 *Quant' è bella . . . certezza*: '"Beauteous is life in blossom! | And it fleeteth—fleeteth ever; | Whoso would be joyful—let him! | There's no surety for the morrow." *Carnival Song by Lorenzo de' Medici.*' [GE] It is appropriate that Tito should choose these particular lines, which form the opening of Lorenzo's song 'The Triumph of Bacchus and Ariadne' (see p. 177).

as the sublime poet says: cf. Dante, *Purgatorio*, 21. 37–8: '. . . la cruna | del mio disio' ('the needle's eye of my desire').

young Bernardo Dovizi of Bibbiena: Dovizi (1470–1520) was a tutor to Lorenzo's son the 'boy-cardinal' Giovanni de' Medici (see n. to p. 129), though he was barely five years older than his pupil—on whose election to the papacy in 1513 he himself was created a cardinal.

127 *carry a net out to catch the wind*: a translation of the Tuscan proverb 'pigliare il vento con le reti' ('to catch the wind with a net').

Ser Piero: Piero Dovizi da Bibbiena had been chancellor to Lorenzo de' Medici, and subsequently acted in the manner of a vizier to Piero de' Medici. His arrogance and high-handed behaviour made him widely unpopular.

touch the sky with your forefinger: a literal translation of the Italian expression 'toccare il cielo con un dito' (meaning to be beside oneself with joy).

ears double-waxed: a reference to Ulysses' device of filling his companions' ears with wax to prevent them from hearing the song of the sirens.

overthrown . . . like cavaliers in heavy armour: the origin of this remark is probably to be found in Tacitus (*Histories*, 1. 79), describing a battle in which the Sarmatian cavalry suffered just such a fate at the hands of the Romans. The phrases 'not a herb out of his own garden' and 'feeding one with an empty spoon' are from the Italian expressions 'non è erba del suo orto' and 'imboccare col cucchiaio vuoto'.

128 *win my Alcestis . . . a Pleiad*: according to Greek mythology, when Admetus asked for the hand of Alcestis he was told that she would be given only to a man who arrived at her father's court in a chariot drawn by a lion and a boar. Admetus accomplished this feat with the aid of Apollo. Alcestis later gave up her life for her husband. The Pleiades were the seven daughters of Atlas, who were transformed into stars. One of them, Merope, is invisible, supposedly out of shame at having married a mortal.

'prettier than the turnip-flower,' 'with a cheek more savoury than cheese': Nello's quotation is from the 25th octave of Lorenzo de' Medici's *Nencia da Barberino*.

the mountains of Pistoia: the town of Pistoia is some 20 miles to the north-west of Florence; a range of hills begins just to the north of it.

the Fierucola: 'The Little Fair.' [GE]

129 *Giovanni de' Medici . . . Pope Leo the Tenth*: Giovanni, the second son of Lorenzo the Magnificent, became a cardinal at the age of 13 in 1489, and was elected Pope in 1513. His 'broad dark cheek' is most famously represented in Raphael's portrait of him as Leo X.

131 *as old as Sant' Anna*: St Luke (2: 36–7) records that the prophetess Anna, a widow, was 84 years old.

a sign of reverence rarely made: in his *Storia fiorentina*, in a passage marked by GE in her own copy, the historian

Benedetto Varchi records that the 'reverenza' of raising the 'cappuccio' was commonly accorded only to the Gonfaloniere or to a bishop or cardinal.

134 *Maestro Gabbadeo*: the comic exploits of a quack doctor from Prato called Maestro Gabbadeo are described in nos. 155 and 168 of Sacchetti's *Trecentonovelle*.

135 *a pumpkin on my shoulders*: the phrase 'testa di zucca' (literally 'pumpkin-head') is commonly used to signify a fool.

137 *Alexander the Sixth . . . peculiar piety*: Rodrigo Borgia—'a lustful, greedy, lying, and murderous old man' (p. 431)—was elected Pope in 1492.

138 *youth of seventeen . . . Mariotto*: GE is probably thinking of the Florentine painter Mariotto Albertinelli (1474–1515), who was indeed aged 17 in 1492.

139 *dark with the excess of light*: the phrase is almost certainly borrowed from Dante: either *Purgatorio*, 17. 55–7 ('a divine spirit which hides itself with its own light') or *Paradiso*, 5. 133–4 ('like the sun which conceals itself by too much light').

140 *altar-piece*: surprisingly, perhaps, it would seem that GE has invented this. The only altarpiece in the church with an image of St Michael was the one by Antonio del Ceraiuolo in the eighth chapel of the circular Tribune at the east end—a long way from the 'sacred image' of the Annunciation, and at the opposite end from the cloisters through which Tito leads Tessa. In fact, the description here of St Michael 'in his armour, with young face and floating hair, amongst bearded and tonsured saints' is strikingly reminiscent of Perugino's altarpiece of the Assumption, to which GE had apparently referred earlier in the novel (see n. to p. 80), though this was never in the Annunziata and was not executed until *c.*1500.

141 *cloisters surrounding the atrium . . . Andrea del Sarto*: there are 12 frescoes in the atrium, or Chiostrino dei Voti, of the Santissima Annunziata, all dating from the carly 16th cent. Seven of them are by Andrea del Sarto (1486–1530). The cloisters were roofed over in the 1830s.

142 *Saint Christopher . . . little Gesù*: the story goes that St Christopher was a giant who one day carried a little child across a river. The child was Jesus, and when Christopher [= Christ-bearer] exclaimed that had he carried the whole world upon his shoulders the load could not have been heavier, the

child replied that this was because he was in fact carrying him who made the world. The St Christopher sighted by Tessa in the streets was evidently one of the 'saints of gigantic size . . . balancing themselves on stilts' who formed part of the procession in honour of San Giovanni described in Ch. 8. The St Christopher 'on the wall of the church' was probably the twenty-foot-high painting by Pollaiuolo on the side of the church of San Miniato-tra-le-torri.

149 *roll myself among thorns*: when St Benedict, a hermit, was tempted by the memory of a beautiful woman he had once known, he took off his clothes and flung himself into a thicket of thorns until his whole body was lacerated—to rid himself of the impure mental image by physical pain.

157 *ordeal of swallowing bread and cheese pills*: the allusion is to the medieval superstition (to which Tito clearly does not subscribe) that men who know themselves to be guilty will be unable to swallow, and may therefore be tested by being given bread and cheese to eat.

ortolans: an ortolan is a small bird, a species of bunting, found in southern Europe and prized for its delicate taste.

160 *got your Fra Girolamo back again*: a reference to Savonarola's visit to Venice during the summer of 1492.

new Jonah: Jonah was the prophet who warned Nineveh of impending destruction if it did not mend its wicked ways. Savonarola himself invokes this parallel on p. 201.

non oratorem, sed aratorem: 'not an orator, but a ploughman.' The remark is from a letter of Filelfo about the Roman author Quintilian.

161 *Dombruno's sharp-cutting scimitar*: Don Bruno was a fearsome Saracen giant in Luigi Pulci's *Il morgante maggiore*. The words quoted by Nello about his 'scimitarra incantata' ('enchanted scimitar') are from canto 17, stanza 101.

Bucephalus: an ironic reference to the famous war-horse of Alexander the Great.

Boccaccio's Maestro Simone: *Decameron*, 8. 9 concerns the exploits of a Florentine doctor called Maestro Simone who is eventually thrown into a sewerage ditch by the townspeople.

162 *Laudamus*: Latin: 'praise be'.

163 *batrachian*: from the Greek *batrachos*, a frog: a member of the frog or toad family.

Antonio Benevieni: Ben*i*vieni (1443–1502) was a celebrated Florentine doctor and author of a treatise on the causes of disease.

164 *Hippocrates, Galen, and Avicenna*: it is in honour of Hippocrates (5th cent. BC), the most famous of all ancient physicians, that the 'Hippocratic oath' is still taken by doctors upon qualification. Galen, a Graeco-Roman of the 2nd cent. AD, wrote treatises on almost all aspects of medicine and was widely influential in medieval and Renaissance times. Still more important to the development of the modern science was the great Arab physician Abu Ibn Sina (980–1037), who was known in the west as Avicenna.

carry a large nail ready to fasten in the wheel of Fortune: GE is probably thinking of no. 193 of Sacchetti's *Trecentonovelle*, which tells the story of Valore Buondelmonte who turned up uninvited at a feast carrying a large nail and suggested that the host, a very successful man, should fasten it in the wheel of Fortune while he was still at the top, thereby preventing himself from coming down in the world as the wheel continued to turn.

San Cosmo and San Damiano: Cosmas and Damian were twin brothers who practised medicine in Cilicia. Christians, they were martyred in the year 303 during the persecutions of Diocletian. They are patron saints of barbers, druggists, dentists, and doctors (and hence of the Medici family). San Stefano is of course St Stephen, the first Christian martyr, whose death by stoning is recorded in the Acts of the Apostles.

165 *Cecco d'Ascoli*: Francesco (or Cecco) Stabili, known as d'Ascoli from his birthplace, was an astrologer who was burned at the stake for heresy in Florence in 1327.

tussis: Latin: a cough.

166 *Frate Minore who preached against the Jews*: as Bratti had explained to Tito in Ch. 1, the Franciscans (the *Frati Minori*) were implacable enemies of the Jews and had frequently urged their eviction from the city. The specific event to which Nello alludes here is presumably the expulsion from Florence in 1488 of the rabble-rousing Franciscan Bernadino da Feltre, who denounced the government for permitting Jews to live in the city and practise usury.

wondrous Florentine device: in *BL* GE notes that spectacles were invented by a Florentine named Salvino d'Armato, who died in 1317. In fact, though the earliest recorded comment on the use of optical lenses in the West is by Roger Bacon in 1268, it is now generally believed that eyeglasses were introduced into Europe in the late 13th cent. by Alessandro di Spina, also a Florentine.

168 *a scene such as Florentines loved*: writing to Alexander Main in 1871, GE noted: 'The general ignorance of old Florentine literature, and the false conceptions of Italy bred by idle travelling . . . have caused many parts of "Romola" to be entirely misunderstood—the scene of the quack doctor and the monkey for example, which is a specimen, not of humour as I relish it, but of the practical joking which was the amusement of the gravest old Florentines, and without which no conception of them would be historical. The whole piquancy of the scene in question was intended to lie in the antithesis between the puerility which stood for wit and humour in the old Republic, and the majesty of its front in graver matters.'

potent and reverend signor: cf. *Othello*, I. iii. 76: 'potent, grave, and reverend signiors'. GE had already alluded to this line in the Proem (see p. 6). The *MS* here originally read 'grave signor'.

licking marble: 'as vain as licking marble' is a proverbial Florentine expression of the 15th cent.

171 *theosophy . . . the New Platonists*: theosophy is divine illumination claimed to be possessed by specially inspired men. The 'New Platonists' were a group of writers such as Plotinus, Porphyry, and Iamblichus, originating in Alexandria in the 3rd cent. AD, who combined the tenets of Platonism, Eastern mysticism, and Christianity.

172 *Aurora*: though Aurora was the Roman goddess of the dawn, Tito is plainly alluding here to a Greek source—the 'fair-tressed Dawn' of *Odyssey*, 5. 390.

174 *'ingenia acerrima Florentina'*: 'very sharp Florentine minds'. The quotation is from a letter of Filelfo.

176 *a basket of eggs*: Vasari notes that when he was working Piero would often live off nothing but hard-boiled eggs for days on end. Most of the details in the following pages about Piero's studio, garden, sketches, and props are taken from Vasari's biography.

177 *the triumph of Bacchus and Ariadne . . . a story in Ovid*: in Greek mythology, Dionysus (with whom the Romans identified Bacchus) found and married the Cretan princess Ariadne on the island of Naxos, where she had been abandoned by Theseus after helping him escape from the Minotaur's labyrinth. The marriage is described in book 8 of Ovid's *Metamorphoses*, though the image of Bacchus in his ship, exactly as outlined by Tito, is taken from *Metamorphoses*, 3. 664–9.

178 *mænads . . . Saint Margaret's resurrection out of the devouring dragon; Madonnas with the supernal light upon them*: maenads were female votaries of Bacchus who became possessed by the god. Legend has it that St Margaret (or Marina) of Antioch was swallowed by the devil in the form of a dragon but promptly disgorged when she made the sign of the cross in its stomach. GE is probably thinking of Piero's tiny painting of the scene on the base of an altarpiece for the Santissima Annunziata, depicting a Madonna who, in Vasari's description, 'turns her head towards the heavens . . . by whose light she is illuminated'.

179 *the picture of Mars and Venus*: the painting, once owned by Vasari himself, is now in the Staatliche Museen in Berlin.

Giovanni Vespucci . . . Colonos: though the portrait of the blind Oedipus and his daughter Antigone is an invention of GE, its hypothetical patron is carefully chosen, for Piero had been commissioned to paint two Bacchanalian scenes for the Vespucci palace in Florence.

182 *"sitting with a certain grandeur . . . queenliness"*: '"Quando una donna e grande, ben formata, porta ben sua persona, siede con una certa grandezza, parla con gravita, ride con modestia, e finalmente getta quasi un odor di Regina; allora noi diciamo quella donna pare una maesta, ella ha una maesta."—FIRENZUOLA: *Della Bellezza delle Donne*.' [GE] The *Discorsi delle bellezze donne* by the Floretine writer Agnolo Firenzuola (1493–1543) offers a portrait of the ideal Renaissance woman. The quotation here is from the first of the *discorsi*.

190 *young faun . . . by a promising youth*: Michelangelo was born in 1475. Vasari records that at the age of 14 he was encouraged by Lorenzo de' Medici to copy the head of an 'old Faun' from a classical statue in the Medici gardens. A later work of which GE may be thinking (not inappropriately in the light of

one of the novel's most persistent metaphors) is the statuette of Bacchus commissioned by Jacopo Galli in Rome *c.*1497 and subsequently brought to Florence by the Medici (it is now in the Bargello).

192 *that scholarly Benedict, Leonardo Bruno*: Leonardo Bruni (1370–1444), who served as Chancellor of the Florentine Republic from 1427 until his death, was one of the most learned men of his time. He thought of taking holy orders, but in his early forties renounced his canonry and married. His wife brought him a large dowry—some compensation for the cost of their wedding celebrations, of which he remarked, 'In one night I have consummated my marriage and consumed my patrimony.' The term 'Benedict', from the character Benedick in *Much Ado About Nothing*, denotes an erstwhile confirmed bachelor now married.

193 *a Miserere*: a penitential prayer, more specifically the opening of Psalm 50 in the Vulgate: 'Miserere mei, Deus' ('Have mercy upon me, O Lord').

an invention of Piero di Cosimo: Tito is correct in his attribution of the origin of the procession, but GE is anticipating the event. The details of the scene are taken from Vasari's account of an 'extraordinary spectacle' mounted by Piero di Cosimo for the Florentine Carnival in 1511.

194 *Care-dispeller*: one of the many names by which Dionysus/Bacchus was known was Luaios or Lyaeus—the 'loosener' of care.

196 *Charlemagne, reputed rebuilder of Florence . . . Cyrus, liberator of the chosen people, restorer of the Temple*: Charlemagne is supposed to have rebuilt the city around the year 800, following its destruction by the Goths, while on his way to Rome to be crowned first Holy Roman Emperor. The parallel between Charles VIII and Charlemagne was invoked by numerous French and Italian politicians of the time as well as by the King himself. Following his conquest of Babylon in 538 BC, Cyrus the Great, King of Persia, allowed the captive Israelites to return to their homeland and rebuild the temple at Jerusalem. Savonarola himself was one of the many who hailed Charles as a 'new Cyrus'.

197 *Most Christian King*: the title 'Rex Christianissimus' had been granted to Charles's father Louis XI by Pope Paul II in 1469.

widely spread conviction . . . monstrous births: GE follows the account of the 16th-cent. historian Francesco Guicciardini, who reports that 'an infinite number of armed men on enormous horses were seen for many days passing through the air with a terrible clamour of drums and trumpets. In many places in Italy the sacred images and statues had openly sweated. Everywhere monsters of men and other animals were being born.' In one phrase at least her precise wording also recalls Shakespeare's *Julius Caesar*: 'Fierce fiery warriors fought upon the clouds | In ranks and squadrons and right form of war' (II. ii. 19–20).

"Behold . . . upon the earth." . . . supreme guidance . . . listened with shuddering awe: Genesis 6: 17, the text of Savonarola's sermon on 21 September 1494. Savonarola himself asserted that it was 'by God's will and guidance' that he should have reached this point in his exegesis of Genesis at the fateful moment when Charles VIII was approaching Florence, and noted that among his audience was Pico della Mirandola—'a man unique in our times for his intellect and breadth of learning, who was terrified upon hearing these words and later told me that his hair had stood on end'.

198 *the fear of the Turk had ceased to be active . . . a little prospective poisoning*: fear of the Turks had reached its zenith in 1480, when a Turkish army landed at Otranto in southern Italy, sacked the city, and massacred the inhabitants. In the following year, however, the city was retaken by the Duke of Calabria, and the Turks expelled from Italy. Prince Djem, the brother of the Turkish Sultan Bajazet II, had been captured by Pope Innocent VIII and was subsequently held by his successor Alexander VI, to whom the Sultan paid 40,000 ducats a year to keep him prisoner, though offering much larger sums for his murder. Djem died in 1494, reportedly having been given slow poison by the Pope in return for a vast bribe of 300,000 ducats.

199 *a sword hanging*: in his book *Compendium Revelationum* Savonarola records that the night before his last Advent sermon of 1492 he had a vision, which he took to be a divine revelation, of a sword in the sky inscribed with the words '*Gladius Domini super terram cito et velociter*' ('the sword of God upon the earth, swift and sudden': see p. 216). He heard voices threatening that the wrath of God was about to descend on a corrupt world, which would be given over to

war, famine, and pestilence. Finally, he was commanded to warn his flock of the impending scourge and to enjoin them to pray that good shepherds might be sent to purify God's Holy Church.

200 *Ludovico Sforza*: when Galeazzo Maria Sforza, Duke of Milan, was murdered in 1476, he was succeeded by his son Gian Galeazzo, a minor. His uncle Ludovico, however, under the pretence of protecting him, usurped the power and property of the ducal crown, which he retained even after his nephew's majority. But Gian Galeazzo had married a granddaughter of Ferdinand of Aragon, King of Naples, and her father, the Crown Prince Alfonso, was understandably unhappy with the situation in Milan. In time his remonstrances and threats became such that Ludovico realized he would be unable to maintain his position unless he could find a way of disabling Ferdinand and Alfonso. It was with this in view that he encouraged Charles VIII to invade Italy and claim his dubiously inherited right to the throne of Naples. His unfortunate nephew died in 1494, though probably from natural causes.

a recusant Cardinal: Giuliano della Rovere, Cardinal of St Peter in Vincoli, had been defeated by his sworn enemy Rodrigo Borgia in the papal election of 1492. Having defied the new Pope, he took refuge in France, where he urged Charles VIII to invade Italy in order to embarrass and weaken his rival.

201 *repent . . . like Nineveh*: Jonah was commanded by God to give Nineveh forty days' notice of destruction if it did not abandon its evil ways. The people repented and the city was spared.

"orators," even with a prophet at their head: on 5 November 1494 Savonarola had led an embassy to Charles VIII at Pisa to ascertain what his intentions were toward Florence.

203 *Galli*: the speaker is punning on the word *Gallo* (plural *Galli*), which means both 'a cockerel' and 'a Gaul' (i.e. Frenchman).

204 *the old cow lowed*: '"*La vacca muglia*" was the phrase for the sounding of the great bell in the tower of the Palazzo Vecchio.' [GE]

Ciompi: 'The poorer artisans connected with the wool trade—wool-beaters, carders, washers, &c.' [GE]

Lorenzo Tornabuoni: the Tornabuoni were a prominent Florentine family with strong Medicean connections (Lucrezia Tornabuoni was the mother of Lorenzo the Magnificent). Young Lorenzo Tornabuoni, though indeed 'a Medicean in his heart' (he was one of the five conspirators executed in 1497 for plotting the return of Piero de' Medici—see Ch. 60), 'pretends to look well satisfied' since he feigned adherence to Savonarola and the popular party, who had invited the French into Florence.

205 *Signa*: six miles to the west of Florence.

hoof-shaped shoes . . . royal superfluity in toes: Charles VIII had an extra toe on one foot and wore peculiarly shaped shoes to disguise this deformity. His soldiers adopted the same ungainly style in deference to him.

206 *prisoners in Lunigiana*: GE has based the climactic scene that follows on documented fact. Several of the contemporary chroniclers relate that some Italian prisoners taken in Lunigiana (a province in northern Tuscany) were brought into the city by French soldiers to beg their ransom money, that their ropes were cut by the angry crowd, and that they escaped in the ensuing mêlée.

210 *Fivizzano*: a town some 90 miles to the north-west of Florence. It was assaulted and sacked by the French in October 1494.

215 *the Shechinah*: the visible glory of God, a manifestation of the divine presence, often symbolized by a refulgent light, as in the light over the 'mercy-seat', or cover, placed above the Ark of the Covenant.

it is written: cf. Amos 3: 7: 'Surely the Lord God will do nothing, but he revealeth his secret unto his servants the prophets.'

smote the sons of Eli: Hophni and Phinehas, the sons of the High Priest Eli, and priests themselves, were killed for abusing their position and showing contempt for God (see 1 Samuel 2–4).

216 *there was a pause*: in AD 66 the Jews rebelled against Rome. Nero sent Vespasian to subdue them and he duly reconquered most of Judaea, but before he could take Jerusalem itself his campaign was interrupted by Nero's death and his own promotion to the throne. This gave Jerusalem a respite of almost

two years before it was again besieged and eventually destroyed by Vespasian's son Titus in AD 70.

217 *while you suffer the accursed thing to lie in the camp*: following Joshua's destruction of Jericho, a ban was placed upon bringing anything from the ruins of the city into the Israelite camp. Achan, however, disobeyed the order and hid some plunder among his own possessions, as a result of which God caused the Israelites to be defeated in battle. Achan confessed his sin and was stoned to death; the offending items were thrown out of the camp, and the Israelites immediately triumphed over their enemies. (See Joshua 6–7.) In his sermon on 14 December 1494 Savonarola urged that the Signoria should extirpate from Florence everything hostile to religious devotion: vices should be suppressed, gaming and drinking banned, and women forced to reform the manner of their dress.

218 *. . . prosper for ever*": 'The sermon here given is not a translation, but a free representation of Fra Girolamo's preaching in its more impassioned moments.' [GE]

220 *Bacco trionfante*: i.e. Bacchus in triumph, referring to the picture commissioned by Tito. Piero describes Romola as Antigone rather than Ariadne (having painted her in both roles) to indicate that her marriage to Tito is as incongruous as one between the daughter of Oedipus and the god of wine.

221 *faces such as Masaccio had painted*: GE is probably thinking of the frescoes (1428) by Masaccio (1401–28) in the Brancacci Chapel in Santa Maria del Carmine. For Ghirlandaio see n. to p. 20.

Samuel: the Old Testament prophet who became also a civil ruler and law-giver.

Soderini: Pagolantonio Soderini, a doctor of law, had been Lorenzo de' Medici's ambassador to Venice. It was he who first proposed the scheme of a 'Great Council' for Florence along Venetian lines.

Piero Capponi: a wealthy merchant and erstwhile supporter of Lorenzo de' Medici, Capponi became a republican in opposition to the would-be despotism of Lorenzo's feeble and vacillating son Piero. His further exploits in defence of Florentine liberty are described in Ch. 29. He died fighting against Pisa in 1496.

Accursius: the Latinized name of Francesco Accorso (1182–1260), professor of Law at Bologna and author of the *Glossa Magistralis*, a commentary on the laws of Justinian.

Luca Corsini . . . the Frate: Corsini, a nobleman and scholar, was a prominent supporter of Savonarola. The 'memorable occasion' refers to the burning of the Pyramid of Vanities (see Ch. 49), when Corsini is reported to have thrown stones at the *Compagnacci* who were attempting to disrupt the procession of Florentine boys organized by Savonarola.

join the community of San Marco: Savonarola's rule attracted numerous recruits to the Dominican order at San Marco, many of them from Florence's most distinguished families—including the scholars Alessandro Strozzi and Zanobi Acciajoli.

young painter . . . Fra Bartolommeo: the Florentine painter Baccio della Porta (1475–1517) was a lay follower of Savonarola, and was with him at San Marco when the convent was besieged in 1498 (see Ch. 66). According to Vasari's account, he was so frightened by the mob that he swore he would himself take holy orders as a Dominican if he was safely delivered. He was, and he did; he is better known to history by his religious name of Fra Bartolommeo. Not being allowed access to San Marco herself, GE relied on Lewes's account for her description of its interior. In his journal for 22 May 1860 Lewes made notes on the Madonna and Child by Fra Bartolommeo in one of the rooms that had been occupied by Savonarola, remarking that the child 'was more life-like and noble than any but Rafael's Sistine children'.

222 *Girolamo Benevieni . . . Pico della Mirandola, who was never to see the light of another morning*: like Pico a zealous supporter of Savonarola, Benevieni wrote many of the hymns sung by the youth of Florence on the occasion of the burning of the vanities (see Ch. 49). Pico died on 17 November 1494, the day of Charles VIII's entry into Florence. On the 16th Savonarola had visited his bedside, received his vows, and accepted him into the Dominican order. The '*Frate*'s speedy coming'—a further (undocumented) visit which GE suggests that Benevieni may be going to announce—would have been in vain.

Dolfo Spini: Ridolfo (known as Dolfo or Doffo) Spini, leader of the *Compagnacci*, a violent faction of the aristocratic party opposed to Savonarola and the Medici alike. Savonarola's biographer Pasquale Villari, one of GE's principal sources, describes him as a 'depraved . . . youth of noted audacity' whose 'band met together at nightly banquets, and amid the cheerful clinking of wine cups, laid fresh plots against Savonarola'.

224 *fù gran magnificenza*: the 'old diarist' is Giovanni Cambi, whose archaically spelled and colloquially expressed account records that the King's entry 'fu gran magnifice*mza*' (was a magnificent spectacle).

225 *Luca Corsini . . . Francesco Gaddi*: the contemporary chroniclers relate that just as Luca Corsini began to read his written address it began to rain; the horses grew restless and the company was thrown into confusion. At this point Francesco Gaddi, one of the two secretaries of the department of external affairs, pushed his way forward and made an impromptu but appropriate speech in French.

227 *Niccolò Caparra . . . iron-work*: the celebrated smith Niccolò Grosso was given the sobriquet 'Caparra' ('earnest-money') by Lorenzo de' Medici since he refused to do any work on credit. The burning books on the sign over his shop (see p. 228) were to signify that he could inscribe the names of no more debtors therein. Vasari describes him as 'an upright and religious man, but very whimsical and obstinate', and as one who refused to do business with anyone whose motives he suspected.

block or "isle" of houses: the Italian for block (of houses) is *isolato*.

228 *Brescia*: the northern Italian city of Brescia was renowned for the manufacture of arms.

233 *a lien on the collection as a security*: a lien is the right to retain possession of another's property until the owner repays his debt.

the Cardinal: presumably the cardinal Giovanni de' Medici (see n. to p. 129), to whom, following the death of Lorenzo, Bardo has apparently transferred his hopes for the establishment of a Bardi Library.

the Pnyx and the Forum: places of public assembly in ancient Athens and Rome respectively.

240 *Mysteries*: i.e. mystery plays, as performed by trade guilds.

On 23 November 1494 the traditional Florentine mystery play of the Annunciation was performed for Charles VIII at the church of San Felice in Piazza.

his lance in rest: according to French military conventions of the time, by entering Florence with his lance at the ready (i.e. stowed in the 'rest' by the side of his saddle), Charles could legitimately claim dominion over the city.

242 *Chi promette . . . maì bene*: 'The soul of one who promises and fails to keep his word does not prosper': Lippi, *Il malmantile racquistato*, I. 5.

244 *swan-egg*: a variety of pear.

245 *seemed to be planting a vine*: from the Italian expression 'piantare una vigna', roughly equivalent to the English 'to be miles away'.

246 *well-authenticated vision . . . piece of honeycomb*: in its context here, and the speaker being Francesco Cei—a particularly vicious enemy of Savonarola—I take this 'vision' (unauthenticated by any of the contemporary biographers or historians) to be made up by GE, and Cei's remark to be intended sarcastically. Besides being the god of war, Mars would carry an added symbolic value for Florentines as their erstwhile patron deity, as would a liaison with his successor, San Giovanni, above their principal civic building. The 'piece of honeycomb' may be a reference to the Baptist's famous diet of locusts and wild honey.

247 *hide . . . as soon as a storm comes on*: Vasari reports that Piero was terrified of lightning, and that during storms he would cover himself with a cloak and hide in a corner.

not two months since: Poliziano died in late September 1494. The Malebolge (literally, the 'evil pits') are the ten galleries which comprise the lowest circle of hell in Dante's *Inferno*. According to Paulus Jovius, whose account is generally agreed to be preposterously inaccurate in detail (though probably based on a vestige of truth), Poliziano died from a paroxysm of amorous fever while singing the praises on a lute of a male pupil for whom he had conceived a passionate attraction. (Nello has already shown himself susceptible to the kind of prurient gossip in which Jovius dealt—in his reference to Piero Crinito: see n. to p. 30.)

Camilla Rucellai: a Florentine noblewoman who, under the

influence of Savonarola's preaching, divorced her husband and became a sister of the third order of Dominicans. She soon acquired a considerable reputation as a prophetess. Her prophecy about Pico della Mirandola's death 'in the time of lilies' is widely reported by the contemporary chroniclers.

248 *Euge*: Greek (and Latin): 'bravo', 'well done'.

Dido's bull's hide: the story goes that Dido was sold as much land as could be measured by the hide of a single bull. By cutting the hide into strips, joining them together, and stretching them out, she was able to enclose a sufficient area to found what would become the city of Carthage.

Franco Sacchetti says: In *Trecentonovelle*, no. 164.

249 *sent from Herod to Pilate*: the phrase means something like 'sent from pillar to post'. According to St Luke (23: 7–12), Pontius Pilate sent Jesus to King Herod, relieved to find that Galileans came under his jurisdiction. Herod, however, irritated at Jesus's refusal to answer questions, promptly sent him back to Pilate.

257 *men love their own delights*: possibly an echo of Virgil, *Eclogues*, 2. 65: 'each is led by his own delight'.

261 *the Milanese Count . . . and the Seneschal de Beaucaire*: the Milanese Count is probably Galeazzo di Sanseverino, a lieutenant of Ludovico Sforza and a favourite of Charles VIII. Etienne de Vesc, Seneschal of Beaucaire, was one of Charles's most trusted advisers.

264 *the mastiff of the city*: an allusion to Savonarola as leader of the Dominicans—the 'hounds of the Lord' (see n. to p. 83). Alarmed that Charles showed no sign of departing from Florence, in late November the Signoria asked Savonarola to intercede. By threatening him with the wrath of God if he failed to obey, Savonarola persuaded the King to leave the city.

268 *a Bacchante*: a female votary of Bacchus.

great subsidy: one of the provisions of the treaty whose signing is described in Ch. 29 was that Florence should loan Charles the sum of 120,000 gold florins.

270 *the Medici collections*: the Medici collections of books and antiquities, with the exception of those that had been transferred to San Marco, were plundered by the French.

278 *sin that's hidden's half forgiven*: '"Peccato celato è mezzo perdonato."' [GE] The expression, from Boccaccio, *Decameron*, i. 4, signifies—ingeniously—that such a transgression is more worthy of forgiveness than one that is generally known about.

281 *the Natività*: Tessa was 'married' on the feast-day of the Nativity (*Natività*) of the Blessed Virgin Mary (see p. 133), i.e. 8 September, in 1492. Lillo, who is clearly an infant at this point in the novel, and who is described as 'not more than three' in late July 1497 (see p. 433), was presumably born exactly two years later.

289 *Fra Lippo Lippi's round-cheeked adoring angels*: GE may be thinking of the angels in the *Coronation of the Virgin* or in the *Madonna and Child* by Filippo Lippi (*c.*1406–69).

298 *"ginger is hot in the mouth"*: cf. *Twelfth Night*, ii. iii. 116–17 ('ginger shall be hot i' th' mouth too').

300 *'Do not wonder . . . few and great'*: '"Se vi pare che io abbia detto poche cose, non ve ne maravigliate, perchè le mie cose erano poche e grandi."' [GE] The words are from Savonarola's interrogation on 21 May 1498—two days before his execution.

302 *San Gaggio*: a village barely a mile to the south of the city.

San Piero: a town some eight miles north-west of Florence.

Trespiano: about two-and-a-half miles from Florence on the road to Bologna.

305 *She had endured and forborne*: GE is alluding to Epictetus, in the 'grand severity' of whose 'Stoical philosophy', as the previous sentence reminds us, Romola had been instructed by her father. More specifically, the reference is to the account of Epictetus' maxims given by the Roman author Aulus Gellius (2nd cent. AD) in his *Noctes Atticae* (17. 19. 5–6)—to the effect that endurance and self-restraint ('to bear and forbear') are the two essential qualities required for a pure and peaceful life.

309 *the Suora Maddalena*: Maddalena de' Medici, the youngest daughter of Lorenzo the Magnificent.

313 *Pietra*: the village of La Pietra is about a mile north of the Porta San Gallo.

315 *under certain circumstances*: in the notes to his edition of Agostino Ademollo's novel *Marietta de' Ricci* (1841: almost certainly GE's source) Luigi Passerini explains that to produce the dye the lichen had to be mixed with urine.

our Bernardo: the prosperous merchant, diplomat, scholar, and poet Giovanni Bernardo Rucellai (1448–1514) had been one of Lorenzo de' Medici's most trusted advisers. His marriage to Lorenzo's sister Nannina was a splendid affair—at which 500 guests feasted in the piazza in front of the Rucellai Palace beneath a sumptuously decorated awning of dark blue cloth (hence, presumably, the reference to 'Florentine upholstery'). It was in fact Bernardo's father, Giovanni de Paolo (1403–81) who built the Rucellai Palace in the Via della Vigna Nuova (*c.*1446–51) and commissioned the completion of the façade of Santa Maria Novella (1456–70), both designed by the great Florentine architect Leon Battista Alberti. As GE explains, Bernardo was responsible for the remarkable gardens to the palace, in which he tried to represent all species of trees mentioned in classical literature. His 'excellent, learned book', *De Urbe Roma*, on the classical antiquities of Rome, was one of the first topographical studies of its kind.

316 *laudatory epitaph . . . tear their hair*: GE has appropriated the Latin epitaph on the monument in Santa Croce to the scholar Carlo Marsuppini (1398–1453), which she herself translates (in her notes in *Pf*) as 'Tear your hair, O Greek and Ausonian Muses'. The adjective 'Ausonian' refers both to ancient (i.e. Roman) and contemporary Italy.

318 ΜΕΣΣΗΝΙΚΑ. ΚΒ': Messenica. XXII—ch. 22 of bk. 4 of Pausanias' *Periegesis*, concerning the treachery and death of Aristocrates.

the traitor Aristocrates: Aristocrates, the leader of the Arcadians, formed an alliance with the Messenians against Sparta. Bribed by the Spartans, however, he fled the battlefield and brought about a crushing defeat of his allies. Later, when his treachery was revealed, he was stoned to death by his own people, who set up a tablet inscribed: 'Truly time hath declared justice upon an unjust King and with the help of Zeus hath easily declared the betrayer of Messene. Hard it is for a man forsworn to hide from God.'

319 *hecatomb*: the sacrifice of a large number of victims.

the Mænad . . . on the mountain top: the allusion is presumably to Horace's ode 'Quo me, Bacche, rapis tu' ('Whither dost thou lead me, Bacchus'): 'just so does the sleepless Bacchanal stand rapt on the mountain-tops' (*Odes*, 3. 25).

321 *Madonna della Gozzoviglia and San Buonvino*: 'Our Lady of Feasting and Saint Good-Wine.'

the Platonic Academy: an informal group of kindred spirits who gathered to celebrate and discuss the master, the Academy had met both at Lorenzo de' Medici's villa at Careggi and at the neighbouring one of Marsilio Ficino. At the banquets on Plato's birthday each of the guests made a philosophical oration or read aloud from Plato's works.

322 *astonishing Rome with heterodox theses*: in December 1486 Pico caused a sensation in Rome by proclaiming 900 conclusions or theses of a controversial nature, and offering to pay the travelling expenses of anyone who wished to debate them publicly. The theses ranged from Arabic, Hebrew, Egyptian, and Greek and Latin quotations imparting what he termed 'perennial' truths, to opinions of his own on subjects as diverse as magic and mathematics.

Leon Battista Alberti: an accomplished Florentine mathematician and classical scholar, a poet and author of several books on architecture and painting, Alberti (1404–72) is best known as an innovative architect. GE's description of his cast of mind follows that of Vasari, who suggests that in him 'theory and practice [were] happily united in the same person'.

says Erasmus: in book 8 of his *Apothegms*, referring to his meeting with Rucellai in Venice. Erasmus (?1466–1536) spoke no Italian and Rucellai obstinately refused to speak Latin: 'Verbum latinum nunquam quivi ab eo extundere' ('Not one word of Latin could I squeeze out of him').

Dante's pattern old Florentine: a reference to Dante's own great-great-grandfather Bellincion Berti, whose 'cinto di cuoio e d'osso' ('belt of leather and bone') is mentioned in the *Paradiso* (15. 112–13). The custom of eating with forks, as opposed to one's fingers, was a late 15th-cent. development.

323 *Antonio Pollajuolo . . . seduced . . . to more gorgeous Rome*: the Florentine sculptor, silversmith, and painter Antonio Benci (1433–98), known as Pollaiuolo, went to Rome in 1484 to work on the tomb of Sixtus IV and on the trappings of the coronation of Innocent VIII.

the artist who puts . . . melting-pot: Ridolfi's 'quotation' from Pollaiuolo is probably based on Vasari's account of the artist's life, which records that he decided to forsake the sculpting of precious metals for painting since the former activity produced works that could all too readily be melted down to raise money. The 'silver saints round the altar of San Giovanni' are probably a reference to Pollaiuolo's panel (1477–85), depicting the birth of John the Baptist, in the silver altar in the Baptistery in Florence.

324 *Luigi Pulci . . . Matteo Franco*: Pulci's characteristic scepticism is alluded to in the Proem. His quarrel with the minor poet and philosopher Matteo Franco dates from the 1470s, when he apparently felt himself supplanted by Franco in Lorenzo de' Medici's affections. GE was evidently familiar with the details of their antagonism, though Pulci's precise words as 'quoted' here seem to be of her own invention. The 'preaching friar' (i.e. a Dominican) may well be a disdainful reference to Savonarola himself before his rise to power.

a mere blowing of soap bubbles: the phrase *bolla di sapone* (a soap-bubble) is commonly used in Italian to signify something insubstantial.

dithyrambs: raptures (literally, a hymn sung in honour of the god Bacchus).

the receipt of Apicius: Apicius was the proverbial cognomen of several Roman gourmets, most notably of Marcus Gavius Apicius who lived during the reigns of Augustus and Tiberius. GE's description of the recipe for partridge is taken from *De Re Coquinaria*, a collection of recipes ascribed to a certain Caelius Apicius, probably compiled in the 4th cent. AD.

Tito quoted Horace: presumably *Satires*, 2. 2. 23–30: about the folly of thinking a peacock tastes better than a pullet because it costs more and looks exotic with its (inedible) tail-feathers spread out.

a favourite story of Luigi Pulci's: the episode provides the story for Pulci's *Novella dello sciocco senese* ('Tale of the Sienese Fool'); it is also referred to in *Il morgante maggiore* (14. 53).

325 *kneaded in the same trough*: a literal translation of the Italian expression for 'made in the same mould'—*impastati nella stessa madia*.

326 *studied the Venetian Council . . . indebted to a monk*: Soderini had been Florentine ambassador to Venice, and the *Consiglio Maggiore* (Great Council) he proposed for Florence was based on that of the Venetians. The council was empowered to appoint the city's chief magistrates and approve all laws, thus making it the sovereign body of the State.

the general amnesty: along with his advocacy, early in 1495, of a law of appeal against the condemnation of citizens by 'a majority of black beans' (see p. 451), Savonarola successfully urged a general pardon for all political crimes.

Arrabbiati: literally, the furious or rabid ones.

328 *a fine net to catch reasons in the air*: probably an adaptation of the Tuscan proverb 'pigliare il vento con le reti' (see n. to p. 127).

329 *Ulysses often made himself disagreeable*: it was Ulysses who, with Sinon, devised the ruse of the Trojan horse—a scheme to which Pucci may be alluding here (cf. *3 Henry VI*, III. ii. 189–90: 'Deceive more slily than Ulysses could, | And, like Sinon, take another Troy'). As for his being 'disagreeable', though characterized by Homer as being tactful, energetic (and at times cunning), Ulysses is less favourably represented by Horace: in *Satires*, 2. 5 Ulysses in the underworld is instructed by the blind seer Tiresias on the lucrative ways of fortune-hunting in polite society.

'in commendam': an ecclesiastical benefice is held *in commendam* by a temporary stand-in until a full-time incumbent is appointed. Tito here alludes to the common practice of a layman being granted the income of a benefice without having to undertake any of the duties.

331 *Montepulciano*: a wine from the Montepulciano region, south of Florence.

Ciascun segua, o Bacco, te: 'Let everyone follow thee, O Bacchus.' *Evoè* (from the verb *evoeggiare*: to cry out) was used specifically as an invocation to Bacchus. Poliziano's *Orfeo* (1480) was designed as an entertainment to be performed during a banquet.

334 *sard*: a type of cornelian, varying in colour from pale yellow to reddish orange.

336 *the Stinche*: 'The largest prison in Florence.' [GE]

341 *those who sit on a hill aloof . . . fellow-men*: since Savonarola is criticizing scholars like Bardo whose vain sense of superiority derives from their familiarity with the classics, it is ironic that the form of words he uses should be an allusion to just such an ancient writer—Lucretius (*De Rerum Natura*, 2. 7 ff.): 'nothing is more delightful than to possess lofty and serene sanctuaries, well fortified by the teachings of the wise, whence

you may look down upon others and behold them all astray, wandering abroad and seeking the path of life.'

347 *Fra Salvestro . . . somnambulism*: properly Fra Silvestro Maruffi, an extraordinary colleague of Savonarola's, given to sleep-walking and the uttering of mysterious prophecies while in a trance. He was executed beside Savonarola in 1498.

349 *grief for the loss of a new-born son*: Charles's son, born in September 1496, died when barely a month old. The King was so overwhelmed by grief that he lost all interest in his Italian campaign.

A league had been formed: Ludovico Sforza's plan to use the French invasion to secure his own position (see n. to p. 200) had backfired, and he saw their continued presence in Naples as a threat to his interests. Accordingly, in March 1495 he had engineered an alliance between Milan, Venice, Spain, the German Emperor Maximilian, and the Pope—supposedly against the Turks (hence a 'Holy League'), but really designed to expel the French from Italy. In advocating the league, Sforza announced that its purpose was 'to drive away the barbarians'.

352 *San Jacopo del Popolo*: one of Florence's charitable religious societies, dating from the 13th cent.

two or three bracci foremost: *Braccio* (= arm) was a common Florentine unit of measurement. The phrase here seems to mean something like 'at two or three arms' lengths'.

354 *preaching to the birds, like Saint Anthony*: it was in fact St Francis who is reported to have preached to the birds. St Anthony of Padua (1195–1231), a friend of St Francis, is said to have preached to fishes in the river at Rimini after the heretics in the city had refused to listen to him. This is clearly not a slip by GE, but a deliberate indication by her of the ignorance about such matters of the well-to-do young man who speaks the words.

357 *Companies of Discipline*: lay fraternities, dating from the 13th cent., some devoted simply to communal prayer, others to tending the sick and performing acts of charity.

358 *reformed Benedictines . . . zoccoli, or wooden sandals . . . when learning was rarer . . . forsook their gains to adore the Divine Mother*: the Benedictine order was reformed on a number of occasions during the Middle Ages in order to make its rules

stricter. Most Benedictines wore black; certain 'reformed' branches of the order, such as the Cluniacs, wore white; the Vallombrosans wore grey; the *Umiliati* first grey, then white. The *Zoccolanti* were a reformed branch of the Franciscan order instituted in the mid-14th cent. In the late 14th cent. a regular colloquium had been held at the Augustinian monastery of San Spirito (to which Boccaccio had bequeathed his library), at which scholars and citizens debated moral and philosophical issues. In 1394 leadership of the group was assumed by Coluccio Salutati, an early champion of the classics in Florence and a leading figure in the city's development as a centre of the new learning. The Servite order of mendicant friars was founded in 1233 by St Bonfilius of Florence and six fellow Florentine merchants who renounced the vanities of the world to live in poverty and sing praises to the Virgin. They came to be known as *Serviti* since they were *servants* of the Blessed Virgin Mary.

359 *Frati Umiliati . . . Vallombrosan*: founded as an independent order in the 12th cent. devoted to a life of penitence and piety, the *Umiliati* later came under Benedictine rule. They were skilled in the manufacture of woollen goods and founded the Church of Ognissanti in 1256. The Vallombrosans were an order of Benedictines founded by San Giovanni Gualberto in the 11th cent. The town of Vallombrosa, where their monastery was located, is some 20 miles to the east of Florence.

the twenty-one incorporated Arts of Florence: these 'Arts' or guilds comprised: cloth dealers, bankers and money-changers, wool merchants, silk merchants, lawyers and notaries, physicians and apothecaries, furriers, armourers, locksmiths, shoemakers, strapmakers, leather-workers and tanners, linenmakers and second-hand dealers, blacksmiths, stone- and wood-carvers, carpenters, bakers, butchers, wine merchants, olive-oil dealers, and innkeepers.

San Zenobio: d. 424, Bishop of Florence and one of the city's patron saints. His prayers are reputed to have saved Florence from the Goths in the year 405. His skull was discovered beneath the apse of the Duomo in 1331; it is kept in a reliquary in the Duomo.

image of the Pitying Mother: a miraculous painting of the Virgin, attributed to St Luke, ploughed up in a field near the village of L'Impruneta and taken into Florence to help the city in times of trouble.

367 *believing utterance*: 'He himself had had occasion enough to note the efficacy of that vehicle. "If," as he says in the *Compendium Revelationum*, "you speak of such as have not heard these things from me, I admit that they who disbelieve are more than they who believe, because it is one thing to hear him who inwardly feels these things, and another to hear him who feels them not; . . . and, therefore, it is well said by St. Jerome, 'Habet nescio quid latentis energiae vivae vocis actus, et in aures discipuli de auctoris ore transfusa fortis sonat.'"' [GE] As its title implies, the *Compendium Revelationum* comprises a summary of its author's visions and prophecies. It was published in 1495, in both Latin and Italian. Savonarola's quotation, from an epistle of Jerome to Paulinus, may be translated: 'The effect of the living voice has an indefinable hidden force, and sounds more strongly in the ears of a disciple when it comes from the mouth of the author himself.'

368 *avowed embassy . . . the League*: Rucellai, entrusted by the new government with its most crucial diplomatic missions, was sent to Milan to persuade Ludovico Sforza (who had convened the League) to exert his influence with Charles VIII against any plan to restore Piero de' Medici to Florence.

370 *Compagnacci*: a derivative of *compagno* (comrade) used specifically to refer to the younger *Arrabbiati*, who went about the streets armed, provoking quarrels and committing acts of violence.

great house . . . Santa Trinità: in the Via Tornabuoni, overlooking the Ponte Santa Trinità, the Palazzo Spini-Feroni is one of the largest medieval houses in the city, built for Geri degli Spini in 1289.

372 *that fainting Madonna of Fra Giovanni's*: Nello is referring to the figure of the Virgin in the fresco of the Crucifixion by Fra Angelico (Giovanni de Fiesole, 1387–1455) in the chapter-house at San Marco. GE sat admiring the work while Lewes toured the monastery taking notes for her on 22 May 1860. In her journal GE described the 'inimitable group of the fainting mother' as one of 'the frescoes I cared for most at Florence'.

373 *our forefathers resisted Pope Gregory the Eleventh*: during the famine of 1374, Pope Gregory, in an attempt to gain control over Tuscany, refused Florence's request for grain and attacked the city. Florence, however, bribed his army to raise

the siege and then allied itself with numerous other cities in a war which lasted for three years and ended only with the Pope's death.

false prophets in the Inferno: see Dante, *Inferno*, 20.

375 *in the world or in the wolds*: '"Del mondo o di maremma."' [GE] The phrase is taken from the summary at the beginning of *Decameron*, 6. 6. GE's translation is ingenious: *Maremma* is the marshland in southern Tuscany; its juxtaposition with *mondo* is jocular, and GE has effectively reproduced the word-play in English.

376 *'painted with fear,' as our sour old Dante says*: possibly *Inferno*, 4. 20–1: '. . . nel viso mi dipigna | quella pietà che tu per tema senti' ('. . . the anguish of the people down here paints my face with that pity which you take for fear'). The more likely source, however, is *Purgatorio*, 2. 82: 'Di maraviglia, credo, mi dipinsi' ('wonder, I think, was painted on my face'). Despite the unusual translation of 'maraviglia' as 'fear', there is strong circumstantial evidence for this latter line being the source, for in both *Bod* and *WN* GE jots down 'My visage was painted with fear' in a long sequence of quotations drawn exclusively from the *Purgatorio*.

trumpets . . . in a bag: the proverbial expression 'tornare con le pive nel sacco' ('to come back with one's bagpipes in a bag', i.e. empty-handed, deflated) has a variant which substitutes *trombe* (trumpets) for *pive*. Capo d'Oca means 'Goose Head'.

380 *Beoni*: one of Lorenzo de' Medici's Carnival Songs was entitled 'I Beoni' ('The Winebibbers'); it is possible that this accounts for the capital B on the word here.

381 *Ser Saccente*: 'Mr Know-All.'

know where the devil keeps his tail: by tradition, a tail is a sign by which the devil may be recognized. The better to disguise himself, therefore, he carefully hides his tail. A man who knows where the devil keeps his tail (from the Italian 'sapere dove il diavolo tiene la coda') is one who is particularly astute. GE may have come across the expression in Boccaccio (*Decameron*, 8. 7).

Trebbiano: a white wine from east central Italy.

Vicario dell' Arcivescovo: the Archbishop's vicar, or vicar-general, in charge of the legal affairs of the Florentine archdiocese.

388 *Ser Ceccone*: originally a Medicean, on the discovery of Piero de' Medici's conspiracy Ser Francesco (or Ceccone) di Ser Barone, a Florentine notary of some ability, had sought refuge at San Marco, where he pretended to support the *Piagnone* party while in fact acting as a Milanese spy and an agent of the *Arrabbiati*. He declared his true colours publicly only after Savonarola's arrest (see Ch. 71).

391 *turn a plum into an orange*: the phrase is taken from Boccaccio (*Decameron*, 4. 8).

392 *cool the baths of Nero*: the phrase is taken from Martial (*Epigrams*, 3. 25. 4).

394 *threatening German Emperor*: following the unexpected arrival of the French galleys in Leghorn and the subsequent wreck of his own fleet, in late November 1496 the Emperor Maximilian declared himself weary of fighting 'against God and man' and hastily retreated from Italy.

395 *Christ had been declared King*: in the last of his Advent sermons in 1494, Savonarola had declared that it was God's will that Florence should have a new ruler, and that the ruler was to be Jesus Christ. The city then struck a new coin, on one side of which was the Florentine lily, and on the other a cross and the words 'Jesus Christus Rex Noster'.

397 *reddened balls . . . "dead hair"*: the contemporary chroniclers report that among the *Anathema* (i.e. cursed or evil things) collected by the children were women's false hairpieces ('dead hair' is from the Italian *capelli morti*) and *pezzelle di Levante* (cotton balls coloured red for rougeing the cheeks).

398 *the last struggle of their Republic*: the Florentine Republic finally fell to the forces of Pope Clement VII in 1530. The Pope re-established the Medici as rulers of the city.

Ninferno: a colloquial alternative to *l'inferno* ('hell'), found in Boccaccio and other writers of the 14th cent.

Lorenzo di Credi and young Baccio: the Florentine artists Lorenzo di Credi (*c.*1458–1537) and Baccio della Porta (Fra Bartolommeo: see n. to p. 221) were both devoted followers of Savonarola. Vasari records that the latter burned his sketches of nudes on the Bonfire of Vanities, and that his example was followed by Lorenzo di Credi and other *Piagnoni* painters.

Laura: the woman to whom Petrarch addressed many of his most passionate love poems.

399 *wise Saint Catherine of Egypt*: St Catherine of Alexandria (supposedly 4th cent. AD) was renowned for her learning and beauty. She thus became the patron saint both of young girls and of philosophers. GE had seen Titian's painting of *The Marriage of St Catherine* in the Pitti Palace, and had described it as 'a work of supreme beauty'.

405 *An ass may bray . . . shakes the stars down*: from the Tuscan proverb 'raglio d'asino non arrivò mai in cielo' ('the braying of an ass never reaches as far as heaven').

biting the man in San Giovanni: depicted in the mosaic of the Last Judgement on the interior of the Baptistery roof (see n. to p. 7).

412 *her beloved crimson-velvet berretta*: among the items GE listed from the 'Trousseau of Ginevra' (see n. to p. 117) was a 'cap of Alexandrian velvet, embroidered with pearls and silver'. In a letter to Frederic Leighton (who illustrated *Romola* for the *Cornhill Magazine*) about women's costume in the 1490s, GE talks of 'the woman's *berretta*, frequently of velvet embroidered with pearls, and apparently almost as prevalent as our bonnet'.

embonpoint: plumpness.

413 *an angel loosing prison bolts*: cf. Acts 5: 19: 'the angel of the Lord by night opened the prison doors, and brought them forth'.

414 *better fall from the window than the roof*: probably an adaptation of the Tuscan proverb 'meglio cascar dall' uscio, che dalla finestra' ('better fall from the doorstep than the window').

415 *body of Lazarus trembled . . . sepulchre*: the story of Jesus raising Lazarus from the dead is told in John 11, but makes no mention of the body trembling. In one of his Lenten sermons in 1497, however, Savonarola promised to 'send forth a mighty cry that shall resound throughout Christendom, and make the corpse of the Church to tremble even as trembled the body of Lazarus at the voice of our Lord'.

419 *Filippino Lippi's serene Virgin appearing to St. Bernard*: in fact this painting, dating from the early 1480s, was at this time in the convent at Campora outside the city. It was not removed to the Badia until 1529.

420 *a sort of Agag*: Agag was the King of the Amalekites 'hewed in pieces before the Lord' by Samuel (see 1 Samuel 15: 33).

429 *Piero de' Medici, with thirteen hundred men*: when word reached Piero that Bernardo del Nero, a noted Medicean, had been elected Gonfaloniere for the months of March and April 1497, he rashly decided to return to Florence, arriving with 1,300 troops early on 28 April. Finding the gates barred against him, he waited outside the city all day, and then marched back to his base at Siena.

444 *Lamberto dell' Antella . . . his friends*: a prominent Medicean, Lamberto dell' Antella had been banished along with Piero de' Medici in 1494. On 1 August 1497 he was arrested near Florence with a letter on his person giving details of a plot to restore Piero and incriminating numerous leading citizens. Most of those implicated promptly fled the city, but Bernardo del Nero, Niccolò Ridolfi, Lorenzo Tornabuoni, Gianozzo Pucci, and Giovanni Cambi were arrested. The letter, and the subsequent revelations made by Antella under torture, were crucial to the condemnation of the conspirators.

448 *another plot*: as elsewhere in the novel (e.g. the arrival of the messenger in Ch. 43, olive-branch in hand), GE attributes to Tito an action which history gives to another (minor) character. Following his arrest and torture, and in return for a free pardon, Lamberto dell' Antella revealed details of a further plot, by which Piero was to be secretly brought into Florence on the night of 15 August.

memorable transaction . . . unscrupulousness: presumably a reference to the trial of Savonarola and the manipulation of the evidence therein (see p. 535).

Il tradimento . . . piacque mai: 'Treason is very pleasing to many, but a traitor has never pleased anyone' (Pulci, *Il morgante maggiore*, 17. 69).

452 *the smaller council or senate of eighty*: the Great Council instituted by Savonarola had over 1,000 members. The 'Senate of Eighty' was an executive body elected by the Council to be in permanent attendance on the Signoria.

453 *Piero Guicciardini . . . Giovan Battista Ridolfi*: a Florentine aristocrat and father of the historian Francesco Guicciardini, Piero had known the five conspirators from his days as a prominent official in the government of Lorenzo de' Medici. Tito is incorrect in his assumption about Ridolfi's future behaviour; despite the execution of his brother Niccolò he remained a loyal supporter of Savonarola, and during the

attack on San Marco (Ch. 66) he narrowly escaped being murdered by an anti-*Piagnoni* mob.

454 *it was he who got the law passed*: 'The most recent, and in some respects the best, biographer of Savonarola, Signor Villari, endeavours to show that the Law of Appeal ultimately enacted, being wider than the law originally contemplated by Savonarola, was a source of bitter annoyance to him, as a contrivance of the aristocratic party for attaching to the measures of the popular government the injurious results of licence. But in taking this view the estimable biographer lost sight of the fact that, not only in his sermons, but in a deliberately prepared book (the *Compendium Revelationum*) written long after the Appeal had become law, Savonarola enumerates among the benefits secured to Florence, "*the Appeal from the Six Votes, advocated by me, for the greater security of the citizens.*"' [GE]

457 *Andrea Cambini*: a prominent political supporter of Savonarola and the popular government, his house—like that of his friend Valori—was sacked and burnt by the mob following the attack on San Marco (see Ch. 71).

458 *sad frescoed figures*: another reference to Fra Angelico's *Crucifixion* (see n. to p. 372).

459 *his "Triumph of the Cross"*: a treatise in four books, published in both Italian and Latin in 1497, designed to demonstrate the truth of the Christian faith.

460 *knew beforehand*: Savonarola was said to have foretold the Dauphin's death, as well as those of Lorenzo de' Medici and Pope Innocent VIII.

465 *the Florentine Cato*: the phrase is not GE's own. Valori was commonly thus referred to by the contemporary chroniclers, in allusion to Marcus Porcius Cato (95–46 BC), a staunch Republican and opponent of Julius Caesar, who argued for the execution of the Catiline conspirators in 63 BC.

467 *blows that are too heavy to be avenged*: Machiavelli's remark here is based on a statement in ch. 3 of *The Prince* (marked by GE in her own copy of the book): 'One has to point out that men should either be well treated or totally crushed, because they can avenge themselves of lighter injuries but not of more serious ones. Therefore the injury that is to be done to a man should be of such a kind that one does not fear revenge.'

471 *Viareggio*: some 50 miles from Florence.

473 *naiad*: a water-nymph.

fair Gostanza: see *Decameron*, 5. 2. Believing that the man she loves is dead, Gostanza decides to kill herself, but lacking the strength to do the deed by violent means she resolves to drift out to sea—with the expectation of being drowned. She goes to a port, finds a small fishing boat, and rows away from land, but is carried by the wind to the coast of North Africa.

476 *This man had said*: in his sermon in the Duomo on Septuagesima Sunday (11 February) 1498—though the words given to Savonarola in the novel are a paraphrase rather than a direct quotation of his actual address. In this instance, for example, the phrases 'broken swords' and 'a hilt without a blade' are representations of Savonarola's repeated characterization of the Pope as '*ferro roto*'—a broken iron, tool, or sword: powerless because he was not acting as the instrument of God.

478 *Misereatur vestri . . . Benedicat vos omnipotens Deus*: 'May He have mercy upon you . . . May Almighty God bless you.'

479 *"Without preaching I cannot live"*: the words are from one of Savonarola's sermons on the books of Ruth and Micah in May 1496: 'Senza predicara, io non posso vivere.'

hold this Sacrament . . . send a fire and consume me: Savonarola's words here are a direct translation from his sermon on Quinquagesima Sunday (i.e. Shrove Sunday), 25 February 1498.

481 *this "wretched worm" and "monstrous idol"*: the words quoted (*isto vermiculo . . . isti monstruoso idolo*) are from a letter of the Pope of March 1498 to the Florentine Signoria.

482 *spelling . . . read and write*: 'The old diarists throw in their consonants with a regard rather to quantity than position, well typified by the *Ragnolo Braghiello* (Agnolo Gabriello) of Boccaccio's Ferondo.' [GE] See *Decameron*, 3. 8, in which the foolish Ferondo, with his slurred speech, talks of a revelation made '*per la bocca de ragnolo Braghiello*' ('by the mouth of the Angel Gabriel').

483 *fibula*: a clasp or buckle.

484 *the Mugnone*: a tributary flowing into the Arno just to the west of Florence.

485 *get the wool from England as we used to do*: throughout the Middle Ages Florence, as a major cloth-producing centre, had imported English wool, but in the late 15th cent. Edward IV had imposed export restrictions to protect English weavers from foreign competition.

487 *Alcibiades*: wealthy, dissolute, unscrupulous, and untrustworthy, Alcibiades (*c.*450–404 BC) was an Athenian general and statesman who provoked the sharp political antagonisms which led to the final defeat of Athens in the Peloponnesian War.

the Salviati and the Albizzi: Marcuccio Salviati commanded the armed guard that protected Savonarola at the trial by fire (see p. 501); Francesco Salviati was one of the two Dominicans flanking Savonarola as he arrived for the trial. Francesco degli Albizzi's was among the loudest voices to demand the execution of the five Medicean conspirators; Luca degli Albizzi urged the armed defence of San Marco despite Savonarola's insistence on non-violence.

an incubus: here used in the sense of 'an oppressive force'.

488 *maglio*: the word literally means 'mallet'. Here it is short for *pallamaglio* (English: pall-mall), a precursor of croquet. The mallet is used to hit a wooden ball (*palla*) through an iron ring. The street in London so named was originally an alley where the game was played in the 16th cent.

491 *his provisional substitute*: Machiavelli became Secretary to the Ten early in 1498, succeeding the grammarian Marcello Virgilio Adriani.

492 *Fra Benedetto*: a prominent socialite and successful miniaturist who was inspired by Savonarola's sermons to take holy orders as a Dominican in 1495. GE may have seen an example of his illumination in the Rinuccini codex in the National Library in Florence. In his autobiographical poem *Cedrus Libani* he recounts that during the assault on San Marco it was he who was ordered by Savonarola to lay down his arms (see p. 508).

Cor mundum crea in me: 'Create in me a clean heart' (Vulgate, Psalm 50, verse 10).

497 *Philippe de Comines*: Philippe de Commynes (*c.*1446–1511) had first been sent to Florence as an ambassador of Louis XI in 1478. He subsequently accompanied Charles VIII on his Italian expedition, of which he became one of the most important chroniclers.

library of the Medici, which we purchased: for all his wealth Lorenzo the Magnificent left heavy debts. His library was sold to help pay his creditors and Savonarola was instrumental in its purchase by the convent of San Marco.

498 *Hungary, where scholars are eminently welcome*: Tito's information is somewhat out of date: the scholar-King of Hungary, Matthias Corvinus, who had made his court a centre of European learning, had died in 1490, and his successor, Ladislas VI, had failed to continue the tradition.

499 *still to be seen*: two of Savonarola's Bibles, thus annotated, are preserved in Florence, one in the Riccardi Library, one in the National Library. GE examined the latter while in Florence in May 1861.

500 *every coign of vantage or disadvantage*: cf. *Macbeth*, I. vi. 6–8: 'No jutty, frieze, buttress, nor coign of vantage, but this bird hath made his pendent bed and procreant cradle.'

rustic stone-work: 'rustication' is the architectural style—common in Renaissance Italy—of cutting stone in large blocks separated by deep joints.

501 *"Let God arise, and let his enemies be scattered"*: the opening of Psalm 68.

504 *Elijah to the priests of Baal*: Elijah challenged King Ahab to a public contest to determine whether Baal or Jehovah were the true God. Two bulls were slaughtered and placed on altars on Mount Carmel, and the priests of Baal invited to call upon their god to light the fire. All morning they invoked Baal, but with no response, whereupon Elijah taunted them sarcastically about the delay before successfully calling upon Jehovah to ignite the other altar, thus proving his case (see 1 Kings 18).

505 *Accidents . . . Substance*: the accidents are the material form of the bread used in the sacrament, the substance that essence which through transubstantiation becomes the body of Christ.

506 *Tetto de' Pisani*: a projecting roof built by Pisan prisoners on the west side of the Piazza della Signoria in 1362. It was demolished in 1866.

508 *Knights Templars*: the knights Templar (also known simply as 'the Templars') were a military order founded in the early 12th cent. to protect pilgrims on their way to the Holy Land. The name derived from their headquarters on the site of Solomon's Temple at Jerusalem. They were renowned for their bravery—and savagery—in battle.

509 *men named Ridolfi and Tornabuoni*: Valori was killed by Vincenzo Ridolfi and Simone Tornabuoni in revenge for their kinsmen who were executed along with Bernardo del Nero.

512 *San Miniato*: the ancient Benedictine monastery of San Miniato al Monte, located on the hill to the south-east of the city where Romola and Baldassarre had met in Ch. 53.

515 *the last bridge*: in the 15th cent. the Ponte alla Carraja (now spelled Carraia) was the last bridge downstream, though several more have since been constructed.

518 *Lethe*: a river in the underworld which induced forgetfulness in those who drank from it.

520 *the Inquisition*: an ecclesiastical body charged with the prosecution of heresy. In 1492 the Jewish community was banished from Spain on the orders of the Grand Inquisitor Torquemada. Many of its members took refuge in Portugal, whence they were in turn expelled in 1497.

524 *pievano*: 'Parish priest.' [GE]

535 *the New Eight prematurely elected, in order to load the dice*: the 'new Eight' (i.e. the 'Magnificent Eight': see n. to p. 6) were elected at the beginning of March 1498, before the expiry of the existing Eight's term of office in order to remove supporters of Savonarola from this, the judicial body of the Signoria that would pronounce sentence on him. It is reported that on hearing of Spini's election Bartolo dei Zati, one of the sixteen examiners, indignantly resigned his appointment declaring that he would have 'no share in this homicide'.

536 *one who had formerly been his secretary*: GE is referring to Pacifico Burlamacchi, though in fact he became a Dominican monk only after Savonarola's death. The 'testimony' as recounted here 'to an unimpeachable purity and consistency in his life, which had commanded their unsuspecting veneration' is a direct translation of Burlamacchi's description of Savonarola's conduct.

537 *he would not obey the devil*: probably a reference to Savonarola's sermon on Quinquagesima Sunday 1498, when he declared: 'This excommunication is hostile to godly living, and therefore proceedeth from the devil . . . it then becomes thy duty to disregard it.'

538 *one memorable passage*: as the context implies, this quotation is a direct translation of part of Savonarola's 'confession', as taken down by Ser Ceccone.

542 *if he suffered, he would suffer for the truth—"The things that I have spoken, I had them from God" . . . "I said it that I might seem good; tear me no more, I will tell you the truth"*: these words too are direct translations from Ser Ceccone's account of Savonarola's confession.

543 *Jacopo Nardi*: (1476–1563). The author of several political discourses, a collection of carnival songs, and a popular translation of Livy, his most important work was the posthumously published *Istorie della città de Firenze*, which analysed Florentine affairs between the years 1494 and 1538 from the viewpoint of an anti-Medicean, pro-Savonarolian republican.

546 *"Spirto gentil"*: the opening words of the fifty-third poem of Petrarch's *Rime sparse*: 'Noble spirit, you who control those limbs within which, on his pilgrimage of life, dwells a man who is valorous, knowing, and wise'.

GLOSSARY OF ITALIAN WORDS

addio good-bye
amico mio my friend
andate con Dio 'good day to you' (literally, 'go with God')
anima mia my soul

babbo daddy
baie 'don't be silly', 'you're joking'
bambino/bimbo baby
bellissimi 'how very beautiful'
bello/a beautiful
bembè 'well, well'
berlingozzi ring-shaped cakes
bestia beast, animal
bracca hunting-dog
buon fortuna good-luck charm

capo d'opera masterpiece
cavallo horse
che miracolo what a miracle
chiaroscuro effects of light and shade
cicalata chatter
cieli 'Heavens'
condottieri commanders of foreign mercenaries
confetti sweets (more specifically, sugared almonds)
contadino/i/a/e peasants/s / peasant girl/s
cugina cousin

damigella damsel
deh ah, alas
demoni devils, demons
diavolo 'the Devil'
donna lady
dunque so, therefore

è falso it's false
è vero it's true
ebbene 'well then'
ecco 'there'
erudito scholar

fediddio 'God's faith'
festa festival
figliuola mia my little daughter
frate/i brother/s
fù tutt'uno it was all at once

giostra joust
giovane young man
giovanetti lads
gnaffè 'faith'
gozzoviglia debauchery

in coro in the choir, in church

lasso alas

madesì 'yes indeed'
madonna my lady (also the Virgin Mary)
madre mother
maledizione 'curses'
maniera Tedesca German style
marzolino sheep's-milk cheese made in the month of March
messer/messere sir
Messer Domeneddio God Almighty
mi pare it seems to me
monna a familiar (period) form of *madonna*, used for married women, roughly equivalent in this context to the English word 'mistress'
muoio di fame I'm dying of hunger

novità innovation, novelty

oimè alas
olà 'hey there'
orgogliosa proud, haughty
orsù 'come now', 'come on'

padre father, priest
padrone master
palio banner
panno di garbo stylishly cut cloth
paradiso paradise

parentado literally 'parentage', here meaning an arranged marriage
Pasqua Easter
pazzarella 'you silly thing'
pestilenza 'a plague on it'
pian piano softly, softly
piazza/e square
piccina little one
polenta porridge made of maize meal
popolani the middle classes
Popolo the people
poverina 'poor little thing'

ragazza girl
regina mia my queen
rigattiere old clothes dealer, junk merchant

salotto reception room
santa madonna 'holy lady', 'heavens'
santiddio 'good lord'
Satanasso Satan
sbirro police agent or spy
segretario secretary
sgherro hired ruffian, bully boy
sia so be it
sposi betrothed couple
suora sister, nun

Tedesco German
transmarini people from across the sea
trovatore troubadour

va via 'go away', 'clear off'
vermocane a disease of horses
vernaccia a dry white wine
vino di sotto cheap wine

zazzera (long) hair

THE WORLD'S CLASSICS

A Select List

HANS ANDERSEN: Fairy Tales
Translated by L. W. Kingsland
Introduction by Naomi Lewis
Illustrated by Vilhelm Pedersen and Lorenz Frølich

JANE AUSTEN: Emma
Edited by James Kinsley and David Lodge

Mansfield Park
Edited by James Kinsley and John Lucas

J. M. BARRIE: Peter Pan in Kensington Gardens & Peter and Wendy
Edited by Peter Hollindale

WILLIAM BECKFORD: Vathek
Edited by Roger Lonsdale

CHARLOTTE BRONTË: Jane Eyre
Edited by Margaret Smith

THOMAS CARLYLE: The French Revolution
Edited by K. J. Fielding and David Sorensen

LEWIS CARROLL: Alice's Adventures in Wonderland
and Through the Looking Glass
Edited by Roger Lancelyn Green
Illustrated by John Tenniel

MIGUEL DE CERVANTES: Don Quixote
Translated by Charles Jarvis
Edited by E. C. Riley

GEOFFREY CHAUCER: The Canterbury Tales
Translated by David Wright

ANTON CHEKHOV: The Russian Master and Other Stories
Translated by Ronald Hingley

JOSEPH CONRAD: Victory
Edited by John Batchelor
Introduction by Tony Tanner

DANTE ALIGHIERI: The Divine Comedy
Translated by C. H. Sisson
Edited by David Higgins

CHARLES DICKENS: Christmas Books
Edited by Ruth Glancy

FEDOR DOSTOEVSKY: Crime and Punishment
Translated by Jessie Coulson
Introduction by John Jones

The Idiot
Translated by Alan Myers
Introduction by W. J. Leatherbarrow

GEORGE ELIOT: Daniel Deronda
Edited by Graham Handley

ELIZABETH GASKELL: Cousin Phillis and Other Tales
Edited by Angus Easson

KENNETH GRAHAME: The Wind in the Willows
Edited by Peter Green

THOMAS HARDY: A Pair of Blue Eyes
Edited by Alan Manford

JAMES HOGG: The Private Memoirs and Confessions of a Justified Sinner
Edited by John Carey

THOMAS HUGHES: Tom Brown's Schooldays
Edited by Andrew Sanders

HENRIK IBSEN: An Enemy of the People, The Wild Duck, Rosmersholm
Edited and Translated by James McFarlane

HENRY JAMES: The Ambassadors
Edited by Christopher Butler

JOCELIN OF BRAKELOND: Chronicle of the Abbey of Bury St. Edmunds
Translated by Diana Greenway and Jane Sayers

GWYN JONES (Transl.): Eirik the Red and Other Icelandic Sagas

CHARLOTTE LENNOX: The Female Quixote
Edited by Margaret Dalziel
Introduction by Margaret Anne Doody

JACK LONDON: The Call of the Wild, White Fang, and other Stories
Edited by Earle Labor and Robert C. Leitz III

KATHERINE MANSFIELD: Selected Stories
Edited by D. M. Davin

KARL MARX AND FRIEDRICH ENGELS: The Communist Manifesto
Edited by David McLellan

HERMAN MELVILLE: The Confidence-Man
Edited by Tony Tanner

PROSPER MÉRIMÉE: Carmen and Other Stories
Translated by Nicholas Jotcham

MYTHS FROM MESOPOTAMIA
Translated and Edited by Stephanie Dalley

EDGAR ALLAN POE: Selected Tales
Edited by Julian Symons

PAUL SALZMAN (Ed.):
An Anthology of Elizabethan Prose Fiction

OLIVE SCHREINER: The Story of an African Farm
Edited by Joseph Bristow

TOBIAS SMOLLETT: The Expedition of Humphry Clinker
Edited by Lewis M. Knapp
Revised by Paul-Gabriel Boucé

ROBERT LOUIS STEVENSON: Kidnapped and Catriona
Edited by Emma Letley

The Strange Case of Dr. Jekyll and Mr. Hyde
and Weir of Hermiston
Edited by Emma Letley

BRAM STOKER: Dracula
Edited by A. N. Wilson

WILLIAM MAKEPEACE THACKERAY: Barry Lyndon
Edited by Andrew Sanders

LEO TOLSTOY: Anna Karenina
Translated by Louise and Aylmer Maude
Introduction by John Bayley

ANTHONY TROLLOPE: The American Senator
Edited by John Halperin

Dr. Wortle's School
Edited by John Halperin

Orley Farm
Edited by David Skilton

VIRGIL: The Aeneid
Translated by C. Day Lewis
Edited by Jasper Griffin

HORACE WALPOLE : The Castle of Otranto
Edited by W. S. Lewis

IZAAK WALTON and CHARLES COTTON:
The Compleat Angler
Edited by John Buxton
Introduction by John Buchan

OSCAR WILDE: Complete Shorter Fiction
Edited by Isobel Murray

The Picture of Dorian Gray
Edited by Isobel Murray

VIRGINIA WOOLF: Orlando
Edited by Rachel Bowlby

ÉMILE ZOLA:
The Attack on the Mill and other stories
Translated by Douglas Parmée

A complete list of Oxford Paperbacks, including The World's Classics, OPUS, Past Masters, Oxford Authors, Oxford Shakespeare, and Oxford Paperback Reference, is available in the UK from the Arts and Reference Publicity Department (BH), Oxford University Press, Walton Street, Oxford OX2 6DP.

In the USA, complete lists are available from the Paperbacks Marketing Manager, Oxford University Press, 200 Madison Avenue, New York, NY 10016.

Oxford Paperbacks are available from all good bookshops. In case of difficulty, customers in the UK can order direct from Oxford University Press Bookshop, Freepost, 116 High Street, Oxford, OX1 4BR, enclosing full payment. Please add 10 per cent of published price for postage and packing.